Adventures in the Ancient World: 1

Adventures in the Ancient World: 1

Queen of the Dawn
★
Moon of Israel

H. Rider Haggard

LEONAUR

Adventures in the Ancient World: 1
Queen of the Dawn & Moon of Israel
by H. Rider Haggard

Leonaur is an imprint of Oakpast Ltd

Material original to this edition and
presentation of text in this form
copyright © 2009 Oakpast Ltd

ISBN: 978-1-84677-986-2 (hardcover)
ISBN: 978-1-84677-985-5 (softcover)

http://www.leonaur.com

Publisher's Notes

The views expressed in this book are not necessarily
those of the publisher.

Contents

Queen of the Dawn

CHAPTER 1

The Dream of Rima

There was war in Egypt and Egypt was rent in two. At Memphis in the north, at Tanis, and in all the rich lands of the Delta where by many mouths the Nile flows down to the sea, a usurping race held power, that whose forefathers, generations before, had descended upon Egypt like a flood, destroyed its temples and deposed its gods, possessing themselves of the wealth of the land. At Thebes in the south the descendants of the ancient Pharaohs still ruled precariously, again and again attempting to drive out the fierce Semitic or Bedouin kings, named the Shepherds, whose banners flew from the walls of all the northern cities.

They failed because they were too weak, indeed the hour of their final victory was yet far away and of it our tale does not tell.

Nefra the Princess, she who was named the Beautiful and afterwards was known as Uniter of Lands, was the only child of one of these Theban Antefs, Kheperra, born of his Queen, Rima, daughter of Ditanah, the King of Babylon, who had given her to him in marriage to strengthen him in his struggle against the Shepherds, also called the *Aati* or "Plague-bearers." Nefra was the first and only child of this marriage, for shortly after she was born Kheperra the King, her father, with all the host that he could gather, went down Nile to fight the Aati who marched to meet him from Tanis and from Memphis. They met in a great battle in which Kheperra was slain and his army defeated, though not before it had slaughtered such numbers of the enemy that, abandoning their advance on Thebes, the generals of the Shepherds returned with the remnant of their troops whence they came. Yet by this victory Apepi, the King of the Shepherds, became in fact Pharaoh of all Egypt. Kheperra was dead, leaving behind him but one infant girl, and so were numbers of the great Theban lords, others of whom hastened to submit to the ruler of the North.

The Shepherd people too, like the Egyptians of the South, were weary of war and would not fight again. Therefore, although they were defeated, no cruelties were inflicted upon the followers of Kheperra, nor was great tribute asked of them; also they were allowed to worship their ancient gods in peace, and this in the northern as well as the southern lands. Indeed, by now, although the god of the Shepherds was Baal, to whom they gave the name of Set because already it was well known upon the Nile, the Shepherd kings re-built the temples of Ra and Amen and Ptah, of Isis and of Hathor, that their forefathers had destroyed when first they invaded Egypt, and themselves made offerings in them, acknowledging these divinities.

Only one thing did Apepi demand of the conquered Thebans, namely that Rima the Queen of dead Kheperra, and the babe Nefra, his daughter and lawful heiress of Upper Egypt, should be given up to him, hearing which Rima hid herself away with the child, as shall be told.

****

Now of the birth of Nefra the Princess there were strange stories. It was said that after she came into the world, a very fair babe, grey-eyed, light-skinned, and black-haired, and the rites had been accomplished, she was laid upon her mother's bosom. When Rima had looked upon her and she had been shown to the King her father, in a weak voice, for she had suffered much, the Queen demanded to be left alone, so earnestly that the physicians and women thought it best to appear to obey her and withdrew themselves behind certain curtains that divided the birth-chamber from another, where they remained silent.

The night had fallen and the birth-chamber was dark, for as yet Rima could bear no light near her. Yet of a sudden one of the women, a priestess of Hathor named Kemmah, who had nursed the King Kheperra from his birth and now was to fill that office to his child, having remained awake, saw a light glowing through the curtains, and being frightened, peeped between them. Behold! in the birth-chamber, looking down on the Queen, who seemed to be asleep, were two royal and glorious women or so Kemmah swore and believed, from whose robes and bodies flowed light and whose eyes shone like stars. Queens they seemed to be, no less, for there were crowns upon their heads and they glittered with jewels which only queens could wear. Moreover, one of them held in her hand the Cross of Life fashioned in gold, and the other a looped *sistrum* with gems strung on golden wires, such as is used to make music when the priestesses walk in procession before the statues of the gods.

This glorious pair, at the sight of whom the knees of the watcher trembled and the power of speech left her, so that she could say no word to wake the others, bent down—first she who held the Cross of Life and then she who held the *sistrum*—and whispered into the ear of the sleeping Queen. Then she who held the Cross of Life very gently lifted the babe from the mother's breast, kissed it, and laid the Cross upon its lips. This done she gave it to the other goddess, who also kissed it and shook above its head the *sistrum*, which made a tinkling music ere she laid the infant back upon its mother's breast.

Next instant both were gone and the room that had been filled with brightness grew black with night, while the priestess who had seen, being overcome with fear, swooned away until the sun was risen.

Nor was she the first to speak of this matter which she deemed holy and fearful, being afraid lest she had but dreamed or should be held a teller of tales who took the names of the gods in vain. Yet on the morrow the Queen called for her husband and said that a very strange vision had come to her during the night which she described in these words:

"It seemed to me that when weak with pain I had fallen asleep, two glorious ladies appeared to me clothed in the garments and wearing the emblems of goddesses of Egypt. One of these, who bore in her hand the symbol of Life, spoke to me in my dream, saying, 'O Daughter of Babylon, by marriage Queen of Egypt and mother of Egypt's heiress, hear us. We are Isis and Hathor, ancient goddesses of Egypt, as you know, who of late, since you came to this land, have worshipped in our temples and made offerings on our altars. Be not afraid, for although you were bred to the service of other gods we come to bless her who is born of you. Know, O Queen, that great troubles await you and bitter loss that shall leave you desolate, nor with all our strength can we save you from these, for they are written in the book of fate and must befall. Nor, for a while, that to mortals must seem long, can we free Egypt from the bonds with which the Shepherds have bound her, as they bind the feet of their own sheep for slaughter, though the time shall come when she shall shake them loose, like a bull breaking through its net, and grow greater than ever she has been. As every living thing suffers for its sins, so must Egypt suffer for her sins who has not been loyal to herself, her faith, or the lessons of the past. Yet in the end, if only for a while, her troubles shall pass like summer clouds, and from behind them shall shine out the bright star of her glory.'

"Now I answered that vision or that goddess, saying: 'These are heavy words you speak to me, O divine Lady. With Egypt indeed

I have little to do, who am but the wife of one of its kings, a princess sprung from another land. Egypt must find the fate that she has shaped, but as a woman I would learn that of my lord whom I love and of the child that has been given to us.'

"'The fate of this lord of yours shall be glorious,' answered she who bore the symbol of Life—'and in the end, that of your child shall be happy.'

"Then she seemed to bend down and to take the babe in her arms and to kiss it, saying: 'The blessing of Isis the Mother be upon thee. The strength of Isis be thy strength, and the wisdom of Isis be thy guiding star. Fear not! Be not faint-hearted, O Royal Child, since always Isis is at thy side, and however great thy danger, never shalt thou come to harm. Long shall be thy day and peaceful at the last, and thou shalt see thy grandchildren playing round thy knees. If only for a while, thou shalt bind together that which is divided and thy name shall be Uniter of Lands. Such are the gifts that Isis gives to thee, O Lady of Egypt.'

"So that goddess spoke, holding out the babe in the hollow of her shining arm to the divine sister who stood at her side. She took the child; she too kissed her on the brow and said: 'Behold! I, Hathor, goddess of Love and Beauty, bestow upon thee, the Princess of Egypt, all that I have to give. Beautiful exceedingly shalt thou be, and through love thou shalt make smooth the path of millions. Turning neither to right nor left, forgetting crookedness and policies, follow thou Hathor's star and thine own heart, rejoicing in Hathor's gifts and leaving all else to heaven that sees what thou canst not see and works to ends thou dost not know. Thus, O Royal Child, shalt thou sow happiness upon the earth and beyond the earth garner its harvest to thy breast.'

"Thus in my dream those goddesses seemed to speak, and lo! they were gone."

Kheperra the King listened to this tale and made light of it.

"A dream indeed," he said, laughing, "and a happy dream since it prophesies naught but good to this babe of ours, who it seems is to be beautiful and wise, a very Flower of Love and a Uniter of Egypt, if only for a while. What more could we wish for her?"

"Yes, Lord," answered Rima, heavily, "it prophesies good to the child, but, as I fear, ill to others."

"If so, what of it, Wife? One crop must fall before another can be sown and in every crop there are weeds as well as wheat. Such is the law to which all that lives must bow. Nay, do not weep over a fantasy born of pain and darkness. They call me, I must go, for soon the army starts to fight those Shepherds and to conquer them."

Yet Kheperra thought more of this tale than he chose to say, so much indeed that he went to the high priests of Isis and of Hathor and repeated it to them, word for word. These priests, not knowing what to believe, inquired if any had seen aught in the birth-chamber, and thus came to learn of the vision of the Lady Kemmah for, to them, as her superiors, she must tell all.

Now they were astonished indeed, and rejoiced, because they were sure that such a wonder had happened as was not told of in Egypt for generations. Moreover, they caused the words of the dream and the vision of Kemmah to be written down in full and sealed by the Queen and Kemmah, also by themselves as witnesses, in three different rolls, one of which was given to the Queen to keep for the Princess Nefra, while the others were hidden away in the archives of Hathor and Isis. Yet both they and the magicians whom they consulted were frightened at that part of the dream which told of great troubles and bitter loss that were to befall the Queen and leave her desolate.

"What loss," they asked, "could befall her, when happiness and prosperity were promised to her child, save that of the King her husband?—unless, indeed, other children were to be born to her whom Heaven would take away."

Still of these terrors they said nothing, only letting it be known that Isis and Hathor had appeared and blessed the new-born Princess of Egypt. Yet they were true enough, for very soon King Kheperra marched to the war and within two moons came the evil tidings that he was slain, fighting gallantly in the van of his troops, and that his army, although not crushed, was too weak from loss of men and generals to renew the battle and was retreating upon Thebes.

Rima the Queen heard the tidings, which indeed her heart seemed to have taught her before they were spoken. When she had listened to them, all she said was:

"That has happened which the great goddesses of Egypt foretold to me, and so without doubt shall the rest of their words be fulfilled in due season."

Then, according to the Babylonian fashion she withdrew herself to her chamber with the child, and there mourned many days for the husband whom she loved, seeing none save the Lady Kemmah who tended the babe.

At length the army reached Thebes, bringing with it the body of King Kheperra, that had been embalmed, though rudely, on the field of battle. She caused the wrappings to be loosed and for the last time looked upon her lord's face all shattered and marred with wounds.

13

"The gods have taken him and he died well," she said, "but my heart tells me that as he has died in blood, in a day to come, so in blood shall perish that usurper who brought him to his death."

These words were repeated to Apepi and caused him to go in fear through all his life, for his spirit told him that they were inspired by the god of Vengeance, as did the magicians whom he consulted. Indeed, when he remembered that Queen Rima was by birth of the royal Babylonian House, he grew more afraid than he had been before, because in his family, the Babylonians, to whom once his forefathers had been subject, were held to be the greatest wizards in the world. Therefore he was not surprised at the tale of the vision of Rima which came to her in the night of the birth of her child, though he could not understand why the goddesses of Egypt should appear to a Babylonian.

"If Babylon and Old Egypt come together, what chance will there be for us Shepherd kings who sit astride of the mouths of Nile? Surely our state will be as that of the corn between the upper and the nether millstone and we shall be ground to fine flour," he said to his wise men.

"Those stones grind slowly, and after all flour is the bread of peoples, O King," answered the chief of them. "Did not the dream of the wife of dead Kheperra tell—if report be true—that long years would go by before the Egyptians shake off our yoke, and did it not say that this Princess of Egypt who has been born to dead Kheperra and the Babylonian should be a Uniter of Lands? Bring hither the Babylonian widow and her daughter, the Royal Princess, O King, that these things may be accomplished in their season, though as yet we know not how."

"Why should I admit to dwell in my house one who, inspired by the devils of Babylon, has prophesied that I shall die in blood? Why should I not rather kill her and be done, and her babe with her?" asked Apepi.

"Because, O King," answered the chief of the Wise Men, "the dead are stronger than the living, and the spirit of this royal lady will smite more shrewdly than can her flesh. Moreover, we think that if the oracle of those Egyptian goddesses be true, this child of hers cannot be killed. Make them captives, O King, and hold them fast, but do not leave them at large to move mighty Babylon and the world against you."

"You are right," said Apepi. "It shall be done. Let Rima, the widow of King Kheperra, and her daughter Nefra, Princess of Upper Egypt, be brought to my Court, even if an army must be sent to fetch them. But first try to lead them hither by peaceful words and promises, or if these fail, bribe the Thebans to deliver them into my hand."

CHAPTER 2

The Messenger

Rima the Queen heard through her spies that Apepi, King of the Shepherds, purposed to take her and her child and to hold them captive. Having learned that this was the truth, she summoned a council of such lords as remained in Upper Egypt, and of the high priests of the gods, to ask them what she should do.

"Behold," she said, "I am a widow. My lord and yours fell fighting bravely against the North, leaving his heir, this royal infant. When it became known that he was dead, his army would fight no more but fell back on Thebes, and therefore the Shepherds claim the victory. Now, as I hear, they claim more: namely, that I who was the wife of your king, and our daughter who is your Royal Princess, should be delivered up to them, saying that if this is not done, an army shall be sent to take us. What is your mind, O Lords? Will you defend us from Apepi, or will you not?"

Now some answered one thing and some another. They showed that the people would fight no more, since the King of the Shepherds offered them better terms than ever they could hope to win in battle, and that after the sight of so much blood they longed for peace whoever might be called Pharaoh of Egypt.

"I perceive that I and your Princess have naught to hope from you, Lords, for whom and for whose cause my husband and her father gave his life," said Rima quietly, adding, "But what say the priests of the gods he worshipped?"

Now these answered with many smooth words. One declared that the will of Heaven must be obeyed; another that perchance she and the Princess would be safer in the court of King Apepi, who swore to treat them both with all honour; a third, that it might be well if she would appeal to her mighty father, the King of Babylon, for succour, and so forth.

When all had finished, Rima laughed bitterly and said:

"I perceive, O Priests, that the gold thrown by the Shepherd king is so heavy that it can travel many leagues of air into the treasuries of your temples. Let me be plain. Will you help me and your Princess to escape from bondage, or will you not? If you will stand by me, I will stand by you to the last, and so I swear will my daughter when she comes to the years of knowledge. If you reject us, then we wash our hands of you, leaving you to go your ways while we go ours, to Babylon or anywhere, save to a prison in the house of the Shepherd kings, where certainly your Royal Princess would be done to death that Egypt might be left without a lawful heir. Now I pray you consult together. I withdraw myself that you may talk freely. But at noon, that is within an hour, I will return to you for your answer."

Then she bowed to that company, who bowed back to her, and went away.

At the appointed time of noon, accompanied only by Lady Kemmah, the nurse who bore the Princess in her arms, she returned to the Council Hall entering it through the side door by which she had departed. Lo! it was quite empty. The lords and priests had gone, every one of them.

"Now it seems that I am alone," said Rima the Queen. "Well, such is often the lot of the fallen."

"Not altogether, Queen," answered the Lady Kemmah, "since the Royal Princess and I are still the companions of your Majesty. Moreover, I think that in yonder empty chairs I see the shapes of certain of the gods of Egypt who perchance will prove better councillors than those who have deserted us in the hour of need. Now let us talk with them in our hearts and learn of their wisdom."

So there they sat awhile, gazing at those empty chairs and at the painted pictures of divinities upon the walls beyond, each of them putting up supplications in her own fashion for help and guidance. At length the Lady Kemmah lifted her head and asked:

"Has light come to you, Queen?"

"Nay," answered Rima, "naught but darkness. This only do my gods tell me—that if we stay here those false lords and priests certainly will seize us and deliver us into the power of Apepi, as I think that they have been bribed to do. Have yours aught else to say to you, nurse Kemmah?"

"Something, Lady. It seems to me that the divine queens of Heaven, godmothers of this royal babe, Isis and Hathor whom I serve, have been whispering in my ears. 'Fly,' said the whisper, 'fly fast and far.'"

"Aye, Kemmah, but whither shall we fly? Where can the Queen of the South and her babe, the Royal Princess of Egypt, be hidden away from Apepi's spies? Certainly not here in the South where, being fearful or suborned, all would betray us."

"Nay, Queen, not in the South, but in the North where perhaps none would search for us, since the lion does not seek for the buck at the door of its own den. Hearken, Queen. There is a certain aged holy man named Roi, a brother of my grandfather, sprung from an old line of Theban kings. This great-uncle of mine, whom, when a girl, I knew well, was inspired by the gods and became the prophet of a secret brotherhood called the Order of the Dawn, which has its home by the pyramids that stand near to Memphis. There he and his brotherhood, which is very powerful, have dwelt these thirty years or more, since none now dares to approach those pyramids, and least of all any of the Shepherds, because they are haunted."

"By whom?" asked Rima.

"It is said by a spirit that appears as a beautiful bare-breasted woman, though whether she is the *Ka* of one who is buried in the tombs where my uncle lives, or a ghost from hell, or the shadow of Egypt itself shaped like a woman, is not known. At least because of her no man dares approach those ancient pyramids after night has fallen."

"Why not? Since when have men been afraid of beautiful unveiled women?"

"Because, Queen, if any looks upon her loveliness he goes mad and wanders off to perish miserably in the wilderness. Or perchance he follows her up to the crest of one of the pyramids, and falling thence, is crushed to powder."

"An idle tale, as I think, Kemmah. But what of it?"

"This, Queen: that there in those tombs, could we come to them, we might dwell safely enough with my uncle, the Prophet Roi. No man has courage to approach the place, save from time to time some young fool who longs to look upon the loveliness of the ghost and meets his death, or having seen her goes thence a raving madman. Even the wildest Bedouin of the desert dare not pitch his tent within a mile or more of those pyramids, while the Shepherd kings and their subjects hold the place accursed because two of their princes have found doom there; nor would they draw near to it for all the gold in Syria. Also they fear the magic of this brotherhood which is protected by spirits and have sworn to leave it unharmed. At least, such is the tale that I have heard, though doubtless there is more of it that I have not heard."

17

"Here then it seems we might rest in peace," said Rima with a little laugh, "at any rate, for a while until we found opportunity to escape to Babylon, where doubtless the King my father would welcome us. Yet how can we do so, bearing a babe with us, now when there is war all along the frontiers and none can cross the Arabian deserts. But, Kemmah, how are we to know that your uncle would receive us, and if he will, how are we to reach him?"

"As to the first question, Queen, the answer is easy. Strangely enough it chances that only this day I have received a message from the holy Roi. The captain of a corn boat sailing from Memphis to Thebes brought it to me. He told me that his name is Tau."

"What did he say to you and where did you meet him, Kemmah?"

"Last night, Queen, I could not sleep, being full of fears for you and the babe, so I rose before the dawn and going out, I stood on the private quay in the palace garden watching the sun rise, that I might make my prayer to Ra when he appeared in the heavens. Presently, as the mist thinned, I saw that I was not alone, for quite close to me a stalwart man who had the air or at least wore the dress of a seafarer, was leaning against the trunk of a palm, staring at the Nile beneath, near to the bank of which was moored a trading ship. He spoke, saying that he waited for the mist to clear and the wind to rise, that he might sail on to the trading quay and there deliver his cargo. I asked him whence he came and he answered—from Memphis of the White Walls, having permission from the Governor of Thebes and from him of Memphis to trade between the two cities. I wished him good fortune and was about to leave to make my prayer elsewhere, telling him my purpose, when he said:

"'Nay, let us pray together, for I too, whose name is Tau, am a worshipper of Ra, and see, the god appears,' and he made certain signs to me which I who am a priestess understood.

"Our prayer finished, again I prepared to go, but he stayed me, asking me for news as to the state of Thebes and whether it were true that the Queen Rima had died of grief because of the loss of her husband Kheperra, who fell in the battle, or as some said, had been killed with her child. I answered that these things were not true, words at which he seemed glad, for he thanked the gods and said that without doubt the Princess Nefra was the lawful heiress of all Egypt, North and South together. I asked him how he knew the name of this princess. He replied:

"'A learned man told it to me, a holy hermit to whom I confess my sins, which alas! are many, who dwells in the wilderness nigh to the Great Pyramids and among the tombs. He told me also that he knew the name of this royal child's nurse who was a kinswoman of his, and that it is Kemmah, a lady of high blood. Yes, and he charged me with a message for this Lady Kemmah, if I could find her in Thebes, because he said he dared put nothing in writing.'

"Here this Tau, the captain of the ship, stopped and stared at me and I stared back at him, wondering whether he were setting any trap for my feet.

"'It would be very dangerous, O Tau,' I said to him, 'if perchance you gave this secret message to the wrong woman. There may be many Kemmahs in Thebes. How will you know that you find the right one, or that she whom you are told is the nurse of the princess is in truth that nurse?'

"'It is not so difficult as it seems, Lady. As it chances, the holy hermit gave to me the half of an amulet of lapis lazuli on which is cut a charm or spell or prayer. He said that on this half the signs read, "May the living Ra protect the wearer of this holy thing at the last nightfall. May that protected one travel in the boat of Ra and——" Here, Lady, the writing ceases but the holy hermit said that the Lady Kemmah would know the rest,' and again he looked at me.

"'Does it perchance run,' I asked, '"and may Thoth find the balance even and may Osiris receive this protected one at his table to feast with him eternally"?'

"'Yes,' he said, 'I think that those were the words, or something very like them, that the Holy One repeated to me. Still I cannot be sure because my memory is bad, especially where prayers or writings about the gods are concerned. Since you, Lady, a stranger, know the end of the charm, doubtless it is a common one worn by thousands between Thebes and the sea. She whom I have to find not only knows the charm, but wears its other half, and how to seek her out I cannot think. Can you help me, Lady?'

"'Perhaps,' I answered. 'Show me this amulet, O Tau.'

"He looked round him to see that we were alone. Then he thrust his hand into his garments and from somewhere drew out the upper half of a very ancient tablet carven over with writing, that was fastened about his neck by a woven string of woman's hair. This tablet was broken or sawn asunder in the middle, not straight across but so as to leave a jagged edge with many points and hollows. I looked at it and knew it at once, since years before Roi the Hermit and my great-uncle had given me its counterpart, bidding me send it to him as a token if ever I had need of help. Then from where it hung upon my breast, I drew out that counterpart and set it against the half that Tau the Sailor held before me. Lo! they fitted exactly, since the stone being very hard had worn but little during the passage of the years.

"Tau looked and nodded his head.

"'Strange that I should meet you thus, Lady Kemmah, and quite by chance—oh! quite by chance. Still, the gods know their own business, so why should we trouble ourselves about such things? Yet there might be another half that fitted on to this broken charm that has been lent to me. So before we go farther, tell me the name of the sender and where he dwells and aught else that you know about him.'

"'His name is Roi,' I answered, 'who in the world was known as Roi the King's son, though that king died long ago, and as you have said yourself, he lives beneath the shadow of the pyramids. For the rest he is the holy Prophet of a great brotherhood, has a long white beard and hair, is very handsome and pleasant-spoken; can see in the dark like a cat because he has dwelt so much among shadows, has knees that are hornier than the feet of a desert man, because of his continual kneeling in prayer, and when he thinks that he is alone, converses much with his own double, the *Ka* that is always at his side, or perchance with other ghosts, which tell him everything that passes in Egypt. At least, such were his appearance and custom many years ago when he gave me this half of the amulet, but what they are now, I cannot say.'

"'The description will serve, Lady. Yes, it will serve well enough, though now the holy Roi has lost most of the hair from the top of his head and is too thin to be called handsome, having something of the air of an ancient and half-famished *halk*. Yet without doubt we speak of the same man, as the joined amulet bears us witness. Therefore, Lady Kemmah, whom I have met by chance, yes, quite by chance, just by waiting for you where the holy Roi told me I should do, hearken to my message!'

"Here, Queen, the manner of this seaman changed, and from being light and easy like to that of one whose words conceal a jest, became quick and intent. His pleasant, smiling face changed also, for of a sudden it seemed to grow fierce and eager, the face of one who has great things to carry through and whose honour hangs upon their doing.

"'Listen to me, Nurse of Royal Ones,' he said. 'The king whom once you dandled on your knees lies in his tomb, slain by the Shepherd spears. Would you see her who is sprung from him and the lady who gave her birth follow by the same road?'

"'Your question seems foolish, Tau, seeing that where they go, I must accompany them,' I answered.

"'I know that you would not,' he went on, 'and not for your own

20

sake only. Yet the danger is great. There is a plan to take all three of you; it was revealed to the holy Roi. In this city dwell traitors who are parties to the plot. Soon, to-morrow mayhap, or the next day, they will come to the Queen and tell her that she is in peril and that they purpose to hide her away in some safe place. If she is persuaded by them, soon she will find that this safe place is in the prisons of Apepi at Tanis, if ever she lives to reach them—and then—do you understand? Or if she is not persuaded, then they will drag her away by force with the babe and deliver them up to the Shepherds.'

"I nodded my head and answered:

"'It would seem that time presses. What is your plan, Messenger?'

"'This: Presently I sail on to the city and there deliver a certain cargo to merchants who await it. Also I have passengers on board, travellers from Siout, farmer folk flying from the Shepherds. There are three of them: a woman of middle age not unlike to you in face and form, Lady Kemmah, who passes as my sister; a fair young woman who passes as my wife and nurses in her arms a baby girl of some three months. As such at least I shall describe them to the officers on the quay, nor will those two women question my words. Yet being changeable, they will desert me here for other friends and the place where they slept will be empty. Again, do you understand, Lady Kemmah?'

"'I understand that you propose that the Queen and I and the babe should take the place of the three upon your boat. If so, when and how?'

"'To-night, Lady Kemmah, I am told there is a religious feast in this city in honour of the god of Nile, to celebrate which hundreds will row out upon the river bearing lanterns and singing hymns. To avoid all these craft I purpose to bring my ship back to this wharf, since I must sail down Nile with the south wind that springs up ere the dawn. Shall I perchance find two peasant women and a babe waiting among those palms an hour before the rising of Ra?'

"'Perchance, Messenger. But tell me, if so, where would that journey end?'

"'In the shadow of the Great Pyramids, Lady, where a certain Holy One awaits them, since he says that although the lodging be poor, there alone they will be safe.'

"'That thought has come to me also, Tau. Yet this flight is very dangerous, and how know I that in it there is not some trap? How know I that you yourself are not in the pay of the Shepherds, or in that of the Theban traitors, and sent to tempt us to our doom?'

"'A wise question,' he answered. 'You have the message and you have the token of the amulet and you have my oath sworn upon the holy name, to break which will consign me everlastingly to hell. Still, a very wise question when there is so much at stake, and by the gods, I know not how to answer it!'

"We stood still awhile, staring at each other, and my heart was full of doubt and fear. Once we were in this man's power, what might not befall us? Or rather what might not befall you, O Queen, and the royal child, since it is true, Queen, that for myself I cared and care little."

"I know it, Kemmah beloved," answered Rima. "But to your tale. What happened?"

"This, Queen. Of a sudden Tau the Messenger seemed to grow uneasy.

"'This place is quiet and lonely,' he said, 'yet certainly I feel as though we were being watched.'

"Now, Queen, we stood back from the private quay by the single palm that stands in the open place, whither we had withdrawn when we began to talk, for there we could not be seen from the river and I knew that none could overhear us. In the hollow to my left stands that old shrine surmounted by the shattered statue of some god, which once, it is said, was the gateway of a fallen temple; the same, Queen, in which you often sit."

"I know it well, Kemmah."

"This shrine, Queen, was still half hidden by the morning mist, and although it was out of earshot, Tau gazed at it earnestly. As he gazed the mist departed from it like a lifted veil, and following his glance, I saw that the shrine was not empty, as I had thought. For there, Queen, kneeling in it as though lost in prayer, was an aged man. He lifted his head and the full light fell upon his face. Lo! it was the face of the holy Roi, my great-uncle, somewhat changed since last I had seen him many years ago when he gave me the half of the broken amulet, but without doubt Roi himself.

"'It seems that here also dwells a hermit, Lady Kemmah, as well as in the shadow of the pyramids,' said Tau, 'and one whom I think I know. Is yonder man perchance the holy Roi, Lady Kemmah?'

"'The holy Roi and no other. Why did you not tell me that you had brought him with you on your ship? It would have saved me much trouble of mind. I will speak to him at once.'

"'Aye, speak with him and satisfy your heart as to whether I be a true man or a false, Lady Kemmah.'

"I turned and ran to the shrine. It was empty! The holy Roi had gone, nor was there anywhere that he could have hidden himself.

"'The ways of prophets and hermits are very strange, Lady Kemmah,' said Tau. 'Alone of all men, they, or some of them, can be in two places at once. Now perchance I shall find you here to-night, here by this shrine?'

"'Yes,' I answered, 'I think that you will find us. That is, if the Queen consents and nothing hinders us, such as death or bonds. But stay! How can we come by those country women's garments? There are none such in the palace, and to send out to buy them might awake doubts, for the Queen is well watched.'

"'The holy Roi is very foreseeing,' said Tau with a smile, 'or I am; it matters not which.'

"Then he went to where I first met him and from behind a stone drew a bundle.

"'Take this,' he said. 'In it I think you will find all that is needful, clean clothes though rough, that it will be safe even for a royal babe to wear. Farewell, Lady Kemmah; the river is clear of mist and I must begone. Guided by the spirit of the holy Roi which, as he can be in two places at once, doubtless will companion you also, I will return to find—my sister, my wife, and her infant babe—one, nay, two hours before to-morrow's dawn.'

"Then he went, and I went also, full of thoughts. Yet I determined to say nothing of the matter to you, O Queen, till I heard what answer those lords made to your prayer to-day."

"Have you looked in the bundle, Kemmah?" asked the Queen.

"Yes," answered Kemmah, "to find that all is as this Tau said. There are two cloaks and other garments such as farmer women use in travelling, suited to your size and mine, also the winter dress of a little child."

"Let us go to look at them," said the Queen.

CHAPTER 3

The Escape

They stood in the private apartments of the palace. Eunuchs guarded, or were supposed to guard, the outer gates, for the Queen Rima
was still surrounded by the trappings of royalty, and at the door of her
chamber stood the giant Nubian, Ru, he who had been the body-
servant of King Kheperra, he who after slaying six of the Shepherds
with his own hand had rescued the body of his master, throwing it
over his shoulder and bearing it from the battle as a shepherd bears
a lamb. The Queen Rima and the Lady Kemmah had examined the
garments brought by Tau the Messenger, and hidden them away. Now
they were consulting together, near to a little bed on which the infant
princess lay asleep.

"Your plan is very dangerous," said the Queen, who was much
disturbed and walked to and fro with her eyes fixed upon the sleeping
babe. "You ask me to fly to Memphis, that is, to walk into the jaws
of the hyena. This you do because a messenger is come from an aged
uncle of yours who is a hermit or a high priest, or a prophet of some
secret sect, and who, for aught you know, may have been dead for
years and now be but a bait upon a hook to catch us."

"There is the cut amulet, Queen. See how well the pieces fit and
how that white line in the stone runs on from the one to the other."

"Doubtless they fit. Doubtless they are the halves of the same talisman. But such holy things are famous and so is their story. Mayhap
someone knew that the priest Roi had given you one half of this
charm and took the other from his body, or stole it to be used to
deceive you and to give colour to the offer of a hiding place among
the dead. Who is this Tau of whom you never heard before? How
came he to find you so easily? How is it that he can pass in and out of
Thebes without question, he who comes from Memphis, holding all
the threads of these plots between his fingers, if plots there be?"

"I do not know who he is," said Kemmah. "I know only that when these same doubts crossed my mind, this messenger showed me the holy Roi himself in proof of the truth of his message, and that then I believed."

"Aye, Kemmah, but bethink you. Are you not a priestess, one soaked in the mysteries and magic of the Egyptians from your childhood, like to this uncle of yours before you? Did you not see the vision of the Egyptian goddesses Isis and Hathor blessing my child, which after all is but an old tale retold of those who spring from the bodies of kings? How comes it that no one else saw those goddesses?"

"How comes it that you dreamed of them, O Queen?" asked Kemmah drily.

"A dream is a dream. Who can give weight to dreams that come and go by thousands, flitting round our heads like gnats in sleep to vanish into the darkness whence they rose? A dream is a dream and of no account, but a vision seen with the waking eye is another matter, something that springs from madness—or perchance from truth. And now you have another vision, that of an old man who, if he lives at all, dwells far away, and on this unstable cloud you ask me to build a house of hope and safety. How can I be sure that you are not mad, as indeed the wise men of my country say that most of us are in this way or in that? You behold gods, but are there any gods, and if so, why are the gods of Egypt not the same as those of Babylon, and the gods of Babylon not the same as those of Tyre? If there be gods, why are they all different?"

"Because men are different, Queen, and every nation of them clothes God in its own garments: aye, and every man and woman also."

"May be, may be! Yet a stranger's tale and a vision are poor props to lean upon when life and safety hang in the balance and with them the crown of Egypt. I'll not trust myself and the babe to this man and his boat lest soon both of us should sleep at the bottom of the Nile, or lie awaiting death in some Shepherd dungeon. Let us bide where we are; your gods can protect us as well here as by the Pyramids of Memphis, should we live to reach them. Or if we must go, let these gods send us some sign; they have still many hours in which to travel from their heaven."

Thus spoke Queen Rima wildly in her doubt and despair. Kemmah listened and bowed her head.

"Let it be as the Queen pleases," she said. "If the gods desire, doubtless they will show us a path of escape. If they should not desire so to do, then we can remain here and await their will, since the gods are still the gods. Now, Lady, let us eat and rest, but let us not sleep till that hour is past when we should have embarked upon the ship of Tau the Messenger."

So they ate, and afterwards, taking a lamp, Kemmah walked through the palace and found it strangely silent. All seemed to have departed; as one weak old slave told her, to attend the feast of the god of the Nile and to sail in boats upon the river.

"Such things would not have been allowed to happen in the old days," he said querulously, "for then, who ever heard of a palace being deserted by those who were in attendance upon Majesty in order that they might enjoy themselves elsewhere? But since the good god Kheperra was killed by those Shepherd dogs in the battle everything seems to have changed. Nobody thinks anything of service; everybody thinks of himself and what he can get. And there is money going, Lady Kemmah, I tell you there is money going. Oh! sitting in my corner I have seen plenty of it being passed from hand to hand. Where it comes from I do not know. I was even offered some myself, what for I do not know, but I refused it, for what do I want with money who am so old and draw my rations from the stores, as I have done these fifty years, also my summer and winter garments?"

Kemmah contemplated him with her quiet eyes, then answered:

"No, old Friend, you want nothing with money, since I know that your tomb is provided. Tell me, you are acquainted with all the palace doors, are you not, and the gates also?"

"Every one of them, Lady Kemmah, every one of them. When I was stronger it used to be my office to lock them all, and I still have the second set of keys, which no one has taken from me, and remember the tricks of the inner bolts."

"Then, Friend, grow strong again; even if it be for the last time, go lock those doors and gates and shoot those bolts and bring the keys to me in the private apartments. It will be a good trick to play upon those revellers who are absent without leave when they return and find that they cannot get in to sleep off their drink until after the sun has risen."

"Yes, yes, Lady Kemmah, a very good trick. I will get the keys and go, following the round as I used to do and shooting the inner bolts that I named after all the gods of the Underworld, so that I might never forget the order in which they came. Oh! I will light my lantern and go at once, as though I were young again, and my wife and little children were waiting to receive me at the end of my round."

The half of an hour later the old man reappeared at the private chambers, announcing that all the gates and doors were locked, and that strangely enough he had found every one of them open and the keys missing.

"They forgot that I had their twins," he said, chuckling, "also that I knew how to shoot the inner bolts; I whom they look upon as a silly old fool only fit for the embalmer's bath. Here are the keys, Lady Kemmah, which I shall be glad to be rid of for they are a great weight. Take them and promise not to tell that it was I who locked the doors and forced all those idle people to sleep out in the cold. For if you do they will beat me to-morrow. Now if you had a cup of wine!"

Kemmah fetched drink and gave it to the aged man, mixed with water that it might not be too strong for him. Then, while he smacked his lips refreshed by the liquor, she bade him go to the little gatehouse of the private apartments and watch there, and if he should see any approaching the gate, to make report to Ru, who kept guard at the door which was at the foot of the eight stairs that led to the ante-chamber of the apartments.

This, encouraged by the wine and by a sense that once more he was taking part in the affairs of life, though what these might be he did not understand, the old fellow said that he would do and departed to his station.

Then Kemmah went and talked earnestly with the giant Ru, who listened, nodding his head and as he did so girt his armour of bull's hide upon his mighty frame. Moreover, he looked to see that his javelins were loose in their sheath and that the edge of his great bronze battle-axe was sharp. Lastly, he set lamps in the niches of the wall in such fashion that if the door were forced their light would fall upon those coming up the stair, while he, standing at the head of it, would remain in shadow.

These things done, Kemmah returned to the Queen, who sat brooding by the bed of the child, but of them to her she said nothing.

"Why do you carry a spear in your hand, Kemmah?" asked Rima, looking up.

"Because it makes a good staff to lean upon, Queen, and one that at need may serve another purpose. This place seems very still and fateful and who knows but that in the stillness we may hear some god speaking ere the dawn, telling us whether we should take ship with Tau, or bide where we are?"

"You are a strange woman, Kemmah," said the Queen, and once more fell to her brooding till at length she sank to sleep.

But Kemmah did not sleep; she waited and watched the curtains that hid the stair on which Ru kept guard. At length in the intense silence of the night that was broken only now and again by the melancholy note of some dog howling at the moon, for all the inhabitants of the city seemed to be absent at the festival, Kemmah thought she heard the sound as of gates or doors being shaken by someone trying to enter them. Rising softly she went to the curtains beyond which Ru was seated on the topmost stair.

"Did you note anything?" she asked.

"Aye, Lady," he answered. "Men try to enter by the gates, but find them closed. The old slave reported to me that they were coming and has fled to hide himself. Now go up to the top of the little pylon above this door and tell me if you can see aught."

Kemmah went, climbing a narrow stair in the dark, and presently found herself on the roof of the pylon some thirty feet above the ground, where in times of trouble a watchman was stationed. Round it ran a battlement with openings through which arrows could be shot or spears thrown. The moon shone brightly, flooding the palace gardens and the great city beyond them with silver light, but the Nile she could not see because of the roofs behind her, though she heard the distant murmur of those who kept festival upon its waters, from which they would not return until the sun had risen.

Presently in the shadow of one of the great gateways she saw a group of men standing and, as it seemed to her, taking counsel together. They moved out of the shadow and she counted them. They were eight in all, armed every one of them, for the light shone upon their spears. They came to some decision, for they began to walk across the open court towards the private door of the royal apartments. Kemmah ran down the stairs and told Ru what she had seen.

"Now were I standing on that roof perhaps I might put a javelin into one or more of these night birds before they come to the doors," he said.

"Nay," answered Kemmah. "They may be messengers of peace, or soldiers who will guard the Queen. Wait to smite till they show themselves otherwise."

He nodded and said:

"Yonder door is old and not of the strongest. It can soon be battered in and then perhaps there will be fighting—one man against eight, Lady Kemmah. What if aught should happen to me, Lady Kemmah? Is there any other way by which the Queen and the royal babe may escape?"

"Nay, for the doors into the great hall where the Council are held are barred; I have tried them. There is no way save by leaping from the palace wall at the back, and a babe's bones are tender. Therefore, Ru, nothing must happen to you. Pray the gods to give you strength and cunning."

"Of the first I have plenty, of the second I feat but little. Still I will do my best and may Osiris be good to him on whom my axe falls."

"Hearken, Ru. Should you scotch those snakes or cause them to run, make ready to fly with us and be not astonished if instead of a Queen and a waiting-lady, you see two peasant women and a peasant's babe."

"I am not easily astonished, Lady, and I weary of this Thebes since the good god my master fell and all these upstarts began to plot with Apepi, as plot they do. But whither will you fly?"

"I think that a ship waits us by the private quay, and its captain, one Tau, will meet us two hours before the dawn, that is before so very long, in the shadow of the old shrine. You know the place."

"Aye, I know it. Hush! I hear footsteps."

"Parley with them as long as you may, Ru, for there are things to be done."

"Yes, there is plenty to be done," he answered as she fled back through the curtains.

The Queen woke at her step.

"Your gods have not come, Kemmah," she said, "or given any sign. So I suppose it is fated that we should stop here."

"I think that the gods—or devils—are coming, Queen. Now off with those robes and be swift. Nay, talk not, I pray, but do as I bid you."

Rima glanced at her face and obeyed. Within a very little time, all being prepared to their hands, the three of them were changed into farmer women and a farmer's babe. Then Kemmah took a sack and thrust into it all the ancient priceless jewels, the regalia of the old Pharaohs of Egypt, and these were not few; also a sum in gold.

"This gear of crowns and sceptres and gems and gold which you have got together so carefully will be too heavy for us to carry, Kemmah, who have that which is more precious to bear between us," and she glanced at the child.

"There is one yonder who will carry it, Queen, one who carried something else on his shoulder out of the battle. Or if he cannot, then I think it will not matter who takes the gathered wealth of the Pharaohs of the South."

"You mean that our lives are at hazard, Kemmah?"

"That is what I mean, no less."

Rima's beautiful but sorrow-stricken face and eyes seemed to take fire.

"I would that they might be lost," she said. "Have you ever thought, Friend, of the wonderful things that may lie behind the gates of death, the glories and the harmonies and the eternities, or failing these, the rich darkness of everlasting sleep? Life! I weary of life and would put all to the hazard. Yet there is the babe born of my body, the Royal Princess of Egypt, and for her sake——"

"Yes," said the quiet Kemmah, "for her sake!"

****

There came a thunder of noise upon the door beyond the curtains.

"Open!" shouted voices.

"Open for yourselves. But know that death waits those who would violate her Majesty of Egypt," answered the deep guttural voice of Ru.

"We come to take the Queen and the Princess to those who will guard them well," cried one without.

"What better guard can they have than death?" asked Ru in answer.

There was a pause. Then came blows upon the door, heavy blows as of axes, but still it held. Another pause and a tree trunk or some such weighty thing was brought and driven against it, and presently with a crash it fell, burst from its hinges. Rima seized the child and ran into the shadows. Kemmah leapt to the curtains and stood there looking between them, the spear she carried raised in her right hand. This was what she saw.

The giant Nubian stood on the topmost stair in the shadow, for the light of the lamps in the niches struck forward. In his right hand he held a javelin, in his left he grasped the handle of his battle-axe and a small shield made of the hide of a river horse. Grim and terrible looked the Ethiopian giant outlined thus against the shadow.

A tall man with a sword in his hand scrambled over the fallen door, the moonlight shining on his armour. The javelin flashed and the man fell in a heap, his mail clattering upon the bronze hinges of the door. He was dragged aside. Others rushed in, a number of them. Ru shifted his battle-axe into his right hand, lifted it, leaned forward and waited, advancing the shield to cover his head. Blows fell upon the shield. Then the axe crashed down and a man sank in a heap. Ru began to sing some wild Ethiopian war chant and as he sang he smote, and as he smote men died beneath the blows of that terrible axe driven with the weight of his mighty arm. Yet they pressed forward, for they were desperate. Death might be in front of them, but if they failed death was also behind at the hands of their confederates.

The stair was too wide for Ru to cover. One ran under his arm and appeared between the curtains, where he stood staring. Kemmah saw his face. It was that of a great Theban lord who had fought with Kheperra in the battle and now had been suborned by the Shepherds. Rage seized her. She sprang at him and with all her strength drove the spear she held through his throat. He fell, gasping. She stamped upon his face, crying, "Die, dog! Die, traitor!" and die he did.

On the stairway the blows grew fewer. Presently Ru appeared, laughing and red with blood.

"All are dead," he cried, "save one who fled. But where is the knave who slipped past me?"

"Here," answered Kemmah, pointing to a still form in the shadows.

"Good. Very good!" said Ru. "Now I think better of women than ever I did before. Yet, hurry, hurry! One dog has escaped and he goes to call the pack. What is that? Wine? Give me to drink. Aye, give me wine and a cloak to cover me. I am no seemly sight for queens to look on."

"Are you hurt?" said Kemmah as she brought the goblet.

"Nay, not a scratch; still no seemly sight, though the blood be that of traitors. Here's to the gods of vengeance! Here's to the hell that holds them! This garment is scant for one of my size, but it will serve. What's that sack you drag to me?"

"No matter what it is. Carry it, Ru. You are no warrior now, you are a porter. Carry it, O glorious Ru, and lose it not, for in it lie the crowns of Egypt. Come, Queen, the road is clear, thanks to the axe of Ru."

Rima came, bearing her babe, and at the sight of the red stair and of those who lay upon it or at its foot, shrank back and said in a wavering voice, for she was almost bemused with doubts and terror:

"Is this the message of your gods, Kemmah?" and she pointed to the stains upon the floor and walls. "And are these their messengers? Look at them! I know their faces. They were the friends and captains of dead Kheperra, my lord. Why, O Ru, do you slay the friends of him who was Pharaoh, who came here doubtless to lead me and his child to safety?"

"Aye, Queen," said Kemmah, "to the safety of death or of the prison of Apepi."

"I'll not believe it, woman, nor will I go with you," said Rima, stamping her foot. "Fly if you will, as well you may do with all this blood upon your hands; here I stay with my child."

Kemmah glanced at her, then as though in thought she looked down at the ground while Ru whispered in her ear:

"Command me and I will carry her."

The eyes of Kemmah fell upon that great lord whom she had slain with her own hand, and she noted that from beneath his breastplate there projected the end of a papyrus roll that had been thrust upwards when he fell. She bent down and took it. Opening it swiftly she read, as she who was learned could do well enough. It was addressed to the dead man and his companions and sealed with the seals of the high priest and others. This was the writing:

"In the names of all the gods and for the welfare of Egypt, we command you to take Rima the Babylonian, wife of the good god Pharaoh who is not, and her child, the Royal Princess Nefra, and to bring them to us, living if may be, that they may be delivered to King Apepi in fulfilment of our oath. Read and obey."

"Can you read the Egyptian writing, Queen?" asked Kemmah. "If so, herein is a matter that concerns you."

"Read you. I have little skill," answered Rima indifferently.

So she read, slowly, that the words might sink into the mind of the Queen. Rima heard and leaned against her, trembling.

"Why did I ever come to this land of traitors?" she moaned. "Oh! would that I were dead."

"As you will be if you stay here longer, Queen," said Kemmah bitterly. "Meanwhile it is the traitors who are dead, or some of them, and now tell their tale to Kheperra, your lord and mine. Come. Come swiftly, there are more villains left in Thebes."

But Rima sank to the ground, swooning. As she fell Kemmah snatched the child from her and looked at Ru.

"It is good," said the giant. "Now she can talk no more and I will carry her. But what of that sack? Must we leave it behind? Life is more than crowns."

"Nay, Ru, set it on my head, for thus peasants bear their burdens. I can hold it with my left hand and clasp the child with my right."

He did so and lifted the Queen in his great arms. Thus they passed down the stair, stepping over the dead and out into the night.

Across the open space they went, heading for the palm trees of the garden. The babe wailed feebly but Kemmah stifled its cries beneath her cloak. The weight of the treasures in the sack pressed her down and the sharp edges of the jewelled crowns and sceptres cut into her brow. Still she staggered on bravely. They reached the shadow of the palms where she paused for a moment to look back and get her breath. Behold! Men—numbers of them—were running toward the doors of the private apartments.

"We did not leave too soon. Forward!" said Ru.

On they went, till at length before them in the glade they saw the ruined shrine. Kemmah staggered to it and sank to her knees, for she was spent.

"Now, unless help comes, there is an end," said Ru. "Two half-dead women I might carry, also the sack upon my head. But how about the babe? Nay, that babe is the Princess of Egypt. Whoever dies, she must be saved."

"Aye," said Kemmah faintly. "Leave me, it matters not, but save the child. Take her and her mother and go to the quay. Perchance the boat is there."

"Perchance it is not," grumbled Ru, staring about him.

Then help came. For as before from behind a palm appeared the sailor Tau.

"You are somewhat early, Lady Kemmah," he said, "but fortunately so am I and so is the down Nile wind. At least here you are, all three of you. But who is this?" and he stared at the giant Nubian.

"One who can be vouched for," answered Ru. "If you doubt it, go look at the stair of the royal apartments. One, too, who, if there be need, can break your bones as a slave breaks sticks."

"That I can well believe," said Tau, "but of bone-breaking we can talk afterwards. Now follow me, and swiftly."

Then he threw the sack over his shoulder, and putting his arm about Kemmah, supported her forward to the quay. At the foot of the steps was a boat, and at a distance on the Nile appeared a ship riding at anchor, her sail half hoisted. They entered the boat, and seizing the oars Tau rowed them to the ship. A rope was cast which he caught and made fast to the prow of the boat, drawing on it till they came alongside the ship. Hands were stretched out to help them; soon they were all aboard.

"Up anchor!" cried Tau, "and hoist the sail."

"We hear you, Lord," answered a voice.

Three minutes later that ship was gliding down the Nile before the strong south wind. Nor was it too soon, for as they passed silently into the night they caught sight of men, some of whom bore lanterns, searching the palm grove that they had left. They laid the women and the child in the cabin. Then Tau said:

"Now, Breaker of Bones, you may have a tale to tell me, and perchance a cup of wine and a bite of food will loose your tongue."

****

Thus did Queen Rima, Nefra, Royal Princess of Egypt, and Lady Kemmah and Ru the Ethiopian escape from Thebes and from the hands of traitors.

CHAPTER 4

The Temple of the Sphinx

For day after day the ship of Tau journeyed on down Nile. At night, or when the wind would not serve, it was tied up to the bank, always in as uninhabited a place as might be but never near a town. Twice this happened in the neighbourhood of great temples that had been wrecked by the Shepherds in the first fury of their invasion and not as yet repaired. Yet after it was dark, out of these desolated fanes or of the sepulchres around them issued men who brought food and other things to sell, but who from the signs that they made, Kemmah, being initiated, well knew to be priests, though of what faith she did not know. These men would talk with Tau apart, showing him much reverence, then on this pretext or on that he would bring them into the cabin where the infant princess lay asleep, whom they would look upon fearfully, and even adore upon their bended knees as though she were divine; then rising, depart blessing her in the names of the gods they worshipped. Moreover, never did they seem to take payment for the food they brought.

All of these things Kemmah noted, as did Ru, although he appeared so simple, but of them Rima the Queen took but little heed. Ever since her lord the Pharaoh Kheperra had been slain in the battle, her spirit had left her, and the discovery of the treason of the lords who had been his counsellors and generals, whereof Ru had slain six and Kemmah one in the fight upon the stairs of the Theban palace, seemed to have crushed her very soul so that now she cared for nothing save to nurse her child.

When she woke from her swoon to find herself upon the ship she asked few questions and from Ru she shrank, although she loved him well, saying that he smelt of blood. Nor would she speak much to Tau because, as she declared, she trusted no man any more. To Kemmah only did she talk freely at times, and then mostly as to how she might escape out of this accursed Egypt with her child, back to her royal father, the King of Babylon.

"So far the gods of Egypt have not served you so ill, Queen," said the Lady Kemmah, "seeing that they brought you and that Royal One"—and she waved her hand toward the babe—"out of the net of traitors, and when escape seemed impossible, safe on to this ship, doing this after you had declared that you had no faith in them."

"Mayhap, Kemmah. Yet those gods decreed that my royal husband should be killed and that those whom he and I trusted should prove themselves the foulest of all men who sought to betray his wife and child into the hands of enemies, whence we were saved only by your wit and the strength and courage of an Ethiopian. Also it is not for me, a stranger, that they work, but for Egypt's royal seed that was born of my body. Nor is this to be wondered at, seeing, although as Pharaoh's wife I made offerings upon their altars, they are no gods of mine. I tell you that I would get me back to Babylon and ere I die bow my knee again in the temples of my forefathers. Take me back to Babylon, Kemmah, where men are not traitors to the bread they eat and do not strive to sell the seed of those who died for them into captivity or death."

"This I will do if I may," answered Kemmah, "but alas! Babylon is far off and all the lands between are ablaze with war. Therefore take heart, Queen, and wait with patience."

"I have no heart left," answered Rima, "who desire but one thing—to find my lord again whether he sits at the table of your Osiris, or rides the clouds with Bel, or sleeps in the deep darkness. Where he is, there would I be and nowhere else, and least of all in this accursed Egypt. Give me my child to nurse, that I may hold her while I may. We love that most that we must leave the soonest, Kemmah."

Then Kemmah gave her the babe and turned away to hide her tears, since she was sure that sorrow was eating out the life of this bereaved widow and daughter of kings.

Once when they were off Memphis which they strove to pass at early dawn before men were abroad, there was danger. Officers came to their ship from a boat, bidding it lie to, a command that Tau thought it best to obey.

"Now play your parts well," he said to Kemmah, "remembering that you are my sister and that the Queen is my wife who lies sick. Go tell her to forget her woes and be as crafty as a serpent. As for you, Ru, hide that great axe of yours, though where you can find it easily, remembering that you are a slave whom I bought for a great sum in Thebes that I may make money by showing off your strength in market-places, and that you can talk little or no Egyptian."

The boat came alongside. In it were two officers, young men who seemed to be sleepy, for they yawned, and a common fellow who rowed it. The two officers climbed to the deck and asked for the captain. Tau appeared, very roughly clad, and in a coarse voice inquired of their business.

"It is your business that we want to know, Sailor," said one of the officers.

"That is easy to tell, sir. I am a trader who take corn up Nile and bring cattle down. There are a number of calves forward there, bred by the best southern bulls. Are you perchance buyers? If so, you might like to look at them. There is one that has the *apis* marks upon it, or something of the kind."

"Do we look like cattle dealers?" asked the officer haughtily. "Show me your writings."

"Here they are, sir," and Tau produced a papyrus sealed by the trade masters at Memphis and other cities.

"A wife and child, a sister—which means another wife grown old—and so many crew. Well, we seek two women and a child, so perhaps we had better see them."

"Is it necessary?" asked the other. "This does not look like a queen's warship such as we were told to search for, and the stench of those calves is horrible after a night of feasting."

"Warship, sir? Did you talk of a warship? Well, there is one following us down the river. We saw her once, but being of such deep draught, she got stuck on a sand bank so that I do not know when she will reach Memphis. She seemed to be a very fine ship with a multitude of armed men on board of her. But it was said that she was going to stop at Siout, the frontier city of the South, or what used to be its frontier city before we beat those proud-stomached Southerns. But come and look at the women, if you will; come and look at them."

This information about the warship seemed to interest the two officers so much that they followed Tau thinking little of the two women. He took a lantern and thrust it through the curtains into the cabin, saying;

"May an evil spirit take this thing! How badly it burns."

"An evil stink has taken it already," answered one of the officers, pinching his nostrils between his finger and thumb as he peered between the curtains. In the low light the place was very dark and all that the officers could see was Kemmah in dirty garments seated on a sack—little did they know that this sack contained the ancient and priceless royal ornaments of Upper Egypt—and engaged in mixing milk and water in a gourd, while beyond on a couch lay a woman with dishevelled hair and holding a bundle to her breast.

Just then the lantern went out and Tau began to talk of finding oil to relight it.

"It is needless, Friend," said the chief officer, "I think that we have seen enough. Pursue your voyage in peace and sell the calves at the best price you can get."

Then he turned to the deck where, as ill luck would have it, he caught sight of Ru squatted on the boards and trying to look as small as he could.

"That is a big black man," he said. "Now did not some spy send a message about a Negro who killed many of our friends up yonder? Stand up, fellow."

Tau translated, or seemed to do so, and Ru stood up, rolling his big eyes till the white showed and grinning all over a silly face.

"Ah!" said the officer, "a very big man. By the gods! what a chest and arms. Now, Captain, who is this giant and what are you doing with him on board your trading boat?"

"Lords," answered Tau, "he is a venture of mine in which I have put most of my savings. He is mighty and performs feats of strength, for the sight of which I hope to get much money down in Tanis."

"Does he?" said the officer, much interested but with suspicion. "Well, fellow, perform a feat of strength."

Ru shook his head vaguely.

"He does not understand your tongue, sir, who is an Ethiopian. Stay, I will tell him."

Then he began to address Ru in unknown words. Ru woke up and nodded, grinning. Next instant he sprang at the two officers, seized one of them with either hand by the neckbands of their garments and lifted them from the deck as though they had been infants. Next, roaring with laughter, he stepped to the side of the ship and held them out over the Nile as though he were about to drop them into the water. The officers shouted, Tau swore and tried to drag him back, yelling orders into his ear. Ru turned round astonished, still holding the two men in the air before him and looking at the belly of the ship as though he meant to throw them into it.

At length he seemed to understand and dropped them to the deck, on which they fell flat.

"That is one of his favourite tricks, sirs," said Tau as he helped them to their feet. "He is so strong that he can carry a third man in his teeth."

"Is it?" said an officer. "Well, we have had enough of your savage and his tricks, who, I think, will land you in prison before you have done with him. Keep him off now while we get into the boat."

Thus was the ship of Tau searched by the officers of Apepi.

****

When the boat had gone and once more the ship was slipping past the quays of Memphis unobserved in the mists drawn by the rising sun from the river, Ru came near to the tiller and said:

"I think, Lord Tau, for a lord or count I hold you to be, although it pleases you to pass as the owner of a small trading boat, that you would have done well to let me drop those two fine fellows into the Nile that tells no stories of those it buries. By and by it will be found that there is no warship such as you talked of so wonderfully, and then——?"

"And then, Breaker of Bones, it may go hard with those officers who chattered of such a ship like finches in the reeds and while they did so let the real prize slip through their fingers. For this, indeed, I am sorry, since those young men were not bad fellows in their way. As for dropping them into the Nile, it might have been well enough, though cruel, had there not been a witness. What would that boatman who rowed them to the ship have reported when he found that they returned from it no more?"

"You are clever," said Ru admiringly. "I never thought of that."

"No, Ru. If my brain were added to your brute strength and un-instructed honesty, why, you would rule the world of brutes. But they are not, and therefore you must be content to serve in the yoke, like a bull, which is as strong as you are, or stronger."

"If it is brains that make a difference, why do you not rule, Lord Tau, who are also a likely man though not so big as I am? Why are you carrying fugitives upon a dirty little merchant ship instead of sitting upon a Pharaoh's throne? Tell me, who am but a simple black man bred to war and honesty."

Tau with much skill steered his ship through a fleet of barges pol-ing up Nile laden with fodder. Then calling to a sailor to take his place, for now the river was open with no craft in sight, he sat himself down in the low bulwark, and answered:

"Because mayhap, friend Ru, I also choose to serve. Being stupid, like most honest men, especially if they are strong and one of a simple

38

race that understands nothing except love from which is born mankind, and war that keeps down its numbers, you may not believe me when I tell you that the only true joy in life lies in service of this sort or of that. Pharaohs are served, which is why they are often so blind and so satisfied at being but vain bubbles blown along by a wind they cannot see, springing, although they know it not, from the poisoned breaths of multitudes; for the most part they do more harm than good and are themselves the slaves of slaves. With him who serves it is otherwise, for, setting aside self-seekings and ambitions, he works humbly for that which is good and in this work finds his reward."

Ru rubbed his brow, then asked:

"But whom does such an one serve, Lord?"

"He serves God, Ru."

"God? There are many gods that I have heard of in Ethiopia, in Egypt, and in other lands. What god does he serve and where does he find that god?"

"He finds him in his own heart, Ru, but what his name may be I cannot tell you. Some call it Justice, some call it Freedom, some call it Hope, some call it Spirit."

"And what do those call it who serve only themselves and their own lusts, careless of all those fine things, Lord?"

"I do not know, Ru, and yet I know that name. It is Death."

"Yet they live as long as other men, Lord, and often reap a finer harvest."

"Aye, Ru, but very soon their day is done and then, if they have not repented, their souls die."

"So you believe that souls can live on, as the priests seem to teach."

"Yes, Ru, I believe that they can live longer than Ra the sun himself, longer than the stars, and from age to age reap the fruits of honest service. Yet of these matters do not ask me but ask one whom you will soon meet and whose disciple I am."

"I don't wish to, Lord, seeing that my brain swims already, but tell me, if it please you, to what end is all this service of yours that causes you to sail up Nile and at great risk to rescue certain ladies and a certain babe?"

"I am not sure, for true service is its own end. Moreover, it is not for me to ask of ends, who am sworn to obey without doubt or question."

"So you also have a master, Lord. Who is he?"

"That you will learn ere long, Ru. Yet do not think to look upon some king or enthroned high priest surrounded with pomps and ceremonies. Ru, I will instruct you, who are so ignorant. Doubtless you

39

believe that Egypt and the world are ruled by the strength you see, by Pharaohs, by armies, and by wealth. Yet it is not so. There is another strength you do not see which is its guide and conqueror, and its name is Spirit. The priests teach that to every man there is given a *Ka* or a double, an invisible something that is stronger, purer, more enduring than he is. Something that perhaps from time to time looks upon the face of God and whispers of God's will. Now if this be a parable, yet in a sense it is true since always such a spirit is at the elbow of everyone who lives. Or rather there are two spirits, one of good and one of evil; one that leads upwards and one that leads downwards."

"I say again that you make my head swim, Lord. But tell me, where and to what is your spirit leading you?"

"Towards the gates of peace, Ru; peace for myself and peace for Egypt; towards a land where you would find little occupation for in it there is no war. Look, yonder are the Great Pyramids, the homes of the dead, and mayhap of their souls which do not die. Come, help me lower the sail since we must drift past them slowly, to return when night has fallen and land certain passengers. There, perhaps, Ru, you will learn more of the meaning of all this talk of mine."

****

Night had come. At its approach he who was called Tau had rowed his ship back to a certain landing place which now, at the time of the rising Nile, was not so very far away from the Great Pyramids and the Sphinx that sits near to them staring eternally into nothingness. Here they disembarked, all of them, under shelter of the darkness and of a bed of reeds.

Scarcely were they on shore when they saw boats, which great lanterns hung at their prow and stern showed to be full of armed men, rowing down Nile. Tau watched them go by and said:

"I think some messenger has told those officers at Memphis that there was no warship following us from Thebes and that now they search for a certain trading boat on which travelled two women and a babe. Well, let them search, for the birds are out of their hands and where they nest no Shepherd will dare to come."

Then, having given directions to the mate of the boat, a very quiet, secret-faced man, as were all those on board of her, he took Rima the Queen by the hand and led her into the darkness, being followed by Kemmah, who bore the child, and by Ru the Ethiopian, who carried upon his shoulder the sack that contained the jewels of the Pharaohs of Upper Egypt.

For a long while they trudged forward, first between groves of palm trees and then over desert sands, till at length the waning moon rose and they saw a wondrous sight. In front of them appeared the enormous shape of a lion cut from the living rock whose face was not that of a beast but of a man, wearing the headdress of a god or king, and staring towards the east with solemn, terrifying eyes.

"What is that?" asked Rima faintly. "Have we reached the Underworld and is this its god? For surely yonder dreadful smiling countenance must be that of a god."

"Nay, Lady," answered Tau, "it is but the symbol of a god, the Sphinx which has sat here for countless ages. Look! Behind it stand the pyramids outlined against the sky, and beneath it are safety and rest for you and for your child."

"Safety for the child, perhaps," she said, "and for me, as I think, the longest rest of all. For know, O Tau, that Death looks at me out of those solemn smiling eyes."

Tau made no answer; indeed, even his calm spirit seemed to be frightened at those words of evil omen, as was Kemmah, who muttered:

"We go to dwell among sepulchres and it is as well, for I think that soon they will be needed."

Even Ru was frightened, though more by the gigantic figure of the Sphinx towering above him than by the Queen's words, which he scarcely seemed to understand.

"Here is that which turns my heart to water and loosens my knees," he said in his savage imagery. "Here is that with which no man, not even I, can fight, and therefore for the first time I am afraid. Here is Fate itself, and what can man do in the face of Fate?"

"Obey its decrees, as all must," answered Tau solemnly. "Forward now, for the temple of this god is open, and leave the rest—to Fate."

They came to some steps about fifty paces from the outstretched paws of this mighty monument, and descending them, found themselves facing what seemed to be a huge granite block in a wall. Taking a stone which lay at hand, Tau knocked upon this block in a peculiar fashion. Thrice did he repeat this rhythmic series of blows, each time with some difference. Then he waited, and behold, presently in a silent fashion the great stone turned, leaving a narrow opening through which he beckoned them to follow him. They entered to find themselves in dense darkness and to hear sounds as of passwords being given and received. Next lamps appeared floating towards them through the darkness and they perceived that these were borne by men clothed as white-robed priests who yet carried swords like soldiers and wore knives thrust through their girdles. There were six of these priests and a seventh who appeared to be a leader of them, for he walked ahead. To this man Tau spoke, saying:

"I bring you that I went forth to seek," and he pointed to the royal child sleeping in the arms of Kemmah and to the Queen and behind her, to the gigantic Ru on whom the priests looked doubtfully.

Tau began to tell them who he was, but the leader of the priests said:

"It is needless. The Holy Prophet has spoken to me of him. Yet let him understand that he who reveals the secrets of this place dies terribly."

"Is it so?" said Ru. "Well, already I feel as though I were dead and buried."

Then one by one the priests made obeisance to the babe, and this done, motioned to them to follow.

On they went, down a long passage that seemed to be built of blocks of alabaster, till they came to a great hall, of which the roof was supported by huge columns of granite, in which hall sat solemn statues of gods or kings. Crossing it, they reached a gallery, out of which opened chambers that served as dwelling rooms, for in them were window-places, which chambers, it seemed, had been made ready for them, since they were furnished with beds and all things necessary, even to clothing such as women wear. Moreover, in one of them a table was set with good food and wine.

"Eat now and sleep," said Tau. "I go to make report to the Prophet. To-morrow he will speak with you."

CHAPTER 5

The Swearing of the Oath

Early on the following morning Kemmah was awakened by a ray of sunshine striking upon her bed through a window-place in the chamber. *At least we are not dwelling in a tomb*, she thought to herself with gratitude, for tombs have no windows; the dead do not need them.

Then she looked at the Queen Rima who lay in another bed with the babe near by, and saw that she was sitting up, staring before her with rapt eyes.

"I see that you are awake, Kemmah," she said, "for the sun shines upon your eyes, for which I thank the gods because it shows me that we are not in a grave. Hearken, a dream has visited me. I dreamed that the good god my husband, Kheperra who is dead, came to me, saying:

"'Wife, you have accomplished all things; you have brought our child to a place where she will be safe, a holy place where the spirits of those who were great in Egypt before her protect and will protect her. Fear not for the child who is safe in their keeping and in that of those about her on the earth. Make ready, Wife beloved, to return to me, your Husband.'

"'That is my desire,' I answered. 'But tell me, Lord, where shall I find you?'

"Then, Kemmah, in that dream of mine the spirit of King Kheperra showed me a wondrous and beautiful place of which the memory has faded from me, saying:

"'Here shall you find me, where are no wars or fears or troubles, and here shall we dwell together happily for many an age, though, what will chance to us in the end I do not know.'

"'But the child. What of the child?' I asked. 'Must we lose the child?'

"'Nay, Beloved,' he answered, 'presently she will be with us.'

"'Then, Lord, is she also doomed to die to the world before she has known the world?'

"'Not so, Beloved, but here there is no time, and soon her hour there will be accomplished and she will be counted of our company.'

"'Yet she will never know us, Lord, who died when she was without understanding.'

"'The dead know everything; in death all that seems lost is found again; in death all is forgiven, even those priests and princes who would have betrayed you to the Shepherds are forgiven, for some of them whom the axe of Ru sent hither, stand by me and ask pardon of you as I speak. In death are life and understanding. Therefore come hither swiftly and without fear.'

"Then I awoke, happy for the first time since Ru bore the body of King Kheperra out of the battle."

"A strange dream. A very strange dream, Queen. But who can put faith in such visions of the night?" exclaimed Kemmah, for she was frightened and knew not what to say, adding:

"Now rise, if it pleases you, and let me dress you in these garments that have been provided. Afterwards we will call the Lord Tau, for I am sure that he is no sailor man but a lord, and explore this place, which it would seem might be worse, for here are good food and light and friends and dark caverns where we may hope to hide ourselves away if foes should come."

"Aye, Kemmah, I will rise, though it should be for the last time, for I would look upon the face of this wondrous Roi the prophet who has brought us here and then commend my child to him ere I pass farther than he can follow."

"From all that I have heard of Roi I think that would be far indeed, Queen," said Kemmah.

A while later, when they were seated at their morning meal that was served by priestesses who now appeared for the first time, came Tau, praying them to follow him into the presence of Roi, the prophet and his master.

They obeyed, Rima leaning on the arm of Tau, for now she seemed too weak to walk alone, Kemmah bearing the babe, and Ru bringing up the rear. Presently they heard sounds of singing, and entering a great hall lit by little window-places set high up near the roof and by an opening to the East, saw that in it were gathered a number of men and women, all clad in white robes, the men to the right and the women to the left. At the head of the hall was an altar and behind the altar, in a shrine of alabaster, a life-sized statue of Osiris, god of the dead wrapped in the trappings of the dead. In front of this altar in a chair of black stone sat an aged man clad in white priestly garments over which hung strange-shaped, mystical jewels of gold and gems.

He was a wonderful old man, or so thought Ru staring at him with round eyes, for his beard was long and white as snow, his hands were thin as those of a mummy, his nose was hooked and his eyes were black, piercing, and full of fire. Though she had not seen him in the flesh for many years, Kemmah knew him at once to be none other than the king's son, her great-uncle, Roi the Prophet, whose fame for holiness, secret power, and magic was told of throughout Egypt. Indeed, she remembered that just so had he appeared to her in the ruined shrine that was in the palace gardens at Thebes when she sought a sign that Tau was a true messenger and not one who set a trap.

They drew near while all the company stared at them in silence. Suddenly Roi lifted his head, studying them with his piercing eyes, then in a strong, clear voice asked of Tau: "Who are these that you bring into the Chapter of the secret Brotherhood of the Dawn, to enter which without authority is death? Answer, O my son in the spirit."

Thrice Tau made reverence and said:

"O Holy One, O Home of Wisdom, greater than all kings, voice of Heaven upon earth, hear me! On the day of full moon before the last you commanded me, saying:

"'Priest of our Brotherhood, become a merchant. Sail up Nile to Thebes, and before dawn on the day that you reach the ancient city enter the garden of the palace and take your stand behind a palm tree that grows near to a forgotten shrine. There you will find a woman, a nurse of kings in whom my blood runs. Speak to her. Show her this half of a broken talisman, and if she can show its other half, declare to her that you are my messenger charged with a certain mission. Set out that mission, and if she doubts, pray to me, sending your prayer through space, and I will hear you and come to your aid. Then when she doubts no more, fulfil that mission as shall be made clear to you.'

"I heard your commands, O Holy One, and behold! the mission is fulfilled. Before you appear Rima the Babylonian, daughter of Ditanah the King of Babylon and widow of Kheperra, Pharaoh of Upper Egypt; Lady Kemmah, the royal nurse, your kinswoman, and the royal babe Nefra, Princess of Egypt."

"I see them, my son, but what of the fourth, the mighty black man, as to whom I gave no command?"

"This, Father: that without his help sent by the gods none of us would be here to-day, seeing that he held the door against traitors and with that axe of his, slew them all, eight in number."

"Not so, my son, unless my spirit told me falsely, the Lady Kemmah, my kinswoman, slew one of them."

Now Ru, who had been listening amazed, could contain himself no longer.

"That is right, O Prophet, or O God," he broke in, in his big voice. "She killed one of them who slipped past me, their captain as I think, with the shrewdest thrust ever driven by a woman's arm—also another escaped. But your sight must be very good, O Prophet, if you can see from here to Thebes and take note of one blow among so many."

A faint smile flickered on the face of Roi.

"Come hither, Ru, for so I think you are named," he said.

The giant obeyed and of his own accord knelt down before Roi, who went on:

"Hearken, Ru the Ethiopian. You are a gallant man and a true-hearted. You slew those who slew your King Kheperra and bore his body from the battle. By your gift of strength and skill in war you saved your lord's child and the Queen her mother from prison and death. Therefore I number you among our Brotherhood into whose company hitherto no black man has ever entered. Afterwards you shall be instructed in its simpler rites and take the lesser oaths. Yet know, O Ru, that if you betray the smallest of its secrets or work harm to any of your fellow servants of the Dawn, you shall die thus," and leaning forward he whispered fiercely into the Negro's ear.

"Have done, I pray you, Prophet," exclaimed Ru in lively terror and springing to his feet. "I have seen and heard of many things but never of such a one as this, in Ethiopia or in Egypt, in war or in peace. Moreover, such threats are needless, since I never betrayed any one except myself, and least of all those whose bread I eat and whom I love," and he glanced towards the Queen and the child.

"I know it, Ru; yet sometimes folly betrays as well as craft. Hearken! You are appointed body servant and guard to the Royal Princess of Egypt as you were to her father before her. Where she goes, there you go; when she sleeps your bed is without her door. If she fights you stand at her side in battle, shielding her with your life. If she wanders by day or by night, you wander with her, and when at last she dies, you die also and accompany her to the Underworld. For this shall be your reward—that the blessing and the strength that are on her shall be on you also, and that you shall serve her to all eternity. Retire."

"I ask no better fate," muttered Ru as he obeyed.

"Kinswoman, bring me the child," said the Prophet.

Kemmah came forward bearing the sleeping babe and at Roi's bidding held it up to be seen of all, whereon everyone in that company bowed the knee and bent the head.

"Brothers and Sisters of the Company of the Dawn, in the person of this child behold your Queen and Egypt's!" cried Roi, and again they bent the knee and bowed the head.

Then he breathed upon the babe and blessed it, making over it certain mystic signs and calling upon gods and spirits to guard it through life and for ever. This done he kissed the infant and handed it back to Kemmah, saying:

"Blessed be you also, O faithful woman. Aye, and you shall be blessed, and later instructed in our mysteries and numbered of our Company. Go in peace."

Now Roi had spoken to all that company save to the chief of them, Rima the Queen, who sat in front of him in a chair that had been given to her, watching him with empty eyes and listening to his words as though they dealt with far-off matters and moved her not. Yet when he had finished she lifted her head, saying:

"Words and blessings for the slave. Words and blessings for the nurse. Words and adoration for the babe in whom run the royal bloods of Egypt and of Babylon. But what words for the Queen and mother, O Prophet, at whose bidding she and that which was born of her have been brought to this darksome place and habitation of conspirators plotting to ends unknown?"

Now Roi arose from his throne before the altar, a tall, ethereal shape, and advancing to the stricken queen lifted her hand and kissed it.

"For your Majesty I have no message," he said, bending his venerable head, "seeing that already you hold communion with one who is greater than I," and he turned and bowed to the solemn statue of the god Osiris which stared at them from beyond the altar.

"I know it," she answered with a sad smile.

"Yet," he went on, "it is reported to me that in this night that is gone, your Majesty dreamed a dream. Is it not so?"

"It is so, Prophet, though who told you I do not know."

"It matters not who told me. What matters is that I am charged to say to your Majesty that this dream was no fantasy bred of human hopes and longings but the very truth. Learn, O Queen, that this world and its sufferings are but a shadow and a show, and that beyond them, like the pyramids towering above the sands and palm trees at their base, stands the eternal verity whose name is Love. The sands are blown away and having borne their fruit, the palm trees are torn up by the tempest or grow old and die, but the pyramids remain."

"I understand and I thank you, Prophet. Now lead me hence for I am weary."

****

On the third night from this day Rima the Queen, knowing that the fever which consumed her had done its work and that the time was at hand for her to bid farewell to the world, sent a messenger to Roi the Prophet saying that she would speak with him. He came and she addressed him thus:

"I know not who you are nor what is this Brotherhood of the Dawn of which you speak, and to what ends it works, nor why you have brought the Royal Princess hither, nor what gods you serve, I who take but little count of the gods of Egypt, although it is true that when my child was born two of them seemed to appear to me in a vision. Yet I will add this: my heart tells me that you are a most righteous man and a prophet of power appointed by Fate to fulfil its will; also that you and those about you plan good and not ill for the Princess, who, if there is justice in the world, should one day be Queen of Egypt. There then I leave this matter in the hands of Heaven; I, who, having done all that I can do, find myself dying, unfortunate and powerless. Those things will happen which must happen and there is no more to be said.

"Now I demand an oath of you, Roi, and of the priest Tau, and of all the Brotherhood under you. It is that when I am dead you will embalm my body with all the skill of the Egyptians, and that afterwards, when there is opportunity, you will cause it to be conveyed to Ditanah, the King of Babylon, my father, or to him who sits in his place, with these my dying words written in a scroll on its breast, accompanied, if may be, by my daughter, the Royal Princess of Egypt.

"I demand an oath of you, further, that those who bear my body shall say to the King of Babylon that I, the dead daughter of Babylon, aforetime wife of the King of Egypt, call upon him in the name of our gods and by our common blood to avenge the wrongs that I have suffered in Egypt and the death of my lord beloved, my husband, King Kheperra. I call upon him under the pain of the curse of my spirit, to roll down in his might upon Egypt and to smite these Shepherd dogs who slew my husband and took his heritage, and to establish my daughter, the Princess Nefra, as Queen of Egypt, and to seize those who were traitors to her and would have given her to doom and me with her, and to slay them. This is the oath which I demand of you."

48

"Yet, Queen," answered Roi, "it is one that is little to my liking, seeing that if fulfilled it may breed war and that we, the sons and daughters of the Dawn—for Harmachis whose image is the Sphinx that watches at our door, is the god of Dawn—seek peace and not war. Forgiveness, not vengeance, is the law we follow. It is true that if may be we desire to depose the usurping Shepherd kings and to restore Egypt to the line of its rightful rulers, of whom the Princess Nefra is the heir, or if as yet this is refused to us by the gods, to unite the North and South so that Egypt may grow greater and cease to bleed from the wounds of war."

"That is what the Shepherds seek also," said Rima faintly.

"Aye, but their ends are other than ours. They would rivet a yoke upon the neck of Egypt; we would loose that yoke and not by the sword. The Shepherds are many, but the people of Egypt are more, and if the two races can be mingled, then the good Nile wheat which we sow will smother the foreign Shepherd weeds. Already something has been done; already these Shepherd kings bend the knee to the gods of Egypt whose altars once they overthrew, and accept Egypt's laws and customs."

"It may be so, Prophet, and in the end all may come about as you desire. But I am of blood different from that of you soft Egyptians and I have suffered grievous wrong. My husband has been slain; those whom he trusted have striven to sell me and my child to slavery and therefore I seek for the justice that I shall never see. Not with soft words and far-sighted plottings would I win that justice, but with spears and arrows. My body is weak and I am near my end, but my soul is aflame. I know, moreover, that all your hopes are centred on this child of mine, as are my own, and my spirit tells me how they may best be brought to harvest. Will you swear the oath? Answer, and quickly. For if you will not swear, mayhap I may find another counsel. What if I take the babe with me, Prophet, to plead our cause in the Courts above, as I think I can still find the means to do?"

Now Roi considered her, reading her mind, and saw that it was desperate.

"I must take counsel of that which I serve," he answered. "Perchance It will give me wisdom."

"And what if I and mayhap another die while you are taking counsel, Prophet? You think that you can remove the babe, who do not know that a mother's will is very strong and that we Babylonians have secrets of our own, especially at the hour of death, with which we have the power to draw after us those who are born of our bodies."

"Fear not, Queen Rima. I, too, have my secrets, and I tell you that Osiris will not take you yet."

"I believe you, Prophet. On such a matter you would not lie. Go, take counsel with your gods and come back quickly."

"I go," he said, and went.

A little before the hour of dawn Roi returned to that death chamber and with him came Tau, also she who was the first priestess of the Order of the Dawn. Rima awaited him, supported with pillows upon her bed.

"You spoke truly, Prophet," she said, "seeing that now I am stronger than when we parted yesterday. Yet be swift, for this strength of mine is but as the brightness of a dying lamp. Speak, and shortly."

"Queen Rima," he replied, "I have taken counsel of the Power I serve, who guides my feet here upon the earth. It has been pleased to send an answer to my prayer."

"What answer, Prophet?" she asked eagerly.

"This, Queen: That I, on behalf of the Order of the Dawn over which I rule, and in the presence of those who stand next to me in that order"—and he pointed to Tau and to the priestess—"should take the oath that you desire, since thus our ends can best be brought about, though how they will be accomplished was not revealed. I swear, therefore, in the name of that Spirit who is above all gods, also by your *Ka* and mine, and by the child who here and now we take for queen, that when there is opportunity, which I think will not be for many years, your body shall be borne to Babylon and your message delivered to its king, if may be—by your daughter's lips. Moreover, that nothing may be forgotten, all your desire and this oracle are upon this roll which shall be read to you and sealed by you as a letter to the King of Babylon, and with it our oath, sealed by me and by Tau who comes after me."

"Read," said the Queen. "Nay, let the Lady Kemmah, who is learned, read."

So with some help from Tau, Kemmah read.

"It is truly written," said Rima. "There on the roll the matter is set out well and clearly. Yet, add this—that if my father, the royal Ditanah the King, or he who sits upon his throne after him, denies this my last prayer, then I call down the curse of all the gods of Babylon upon his people, and that I, Rima, will haunt him while he lives and ask account of him when we meet at last in the Underworld."

"So be it," said Roi, "though these words are not gentle. Yet write them down, O Tau, for the dying must be obeyed."

So Tau sat himself upon the floor and wrote upon his knee. Then wax mixed with clay was brought and drawing from her wasted finger a ring on which was cut the figure of a Babylonian god, Rima pressed it on the wax, while Kemmah took a scarab from her breast and sealed as witness.

"Set one copy of this roll with the ring among the wrappings of my mummy that the King of Babylon may find it there, and hide the other in your most secret place," said Rima.

"It shall be done," said Roi, and waited.

At this moment the first rays of the rising sun shot like arrows through the window-place. With a strange strength Rima took her child and held her up so that the golden light fell full upon her.

"The Queen of the Dawn!" she cried. "Behold her kissed and crowned of the Dawn. O Queen of the Dawn, rule on triumphant through the perfect day, till night brings you to my breast again."

Then she embraced the child, and beckoning to Kemmah, gave it into her arms. A moment later, murmuring, "My task is done. My Lord awaits me," she fell back and died.

CHAPTER 6

Nefra Conquers the Pyramids

Strange, very strange indeed was the book of Life as it opened itself to the child Nefra, Royal Princess of Egypt. Looking back in after years to those of her infancy, all she could remember was a vision of great pillared halls, where stone images stared at her and the carved or painted walls were full of grotesque figures which seemed to pursue each other everlastingly from darkness into darkness. Then there were visions of white-robed men and women who from time to time gathered in these places and sang sad and mellow chants, of which the echoes haunted her sleep from year to year. Also there was the stately shape of the Lady Kemmah, her nurse whom she loved well yet feared a little, and that of the gigantic Ethiopian named Ru, who always seemed to be about her day and night, carrying a great bronze axe in his hand, whom she loved entirely and feared not at all.

Foremost among them, too, was the awful apparition of an aged man with a white beard and black, flashing eyes whom she came to know as the Prophet and whom all worshipped as though he were a god. She remembered waking up at night and seeing him bending over her, a lantern in his hand, or in the daytime meeting her in the dark temple passages and passing by with words of blessing. To her childish imagination, indeed, he was not human but a ghost to be fled from; yet a kindly ghost withal, since sometimes he gave her delicious sweetmeats or even flowers that a Brother carried in a basket.

Infancy passed by and there came childhood. Still the same halls were about her, peopled by the same folk, but now, at times, with Kemmah her nurse and guarded by the giant Ru and others, she was allowed to wander outside of them, most frequently after night had fallen and when the full moon shone in the sky. Thus it was that first she came to know the lion shape of the terrible Sphinx, lying crouched upon the desert. In the beginning she was afraid of this stone creature with its human face painted red, its royal headdress, and its bearded chin, though afterwards, when it grew familiar to her, she learned to love that face, finding something friendly in its smile and its great calm eyes that stared at the sky as though they would search out its secrets. Indeed, at times she would sit on the sand, sending Kemmah and Ru to a little distance, and tell it her childish troubles and ask it questions, furnishing the answers for herself, since from the great lips of the Sphinx none ever came.

Then beyond the Sphinx rose the mighty pyramids, three principal ones that pierced the very sky, with temples at the base of them wherein dead kings had once been worshipped, and others that were smaller which, she fancied, must be their children. She worshipped those pyramids, believing that the gods had made them, till Tau, her tutor, told her that they were built by men to be the graves of kings.

"They must have been great kings that had such graves; I should like to look on them."

"Perhaps you will some day," answered Tau, who was a most learned man and her instructor in many things.

Besides herself there were other children of the Order, born of the wedded brothers and sisters. These were formed into a school, Nefra among them, which school was taught by the Instructed among the Brotherhood. Indeed, nearly all of them had learning, for the full members of the Order of the Dawn were no common folk, although their servants and those who tilled the flat lands not far from the Sphinx having their habitations upon the borders of the great Necropolis were, or seemed to be like, any other husbandmen. To look on them, none would have known that they were partakers in mysteries which they were sworn by solemn oaths not to reveal, and indeed never did reveal, even under the fear of death or torture.

Soon Nefra became the head of this school, not because of her rank but for the reason that she was by far the cleverest of all its pupils, and her quick mind drank up knowledge as a dry fleece of wool drinks up the dew. Yet if any visited that school and watched the children listening to the teacher, or seated on their stools, copying the picture-writing of the Egyptians upon potsherds or fragments of papyrus, save that she sat at the head of a line of them and for something different in her face, they would have found nothing to distinguish her from the other little maidens who were her companions. She wore the same plain robe of white, the same simple sandals to protect her feet from stones and scorpions, while her hair was tied with a stem of dried grass into a single tress after just the same fashion. Indeed, it was a rule of the Order that she should carry on her person no robe or ornament which might reveal that she was not as other children were.

Yet the instruction of Nefra did not end with her lessons in this school, for when these were done or in times of holiday she must learn a deeper lore. Tau, accompanied by Kemmah her nurse, would take her to a little private room that once had been the sleeping place of a priest of the temple in ancient days and there teach her many secret things.

Thus he taught her the Babylonian tongue and writing, or knowledge of the movements of the stars and planets, or the mysteries of religion, showing her that all the gods of all the priests were but symbols of the attributes of an unseen Power, a Spirit that ruled everything and was everywhere, even in her own heart. He taught her that the flesh was but the earthly covering of the soul and that between flesh and soul there reigned eternal war. He taught her that she lived here upon the earth to fulfil the purposes of this almighty Spirit that created her, to whom in a day to come she must return, perchance to be sent out again to this or other worlds; though what those purposes might be were not known even by the wisest men who breathed. And while he taught thus and she listened, watching him with eager eyes, sometimes the old prophet Roi would steal into the chamber and listen also, adding a word here or there, then hold out his hand in blessing and steal away.

Thus, though outwardly Nefra was as are other merry children, inwardly her soul opened like a lotus lily in the sun and she was different from them all.

So the years went on till from a child she grew into a maiden, tall and sweet and very fair. It was at this time in her life that Roi himself and Tau, in the presence of Kemmah only, revealed to her who she was, namely, none other than the Royal Princess of Egypt by right of blood and the appointment of Heaven, and told her the story of her father and her mother and of the kings and queens who went before them; also of the divisions in the land.

When she heard these things Nefra wept and trembled.

"Alas! that it should be so," she said, "for now no longer can I be happy. Tell me, holy Father, whom men name Home-of-Spirits that, they say, hold converse with you in your sleep, what can a poor maid do to right so many wrongs and to bring peace where there is but bitterness and bloodshed?"

"Princess of Egypt," said Roi, for the first time giving her her title, "I do not know because it is not revealed to me or to any. Yet it is revealed to me and to certain others that in some way unforeseen you will do these things. Aye, and it was revealed in a dream to your mother, the Queen Rima, when you were born, for in this dream that part of the Universal Spirit whom here in Egypt we know as Mother Isis appeared to her and amongst other gifts gave to you, the royal child, the high name of Uniter of Lands."

Here Kemmah thought to herself that another goddess appeared as well as Isis and gave to this same child different gifts, and though she said nothing Roi seemed to read her thoughts, for he went on:

"As to this dream and certain mysteries by which it was accompanied, the Lady Kemmah, your nurse and instructress, is commanded to inform you; also to show to you the record of all these matters which at that time was written down and sealed, and with it another record of a certain oath which I and others swore to your mother, the Queen Rima, upon her deathbed, concerning a journey which you must make at the appointed time. Enough of these matters. Now I am commanded to tell you that on a day to come which shall be declared when it is known to me, it is our purpose with such state as we can compass, to crown you, standing as you do on the threshold of womanhood, as Queen of Egypt."

"How can that be?" asked Nefra. "Kings and queens are crowned in temples, or so I have been taught, and in the presence of multitudes of courtiers, with pomp and shoutings. But here————" and she looked about her.

"Is not this a temple and one of the most ancient and holiest in Egypt, Nefra?" asked Roi. "And for the rest, listen. We seem to be but a humble Brotherhood, the inhabitants of tombs and pyramids which few dare approach because they hold them haunted and deadly to the life and soul of any stranger who dares to violate their sanctuary. Yet I tell you that this Order of the Dawn is more powerful and more far-reaching than the Shepherd king himself and all those that cling to him, as you will learn shortly when you are sworn of it. Its disciples are everywhere, from the Cataracts of the Nile down to the sea; aye, and in lands beyond the sea, and, as we believe, in Heaven above; and one and all they obey the commands that issue from these catacombs, accepting them as the voice of God."

"Then if so, Holy Prophet, why do you not sit at Tanis openly, instead of in secret in these tombs?"

"Because, Princess, visible power and the trappings of power can only be won by war, and we are sworn to wage no war, we whose empire is of the spirit. It may be that in the end it is decreed that war must be waged and that thus all will be accomplished. Yet it is not our Brotherhood that will lift its banners or, save in self-defence, bring men to their deaths, for we are sworn to peace and gentleness."

"I rejoice to hear it," said Nefra, "and now, Master, I pray you let me go to rest, for I am overwhelmed."

****

A year or more after this day of the revealing of secrets, but before the ceremonies which it foretold, a terrible thing happened to Nefra.

Now it was her custom to wander about the great graveyard that surrounded the pyramids where in their splendid tombs so many of the ancient nobles and princes of Egypt had been laid to rest a thousand years or more before her day, so long ago indeed that none remembered the names of those who slept beneath these monuments. On these wanderings of hers it was her pleasure to go unaccompanied save by her body-servant, Ru, for Kemmah, who now grew aged, had no strength for such rough journeys over tumbled stones and through deep sand.

Moreover, at this time Nefra loved to be alone, that she might find time to think in solitude over all that had been revealed to her as to her history and fate, and the unsought greatness that had been thrust upon her.

Further, being very vigorous in body as she was in mind, she wearied of being cooped up in the narrow precincts of the temple and its neighbourhood and longed for exercise and adventure. By nature she was a climber, one of those who love to scale heights and thence look down upon the world below. Thus it became her pleasure to scramble to the top of great monuments and even of some of the smaller pyramids, which she found she could do with ease, since her feet were sure and no dizziness ever overtook her.

All of these fancies of hers were reported to Kemmah by Ru and others who watched her, and to Roi and Tau by Kemmah when she found that the young princess would not listen to her chidings, but for the first time in her life turned upon her angrily, reminding her that she was no more a child to be led by the hand and would have her way.

These consulted of the matter, and, it would seem, according to their rule, made divination, taking counsel of that Spirit who, as they declared, guided them in all things.

The end of it was that the Prophet Roi bade his great-niece, the Lady Kemmah, to trouble the Princess no more about this business, but to suffer her to walk where it pleased her and to climb what she would, because it was revealed to him that whoever took harm, she would take none.

"It is not wise to thwart her as to such a little thing, Niece," he went on, "seeing that there is no danger to her and none of the Shepherds or other enemies dare to approach this haunted place. Also, she goes forth guarded by Ru to talk, not with any man, but only with her own heart amid the holy company of the dead."

"There are always some who will dare that of which all others are afraid, and who knows whom she may meet and talk with before all is done?" answered Kemmah.

"I have spoken, Niece. Withdraw," said Roi.

So, having triumphed, Nefra, who was young and headstrong, continued her wanderings and indeed did more.

Now there was a family of Arab blood among those who served and were sworn to the Brotherhood of the Dawn, who from generation to generation had been climbers of the pyramids. These men alone, by following certain cracks in their marble casings and clinging to knobs or hollows that had been worn in them by the blowing of sand during hundreds or thousands of years, had the art and courage to come to the crest of every one of them; nor until they had done so were they counted fit to take a wife. With the Sheik of these men Nefra often talked, and for her pleasure at different times he and his sons scaled every one of the pyramids before her eyes, returning safely from their dizzy journey to her side.

"Why cannot I do as you do?" she asked of this sheik at length. "I am light and surefooted, and my head does not swim upon a height; also I have limbs as long as yours."

The Captain of the Pyramids, for so he was commonly called, looked at her, astonished, and shook his head.

"It is impossible," he said. "No woman has ever climbed those stone mountains; that is, except the Spirit of the Pyramids herself."

"Who is the Spirit of the Pyramids?"

"Lady, we know not," he answered. "We never ask her, and when we see her in the full moon upon her journeyings, we veil our faces."

"Why do you veil your faces, Captain?"

"Because if we did not we should go mad, as men have done who looked into her eyes."

"Why do they go mad?"

"Because too much beauty breeds madness, as perchance you may find out one day, Lady," he answered; words that brought the colour to Nefra's brow.

57

"Who and what is this spirit?" she continued hastily. "And what does she do?"

"We are not certain, but the story tells that long, long ago there was a maiden queen of this land who would not marry because she loved some man of a humble station. Now it came about that strangers invaded Egypt, which was weak and divided, and conquered. Then the king of the strangers, seeing the beauty of this queen and that he might build his throne upon a sure foundation, wished to take her to wife, even by force. But she fled from him and in her despair climbed the greatest of the pyramids, he following after her. Reaching its crest she hurled herself thence and was crushed, seeing which faintness took hold of the king, so that he, too, fell to the ground and died. After this they buried both of them in a secret chamber of one of the pyramids—which is not known, but I think it must have been the second since there the spirit is most often seen."

"A pretty tale," said Nefra, "but is that the end of it?"

"Not quite, Lady, since to it hangs a prophecy. It is that when another king follows another Queen of Egypt up the pyramid whence this one fell, whichever it may have been, and there wins her love, the avenging spirit of her who threw herself thence will find rest and no more bring destruction upon men."

"I would see this spirit," said Nefra. "As I am a woman she cannot make me mad."

"Nor being a woman, Lady, do I think that she will appear to you. Nevertheless, it may be her pleasure to possess your soul for her own purposes," he added thoughtfully.

"My soul is my own and no one shall possess it," answered Nefra in anger. "Nor indeed do I believe that there is such a spirit, who think that what you and other foolish men have seen was nothing but a moon-cast shadow travelling among the graves. So tell me no more such idle tales."

"There are one or two mad fellows living among the tombs who know more of that moon-cast shadow than I do, Lady. Still it may be as you say," replied the Sheik, bowing courteously after the ancient fashion of the East to a superior. "Yes, maybe you are right. Have it as you will," and he turned to go.

"Stay," said Nefra, "it is my wish that you who have more skill and knowledge of them than any other man, should teach me to climb those pyramids. Let us begin upon the third, which is the smallest, and at once. The others we can conquer afterwards when I am more accustomed to the work."

Now the man stared at her and began to protest.

"Have you not the commands of the holy prophet Roi and of the Council of the Order to obey me in all things?" asked Nefra presently.

"That is so, Lady, though why we should obey you I do not know."

"Nor do I quite, Captain, seeing that you can climb pyramids and I cannot, and you are therefore greater than I. Still, there are the orders and you know what happens to those who break the commands of the Council. Now let us begin."

The Sheik reasoned and prayed and almost wept, but all that happened was that Nefra exclaimed at last:

"If you are afraid to go up that pyramid, I will go by myself. Then, you know, I may fall."

So the end of it was that the afflicted Sheik summoned his son, a lissom youth who could climb like a goat, bidding him bring with him a long rope made of twisted palm fibre, which rope he fastened round Nefra's slender waist. But now there was more trouble, for Ru, who had been listening to all this talk amazed, asked him what he was doing binding his lady like a slave.

The Sheik explained, while Nefra nodded assent.

"But it cannot be," said Ru. "My duty is to accompany this Noble One everywhere."

"Then, friend Ru," said Nefra, "accompany me up the pyramid."

"Up the pyramid!" said Ru, puffing out his cheeks. "Look at me, I pray you, Mistress, and say whether I am a cat or a monkey that I can climb up a slope of smooth stone from earth to heaven. Ere we had gone the length of that rope I should fall and break my neck. Rather would I fight ten men single-handed than be so mad."

"It is true. I think that you will make no good scaler of stone mountains, friend Ru," said Nefra, surveying the Ethiopian's mighty form which had grown no smaller with the passage of the years. "Now cease from talking, for we waste time. If you cannot go up the pyramid, stand at the bottom of it, just beneath me, and if I slip and fall, catch me as I come."

"Catch you as you come! Catch you as you come!" gasped Ru.

Without more words Nefra went to the foot of the third pyramid, up which the Sheik, who also seemed to be empty of speech, began to mount by the way he knew, having the end of the rope that was about Nefra tied round his middle. She followed him, her feet bare and her robe tucked up about her knees, as he bade her, while after her came his son watching her every movement.

"Hearken, men," groaned Ru. "If you suffer my Lady to slip, you had better stop on that pyramid for the rest of your lives, for if you come down I will kill you both."

"If she slips, we shall slip also. The gods bear me witness that it is no fault of mine," answered the Sheik, who was lying on his face upon the slope of the pyramid.

Now it is to be told that Nefra proved an apt pupil at this game. She had the eye of a hawk, the courage of a lion, and was sure-footed as an ape. Up she went, setting her hands and feet exactly where her guide had done, till they had conquered half the height.

"It is enough for to-day," said the Sheik. "No beginner of our race comes farther at the first trial; that is the rule. Rest here awhile, and then descend. My son will place your feet where they should go."

"I obey," said Nefra, and turned herself round as her guide had done above her, to see nothing beneath her save a sheer gulf of space and Ru, grown small, standing on the sand at the bottom. Then for the first time she grew dizzy.

"My head swims," she said faintly.

"Turn about again," said the Sheik, nor could his quiet voice quite conceal the agony of his fear.

She obeyed, and her strength came back to her, her flesh obeying the will within.

"I am well again," she said.

"Then, Lady, turn once more, for if you do not do so now you never will."

For the second time she obeyed, and lo! she no longer feared the height, the spirit within her had conquered her mortal tremblings. After this the descent was easy, for she could see where to place her hands and feet in the fissures of that hot and shining marble; moreover, the young man beneath, who, knowing every one of them, was able to keep his face to the pyramid, guided her as to where to set them. So they came safely to the ground, where Nefra sat a little while, panting and smiling at Ru who mopped his brow with his robe, his big eyes starting from his head, for never before had he been so frightened.

"Have you had enough of the pyramids, Lady?" asked the Sheik as he loosed the rope from about her.

"By no means," answered Nefra, springing up and clapping her sore hands. "I love the work and never shall I have had enough of them till I can climb them all alone by moonlight, as it is said that you can do."

"Isis, Mother of Heaven!" exclaimed the Sheik, throwing up his hands, "this is no mortal maid; this is a goddess; this is the Spirit of the Pyramids herself appearing in earthly form."

"Yes," said Nefra, "I think that is what I am—the Spirit of the Pyramids. Now will it please you to meet me here to-morrow at the same time, when I hope that we may be able to reach the top of the smallest of them."

Then having put on her sandals, before the unhappy man could answer, she departed at a run followed by Ru, who was so astonished that he could not speak.

****

This was but a beginning, for what Nefra prophesied, that she performed. At this time all the strength of her young and burning nature was directed to one thing only—the mastery of those pyramids. It was a small ambition, yet to her, in the day of her dawning womanhood, it was everything. She had been told that by birth she was Queen of Egypt. It moved her little, for dwelling amid those deserted temples and tombs the royalty of Egypt seemed to her a dream, or at least something far away. But the pyramids were near, and what she desired was to be Queen of the Pyramids which, she was also told, her far-off ancestors had raised up to be their tombs. Moreover, that story of a spirit which haunted them had stirred her. She did not believe in the Spirit, but since youth is credulous over matters that have to do with love, she believed the story. She saw that fair young queen, such a one as she was, who had also learned to climb the pyramids, flying to the top of the tallest of them and thence hurling herself to doom to escape one whom she hated and who had humbled her country to the dust, thus bringing conquered and conqueror to a common doom. Also she found something beautiful, something that touched the heart in the pendant of this story, namely, that in a day to come another young and lovely queen would fly up one of those pyramids pursued by another alien lover, and that there on the verge of dizzy death, their hate would melt in the fires of passion, thus bringing blessings on the land for the rule of which they fought.

As yet Nefra knew nothing of love, still Nature was at work in her, as it is in the smallest child, and she understood something of the meaning of this beautiful fable, and the dim thoughts that sprang from it warmed her sleeping soul. Meanwhile she had but one desire—to achieve that which seemed to be impossible to woman, to conquer the pyramids, not understanding in those days that the thing was an allegory and that she, whose strong spirit could enable her to dare so many dangers and to overcome them with her young body, might also in time come to meet subtler perils and tread them beneath her conquering feet.

Moreover, at this time the desire of prayer and the mystery of communion with That which is above mankind, That which the dwellers upon earth called God, came home to her, not from any teaching of Roi or Tau, but, as it were, out of her own soul. Above all things she yearned for this communion, and there fell upon her one of the strange fancies, some would call them madnesses, which often enough possess those who are passing from childhood into the fullness of life, or from the fullness of life into the twilight that precedes the darkness of death. This was her particular dream, or illusion, or vision of the Truth, that she could best make her prayer and come into closest communion with the Spirit which brooded over her and all the world, in utter solitude upon the summit of those pyramids. It was a folly, perhaps, yet a noble folly. At least in the end she reaped its fruit, for within a year she learned to climb them all and this quite alone.

The Sheik of the Pyramids and his sons who had instructed her, the art and craft of whose family it had been for generations to scale these stone mountains for praise and reward on days of festival, were astonished and abased to see themselves equalled or outpassed in their peculiar business by a mere maiden.

At the beginning of the adventure they had been summoned before the Council of the Order, who had grown alarmed at the reports of Ru and Kemmah as to this vagary which had seized upon one whose life was precious, and asked as to its peril. They replied that there was none for those to whom the gift was given, since not for six generations had a single man among them come to his death from following this business. Yet, they added, that to those who were not of their family, it was fatal, since many had tried to share their secret and its fruits, but all of them had perished miserably, an answer that frightened the Council. Yet because of the revelations of Roi, they did nothing to restrain Nefra, who went her way about the matter and took no harm at all, till at length by day or even by night when the moon was at its full, she could reach the top of any of the pyramids as quickly as the Sheik or his sons.

Then that family abased themselves before her and, gathering together, prayed her to accept the captaincy and leadership of them all, since she had outpassed them all. But Nefra only laughed and said that it was nothing and she would not, and ordered that they should be given rewards such as she had to bestow. Thereafter she had the freedom of the pyramids and was allowed to climb them when and how she liked without the attendance of the Sheik or his sons.

Yet of this at last came trouble.

CHAPTER 7

The Plot of the Vizier

Nefra, as has been said, when the fancy took her made a custom of climbing one or other of the pyramids, generally at the hour of the rising or the setting of the sun, and, standing there upon the topmost flat coping-stones, of praying in that glorious loneliness. Or perchance she would not pray but content herself with looking down upon the world beneath, reflecting the while upon what fortunes it might have to offer her, or on such other matters as come into a maiden's mind.

Now this habit of hers became known, not only among the members of the Order and their dependents, but to many who dwelt or journeyed beyond the boundaries of what was called the Holy Ground, upon which no stranger dared to set his foot. Nor was this strange, seeing that her slender form thus poised between earth and heaven and outlined against the sky at dawn or sunset could be seen from far away, even from the Nile itself when it was in flood. Most held it to be that of the Spirit of the Pyramids herself whose appearance thus heralded trouble in Egypt, for there were few indeed who believed it to be possible that any woman could adventure herself in this fashion, or find the strength and skill to climb up marble like a lizard.

Soon the story of the marvel spread far and wide, and even came to the Court of King Apepi.

One evening Nefra, having climbed the second pyramid in this fashion, descended as usual and because the light was failing chose a somewhat shorter route that brought her to the ground not by the southern face where Ru was waiting to receive her, but just round the angle on that face which looked towards the west where the light of the dying day still shone. Having leapt lightly to the sand, she looked about for Ru and instead of him saw four men approaching her, of whom at first she took little note, thinking in the fading light that these were the Sheik of the Pyramids and his sons who came to inquire of her about the new road she had found upon the western face of this pyramid. So she stood still and they drew near, then hesitated a little as though they were afraid of her, till presently a voice called out:

"Woman or spirit, seize her! Let her not escape us! Think of the great reward and seize her!"

Thus encouraged, with a bound they came at her. Understanding her peril Nefra turned to fly up the pyramid again and already was some feet above the sand when the first of the men caught her by the ankle and dragged her down.

"Ru!" she cried in a clear and piercing voice. "To my aid, Ru. I am snared, Ru!"

Now as it chanced Ru was very near, only just round the angle of the pile indeed, because having lost sight of Nefra in the shadow as she descended, feeling disturbed, he was advancing to the western face where the light was better to discover if perchance she were there. He heard her cry for help; he rushed forward and, turning the corner, saw Nefra on the ground, while round her were the four men, three of them binding her with a rope while the fourth was tying a linen bandage across her face.

With a roar he leapt upon them holding his great axe aloft. He who had the bandage saw him first, a black, gigantic figure whom doubtless he took for some terrible guardian spirit and strove to leap past him and fly. The axe flashed and down he went, dead, cloven through and through. Then the other men who at first thought that a lion had roared, saw also, and for a moment stood amazed. Instantly Ru was on them. Letting fall the axe he gripped the two who were nearest, seizing each of them by the throat. He dashed their heads together, and putting out his mighty strength, cast them far away to right and left in such fashion that where they fell, there they lay, stone dead. The fourth man had drawn a knife either to stab at Ru or to kill Nefra; but when he saw the fate of his fellows all courage left him and, screaming with fear, he let fall the knife and fled away. Ru snatched the knife from the sand and hurled it after him. A yell of pain told him that his aim was true, though because of the shadows he could no longer see the man. Ru would have started in pursuit, but Nefra, struggling from the ground, cried:

"Nay. Bide here, there may be more of them."

"True," he answered, "and the dog has it."

Then, without more words, snatching up Nefra and holding her to his breast with his left arm as though she were but a babe, he found his axe and, without waiting to look at the dead, sped away with her along the western base of the pyramid, till presently they were among tombs where they could be seen no more.

"This is the end of those tricks of yours, Lady," he said roughly, for he was shaking, not with fear, but at the thought of what she had escaped.

"Had it not been for you, it might have been worse," answered Nefra. "Still, I have learned my lesson. Set me down now, O most dear Ru, for my breath has returned to me."

When presently all this tale was told to Kemmah and to the Council of the Order, fear and dismay took hold of them; even Tau the Wise was dismayed. Only Roi the Prophet remained undisturbed.

"The maid will take no harm," he said. "I know it from those who cannot lie, and therefore it is that I have permitted her to follow her fancy as to the climbing of the pyramids, for it is ill to cross or to coop up such a one as she, as it is good that she should learn to look upon the face of dangers and to overcome them. Still, doubtless this is the beginning of perils and henceforward we must be upon our guard."

Then he sent out men to bring in the dead whom Ru had slain and to search for the wounded man and, if he could be found, to capture him alive. This, however, did not happen, for when the light came again of that man there remained only certain bloodstains upon the sand which after a while were lost, showing that he had been able to staunch his hurt, and, by walking upon stones, to leave no tracks behind him.

The dead, however, told their own story, for they were of the Shepherds race and two of them wore garments such as were used in the Court of King Apepi. The third, it would seem, was a guide, though of what people could not be known, seeing that it was on his head that the axe of Ru had fallen, and who could tell aught of whence he came upon whose head the axe of Ru had fallen?

So the bodies of those woman-thieves were thrown to the jackals and the vultures, that their *Kas* might find nothing to inhabit, and their souls with all solemnity were cursed by Roi in a Chapter of the Order, that from age to age they might find no rest because of their double crime. For had they not violated the pact of generations and entered the Holy Ground which was the home of the consecrated Order of the Dawn, and there striven to steal away or perchance to murder a certain lady who in the world without was not known by any name?

Thence the matter ended for a space, except that at dawn or sunset Nefra was no longer seen standing upon the crests of pyramids.

Yet some while later a sick and sorry man with a bandaged back, who from time to time coughed up blood as though from a pierced lung, staggered into the Court at Tanis, where his face was known, and being admitted, told his tale to a great officer, who listened to it wrathfully and commanded a scribe to write it down word for word. When it had finished that officer cursed this man because he had failed in his mission.

"Is it my fault?" asked the man. "Was it right to send those who are born of women to capture a spirit or a witch?—since no maid in whom warm blood flows can run up and down pyramids faced with smooth and shining stone, as flies run up and down a wall, which we saw this one do. Is it right to expect them to fight and overcome a black devil from the Underworld, larger than any who walks the earth, whose voice is the voice of a lion and whose hands can crush skulls as though they were pomegranates? Is it right to command them to enter a haunted place peopled by gods and wizards and the ghosts of the dead? A fool was I to listen to you and your promises of great reward, and fools were my companions, as doubtless they think in the Underworld to-day, for who is there in Egypt that does not know that to violate the Holy Ground of the Order of the Dawn is to court death and damnation? Now give me my price that I may divide it among my children."

"Your price!" gasped the high officer. "Were you not wounded, it should be rods. Go, dog, go!"

"Where am I to go," asked the man, "I who am accursed?"

"To the home of all who fail—to hell," replied the officer, making a sign to his servants.

So they threw him out, and to hell or elsewhere he went very shortly. For that knife of his which Ru had cast after him with so good an aim was poisoned. Moreover, it had struck him beneath the shoulder and pierced his lung.

The officer went into the private chamber where sat King Apepi with some of his counsellors and his young son, the Prince Khian, the heir apparent to the throne. This Apepi was a big, fleshy man still in middle age, with the hooked nose of the Shepherds and black, beady eyes, one who was violent in his temper, revengeful and fierce-natured like all his people, yet very anxious-minded, a fearer of evil.

Very different from him was his son Khian, born of an Egyptian mother with royal blood in her veins, whom Apepi had married for reasons of policy. More—he had loved her in his fashion, and when she died in giving birth to her only child, Khian, had taken no other queen in her place, though of those who were not queens he had many about him. And now this child Khian had grown up to manhood. He was gentle-natured and soft-eyed, showing but little trace of the Shepherd blood, strong and handsome in body and quick in mind, one, too, who thought and studied, a soldier and a hunter, yet a lover of peace, by nature a ruler of men who desired to heal the wounds of Egypt and make her great.

Before these appeared the old Vizier Anath, and told his tale, reading what had been written down from the lips of the wounded man.

Apepi listened earnestly.

"Do you know, Vizier, who this mad girl is who has a fancy for climbing the Great Pyramid?" he asked at length.

"No, your Majesty, though perhaps I might hazard a guess," answered the Vizier in a doubtful voice.

"Then I will tell you, Vizier. She is no other than the only child of Kheperra, the Pharaoh of the South, who fell in the battle years ago. I am sure of it. It is known that such a child was born, for as you may remember, with the help of certain bribed Theban nobles, we tried to capture her and her mother, the Queen Rima the daughter of the King of Babylon. It would seem that her gods fought for her, since both of them escaped, and of those who went to take them only one was left alive. The rest, he swore, were all killed by a black giant who guarded them. Now there was such a giant for he fought at the side of Kheperra and bore his body out of the battle. More, he was seen upon a trading boat going down the Nile, and with him were two women and a child, doubtless disguised. By craft these three slipped through the hands of my officers at Memphis, who afterwards were degraded for their negligence, and it was reported that they had made their way to Babylon. Yet our spies tell us nothing of their coming to Babylon, which is strange if Queen Rima and her daughter, who is called Princess of Egypt, reached the Court of Ditanah with whom now and again we have been at war for many years. Therefore, either they are dead or they are hiding in Egypt."

"It would seem that this is so, Pharaoh," said the Vizier, and the other councillors nodded assent.

"Of late," went on Apepi, "a wind of rumour has sprung up which blows from the Cataracts to the sea, and whispers in the ears of men in every city and village on the Nile. This rumour says that the Queen of Egypt lives and ere long will appear to take her throne. It says, moreover, that she shelters among that strange Brotherhood of learned folk who have their home in the tombs of the old pyramids near Memphis and who are called the Order of the Dawn. It was to find out the truth of this matter that, somewhat against my counsel, you, Vizier Anath, sent certain bold fellows under promise of great reward to spy upon this Order which has no traitors, and to get sight of this wondrous maiden who can climb the pyramids and who, rumour says, is none other than the Princess of Egypt herself, though for aught I know she may be but a juggler."

"Or a spirit," suggested the Vizier, "since it seems impossible that a woman can perform such feats, and as to this matter there is a legend."

"Or even a spirit, though for my part I put little faith in spirits. Well, the men go; they creep into the Holy Land, as this place is called; they see the climber descending a pyramid; though I gave no such order, they seize her, which shows that she is flesh and blood; she calls aloud, a black giant—mark! again a black giant—rushes roaring to her rescue. He slays three of these men as though they were but children and hurls the man's own knife after the fourth, wounding him sorely, so that the maiden escapes and the Order of the Dawn is put upon its guard. Now I say that this maiden is no other than Nefra, Princess of Egypt, still guarded by that Ethiopian who bore her father's body from the battlefield."

When the murmur of assent had died away, Apepi continued:

"I say also that this business is very dangerous. Let us look it in the face. What are we Shepherds? We are a race that generations ago entered Egypt and took possession of its richest lands, driving the king back to Thebes and usurping the throne of the North. This I still hold, and the South also in a fashion, for we have corrupted its chief nobles and its high priests, binding them with chains of gold. Yet we are in peril, having been much weakened by cease-less wars with Babylon; also, many of our people have intermarried with Egyptians, as indeed I did myself, so that the Shepherds are becoming stained to the colour of the dwellers on the Nile. Now these Egyptians are a stubborn and a subtle folk, also they are loyal to their old traditions and to the blood of the kings that ruled them for thousands of years. If one day they should learn certainly that a queen of that blood lives, it well may be that they will rise like the Nile in flood and sweep us into nothingness. Therefore I say that this queen must be destroyed and with her the Brotherhood that is called the Order of the Dawn."

In the silence that followed the Prince Khian rose from the chair in which he was seated below the throne, and making obeisance, spoke for the first time, saying:

68

"O King my father, hear me. As is known to you I study many things that have to do with the traditions and the mysteries of ancient Egypt, and amongst others from certain instructed men and from old writings I have learned much of this Order of the Dawn. It is an old order and its members are peaceful folk who fight with the spirit and not with the sword, a very powerful order, moreover, for although none know them, it has adherents by the thousand throughout Egypt, perhaps even in this Court, and, it is reported, in far lands as well, especially in Babylonia. Further, it is headed by a mighty prophet, an ancient man named Roi, if indeed he is a man; one who holds commune with the gods, and like all those over whom he rules, is protected by the gods. Lastly, by treaty made with our forefathers, the first of the Shepherd kings, and renewed by every one of them, even by yourself, my Father, this Holy Ground of graves where this order dwells in the shadow of the pyramids, is sacred and inviolate. Under pain of a dreadful curse, which curse it would seem has fallen swiftly upon those four who, somewhat against your counsel, and certainly against mine, broke the pact and entered this land, and there, not satisfied with spying, tried to do violence to a certain lady or spirit. Yet under oath and custom it may not be entered, nor may any harm be worked to the dwellers in the tombs. Therefore, Pharaoh my father, I pray you think no more of bringing destruction on this order and on a maiden whom you believe to be the daughter of Kheperra, since if you attempt it I am sure that you will bring destruction upon yourself and upon many of those who serve you."

Now the King grew angry.

"Almost might one think, Prince," he said with a sneer, "that you yourself had been sworn of this Order of the Dawn. What are oaths and treaties when our throne itself is at stake? There is disaffection in the land. Babylon harasses us continually, and why? Because she says that we have worked wrong to one of her princesses who married Kheperra, or have done her to death. You do not know it, but I have it in a recent letter from her King. I say that all this nest of plotters must be destroyed, whether it be your will or not."

The Prince Khian seated himself again and was silent, but Anath the Vizier said:

"O Pharaoh, a thought has come to me: is there not another way? Can you not walk a gentler road and gain your ends without breaking faith with the Order of the Dawn, which indeed is greatly to be feared, since, like the Prince Khian, I hold that it is protected by Heaven itself? You believe that this Lady of the Pyramids is the lawful child of Kheperra, and it may be so. If this can be established, here is my plan. Send an embassy to Roi the Prophet and demand that this lady should be given to you in marriage and become your lawful queen, as she well may do, seeing that now you have none. Thus would you tie all Egypt together in the bonds of love and keep your hands unstained."

At these words Khian laughed aloud and the councillors smiled. But Apepi stared at Anath, then dropped his fierce eyes and considered awhile. At length he lifted them again and said:

"You are wise in your fashion, Anath. A lion's cub can be tamed as well as killed, although it must be remembered that if tamed, still it grows at last into a lion and longs to walk the desert and fill itself with wild meat, as did its begetters from the first of time. Why should I not wed this maiden—if she lives, as I believe—and thus unite the House of the Shepherd kings and that of the old Pharaohs of the land? It would put an end to many differences and thereafter Egypt might be one and at peace, able also to look Babylon in the face. Only, what says the Prince Khian? I am not so old but that children might be born of such a union, undertaken in the hope that the eldest of them, like to the Pharaohs of old times, should wear the double Crown of North and South without question or dispute; for ever it was the law of Egypt that the right to royalty came through the mother born of the true race of Pharaohs, and thus has dynasty been linked to dynasty from the beginning."

Now the Vizier and all there present looked at Khian, wondering what he might answer, because upon this answer in the end might hang his inheritance to the crown of the North.

For a little while he made none. Then suddenly he laughed again and said:

"It seems that the case stands thus. *If* there lives one who is the heiress of Kheperra, the dead Pharaoh of the South, and therefore of the ancient royal blood of Egypt that ruled for thousands of years before we Shepherds seized a portion of their inheritance, and *if* she consents to wed my royal father, the King, and *if*, having wed him, a child is born of this marriage, I, the present apparent heir, under such a solemn treaty of union may be dispossessed of my heritage. Well, here are many Ifs, and should all of them be fulfilled a score of years or so hence, does it so greatly matter? Do I so much desire to be King of the North and the inheritor of wars and troubles, that for the sake of such a rule I should seek to prevent the healing of Egypt's wounds and the welding together of her severed crowns? Man's day is short, and Pharaoh or peasant, soon he is forgot and perchance, in the end, it will be better for him if he has been a bringer of peace rather than the wearer of a ravelled robe of power that he does not seek."

"Truly I was right when I said that you must belong to yonder Order of the Dawn, for not so in a like case should I have answered the King my father, Khian," said Apepi, astonished. "Still, let that be, for each man dreams his own dream and feeds upon his own follies. Therefore I take you at your word, that as the heir apparent to my throne you have nothing to say against this plan, to my mind wild enough, yet one of which trial may be made, even if in the end it should damage you. Now hearken, Khian, it is my will to send you, the Prince of the North, on an embassy to this prophet Roi and to the Council of the Order of the Dawn. Will you, who are wise and politic, undertake such a mission?"

"Before I answer, Pharaoh, tell me what words would be put in the mouth of your ambassador. Would these be words of peace or war?"

"Both, Khian. He would say to the People of the Dawn that the Pharaoh of the North was grieved that against his will the pact between him and them was broken by certain madmen in his service who every one of them had paid the penalty of their crime, in atonement of which he brought gifts to be laid as offerings upon the altars of whatever gods they worship. He would inquire whether it is true that among them shelters Nefra, the child of Kheperra and of Rima, the daughter of the King of Babylon, and if he discovers that this is so, which may prove impossible, for perhaps she might be hidden away and all knowledge of her denied, he would declare in the presence of their Council, and of the maiden herself, if may be, that Apepi, King of the North, being still a man of middle age and one who lacks a lawful queen, offers to take this maiden, Nefra, to wife with all due solemnities, and having obtained your consent thereto, to swear that a child of hers, should she bear any, shall by right of birth after my death wear the double crown of Egypt as Pharaoh of the Upper and the Lower Lands. All of these things he would prove by writings sealed with my own seal and your own, which would be given to him."

"Such are the words of peace, O King, which I hear and understand. Now let me learn what are those of war."

"Few and simple, it would seem, Khian. If this maiden lives and the offer is refused by her or on her behalf, then you would say that I, the King Apepi, tear up all treaties between myself and the People of the Dawn whom I will destroy as plotters against my throne and the peace of Egypt."

"And if it should be proved that there is no such maiden, what then?"

"Then uttering no threats, you would return and report to me."

"Life at this Court is wearisome to me since my return from the Syrian wars, Pharaoh, and here is a new business to which I have a fancy—I know not why. Therefore, if it pleases you to send me, I will undertake your mission," said Khian after thinking for a while. "Yet is it well that I should go as the Prince Khian, seeing that although the throne is your gift and you can bequeath it to whom you will, hitherto I have been looked upon as your heir, and this Order of the Dawn might be mistrustful of such a messenger, or even make strange use of him? Thus he might remain as a hostage among them."

"Which mayhap I should ask you to do, Khian, as a proof of my good faith until this marriage is accomplished. For understand one thing. If the Princess Nefra lives, it is my will to wed her, because, as I see, she and she alone is the road to safety. He who crosses me in this matter is my enemy to the death; whether he be the prophet Roi or any other man, surely he shall die."

"You are quick of decision, my father. An hour ago no such thought had entered your mind, and now it holds no other."

"Aye, Son, for now, thanks to Anath, I see a ship that will bear me and Egypt over a rising flood of troubles which soon might overwhelm us both, and after the fashion of the great, I embark before it be swept downstream. Vizier, when you espied that ship, you did good service, and for you there is a chain of gold and much advancement. Nay, keep your thanks till it has borne us safe to harbour. For the rest, if you, Khian, think this mission too dangerous—and it has dangers—I will seek another envoy, though you are the one whom I should choose. I doubt whether you will deceive these keen-eyed magicians by taking another name and pretending that you are not Khian, but an officer of the Court, or a private person. Still, do so if you will."

"Why not, Pharaoh?" answered Khian, laughing, "seeing that, if all goes well, it is your purpose to make of me a very private person, for then I who this morning was the heir apparent, or so it pleased you to say, shall be but one of many king's sons. If that chances I would ask whether I who shall have lost much may retain my private estates and revenues that have come to me through my mother or by the endowment of your Majesty? For I who do not greatly care for crowns could wish to remain rich with means to live at ease and follow those pursuits I love."

"That is sworn to you, Khian, here and now and upon my royal word. Let it be recorded!"

"I thank the King, and now by permission I will withdraw myself to talk with that wounded man before he dies, since perhaps he can tell me much that may be useful upon this business."

Then the Prince Khian prostrated himself and went.

When he had watched him go, King Apepi thought to himself:

Surely this young man has a great heart. Few would not have winced beneath such a blow, unless indeed they planned treachery, which Khian could never do. Almost am I grieved. Yet it must be so. If that royal maiden lives, I will wed her and swear the throne to her children, for thus only can I and Egypt sleep in peace. Then he said aloud:

"The Council is ended and woe to him that betrays its secrets, for he shall be thrown to the lions."

CHAPTER 8

The Scribe Rasa

Within thirty days of the holding of this Council, a messenger appeared on what was acknowledged to be the frontier of the Holy Ground that was marked by the highest point to which the Nile rose in times of flood, and called to one who was working in the field that he had a writing which he prayed him to deliver to the Prophet of the Order of the Dawn.

The man came and, staring at the messenger stupidly, asked:

"What is the Order of the Dawn and who is its prophet?"

"Perchance, Friend, you might make inquiries," said the messenger, handing him the roll and with it no small present. "Meanwhile I, who may always be found at dawn or sunset seated at my prayers in yonder group of palms, will bide here and await the answer."

The farmer, for such he seemed to be, scratched his head and, taking the roll and the present, said that he would try to serve one so generous, though he knew not of whom to ask concerning this order and its prophet.

On the following day at sunset he appeared again and handed to the messenger another roll which he declared he had been charged by some person unknown to give to him for delivery to the King Apepi at his Court at Tanis. The messenger, mocking this peasant, said that he had never heard of King Apepi and did not know where Tanis might be; still out of kindness of heart, he would try to discover and make due delivery of the roll after which the two smiled at each other and departed.

Some days later this writing was read to Apepi by his private scribe. It ran thus:

"In the name of that Spirit who rules the world, and of his servant Osiris, god of the dead, greeting to Apepi, King of the Shepherds, now dwelling at the city of Tanis in Lower Egypt.

"Know, O King Apepi, that we, Roi the Prophet and the Council of the Order of the Dawn, who sit in the shadows of the ancient pyramids built long ago by certain kings of Egypt, once members of our order, to serve as tombs for their bodies and to be monuments to their greatness on which all eyes might gaze till the end of the world; we who from age to age drink of the wisdom of the Sphinx, the Terror of the desert, have received your message and given it consideration. Know, O King, that although of late we have suffered grievous wrong at the hands of some who seem to have been your officers, for which wrong those unhappy ones paid with their lives, as all must do who attempt to violate our sanctity and to peer into our secrets; in obedience to the precepts of our Order, we forgive that wrong and having put it aside as a matter of small account, we will receive the ambassador whom you desire to send to us to discuss matters of which you do not reveal the purport. Know, O King, further, that this ambassador, whoever he may be, must come alone, for it is contrary to our rules to admit more than one stranger beyond the borders of the Holy Ground. If after learning this it be still your pleasure to send that ambassador, let him appear before the next full moon in the same grove of palms where this roll was delivered to your messenger. Here one of those who serve us will find him and guide him to where we are, nor shall he suffer any harm at our hands."

When Apepi had heard this letter, he sent for the Prince Khian and asked him privately whether still he dared to adventure himself unaccompanied among the people of the Order of the Dawn and in a place which all men swore was haunted.

"Why not, Father?" asked Khian. "If mischief is meant against me, an ambassador's guard would be no protection, nor are ghosts and spirits to be frightened away by numbers. If I go at all I would as soon go alone as in company. Also it is plain that thus only can this embassy be carried out, because yonder Brotherhood will not receive more than a single man."

"As it pleases you, Son," replied Apepi. "Go now and make ready. To-morrow the writing shall be delivered to you by the Vizier together with my instructions; also a guard will be waiting to conduct you to the place appointed by this prophet. Go and return in safety, remembering our bargain and bringing this maiden with you in charge of women of her own people, if so it may be, for thus shall you earn my favour."

"I go," said Khian, "to return, or perchance not to return, as the gods may direct."

So, everything having been made ready and the roll containing the offers and the threats of King Apepi given into his keeping, together with offerings of gold for the gods of the Children of the Dawn and presents of jewels for the Princess Nefra, if it should be proved that she was the wondrous maiden who dwelt among them, Khian departed. Yet he did not travel as the Prince, but rather as a Scribe of the Court, Rasa by name, whom it had pleased the King to choose to be his envoy upon a certain business. Leaving Tanis so secretly that few discovered he had gone, he sailed up Nile in a ship whose sailors had never seen him, and although they had orders to obey him in everything, took him to be what he said he was, a messenger, Rasa by name, travelling upon the royal business. Even the guard that accompanied him, six in number, were soldiers from a distant city who had never looked upon his face.

His journey ended, he reached the landing place in the afternoon upon the day appointed and was escorted by the soldiers who bore the gold and other gifts, also his travelling gear, to the grove of palms which the messenger had described, as to which there could be no mistake, for no other was in sight. Here he dismissed the guard, who left him doubtfully and yet were glad to go before evening came, for like all Egypt they believed this place to be haunted by the ghosts of the mighty dead, also by the Spirit of the Pyramids whose eyes drove men to madness.

"Now, as we are ordered by Anath the Vizier," said the captain of the guard, "we and the ship in which you have travelled, my Lord Rasa, depart to Memphis where we may be found when we are summoned, though we are not sure that you will ever need a ship again."

"Why not, Captain?" asked Khian, or Rasa.

"Because this place has an evil repute, my Lord Rasa, and it is said that no stranger who crosses yonder belt of sand ever returns."

"If so, what happens to him, Captain?"

"We do not know, but it is reported that he is walled up in a tomb and left to perish there. Or, if he escapes this fate and is as young and well-favoured as you are, perchance he meets the beauteous Spirit of the Pyramids who wanders about in the moonlight, and becomes her lover."

"If she is so fair, Captain, worse things might happen to a man."

"Nay, Lord Rasa, for when he kisses her on the lips, she looks into her eyes and madness takes hold of him, so that he runs after her, till at last he falls on the sand raving and, should he live at all, remains thus all his days."

"Why does he not catch her, Captain?"

"Because she leads him to one of the pyramids, up which, being a spirit, she can glide like a moonbeam but whither he cannot follow. And when he sees that he has lost her, then his brain boils and he is no more a man."

"You make me afraid, Captain. This would be a sad fate to happen to a learned scribe, for such is really my trade, just when he had won favour at the Court. Still, I have my orders and you know the doom of him who disobeys, or even does not carry out, the commands of his Majesty Apepi."

"Aye, Lord Rasa, I know well enough, for this king is very fierce, and if he has set his mind on anything, ill to cross. Such a one, if he is lucky, is shortened by a head, or if he is unlucky, is beaten to death with rods."

"If so, Captain, it would seem better to run the risk of the ghosts, or even of the terrible eyes of the Spirit of the Pyramids, rather than to return with you, as I confess that I should wish. About my neck I have a holy charm which is said to defend its wearer from all tomb-dwellers and other evil things, and to this and to my prayers I must trust myself. Soon I hope to see you again upon the ship, but if you learn that I am dead, I pray of you, lay an offering for my soul upon the first altar of Osiris that you find."

"I'll not forget it, Lord Rasa, for know that I like you well and could have wished you a better fate," answered the captain, who was kind-hearted; adding, as he departed with his company, "Perchance you have offended Pharaoh or the Vizier, and one or other of them has chosen this way to be rid of you."

"That man is as cheerful as a bullfrog croaking in a pool in a night of storm," thought Khian to himself. "Well, perhaps he is right, and if so, what will it matter when those pyramids have seen the Nile rise another hundred times?"

Then he sat himself down upon the ground, resting his back against the bole of one of the palms, and contemplated the mighty outlines of these same pyramids, which hitherto he had only seen from far away, thinking to himself, as Nefra had thought, that those who built them must have been kings indeed. Also he reflected, not without pleasure, for he was a lover of adventures and new things, upon the strangeness of his mission and of the manner in which it had been thrust upon him.

If this royal maiden lives, he thought, and I succeed it means that I lose a crown, and if I do not succeed, then it is also possible that I shall lose the crown, since my father never forgives those who fail. Indeed, it would be best for me if there is no such lady, or that I should not find her. At any rate, there is some girl who climbs pyramids, because before he died that woman-thief swore to me that he saw her. He swore to me also that she was very beauteous, the loveliest lady that ever he beheld, which almost proves to me that she cannot have been the princess, for as the gods do not give everything, princesses are always—or almost always—ugly. Moreover, they do not climb pyramids but lie about and eat sweetmeats. Perhaps after all she whom the dying thief believed he saw, if he saw any one, is a spirit, and if so, may it be given to me to behold her, to do which I would take my chance of madness. Meanwhile, these Children of the Dawn are strange folk, to judge from all that I can learn concerning them, yet it is said, most kindly, so perhaps they will not murder me, even if they guess or know that I am the Prince Khian. What would be the use, seeing there are so many who are princes, or who can be made princes by a decree and a touch of a sceptre?

Reflecting thus, Khian fell asleep, for the afternoon was very hot and he had found little rest upon that crowded boat.

While he was sleeping Roi the Prophet, the lord Tau, and the Princess Nefra were taking counsel together in a chamber of the temple where they dwelt.

"The messenger has landed, Prophet," said Tau; "it is reported to me that he is already seated in the grove of palms."

"Is aught else reported, Tau, that is, as to his business?" asked Roi. "If so, speak it out, since a command has come to me that the time is at hand when our Lady of Egypt here"—and he pointed to Nefra— "should be taken into our full counsel."

"Yes, Prophet. A certain brother of ours who is one of the Court of King Apepi—look not astonished, Princess, for our brethren are everywhere—informs me by the fashion that is known to you that this business is one which concerns a certain lady very closely. To be brief: When four men strove to carry off this lady, Ru the Ethiopian made a mistake, for he killed three of them but suffered the fourth to get away, though wounded to the death. This man reached the Court at Tanis and before he died made a report which, added to other rumours, assured King Apepi that a certain babe who escaped from his hands in Thebes long ago—dwells among us here and is no other than the heiress of the ancient line of the Pharaohs of Egypt."

"It seems that this king is a shrewd man," said Roi.

"Very shrewd," answered Tau, "and quick to decide; so much so that on a hint given to him by his Vizier Anath, also a shred man, he determined at once not to kill a certain lady, as at first he thought to do, but to make her his queen, and thus, by promising their heritage to her offspring, to unite the Upper and the Lower Lands without war or trouble."

Now Nefra started, but before she could speak Roi answered:

"The scheme has merits, great merits, for thus would our ends be attained and many sorrows and perils melt away like morning mist. But," he added with a sigh, "what says Nefra our Princess, who after to-night's ceremony will be our Queen?"

"I say," answered Nefra coldly, "that I am not a woman to be sold for the price of a crown, or of a hundred crowns. This man, Apepi the Usurper, is one of the fierce Shepherds who are the enemies of our race. He is a thief of the desert who has stolen half Egypt and holds it by force and fraud. He, who is more than old enough to be my father, slew my father, the Pharaoh Kheperra, and strove to slay me and my mother, the Queen Rima, the daughter of Babylon. Having failed in this, now he seeks to buy me whom he has never seen, as an Arab buys a mare of priceless blood, and for his own purposes to set me at the head of his household. Prophet, I will have none of him. Rather than enter his palace as a bride I will hurl myself from the tallest pyramid and seek refuge with Osiris."

"Here we have the answer that I foresaw," said Roi with a little smile upon his aged lips; "nor is it one that causes me to grieve, since whatever its gains, such a union would be unholy. Fear not, Princess. While the Order of the Dawn has power you are safe from the arms of Apepi the Wolf. Tell me, Tau, according to the report that has reached you, is this all that the King of the North has to say to us?"

"Nay, Prophet. When the roll that yonder messenger bears is opened, I think that in it will be found written, that if the heiress of Egypt is not delivered to him, then he proposes to take her by force, or if he cannot do so, to send her down to death, and with her, notwithstanding his treaties, every one of the Children of the Dawn from the most aged to the babe in arms."

"Is it so?" said Roi. "Well, if a fool strives to drag a sleeping snake from its hole, that snake awakes, puffs out its head, and strikes, as mayhap Apepi will find before all is done. But these things are not yet; time to talk of them when the royal hand is thrust into the hole to grip the deadly hooded snake. Meanwhile, this envoy from Apepi must be granted the hospitality which we have sworn to him, and brought from the palm grove where he sits alone. Would it please you, Princess, to throw a man's robe over that woman's dress of yours and go to lead him here? Ru and the Lady Kemmah would accompany you, keeping themselves out of sight? If so, being clever, you might learn something from the man, who finding but a gentle youth sent to guide him, would fear no trap, and perhaps even speak freely to such a one."

"Yes," answered Nefra, "I think that it would please me; that is, if you are sure that there is no trap or ambush, since the walk to the grove is pleasant and I have been cooped up of late."

"There is no ambush, Lady," replied Roi. "Since what happened awhile ago by the pyramids our frontiers have been well guarded; also your every step will be watched, although you do not see the watchers. Therefore fear nothing. Learn all you can from this envoy and bring him to the Sphinx where he will be blindfolded and led before us."

"I go," said Nefra, laughing. "To-morrow I shall be called a queen and who knows whether afterwards I shall be suffered to walk alone."

So she went accompanied by Tau who summoned Ru and Kemmah in one of the courts of the temple and there gave certain orders to them and to others who seemed to be awaiting him. This done he returned to Roi and looking him in the face, said in a low voice:

"Do you, O Prophet, who know so much, chance to have learned what may be the name and quality of this envoy from Apepi?"

Now Roi looked him in the eyes and said:

"It comes into my mind, how or whence does not matter, that although he travels as a simple officer of the Court, called I know not what, the man is no other than the Prince Khian, Apepi's heir."

"So I think also," said Tau, "and not without reason. Tell me, holy Prophet, have you learned aught concerning this Khian?"

"Much, Tau. From his boyhood he has been watched by those at Apepi's Court who are our friends, and their report of him is very good. He has his faults like other men in youth, and he is somewhat rash. Had he not been so, never would he have undertaken this mission under strange conditions. For the rest he is more Egyptian than Shepherd, for in him the mother's blood runs strong; and if he worships any gods at all, of which, he being a philosopher, I am not sure, they are those of Egypt. Further, he is learned, brave, handsome of body, and generous in mind; something of a dreamer, one who seeks that which he will never find upon the earth, one, too, who longs to heal Egypt's wounds. Indeed, he seems to be such a man as, had I a daughter, I would choose for her in marriage if I might. This is the report that I have concerning the Prince Khian. Is yours as good?"

"In all things it is the same, Prophet. Yet why does he come hither upon such an errand, seeing that, if it succeeds, it may cost him his succession to the Crown? I fear some trap."

"I think, Tau, that he comes for adventure, and because he seeks new things; also because he is drawn to our doctrines and would study them with his own eyes and ears, not knowing that he may find more than he seeks."

"Is it in the hope that he will do so, Prophet, that you have put it into the mind of the Princess Nefra to meet him yonder in the palm grove?"

"It is, Tau. When I said that such a marriage as this Apepi proposes had many merits, what I meant was, not that she should be thrown to the Shepherd lion, but that a marriage between her and the Prince Khian would have those merits. How could Egypt be better tied together? Even if we were strong enough to wage it, we are haters of war, and would not attain our ends by death and bloodshed. Yet to propose such a thing would defeat itself, since, as she told us, this Lady Nefra is not one to be sold or driven. Her heart and nothing else is her guide, which she will follow fast and far."

"The heart of woman goes out more readily to princes than it does to humble messengers. What if this one who sits among the palm trees does not please her?"

"Then, Tau, all is finished and we must find another road. Let Fate decide after she has judged, not of the Prince but of the man. We cannot. Hearken. This envoy, however named, comes to learn what thousands know already, whether or not the daughter and heiress of Kheperra shelters among us. We can deny or we can confess. Which shall we do?"

"If we deny, Prophet, certainly he will discover the truth otherwise and set us down as liars and cowards. If we confess, he and the world will know us for true men and brave, and that the oath which we swear to the goddess of Verity is no empty form. So whatever we may lose, we shall win honour even from our foes. Therefore, I say confess and face the issue."

"So say I and the rest of the Council, Tau. To-night before the delegates from all Egypt and elsewhere, the Princess is to be crowned its Queen in the great hall of the temple, a matter that cannot be hid, since the very bats will twitter it throughout the land. Therefore it seems wise to me that this messenger should be present at the ceremony and if he will, make open report of it to Apepi. There is another thing of which he must also make report, Tau: namely, whether the new-crowned Queen will take this Apepi as a husband."

"Already we know the answer, Prophet, but after it—what?"

"After it—Babylon. Listen, Tau. Apepi will send an army to destroy us and to capture the Queen, but he will find nothing to destroy, for the Order has its hiding places, and in Egypt are many tombs and catacombs where soldiers dare not come, while the Queen will be far away. If Apepi seeks a curse, let the curse fall upon him, as fall it shall when a hundred thousand Babylonians pour down on Tanis in answer to dead Rima's prayer and to right her daughter's wrongs."

"Be it so," said Tau. "Those who seek the face of War must be prepared to look him in the eyes, for such is the rule of God and man."

****

Nefra, wrapped in a long cloak, approached the grove of palms, followed by Ru and the Lady Kemmah, who grumbled at the business.

"The day is hot," she said, "and who but fools would walk so far in the blaze of the sun? To-night there are ceremonies in which you, Princess, must play the greatest part. Is it fitting that you and I should weary ourselves thus when the work of making ready your robes and jewels is not finished? What is this new madness? What do you seek?"

"That which, as you have instructed me, is sought of all women, Nurse, namely—a man," answered Nefra in her sweet, mocking voice. "I believe that there is a man in yonder palm grove and I go to find him."

"A man, indeed! Are there not men in plenty nearer home, if tombs can be called a home while one is still living beneath the sun? Still, it is true that most of them are grey-bearded dotards and the rest but priests or anchorites who think of nothing but their souls, or husbandmen who toil all day and dream all night of how much mud Nile will yield at its next rising. Well, there are the palms and I see no man, nor can I walk any farther in this accursed sand. Here is the statue of a god, or perchance of some king whose name no one has heard for a thousand years. At least, god or king, he gives shade and in it I will sit as, if you are wise, you will do also while Ru hunts for this man of yours, though when he sees a black giant grinning at him with a great axe in his hand I think that he will run away."

"So do I," said Nefra, "yet, Ru, come with me, as indeed you must."

Then walking somewhat to the right she entered the grove of palms at its end and stepped softly along it, bidding Ru keep himself as much hidden as possible. Presently, seated against the trunk of one of them she saw an officer who wore upon his robe the lion badge of the Shepherd kings, having by his side certain packages, and behold! he was fast asleep. Now a thought took her and she commanded Ru to approach him softly, and having carried off the packages, to go and hide with them behind the statue where Kemmah sat. Then, she said, he was to follow her with Kemmah and the gear in such fashion, if might be, that the officer did not see them as she led him toward the statue of the Sphinx.

This Ru did without awakening Khian, for although he was so large, like all Ethiopians he could move softly enough at need—an art that they learn in tracking enemies and game. He vanished with his burden behind the statue, whence she knew well he was watching her in case of danger, but Nefra, leaning against another palm, studied the sleeper closely. At the first glance she was aware that never before had she beheld such a man as this officer, one at once so handsome and so refined of face.

If his eyes, which I cannot see, are as good as the rest of him, he is beautiful, though Nefra. Also he looks like one whose spirit guides his flesh and not his flesh his spirit; and as she thought, something new, something she had never felt before stirred her serenity and frightened her a little, though in what way she was not sure.

So for many minutes they remained, the weary Khian sleeping and Nefra watching him. At length he stirred, stretched out his arms as though to clasp a dream, yawned, and opened his eyes.

They *are* as good as the rest of him! reflected Nefra as she slipped behind the palm and hid there, which they were, being large, brown, and somewhat melancholy.

Now Khian remembered the packets which contained the presents and the gold and began to search for them eagerly.

"By the gods, they are gone!" he said aloud in a voice that, although anxious, still was soft and pleasant. "How can this have happened and I not know it, seeing that they lay under my hand? Truly they are right who say that this place is the home of ghosts."

Nefra stepped forward, closely muffled in her long cloak, and asked: "Is aught amiss, Sir? And if so, can I aid you?"

"Yes," said Khian, "by restoring to me certain articles which I suppose you have stolen, young man. That is, if you are a man," he added doubtfully, "for your voice——"

"—Is breaking, Sir," replied Nefra, trying to make it as hoarse as possible.

"Then it has broken the wrong way. Breaking voices should grow gruff, not soft as a girl's. But let that be. Restore to me my goods lest I should—well, kill you——"

"And perchance thereby lose them and much else for ever, Sir."

"You do not seem very frightened. Tell me, who are you?"

"Sir, I am the guide appointed to lead you—if you be Apepi's officer—to where you must lodge before you are brought into the presence of the Council of the Order of the Dawn. Knowing that you were alone and thinking that you might be alarmed if armed men came, I, as a young person who can frighten no one, was chosen to fill this office by the Council."

"That is very kind of the Council. But meanwhile, Young Person, where are the goods which my servants set by my side before they departed?"

"Sir, they have gone on before you. As you said just now, this is a home of ghosts and ghosts can carry gold and garments very fast."

"Then they might have carried me also, though on the whole I am glad they did not, for, Young Person, you amuse me. Well, I suppose that I must take your word for it, as to the goods, I mean, and if I find that you have lied, I can always kill you afterwards, or if I don't, the Order of the Dawn can, since they will have lost their presents. What next?"

"Be pleased to come with me, Sir."

"Good, Young Person. Lead on, I follow."

CHAPTER 9

The Crowning of Nefra

So this pair stared upon their long walk, Nefra being careful to lead her companion wide of that overthrown statue behind which hid Kemmah and Ru.

"Do you live in this place?" asked Khian presently.

"Yes, Sir, here and hereabouts," replied Nefra with vagueness.

"And might I ask what is your office when you are not escorting travellers, who must be rare, and arranging for the transport of their baggage by uncommon means?"

"Oh! anything," replied Nefra still more vaguely, "but generally I run errands."

"Indeed! And where to?"

"Oh! anywhere. But tell me, Sir, are you acquainted with the pyramids?"

"Not at all, Friend, except from a distance. The pyramids, it would appear, are now the private property of that Order you mentioned, to which, by the way, I, who also run errands, have a message to deliver. None may approach them. Indeed, I have heard that some unfortunate men who wished to explore their wonders not long ago, came to a terrible end. According to the story a black lion rushed out of one of them, killed three of those men, and mauled the fourth so badly that afterwards he died. Or it may have been one of your ghosts that rushed out. At any rate, the men died."

"What a strange tale, Sir. I wonder that we did not hear of it, but living quite secluded as we do, we hear nothing, or at least very little. But they are beautiful, those pyramids, are they not, standing up thus against the evening sky in majesty? Look how their sharp outlines seem to cut into the heavens. Also from them the great dead seem to speak to us across the gulfs of Time."

"I perceive, Young Person, that you have imagination, which is unusual in those who run errands and guide travellers. Yet I dare to differ from you. These stone heaps undoubtedly are beautiful with a beauty that crushes the mind, though not so much so as are mountains chiselled out by Nature and capped with snow, such as I have seen in Syria. But to me they speak not of the mighty dead whose memories they glorify, but of the thousands of forgotten ones who perished in the toil of their uprearing, that in them the bones of kings might find a house deemed to be eternal and their names preserved among men. Was it worth while to leave monuments to be the marvel of generations at the cost of so much doom and misery?"

"I do not know, Sir, who never thought of the matter thus. Yet there is this to be said. Mankind must suffer, so I have been told who am but an ignorant——"

"—Young person," suggested Khian.

"And generally it suffers to no end," went on Nefra as though she had not heard him, "leaving naught behind, not even a record of its pain. Here at least something remains which the world will admire for thousands of years after those who caused the suffering and those who suffered are lost in darkness. Suffering that has purpose, or that bears fruit, even though we know not the purpose and never see the fruit, may be borne also with joy, but empty, sterile suffering is a desert without water and a torment without hope."

Khian looked at the speaker, or rather at her hood, for he could see nothing else, and remarked:

"The thought is just and finely put. They instruct those who run errands well in this land."

"The brethren of the Order are learned, so even the young can pick up crumbs of knowledge from their feasts—if it pleases them to look for them, Sir—but forgive me, how are you named?"

"Named?—Oh! I am called Rasa the Scribe."

"Is it so? I did not guess your trade because among us scribes carry palettes at the girdle, not swords; also their hands are different. I should have thought that you were a soldier and a hunter and a climber of the mountains of which you spoke, not a copyist of documents in hot palace rooms."

"Sometimes I am these things also," he replied hastily, "especially a climber—when I was in Syria. By the way, my guide, I have heard strange stories of another climber, one who scales these pyramids. It is said at Tanis and elsewhere that they are haunted by a spirit who runs up and down their sides at night, and even in the daytime also. I say by a spirit, for woman she cannot be."

"Why not, Scribe Rasa?"

"Because, or so the tale tells, this climber is so beautiful that those who look upon her go mad, and who could be made mad by the sight of any woman? Also what woman could clamber over those smooth and mighty monuments like a lizard?"

"If you are a scaler of mountains, Scribe Rasa, you will know that such feats are often not so difficult as they seem. There lives a family of men in this place that for generations has been able to conquer the pyramids by day or night," she replied, leaving the first part of his question unanswered.

"Then if I stay here long enough I will pray them to teach me their art, in the hope that at the top of them I might meet this spirit and be made mad by drinking of the Cup of Beauty. But you have not answered me. Is there such a spirit, and if so, can I see her?—to do which I would give my—well, a great deal."

"Here before us is the Sphinx which I thought, Scribe Rasa, being one so curious, you would have noticed as we approached it. Now put your question to that god, for they say that he solves riddles sometimes, if he likes the asker, though never yet have *I* wrung an answer from those stony, smiling lips."

"Indeed? I have sundry problems that I seek to solve and one of them is what may be hidden by that long cloak of yours, my young guide with an instructed mind."

"Then you must propound them at another time, after the needful prayers and fastings. And now, your pardon, but I am commanded to blindfold you because we have come to the entrance of the sanctuaries of the Order of the Dawn, of which no stranger may learn the secret. Will you be pleased to kneel down, for you are very tall, Scribe Rasa, and I can scarcely reach your head."

"Oh! why not?" he answered. "First my packages are stolen; then I am thrown to the crocodiles of curiosity, and now I must be blindfolded, or perhaps beheaded by a 'young person' who has driven me as mad as though she were the Spirit of the Pyramids herself. I kneel. Proceed."

"Why do you talk of a poor youth who earns his bread by following the profession of a guide as 'she,' also as a thief or perhaps a murderer, and compare him to the Spirit of the Pyramids, Scribe Rasa? Be so good as to keep your head still and not try to look over your shoulder as you are doing, lest I should hurt you with the bandage. Fix your eyes upon the face of the Sphinx in front of you and think of all the riddles you would like to ask of its divinity. Now all is ready, I begin"; and very deftly and softly she tied a scented silken cloth, warm from her own bosom, about his head, saying presently:

"It is finished. You may rise."

"First I will answer your question, knowing that you cannot be wroth with one who is blinded. I call you 'she' because by accident I forgot and looked down instead of up and thus saw your hands, which are those of woman; also the ring you wear, which is an ancient signet; also a long lock that escaped from beneath your hood while you bent over me; also——"

"Kemmah," broke in Nefra, "my task is finished and I go to ask my fee from the gatekeeper. Be pleased to guide this scribe or messenger into the presence of the holy Prophet and let the man with you bear his goods, which all the way he has accused me of stealing from him, so that they may be checked in his presence."

****

He who was called the Scribe Rasa sat in the presence of the Prophet Roi, of the Lord Tau, and of the elders of the Council of the Order of the Dawn, venerable, white-robed men. Roi spoke, saying:

"We have read the roll, O Envoy Rasa, which you bring to us from Apepi, King of the Shepherds, at this time sitting at Tanis in the Land of Egypt. Briefly it contains two questions and a threat. The first question is whether Nefra, Royal Princess of Egypt, the child and heiress of the Pharaoh Kheperra, now gathered to Osiris whither he was sent by the spear of Apepi, and of Rima the daughter of the King of Babylon, lives and is dwelling among us. To that question you will learn the answer at a certain ceremony this night. The second question is whether this Royal Nefra, if she still looks upon the sun, will become the wife of Apepi, King of the Shepherds, as he demands that she should do. To this doubtless the Royal Nefra, if she lives, will give her answer when she has considered of the matter, for then there is a queen in Egypt, and a Queen of Egypt chooses whom she will as husband.

"After this comes the threat, namely, that should there be a certain Lady to refuse this offer, and should it be refused, Apepi, King of the Shepherds, violating all treaties made between his forefathers and himself with our ancient Brotherhood of the Children of the Dawn, will in revenge destroy us root and branch. To this we reply at once and afterwards will write it in a roll, that we do not fear Apepi, and that should he attempt this evil thing, every stone of the great pyramids would lie lighter on his head than will the curse of Heaven that he has earned as a man foresworn. Say to Apepi, O Ambassador, that we who seem but a weak band of hermits living in solitude far from the world and there practising our innocent rites, we who have no armies and who, save to defend our lives, never lift a sword, are yet far more powerful than he, or any king upon the earth. We do not fight as kings fight, yet we marshal hosts unseen, since with us goes the Strength of God. Let him attack if he will to find naught but tombs peopled with the dead. Then let him set his ear to the ground and listen to the tread of armies who rush to stamp him down to doom. Such is our message to Apepi, King of the Shepherds."

"I hear it," said Khian, bowing respectfully, "and glad am I to learn, O Prophet, that it is your intention to write it in a roll, for otherwise King Apepi, a violent man who loves not rough words, might make him who delivered it by word of mouth, shorter by a head. Be pleased, therefore, to remember, O Prophet and Councillors, that I, the Scribe Rasa, am but a messenger charged to deliver a writing and to carry back the answer; also to collect certain information if I can. Of the matter of treaties between the Shepherd kings and your Order I know nothing, nor is it one that I am commanded to discuss. Of threats uttered against you, or what may be the end of these threats, I know nothing, whatever I may guess. Be pleased, therefore, to write down at your leisure all you have to say, that it may be delivered to King Apepi in due season. Meanwhile, grant me safety while I dwell among you, and with it as much liberty as you can, since, to speak truth, these temple tombs of yours have something of the air of prisons, nor do I love bandages upon my eyes, seeing that I am an ambassador, not a spy charged to report upon the secrets of your dwelling place."

Roi looked at him with his piercing eyes and answered:

"If you will swear to us upon your soul to reveal nothing that you may learn of these poor secrets of ours that lie outside the matters of your commission; also not to attempt to depart from among us until such time as we think fitting and our written answers are prepared, we, for our part, will grant you liberty to come and go among us as you will, O Messenger, who tell us that you are named Rasa and a scribe by occupation. This we grant because, having gifts of discernment, we believe you to be an upright man, although perchance you have been commanded to travel under another name than that by which you are known at the Court of Tanis, one, too, who has no desire to bring evil upon the innocent."

"I thank you, Prophet," said Khian, bowing, "and all these things I swear gladly. And now I am charged to deliver offerings to your gods in atonement for a crime against you that was wrought recently by certain evildoers."

"Our god, Scribe Rasa, is the Spirit above all gods who rules the earth and whose raiment we behold in the stars of heaven, one to whom we make no offerings save those of the spirit. Nor do we accept presents for ourselves who being a Brotherhood in which each serves the other, have no need of gold. Therefore, Ambassador, be pleased to take back the gifts you bring and on our behalf to pray the King of the Shepherds that he will distribute them among the widows and children of those men who came by their death in seeking, at his command as we suppose, to do violence to one of us and to discover our secrets."

"As regards this new god of yours," answered Khian, "if it be lawful, Priest, I would pray of you, or of any whom you may appoint, to instruct me, a seeker after Truth, in his attributes and mysteries."

"If there is opportunity it shall be done," said Roi.

"As touching the matter of the presents," went on Khian when he had bowed acknowledgment to this promise, "I have naught to say, save that I pray that you will return them with your written answer and, if possible, by another hand than mine. You who are so wise and aged, Prophet, may have noted that great kings do not love to have gifts thrown back into their faces with words like to yours, and, in such cases, are apt to blame their bearer."

Roi smiled a little and without comment on this matter, said:

"This night we invite you to a ceremony, Scribe Rasa. Go now, eat and rest till, at the appointed hour, you are summoned, if it be your pleasure to attend."

"Surely it is my pleasure," answered Khian, and was led away.

****

It was near to midnight, and Khian, having arrayed himself in garments that he had brought with him, such as scribes wear upon occasions of festival, lay upon the bed in his chamber, thinking of the strange place in which he found himself and its still stranger inhabitants. He thought of the wondrous hawk-eyed old prophet, of his grave-miened councillors as they had appeared gathered in that tomb-temple, of the ceremony to which he was to be summoned, if indeed he had not been forgotten, and what might be its occasion. He thought also of how his father, Apepi, would receive the proud answer of these anchorites; of the smile upon the face of the mighty Sphinx which they day he had seen for the first time, and of other things.

But most of all did he think of the guide who had led him from the palm grove and afterwards bandaged his eyes. This guide was a woman, a young woman with beautiful hair and hands, on one of which she wore a royal ring. That was all he knew of her who for aught he could tell might be very ugly, as the ring might be one she had found or stolen. Yet this was certain, that however common her face or humble her station, her mind was neither. No uninstructed peasant girl could harbour her thoughts or clothe them in her words. Much indeed did he long to see that guide unveiled, and to discover the mystery of one who had so sweet a voice.

At this point a deep, gruff voice asked leave to enter, which he gave. As he rose from the bed there appeared before him in the lamplight a black man more gigantic than any he had ever seen, who carried in his hand an enormous axe.

"I pray you tell me, who are you and what is your business with me?" Khian inquired, staring at him and rubbing his eyes, for at first he thought he must be dreaming.

"I am your guide," said the giant, "and I come to take you with me."

"By Set, another guide, and very different from the last!" exclaimed Khian. "Now I wonder if this ceremony is that of my execution," he added to himself. "Surely the man and his axe would be well suited to such a purpose. Or is he but another of the ghosts that haunt these pyramids?" Then he addressed Ru, for it was he, saying:

"Sir Giant on the Earth, or Sir Spirit from the Underworld, for I know not which you are, I feel no wish for a journey in your company. I am tired and prefer to stop where I am. I bid you good-night."

"Sir Envoy, or Sir Scribe, or Sir Prince in disguise, or Sir Soldier, for that at any rate I am sure that you are because of your bearing and the scars on you, which were never made with a stylus, however tired you may be, you cannot remain upon that bed. I am commanded to lead you elsewhere. Will you come or must I carry you as I did your baggage?"

"Oh! So you were the thief who stole my parcels and left a smooth-tongued wench behind you to conduct me across the sand!"

"A wench!" roared Ru. "A wench——" and he lifted his axe.

"Well, Friend, what else was she? Not a man, that I'll swear, and between man and woman there is no halfway house. Tell me, I pray you, for I am curious. Sit down and take a cup of wine, for this place is cramping to one of your stature. These monks of yours seem to have very good wine. I never tasted better in my—in the King's Court. Try it."

Ru took the cup which he proffered to him and drained it.

"I thank you," he said. "The worst of dwelling with hermits is that they are so fond of water, though they have plenty of good stuff stored away in some grave or other. Now let us be going. I tell you I am commanded——"

"So you said before, Friend Giant. By whom are you commanded?"

"By her——" began Ru, and stopped.

"Her, who or what? Do you mean the lady who guided and blind-folded me? Stay. Take one more cup of this excellent wine."

Ru did so, answering as he set it down:

"You are not far from it, but my tongue is tied. Come, Prince."

"Prince!" he exclaimed, holding up his hands. "Friend Giant, that wine must be getting into your head if it can reach so far in so short a time. What do you mean?"

"What I say, though I should not have said it. Don't you under-stand, Prince, that these tomb dwellers are wizards and know every-thing although they pretend to know nothing? They think me a stu-pid Ethiopian, just a black fellow who can handle a battle-axe, which perhaps is all I am. Still, I have ears and I hear, and that is how I come to know that you are a certain Prince, and a soldier like myself, though it pleases you to pretend to be a scribe. Still, I have not mentioned it to any one else, not even to——But never mind. Be sure—she knows nothing. She thinks you are just what you say—a fellow who scribbles on papyrus. Now talk no more; come, come. Time passes. Afterwards you shall tell me what wars go on in Egypt to-day, for in this place I hear nothing of battle who before I became a nurse was a warrior"; and seizing Khian by the hand—he dragged him away down sundry dark passages, till at length, at the end of one of them, he saw light gleaming faintly.

They entered a great hall of the temple. It was roofed and the moon's rays shining through the clerestory windows and the high-set opening at its end, showed Khian that in it were gathered a multitude of men or women—he could not see which because they were all draped in white robes and wore veils upon their faces, that gave them a ghost-like air. At the head of this hall, on a stage lit with lamps, also white-robed but unveiled, sat the Council of the Order of the Dawn. In the centre of their long, curved line was a shrine half hidden by a curtain and in front of this alabaster shrine stood an empty chair with sphinx-headed arms. Nothing more could be seen in that dim light. When Khian entered there was silence in the hall; it was as though his appearance had been awaited for some rite to be begun.

"We are late," muttered Ru and dragged him forward up a kind of aisle, all present turning their veiled heads and staring at him as he went by, through eyeholes cut in the veils. They came to a seat set in front of the stage or dais, but at a little distance, so that he could see everything that happened there. Into this seat Ru thrust him, whispering that he was not to move. Then he departed and presently reappeared upon the dais where he took his stand upon the left-hand side of the shrine to the right of which stood the tall, white-haired Kemmah.

"Let the entrance be shut and guarded," said Roi presently, and movements behind him told Khian that this was being done. Then Roi rose and spoke, saying:

"Brethren and Elders of the holy, ancient, and mighty Order of the Dawn, whereof the Council at this time has its home amid these tombs and pyramids and is sentinelled by the watching Sphinx, the symbol of the rising sun, hear me, Roi the Prophet. You are summoned hither from every *nome* and city in Egypt, from Tyre, from Babylon and Nineveh, from Cyprus and from Syria, and from many another land beyond the sea, being the chosen delegates of our Brotherhood in those towns and countries, among which it dwells to kindle light in the hearts of men and to instruct them in the laws of Truth and Gentleness, to overthrow oppressors by all righteous means and to bind the world together in the service of that Spirit whom we worship, who, enthroned on high, makes of all gods its ministers.

"Why have you been called from so far away? I will tell you. It is that you may take part in the crowning of a Queen of Egypt, the true descendant of the ancient Pharaohs who for thousands of years have sat upon her throne, and a sworn neophyte of our Order, vowed to its faith and to the execution of its duties, the daughter and heiress of King Kheperra and of Queen Rima of the royal House of Babylon, now both gathered to Osiris. We, the Council of the Dawn, among whom this Queen to be has sheltered from her infancy, declare to you upon our oaths that she who presently will appear before you is none other than Nefra, the Princess of Egypt, the daughter and only child of Kheperra and Rima, as her nurse, the Lady Kemmah, who stands before you, can testify, for she was present at her birth and has dwelt with her till this hour. Are you content, Councillors and Elders of the Dawn, or do you demand further proofs?"

"We are content," answered the audience with one voice.

"Then let Nefra, Princess of Egypt and heiress of the Two Lands, appear before you."

As Roi spoke these words the curtain in front of the alabaster shrine was drawn, and standing within it, glittering in the lamplight, appeared Nefra. So lovely did she seem in her coronation robes upon which shone the royal emblems and jewels of the ancient kings, so stately in her youthful, slender grace, so fair of form and countenance, that a sigh of wonder went up from that veiled gathering, while Khian stared amazed, and as he stared became aware that Love had gripped him by the heart.

The figure in the shrine stood quite still, so still that for a while he pondered if she were human, or perchance Hathor, goddess of Love herself, or a statue fashioned by some great artist. Suddenly his doubts were ended, for behold! she smiled, then stepped from the shrine and was led to the carven chair in which she took her seat. Thrice the veiled company bowed to her, Khian with them, and thrice she bowed back to them. Then, advancing to the side of the chair, Roi addressed her.

"Princess of Egypt," he said, "you are brought before this gathering of true and pure-hearted men from many lands that in their presence you may be anointed and crowned the Queen of Egypt. Not thus should this holy rite have been performed, but the times are difficult and dangerous, and a foreign king of desert blood holds half the land and rings it round with swords. Therefore here in secret and at midnight in a place of ghosts and tombs, and not beneath the sun in the presence of thousands at Memphis or at Thebes, must your hand grasp the sceptre and Egypt's crown be set upon your brow. Yet know that presently from the Cataracts to the sea and far away beyond the sea, aye, and in the Court of the Shepherd King himself, the news will fly that once more Egypt has a Queen. Do you accept this royalty, great as may be its burdens and its perils?"

"I accept it," said Nefra in her sweet, clear voice that Khian seemed to know again. "Unworthy as I am, I accept that which comes to me unsought and undesired, brought to me by right of blood. Nor do I fear its perils and its burdens, for the Strength that led me to the throne will safeguard me there."

There was a faint murmur of applause—even Khian found himself murmuring applause—and as it died away, Roi took an alabaster vase of oil and dipping his finger into it, made some sign upon her brow. Then appeared Kemmah and gave to him a circlet of gold from which rose the royal *uraeus*, and an ivory sceptre surmounted with gems. This circlet he set upon her head and the sceptre he placed in her right hand. Then he bowed the knee to her, and said:

"In the name of the Spirit that rules the world, I, Roi the ancient, son of your great-grandsire, appointed prophet of the Spirit during my life days, before this company of brethren and officers of the Order of the Dawn, anoint and declare you, Nefra, Princess of Egypt and sister-elect of the Order of the Dawn, being a woman come to full estate, Queen by right divine and human of the Upper and the Lower Lands, and call down upon you the blessings of the Spirit. As yet you have no Court nor armies and your prerogatives are usurped by others, yet learn, O Queen, that you are acknowledged in a million hearts and that if anywhere your glance falls upon five talking together, three of them in secret are your faithful subjects. Of the future we know nothing because it is hid from men, yet we believe that in it much joy awaits you with length of days, and that the crown which now we set upon your head in secret in time to come shall shine openly before the multitudes of earth. In the name of Egypt and of the Order of the Dawn to which you are sworn, O Queen, I, Roi the Prophet, do you homage."

Then kneeling down, while the company prostrated itself before her as though she were a goddess, Roi touched the new-made queen's fingers with his lips.

With her sceptre Nefra signed that he and all should rise. Then she stood upon her feet and said:

"At such a time as this what can I say to so many great ones who have gathered here to do me honour, and for Egypt's sake to crown me Egypt's queen, I who am but an untaught maiden? Only one thing, I think. That I swear I will live and die for Egypt. I have been told that at my birth Egypt's goddesses appeared in a dream to my mother and gave me a certain title, that of the Uniter of Lands. May this dream come true. May I prove to be the Uniter of the Upper and the Lower Lands, and when I pass to join my fathers, leave Egypt one and great. Such is my prayer. Now I thank you all and ask of you leave to go."

"Not yet, O Queen," said Roi. "An ambassador has come to us from the Court of the Shepherd King at Tanis, he who sits before you, bringing messages that to-morrow must be considered by you in Council. Yet there is one of them to which we think an answer should be given here and now, before all this company. Apepi, King of the Shepherds, being unwed, demands the hand of your Majesty in marriage, promising to your children the inheritance of all Egypt. What says your Majesty?"

Now Nefra started and bit her lip as though to keep herself from the uttering of rash words. Then she answered:

"I thank the King Apepi, but like others, this matter must be considered with the rest, seeing that it is a great one to Egypt and to Egypt's Queen. Let King Apepi's envoy"—here she glanced swiftly at Khian—"be pleased to accept our hospitality in this secret place until once more the full moon shines above the pyramids, while I take counsel with myself and with some that dwell far off. Meanwhile, let messengers be sent to King Apepi to inform him how it comes about that the return of his ambassador is delayed. Or if it pleases him, let that ambassador make his own report at once to his master, the King Apepi."

Now Khian rose, bowed, and said:

"Nay, Lady and Council of the Dawn, the command given to me, Rasa the Scribe, was that with my own hands I should bear back the answers to those questions which were written in the roll of my commission. Here then I bide till these are delivered to me. Meanwhile, if it pleases you to send messages to King Apepi, it is not in my power to say that they shall not be sent. Do as you will."

"So be it," said Nefra.

Then she rose, bowed, and departed, led by the Lady Kemmah and escorted by the Council.

****

Thus ended the midnight crowning of Nefra as Queen of Egypt.

Chapter 10

The Message

On the morrow Khian slept late, being very weary, and in his sleep was visited by dreams. They were fantastic dreams of which, when he awoke, he could remember little, save that they had to do with pyramids and men with veiled faces and with a giant who bore a great axe, and with palm trees through which the wind sighed gently, till presently it changed to the voice of a woman, just such a voice as that of the messenger who had guided him from the grove, just such a voice as that of the royal lady who had sat upon the throne in the temple halls.

Yet, alas! he could not understand what this voice said, and in his dream, growing angry, he turned to the giant with the axe, bidding him interpret the meaning of the song. Behold! the black giant was changed into that Sphinx who sat upon the sands, before which he had been blindfolded. He stared at the Sphinx and the Sphinx stared back at him. Then of a sudden it opened its great stone lips and spoke, and the sound of its voice was like to that of the roll of distant thunder.

"What is it thou wouldst learn of me, the Ancient, O Man?" asked the rolling voice. Now in his dream Khian grew frightened and answered at hazard:

"I would learn how old thou art and what thou hast seen, O Sphinx."

"Hundreds of millions of years ago," answered the lips of stone, "I was shaped in the womb of Fire and cast forth in the agony of the birth of the world. For tens of millions of years I lay beneath deep water, and grew in their darkness. The waters receded and lo! I was a mountain of which the point appeared amidst a forest. Great creatures crept about my flanks, they roared round me in the mists, thousands of generations of them, now of this shape and now of that. The mists departed; I looked upon the sun, a huge ball of flaming red that day by day rose up over against me. In its fierce heat the forests withered and passed away in fire. Sands appeared out of it that, driven by great winds, shaped me to my lion's shape. A river rolled at my feet, the river Nile. New beasts took refuge in my shade in place of the reptiles that were gone; they fought and ravened and mated and bore their young about me.

"More millions of years went by and there came yet other beasts, hairy creatures that ran upon two legs and jabbered. These passed and behold there were men, now of this colour and now of that. Tribe by tribe these men butchered each other for food and women, dashing out the brains of their enemies with stones and devouring them, cooked first in the rays of the sun, and then with fire which they had learned to make.

"These passed away and there appeared other men who wore garments of skins and killed their prey with flint-headed arrows and spears. Yonder in the cliff you may find their graves covered with flat stones. These men worshipped the sun and me, the rock upon which his rays fell at dawn. Thus first I became a god. Again there was war around me and my worshippers were slain, they and their fair-haired children were all slain. Still their dark-hued conquerors worshipped the sun and me. Moreover, they were artists and with hard tools they fashioned my face and form as these appear to-day. Afterwards they built pyramids and tombs and in them kings and princes were laid to rest. For generation after generation I watched them come and go, till at length there were no more of them, and white-robed priests crept about the ruins of their temples as still they creep to-day. Such is my history, O Man, that is yet but begun, for when all the gods are gone and none pour offerings to me or them, still lost in memories I, who was from the beginning, shall remain until the end. Yet was it of this that thou wouldst ask me?"

"Nay, O Sphinx. Tell me, what is the name of that wind among the palm trees of which the sound is as of the voice of woman? Whence comes it and whither does it go?"

"That wind, O Man, blew at the begetting of the world and will blow until its death, for without it no life can be. It came from God and to God it returns again, and in heaven and earth its name is *Love*."

Now Khian would have asked more questions, but could not for suddenly all his dream vanished and his eyes opened to behold, not the face of the Sphinx, mighty and solemn, but the ebon features of the giant Ru.

"What is love, O Ru?" he asked, yawning.

"Love!" answered Ru, astonished. "What do I know about love? There are so many sorts of love; that of men for women, or of women for men, which is a curse and a madness sent into the world by Set to be its torment; that of kings for power which is the father of war; that of merchants for wealth which breeds theft and misery; that of the learned for wisdom, a bird which never can be snared; that of the mother for her child, which is holy; and that of the slave for him or her he serves, which is the only sort I know. Ask it of Roi the Prophet, though I think he has forgotten all love save that of the gods and death."

"It is of the first that I would learn, O Ru, and of it I think that Roi can tell me nothing, who, as you say, has forgotten all. Whom shall I ask of this?"

Ru rubbed his black nose and replied:

"Try the first maiden whom you meet when the moon is rising over the waters of the Nile. Perhaps she can tell you, Lord. Or if that will not serve to so fine a noble, try her whom you saw seated on the throne last night, for she has studied many things and perhaps love may be among them. And now, if it pleases you to rise, the Council awaits you presently, but not, I think, to talk to you of love."

An hour later Khian stood before Roi and his company.

"Scribe Rasa," said the Prophet, for although Ru in his cups had revealed that his true dignity was known, this was not given to him, "we have written in a roll our answers to the letter of the King Apepi, which are such as we told you they would be. As to the matter of the marriage that is offered by the King to that royal lady whom you saw crowned Queen of Egypt but last night, we have added that you, his messenger, shall learn her answer from her own lips on the night of the first full moon after that of her crowning, since she must have time to consider this great business. Now we pray you to add to this letter of ours any that it pleases you to send, making report of what you have heard and seen among us, which report shall be borne faithfully by our messenger to the Court of your master, the King who sits at Tanis."

"It shall be done, Prophet," said Khian, "though what will chance when this report reaches the King Apepi, I cannot tell. Meanwhile, is it still your will that I should abide here among you till that moon shines, having liberty to move to and fro within your boundaries?"

"Such is the will of the Queen Nefra and of us her councillors, Scribe Rasa. That is, unless it pleases you to be gone at once."

"It does not please me, Prophet."

"Then remain among us, Scribe Rasa, remembering the oath that you have sworn, that you will reveal no secret of our hiding places, or our doctrines, or our company, or aught save of that business with which you have to do."

"I will remember it," answered Khian, bowing.

For a while he lingered, talking of little things with the Lord Tau and other members of the Council in the hope that Nefra herself would appear to take part in their deliberations. At length, as she did not come, he went away because he must, and was guided back to his chamber by Ru.

"I am going to write a letter, Friend Giant," he said, "which letter in the end may bring about my end. However, that is some way off, a month away indeed, and meanwhile, after it is finished, I desire to study the pyramids and all the other wonders of this place. Now yesterday a certain youth was my guide who seemed very intelligent. If he can be found I should be willing to pay him well to continue in that office while I remain a guest among these graves."

Ru shook his head and answered:

"Lord, it is impossible. That youth is one of those idlers who stand about waiting for food to fall into their mouths, and if it does not come, move elsewhere. He has moved elsewhere, or at least I have not seen him this morning, and as I do not know his name I cannot inquire where he has gone."

"So be it," answered Khian, "though, friend Ru, you will forgive me if I compliment your honesty by saying that you do not lie very well. Now be pleased to tell me, as this one is lacking, how I can find another guide."

"That is easy, Lord. When you are ready, put your head out of the door and clap your hands. In this place there is always someone listening and watching, and he will summon me."

"That I can well believe. Indeed, here I feel as though the very walls listened and watched."

"They do," replied Ru candidly, and departed.

Khian wrote his letter. It was but short, yet, although so skilled a scribe, it took him a long time, since he knew not what to say or leave unsaid. In the end it ran thus:

"From the Scribe Rasa to His Majesty, King Apepi, the good God:

"As commanded I, the Scribe Rasa, have come to the habitations of the Order of the Dawn who dwell in certain ruined temples and tombs beneath the shadow of the Great Pyramids, and been received by their prophet Roi and the members of their Council. I presented the letter of your Majesty to this Council, also the gifts your Majesty was pleased to send, which gifts they refused for religious reasons. I have learned that the royal Nefra, daughter of Kheperra who once ruled in the South, is living here in the keeping of the Brethren of the Dawn. Last night I saw this princess, who is young, crowned with much ceremony as Queen of all Egypt before a great company of veiled men who, I was told, were gathered from all over the world. The Council of the Dawn send herewith an answer to the letter of your Majesty which has not been shown to me. As touching your Majesty's proposal of marriage, however, the Lady Nefra, seated on a throne and speaking as a queen, said to me that she would consider of the matter and give me her answer to be handed to your Majesty at the time of the next full moon, until when I must abide here and wait in patience. Here then I stay, having no choice in the matter, that I may fulfil the commands of your Majesty and on the appointed day bear back the answer of the Lady Nefra, though whether this will be in writing or by message, I do not know.

"Sealed with the seal of the Envoy of your Majesty, "Rasa the Scribe."

When Khian had copied this letter and done it up into a roll, wondering much what Apepi his father would say and do when he read it and that by which it was accompanied, he ate of the food that was brought to him and afterwards went to the door of his chamber and clapped his hands, as he had been directed to do. Instantly from the recesses of the dark passage appeared Ru accompanied by a white-robed man whom Khian knew for one of the councillors. To this councillor he gave the roll that he had written to be despatched together with the answer of the Council to King Apepi at Tanis. When he was gone Ru led Khian through the great hall where Nefra had been crowned and thence, meeting no one, by a secret doorway to the desert beyond.

"Where have all those gone whom we saw last night?" asked Khian.

"Where do the bats go, Lord, when the sun arises? They vanish away and are no more seen, yet they are not dead but only hidden. So it is with the Company of the Dawn. Search for them among the fishermen of the Nile; search for them among the Bedouins of the desert; search for them in the Courts of foreign kings; search where you will, yet be sure that neither you nor all the spies of the Shepherd king will find one of them."

"Truly this is a land of ghosts," said Khian. "Almost could I believe that those veiled ones were not men but spirits."

"Perhaps," answered Ru enigmatically; "and now, where would it please you to wander?"

"To the pyramids," said Khian.

So to the pyramids they went, walking round all of them, while Khian marvelled at their greatness.

"Is it possible that these stone mountains can be climbed?" he said presently.

Ru led him round the corner of the second pyramid and there, seated on the sand and playing pipes that made a wild music, were three men, the Captain of the Pyramids and two of his sons.

"Here are those who can answer your question, Lord," he said, then turning to the men added, "This lord, who is an envoy and a guest, desires to know whether the pyramids can be climbed."

"We awaited you," said the Captain gravely, "as we have been commanded to do. Is it now your pleasure to see this feat performed?"

"It is," answered Khian. "Moreover, the climber will not lack a present, though I who am a scaler of mountains hold the thing to be impossible."

"Be pleased to stand back a little way and watch," said the Captain.

Then he and his sons threw off their long robes and clothed only in a linen garment about their middles ran to that pyramid which was in front of them and separated. One son disappeared to the north and the other to the south, while the father began to spring up the eastern face as a goat springs up a precipice. Up he went, high and higher yet, while Khian watched amazed, till at last he saw him gain the very crest. Lo! as he did so there appeared with him the two sons who, unseen, had travelled thither by other roads. Moreover, presently there appeared a fourth figure clad in white.

"Who is the fourth?" exclaimed Khian. "But three started to climb, and now, behold! there are four."

Ru stared at the top of the pyramid, then answered stupidly:

"Surely staring at those polished stones has dazed you, Lord. I see but three, doubtless the Captain and his two sons."

Khian looked again and said: "It is true that now I also see but three. Yet there were four," he added obstinately.

Presently the climbers began to descend, following one another down the eastern face. At length they reached the ground safely, and having donned their robes, came to Khian, bowing, and asked him whether he were now satisfied that the pyramids could be climbed.

"I am satisfied that this pyramid can be climbed, though of the others I know nothing," he answered. "Yet before I give you the reward you have earned so well, tell me, Captain, how it comes about that you and your sons, who were three at its base, became four upon its crest?"

"What does my Lord mean?" asked the Sheik, gravely.

"What I say, Captain; neither more nor less. When you stood upon the top yonder, with the three of you was a fourth, a slender figure clad in white. I sweat it by all the gods."

"It may be so," answered the Sheik imperturbably, "only then, as we saw no one, it must have been given to my Lord to perceive the Spirit of the Pyramids herself who accompanied us, invisible to our eyes. Had this chanced when the full moon shines, it would not have been so wonderful, since then she is apt to wander, or so it is reported, but that he should have seen her in the light of day is most strange and portends we know not what."

Now Khian began to ply the man and his sons with questions about this Spirit of the Pyramids and whether she would be visible if they came to look for her when the full moon shone, but from them learned nothing, since to every question they answered that they did not know. Next he inquired of them whether they would teach him how to climb the pyramids as they did, if he paid them well. They replied that except by order of the Council they would not, because the business was very dangerous, and if aught happened to him, his blood would be on their hands. So in the end he made them a large present, for which they thanked him with many bows, and, just as the sun began to set, departed back to the temple.

As they went side by side, Khian, who was lost in thought and wonder, heard Ru mutter:

"A second whom the gods have smitten with the desire to climb the pyramids. Who could have believed that there were two such mad people in the world? What does it mean? Surely such folly must have a meaning, for among my people, the Ethiopians, they say that the maddest are always the most inspired."

Twice or thrice he muttered thus, till at last Khian asked him suddenly: "Who, then, was the other fool to whom the gods gave the desire to climb the pyramids? Was she perchance that one whom I saw standing with the Sheik and his sons upon yonder crest?"

"No, I think not," answered the startled Ru confusedly. "Indeed, I am sure not, since to-day she has other business to attend. Also, I should have known——" Then he remembered and stopped.

"So there is a lady who loves this sport! Well, I have heard as much before, and, friend Ru, as you seem to know her, if you will arrange that I can follow it in her company, you will find yourself growing richer than you are."

"Here is the door to the temple," answered Ru, with a grin, "and, by the way, the second prophet, Tau, bade me to pray you to eat with him and others this night."

"I obey," said Khian, hoping in his heart that one of those others would be the lovely lady whom he had seen crowned as Princess of Egypt. Yet this was not so, for at that meal were only Tau and with him three aged councillors, who, when they had partaken sparingly, slipped away, leaving him and his host together. Then these two began to talk, each of them seeking knowledge of the other.

Soon Khian learned that this Tau, the second Prophet of the order, though not Egyptian by blood, had been born to a high station and great wealth. He had been a warrior and a statesman also, and, it seemed, might have become a king, either in Cyprus or Syria, where he would not say. Far and wide he had travelled about the world, acquiring the languages of many peoples and much learning, and studying religions and philosophies. Yet in the end he had abandoned all and become one of the Priesthood of the Dawn. Khian asked him why he who, as he understood, might have sat upon a throne and mingled with the great ones of the earth while children grew up about him had chosen instead to dwell in tombs with the brethren of a secret order.

"Would you learn? Then I will tell you," answered Tau. "I have done this because I seek peace, peace for Egypt and the world and peace for my own soul, and in pomps and governments there is no peace but only strivings that for the most part end in war to win more wealth and powers that we do not need. Scribe Rasa," he added, looking at him keenly, "were you other than you are, a prince, for instance, I think that perhaps, had you instruction in our philosophy, in the end you might prove to be such another as I am, or even as is Roi the Prophet, and turning your back upon what the world calls greatness, might follow in this same path of peace and service."

"Were I such a one, Priest Tau, it might be so, though other roads run to peace through service than those that lead there by monasteries or tombs, and each must follow that which lies open to his feet."

"That is true and well spoken, Scribe Rasa."

"Yet," went on Khian, "being athirst for knowledge I would learn of these mysteries of yours and of how their servants may attain to this peace and help to call it down upon the world. Is it possible while I sojourn here that one could be found to instruct me in them?"

"I think that it is possible, but of this matter we will talk again. Sleep well, Scribe Rasa, and take counsel with your heart before you enter on this difficult path."

Then he rose and Ru appeared to lead Khian back to his chamber.

CHAPTER 11

The Fall

On the following morning Khian was informed by Ru that orders had been sent to the Captain of the Pyramids to instruct him in the art of scaling them, should he so desire. So presently, accompanied by Ru, he went out and at the foot of the smallest of the pyramids found this man and his sons awaiting him. Awhile later, having been stripped of most of his garments and removed his sandals, he began his lesson, much as Nefra had done, with a rope tied about his middle. Like her, being young, active, and very bold, accustomed to the scaling of heights moreover, he proved an apt pupil, climbing two thirds of the height of the pyramid, that is, as far as he was allowed to go, turning about, as Nefra had done, and descending again with but little help from his guide. Yet trouble came, for when he was within some forty feet of the ground, to which the Sheik who was beneath him had descended already and there stood, talking to Ru, Khian called to him above who held the rope to throw it down as it was no more needed, and at the same time undid the noose from about his middle.

Thus freed the rope slid away, but, although Khian did not notice this, it caught upon the marble but a little below him. Continuing his descent carelessly enough, in setting his foot upon a certain knob of this marble, his heel rested upon the rope that twisted round beneath his weight, causing him to slip and lose his balance.

Next instant he was sliding down the face of the pyramid, and, as he slid he turned so that now his head pointed towards the ground. The Sheik saw, as did Ru. Together they bounded forward to catch him in his fall. In a second he was on them, but the weight of his body struck between them, forcing them apart although they grasped him as he came. Do what they would, his head hit the ground, not so very hard indeed, but, as it chanced, where a stone fallen from the pyramid was hidden just beneath the sand, and though he never felt the blow, of a sudden his senses left him, for he was stunned.

When they returned, dimly and as at a great distance he heard a voice speaking, though who spoke he could not see because his eyelids seemed to be glued together with blood, and for this, or some other reason, he was unable to open them.

"I think that he is not dead," said the voice, which in truth was that of a physician. "The neck does not seem to be broken, nor indeed any limb. Therefore unless the skull is cracked, which I cannot discover for the blood from the cut makes search difficult, I hold that he is but stunned and will come to himself in time."

"The gods send that you are right, Leech," answered another voice, a woman's voice that was full of doubt and fear. "For three long hours has he lain senseless in this tomb and so still that almost I think——Oh! see, he stirs his hand. He lives! He lives! Feel his heart again."

The physician did so, and said:

"It beats more strongly. Trouble not, Lady. I believe that he will recover."

"Pray that he does, all of you," went on the woman's voice, in which now was hope mingled with anger. "Ill did you pyramid-climbers guard him who tangled the rope about his feet. As for you, Ru, was not your great strength enough to hold so light a weight falling from but a little height?"

"It seems not, Lady," answered the deep voice of Ru, "seeing that this light weight of his knocked me down and the Sheik with me, and almost tore my arm out of its socket. Full forty feet he came like a stone from a sling."

At this moment Khian opened his lips and very faintly asked for water. It was brought to him. A soft hand lifted his head, a vase was held to his lips. He drank, sighed, and swooned again.

Once more he awoke or was awakened by the sharp pain that seemed to stab his head from side to side. Now he could open his eyes and, looking about him, saw that he was back in his chamber at the temple, for upon a stool lay possessions of his own. At the foot of the couch a curtain had been drawn and beyond the curtain he heard two women talking.

"How goes he, Kemmah? Has he awakened?" asked a sweet voice that he knew again, for it was the voice of the guide who had led him from the palm grove, the voice, too, of her whom he had seen crowned as Queen of Egypt.

Khian strove to lift his head, to look past the end of the curtain, but could not because his neck was stiff as a stone; so he lay still and listened, his heart beating for joy because this fair, royal lady had been at the pains to visit him that she might learn his state.

"Not yet, child," answered the Lady Kemmah, "though it is true that it is time he did. The learned leech, our brother, said that he can find no great hurt and that he should wake within twelve hours, but twenty have gone by and still he sleeps—or swoons."

"Oh! Kemmah, do you think that he will die?" asked Nefra in tones that were full of fear.

"Nay, nay, I hope not, though when the head is hurt one never can be sure. It would be most sad, for he is a fine man. Never did I see one more perfect in body or more comely in his face, though half his blood is that of the accursed Shepherds."

"Who told you about his blood, Kemmah, and whence it sprang?"

"The birds of the air or the blowing wind. Are you the last to learn what all here know—that this guest of ours is no palace scribe or officer, but the Prince Khian himself, who, if you take Apepi as a husband, will be your stepson?"

"Have done with your talk of Apepi, on whom be the curse of all the gods of Egypt, and of his own as well. For the rest, I guessed, but I did not know, though I was sure that this Rasa could be no common man. Save him, Kemmah! For if he dies—oh! what am I saying? Come, let me look on him. As he sleeps there can be no harm and I will make the sign of health upon his brow and pray for his recovery to the Spirit that we worship."

"Well, then, be swift, for if the leech or Tau should come, they might think it strange to find the Queen of Egypt in a sick man's chamber. Still, have your way, but be swift, I will keep watch without."

Now although Khian shut his eyes close so that he could see nothing, with his ears he heard the curtain drawn aside, heard, too, a light footfall by his bed. More, he felt soft fingers make a sign upon his brow, a loop it seemed to be with a line drawn through it, perchance the Loop of Life. Then she who had drawn the sign seemed to lean over him and, setting her lips close to his face, to murmur holy words of which he could not catch the drift or meaning. And as she murmured, ever those lips drew closer to his own, till at length for one second they touched his own and swiftly were withdrawn. Then came a sigh and silence.

Now Khian opened his eyes, to see other eyes gazing down at him, and in them tears.

"Where am I? What has chanced?" he asked faintly. "I dreamed that I was dead and that some daughter of the gods breathed new life into me. Oh! now I remember, my foot turned on that accursed rope and being careless and over-sure, I fell. It matters not, soon I shall be strong again and then I swear that I will climb those pyramids one by one more swiftly than does the spirit who inhabits them."

"Hush! Hush!" murmured Nefra. "Nurse, come here. This sick one is awake and speaks, though foolishly."

"Soon he will be asleep again for good if you stay at his side talking of pyramids," answered Kemmah who had entered the place unseen by either. "Have you not had enough of pyramids, both of you? Would that those vain fools of kings had never built them to bring trouble to the greater fools who come after."

"Yet I will climb them," muttered Khian.

"Begone, child, and bid Ru bring the leech, and swiftly," went on Kemmah.

With one quick glance at Khian, Nefra glided away. Kemmah watched her go, saying to herself as she turned to minister to him:

"How strange a thing is love that can send so many to their deaths, or by its strength draw the dying back to life again. But of the love of these two what will be born?"

Then she gave Khian milk to drink and bade him lie still and silent. Yet he would not obey who, having drunk, asked her dreamily:

"Think you, good Nurse, that the Spirit of the Pyramids of whom all talk in this holy land is as fair as that lady who has left us?"

"The Spirit of the Pyramids! Can I never be rid of these pyramids? Who, then, and what is this Spirit?"

"That is just what I would find out, Nurse, even if I lose my life in seeking it, as it seems that already almost I have done. My soul is aflame with desire to look upon this Spirit, for something within tells me that until I do so never shall I find happiness."

"Here the story runs otherwise," answered Kemmah. "Here it is said that those who look on her, if there be such a one, find madness."

"Are they not perchance the same thing, Nurse? Are we ever happy except when we are mad? Can the sane be happy, or the wise? Is your holy Prophet Roi happy, who is the sanest of the sane and the wisest of the wise? Are all those death-awaiting Whitebeards who surround him happy? Have you ever been happy, except perhaps years ago when sometimes you were mad?"

"If you ask me, I have not," answered Kemmah, remembering certain things and trembling beneath the thought of them. "Perchance you are right, young sir. Perchance, as drunkards think, we are only happy when we are mad. Yet if you will be guided by me, you will cease to seek a spirit in the skies, or near them, and content yourself with following after woman upon the earth."

"Who knows, Nurse," replied Khian with all the solemnity of one whose brain still reels, "that in seeking after the Spirit I may not find the woman, as in seeking after a woman, some have found a spirit? Who knows that they are not the same thing? I will tell you—perhaps—when I have climbed those pyramids by the light of the full moon."

"Which has already shone," interrupted Kemmah angrily.

"There are more full moons to come, Nurse. The sky is as peopled with full moons unborn as the sea is with oysters that will be eaten, and the pyramids will stand for a long while to welcome climbers," answered Khian faintly.

"To Set with the pyramids and with your silly talk!" burst out Kemmah, stamping her foot. Then she ceased, noting that Khian had once more swooned away.

"A fool!" she thought to herself as she ran to find help. "Indeed, the first of fools who would hunt a ghost when the loveliest of flesh and blood lies to his hand. Yet were I thirty years younger I think that I might find it in my heart to go mad with this spirit-seeking fool, as I think also another is in the way of doing. What did he say? That in searching for the Spirit he might find the woman? Well, perhaps he will; perhaps after all this moonstruck prince is not such a fool as he seems. Perhaps those who climb the pyramids find joy at the top of them, and joy is better than wisdom. So at least some come to believe when we grow old and have left it far behind."

Very soon Khian, who was young and strong and though shaken by the shock of his fall, as the physician said, quite unhurt in his brain or his bones, rose recovered from his bed. Indeed, within five days, once more he was climbing the pyramids by the help of the Captain and his sons, for it would seem that this passion had grown upon him during his swoon. Also that swoon, when he shook off the last of it, left no memory of what he had said or done while it endured. From the moment when he set his foot upon the cord and slipped, until at last he rose from his bed, he remembered nothing, not even the visit of Nefra to his chamber or his talk with Kemmah, though it is true that these came back to him in after days. So where he had left off, there he began again, namely, on the slope of the pyramid, which very soon he mastered, as in due time he did the others, like Nefra before him.

109

Day by day, from dawn until the sun grew too hot for the work, he laboured at those pyramids, so hard that at last the Captain and his sons were almost outworn and declared that they had to do with a devil, not a man. Yet they spoke well of him, as did all others, holding that he who after such a fall dared to persevere and conquer, must be great-hearted. For they did not understand that, from the moment of his slip, of his fall he remembered nothing.

Meanwhile, though he knew it not, at the Court of King Apepi it was believed that he was dead. The tidings of his fall from the pyramid and, it was added, of his death, for dead he seemed to be, had overtaken that messenger, a Brother of the Dawn named Temu, who bore the answer from the Council of the Dawn and Khian's own letter, as he embarked upon the Nile, and he had spread it abroad and carried it to the Court at Tanis. When Apepi heard this news he was grieved in a fashion, since he had loved his son a little, at least when he was younger, though not much because in his fierce and selfish heart there was small room for any love save of himself.

Soon, however, his grief was swallowed up in wrath at that which was written in the letter from the Brotherhood of the Dawn, which he swore to destroy root and branch unless Nefra, whom they had dared to crown Queen of Egypt, were given to him in marriage. Moreover, he believed that Khian had not come to his end by a chance tumble from the pyramid, but that he had been done to death at the decree of this Brotherhood, that the heir to the Crown of the North might be removed because he stood in the path of her who had been consecrated Queen of all Egypt. But of all these things Apepi wrote nothing to the Council of the Dawn. Indeed, he seized their messenger, Temu, and kept him in a safe place where he could communicate with none, and meanwhile made certain plans and preparations.

****

During the weeks which followed his recovery Khian did more than climb the pyramids. Thus he received instruction in the faith and worship of the Brotherhood of the Dawn, as it had been promised that he should do. In the evening, in a little lamp-lit hall, he was taught by Tau, or by Roi the Prophet, or sometimes by both of them together. Moreover, he shared this instruction with another pupil, Nefra the neophyte.

There he sat at one end of a table with ink and papyrus in front of him, while at the other end, with Kemmah behind her and the gigantic Ru standing in the shadow as a guard and sentinel, sat the young Queen simply clothed in white as a neophyte should be, so placed that he could see her face in the rays of the lamp and she could see his, and yet too far away for them to talk together. At the centre of the table in carved seats sat Roi and Tau, or one of them, expounding the secret mysteries of their Order, and from time to time asking or answering questions.

So pure and beautiful was the faith they taught that very soon it possessed the heart of Khian. In its outlines it was simple, that of the existence of one great Spirit, of whose attributes all the gods they knew were ministers, a Spirit who for its own purposes sent them forth into the world, whence in due time it would draw them back again. Moreover, these holy and learned men taught their pupils of those purposes, declaring that the greatest of them was to promote peace upon the earth and to do good to all that breathed. Yet there were other parts of this doctrine which were not so plain and easy, for these had to do with the methods by which that Spirit could be approached of those who still dwelt upon the earth, with forms of prayer and hidden rites also, that would bring the Worshipped into communion with the worshipper. Further, there were many rules of life and great principles of politics and government, all of which were a part of the law.

Khian hearkened and found this doctrine good, for therein was that which fed if as yet it did not satisfy his hungry soul. On a certain day at the end of the last lesson, he rose and said:

"O holy Prophets Roi and Tau, I accept your teaching; I would be sworn as the humblest of the Brethren of the Order of the Dawn. Only for a certain reason which I must keep secret, of your temporal politics I say nothing either good or ill, neither do I bind myself to them. In the spirit I am yours; in the flesh and for the purposes of the flesh, as yet I am the slave of others. Is it enough?"

Roi and Tau consulted together while Nefra watched them curiously and Khian sat lost in thought, his head bowed between his hands. At length the old prophet spoke, saying:

"Son, the time you can give to study and preparation being short and your heart being set upon the truth, it is enough. Here in these tombs also we learn many things, and amongst them that men are not always what they seem to be. Thus it well may chance that by blood, birth, and duty you are bound with chains you cannot break, even to satisfy your soul. It well may chance, moreover, that it is not for you to take the vows of celibacy and abstinence, or to swear that you will lift no sword in war, since perhaps it is decreed that your mission in the world must be otherwise fulfilled. Further, what we say to you, we say to our sister who with you has listened to the words of Life. Her feet also are set upon a road that is high and difficult. Therefore, exempting both of you from much to which others must bow their heads, to-morrow we will absolve you from your sins, swear you to our precepts, to break which will bring a curse upon your souls, and number you among our company in earth and Heaven."

So it came about that on the next day at a great ceremony in the temple hall, Khian the Prince and Nefra the Queen received at the hands of Roi the Ancient absolution of all evil that they had thought or done, and thereafter were sworn as full members of the Order of the Dawn, vowing themselves to accept its law as their guiding star and to pursue its holy ends eternally. Separately they knelt before its white-robed High Priest while far off on the confines of the great hall and out of hearing of their speech the brethren watched them as witnesses, and received forgiveness and benediction with words of whispered counsel, then withdrew and seated themselves side by side while all that company chanted the ancient hymn of welcome to their souls reborn. By slow degrees the loud, triumphant music grew less and died away, as, headed by Roi, those who sang departed from the temple, till at last there was a great silence, and in the si-lence they sat alone.

Khian looked about him and noted that even Ru and Kemmah were gone; in that great and solemn place they were quite alone, stared at by the cold statues of gods and ancient kings.

Khian looked at Nefra and asked:

"Of what are you thinking, Sister?"

"I am thinking, Brother, that I have heard wonderful words and received holy blessings which should have changed me from a sinful maiden into a saint like Roi, and that yet I feel much the same as I did before."

"Are you sure that Roi is so great a saint, Sister? I have seen him once or twice grow wrath like others. Also does the absence of temp-tation, of which there can be little after ninety, make a saint? For the rest, doubtless you feel as you did before, because it is not possible for snow to grow whiter than snow."

"Or fire hotter than fire. But have done, Brother. Is this a time or place for pretty speeches? Hearken, for as we are now both bound in the bonds of the same great oath we can speak our minds to each oth-er, fearing no betrayal. These rites have changed me little, if at all, who always have known the doctrines of the Dawn that from childhood were instilled into my heart, although, until I attained my present age, under its law I could not be admitted to the full fellowship of the order. Behold! I am still no spirit but a woman as before, full of mortal purposes. Thus," she added slowly, considering him with her large eyes, "my father was slain by one I hold to be the usurper of his rights; one, too, who, I think, would have murdered me if he could, and for those deeds I desire to repay him. Also to them of late he has added deadly insult, for now this slayer of my father and would-be murderer seeks to take me, the orphaned child, in marriage, and for that affront, too, I would repay him."

"Bad, very bad, Sister," answered Khian, shaking his head sadly, perhaps to hide a certain twitching of the corners of his mouth. "But, if I may ask, did you confess these black sins to the holy prophet Roi, and if so, what did he say of them, Sister?"

"I did, Brother, who could think of nothing else to confess, or at least not much, and what he answered makes me believe that you are right in holding that the holy Roi is still not so holy as he might be. He said, Brother, that such thoughts were born of my ancient blood and natural, and that it was right that those who committed great crimes for cold, base purposes should suffer for the crimes, and that if I were the means of bringing punishment upon this man, it would be because it had been so decreed by Heaven. Therefore he did not set me down as sinful in this matter. But enough. Tell me, Brother, if it pleases you, do you find yourself changed at heart?"

"I find my feet set upon a better and a higher road, Sister, for now I know what to worship—I who worshipped nothing because I could believe in nothing—also, how this new god should be worshipped. For the rest, no one killed my father or sought to murder me and therefore I do not wish to be avenged upon any one—at present. Yet, Sister——" and he paused.

"I am listening, Brother, who feel sure that you cannot be quite so good as you would have me understand."

"Good! No, I am not good; I only hope to become good if I can find someone to help me—no, not Roi, or Tau, or Kemmah, or the whole Council of the Dawn—someone quite different."

"A goddess from on high," suggested Nefra.

"Yes, that is well said—a goddess from on high—we will talk of her presently. But first what I want to say is that in following after righteousness I have fallen into a very deep pit."

"What pit, Brother?" asked Nefra, looking up at the roof of the temple.

"One out of which I think you alone can help me. But I must explain. First you should know that I am a liar. I am not the Scribe Rasa. The Scribe Rasa, an excellent man and a master of his trade, died many years ago when I was a boy. I am——" and he hesitated.

"——The Prince Khian, son of Apepi and heir apparent to the Crown of the North," suggested Nefra.

"Yes, you have got it quite right, except that I do not think I am any longer heir apparent, or at any rate I shall soon cease to be so. But may I ask, Sister, how you came to know my style and title?"

"We know everything in the House of the Dawn, Brother, also, as it chances, you told me them yourself when you were sick—or was it Kemmah?"

"Then it was very wrong of you to listen, Sister, and I hope that you confessed that sin with the others. Well, now perhaps you see the pit. The Prince Khian, the only lawful son of King Apepi—at present—has been sworn a member of the Order of the Dawn, which order it is the purpose of King Apepi to destroy, as is not wonderful, kings being what they are, seeing that it has just crowned a certain lady Queen of Egypt and thereby in a sense declared war against him, the usurper. Now tell me, what can I do who on the one hand am the Prince Khian and on the other something much higher and better—a brother of the Order of the Dawn?"

"The answer is simple, Brother. You must make peace between Apepi and the Order of the Dawn."

"Indeed, and how? By praying a certain sister to become the Queen of King Apepi? Thus only can such a peace be made, as you know well."

"I never said it," answered Nefra, flushing. "Moreover, it does not please me to listen to such counsel—even from a brother."

"Nor would it please even a brother to give such counsel, for if it were taken, that brother would soon be numbered among those who make their prayers and swing their censers in the heavenly shrine whereof we are instructed in the mysteries."

"Why?" asked Nefra innocently. "If he gave it not, I could under-stand, for then a certain king might be wrath. But if he gave it, why?"

"Because then a certain queen might be wrath, one who, as you, Sister, have told me, loves vengeance. Or at least, because he himself, if that counsel were taken, would be so weary of the world that he could tread it no more."

Now for a while there was silence between them and, beneath the shadow of their white hoods, each of them sat staring at the ground.

"Sister," said Khian at last, and as she made no answer, repeated in a louder voice, "Sister!"

"Forgive me, I had almost fallen asleep after last night's vigils. What is it, Brother?"

"Only this. Would you be minded to help a poor prince out of the pit of which I have spoken by dragging him up with a silken rope of—well, of love which all members of this company owe to one another—and making him a king?"

"A king? A king of what? Of these tombs and the dead in them?"

"Oh, no! Of your heart and the life in it. Hearken, Nefra. Together we may stand against my father Apepi, but apart we must fall, for when he comes to learn the truth he will kill me, and if he can lay his hands on you, drag you whither you do not wish to go. Moreover, I love you, Nefra. From the moment when I heard your voice yonder by the palm trees and knew you for a woman beneath your cloak, I loved you, though then I thought you but some simple girl. What more is there to say? The future is dark; great dangers lie ahead. Mayhap it will be necessary to fly to far lands and leave all these pomps behind us. Yet together would they not be well lost?"

"Then what of Egypt, Prince Khian? What of Egypt and the mission laid upon me and the oath you heard me swear in this very hall?"

"I do not know," he answered confusedly. "The road is dark. Yet with love to light our feet we shall find a way. Say that you love me, and all will be well."

"Say that I love you, the son of him who slew my father, that murderer who seeks to make me his. How can I say this, Prince Khian?"

"If you love me, Nefra, you can say it, because it will be the truth, and have we not heard that to hide the truth is the greatest of sins? Do you love me?"

"I cannot answer. I will not answer. Ask it of the Sphinx. Nay, ask it of the Spirit of the Pyramids, and by her word I will abide, for that spirit is my spirit. One day still remains to us. Ask it to-morrow of the Spirit of the Pyramids, if you dare to seek and find her beneath the moon."

Then suddenly she rose and fled away, leaving him alone and wondering.

CHAPTER 12

The Spirit of the Pyramids

That night Khian slept little; his thoughts would not let him sleep. They filled his mind with problems and as in a mirror showed him the pitfalls that lay about his feet. He, the Prince of the North, was sworn a brother of the Order of the Dawn, which his father, the King, threatened to destroy, and how did these two offices agree? Could he smite with the one hand and defend with the other? Nay, it was impossible. Therefore he must cease either to be a prince, or to be a brother. There his path was clear. Let the rank go; indeed, had it not already been taken away from him with his own consent? Therefore, why should he trouble about it now? Henceforth he was nothing but Brother Khian of the Order of the Dawn. Nay, he was something more—an ambassador who awaited a certain answer which must be conveyed to the King who sent him on his mission. It was as to a matter of marriage; as to whether a royal lady would become the wife of that king or would choose to face his wrath.

Here again his task was easy. He must deliver the answer, whatever it might be, after which his duty came to an end and he would remain nothing more than a Brother of the Order of the Dawn, and perhaps a Prince. If that answer were such as the King desired, then doubtless he, the ambassador, would be allowed to go his ways in peace, though no more as heir to the throne of the North. But if it were very different; if, for example, it announced that this lady refused the King in favour of the ambassador who chanced to be his son—what? Why! Death— no less—death or flight!

Yet at this thought Khian was not dismayed, he even smiled a little as it crossed his mind, remembering the teachings of his new philosophy, that all was in the hands of Heaven and that naught happened save that which must happen. He did not desire to die who now had so much for which to live, but if death came that philosophy taught him not to be afraid. Nor did he write himself down a traitor to his duty, because he knew that in any case Nefra would have refused this monstrous marriage, of which she had spoken to him as an insult. Moreover, as yet he did not know that any thought of him would weigh with her. He had offered her his love, but she had not accepted this gift. She had said that she could not answer, that he must ask the "Spirit of the Pyramids" whether she, Nefra the Queen, loved or did not love him, Khian the Prince. What could such words mean? There was no Spirit of the Pyramids; everywhere he had inquired of this legend and learned that it was built of air. How could he ask of a spirit that which a woman refused to tell, and where should he find this oracle?

He was told to seek it by the light of the full moon among the ancient graves. Well, that on his part nothing might be lacking, he would seek like any simple fool, and if he found nothing, would understand that Nothing was his answer. Then, seeking no more, he would demand from Roi the writing that he must bear to King Apepi and depart sore-hearted to accomplish its delivery. This done he would abide the wrath of the King and, should he escape, would wander away to such distant place as Roi or the Council might appoint and there preach the doctrines of the Dawn or do such things as he was commanded, turning his heart from woman and the joys of life.

Soon he would know; soon all would be finished in this way or in that, for on the morrow of the night of full moon the young Queen must give her answer to the demand of Apepi and he, the ambassador, must bear that answer back to Tanis. Meanwhile this was certain—he who had never loved before worshipped the maiden Nefra with body and with spirit and above all earthly things desired her as his wife; so much so that if he were to lose her he cared not what else he might lose, even to life itself.

****

It was the appointed time and Khian, quite alone, for as an admitted brother now he could pass where he would, unquestioned and unwatched, wandered to and fro among the tombs which surrounded the greatest of the pyramids. He was sad-hearted who believes his to be but a fool's errand; moreover, all his troubles weighed upon his soul. The vast solemnity of the place, too, with its endless streets of graves above which the pyramids towered eternally, crushed him. What a spot was this for a love quest, here surrounded by the monuments which told of the end of all human things. Hundreds of years ago those who slept within these tombs had ceased from mortal loves and hates, and as they were, soon he would be also, perchance before another full moon shone in yonder sky. He wondered whether they looked upon him now with calm, invisible eyes; not one, but ten thousand spirits of the pyramids.

He sat him down upon a stone in the midst of that deep silence which was only broken from time to time by the melancholy howlings of some jackal seeking food, and watched the shadows creep across the sand. At length, growing weary, he covered his face with his hands and brooded on the mystery of all things, as was natural in such a place, and whence men came and whither they must go, a problem that not even Roi could solve.

He heard nothing, yet suddenly, why he did not know, he was moved to let fall his hands and look about him. Surely something stirred yonder in the shadow of a great tomb. Perhaps it was a night-haunting beast. Nay, it seemed too tall. It came out of that shadow and for a moment could be seen flitting to the shelter of another tomb where it vanished. Surely it was a white-veiled woman or a ghost.

Khian was frightened, his hair rose upon his head. Yet springing to his feet he followed it. He came to the tomb where it had disappeared. It was gone. Nay, there it was far away, shaping a course, it would seem, toward the second pyramid, that of the Pharaoh Khafra. Again he followed, but fast as he went, that figure went faster, now hidden and now seen, so that when at length it reached the north face of the second pyramid called *Ur-Khafra*, or "Greatest Khafra," it was a spear's cast in front of him.

Surely, he thought, it would halt there. But it did not. It began to glide up the face of the pyramid and then, at the height of a tall palm tree, it disappeared.

Now Khian more than once had climbed this second pyramid by its northern face and knew that there was no opening in it. Therefore it would seem that what he had seen was indeed a ghost which had melted away as ghosts are said to do. Still, to satisfy himself, though fearfully, he climbed after it and when he had scaled some fifty feet of the steep side, stopped astonished, for behold! there in the pyramid was what seemed to be an open door beyond which a passage ran downwards. Moreover, in that passage lamps were set at a distance from each other. He hesitated, for he was much afraid, but at length, thinking to himself that ghosts need no lamps and that but one, man or woman, had entered in front of him, he grew courageous and followed.

For some five and thirty paces this passage ran downwards steeply between walls of granite, then for another thirty paces it ran on upon the level, ending at last in a large chamber hewn from the living rock and roofed with great painted slabs of stone leaning against each other to bear the mighty weight of the pyramid above. In this darksome place, sunk into the rock, stood a sarcophagus of granite and naught else.

Khian crept down the passages by the light of the lamps, his footsteps echoing against their walls of stone, and from the shelter of a huge half-opened granite door peeped into the tomb chamber. It was lit by one lamp that stood upon the sarcophagus whereof the feeble rays shone like a star in the black gloom of the vaulted hall. This gloom he searched with his eyes. In vain; he could see no one, the veiled shape he had followed was not; or perchance it had departed by some farther door into the bowels of the pyramid.

Muttering a prayer for protection against the spirit of the Pharaoh upon whose rest he broke, and drawing his bronze sword lest he should find that he had been lured into this dreadful place by evildoers, Khian crept forward through the gloom, very carefully, for there might be pitfalls in the rocky floor. Coming at length to the sarcophagus he stood irresolute, for of a sudden his courage seemed to fail him.

What if in truth he had been following a ghost and that ghost should spring upon him from behind! Nay, he would be brave. Did ghosts set lamps in niches? Their shapes showed that they were ancient lamps, it was true; perhaps the same that were used by the builders of the pyramid a thousand years before, or by those who bore the body of the king to its last resting place. Yet lamps did not burn eternally, unless indeed they were ghostly lamps; the oil in them must be new and set there by human hands. The thought gave him courage and he stood still who had meditated flight. There was a sound at the far end of the hall, a rustling sound that checked the beating of his heart. In the darkness appeared a cloud of white which floated forward. The ghost was upon him!

He stood where he was—perchance because he could not stir. The white-veiled shape drew near and halted. Now only the width of the tomb was between them and he stared at it over the flame of the lamp but could see nothing because the face was covered, like the face of one new-dead. In his terror he lifted the sword as though to stab at this unearthly thing. Then a soft voice spoke, saying:

"O Seeker of the Spirit of the Pyramids, would you greet her with a sword-thrust, and if so, why?"

"Because I am afraid," he answered. "That which is veiled is always terrible, especially in such a place as this."

As he spoke the veil fell, and in the lamplight he saw the form and the beautiful, flushed face of Nefra.

"What is the meaning of this play, O Queen?" he asked faintly.

"Does Khian, the heir of the King of the North, name me Queen?" she asked in a mocking voice. "Well, if so, he is right, since here above the bones of him who, history tells, was my forefather and of whose throne I am the heritor, so I should be called. Prince Khian, you sought the Spirit of the Pyramids who never was except in fable, and you have found a queen who is both flesh and spirit. If still you have aught to say to her, speak on, since time is short and soon she may be missed."

"I have nothing to say except what I have said already. Nefra, I love you well and I would learn of you whether you love me. I pray you play with me no more, but let me hear the truth."

"It is short and simple," she answered, raising her head and looking straight into his eyes. "Khian, if you love me well, I love you better, for of this treasure woman has more to give than man."

His mind reeled beneath the weight of her words and his body with it, so that he must rest his hand upon the stone of the tomb to save himself from falling. Yet his first thought was angry and broke from his lips in a sharp question.

"If that be so, Nefra, what need to bring me to this dreadful place of death to tell me that it is so? What need to make me follow a dream and a ghost that I might find a woman? Surely the jest is ill-conceived."

"Not so much so as you think, Khian," she answered gently. "Yesterday I could not tell you what I longed to speak, because, being what I am, I must lay the matter before others, I, who am not a mistress of myself, but the servant of a cause. Therefore I sought time till I had learned that what I desired was the will of those who are set above me and, as they declare, of Heaven which is set above them. Had it been otherwise, you would have seen no Spirit of the Pyramids to-night and no Queen Nefra ere you departed to-morrow morning, and thus would have had your answer which I should have been spared the pain of speaking."

"Then Roi and the rest approve, Nefra?"

"Aye, they approve; indeed, it seems that from the first they hoped for this and therefore brought us together as much as might be, because they trust that so Egypt may once more be united and that thus their policy may prosper through our love."

"Much must happen before that can be," said Khian sadly.

"I know it, Khian. Great dangers threaten us. Indeed, I think that they are near. It is for this reason that, playing the part of a ghost, I have led you to this ancient sepulchre, believed of all to be haunted by the dead, that you may learn its secret and at need make of it your hiding place, Khian. Now I will show you the trick of the door in the casing of the pyramid, revealed to me by right of birth and to certain others by right of office, for from generation to generation this secret has descended as an inheritance in the family of the Captain of the Pyramids who are sworn not to disclose it, even under torture. Look, Khian."

Lifting the lamp Nefra held it above her head and pointed to the end of the tomb chamber, where by its light he saw a large number of great jars set against the wall.

"Those vessels," she added, "are filled with wine, oil, grain, dried flesh, corn, and other sorts of food; also, nearer to the entrance, as I will show you, are more jars of water which from time to time is renewed, so that here a man, or indeed several men, might live for months and yet not starve."

"The gods defend me from such a fate!" he said, dismayed.

"Aye, Khian, yet who knows? That jackal is safest which has a hole to run to when its hunters are afoot."

"Sooner would I be killed in the open than go mad here in the darkness with the dead for fellowship," he answered doubtfully.

"Nay, Khian, you must not be killed; now you must live on—for me and Egypt."

She set down the lamp in its place and moved to the foot of the tomb. He did likewise, so that there they met and stood a little while, gazing at each other in the midst of a silence that was so deep that they could hear the beating of their hearts. Speech had left them, as though they had no more words to say, yet their eyes spoke in a language of their own. They bent towards each other like wind-swayed palms, nearer and nearer yet, till of a sudden she lay in his arms and her lips were pressed upon his own.

"Beloved," he said presently, "swear that while I live you will wed no man but me."

She lifted her head from his shoulder and looked at him with her large and beautiful eyes that were aswim with tears.

"Is it needful?" she asked in a new voice, a deep, rich voice. "You have little faith, Khian, and I ask no such oath from you."

"Because it would be foolish, Nefra, for who, having loved you, could turn to others? Yet there are many who will seek the fairest lady on the earth and Egypt's Queen. Indeed, has not one sought her already? Therefore, I pray you, swear."

"So be it. I swear by the Spirit that we worship, both of us; I swear by Egypt which, if Roi be right, we shall rule in the days to come; and I swear by the bones of my forefather who sleeps within this tomb that I will wed none but you, Khian. While you live I will be faithful to you, and if you die then swiftly I will follow you, that what we have lost on earth, we may find in the Underworld. If I break this, my oath, then may I become as is he who sleeps beneath my hand to-day," and she touched the tomb with her fingers. "Aye, may my name be blotted from the roll of Egypt's royal ones and may Set take my spirit as his slave. Is it enough, O faithless Khian?"

"Enough and more than enough. Oh! how shall I thank you who have given life to my heart? How shall I serve you whom I adore?"

She shook her head, making no answer, but he, loosing her from his arms, sank to his knees before her. He abased himself as a slave; he lifted the hem of her robe and kissed it, saying:

"Queen of my heart and rightful Queen of Egypt, I, Khian, worship you and do you homage. Whatever I have or may have, I set beneath your feet, acknowledging your Majesty. Henceforth I, your lover who hope to be your husband, am the humblest of your subjects."

She bent down and raised him.

"Nay," she said, smiling, when once more he stood upon his feet, "you are greater than I and it is the woman who serves the man, not the man the woman. Well, we will serve each other and thus be equal. But, Khian, what of Apepi who is your father?"

"I do not know," he answered. "Yet, father or not, I pray that he may not try to come between us."

"I pray so also, Khian. To-night is happy, never was there so happy a night; but to-morrow—oh! what of to-morrow?"

"It is in the Hands of God, Nefra, therefore let us fear nothing."

"Aye, Khian, but often the paths of God are steep and rough, or so my father and my mother found. Like us they loved each other well, yet this Apepi was their doom. Come, we must go, for alas! all sweet things have their end."

So once more they clung and kissed, and then hand in hand went down the darksome ways of that House of Death to the moonlit world without.

When they had climbed the steep ascent and were come to the mouth of the passage, Nefra stopped and by the light of the last lamp, for she had extinguished the others as they went, taught Khian how, by pressing a certain stone which swung upon a pivot, the place could be closed at will and, if need were, made fast from within by the aid of a bar and pins of granite, which the builders of the pyramid had used to shut out the curious while they went about their work upon the secret burial chambers at its heart. Also she showed him a great hanging door of granite that those who brought the Pharaoh to his burial a thousand years before had forgotten or neglected to let fall as they departed, leaving him to his eternal rest.

"See," she said, "if that wedge of stone were knocked away the great door would fall. Therefore touch it not, lest we should be shut into this Pyramid of Ur and lay our bones with those of the mighty Khafra, its architect. Look, yonder in that niche, where perhaps once stood the priest or soldier who was guardian of the door, are the jars of water of which I spoke, and by them oil and lamps and wicks of reed and fuel and means of raising fire, with other needful things."

Having shown him all and made sure that he understood, Nefra quenched the last lamp and set it in the niche. Then they crept out on to the side of the pyramid where thrice she made Khian close and open the swinging stone, until he had mastered the trick of it, after which, with a wedge of marble that fitted in a socket hollowed to receive it and yet could be withdrawn in a moment, she made the stone fast, so that now none could tell it from those around unless they had the secret and knew in which course of the casing blocks it lay. This done, they descended to the ground just by a fallen block that marked where the seeker for the swinging stone must mount. Crossing the paving that surrounds the pyramid, they reached the temple of the Worship of Khafra to the east and kept in its shadow lest they should be seen by some night wanderer. Here, too, they parted with sweet murmured words of farewell, Nefra taking one path homewards and Khian another.

Slowly he made his way through the vast, moonlit wilderness of tombs, his heart filled with a great joy, for had he not won all that he desired? Yet with this joy was mingled fear of what the morrow might bring forth. Then would be handed to him, the ambassador, the written answer of Nefra to the demand of Apepi, his father, that she should give herself to him in marriage. Now he knew well what that answer would be, but what he did not know was how Apepi would receive him when, as duty demanded, he delivered it to him. There was but one hope—that he might prove content that his son should wed this queen without a throne instead of himself, seeing that the reason of such a marriage was political and nothing else, and he, Khian, was his father's heir. Had Apepi seen Nefra, almost certainly things would befall otherwise, for he knew his father's nature and that he would desire to possess himself of beauty such as hers. Happily, however, he had not seen her and therefore might be content to let her go, who was naught to him if he could secure her heritage for the House of the Shepherd kings.

Yet Khian doubted whether events would thus shape themselves. It well might be that when he learned, as learn he would certainly through his spies or otherwise, that his son was betrothed to the high lady whom he had sought for himself, that he would hold that his son, who was also his ambassador, had played the traitor to him, which in a sense was true. If so, he might be very wrath and terrible in his rage, who was cruel-hearted. Moreover, he might desire vengeance. What vengeance? Perhaps the death of the traitor, no less, and if still she would not marry him, the death of Nefra also. For was she not Egypt's lawful Queen and, while she lived, could he sit safe upon his stolen throne?

As he picked his way among the tombs by the moonlight Khian knew in his heart that he and Death were face to face. Dark imaginations possessed him. Almost could he see that grisly shape stalking ahead of him while, wrapped in the long, hooded cloak that he used as a disguise, his shadow, cast by the moonlight on the sand, to his sight took the very shape of Osiris in his mummy wrappings—yes, of Osiris the god of death. Yet if so, was not Osiris also the god of resurrection and the king of life eternal? If indeed doom awaited him and Nefra, at least beyond the grave lay joy and peace for thousands of thousands of years.

So Roi taught and so he believed. Still, coming fresh from the lips of his love, those warm and human lips with her sweet words echoing in his ears, he shivered at these sad and solemn thoughts. For who could be sure of what lay over the edge of the world? Oh! who could be quite sure?

****

Khian came to the private door of the Temple of the Sphinx. As he approached it, from beneath its arch appeared the gigantic shape of Ru who looked at him with curious eyes.

"Have you been seeking the Spirit of the Pyramids, Lord, that you wander abroad so late?"

"Who else?" asked Khian.

"And did you find her, Lord, and look upon her face that men say is so beautiful?"

"Yes, Ru, I found her and looked upon her face. Nor does rumour lie as to her beauty."

"And are you already mad, Lord, as they say those become on whom that Spirit smiles?"

"Yes, Ru, I am mad—mad with love."

"And being mad, Lord, are you prepared to pay the price of her embrace and to follow her into the Underworld?"

"If need be, I am prepared, Ru."

The giant stood pondering, his eyes fixed upon the sand. At length he lifted his head, saying:

"Lord, I am but a fool of a fighting man, yet to us of the Ethiopian blood foresight comes at times. I tell you because I like you well that I see it written upon this sand that for your own sake and that of another, you would be wise this very night to fly fast and far across the sea to Syria or to Cyprus, or up Nile to the south, and there lie hid awaiting better days."

"I thank you, Ru. But tell me, at the end of that writing on the sand, do you see the symbol of Osiris?"

"No, Lord, not that for you or for another. Yet I do see the signs of blood and many sorrows near at hand."

"Blood dries and sorrows pass, Ru," and leaving the Ethiopian still staring at the ground, Khian entered the temple and sought his chamber.

CHAPTER 13

The Messenger from Tanis

The Council of the Order of the Dawn was summoned to meet early in the morning on the morrow of that night of full moon when the Prince Khian, in searching for a spirit, had found a woman and a lover. At daybreak, those who watched the frontier of the Holy Field had reported that a messenger had come by boat from King Apepi and waited in the grove of palms to be escorted under safe-conduct into the presence of the Council. It was added that when he was asked what had chanced to the priest Temu who had been sent bearing writings from the Council to the King of the North at Tanis, this messenger replied that he had died of sickness at the Court, and therefore could return no more, or so he had heard. Then it was ordered that the man should be led before the Council at its meeting, there to deliver his message or the writings that he bore.

At the appointed hour Roi the Prophet and all the Council of the Dawn assembled in the temple hall, whither came also every member of the Order to hear the answer of Nefra the Queen to the demands of the King Apepi, and with them Khian under his name and title of Rasa the Scribe, the envoy from the King of the North. Lastly, royally arrayed and for the first time wearing the crowns of Upper and Lower Egypt, appeared Nefra herself attended by the Ethiopian, Ru, for a body-servant, and Lady Kemmah, her nurse. She took her seat upon the throne that was set to receive her, the same throne that she had filled upon the night of her coronation, whereon the Council and the company rose and made obeisance to her.

At this moment it was announced that the messenger from King Apepi waited without with the letters of the King. It was ordered that he should be admitted, and he entered, guarded by two priests.

Khian looked at him as he came up the dusky hall, thinking that he might know him again as one of the King's Court at Tanis, and saw a thickset man of middle-height who limped as he walked, and was wrapped round with shawls that even covered the lower part of his face, as though to protect himself against the cold of the winter morning. Suddenly this man's glance fell upon Khian watching him, whereon he started and turned his head. Next it fell upon Nefra seated in pomp and youthful beauty upon the throne and illumined by a ray of light that struck full upon her through one of the high-placed window openings of the hall. Again the man started as though in wonder, then limped on towards the dais. Arriving in front of it he bowed humbly, drew from his robe a papyrus roll which he laid against his forehead before handing it to one of the priests who mounted the dais and gave it to Nefra. She received the writing and passed it on to the Prophet Roi who sat upon her right hand.

Having opened and studied it, Roi read the writing aloud. It was short and ran thus:

"From Apepi the Pharaoh to the Council of the Order of the Dawn:

"I, the Pharaoh, have received your letter, also one from my envoy, the Scribe Rasa. Your messenger, who gave the name of Temu, reached this Court sick and after lingering for many days, has died. Yet before he died he told my officers that the envoy whom I sent to you, Rasa the Scribe, was dead, having fallen from a pyramid. I demand to know the circumstances of the death of this scribe, my servant, holding that he has been murdered among you.

"Of what is written in your letter I say nothing till I learn the answer of the Lady Nefra to the offer of marriage with me, the Pharaoh, which I have made to her, for according to that answer I shall act. This roll I send by a faithful man but one who, being humble in his station, knows nothing of the matter with which it deals, for the reason that I will not trust another of my high officers among you. Deliver your answer to this man and let him return at once, for if accident overtakes him also, I, the Pharaoh, shall smite.

"Sealed with the seal of Apepi, the good god, Pharaoh of the Upper and the Lower Lands, and with the seal of his Vizier Anath."

Having read Roi cast down the writing, for his rage was great, and motioned to the messenger to fall back. This he did readily, as though afraid, taking his stand among the shadows of the lower part of the hall where he leaned against a pillar after the fashion of one who is lame and weary.

Then Roi spoke, saying:

"The King Apepi sends us no answer to those things that we wrote to him, but accuses us of the murder of his envoy, the Scribe Rasa, and tells us that our messenger Temu is dead of sickness, which we do not believe, to whom it is given to know if aught of ill befalls one of our brethren. Be pleased to appear, Scribe Rasa, that this messenger from King Apepi and all here gathered may see that you are not dead, but living. Come hither, Scribe Rasa, and take your stand by the throne that all may behold you."

So Khian mounted the dais and stood by the throne, and as he came Nefra smiled at him, and he smiled at her. Then Roi went on:

"Queen Nefra, the time has come when you must make answer to the demand of King Apepi that your Majesty should give yourself to him in marriage. What say you, Queen Nefra?"

"Holy Prophet and Council of the Dawn," answered Nefra in a clear and quiet voice, "I say that I thank the King Apepi, but that I will not give myself in marriage to him who brought my father to his death and by treachery would have taken my mother and myself that he might bring us also to our deaths. It is enough."

"Let the words of her Majesty be written down that she may seal them with her seal and that certain of us may seal them as witnesses. Let them be written down forthwith and given to the envoy of King Apepi, Rasa the Scribe. Also let a copy of them be given to this messenger, that thus we may be certain that they come to the eyes of King Apepi."

It was done, Tau writing them with his own hands, after which they were sealed, copied, and made fast in rolls. Then Roi commanded that the messenger of King Apepi should advance and receive the copy.

But when they searched for him that messenger was gone. During the long writing and sealings he had slipped away un-noted, telling those who guarded the door that he had his answer to the message and was dismissed. There was talk of following him, but Tau said:

"Let him be. The man grew frightened and ran, thinking that if he stayed here he might die, as our brother Temu is said to have died at Tanis. That he has left the roll matters nothing, since what his ears have heard his tongue can tell."

So that messenger departed and, save Roi, none thought of him more.

****

Khian was summoned to a private chamber, that of Roi. There he found the prophet himself and with him the lord Tau, some of the elders of the Council, and Nefra attended by the Lady Kemmah. When he was seated Roi spoke, saying:

"Our Queen has told us a story, Prince Khian, for so you are, as we have known from the first. She says that while wandering among the tombs last night, as at times it is her fancy to do, she chanced to meet you, Prince Khian, who were taken with a like desire, and that you spoke together alone. If so, what did you say to the Queen and what did she say to you?"

"Holy Prophet, I said that I loved her and desired to be her husband, which were the truest words that ever passed my lips," answered Khian boldly. "As to what she said to me, let her tell you if she will."

Now the blood came to the brow of Nefra, and looking down, she murmured:

"I said to the Prince Khian that I gave gift for gift and love for love, desiring him and no other man to be my lord. Now I pray your blessing on this choice of mine, my Master in the spirit, and with it the consent of the Council of the Order to our betrothal."

"The blessing you have in full measure, Sister and Queen, and the consent I think will not be withheld. Know that we have hoped and prayed that so it would befall, and even made the happening easy, in the trust that thus, without war or bloodshed, Egypt that is severed in twain may once more become one land, acknowledging one throne. Moreover, it seemed to us who have watched you both that you two are well-fitted to each other, and we believe that you were appointed to come together. That is our answer."

"I thank you, Father," said Khian, and Nefra also murmured, "I thank you."

"Aye," went on Roi, "doubtless your hearts thank us in their happiness, yet, Prince and Queen, there is more to be said. Troubles are ahead of you and us, nor can you be united until these are overcome. Apepi threatens us. When he learns that he has been rejected, he will be very wrath, and when he comes to understand why and for whom his suit has been refused—and such a matter cannot be long concealed—what then? Is it still your purpose, Prince Khian, to bear our written answer which that messenger has left behind him, to your father, King Apepi, or will you choose to bide on with us, or to fly the land and hide awhile?"

Khian thought a little, then replied:

"Before I knew what fate held in store for me, I accepted this embassy and, according to custom, swore the envoy's oath of loyal service, namely, that I would bear my message and return with its answer, if I lived, making a true report of those to whom it was sent. This oath I must fulfil or be shamed, and therefore I cannot hide away disguised here or elsewhere because my task has become dangerous. That I have adopted the doctrines of the Dawn and am affianced to a certain high lady are my private matters, or so I hold; but to sail in that ship which has been summoned from Memphis to await me in the river, and to deliver your answer to the King Apepi, is my public duty. If ill comes to me in the performing of that duty, it must be so, but if I left it un-performed I should be no honest man. I will deliver the letters and, if need be, tell King Apepi the truth, leaving the end of all to fortune, or rather to the will of That which we worship."

Now Nefra looked at him proudly, while the others murmured: "Well spoken."

"These are high-hearted words," said Roi, "and they please me, Prince Khian, who know from them that our Queen has given her love to no base man. The danger is great and until it be overcome you may not marry lest your bride should be widowed almost as soon as she was wed. Yet I believe that it will be overcome and that in the end the Spirit whom we serve will guide your feet to joy and safety."

"May it be so," said Khian.

"Hearken both of you," went on Roi. "I am very old and it is re-vealed to me that soon I must pass hence, how as yet I do not know. Yes, I, the seeker after light, must enter into the darkness where, as I trust, I shall find light. Prince Khian, you look upon my face for the last time. All my days I have striven to bring about the unity of Egypt, without bloodshed if that might be. Now perchance in the persons of you, Prince and Queen, this unity will be accomplished and Egypt will be one again, if only for a while. That accomplishment I shall not live to see, though I trust that in after days I may hear of it from your lips else-where. Yet being dead I trust also that my spirit may still guide you both upon the earth although you see it not. Come hither, Khian, Prince of the North, and Nefra, anointed Queen of Egypt, that I may bless you."

They came and knelt before the ancient priest who already seemed more a spirit than a man. He laid his thin hands upon their heads and blessed them in the name of Heaven and in his own, calling down joy and fruitfulness upon them and consecrating them to the service of Egypt—of the order of the Dawn, and of that universal Soul whom they worshipped. Then suddenly he rose and left them.

One by one, according to their degree, the members of the Coun-cil followed, and with them went Kemmah and the giant Ru, so that presently Khian and Nefra found themselves alone.

"The hour of farewell is at hand," said Khian sadly.

"Yes, Beloved," answered Nefra, "but oh! when and where will come the hour of re-union?"

"I do not know, Nefra. None knows, not even Roi, but be brave, for assuredly it will come. I must go; but now I saw it in your eyes that, like myself, you thought that I must go."

"Yes, Khian, so I thought, and think. Therefore go, and swiftly, before my heart breaks. Remember all, Khian, and every word that has passed between us. Now one thing more. I charge you by our love that whatever you may hear concerning me, even if they tell you that I am wed elsewhere, or faithless, that you believe nothing, save that while I live, here or in the Underworld, I am yours and yours alone, and that rather than pass into the hands of another man I will surely die. Do you swear this, Khian?"

"I swear it, Nefra; also that as you are to me, so I will be to you."

Then with murmured words of love again they clung and kissed till soon, at a sign, for she could speak no more, Khian loosed her from his arms. He loosed her, he bowed to her, and she bowed back to him. Then he went. At the doorway he turned to look on her. There robed in the virginal white of the Sisters of the Dawn, wearing no ornament or mark of rank and yet looking most royal, she stood still as a statue, gazing after him while one by one the heavy tears welled from her deep eyes. Another instant and like some gate of doom the door swung to behind him and she was seen no more.

****

In his chamber Khian found Tau, the second Prophet of the Order, awaiting him.

"I come to tell you, Prince, that your ship is ready at the river bank, to which your goods with the presents sent by King Apepi have been borne," he said, adding, "Ru will escort you thither."

"Yes, Tau, but who will escort me back?" he asked, sighing heavily. "I feel like one who has dreamed a happy dream and awakened to the world and know it but a dream which will never be fulfilled."

"Take courage, Prince, for I hold otherwise. Yet I will not hide from you that the peril of all of us is great. We learn that Apepi masses troops, as he says, to protect himself against the Babylonians who threaten him, but who can be certain? I would that we had questioned that messenger as was my purpose. But he slipped away while we thought that he was waiting for our letter."

"So would I, Tau, but he is gone and now it is too late."

"Prince," went on Tau in a low voice, "it may be that for a while the Order of the Dawn, and with it a certain lady, must vanish from Egypt. Yet if this comes about, do not believe that we are lost or dead who shall but have gone to seek help, whence as yet I may not reveal even to you, though perchance you may guess. We hate war and bloodshed, Prince, but if these are forced upon us, we shall fight, or certainly I shall fight who in my youth was as you are, a soldier and have commanded armies. Therefore, remember that while I live and indeed while a Brother or Sister of the Dawn lives throughout the world, and as you saw on the night of the Crowning, they are many, dwelling in many lands, that lady will not lack a defender or a home. And now, farewell till perchance in a day to come I see you and that lady wed and afterwards crowned as King and Queen of the Land of the Nile, reigning from the Cataracts to the sea. Again, Brother, fare you well."

****

Once more Khian walked across the stretch of desert that lay between the Sphinx and the palm grove by the bank of the Nile, but this time his companion was no hooded youth with the voice and the hands of a woman, but the Ethiopian Ru who, as he went, addressed him in a kind of soliloquy, after this sort:

"So, Lord, you really are the Prince Khian, as rumour said and the Lady Kemmah and I guessed from the first, and now you are affianced to my Queen, for which I hate you because ever since you came she has hardly had a look or a word for me. Yet to be honest, as such things must happen, I would rather it was to you than to any one else, because you are a soldier and I like you, also a man of courage, as you showed when you learned to climb those pyramids which I should never have dared to do. So I shall be glad to serve you when you are married, though if you do not treat my Queen well, beware of this axe, for then, if you were fifty Pharaohs and a hundred gods, with it I would still cleave you to the chin. No doubt you think that you are very clever to win her love, as certainly you have done, but there you are mistaken. You did not win her love and she did not win yours. It was those old priests of the Dawn who arranged everything and by their magic threw a spell upon both of you because they wished to bring all this about for purposes of their own. Believe me, that as they have joined you together, so they can separate you if they choose, and by their incantations, make you hate each other. Only I don't think they will as that would not suit them, and you see you are both of you members of the Order of the Dawn, and therefore will be supported by them in all things that you may desire."

"I am glad to hear that," interrupted Khian, when at length Ru paused to take breath.

"Yes, yes. Lord, it is a very good thing to be one of the Order, or even its servant as I am, because then everywhere you have a friend. Therefore never be afraid, however desperate your case may be, even if the hangman is putting his rope about your neck; for certainly Roi, or another far away, will utter one of the spells, or speak a word of power, and someone will appear to help you. That is why I am quite sure that in the end you will marry my Queen if both of you continue to want each other, and that all of us will escape from the jaws of that roaring lion, your father the King Apepi, although he does think that he has our heads in his mouth."

"How will you all escape, Ru?"

"Why, Lord, by finding friends who are stronger than Apepi. There is the King of Babylon, for instance, our Lady's grandfather who can put two spearmen in the field for every one of Apepi's, to say nothing of a multitude of chariots drawn by horses, which Apepi has not got. The Order has plenty of brothers at the Court of the King of Babylon; some of them were here on the night of the Crowning, and I know that messages have been going to them almost every day. Never mind how they went—that's a secret. I should not wonder if we went, too, before long, and then perhaps I may see some more fighting before I grow too old and fat to use my axe. As you are affianced to our Queen, I do not mind talking of these things to you."

"No, of course you don't," answered Khian.

"Talking of messages reminds me of messengers," went on Ru, "or rather of one messenger. I mean that fellow who came from Apepi this morning and slipped away afterwards, which he would never have done had I been guarding him instead of those silly priests."

"What of him?" asked Khian.

"Oh! only that he was a queer sort of fellow, and more, I think, than he seemed to be. Did you see his eye, Lord? It was like that of a hawk, very proud, too, such an eye as a great noble might have, and when he heard the Queen's answer, it grew full of rage and all his body shook beneath those shawls. More—there were other strange things. Thus, when he came to the hall he limped as though he were very lame, but some people who were working in the fields told me that they saw him running down to the Nile like a hunted jackal.

"Now how can a lame man run like a jackal? Also I hear that when he came to the boat which was waiting for him, those who were in the boat or watching on the shore, prostrated themselves as though he were some Great One, but he leapt aboard and cursed them, calling them slaves—as a Great One does. That is why I think he was more than he seemed to be, just like yourself, Lord, who were announced as the Scribe Rasa and yet are really the Prince Khian. But here we are at the palm grove where more than a month ago I stole your baggage while you were asleep, as the Queen, who was only a princess then, put it into my head to do, for from childhood she has loved such jests. And look, there is your ship, the same that brought you hither, and there are the priests with your packages."

"Yes, Ru, there they all are who I wish were somewhere else. And now here is a present for you, Ru, a chain of fine gold that I have worn myself. Keep it in memory of me and hang it about your neck when you attend upon the Queen, that it may make her think of one who is absent."

"I thank you, Lord, though it seems that you seek to kill two birds with this stone of a gift, which I may show but may not sell. Well, lovers will think of themselves first, and I hope that one day if we should stand together in war——Why, look! Here comes the Lady Kemmah, walking faster than I have seen her do for years. I think she must have some words for you."

As he spoke Kemmah arrived.

"So I have caught you, Prince," she said, puffing. "A pretty task for an old woman to toil across that sand in the heat like a cow after a lost calf, just to please a maiden's fancy."

"What is it, Kemmah?" asked Khian anxiously.

"Oh! little enough. To give you this which a certain one might as well have done herself, had she thought of it, and to pray you to wear it always for her sake, remembering that thereby she acknowledges you as her king as well as her lover, which of course she has no right to do, any more than she has a right to send you what she does. I told her so but she flew into a rage and said that if I would not take it, she would bring it herself as she could trust it to no one else. A pretty sight indeed that a Queen should be seen tearing across the desert after a departing scribe, for so the common people still believe you to be. Therefore come I must or bear her wrath."

"I understand, Lady Kemmah, but what do you bring? You have given me nothing save words."

"Have I not? Well, here it is," and she produced from her robe some small object wrapped in papyrus on which was written, "The gift of a Queen to her King and Lover."

Khian undid the papyrus. There within lay the royal signet of Nefra, the same which he had seen set upon her hand on the night of Coronation.

"This is the Queen's ring," said Khian, astonished.

"Aye, Prince, and the King her father's ring before her, that which was taken from his finger by the embalmers after the battle, and his father's before him, and so on back and back for ages. Look, on it is cut the name of Khafra whose tomb I think you saw the other night, though if he ever wore it I cannot tell. At least it has descended through countless generations from Pharaoh to Pharaoh, and now it seems must pass as a love gift to one who is not Pharaoh but yet is charged to wear it as though he were."

"As perchance he may be yet, by right of another, Lady Kemmah, though the matter does not trouble him overmuch," answered Khian, smiling. Then he took the ancient hallowed thing and, having touched it with his lips, set it on a finger of his right hand that it fitted well, removing thence, to make place for it, another ring on which was engraved a crowned and lion-headed sphinx, the symbol of his house.

"A gift for a gift," he said. "Take this to the Lady Nefra and bid her wear it in token that all I have is hers, as I will wear that she sends to me. Say to her also that on the day when we are wed each shall return to the other that ring which belonged to each and with it all of which it is the symbol."

So Kemmah took the ring and as she hid it away there came that Captain of the Guard who had accompanied him from Tanis.

"Welcome, my Lord Rasa, who I rejoice to see have not fallen a victim to the Spirit of the Pyramids of which we talked when we parted here some five and thirty days ago, or was it more? for time passes quickly in yonder gay city of Memphis. You seem to have found strange company in this holy haunted land," and he glanced with awe at the ebon form of the giant Ru who stood by leaning on his great axe, and at the white-veiled, stately Lady Kemmah who stood near him. "You look thin and changed, too, as though you had been keeping company with ghosts. Well, the steersman says that if you are ready, my Lord Rasa, he desires to sail before the wind changes, or because the sailors are afraid of this place, or for both reasons. So if it pleases you, come."

"I am ready," answered Khian, and while Kemmah bowed to him and Ru saluted him with the axe in farewell, he turned and went to the river bank where the sailors bore him through the shallow water to the ship. Presently he was far out upon the Nile, watching the palm-grove, where first he had met Nefra, fade in the gathering gloom. Still there he sat upon the deck till the great moon rose shining upon the pyramids, and thinking of all the wondrous things that had befallen him in their shadow, until these at last grew dim and vanished, leaving him wondering, like one who awakens from a dream.

135

CHAPTER 14

The Sentence of Pharaoh

Khian came to Tanis safely, landing at dawn.

Having reached the palace, he went to his private chambers and, putting off his scribe's attire, clothed himself in the robes of his rank. As soon as men began to stir he reported his arrival through an officer to the Vizier, and waited.

From the window-place of his chamber he saw that troops were moving on the plain beneath, also that many vessels flying the royal banner were unmooring from the quays and sailing away up Nile. While he marvelled what this might mean, the cunning-faced old Vizier, Anath, came and welcomed him with bows.

"Greeting, Prince," he said. "I rejoice to see that you have accomplished your mission in safety, for know that here we heard that you were dead by a fall from a pyramid, which we took to mean that you had been murdered by those strange zealots of the Dawn."

"I know that story, Anath, for it was written in a letter which was brought by a messenger from my father, whereon I stepped forward to show myself alive and well, though it is true that I did fall from a pyramid and was senseless a while. Has that messenger returned? He fled away suddenly before I could have speech with him."

"I do not know, Prince," answered Anath. "The man has not been reported to me, but I have only just risen and he may have come in the night."

"I hope he has, Anath," said Khian, laughing, "seeing that although he did not wait for the writing which I bear, he had news that I fear will scarcely please my father who I prefer should learn it from him, not from me."

"Is it so, Prince?" asked Anath, eyeing him curiously. "Already there has come news from these people of the Dawn, enough and more than enough to make His Majesty very wrath, and should it be added to by other tidings of the same sort, I think he will be mad with rage. Would it please you to tell me this news?"

"I think not, Anath, although you are his Vizier and the holder of his secrets, as you know, Pharaoh my father is strange-tempered and might take it ill if I reveal to any one what I am charged to deliver to himself."

Anath bowed and answered:

"As to the temper of his Majesty, you are right, Prince, for since you went away it has been terrible. Would that some evil god had never moved me to put a certain thought into his mind: would that we had never heard of the Order of the Dawn. Because of that thought and them he has even threatened me with the loss of my office, though he knows well that if I were driven from it, evil would come to himself, seeing that for years I have been the shield that has turned arrows from his head and by my foresight have saved him from conspiracies."

"I know that this is so," answered Khian.

Anath thought a little while, then went on in a low voice:

"Prince, even Pharaohs fall or die at last. The dust awaits their crowns, the grave their greatness. Prince, I have watched you from a child and made a study of your heart, which I know to be honest and true. Now I will ask you a question, promising to believe your answer as though it were that of a god. Are you friendly towards me and if a time should come when you sit where another sits to-day, would you continue me in my offices, especially in that of Vizier of the North? Weight the matter and tell me, Prince."

Khian reflected for a moment, then answered:

"I think that I would, Anath; indeed I am sure that I would."

"And of the South also if that great land should chance to be added to your heritage?"

"Yes, I suppose so, Anath, though here another—I mean others— might claim a voice. Why not? If you have watched me, I have watched you, and forgive me if I say I know your faults, namely, that you are cunning and a great seeker after wealth and power. But I know also that you are faithful to those you serve and to your friends, and in your own way the cleverest man in Egypt, also the most far-seeing, as you showed when you schemed that Pharaoh should wed the Princess of the South, though that plan has bred more trouble than you know. So there you have my answer, and, as you said, I am not one who breaks his word."

Anath took the Prince's hand and kissed it, saying:

"I thank you, Prince." Then he paused and added: "The day when you are Pharaoh of the North and South I may remind you of these words which from your lips are a decree that may not be broken."

"What does all this mean, Anath?" asked Khian impatiently. "You are not making me party to some plot against my father, are you?"

"By all the gods of the Shepherds and the Egyptians, no, Prince. Yet hearken. I have noted that if he is crossed in his will, his Majesty of late goes mad, and those who go mad seek ruin, especially if they be kings. Moreover, he is very rash and the rash fall into pits from which other men escape. Also in his body he is not as strong as he thinks and rage sometimes stops the heart. If Pharaoh's heart stops, what is Pharaoh?"

"A good god!" replied Khian, laughing.

"Yes, but one who attends no more to the affairs of earth. A month or so gone your father asked your consent to his disinheritance of you and you gave it without a thought. Perchance since then, Prince, you may have found reason to change your mind upon this matter."

Here he glanced at Khian shrewdly and went on: "But whether you have changed it or not, know that heirs apparent cannot be so lightly dispossessed of their acknowledged rights."

"You seemed to agree at the time, Anath; indeed you did more: it was you who set afoot that new scheme of a certain marriage."

"The rush bends before the wind, Prince, and as to this marriage, perchance I wished to save the People of the Dawn, of whose doctrines I think well, or perchance I wished to save Egypt from another war, or both. The one thing that I did not wish to do was to hurt you, Prince. And yet this came about, and now that knot must be undone."

"Yes, Anath, it came about, or seemed to, for which the gods be thanked, since otherwise I should never have been sent upon a certain mission and certain things would never have happened to me which have made me the happiest man in all the world. I will tell you of them afterwards, perhaps—if I dare. Meanwhile, when will my father receive me? Also, why are those troops gathered yonder and whither do the ships sail up Nile? Is it to make another war upon the South?"

"His Majesty has been upon some pilgrimage of his own, Prince, as he said to make a sacrifice in the desert after the custom of our forefathers, the old Shepherds. He only returned thence last night, so weary or so angered about I know not what that he would not receive me. I believe that he still sleeps but there will be a Court before noon, at which you must appear. As for the soldiers and the ships——"

At this moment there rose a cry without.

"A messenger from Pharaoh!" said the cry. "A messenger from Pharaoh to the Prince Khian. Way for the messenger of Pharaoh!"

The doors burst open, the curtains were torn apart, and there entered one of Apepi's heralds clad in his livery and wearing a sheepskin on his back, after the ancient fashion of the shepherds. He sprang forward and, prostrating himself before the Prince, said:

"Having heard that your Highness has returned to Tanis Pharaoh Apepi summons you to his presence in the Hall of Audience instantly, instantly, instantly! O Prince Khian. And you also He summons, O Vizier Anath. Come, come, come, O High Prince, and O great Vizier."

"It seems that my father is in a hurry."

"Yes," answered Anath, "in such a hurry that we had best not keep him waiting. Afterwards we will talk again, Prince. Herald, lead on."

So they followed the man down the passages and across the courtyard to the door of the Hall of Audience through which were speeding sundry of the counsellors and nobles who were called "The King's Companions," and as it seemed, also had been summoned hastily. At the end of the hall, seated in a chair of state and surrounded by priests, scribes, and a guard of soldiers, was Apepi. Glancing at him, Khian noted that he seemed to be weary and dishevelled in his dress, for he wore no crown, while in place of the royal mantle and apron of ceremony, a coloured shawl was thrown round him which reminded Khian of something, though at the moment he could not remember what it was. Moreover, his face seemed drawn and thin and his eyes were very fierce.

Khian advanced up the hall and, after uttering the customary salutation, prostrated himself before the King, while having made obeisance, Anath the Vizier took his place on the left of the throne.

"Rise," said Apepi, "and tell me, Prince Khian, how it comes about that you whom I sent upon a certain embassy did not report your return to me."

"Pharaoh and Father," answered Khian, "I disembarked at dawn and at once, according to custom, caused the Vizier to be informed of my arrival. The Vizier Anath rose from his sleep and visited me. He told me that your Majesty was still resting on your bed after some journey that you had made."

"It matters not what he told you, and is the Vizier Pharaoh that you should report yourself to him and not to me, so that I must learn of your coming from the Captain of the Guard, whom I sent with you? Surely you lack respect and he takes too much upon himself. Well, what of your mission to those People of the Dawn? Have you made report of that also to the Vizier? Know that I thought you dead, as my messenger may have told you yonder at the pyramids. Should you not therefore have hastened to advise me that you still lived? Is it thus that a son should treat his father or a subject his king?"

Once more Khian began to explain but Apepi cut him short.

"I received the letter from the Council of the Dawn, an insolent letter giving me back threat for threat, and with it another from yourself, Khian, saying that you had seen this Nefra at some ceremony when and where she purported to be crowned as Queen of Egypt. But I have received no answer to my question as to whether this lady accepts or refuses my offer of marriage. Do you bring that answer, Khian?"

"I do," answered Khian, and drawing out the roll he handed it to the Vizier who on bended knee passed it on to the King.

Apepi undid the writing and read it through carelessly, like to one who already knew what was written there. As he read his brow grew black and his eyes flashed.

"Hearken," he said. "This mock queen refuses to be my wife, as she says because years ago her father Kheperra was killed in battle with my armies. Yes, that is what she says. Now, Khian, do you who have dwelt all this while among the People of the Dawn tell me of her real reasons."

"How am I to know a woman's reasons in such a matter, your Majesty?"

"In sundry ways, I think, Khian, otherwise you are but a poor envoy. Yet before you search your mind for them, stretch out your right hand."

Thinking that he was about to be asked to take some oath, Khian obeyed. Apepi stared at it, then once more stared at the letter and asked in a quiet voice:

"How comes it, Khian, that you wear upon your hand, where I remember used to be a certain ring that I gave to you engraved with the symbol of our House and your titles as Prince of Egypt, another ring, an ancient ring inscribed with the name of Khafra, Royal Son of the Sun, who once a thousand years ago was Pharaoh of Egypt? And how does it chance that this letter of refusal is sealed with that same ring by Nefra who describes herself as Queen of Egypt?"

Now all present stared at Khian, while for a moment a little smile flickered on the withered face of the Vizier Anath.

"It was a parting gift to me," said Khian, looking down.

"Oh! So this puppet queen makes a parting gift of her royal ring to you, my envoy. And did you perchance make a parting gift to her of the ring of the heir apparent to the Crown of the North?"

Apepi paused, watching Khian, but he made no answer.

Then the King his father went on in a low, roaring voice like to that of an angry lion:

"Now I understand all. Know, Son, that *I* was that messenger who visited the habitations of the Brethren of the Dawn some few days ago. Yes, since he could trust no one else, not even his own son, Pharaoh himself filled that humble office and came for his own answer. See, do you know him now?" and rising from the throne with a quick motion he wound the coloured Bedouin shawl about him so that it hid his face up to the eyes, and limped forward a few paces.

"Yes," answered Khian, "and, my Father, the disguise is as excellent as the plan was bold, for had you but known it, you ran a great risk among people who are worshippers of truth and look for it in others."

Apepi returned to his throne and spoke again in the same roaring voice:

"Aye, I ran a risk because I, too, love truth and desired to know what was passing yonder by the pyramids, also to behold this daughter of Kheperra with my own eyes. So I came and saw that she is very fair and royal, such a one as I desire above all women for my queen. Other things I saw also, among them that again and again she looked sweetly at one clad in the white robe of a Brother of the Dawn, one who presently I discovered to be no other than yourself, my envoy that I believed was dead. Moreover, I heard from a fisherman that there were strange sayings in those parts: namely, that the 'Daughter of the Dawn' had promised herself to the Son of the Sun and that the Spirit of the Pyramids had been unveiled by a man, of which sayings he swore he did not know the meaning, though now to me it is clear enough. Tell me, therefore, Khian, who come from the House of Truth, first—are you wed or affianced to the Princess Nefra, daughter of Kheperra whose ring you wear upon your hand? and secondly, are you sworn a Brother of the Dawn?"

Now his courage came back to Khian and, looking his father in the eyes, he answered boldly:

"Why should I hide from your Majesty that I am betrothed to the royal lady, Nefra, whom I love and who loves me, also that after thought and study I have adopted the pure doctrines of the Dawn and am sworn of its holy Brotherhood?"

"Why, indeed," asked Apepi with bitter irony, "seeing that these things have been discovered before it pleased you to announce them. So, my son Khian, you whom I sent as my ambassador to ask a wife for me, have stolen that wife for your own, and you whom I set to watch my enemies, have adopted their doctrines and been sworn of their secret fellowship. Why have you done these things? I will tell you. You have broken your trust and robbed me of the woman because, did I marry her, her son might thrust you from your heirship, whereas, if you marry her, you keep it, as you think, and add to it whatever claims this princess may have on the throne of Egypt. It is clever, Khian, very clever."

"I became affianced to the Lady Nefra because we love each other and for no other reason," answered the Prince hotly.

"If so, Khian, your love and your advantage go hand in hand, as do her love and her advantage, wherein I think I see the cunning of that old prophet, Roi. For the rest, you swear yourself of this Order because you believe it to be powerful, having friends in many lands, and think that by their help in days to come you will buttress up your throne or win mine from me. Khian, I say that you are a thief, a liar, and a traitor, and that as such I will deal with you."

"Your Majesty knows well that I am none of these. In order to bring about a certain alliance, your Majesty was pleased to reduce me from my rank of heir apparent to that of a private person and as such to send me on an embassy. As envoy I did my duty, but those to whom I was sent would not listen to your Majesty's proposal which I could not help. Afterwards, as a private person I chanced to become attached to a certain lady who, if I had not lived, for reasons of her own would never have listened to the offer of your Majesty. That is all the tale."

"That perhaps we shall know when you have ceased to live, Khian. Learn now how I will deal with these tomb rats of the pyramids who have defied and insulted me. I will send an army—already it is on its road—to knock them on the head, all of them. Only one will I spare—the Lady Nefra; not because she is born of a royal House, but because I have looked upon her and seen that she is beautiful, for, Khian, you are not the only man who can worship beauty. Therefore I will bring her here and make her mine, and for a marriage gift I will give her your head, Khian; yes, you, the traitor, shall die before her eyes."

Now when they heard this decree the high officers who were named Companions of the King stared at each other dismayed, for never before had such a thing been told of, as that a Pharaoh of Egypt should kill his own son because both of them loved the same woman. Even Anath the Vizier started and paled; yet all that came from his lips was the ancient salutation:

"Life! Health! Strength! Pharaoh's word is spoken, let Pharaoh's will be done!"

As this hideous sentence fell upon his ears and a vision of all it meant rose before his eyes, for a moment Khian felt his heart stop and his knees tremble beneath him. He saw his Brethren of the Dawn slaughtered and lying in their blood wherever they were trapped in their hiding places. He saw the giant Nubian, Ru, overcome at last and falling dead upon a mat of foes that he had slain. He saw the Lady Kemmah butchered and Nefra seized and dragged a prisoner to Tanis, there to be wed by force to a man she loathed. He saw himself led out to death before her eyes and his gory head laid at her feet as an offering. All these things and others he saw with the eye of his mind and was afraid.

Yet of a sudden that fear passed. It was as though a spirit spoke to his soul, the spirit of Roi, or so he thought, because for an instant he seemed to appear before him seated where Apepi sat, venerable, calm, and holy. Then he was gone, and with him went the terrors of Khian. Moreover, now he knew what to answer; the words welled up within him like water welling in a spring.

"Pharaoh and my Father," he said in a bold, clear voice, "speak not so madly, for I say that you cannot do these things which you have decreed. Did not the Prophet of the Dawn repeat to you in his letter his answer to your threat? Did he not say that he had no fear of you and that should you attempt harm against the Brotherhood, every stone of the pyramids would lie lighter on your head than will the curse of Heaven which you would earn as a butcher and one forsworn? Did he not tell you that the Order of the Dawn marshalled hosts unseen and that with it goes the Strength of God? If not, I, your son, who am to-day a Brother of the Dawn and its consecrated priest, deliver to you this, his message. Try to do the wickedness that you have decreed, O Pharaoh, and speaking with the voice of the Order of the Dawn, as I am taught by the Spirit which it worships, I warn you that you will draw down upon yourself disaster and death on earth, and after you have left the earth, woe untold in the Underworld. Thus say I, speaking not with my own voice but with that of the Spirit within me."

When Apepi heard these dreadful words, he bowed his head and with trembling hands drew the coloured robe more tightly about him, like to one who in the midst of great heat is struck suddenly by a blast of icy wind. Then again his rage possessed him and he answered:

"Now, Khian, I am minded to send you, the traitor, to your gods, your king, your father, and your blood, down to that Underworld of which you speak, there to discover whether this wizard Roi is or is not a liar. Yes, I am minded to do this instantly here in the presence of the Court. And yet I will not, since to you I appoint a punishment more worthy of your crime. You shall live to see your fellow knaves dead, every one of them; to see this maiden whom you have beguiled, not yours but mine. Then, Khian, you shall die and not before."

"Pharaoh has spoken, and I, an ordained Brother and Priest of the Order of the Dawn, have spoken also," answered Khian in the same clear and quiet voice. "Now let the Spirit judge between us and show to all who have heard our words, and to the whole world, in which of us shines the light of Truth."

Thus said Khian, then bowed to Apepi and was silent.

Pharaoh stared at him awhile, for he was amazed, wondering whence came the strength that gave his son power to utter such words upon the edge of doom. Then he turned to Anath and said:

"Vizier, take this evildoer who is no longer Prince of the North or son of mine, and make him fast in the dungeons of the palace. Let him be well fed that life may remain in him till all things are accomplished."

Anath prostrated himself, rose, and clapped his hands. There appeared soldiers. Khian was set in the midst of them and led away, Anath walking before them.

CHAPTER 15

Brother Temu

Through long passages and down flights of steps, at the head of which stood guards, the melancholy procession descended almost to the foundations of the vast building of the palace. As they went Khian remembered that, when he was a child, some captain of the guard had led him by this path to certain cells where, through a grating in the door, he had looked upon three men who were condemned to die upon the morrow for the crime of having conspired to murder Pharaoh. These men, whom he expected to see groaning and in tears, he recalled, were talking together cheerfully, because, they said, for he heard it through the grating, their troubles would soon be over and either they would be justified in the Underworld or fast asleep for ever.

The three of them took different views upon this matter; one of them believed in the Underworld and redemption through Osiris, one rejected the gods as fables and expected nothing save eternal sleep, while the third held that he would be re-born upon the earth and rewarded for all he had endured by a new and happier life.

The next day Khian heard that all three of them had been hanged and awhile after he learned from his friend, the captain of the guard, that they had been proved to be innocent of the offence with which they were charged. It seemed that a woman of the House of Pharaoh, having been rejected by one of them, had avenged herself by a false accusation and for certain reasons had denounced two other men, whom she hated, as partners in a plot against Pharaoh. Afterwards, when at the point of death from a sudden sickness, she had revealed all, though this did not help her victims who were already dead.

The sight of these men and the learning of their story, Khian recollected as once more he trod those gloomy stairs, had bred in his mind doubts as to the gods which the Shepherds worshipped and of the justice decreed by kings and governors, with the result that in the end he turned his back upon his people's faith and became one of those who desired to reform the world and to replace that which is bad if ancient, by that which is good if new. So indeed he had remained until fate brought him to the Temple of the Dawn, where he found all he sought, a pure faith in which he could believe and doctrines of peace, mercy, and justice such as he desired.

Now, as innocent as those forgotten men, he, the proud Prince of the North, disgraced and doomed, was about to be cast into the same prison that had hid their sufferings and those of a thousand others before and after them. He recalled it all—the stone-vaulted place lit only by a high-set grating of bronze to which none could climb because of the curve of the walls; the paved floor damp from the overflowings of the Nile which, in seasons of flood, rose high above the foundations of the palace; the stools and table, also of stone; the bronze rings to which the officer had told him prisoners were tied if they became violent or went mad; the damp heaps of straw whereon they slept, and the worn skin rugs that they used for covering against the cold; yes, even the places where each of the three victims lay or stood and the very aspect of their faces, especially that of the young and comely man upon whom the rejected woman had avenged herself. Though to this hour it had never been re-visited by him, his mind pictured that horrid hole with all its details.

Now they had trodden the last flight. There was the massive door and in it the grating through which he had looked and listened. The bolts were drawn by the jailer who had joined them; it opened. There were the table and the stone stools, the rings of bronze, the coarse earthenware vessels, and the rest. Only the men were gone—of these nothing remained.

Khian entered the dreadful place. At a sign from Anath the guards saluted and withdrew, looking with pity at the young prince under whom they had served in war and who was beloved of all of them. Anath lingered to give certain instructions to the jailer, then as they were both departing he turned back and inquired of the Prince what garments he required to be sent to him.

"I think such as are thick and warm, Vizier," replied Khian, shivering as the damp cold of the dungeon got a hold of him.

"They shall be sent to your Highness," said Anath. "May your Highness forgive me who must fill this sorry office towards you."

"I forgive you as I forgive all men, Vizier. When hope is dead, forgiveness is easy."

146

Anath glanced behind him and saw that the jailer was standing at a distance from the door with his back towards them. Then he bowed deeply as though in farewell, so that his lips came close to the ear of Khian.

"Hope is *not* dead," he whispered. "Trust to me, I will save you if I can."

Next moment he, too, was gone and the massive door had shut, leaving Khian alone. He sat himself down upon one of the stools, placing it so that the faint light from the grating fell upon him. Awhile later, he did not know how long, the door opened again and the jailer appeared accompanied by another man who brought garments, among them a dark, hooded cloak lined with black sheepskin; also food and wine. Khian thanked him and put on the cloak gratefully, for the cold of the place was biting, noting as he did so that it was not one of his own, which made him wonder; also, that in such a cloak a man might go anywhere and remain unknown.

The jailer set out the food upon the table and prayed his prisoner to eat, addressing him as Prince.

"That title belongs to me no more, Friend."

"Oh, yes! your Highness," replied the man kindly. "Trouble comes to all at times but it cannot change the blood in the veins."

"No, Friend, but it can empty the veins of the blood."

"The gods forbid!" said the jailer, shuddering, from which Khian learned that he had rightly named him friend, and again thanked him.

"It is I who should thank your Highness. Your Highness has forgotten that when my wife and child were sick in the season of fever three years ago, you yourself visited them in the servants' huts and brought them medicines and other things."

"I think I remember," said Khian, "though I am not sure for I have visited so many sick, who, had I not been what I am, or rather was, would, I think, have turned physician."

"Yes, your Highness, and the sick do not forget, nor do those to whom they are dear. I am charged to tell you that you will not be left alone in this place, lest your mind should fail and you should go mad, as many here have done before you."

"What! is another unfortunate to be sent to join me, Friend?"

"Yes, but one whose company it is believed will please you. Now I must go," and he departed before Khian could ask him when this other prisoner would come. After the door had shut behind him Khian ate and drank heartily enough, for he was starving, having touched no food since the afternoon before upon the ship which brought him to Tanis.

When he had finished his meal he fell to thinking and his thoughts were sad enough, for it was evident that it was in his father's mind utterly to destroy the Brotherhood of the Dawn, and to drag Nefra away to be made his wife by violence, for, having by evil fortune looked upon her beauty, nothing now would turn him from his purpose of making her his own. This, however, Khian knew would never happen, for the reason that first Nefra would choose to die. Therefore it would seem that both of them were doomed to death. Oh! if only he could warn them by throwing his spirit afar, as it was said that Roi and some of the higher members of the Order had the power to do. Indeed, had he not felt the thought of Roi strike upon him that morning when he stood before the Pharaoh in the hall of audience? He would try, who had been taught the secrets of the "Sending of the Soul" as it was called, though he had never practised them before.

Try he did according to the appointed form and with the appointed prayers as well as he could remember them, saying:

"Hear me, Holy Father. Danger threatens the Queen and all of you. Hide or fly, for I am in the toils and cannot help you."

Again and again he said it in his heart, fixing the eyes of his mind upon Roi and Nefra till he grew faint with the soul struggle and even in that bitter place the sweat burst out upon him. Then of a sudden a strange calm fell on him to whom it seemed that these arrows of thought had found their mark, yes, that his warnings had been heard and understood.

An utter weariness fell upon him and he slept.

He must have slept for long, for when he woke all light had faded from the grating and he knew that it was night.

The door opened and through it came the jailer bearing more food, quantities of food, and bringing with him another man clothed like Khian himself in a dark, hooded cloak. The stranger bowed and without speaking took his stand in a corner of the cell.

"Behold your servant, Prince, who is appointed to wait upon you. You will find him a good man and true," said the jailer. Then he removed the broken meats and went, having first lit lamps which he left burning in the prison.

Khian looked at the meats and wine; then he looked at the hooded figure in the corner and said:

"Will you not eat, my brother in misfortune?"

The man threw back his hood:

"Surely," said Khian, "I have seen that face before."

The man made a certain sign, which, by habit as it were, Khian answered. The man made more signs and Khian answered them all, then uttered a secret sentence which the man, speaking for the first time, completed with another sentence still more secret.

"Will you not eat, Priest of the Dawn?" he asked again meaningly.

"In hope of the Food Eternal I eat bread. In hope of the Water of Life I drink wine," replied the man.

Then Khian was sure, for in these very words those of the Order of the Dawn were accustomed to consecrate their meat.

"Who are you, Brother?" he asked.

"I am Temu, a priest of the Order of the Dawn whom you saw but once in the Temple of the Sphinx, Scribe Rasa, when you came thither on a certain embassy, though then I did not know that you were sworn of the Brotherhood, Scribe Rasa, if that indeed be your name."

"It is not my name and at that time I was not sworn of the Brotherhood, Priest Temu, who, I think, are the messenger sent by the holy Roi with letters for Apepi, King of the North. We heard that you were dead of sickness, Priest Temu."

"Nay, Brother, it pleased Apepi to keep me prisoner, that is all. Had I died, my spirit, as it departed, would have whispered in the ear of Roi."

"I remember now that so the Prophet said. But how come you here, and why?"

"I come because I am sent to help another in distress, by some Great One who visited me in my prison. He gave no name, or if he did I have forgotten it, as we of the Order forget many things. Nor did he tell me whom I was to help, yet I can guess, as we of the Order guess many things. I see that you wear a royal ring, Scribe Rasa. It is enough."

"Quite enough, Priest Temu. But tell me, why were you sent to me? In such a hole as this even a Pharaoh would need no servant."

"No, Brother, yet he might need a companion and—a deliverer."

"Very much indeed, both of them, especially the last. But, Temu, how could even Roi himself open that door or break through these walls?"

"Quite easily, Scribe Rasa, by means of which we know nothing, and if only we have faith perhaps I can do the same, though not so easily and in another fashion. Hearken. During the many days I have spent in prison, bettering my soul with prayers and meditations, from time to time I have given instructions to that humble man who is our jailer, setting his feet in the way of truth. Thus in the end he has become well affected to those who profess our faith, to which I have promised that he shall be gathered in days to come. In reward he has imparted a certain secret to me which, as neither he nor any other will visit this place again to-night, I will now show to you, Brother Rasa. Help me, if it pleases you, to move this table."

With difficulty it was dragged aside, for it was of massive stone. Then Temu took from his robe a piece of papyrus on which were marks and lines. By aid of these he made certain measurements and at length in the roughly paved floor found a stone for which he seemed to have been searching. At this stone he pushed from left to right, for there was a roughness on it against which he could rest the palm of his hand, thereby, it would appear, loosing some spring or bolt. Suddenly a section of the floor, a pace wide or more, tilted up, revealing a shaft cut in the rock, of which the bottom could not be seen, and against its side, also cut from the rock, stone bars set at intervals one above the other, down which it would be possible for an active man to climb.

"Is it a well?" asked Khian.

"Aye, Brother, a well of death, or so I think, though perhaps of that we shall learn more later. At least all is as the Great One whose face was veiled, told me, for it was he who gave me the plan and bade me trust the jailer and do as he instructed me."

"And what is that, Temu?"

"Descend by this ladder, Brother, until at the foot of it we come to a tunnel; then follow the tunnel until it ends in what seems to be the mouth of a drain in the stone embankment of the river. Beneath this hole or drain-mouth a boat should be waiting, and in it a fisherman following his trade by night when the largest fish are caught. Into that boat we must enter and be gone swiftly before it is discovered that this place is empty."

"Do we fly at once?" asked Khian.

"No, Brother, not for another hour, for so I was instructed; why I do not know. Help me now to close the trap, but not quite lest the spring should refuse to work again, and to replace the table over it exactly as it stood before. Who knows that some officer or spy might not be moved to pay us a visit, although the jailer said that none would come."

"Aye, who knows, Temu?"

So they closed the trap, setting a piece of reed from a food basket between its edges so that it did not shut altogether, and dragged back the table to its place. Then they sat down to eat. Scarcely had they done so when Temu pressed Khian's foot and looked towards the door.

He looked also and, though he heard nothing, saw, or thought that he saw, a white face and two glowing eyes set against the grating and watching them, a sight that made his blood turn cold. In an instant it was gone again.

"Was it a man?" whispered Khian.

"A man, or perchance a ghost, Brother, for I heard no footfall, and of such this place may well be a home."

Then he rose, and taking a linen cloth that had been laid over the food, he thrust it into the grating.

"Is that not dangerous?" asked Khian.

"Aye, Brother, but to be watched is more dangerous."

To Khian it seemed as though that hour would never end. Moment by moment he feared lest the door would open and all be discovered. Yet no one came, and indeed they never learned whether they had seen a face at the grating or whether its appearance was but a trick of their minds.

"Whither would you fly, Brother?" asked Temu.

"Up Nile," whispered Khian, "to warn our brethren who are in great danger."

"I felt it," said Temu. Then he rose and packed the most of the food, of which, as has been said, there was much more than they could eat, into two of the baskets wherein it had been brought which were made of reeds and had handles that could be slipped on to the arm.

"It is time to go, Brother. Faith, have faith!" said Temu.

They rose and for a moment stood still to put up a prayer to the Spirit they worshipped for help and guidance, as was the custom of their Brotherhood before they entered on any undertaking.

"I will go first, Brother, carrying one of the lamps in my teeth—the second we must leave burning—and one basket on my arm. Do you follow with the other."

Then he stepped to the door, pulled out the food-cloth from the grating, and having listened awhile, returned, and taking the smaller of the lamps, set its flat handle between his teeth. Next he crawled beneath the table, pushed upon the stone so that it tilted up and stood edge in air, climbed through the hole on to the stone ladder, and began to descend. Khian followed. As it chanced when he had taken some three steps down the ladder, the peaked hood of his cloak touched the stone, disturbing its balance. Instantly it swung to, releasing the spring or catch, so that now there was no hope of return, since this could not be opened from beneath. Even then the purpose of this trap came into Khian's mind. When it was desired to destroy some unhappy captive, unknown to him the spring or bolt was set back. Then shortly, as the doomed one tramped that gloomy cave he would tread upon the swinging stone and vanish into the gulf beneath, for when this was purposed doubtless the heavy table stood elsewhere. Or if his secret end was desired very swiftly, jailers would hurl him down the pit. Khian shuddered as he thought of it, remembering that this fate might well have been his own. Down, down he climbed, the feeble little lamp which Temu carried in his teeth lighting his way. It seemed a long journey, for the pit was deep, but at length Temu called to him that he had reached its bottom. Presently he was at his side perched upon a white and moving pile that crackled beneath his feet. He looked down and by the lamplight perceived that they stood upon a pyramid of bones, the bones of the victims who in past days had fallen or been cast down the shaft. Moreover, some of them had fallen not so very long before, as his senses told him, which caused him to remember certain friends of his own who had incurred the wrath of Pharaoh and, as it was said, were banished. Now he guessed to what land they had been banished.

"Lead on, Temu," he said. "I choke and grow faint."

Temu obeyed, turning to the right as he had been told that he must do, and holding the lamp near the ground lest there should be pitfalls in the path, which ran down a tunnel so low and narrow that they must walk it doubled up with their shoulders brushing against its walls. For forty or fifty paces they followed this winding burrow, till at length Temu whispered that he saw light ahead, whereon Khian answered that it would be well to extinguish the lamp lest it should betray them. This was done, and creeping forward cautiously for another ten or twelve paces, they came at last to an opening in the great embankment wall built of granite blocks, upon which the palace stood, so small an opening that few would notice it in the roughness of the blocks, and, twice the height of a man beneath them, saw the waters of the Nile gleaming blackly in the starlight.

They thrust their heads out of the hole and looked down, also to right and left.

"Here is the river," said Khian, "but I see no boat."

"As all the rest of the tale has proved true, Brother, doubtless the boat will appear also. Faith, have faith!" answered Temu to whom the gods had given a trusting soul, and when they had waited half an hour or more, he repeated his words.

"I hope so," answered Khian, "since otherwise we must swim before dawn and hereabout are many crocodiles that feed upon the refuse from the palace."

As he spoke they heard the sound of oars and in the deep shadow of the wall saw a small masted boat creeping towards them. This boat came to a halt beneath their hole. There was a man in it who threw out a fishing line, looked upwards and whistled very softly. Temu whistled back, whereon the man began to hum a tune, such as fishers use, then at the end of it sang softly:

"Leap into my boat, O Fish."

Khian scrambled out of the hole and climbed down the surface of the rough wall, which, being accustomed to such work, was easy to him, and presently was safe in the boat. Temu, having first thrown the lamp into the Nile lest it should be found in the tunnel, followed after him, but more awkwardly; indeed, had not Khian caught him he would have fallen into the river.

"Help me to hoist the sail. The wind blows strongly from the north, therefore you must fly southwards; there is no choice," said the man.

As he obeyed, Khian saw his face. It was that of the jailer himself.

"Be swift," he went on. "I see lights moving; perhaps the dungeon has been found empty. Many spies are about."

Then Khian bethought him of the glowing eyes he had seen at the grating.

With an oar the jailer pushed the boat away from the wall; the wind caught the sail and it began to move through the water, so that presently they were in the middle of the Nile and gliding up it swiftly.

"Do you come with us?" asked Khian.

"Nay, Prince, I have my wife and child to mind."

"The gods reward you," said Khian.

"I am already rewarded, Prince. Know that for this night's work I have earned more than I have done in ten long years—never mind who paid. Fear not for me who have a sure hiding place, though it is not one that you could share."

As he spoke, with the oar he steered the boat near to the farther shore of the river, where at this spot were hundreds of mean dwellings.

"Now go your ways and may your Spirit be your guide," said the jailer. "There is fishing gear in the boat, also you will find such garments as men use who live by it. Put them on ere dawn, by which time with this wind you should be far away from Tanis, for she sails swiftly. Farewell and pray to your gods for me as I will pray for you. Prince, take the steering oar and stand out into the middle of the river where in this stormy night you will not be seen."

As he spoke the man slipped over the stern of the boat. For a moment they saw his head a dark blot on the water, then he vanished.

"At last I have found one who is good and honest, although of an evil trade," said Khian.

153

CHAPTER 16

The Passing of Roi

All that night Khian and Temu sailed on, for the north wind held strong and steady, and by daybreak were many leagues from Tanis. Once they saw lights upon the water behind, such as might have been borne by following boats, but soon these vanished. At daybreak they found the fisher's clothes of which the jailer had told them, and put them on, so that for the rest of that journey all who saw them believed them to be two fishermen plying their trade; such men as were to be found by hundreds on the Nile, taking their catch to market, or having sold it, returning to their homes in some distant village. Thus it came about that, Khian being accustomed to the handling of boats, they accomplished their journey safely, though during the second night a number of great ships passed them going down Nile.

Catching sight of these ships they lowered their sail and rowed in-shore where they hid among some reeds in shallow water until they were gone by, a whole fleet of them. What these might be they could not discern because of the darkness, but from the lanterns at their prow and stern, the words of command that reached them, and the singing of those on board Khian thought they must be war vessels full of soldiers, though whence such came he did not know. Only he remembered what he had heard at Apepi's Court and that on his return to Tanis he had seen armed vessels sailing up Nile, and remembering, grew afraid.

"What do you fear, Brother Rasa?" asked Temu, reading his mind.

"I fear lest we should be too late to give a certain warning, Temu. Oh! let us play no more with words. I, whom you call the Scribe Rasa, am Khian, once Prince of the North, the affianced of Queen Nefra, whom my father Apepi would seize to be his wife. When he discovered that I, his envoy, had become his rival, the King imprisoned and would have killed me, and that is why we came together in yonder darksome vault."

"All this I have guessed, Prince and Brother, but what now?"

"Now, Temu, I would warn the Queen and our brethren of the dangers that threaten them; namely, that Apepi would steal her and kill out the rest of the Order to the last man and woman, for so he has sworn to me that he will do."

"I think that there is no need to take them that message, Prince," answered Temu lightly, "since Roi would learn such tidings quicker than men could carry it. Still, let us go on, for God is with us always. Faith, have faith!"

So they sailed forward and shortly after daylight saw the pyramids and at last came to the strand that was near to the palm grove where first Khian had met Nefra disguised as a messenger.

Here they hid away their boat as best they could and wearing the long cloaks that had been given to them in the prison, beneath which were swords that they had found in the boat, set there doubtless for their use, made their way across the sand to the Sphinx, and thence to the temple, meeting no man. Indeed, they noted that those who cultivated the fertile belt of land were not to be seen and that the crops were trodden down by men and wandering beasts. Filled with fear they entered the temple by the secret way they knew and crept down its passages into the great hall where Nefra had been crowned. It was silent and empty, or so they thought at first, till suddenly, far away at the end of the hall Khian perceived a white-robed figure seated in the throne-like chair upon the dais, behind which stood the ancient statue of Osiris, god of the dead. They advanced swiftly. Now they were near and Khian saw that it was the figure of Roi or—the ghost of Roi. There he sat in his priestly robes, down which flowed his long white beard, his head bent upon his breast, as though he slept.

"Awake, holy Prophet," said Khian, but Roi did not stir or answer.

Then they went to him, trembling, climbed the dais, and looked into his face.

Roi was dead. They could see no wound on him, but without doubt he was dead and cold.

"The holy Prophet has been taken away," said Khian hoarsely, "though I think that his spirit remains with us. Let us search for the others."

They searched but could find no one. They went into the chamber of Nefra. It was undisturbed but she was gone; even her garments were gone, and so it was with all the others.

"Let us go out," said Khian; "perchance they are hidden in the tombs."

They left the temple and wandered far and wide, but all was silence and desolation. They looked for footprints, but if there were any, the strong north wind had covered them up with sand. At length in the shadow of the second pyramid they sat down in despair. Roi was dead and the rest were gone, Khian could guess why. But whither had they gone? Were they perchance on board those ships which had passed them in the night? Or were they slain? If so, how came it that they had seen no bodies or signs of slaughter? So they asked of themselves and each other, but found no answer.

"What shall we do, Prince?" asked Temu. "Doubtless all will be well in the end. Still, our food and water are almost gone, nor can we stay here without shelter."

"Hide in the temple, I think, Temu, at least for the coming night. Listen. I am sure that the Brotherhood of the Dawn have fled, being warned that Apepi was about to fall upon them."

"Yes, but whither?"

"To seek the aid of the King of Babylon. The Lord Tau hinted to me, as did the giant Ru, that if it were needful they might go thither, and this doubtless they have done. If so we must follow them, though without guides and beasts to carry food and water, the journey is desperate."

"Fear not, Prince," answered Temu the hopeful. "Faith, have faith! We of the Brotherhood are never deserted in our need. Were we deserted in the prison of Tanis, or on our journey up the Nile? And shall we be deserted though we travel from one end of the world to the other? I tell you nay. I tell you that always we shall find friends, since in every tribe there are Brothers of the Dawn to whom we can make ourselves known by signs, which friends will give us all they have, food and beasts of burden and whatever is needful, passing us on to others. Moreover, I have about me a great sum in gold. It was given to me by that high One whose face was veiled, he who visited me in my cell at Tanis and sent me to join you. Yes, and when he gave me the gold and the jewels, for there are jewels also, he said with meaning that I and another of my fellowship might be called upon to journey into far lands, and that if this were so, the treasure would be needed for our sustenance till we found shelter far from the wrath of a certain king."

Now as he listened the heart of Khian grew bold again, for it seemed to him as though this happy-minded Temu had been sent to him as a very messenger from heaven, which indeed perhaps he was, after a fashion.

"I find your fellowship good in trouble, Temu," he said, "though I know not whence you win such calm and strength of soul."

"I win it from faith, Prince, as you will do also when you have been longer of our Brotherhood. Since Apepi seized me yonder at Tanis and threw me into prison, not once have I been afraid, nor am I now. Never yet have I known harm to come to a Brother of the Dawn going about his duty. The prophet Roi is dead, it is true, but that is because his time had come to die, or perhaps he who was too old to travel chose to withdraw himself from the world. But his mantle has fallen upon Tau and others, and with us will go his spirit, and who shall stand against the freed spirit of the holy prophet Roi who walks with God to-day?"

Then, having determined that they could do nothing more that day, for they were weary and first must rest, also get food if they could from the stores that were hidden away by the Order in case of trouble, of which Temu knew the secret, they set out to return to the Temple of the Sphinx where the dead Roi still ruled as he had done when he was alive. At the edge of the great rock platform upon which was built the Pyramid of Khafra, Khian halted suddenly, for in the midst of the deep silence of the tomb he thought that he heard voices. Whilst he was wondering whence they came, from behind a little neighbouring pyramid that marked the grave of some king's son or princess appeared a Negro running with his head bent down and his eyes fixed upon the ground, as do black people when they track game.

"They have gone this way, both of them, Captain," he called out, "and not an hour ago."

Then Khian understood that the man was following the footsteps of Temu and himself, who indeed had come round that same little pyramid. Whilst he stood wondering what to do, for this discovery seemed to freeze his blood, round the corner of the small pyramid came a whole company of men who by their dress and arms he knew to be soldiers of Pharaoh's guard, forty or fifty of them.

"We have been followed up Nile; they are hunting us, Prince. Now we must escape from them, or we shall be killed," said Temu calmly.

As he spoke the black tracker caught sight of them and pointed them out with his spear, whereon the whole company broke into a run, uttering shouts like hunters when at last they view their game.

Then in his extremity a memory came to Khian.

"Follow me, Temu," he said, and turning, fled back towards the Pyramid of Khafra, though to do so he must pass even closer to the pursuers.

Temu saw this and stared, then muttering, "Faith! Have faith!" bounded after him.

For a moment the soldiers halted, thinking that they were coming to surrender, but when they saw the pair speed past them they began to run again. Khian, followed by the long-legged Temu, sped along the south face of the great pile and, as their pursuers reached it from the west, were just seen turning the corner of the east face. So swiftly did Khian and Temu run that when the soldiers reached this east face they lost sight of them, who already were speeding along the north face, and not knowing which way they had gone, waited till the tracker came up to guide them by his art.

Meanwhile Khian, rushing along the north face, sought with his eyes for that fallen block of stone which marked where it must be mounted. There were many such blocks, but at last he saw this one and knew it again. Calling to Temu to keep close, he began to scale the pyramid, which to him was easy.

"Ye gods! am I a goat?" gasped Temu. "Well, faith, faith!" and up he went as best he could. Once he would have fallen, but Khian, glancing back, saw and caught him by the hair.

Which was the course of stones? He had found no time to count them as he climbed and each was like to the other. He thought that he must have over-shot it and stopped, trying to remember all that Nefra had told and shown him. Whilst he stood thus, suddenly and as though by magic a great block of marble stirred and swung round in front of him, revealing the mouth of the passage beyond, in which he saw a light burning. Not staying to think how this marvel came about, he leapt into the hole dragging Temu after him, for now the tracker had rounded the corner and, though still far away, had caught sight of them on the side of the pyramid, though this afterwards the soldiers would not believe. Therefore, guessing by the shouting of the man that they had been seen, in went Khian, though to what fate he did not know, since he could not guess how the swinging block had opened of itself and feared some snare.

Scarcely had they passed the stone when it closed as swiftly and as silently as it had opened, and he heard the clank of the bar. Then panting he turned to look about him and by the faint light of the lamp that was far off, perceived a figure standing in the mouth of the recess which Nefra had shown him was used as a storehouse. The figure came forward, bowing.

"Welcome, Lord," it said. "Wonderful is the wisdom of the Prophets of the Dawn, for they warned me that you might return here thus about this time, and therefore I kept good watch."

Now as his eyes grew accustomed to the light Khian knew the man again to be no other than the sheik who had taught him to climb the pyramids and was called their Captain.

"How could you watch through a stone wall, Friend?" he asked, amazed.

"Oh! easily enough, Lord. Come here and I will show you. Now lie down on the floor and look through that hole, or if you would see higher up, through that one."

Khian obeyed and perceived that the holes were tubes which ran slantwise to the face of the pyramid, so cunningly contrived that a watcher within could see what was passing at its base, or if he used others, farther away. Thus Khian saw the soldiers arrive panting and the black tracker with many wavings of his arms, explaining to them that the fugitives had run up the pyramid. This tale seemed to make their captain angry—for clearly he believed it to be a lie—so angry that he struck the tracker with the handle of his spear, whereon the man grew sullen, as negroes do who are beaten unjustly, and throwing himself on to the sand would say no more. After this the soldiers began to search for themselves. Some of them even began to climb the side of the pyramid, till one of them rolled down and hurt himself and was carried away groaning. Then others of them went on and vanished, to hunt among the tombs beyond, or so Khian supposed. But the Captain and some officers sat down on the sand at the base and took counsel together, for they were bewildered. So they remained till nightfall when they lit a fire and camped there.

Having seen these things, or certain of them, Khian bade the sheik tell him what had become of the Brotherhood of the Dawn and why he was here alone inside the pyramid.

"Lord, this is the story," answered the man. "Some hours after you had sailed away down Nile, bearing letters for the King of the North, news reached the Council of the Dawn. Whence or how it came I do not know who am not in their secrets; a spy may have brought it or it may have been revealed from Heaven, I cannot say. At least this happened: all of the Brotherhood were gathered together; then the women and children and some men who were too old to travel far were sent away across the desert southwards in the direction of the other pyramids where is the burial-place of the *Apis* bulls, though whether they were to stay there or to go further I did not hear. At least they departed quietly that very night, and next morning had vanished, doubtless to seek shelter with friends of the Order in some appointed place where they will be safe."

"But what happened to the Lady Nefra and the rest, Captain?"

"Lord, all that night they made preparations, and the next morning before the dawn they started eastwards, bearing with them tents

159

and much provision laden upon asses. Also they took a mummy case from the burial vault, which I understood contained the embalmed body of that queen who was the mother of our Lady Nefra. Only one remained behind, save myself, and that was the holy prophet Roi."

"Why did you not go also, Sheik?"

"For two reasons, Lord. First because the Captain of the Pyramids is sworn, whatever chances, never to leave them. Here my forefathers have lived and died for countless generations, and here my descendants will live and die till the sun ceases to rise or the pyramids crumble into dust. This is promised to our race so long as we guard them and keep our trust, but if we break it, then it is promised that our family will die out."

"You give a good reason for staying where you are, though in danger and loneliness, Sheik."

"Yes, Lord, and there is a second, just as good. Before she went the Lady Nefra sent for me and, speaking as Queen, laid her commands upon me. These were that I should forthwith see to it that the tomb chamber in this Pyramid of Ur, of which like her I had the secret, was full provisioned with food, fresh water, wine, oil, means of making fire, and all other needful things. That this done, I should take up my abode here and watch all that passed, and if you came, for, Lord, she seemed to be sure that you would come, that I should hide you in the pyramid and tend you there, thus protecting you from all foes. Moreover, she commanded me, as also did the Lord Tau, to tell you that she with all the Brotherhood had fled to Babylon, there to seek the aid of her grandsire, the great King Ditanah, who it seems still lives and had sent messengers to greet her as Queen of Egypt and, if need were, to guide her and all her company to Babylon where, it is believed, he will give her a great army to make war upon Apepi and to establish her upon the throne of Egypt. She said also that I was to bid you, so soon as you could escape, to fly to Babylon where you would find shelter from the wrath of Apepi."

"I thank the Queen for her messages and forethought," said Khian, "though how she learned that I was fated to revisit this place, I cannot guess."

"I think that the holy prophet Roi knew and told her, Lord, for to him at the last the future seemed to be as open as the present, the only difference being that he saw the one with the eyes of his soul and the other with the eyes of his body."

"Mayhap, Sheik. But how comes it that Roi sits dead in the temple hall? Do you know aught of his end?"

"Lord, I know everything. I was present when, after the departure of the aged, the women, and the children, the Prophet summoned all the Order before him in the great hall, and with them Nefra the Queen and the Lord Tau. There he addressed them in wonderful words, telling them that they must make the journey to Babylon without him as now he was too old to travel. They answered that they would bear him with them in a litter; but he shook his head, saying:

"'Not so, the time has come for me to die to this world and to pass to another whence I will watch over you and where I will await you all when your hours are fulfilled. Here, then, I bide till I am called away.'

"Then, while they wept he called Tau to him and, causing him to kneel, with secret and mystical words ordained him to be Prophet of the Order of the Dawn after him, giving him authority over the bodies and souls of men, after which he breathed upon and kissed him. Next he summoned our Lady Nefra, the Queen, and bade her be of a good heart, since it was given to him to know that all things should befall according to her desire, and that, however great his dangers, he whom she loved would be protected and brought back to her at last. Then he kissed and blessed her also, and after her he blessed all the Order, those of the Council by name, charging them to guard its secrets and to keep its doctrines to which they were sworn, pure and undefiled. Moreover, should they shed blood in pursuit of its righteous aims and in defence of their Queen and sister, he absolved them of its guilt, saying that sometimes war was necessary to peace, but that when war was ended, they must show mercy and become poor and humble as before. After this he dismissed them, nor would he speak with any of them again, save to give Tau a writing for the King of Babylon, and another writing addressed to all the members of the Order throughout the world."

"And what happened then, Sheik?"

"Then, Lord, they bent the knee to him one by one and went away, who by dawn were marching for Babylon. When all had gone Roi looked up and, perceiving me left alone, asked why I was not with them. I told him what I have told you, and he said that it was well and that I must tend him till his death. After this he left the throne and laid him down in a chamber near at hand, and there I visited him night and morning, for all the day I was busy preparing this place to which I carried food and water and the rest from the temple stores and, lest I should be seen, hid them here in the hours of darkness. I think it was on the fourth afternoon from the departure of the Brotherhood that, all my tasks being finished, I went to the holy Prophet to give him water to drink, for now he would touch no food. He drank and commanded me to help him to rise and to array him in all his priestly garments. Then at his bidding I led him to the hall and sat him down on the throne with his rod of office in his hand.

"'Hearken,' he said to me. 'Our foes come, thinking to destroy us according to the command of Apepi. I see them landing on the shore; I see the shining of their spears. Man and brother, hide you there and watch, knowing that no harm shall come to you, and afterwards go do as you were bidden.' Now, as the Brother Temu will know if you do not, Lord, all the temple yonder is full of places where only fire or hammers could find a man, into the secrets of which we of the Order have been instructed in case of need. To one of these I went and hid myself, but a little way from the platform on which Roi sat, nor would any have guessed that the calm statue of an ancient god held a living man who could see all through its hollow eyes of stone.

"A while went by, perhaps an hour, for when I came into the temple the sun was still high, but now its beams, striking through the western window-place, began to fall upon Roi and the throne upon which he sat, in shafts of light that clothed him in a robe of flame. Suddenly the silence was broken by sounds that grew ever nearer, sounds of running feet, sounds of rude voices shouting.

"'Here is the path,' they shouted. 'Here is the nest of the white rats of the Dawn, who soon shall be red. Now let us see if their spells can turn Pharaoh's spears.'

"Roaring such words as these, a mob of soldiers burst into the hall through the great entrance, glittering with armour and with lifted swords. The silence of the ancient place seemed to strike and chill them, for their tumult ceased, and after a pause they came on slowly, clinging together like bees. Then it was, Lord, that the red rays of the westering sun fell full upon Roi, revealing him seated, white-robed, upon the throne, his golden-headed staff held like a sceptre in his hand. They stared, they halted.

"'It is a spirit!' cried one.

"'Nay, it is the god Osiris holding the Rod of Power,' answered another.

"The officers consulted together doubtfully, till some captain who was bolder than the rest said:

"'Shall we be frightened by magic tricks? Let us look.'

"He marched up the hall followed by others, and halted in front of the platform.

"'This old god is dead,' he cried. 'Do you fear a dead god, Comrades?'

"Now Roi spoke in a hollow echoing voice, saying:

"'What is life and what is death? And how know you the difference between a dead and a living god, O Violator of Sanctuaries?'

"The officer heard and fell back, but made no answer, for he was afraid.

"'What seek you in this holy place, O men of blood, and who sent you here?' went on Roi.

"Then the officer found courage to answer.

"'Apepi the Pharaoh, whose servants we are, sent us, and our mission is to capture Nefra, the daughter of Kheperra, once King of the South, and to put to the sword the company of the Priests of the Dawn.'

"'Capture Nefra, the anointed Queen of the Two Lands, if you can find her, Man, and put the priests of the Order of the Dawn to the sword, if you can find them. Search the tombs and search the desert, and when you find them put them to the sword, and bear back the heads of the dead to Apepi, the Shepherd dog whom you call a king, and with them the living beauty of Nefra, her Majesty of Egypt.'

"They made no answer and Roi went on:

"'Search, search, to find naught but wind and sand. Search till the Sword of God falls upon you, as fall it will.'

"Now, Lord, it would seem as though that officer drew courage out of the depths of his terrors, for he shouted back:

"'At least, old Prophet, you are neither God nor his Sword, and for you there is no need to search. You we will take to Pharaoh Apepi, that, yet living, he may hang you as a cheat and a wizard above the gates of Tanis.'

"Now Roi arose from this throne and, terrible to behold, stood in the fierce light of the setting sun. Slowly he raised his wand and pointed with it at that officer, saying in a cold, clear voice:

"'Prophet you name me, and now at the last, if never before, Prophet I am. Hearken, Man, and bear back my words to your master, the Shepherd thief Apepi, and lay them to your own heart. It is you and not I who shall hang from the pylon gate of Tanis. Yea, I see you swinging in the wind, you who have suffered that flock to escape on which the Shepherd dog would feed, and must feel his rage, as this Apepi must feel the wrath of God. Say to him from Roi, the Prophet of the Order of the Dawn, that death draws near to him, the breaker of oaths, the seeker of innocent blood, and that soon he shall talk with Roi, not at Tanis but before the Judgment seat in the Underworld. Say to him that his armies shall go down before the sword of the Avenger as corn is reaped by the sickle, and that one whom he would murder shall sit upon his throne and cherish her whom he desired. Say to him that when he stood here in this hall disguised as a messenger, I knew him well, but spared him because his time was not yet and because the humble Brethren of the Dawn, unlike to the King of the Shepherd pack, remember the duties of hospitality and do not seek to stain their hands with the blood of envoys. Say to him, the oath-breaker who would practise treachery, that he shall drink of the cup of treachery and that from the evil he has sown others shall reap the harvest of righteousness and peace.'

"Thus, Lord, spoke Roi and sank back upon the throne.

"'Seize him!' shouted the officer. 'Beat him with rods; torment him till he tells us where he has hidden the royal Nefra, for ill will be our welcome at Tanis if we return without her upon whom the King has set his heart.'

"Now, Lord, very slowly some of the soldiers crept forward, two paces forward and one back, for they were much afraid. At length they came to the platform and climbed it. The first of them, not touching him, stared into the face of the holy Roi, then reeled back, crying:

"'He is dead! This Prophet is dead; his jaw has fallen!'

"'Aye,' answered one in the hall, 'but his curse lives on. Woe! woe to Apepi and woe to us who serve him! Woe! Woe!'

"While the cry still echoed from the walls, of a sudden the sun sank and the hall grew dark. Then, Lord, there arose another cry of 'Flee! Flee swiftly ere the curse strikes us in this haunted place.'

"Lord, they turned, they fled. The narrow passages were choked with them. Some fell and were trampled of their fellows, for I heard their groans, but these they dragged away, dead or living, I know not which. Presently all were gone. I crept from my hiding place, I lifted the hand of the holy Roi. It grew cold and, when I loosed it, fell heavily; I listened at his heart; it did not beat. Then I followed the soldiers, and hiding as I know how to do, saw them embark upon their ships, fighting in their mad haste, and push out into the Nile although a great wind blew. When I came again at dawn they were all gone, only I think that some boat had been overturned, for on the shore were three bodies which I thrust back into the water.

"Such, Lord, was the end of Roi our Master, who now sleeps in the bosom of Osiris."

"A strange tale and a terrible," said Khian.

"Aye," broke in Temu, "but one in which I see the hand of Heaven. But if such is the beginning, Prince, what of the end? Ill for Apepi, I think, and for those who cling to him. Faith! Have faith!"

Chapter 17

The Fate of the Cliff-Climbers

That night, Khian, Temu, and the Sheik of the Pyramids, after they had eaten and drunk, laid themselves down to sleep in the burial chamber of the Pharaoh Khafra, Khian lying on one side of his sarcophagus, Temu on the other, and the Sheik, who said that he would not profane the sacred place with his humble presence, just outside the doorway. But as Khian discovered that night, often enough it is one thing to lie down and another to sleep.

Sleep, indeed, he could not. Perchance he was over-weary, who had rested little for many nights, for on the boat he had laboured hard and scarcely dared to shut his eyes. Perchance all the dangers that he had passed, all that he had suffered, seen, and heard, so filled his mind that it would not cease from troubling. Perchance the hot, still air of the tomb lying at the heart of a mountain of stone oppressed him and took away his breath.

Or there may have been other reasons. Within the great chest against which he lay, silent and stern, reposed the bones of a Pharaoh, the builder of this pyramid, who had been mighty in the world uncounted years before, but of whom now there remained no history and nothing upon earth, save those bones, the pyramid, and, in the temple without, certain statues portraying his royal presence. Such a one as this was no good bedfellow, thought Khian, especially for a man who, as suddenly he remembered, wore to-day the very ring with which, ages past, that departed monarch had sealed his documents of state.

Khian wondered in his wakefulness whether the *Ka* or Double of this Pharaoh, which, as was well known, or so swore all the priests and learned men, dwelt with his body in the tomb till the hour of resurrection, was now looking at that ring and wondering how it came to be on this stranger's hand. As he remembered, already it had brought him trouble, since through it his father, Apepi, with all the cunning of the jealous, had guessed that he and Nefra were lovers, and thereon cast him into prison. He had escaped from that prison to find another, but if this was to be shared with the *Ka* of the mighty Khafra, the second would be no better than the first, for who could deceive a *Ka*? Had he thought of the matter, which in his folly he did not, he might have hidden the ring from Apepi, but where was the pouch that would hide it from the eyes of a *Ka*? Perhaps, however, Khafra had given the ring to him who came after him, from whom it had descended generation by generation, until it came to his hand lawfully enough, in which case the *Ka* might pardon him who wore it to-day.

Oh! his brain grew weak and foolish; he would think no more of *Kas* and rings; he would think of that sweet and lovely lady with whom he had plighted troth in this very sepulchre. Where was she now, he wondered, and when should he find her again? The Sheik said that almost with his last breath Roi had prophesied that they would come together once more, which were comfortable words. Yet Roi might have meant that this would chance in another world since to Roi, especially at the last, there seemed to be little difference between the live and the dead. But he, Khian, desired the breathing woman, not her ghost, for who knew how shadows loved, if indeed they loved at all? How wondrous was the tale of this death of Roi, hurling curses with his last strength upon Apepi and those who violated the sanctuary of the Brethren of the Dawn and strove to steal away their sister and their Queen. He thanked the gods that Roi had not cursed him in such fashion. Nay, he had blessed him, and Nefra also. Therefore, surely, they would be blessed, for he was holy, a minister of Heaven who knew its mind.

Even in that dread habitation and surrounded by so many perils, he would remember that Roi had blessed them, and that his spirit, purified eternally, was watching him, stronger than the *Ka* of Khafra or than any evil ghost or demon that makes its home in tombs. Yes, comforted by that blessing he would cease to stare at the wavering shadow that the lamplight threw upon the arched roof, and sleep.

Sleep he did at last, though fitfully and haunted by bad dreams, for that place was foul-aired, till at length he was awakened by the sound of Temu, who stirred upon the farther side of the tomb and yawned loudly.

"Arise, Prince," said Temu, "for though one would not guess it here, it must be day."

"What is day to those who live in the eternal blackness of a pyramid as though already they were dead?" asked Khian gloomily.

"Oh! a great deal," replied Temu cheerfully, "because one knows that the sun is shining without. Also darkness has its comforts; thus in it, having nothing else to do, one can pray longer and with a mind more fixed."

"But that the sun is shining on others does not comfort me in a stifling gloom, Temu, and I can pray best when I see the heaven above me."

"As doubtless you will soon again, Prince, for be sure that by now, having lost us, those soldiers have departed to report to his Majesty that we have melted away like spirits."

"In which case his Majesty will make *them* into spirits, Temu, that they may search for us elsewhere. Certainly, wherever those soldiers go, it will not be back to Tanis unless they take us with them. Think now. We have escaped from Pharaoh's strongest dungeon which none has ever done before. The Queen Nefra and all our brethren, save Roi who chose to stay behind to die, have escaped his army. What would his mood be, then, towards those who reported to him that they had tracked and hunted us, only at the last to let us slip through their fingers? No, Temu, unless we accompany them, I think that they will not return to Tanis."

At this moment the Sheik appeared bearing a lamp.

"Have the soldiers gone?" asked Temu.

"Come and see," said the Sheik, and turning, led them down the passages. "Now look," he added, pointing to the eyeholes.

Khian looked, and when his sight grew accustomed to the bright light that flowed from without, perceived the soldiers, fifty or more of them, engaged in building themselves huts or shelters of the loose stones that lay about. Moreover, by setting his ear to the hole, he heard an officer call to someone whom he could not see, asking if all were well with the companies that watched the other faces of the pyramid. Then understanding that these men were sure that their quarry lay hid within the pyramid and intended to guard it day and night until starvation or lack of water forced them to come out, Khian motioned to Temu to look for himself and sat down upon the passage floor and groaned.

"Certainly," said Temu after a while, "it seems as though they were going to stop here a long time, for otherwise they would not be building themselves houses of stone. Well, we will outwit them somehow. Faith—have faith!"

"Yes," said Khian, "but meanwhile even faith needs food, so let us eat."

****

167

Thus for these three there began a time of terror. Day added itself to day and still the soldiers remained, watching as a cat watches; also others came to join them, and among these, men who were skilled at the climbing of cliffs and other heights, and set themselves to scale the pyramid with the aid of ropes and spikes of bronze, hoping thus to discover the hiding place of the Prince. It was but lost labour, since although often they crept over it, never did they find the secret stone, nor if they had, could they have opened it that was barred within. Still there they remained, believing always that the prisoners must come out, unless indeed they were already dead.

Khian and his companions slept no more in the tomb chambers; the place was too close and dreadful; they could not rest there. So after that first night they laid themselves down in the passage near to the entrance stone, for there some air reached them through the peep-holes, also a little light. Indeed, by setting his eye to one of these holes that slanted upwards, apparently to make it possible for any looking through it from within to see the southern face of another of the pyramids, Khian found that he could behold a certain star. For hours at night he would lie watching that star, until at length it passed from his vision, as the sight of it seemed to give him comfort, though why he did not know. For the rest they must lie in the dark, or with the peepholes blocked, lest the lamplight flowing through these should betray them, and therefore were obliged to eat farther down the passage. Soon, however, although there was plenty of it, food began to grow distasteful to them, who must stay still, or nearly so, day after day. The water, too, became flat, stale, and nauseous to the taste, and of the wine they dared not drink too much.

Thus it came about that at length courage and spirit began to desert Khian, who would sit for hour after hour silent, sunk in a gloom as deep as that of the bowels of the pyramid. Even Temu, though still he talked much of faith, reminding his companions of Roi and his prophecy, and prayed for hours at a time, became less happy-hearted and declared that the prison vaults at Tanis were as a palace compared to this accursed tomb. The Sheik, also, grew so wild in his manner that Khian thought that he was going mad. What angered him most was that strangers should dare to scramble about the pyramid of which he was the captain, for of this he talked continually. Khian tried to soothe him by saying that he was sure they dared not climb so very high, even with the help of their ropes, since never would they know where to set their feet.

These words made the Sheik thoughtful, for after hearing them he grew silent, as though he were considering deeply. On the following night, just before the dawn, he awoke Khian and said:

"Prince, I go on an errand. Ask me not what it is, but to-morrow at sunset unbar the stone and wait. If I do not return before the dawn, bar it up again and think of me as dead."

He would say no more, nor did Khian try to turn him from his purpose, for he knew that then the man would go quite mad. So the stone was opened a little, and having eaten and drunk some wine, the Sheik slipped out into the darkness.

The sound of the bar falling into its place again woke Temu, who sprang up, crying:

"I dreamed that the stone was open and that we were free. Why, where is the Sheik? He was lying by my side."

"The stone was opened, Temu, but we are not free. As for the Sheik, he has gone on some wild errand of his own. What it was he would not tell me. I think that he could bear this place no more and seeks freedom in death, or otherwise."

"If so, Prince, there will be more water left for us two to drink, and doubtless all is for the best. Faith! Have faith!" answered Temu, and lying down went to sleep again.

That day passed as the others had done. Of the Sheik they spoke no more, for both of them believed that he had fled, or hidden himself among the stones of the pyramids to get air. Indeed now their miseries were so great that scarcely could they think of other matters and talked little, but, like two caged owls, sat staring at the darkness with large, unnatural eyes. Towards evening Khian, watching through his peephole, saw that some Bedouins of the desert, who were mounted upon fine horses, had arrived at the camp of the soldiers who were chaffering with them for corn or perhaps milk, which others on foot carried upon their heads in jars or baskets. When the bargaining was done the soldiers talked with the desert-dwellers, telling them why they were camped there, or so Khian guessed, for the latter stared at the pyramids as though the tale moved them, and asked many questions, as he could see by their eager faces and the movements of their hands. Whilst they were still talking the sun began to set, sinking swiftly, as it seems to do in the clear skies of Egypt. Then suddenly one shouted, pointing upwards:

"Look! Look! Yonder stands the Spirit of the Pyramids, there on its very crest, clad all in white."

"Nay," answered another, "it is clad in black."

"There must be two of them," called a third, "one in white and one in black. Without doubt these are no spirits, but those we seek, the Prince Khian and the priest, who all this while have dwelt not in the pyramid but on its crest."

"Fool," cried a voice, "how can men live for weeks in such a place? These are ghosts, I say. Have we not heard that the pyramids are haunted? Look! The thing mocks us, making signs with its arms."

"Ghosts or men," said the first voice, that of the Captain, "we will take them to-morrow. To-night it is impossible, for darkness falls."

Then followed tumult, for all the soldiers spoke at once, and at that distance Khian could not hear their words. He noted, however, that the desert-dwellers did not speak. They sat still upon their horses at a little distance and behind the soldiers, while he who seemed to be their chief made strange signs with his arms, stretching them out wide, then holding them above his head with his fingers touching. After this, very swiftly came the darkness, covering all, and the shoutings died away, though from the encampment below where the soldiers gathered round their fires, still rose the murmuring of eager talk.

"Temu," said Khian later, "what does this sign mean among the Brotherhood of the Dawn?" and first he stretched his arms out wide and then made them into a loop above his head with the fingers touching.

"That, Prince, is the sign of the Cross of Life which members of the Order use for a signal when they are too far apart to speak. It is thus that they know friend from foe or stranger."

"I thought so," said Khian, and was silent. Then he went to the entrance place and took down the bar that closed it.

An hour later or more he heard a sound and for an instant felt the night air blowing sweetly on his face, though because of the darkness he could see nothing. Next he heard the bar fall into its socket and the voice of the Sheik calling him by name. He answered and together they crept up the passage till they came to a spot where a lamp burned and there were food and water.

When the Sheik had drunk deeply Khian asked him where he had been, though he could guess well enough.

"To the top of the pyramid, Lord. I climbed thither in the dark this morning. It was very dangerous; so dangerous that although you are as skilled as I am, I dared not ask you to accompany me. Still, although I am weak from setting so long stirless in this hole, I did not fear who know the road well; also no harm ever comes to the Captain of the Pyramids while he follows his trade of scaling them."

"Why did you go there, Sheik?"

"I will tell you, Lord. First, that I might make those soldier dogs believe that we were living, not in the pyramid, but on or near its crest in some cave among the stones; or if they would not believe this, that I might frighten them, and perhaps cause them to go away. Doubtless they have heard the tale of the Spirit of the Pyramids and that those who look upon it are doomed to death or madness, and if so, having, as they believed, seen it once they will not wish to do so again. Lastly, I had a reason of my own of which perhaps you will not think well. Skilled cliff-climbers have been brought here to scale the pyramid, *my* pyramid and that of my forefathers, on which none has set foot unless he was of my blood, except only a certain lady and yourself by order of the Council of the Dawn. Yet these bunglers have never yet reached the crest; of that I am sure. Now they will try to do so, for the soldiers will force them to the task, and I think that what will happen to them will cause strangers for many a generation to leave the pyramids to be climbed by my race alone."

"That is revenge which would have been displeasing to Roi," answered Khian, shaking his head. Then remembering that to this man the pyramids were as holy as is a temple to its priest, and that to him he who dared to try to conquer them deserved to die as much as he does who violates a sanctuary, he said no more of the matter, but bade the Sheik to continue his tale.

"Lord, I reached the summit in safety just as the dawn began to break, and there lay flat all day in the little hollow that you know, where part of the cap stone is broken off. It was very hot there, Lord, with the sun beating full upon me, nor did I dare to move lest I should be seen. Yet I endured till at last came the hour of sunset. Then I rose up and stood upon the very point clad in my white robe, so that all the soldiers could see me. While they gazed astonished I slipped back to the hollow and covered up the white robe with my black cloak of camel hair, and thus clad, appeared again, bending my knees so as to make it seem as though I were a second man of a different stature. This I did more than once, Lord, and thus those watchers came to believe that unless they saw ghosts, both you and the priest Temu were on the summit of the pyramid."

"A clever trick," said Khian, laughing for the first time for days, "though I know not how it will serve us."

"Thus, Lord. If the soldiers believe that you are on the summit of the pyramid, they will cease to search and watch its slopes, and all night long the eyes of their sentries will be fixed upon that summit. But listen, there is more to tell. While I stood thus on high I perceived certain men mounted on very fine horses who seemed to be Arabs of the desert and who were, or had been, engaged in chaffering with the soldiers, selling them milk or grain. Now the presence of these men caused me to wonder, for I knew well that no Arabs dared to set foot within the boundaries of this, the Holy Ground of Dawn, fearing lest, if they do so, the curse of Heaven and of the Prophets of the Dawn should fall upon them. Then a thought came to me, sent as I think from on high, and seeing him who seemed to be the headman of the Arabs watching me with uplifted face, with my arms I made certain signs that are known to our Order, and perhaps, Lord, to you also who now are one of them."

Khian nodded, and he went on:

"Lord, that man answered the signs and so did another who was near to him, to show me as I think that this was not done by chance. Then I knew that they were friends sent here for a purpose and understood why my Spirit had moved me to climb the pyramid."

"And if so, what of it, Sheik?" asked Khian in a hoarse voice, for his heart beat high with hope and choked him.

"This, Lord. To-morrow at the sunset once more I shall stand upon the crest of the pyramid, and if as I think those Arabs still are there, I shall make other signs to them, showing them where they must wait at midnight, having horses in readiness. Then I shall return and guide you to them, for I think that they will know which way to ride."

"It is dangerous," said Khian, "but so be it, for if I bide here much longer I think that I shall die. Therefore, better meet fate in the open and swiftly than perish here in this hole by inches."

Then he called Temu and the three of them took counsel together. Also the Sheik and Temu talked much of the secret signs of the Order, and practised them by the lamplight.

Next morning ere dawn the Sheik departed again as he had done before. As soon as it was light, watching through their spyholes, Khian and Temu saw that there was much disturbance in the camp of the soldiers, saw also that the skilled cliff-climbers, six or more of them with their ropes and metal spikes, were collected together, talking with the officers.

At last, as it seemed to Khian somewhat against their will, they advanced to the foot of the pyramid, and setting his ear to the hole Khian heard them scrambling up the face of it. For a long while he heard no more, but noted the soldiers watching eagerly, talking together and pointing with their hands, now in this direction and now in that.

Suddenly there rose a scream of horror. Some of the soldiers stared as though fascinated, others turned their backs, and others hid their eyes. The spyhole was obscured for a moment as though by something passing between it and the light. Then soldiers ran forward and presently Khian and Temu saw them returning towards the huts bearing three shapeless things that had been men. A while later they saw the remainder of the cliff-climbers staggering much as the drunken do, towards the same huts where they cast down their ropes with the air of those who have done with them, and departed out of the sight of the watcher.

"The pyramids are avenged on those who thought that they could master them, and their captain will rejoice," said Khian sadly, thinking to himself that had not some power protected him they would have been avenged upon him also, as indeed very nearly happened.

****

Once more it was sunset and again the Arabs, mounted on fine horses, appeared at the camp. Again, too, there were shoutings and pointings with much disturbance, in the midst of which he who seemed to be the chief of the Arabs drew a little to one side of, also behind, the soldiers, so as not to be seen of them, and from time to time made motions with his arms, as those do who, at its rising or its setting, worship the sun in the desert. Then followed darkness and in it shone the fires round which the soldiers were seated.

Presently they stood up holding their hands behind their ears as though to listen to some sound in the air; then by twos and threes departed like men who are frightened and hid themselves in the huts or elsewhere. A while later the stone turned and the Sheik glided into the passage, but this time he asked for wine, not water.

"I have been near to Osiris," he said, "who slipped upon the blood of one of those cliff-climbing fools and almost fell. Yet I did not fall who I think was guarded, and for the rest all goes well."

"Except for the three who are dead," said Khian, sighing.

"If they died, it was by no fault of mine, Lord. Without knowledge of the road, in their madness, having scaled two-thirds of the height they came to smooth marble where is no holding place for hands or feet. Then one slide down, dragging the others with him, for they were roped together, after which the rest, seeing the fate of their fellows, gave up the venture and returned. Now, as I think, the pyramids will be safe from these common cliff-climbers for many a year."

"What chanced afterwards?" asked Khian.

"I appeared at sunset as before, and making pretence to toss my arms about, as a ghost or a devil might do, I signalled to him who seems to be the captain of the Arabs. He answered me. We understood each other. After dark I shouted curses at the soldiers telling them that I was the Spirit of Roi the Prophet, and that doom was near to them. They grew frightened at what they held to be a voice from Heaven, and crept away to hide themselves from the words of evil omen, nor, as I think, will they come out of their holes again until the sun is high. Now drink a cup of wine and follow me, both of you."

CHAPTER 18

How Nefra Came to Babylon

After he who was known as the Scribe Rasa, the envoy of Apepi, King of the North, had received the betrothal ring from his affianced, Nefra the Queen, and sailed down Nile to Tanis, there to undergo many evil things, at the Temple of the Dawn all came about as the Captain of the Pyramids afterwards described to him and the priest Temu.

Scarcely had this Rasa, who was Khian the Prince, departed, than there arrived at the temple, disguised as Arabs, an embassy from Ditanah, the old king of Babylon. These men, nobles of Babylon, were received in secret by the Council, and bowing before Roi the Prophet, presented to him tablets of clay covered with strange signs.

"Read the writing, Tau," said Roi, "for my sight grows feeble and I forget this foreign tongue which is your own."

So Tau took the tablets and read:

"From Ditanah the aged, Lord of Babylon and King of Kings, whose glory is as that of the Sun, the Mighty One. To Roi the holy Seer, the Friend of Heaven, the Prophet of the Order of the Dawn, and to him who sits under Roi, the first of the Brothers of the Dawn, who in Egypt is named Tau, but who, as I, Ditanah, have heard, in Babylon aforetime was named the High Prince Abeshu, the lawful son of my body, with whom I quarrelled because he rebuked my Majesty as to a certain vengeance which I took upon a subject people, and who thereafter fled away and as I believed was long dead—Greetings.

"Know, O Roi and O Tau or Abeshu, that I have received your letters informing me of all that passes in Egypt, and that you, Abeshu, still live. Also that it was the desire of my daughter Rima whom I gave in marriage to Kheperra, the Pharaoh of the South and by right of descent the King of all Egypt, that her bones should be brought back for burial to Babylon. Also I have read that her daughter Nefra has in secret been crowned Queen of Egypt and seeks my help to win her throne out of the hands of my enemy, Apepi the Usurper who rules at Tanis.

"Now I, Ditanah, say to you, Roi the Holy, and to you, Queen Nefra my grandchild, 'Come to me at Babylon with all your company. Thither I swear you safe-conduct in the name of my god Marduk, Ruler of Heaven and Earth, in the name of the gods Nebo and Bel, and of all the other gods who are my lords. There, also, you shall be guarded from all harm by the strength of my hands, and there we will talk together of all these matters.'

"And to you who are called Tau, I say, 'Come also, and if you can prove to me that you are in truth my son, the Prince Abeshu, I will give you all things that you desire, who have mourned over you for many years, save one thing only, the succession to my throne after me which is promised to another. But if you have lied to me in this matter, then do not come, for surely you shall die.'

"To the bones, also, of my daughter Rima, whose husband Kheperra, the wolf, Apepi, brought to his death, I will give honourable burial in the sepulchre of kings, where it was her desire to lie at last. Nor do I think that I shall refuse her death-prayer, if Nefra, my grandchild the Queen, will obey me in a certain matter.

"Sealed with the seal of Ditanah, the Great King and with the seals of his Councillors."

When Tau had read he touched his forehead with the tablet and gave it to Nefra who sat upon her throne in the centre of the Council. She also laid it against her forehead, then turned to Tau and said:

"How comes it, my Lord Tau, that all these years you have kept this secret from me, who if the tale that is written here be true, must be a brother of my mother and my uncle?"—a question which caused the envoys to stare at him.

Tau smiled and answered:

"O Queen and Niece, the tale is true enough, as should we live to come at Babylon, I will prove to my royal father Ditanah and his Councillors. I am Abeshu and the half-brother of Queen Rima. But when I left Babylon she was but a little child born of another mother whom I had scarcely seen, since she dwelt with the royal women. Nor did I reveal myself to her afterwards when we met again and I saved her from the plots of Apepi at Thebes, or to you when you grew to womanhood, because of oaths that I had taken when I became a Brother of the Dawn, which oaths bound me to lay down all my earthly rank and to forget that I had been a prince. Yet in those oaths there was a loophole—namely, should it ever become needful to declare myself and my true name and history thereby to help the Order of the Dawn, I was free to do so. To all of which our father the Prophet can bear me witness."

"Aye," said Roi, "it is true. Hearken, Queen and Sister, and you, the envoys of Ditanah. Many years ago a brother of our Order, now long dead, brought to me a man who said that he desired to become one of us, a noble-looking warrior man, stalwart and square-bearded, who, I judged, had drunk of the water of Euphrates. I asked him his name and country, also why he sought the shelter of the Dawn. He told me, and proved his words, that he was Abeshu, a Prince of Babylon, who had quarrelled with his father, Ditanah the Great King, whose General he had been, over the matter of a subject people whom he had been ordered to massacre, but would not for mercy's sake, and because of his disobedience had been banished or left the land. Afterwards he had served under other kings, those of Cyprus and of Syria, as a captain of their armies, but in the end grew weary of fighting and ambitions, of loves who betrayed him also, and determined to bid farewell to the vanities of the world and in solitude and silence to feed and purify his soul.

"Therefore, having heard of the Order of the Dawn, he came to knock upon its gate. I answered to him that among us there was no room for one who only sought salvation for himself and rest from earthly toil, since those of our Brotherhood must be the servants of all men and more particularly of the poor and those bound with the chains of sin, sworn to bring peace to the world, even at the cost of their own lives, sworn, too, to poverty and, except for special purposes, to celibacy and the renouncement of all earthly honours. For thus only, as we held, could the soul of man come into union with its god. Therefore, if he became one of us, it must be as the slave of the humblest and he must forget that he had been a Prince of Babylon and a General of her hosts, he who henceforward would be but a minister of Heaven appointed to tasks, mayhap, that the meanest idolator would refuse.

"In the end, Queen, this suppliant bowed his neck beneath our yoke and laying down all his titles, became known under the humble name of Tau. Yet from Tau the Servant he grew to be Tau the spiritual Lord, and after me, its aged Prophet, the greatest in our Brotherhood, and so acknowledged throughout the world, though until it became necessary to proclaim it to the Great King Ditanah but the other day, none knew that he was Abeshu, the Prince of Babylon."

Now when they heard this strange story the members of the Council rose and bowed to Tau, as did the envoys from Babylon, setting their hands upon their hearts. But Nefra did more, for she rose also and kissed him on the brow, calling him her beloved uncle and saying that now she understood why she had always loved him from a child.

Then Tau spoke, saying:

"All is as has been told, but because of it I neither seek nor deserve your praise. What I have done I did for my own soul's sake who came to know that there is no true joy save in the service of others and in the seeking to draw near to God. Now for a while it seems that, still in the service of others, I must once more be known as a prince and perhaps as a captain in war. If so, let not my royal Father have any fear lest I should seek to claim the heritage of those whom he has appointed to succeed him, I whose only hope and purpose is that I may live and die a Brother of the Dawn."

At this moment he who kept the door advanced and whispered into the ear of Roi, who said:

"Admit them."

There came in three men, travel-stained and weary, who when they threw open their cloaks and made the signs, were seen to be Brothers of the Order.

"Holy Prophet," said one of them, "we come from Tanis and from the camp of Apepi's army. We have it from those in authority who in secret are the friends of our Order, that Apepi makes preparation, should a certain request of his be refused, to attack you here; to put every one of the Brotherhood to the sword and to drag away yonder royal lady to be his wife. His troops are gathered and in a few days he will be upon you."

"I know it well," answered Roi. "Let those mad servants of Apepi come, for I have words to say to them."

Then he commanded Tau to call together all the people of the Dawn, that he might take counsel with them.

They gathered together and in their presence Roi the Prophet laid down his office and consecrated Tau as his successor, as the Sheik of the Pyramids had told Khian and Temu. Then, too, he bade them farewell and blessed them, and they departed, weeping, after which all things happened as the Sheik had said. There were some among the Council—Nefra the Queen was one of them—who would have seized Roi and borne him away by force. But he read their minds and forbade it. So at last they went, leaving him alone according to his commands. Yet that was a sad parting and at it many tears were shed. Thus Nefra wept much, for she loved Roi who from her infancy had watched over this orphan child as though he were her father. He noted her grief and called her to him:

"Lady of Egypt," he said, "you who to-day are a queen in name and ere so very long, unless my wisdom fails me, will be so indeed, wide seems the gulf that is set between you and the old hermit, the Prophet of a secret faith whose name will vanish away and who ere long will be utterly forgotten upon the earth. Also between you and me lies the span of many years, for I am very, very old, while but yesterday you came to womanhood. Moreover, your lot in life is far different from that which I have trod and that now is ending, so it would seem as though there were little in common between us. Yet it is not so, because we are tied together by the bond of love which, did you but know it, is the one perfect, eternal thing in Heaven and earth. Time is nothing; it seems to be and yet is not, for in everlastingness what place is there for time? Pomp and glories, beauty and desire, wealth and want, things lost and things achieved, all we seek and all we gain, our joys and griefs, yes, birth and death themselves, are but bubbles on the stream of being which appear and disappear. Only love is real and only love endures. For love is God, and being God, is King of the world; a King with a thousand faces, who in the end will conquer all and make of hate a footstool and of evil the oil within his lamp. Therefore, Child, follow after love, not only that love which you know to-day, but the love of all, even of those who do you wrong, for this is the true sacrifice, and through it only shall your soul be fed. Now for an hour, farewell."

Then he kissed her on the brow and bade her leave him.

Such was the parting of Roi the ancient Prophet and Nefra the royal maid who all her life through remembered this his last message, though perhaps its full mystery and meaning never came home to her until at last she was about to follow him into the shadows. Never did she forget the sight of him, white-robed and bearded, hawk-nosed and wrinkled, seated alone upon his chair of state within that dusky hall, staring with steady eyes out into the farther gloom, as though there he sought some beckoning hand of light and awaited the signal to follow whither it might lead.

****

Ere the dawn they marched, fifty or more of them, besides those who bore the coffin of Rima the Queen. Swiftly they marched by secret ways, for already the sick, the young, and the aged had departed to their appointed hiding places, so swiftly that when the sun rose the pyramids were already distant. Then it was that Nefra bade farewell to the Sheik who had accompanied them thus far, and gave him those commands of which he had spoken afterwards.

For always she believed that Khian would return to seek her there, as did Tau and others of the Brotherhood, who perchance had received some message or spiritual instruction on this matter, and bitterly she grieved that it was not possible to await his coming that he might fly with her. The Sheik bowed and went his way, swearing to fulfil her words, and by degrees the pyramids that had been her only home faded and were lost to sight. Then for the first time Nefra wept a little, for she loved those pyramids which she had conquered and where her joy had found her, and did not know whether she would ever see them more. They came unharmed to the borders of Egypt, and leaving the great gulf of the Red Sea to the south of them, passed safely into the deserts of Arabia. Indeed, on all that journey through Egypt, avoiding towns and villages, they met few in the war-wasted lands, and those few either fled away or made pretence not to see them. It was almost as though some command had gone out that they should not be observed, though whence it came Nefra did not know. Not until she made that journey did Nefra learn how great was the secret power of the humble Order of the Dawn.

At length they were out of Egypt and camped one night by a well in the desert. Next morning when Nefra looked at dawn out of the tent in which she slept with Kemmah, she perceived a caravan of camels and horsemen advancing upon them and was afraid.

"Now I think that Apepi has us in his net," she said to Kemmah, who looked also, then left the tent, making no answer. Soon she returned accompanied by two of the envoys from Babylon, with whom came the Lord Tau himself.

"Have no fear, Queen," said Tau, "all has gone well. Those whom you see are not Shepherds, but troops of your grandsire, the great King Ditanah, sent by him to escort you to his city of Babylon. Behold the banner of the Great King blazoned with the symbols of his gods."

"Thanks and praise be to Heaven," answered Nefra. Then a thought took her and she led Tau aside and said to him: "I believe and you believe that the Prince Khian will return to the pyramids to seek us and to give us warning. There he may be driven into hiding, being pursued. If so he will need help. Cannot some be found to give it to him in his extremity?"

"I will consider the matter and take counsel; indeed, I have already begun to do so," answered Tau.

The end of it was that certain high-bred men of the desert, disguised as Bedouins and mounted on swift horses, Brethren of each other and of the Dawn every one of them, and sworn to its service to the death, were sent back to watch the pyramids with certain instructions, of which men we have already heard.

Then came the General of Ditanah and his officers who kissed the ground before Nefra, greeting her, she noted, not as Queen of Egypt, but as a Princess of the House of Babylon. Also they were led to the tent where rested the body of Queen Rima, before which they knelt while a priest of their worship made prayers and offerings. These things done, camels were brought, a great herd of them, on which were mounted all the Company of the Dawn, and with them a chariot wherein were set Nefra and the Lady Kemmah. Then they departed, guarded by squadrons of Babylonian horsemen and led by guides mounted on fleet camels.

Thus they travelled forward very swiftly across the burning deserts of Arabia by the great military road, halting where there were wells of water, or if there were none, carrying it with them in bags of hide. Moreover, at certain places, oases in the desert, fresh camels and horses awaited them, so that bearing the mummy of Queen Rima with them they advanced almost at the speed of the King's post, helped by all and unharmed by any, and within some five and thirty days beheld before them the mighty walls of Babylon.

Built upon either side of the great river Euphrates, filled with towering temples and glittering palaces, there stood the vast city, the wonder of the world, so huge a place that for a whole day they journeyed through its outskirts before they came to its inmost walls. Then brazen gates rolled back, and as night fell they were conducted down broad, straight streets filled with thousands upon thousands of people, who stared at them curiously, half seen in the twilight, till at length they halted before a palace.

Slaves came forward and led Nefra up steps and through doorways guarded by winged figures of bulls with the heads of men, into a wonderful place such as she had never seen, whose home had been in sepulchres and ancient temple halls. Chamberlains received her, princes bowed before her, eunuchs and women surrounded her and Kemmah, bringing them to a chamber that was hung with tapestry and furnished with vessels of gold and silver. Then they were led to a heated marble bath, welcome indeed after their long journeyings, though never before had Nefra seen such a place, and when they had bathed and been rubbed with oils, were brought back again to their chamber where delicate foods and wines awaited them. Having eaten and being very weary, they laid themselves down upon silken, broidered beds and slept, watched by women slaves and guarded by armed eunuchs who stood without the door.

Nefra was awakened at the dawn by the sound of women's voices singing some hymn to Sames the Sun god, at his rising. For a while she lay contemplating the splendours by which she was surrounded, and already hating them in her heart. By rank she was a queen indeed, but by upbringing only a simple country girl accustomed to the free air of the desert, to the exercise and dangers of scaling rocks and pyramids, to narrow sleeping chambers that once perhaps were tombs, and to the hard, rough fare of the Brethren of the Dawn which she had shared with the humblest of the Order. These silks and broideries, these gorgeous chambers, these scented waters, these crowds of obsequious slaves, these foreign, delicate foods, this pomp and state, crushed and overwhelmed her; she loathed it all.

"Nurse," she said to Kemmah whose bed was near, "I would that we were back upon the banks of Nile, watching the first rays of Ra gild the Sphinx's brow."

"If you were back upon the banks of Nile, Child," answered Kemmah, "and continued to watch Ra at all, it would be to see his first rays gilding the gates of your palace prison at Tanis and to hear the voice of old Apepi calling you by hateful names of love. Therefore be thankful to find yourself where you are."

"Nurse, I have dreamed a dream. I dreamed that Khian, my betrothed, lay in danger of his life and called to me to come to save him."

"Doubtless, Child, he calls to you wherever he is and doubtless he is in danger of his life, as all of us are in this fashion or in that. But what of it? Have we not the promise of my great-uncle, the Prophet, that no harm shall come to him? Listen. I, too, dreamed a dream. It was that Roi himself, clothed in light, as I am sure he is, for doubtless he has been dead for many days, stood beside me.

"'Bid Nefra,' he seemed to say, 'to calm her heart, for though dangers are many they shall be driven away like storm clouds by the keen desert winds, leaving her sky clear and in it twin stars shining.'"

"Those are happy words, Nurse, that is, if you dreamt them at all, which you know alone; words that give me comfort in this strange and gorgeous place. But look, here come those fat, large-eyed women, bearing gifts I think. Nurse, I will not be touched by them. I will clothe myself or you shall clothe me."

The women came, prostrating themselves almost at every step, and

182

laid the gifts upon a table of jasper stone: wonderful and gorgeous garments, royal robes, collars and belts of jewels, and a crown of gold set with great pearls.

"The gifts of Ditanah the mighty King to his granddaughter, Princess of Babylon and Queen of Egypt," said the chief of the women, bowing and speaking in the Egyptian tongue. "Be pleased to array yourself in them, O Princess of Babylon and Queen of Egypt, that Ditanah, the Lord of lords, may behold your beauty suitably adorned. We, your slaves, are here to serve you."

"Then be pleased to bear my thanks to the mighty Ditanah, my grandsire, and to serve me without the door," answered Nefra, throwing the coverlet over her face so that she might see no more of them.

When they were gone, with many protestations and even tears, Nefra arose and by the help of Kemmah, set to clothing herself in these glittering garments. Yet before all was done that chief of the women must be called back again to show them how they should be worn.

At length she was attired after the fashion of a Babylonian royal lady, marvellously attired, and a mirror was brought that she might behold herself. She looked and cast it down upon the bed, crying:

"Am I Nefra, the Egyptian maid, or the woman of some Sultan of the East? Look at this outspread hair sprinkled with gems! Look at these garments in which I can scarcely walk! Smell these unguents with which my face and flesh are smeared! Nurse, rid me of this truck and give me back my white robe of a Sister of the Dawn."

"It is too travel-stained, Child," answered Kemmah drily, adding with satisfaction, "moreover, you look well enough as you are, though somewhat sunburned, and that crown becomes you. Oh! complain no more; in the spirit you may be a Sister of the Dawn, but here you are a Princess of Babylon. Would you anger the Great King from whom you ask so much? See, they summon us to eat. Come, eat, for you will need food."

"Mayhap, Nurse. But what is it that the Great King asks of *me*? Something, as we have heard, of which none will tell us, not even my Uncle Tau, though I think he knows."

Then, sighing and pouting her lips, Nefra gave way and ate, but to her question Kemmah made no answer, either because she could not, or for other reasons.

A while later there came the chief of the eunuchs, a fat, vainglorious person, and cringing chamberlains wearing tall caps, musicians fancifully attired, and women of the Household, and officers, and a guard of swarthy soldiers. All these, gathering together in an appointed

order, set Nefra and the Lady Kemmah in the midst of them surrounded by the fan-bearers, the women, and the eunuchs and preceded by the musicians. Then at a word of command they marched
and though they never left the precincts of the palace, that walk was
long. Down sculptured passages they went, through great chambers,
across courtyards where fountains played and gardens that grew beyond them, till at last they reached a flight of many steps and up these
climbed to the bull-guarded doorway of a vast hall.

This hall was roofless, but at the farther end, for a third of its
length perhaps, awnings were stretched over it, from one side to the
other. The place was filled with people, more people than Nefra had
ever seen; thousands of them there seemed to be, all of whom stared
at her, and as she passed, bowed low. Up a wide pathway between
the crowd to the right and the crowd to the left went Nefra and
her company, till they came to that part of the hall over which was
stretched the awning.

Here the shadow was so deep by contrast with the brilliance without that at first she could see nothing. Presently, however, her eyes
grew accustomed to the gloom and she perceived that before her was
gathered the glittering Court of the King of Babylon. There were
lords; there were ladies seated together by themselves; there were soldiers in their armour, there were square-bearded councillors and captains; there were shaven priests; there were officers of the Household
with wands; there were slaves, black slaves and white slaves, and she
knew not who besides. Moreover, above all this splendour, its centre
and its point, seated on a jewelled throne, was an aged, white-bearded,
wizened man, wearing a strange headdress who, she guessed, must be
her grandsire, Ditanah the Mighty, the King of kings.

As they entered the line of shadow a trumpet blew, whereon all
the Court and all the company about her prostrated themselves before
the majesty of the King and lay with their foreheads touching the
pavement, yes, even Kemmah prostrated herself. But Nefra remained
upon her feet, standing alone like one left living among an army of
dead men; it was as though some spirit within her told her to do so. At
least thus she stood looking at the little wizened man upon the throne,
while he looked back at her.

Again the trumpet blew, whereon all rose, and once more her
company advanced, to halt near to the throne, on either side of
which stood massed a number of gorgeous nobles who afterwards
she learned were kings' sons, princes, and satraps of the subject peoples. For a while there was silence, then the King upon the throne

spoke in a thin, clear voice, an interpreter rendering his words sentence by sentence into the Egyptian tongue.

"Does my Majesty behold before me Nefra, the daughter of my daughter Rima, the Princess, wife of Kheperra, once Pharaoh of Egypt?" he asked, studying her with his sharp and bird-like eyes.

"That is my name, O Grandsire and Great King of Babylon," answered Nefra.

"Why, then, O Granddaughter, do you not prostrate yourself before my Majesty as all these great ones are not ashamed to do?"

Now again something within her seemed to tell Nefra what to say, and while all stared and listened, she answered proudly:

"Because, Grandsire, if you are King of Babylon, I am Queen of Egypt, and Majesty does not kiss the dust to Majesty."

"Well and proudly said," answered Ditanah. "Yet, Granddaughter, I think that you are a queen without a throne."

"That is so, and therefore I come to you, O Father of my Mother, O Mighty King of Kings, O Fount of Justice, seeking your aid. Apepi the Shepherd usurped my throne as his forefathers did before him, and now seeks to make a wife of me, the Queen of Egypt, and thereby to gain my heritage. But by a little I have escaped out of his hands, helped of your Majesty, and now here I stand and make my prayer to you, the King of Kings from whose body I am sprung."

"Well spoken again," answered the old monarch. "Yet, my Daughter of Egypt, you ask much. Apepi I know and hate; for years I have waged a frontier war against him, yet to cross the waterless deserts with a mighty host to invade him in his territory and drag the stolen crown from off his head would be a great venture that might end ill for Babylon. What have you to promise in return, Lady of Egypt?"

"Nothing, O King, save lord and service."

"Aye, thus it stands: you ask much and have nothing wherewith to pay. I must take counsel of this matter. Meanwhile Mir-bel, my grandson, the King of Babylon to be, lead this lady hither and place her where as a Queen she has a right to sit, near to my throne."

Now from among the throng of princes came forward a tall man of middle age, gloriously apparelled and wearing a diadem upon his head; a strong-faced man with black and flashing eyes. He bowed before her, searching her beauty with those hawk-like eyes in a fashion that pleased her little, and saying in a smooth, rich voice:

"Greeting, Queen Nefra the Beautiful, my cousin. Glad am I to have lived to look upon one so fair and royal."

Then he took her by the hand and led her up the steps of the dais to a chair of state that had been made ready for her upon the right of the throne. There he bade her be seated and with bows to her and to the King, returned to his place among the princes.

Nefra sat herself down and for a while there was silence.

At length the old King spoke:

"You say that you have nothing to give, Daughter. Yet it seems to me that you have much, for you have yourself to give, who are, I hear, unwed. If the Queen of Egypt," he went on, speaking slowly and in a fashion which told her that the words had been prepared, "were to take as her lord the heir of Babylon, so that thereafter, if all went well, these two great lands were joined into one empire, then perchance Babylon might be ready to send her armies to conquer Apepi and set that Queen upon the throne of her forefathers. What say you, Daughter?"

Now when Nefra heard and understood at length what was sought of her, the blood left her face and her limbs turned cold. For a moment she hesitated, in her heart putting up a prayer for guidance, as Roi had taught her to do when in difficulty or trouble. It seemed to come, for presently she answered very quietly:

"It may not be, O King and Grandsire, for thus Egypt would be set under the heel of Babylon, and when I was crowned I swore an oath to keep her free."

"That trouble might be overcome, Daughter, in a fashion pleasing to both our countries of which we can speak hereafter. Have you any other reason against this alliance? He who is offered to you is not only the heir to the greatest kingdom in the world; he is also, as you have seen, a man among men, in the flower of his age, a soldier, and one who, as I know, is both wise and kind of heart."

"I have another reason, King. Already I am affianced."

"To whom, Daughter?"

"To the Prince Khian, King."

"The Prince Khian! Why, he is Apepi's heir, and yet you told me that Apepi would have married you."

"Yes, Sire, and therefore Apepi and Khian do not love each other, but"—here she looked down—"but Khian loves me and I love Khian."

At these words a whisper went round the Court and old Ditanah smiled a little, as did many others. Only Mir-bel did not smile; indeed, he looked angry.

"Is it thus?" said the King. "And where, now, is the Prince Khian? Have you brought him here in your company?"

"Nay, Sire. When last I heard of him he was at the Court of Tanis, and, it was said, in prison."

"Where I think he will certainly remain, if, as I doubt not, your story be true, Child," answered Ditanah, and was silent.

Just then, when Nefra thought that all was finished and that her prayer for succour was about to be refused, swelling sweet and solemn she heard a familiar sound, that of a certain funeral chant of the Order of the Dawn. She looked to discover whence it came and perceived Tau followed by all the Brotherhood who had accompanied her from Egypt, and certain others who were strangers to her, clad in simple white robes, every one of them, advancing into the hall by a side entrance to the right. Nor did they come alone, for in the centre of their company, borne upon a bier by eight of the brethren, was a coffin which Nefra knew covered the mummy of her mother, Queen Rima. The coffin was brought and set down before the throne. Then suddenly the lid, which had been loosened in readiness, was lifted, revealing a second coffin within. This also was opened by the priests who very reverently took from it the embalmed and bandaged body of Queen Rima and stood it on its feet before the King, holding it thus, a sight from which all that saw shrank away, for the Babylonians did not love to look upon the dead.

"Whose corpse is this and why is it brought into my presence?" asked the King in a low voice.

"Surely your Majesty should know," answered Tau, "seeing that this dead flesh sprang from your flesh and that here before you, within these wrappings, stands all that is left of Rima your daughter, aforetime Princess of Babylon and Queen of Egypt, who thus comes home again."

Ditanah stared at the mummy, then turned his head aside, saying:

"What is that which hangs about the neck of this royal companion of the gods, as doubtless she is to-day?"

"A letter to you, O King, sealed with her seal while she was still one of the company of the living."

"Read it," said Ditanah.

Then Tau cut the fastenings and unrolled the writing from which fell a ring. This ring he took, and gave it to the King, who sighed when he looked upon it, for well he remembered that he had set it upon his daughter's finger when she left him to journey into Egypt, swearing to her that he would refuse to her no request which was sealed with this seal.

Next Tau read from the scroll in the Babylonian tongue thus:

"From Rima, aforetime Princess of Babylon, aforetime wife of Kheperra, Pharaoh of Egypt, to her sire Ditanah, the King of Babylon, or to him who sits upon his throne. Know, O King, that I call upon you in the name of our gods and by our common blood, to avenge the wrongs that I have suffered in Egypt, and the slaying of my lord beloved, the King Kheperra. I call upon you to roll down in your might upon Egypt and to smite the Shepherd dogs who slew my husband and took his heritage, and to establish my daughter, the Princess Nefra, as Queen of Egypt, and to slay those who were traitors to her and would have given her and me to doom. Know also that if you, my father, Ditanah the King, or you, that King my kinsman, who sit upon his throne after him, deny this my prayer, then I call down the curse of all the gods of Babylon and Egypt upon you and upon your people, and I, Rima, will haunt you while you live, and ask account of you when we meet at last in the Underworld.

"Sealed by me Rima with my seal upon my deathbed."

These solemn words which seemed almost as though they were spoken by the royal woman whose corpse was set upon its feet before the throne, went to the hearts of all who heard them. For a while there was deep silence. Then Ditanah the King lifted his eyes which had been fixed upon the ground, and it was seen that his withered face was white and that his lips quivered.

"Terrible words!" he said, "and a terrible curse decreed against us if we shut our ears to them. She who spoke the words and sealed them with this seal that once I gave to her together with a certain solemn promise, she who stands there dead before me, was my beloved daughter whom I wed to the lawful Pharaoh of Egypt. Can I refuse the last prayer of my daughter, who suffered so many wrongs at the hand of Apepi the Accursed, and who doubtless stands among us now awaiting its answer?"

He paused and from all who heard him there went up a murmur of "You cannot, O King."

"It is true, I cannot who soon must be as is the royal Rima; whate'er the cost, I cannot. Hearken, priests, councillors, princes, satraps, officers, and people. I, Ditanah the King, make a decree. In the name of the Empire of Babylon I declare war by Babylon upon Apepi the Shepherd usurper who rules in Egypt; war to the end! Let my decree that cannot be changed be recorded and proclaimed in Babylon and all her provinces."

Again rose the murmur of assent. When it had died away the King turned to Nefra, saying:

"Fair Queen and grandchild, your prayer and that of your mother who begat you is granted. Therefore rest you here in peace and honour till all things are made ready for this war, and then go forth to conquer."

Nefra heard. Rising from her seat, she cast herself upon her knees before the King and, seizing his hand, pressed it with her lips, for speak she could not. Drawing her to her feet, he bent forward, touched her with his sceptre, and kissed her on the brow.

"I add to my words," he said. "Knowing your errand, Child, I made a plan that as a price for the aid of Babylon you should give yourself in marriage to Mir-bel, the heir of my throne. Now I put aside that plan, for so my heart is moved to do, whether because you ask it or for other reasons. You tell me that you are affianced to the Prince Khian of whom I have heard good report, although on his father's side he comes of an evil stock. Mayhap the Prince is dead already at the hands of Apepi, or thus will die. If so, mayhap also you will turn to Mir-bel because it is my wish and his, though on this matter I make no bargain with you. Yet if Khian lives and you live to find him, then wed him if you will and take my blessing on you both. Look not wrath, Mir-bel, for in the end who knows what the gods may bring to pass. Learn also from this thwarting of your desire that they do not give everything to any man, who to you have given so much. Should this Queen slip through your hands, the heir to Babylon can find another to share his throne. It is my will, Prince Mir-bel, that when the army marches against Apepi, you bide here to guard me, lest some evil god should tempt you to do wrong."

When Mir-bel heard this command, knowing that it could not be altered under the ancient law of Babylon, he bowed first to the King and next to Nefra. Then he turned and left the Court followed by his officers. Nor did Nefra see him again till after many years; for at once he took horse and rode for his own Governorship far away, where he remained till all was finished. When he had gone the King fixed his gaze upon Tau, considering him.

"Who are you, Priest?" he asked.

"I am named Tau, a prophet of the Order of the Dawn, O King."

"I have heard of that Order and I think that certain of its brethren dwell in Babylon and even in my Court. I have heard also that it gave shelter to my dead daughter, Rima the Queen, and to this lady, her child, for which I thank it. But tell me, Prophet Tau, have you any other name?"

"Yes, O King. Once I was named Abeshu, the eldest lawful son of his Majesty of Babylon. Yet many years ago I quarrelled with his Majesty and went into exile."

"I thought it! And now, Prince Abeshu, do you return out of exile to claim your place as the eldest born of his Majesty of Babylon?"

"Not so, O King, I claim nothing, as your envoys may have told your Majesty, save perchance the forgiveness of the King. I am but a Brother of the Dawn and as such dead to the world and all its glories."

Now Ditanah stretched out his sceptre to Tau in token of peace and pardon, and Tau touched it according to the custom of Babylon.

"I would hear more of this faith of yours which can kill ambition in the heart of man. Wait upon me, Prophet, in my private chamber, and we will talk together."

Then waving Tau aside, Ditanah addressed himself to a gorgeous high priest, saying:

"Let this dust that once was my daughter and a Queen, be re-coffined and borne hence to the sepulchre of kings, where to-morrow we will give it royal burial."

Presently it was done, and as the coffin passed away Ditanah stood up and bowed towards it, as did all in that great place. When it had gone he waved his sceptre and a herald blew upon his trumpet, signifying that the Court was ended. Next the King descended from the throne and, taking Nefra by the hand, led her away with him, beckoning to Tau to follow them.

CHAPTER 19

The Four Brothers

Very carefully the Sheik of the Pyramids undid the swinging stone and crept out, followed by Khian and Temu, wrapped, all three of them, in their dark cloaks. They closed the stone again and waited, watching. Save one man, a sentry who sat by the embers of a fire, all the soldiers, frightened by what they had seen upon the crest of the pyramid, were gone into the huts that they had built. Whilst this man remained there they dared not descend, fearing lest he should see or hear them and give warning to the others. So there they crouched, among the stones on the slope of the pyramid, drawing in the sweet air in great gasps and gazing at the stars with dark-widened eyes, while Khian wondered what they should do.

"Bide here," said the Sheik, "I will return."

He crept away into the darkness and presently from somewhere above them arose a sound of hideous howling, such as a ghost or a demon might make, that in the darkness of that solemn place might well curdle a listener's blood. The sentry heard it echoing among the tombs behind him. He rose, hesitated, then of a sudden fled away affrighted and vanished into the huts.

The Sheik reappeared.

"Follow me," he whispered. "Be swift and silent."

They descended the pyramid, Temu, who was no climber, half-blinded, moreover, by many days of dwelling in the gloom, awkwardly enough, and reached the ground in safety. The Sheik turned to the right and ran along its base where the shadows were thick. Now they were clear and darting across an open space towards some tombs. As they reached the tombs a shout told them that they had been seen, by whom they did not know. Following the Sheik, who turned this way and that, they ran on. They came to a hollow in the drifted sand behind a little ruined pyramid, where stood four Arabs holding six horses. Khian felt himself seized and thrown rather than helped on to one of the horses. Glancing round he saw Temu upon another horse, also the Arabs leaping to their saddles. The horses began to move forward, as it seemed to him at some word of command; the Sheik was running at his side.

"What of you?" asked Khian.

"I bide here, as is my duty; fear not, I have hiding places. Say to the Lady Nefra that I have fulfilled her command. Ride fast, for you have been seen; these men know the road. They are our brethren and may be trusted. Prince, farewell!" he said, or rather gasped, and loosing the horse's mane, vanished into the shadows.

They came to open desert and rode on at great speed. All that night they rode, scarcely drawing rein, and at the dawn halted among some palm trees, a place where there was a well of water and hidden away beneath stones, food and forage for the horses. Very glad was Khian to dismount, since, after weeks spent in that tunnel, he was in poor case for hard riding, while that of Temu, at the best no horseman, was worse. They ate a little food, dates for the most part, and drank much water.

"Surely, Brother," said Temu, as he emptied his fourth cup, "we should thank Heaven and our guardian spirits for these mercies. How beautiful is the rising sun; how sweet the fresh air after the heavy heat and blackness of that accursed grave hole. Oh! I pray that I may never again look upon even the outside of a pyramid, and much less upon its tomb chambers. Now we have done with them, thanks to my prayers, and all will be well."

Thus spoke Temu, cheerful as ever, though already he was so sore and stiff that it hurt him even to sit upon the ground. Khian thought to himself that they had more to thank than Brother Temu's prayers; namely, the wit and courage of the Sheik of the Pyramids, also those, whoever they might be, that had sent these Arab horsemen to their succour, if they were Arabs, which as yet he did not know. But he only answered:

"I trust that you are right, Brother, and that all will be well. Yet remember that if we were seen as we left the pyramid and that if we escape a second time heads will pay the price of it. Therefore surely we shall be followed, even to the end of the world."

"Faith, Brother! Have faith!" exclaimed Temu as he shifted his seat to find one that was softer.

Just then Khian saw him who seemed to be the leader of the four Arabs, a tall and noble-looking man, standing at a little distance as though he desired speech with him, and alone.

He rose to go to him, and as he came the Arab bowed humbly in salutation and made a certain sign which Khian knew.

"I see that you are of the Brotherhood. Tell me your name and those of your companions; also who sent you in so fortunate an hour to help us, and whither we go."

"Lord, we are four brethren. I, the eldest, am named *Fire*. He who stands there is named *Earth*: the next to him is named *Air*, and the fourth and last is named *Water*. We have no other names, or if there are any we forgot them when we were sworn Brethren of the Dawn, and especially when we were despatched upon a certain duty."

Now Khian understood that for their own reasons, or because of some command laid upon them, these men desired to remain unknown, as was common among the Brethren when they were sent upon any secret service.

"Is it so, Fire?" he said, smiling. "But what answer to my other questions?"

"Lord, we were commanded to take six good horses and, disguised as you see us, to go to the Great Pyramids and there bargain with soldiers, if we found any, over such wares as Arabs have to sell. Also we must make ourselves known to the Sheik of the Pyramids, if we could, and give aid to a scribe, Rasa—perchance you are he, Lord—and to his companion, a priest whose name was not mentioned, but whom we have heard you call Temu, if he be the same."

"And then, Fire?"

"Then, Lord, we were to say to the Scribe Rasa that a certain Lady—we know not and, lest we should be captured and questioned, do not seek to know, what lady—with all her following, has passed safely out of Egypt and that the Scribe Rasa and his companion must follow by the road she took. Lastly, we were sworn to bring both of you safely to Babylon, or die at the task, which, Lord, we purpose to do. Now, Lord, we must ride again. These horses are of the most swift and purest desert blood but we have far to go before we can find others, and certainly we shall be pursued. Moreover," he added, eyeing Temu doubtfully, "I think that yonder priest is more wont to travel on two feet than on four, and until he learns the trick of horsemanship, we must go with care lest he should fall or faint. Lastly, both of you are weak who have, I think, lain for many days in an evil prison."

"True words, Fire," said Khian as he sought his horse.

****

193

All that day they rode forward, resting while the sun was high and sleeping at night among some rocks where once more they found food and water for man and beast, and at length Temu, who was brave and active, began to lose his soreness and to win something of that trick of horsemanship of which he who was called Fire had spoken. Also in the strong and wine-like desert air their tomb-bred weakness and languor passed away from both of them, and they grew strong again, as young men do.

One night they slept upon a mound by water where once had stood some village, both men and horses being well hidden by a grove of thorn and other trees that flourished in the rich soil of the mound. As the sun sank behind them, he who was called Fire came to Khian and bade him look through the trees towards the east. He did so and to their right saw that at a distance of perhaps a league, a broad canal or natural sheet of water that may have been the head of a lake was crossed by a ford, beyond which stood an old and crumbling fort built of sun-dried bricks, while in front of them there was no ford and the water seemed to be wide and deep. Beyond this water was a great flat plain that stretched away and away, till very far off upon the horizon it seemed to end in a line of stony hills.

"Listen now, Lord," said Fire. "That water is the boundary of Egypt. That plain is Arabia, and among those hills is the first desert outpost of the army of the King of Babylon, to reach which will be to win to safety. But I tell you, Lord, that we are in great danger. I am certain that yonder old fort is held by the horsemen of King Apepi, for I have seen their tracks in the sand, a number of them, fifty men perhaps, and that they watch for us, believing that if we would leave Egypt, we must do so by this ford."

"Why?" asked Khian. "Can we not find another?"

"There is no other, Lord, since below, this water grows into a gulf, and above it is deep for many miles, so that to pass round it we must ride through a peopled country guarded by the border garrisons."

"Then it would seem that we are trapped or must fly back into Egypt."

"Where we should be trapped indeed, Lord, for by now the whole land is searching for us."

"What then, Fire? Know that I would sooner look upon the face of Death than upon that of Apepi."

"I have guessed as much. Listen, Lord. All is not lost. These fleet horses of ours were bred in Arabia, yonder among the mountains, and they scent their home and the troops of mares that wander there. The water in front of us will be unwatched because it is so wide and deep and the current runs so swiftly. Yet I think that the horses will not fear to face it, and once across, with good fortune we may ride far before we are seen and perhaps even reach the pass of the hills in safety. It is a narrow pass, Lord, where one man can hold back a number for a long while, so that some of us, at least, should win though to the heart of the hills and find shelter among the scouts of Babylon," he added slowly and with meaning.

Then speaking very rapidly, he explained to Khian all the details of the plan which he and his brethren had prepared. He told him, and Temu, who had joined them, how they must move down to the water edge before the dawn and at the first light ride the horses into it, and as soon as it grew deep, slip from the saddles and swim with them, clinging to their manes.

Here Temu explained that he could not swim, whereon Fire answered that he must hang to his horse as best he might, or drown. He went on to say that those of them who lived to reach the farther shore must mount at once and ride for a certain bay in the hills where the pass began, which bay would become visible to them before noon. The pass they must climb, on foot if the horses had failed them, and descend its farther side to the entrenched camp of the Babylonian company who had orders to succour all fugitives from Egypt.

Having set out these and other matters, he bade them drink and sleep while they could, for none knew what might be their resting place on the morrow.

Khian obeyed, knowing that he must harbour his strength. The last thing he saw ere his eyes closed was the four strange brethren grooming the horses and with set faces talking to each other in whispers as they worked, also, nearer to him, Temu on his knees, lost in earnest prayer. For with all his faith Temu remembered that this water was said to be broad and deep, and that—he could not swim.

It seemed that but a few minutes had gone by when one of the brethren woke Khian, saying that it was time to be stirring. They rose by the starlight, set the bridles and the saddles on the horses which had been fed already, mounted them, and followed the brethren down towards the water. They reached it in safety just at the first glimmer of dawn, by the light of which Khian saw that it was indeed wide—scarce could the strongest bowman have shot an arrow from one bank to the other. Also some tide or current seemed to run very strongly through it towards the ford below, which was to this water as is the neck of a wine-skin to the bottle.

"Would it not be safer to risk the ford?" he asked of Fire doubtfully.

"Nay, Lord, for there we should certainly be seen and perhaps killed upon the bank, whereas here, where no man crosses, they may not note us from so far away. Follow me now, before the light strengthens."

Then, having patted his horse and whispered into its ear in the Arab fashion, he rode into the flood. After him came Khian, followed by another of the brethren and by Temu. Last of all rode the remaining two brethren, those who were known as Air and Water.

The horses went in bravely enough, and soon Khian saw that Fire's was swimming while its rider had slipped from its back and floated alongside, holding fast to the mane or saddle. Presently Khian's horse also lost foothold and as Fire had done, so did Khian. The swim was long and rough, for the swiftly running water, chilled by the night air, drove them downstream and sometimes broke over their heads. Yet those trained horses held on bravely, smelling the pastures where they were born beyond the desert, and being, as Fire had said that they would be, eager to reach them.

At last they touched the farther shore and Khian, still clinging to the horse, was dragged through the rushes to firm ground. As he came there he heard a shout of "Help!" and looking round, saw Temu's horse struggling up the bank, but unaccompanied by Temu, who indeed, having let go, was floundering in the deep water and being swept down by the current at a distance from the shore. All this the strengthening light showed to them, whereon without a word two of the brethren plunged into the stream and swam to Temu whose shouts grew ever louder. They reached him and with difficulty between them dragged him to the shore, much frightened, but unharmed and still calling to gods and men to save him.

Then one of those strange, fierce brethren drew a knife, saying:

"Will you be silent? Or shall I make you so, who are bringing us all to death?"

"Your pardon," said Temu when he understood, "but my mother always taught me that he who drowns in silence, drowns the most quickly; also I ask you to note that my prayers have saved me."

Muttering words that Temu would have thought evil, Fire helped to thrust him on to his horse and signed to the others to mount theirs.

"Hearken, Lord Rasa," he said, as they pushed their way through the thorn bushes that grew on the bank of the water, "ill-fortune is our companion. The shouts of that mad priest will almost certainly have been heard. Would that he had choked before his throat shaped them. Moreover, he has delayed us, so that the morning wind blows

196

away the mist which I hoped would shroud us for a while. Now there is but one thing to be done—ride straight for the gap in the hills and through the pass. Our horses are better than any the Shepherds have, though theirs will be more fresh, and we, or some of us, may outpace them. At the least, remember this, Lord Rasa, if so in truth you are named, we four brethren will do all that men can do to save you, and we pray you, if we meet no more, so to report to a certain Lady whom we serve, and to the Prophet and Council of the Dawn, that our memory may be honoured among men."

Then without waiting for an answer he spoke to his horse which leapt forward, followed by that of Khian and the others, and sped away.

When they had ridden thus for some minutes and the sun was up, Fire turned and pointed back towards the ford. Khian turned also and saw the bright light glancing on the spears of a great company of mounted men, some of whom were splashing through the ford, whilst others, not more than the half of a league away, were galloping towards them.

They were pursued, and the race for life began.

****

On they rode for hour after hour towards those hills that scarcely seemed to grow more near. Very strong were their horses and well accustomed to these sandy plains over which they swept at a long and steady gallop. Yet the way was far, also for days already they had been ridden across the desert, and that morning they had swum a wide stretch of rapid water, whereas those of the Shepherd troops were fresh from the stable. Still throughout the burning heat of the day those horses held their own, and when it drew towards evening and at length that pass in the mountains was at hand, still they held their own. Yes, parched with thirst, panting, thin-bellied, still they held their own. Long ago most of the Shepherds had fallen out and vanished, so that when at length the pass was reached, not a score of them remained, men who had remounted upon led horses when those they rode were foundered. But now these were hard upon their prey; scarce a bow-shot behind indeed.

Khian and his company stumbled up the pass, for the horses, both of the pursued and the pursuers, had ceased to gallop and at the best could but amble forward. Yet step by step the pursuers gained upon the pursued. The sides of that pass were very steep and the pathway was very narrow; one horse filled it all and therefore they must ride one following the other.

Suddenly at a turn in the road, when the first of the Shepherds was scarcely more than fifty paces away, that Arab or Babylonian, or Brother of the Dawn, whichever he might be, who was pleased to give himself the name of Fire, turned and shouted an order. Thereon the last of those four brethren, he who was called Water, dismounted and with drawn sword took his stand at the turn of the narrow path, while his weary horse followed its fellows, as by certain words and signs he bade it do. Presently those of the party of Khian heard the sound of clashing arms behind them, followed by silence. Then a while later the pursuers appeared again, only whereas there had seemed to be fourteen of them now but eleven could be counted.

Once more they gained, once more they drew near, whereon he who was named Fire shouted a second order, and that brother of his called Air dismounted in another narrow place, leaving a second horse without a rider to follow in the train. Again there was a sound of clashing arms, and, when the pursuers reappeared, there were but nine of them. As before, they gained, and as before, at a narrow place the word of command rang out and the third of the brethren, he who was called Earth, dismounted, waiting. Followed the clash of arms and the shoutings, and when the pursuers reappeared there were but six of them. They gained, they came very near, whereon at a chosen place the first of the brethren, he who was named Fire, halted and leapt from his horse, which he drove forward as the others had done.

"Ride on, Lord," he cried. "Should the god we worship give me strength and skill, for you there is yet a hope of safety. Ride on and forget not the message I gave you by the water."

"Nay," answered Khian wearily, for his head swam and scarce he knew what passed about him. "Nay, here I stay to die with you. Let Temu, who understands nothing, deliver your message."

"Begone, Lord!" cried Fire. "Would you put me to shame and cause me to fail in my trust, making my name a hissing and a reproach? Begone or I fall upon my sword before your eyes."

Then as Khian still stayed swaying in the saddle, that most gallant man called some secret word to the horse he rode and the beast, understanding, stumbled onwards at a trot, nor could Khian stay it.

Once more there came the clash of arms and the sound of shoutings, and presently Khian, looking back, saw that of the pursuers but three remained. He urged his horse but it could do no more. Almost at the crest of the pass it whinnied and stood still.

The three struggled on grimly, for they were afoot, having left their spent beasts behind them. They were strong, soldier-like men, black with dust and sweat, and one of them had been wounded for blood ran down his face and robe, he who seemed to be an officer.

"We are commanded to take you dead or living, Prince Khian, for so you are. Shall we slay you or will you yield?" asked this man hoarsely.

Now when he heard these words Khian's spirit came back to him, and with it some of his lost strength.

"Neither," he answered in a low tone.

Then, changing his sword from the right hand to the left, from his belt he snatched his short javelin and hurled it with all his strength. The officer saw it coming and shrank aside, but in that narrow place it caught the man who stood behind him, piercing him through from breast to back, so that he fell down and died. Then the officer sprang at him and they fought with swords, a well-matched pair, though both were very weary, while the third man who could not come at Khian strove to drag the javelin from the breast of him who had fallen. The officer smote, somewhat wildly, perhaps the blood from his wound had run into his eyes. Khian parried, then bending himself, thrust forward and upward with all his strength, a trick of swordsmanship that he had learned in the Syrian wars. The bronze blade caught the officer in the throat just beneath the chin, and piercing to the neck bone, severed it, so that down he went like a stunned ox, in his fall twisting the sword from Khian's sweating hand. Then it was that the third man, having recovered the javelin, cast it at him, though with no good aim, for it struck him, not in the body, but above the left knee, piercing the leg from front to back.

Khian reeled against the rocky side of the pass, supporting himself there, helpless and unarmed. He who had cast the spear, seeing his state, rushed at him. Perhaps he hoped to take him living, or perhaps he, too, had lost his weapons. At least he seized him with his hands whereon Khian fell backward to the ground with the man above him. Now those hands had him by the throat and were choking the life out of him.

"All is finished," thought Khian.

It was then, just as his senses were leaving him, that he heard the sound of running feet and of a voice crying:

"Faith! Have faith!"

Next there followed the thud of a heavy blow and the grip upon his throat loosened. He lay still, regaining his breath, then sat up and looked about him. There at his side lay the soldier, dead, his head broken like a crushed egg, while over him stood the tall Temu, holding in both hands a great smooth stone.

"None of them will move any more," said Temu in the voice of one who marvels. "Who would have thought that I should live to kill a man in such a fashion, I, a Brother of the Dawn sworn to shed no blood? My brain swam; cooked in the sun; my mind was almost gone; that accursed horse—oh! may I never see another horse—jolted on with me, when I heard a noise, looked over my shoulder, and saw. I could not stop the horse, so I slid over its tail and ran back towards you. I had no weapon—I think I lost the sword in the river; at least, when I looked for it there was nothing but the scabbard. Still I ran, praying, and as I prayed, my eye fell upon that stone. I think that the holy Roi must have sent it there from Heaven. I picked it up and brought it down upon the head of that man of blood, as I used to bring down a flail on corn, and my arms being still strong—well, you see, Brother, the stroke was great and well aimed."

"Very well aimed, most excellent Temu," answered Khian faintly. "Now, if you can, pull this bronze out of my leg, for it pains me."

Temu pulled with goodwill and Khian fainted.

When he came to his mind again, it was to see himself surrounded by tall square-bearded warriors clad in the Babylonian uniform, one of whom supported his head upon his knee and poured water down his throat from a gourd.

"Have no fear, Lord," said the soldier. "We are friends who were warned that fugitives might reach us from Egypt and hearing sounds of war ran towards them, though little we thought to find you thus. Now we will bear you to our camp beyond the pass, there to recover of your wound."

Then Khian fainted again, for he had lost much blood. Yet they carried him to the camp where he was doomed to lie for many a day, for his hurt festered so that he could not be moved and it was thought that he must lose his leg. Moreover, this camp was beleaguered by desert men in the pay of Apepi so that escape from it was impossible.

CHAPTER 20

The March from Babylon

Long must Nefra wait in that scented palace at Babylon before the great army, gathered to set her on her throne, was ready for its work. From all parts of the vast empire troops must be collected, hillsmen and plainsmen and men from the borders of the sea; archers, drivers of chariots, infantry, spearmen, and those who rode upon camels. Slowly they came together and then must be exercised and welded to a whole; also provisions and water for so huge a force must be provided, and companies sent forward with these and to prepare the road. Thus it came about that three full moons went by before ever the vanguard marched out of the brazen gates of Babylon.

To Nefra soon that city grew hateful. She loathed its pomps and ceremonies and its staring crowds. Its religion was not hers, and, unlike her mother, to its gods she put up no prayer; indeed, scarcely could she bring herself to bow when her grandsire led her with him to rituals in its enormous terraced temples, she, the pupil of Roi and the Sister of the Dawn who was sworn to a purer faith.

The unending ceremonies of that ancient Court, the adulation accorded to its king, and even to her, his granddaughter who was known to be a queen; the prostrations, the shouts of "May the King live for ever!" addressed to one who soon must die, wearied and revolted her. Moreover, the confinement and the hot airlessness of the place where she could only move in palace courts or in formal gardens, told upon the spirits of this free daughter of the desert, till Kemmah, watching her, noted that she turned from her food and grew pale and thin.

Lastly her spirit was tormented with fear and doubt. Through the secret service of the Brethren of the Dawn, news reached Babylon that the Prince Khian and the priest Temu had escaped from Tanis and repaired to the pyramids, whence they had again escaped towards Arabia, guided by certain men who had been deputed to aid them.

Then after a while came other news, namely, that both of them, together with those guides, had been cut off by Apepi's outposts beyond the borders of Egypt and either killed or taken captive, as it was thought the former, because the bodies of some of their company were reported to have been seen. After this there was silence which, had Nefra but known it, was not strange.

When the Shepherd captain of the border fort learned that those whom he had been commanded to watch for and snare had slipped from his hand, and having killed certain of his people, had, it was believed, reached the Babylonian outpost in the hills alive, although he did not dare to attack that outpost, which was very strongly placed, first because he had not sufficient strength, and secondly because, in a time of truce, it would be an open act of war upon Babylon for which he had no warrant, still he surrounded it with skirmishers with orders to kill or capture any who set foot on the desert roads. Thus it came about that when messengers were sent bearing news that Khian lay sick and wounded at this camp, they were cut off. Thrice this chanced, and when at last, owing to the recall of the skirmishers at the opening of the war, a letter came in safety to Babylon, the army had marched already by another road to attack Egypt, and with it Nefra and the Brethren of the Dawn. Therefore the letters must be sent after it and never came to Nefra's hands till she was far upon her path.

Meanwhile, when first she heard these rumours at Babylon telling her that Khian was dead or captured, her heart seemed to break within her. For a while she sat silent with a face of stone. Then she bade Kemmah bring Tau to her and when he had come, said to him:

"You have heard, my uncle. Khian is dead."

"No, Niece, I have heard a report that he may be dead or captured."

"If Roi were alive he would tell us the truth, he whose soul could see afar," said Nefra bitterly. "But he is gone and only men remain whose eyes are set upon the ground and whose hearts are filled with matters of the world."

"As it seems that yours is, Niece. Yet Roi being dead, leaving me, all unworthy in his place, still speaks. Did he not tell you that however great your troubles, you and Khian would come together at the last, and was the holy Roi an utterer of empty prophecies?"

"Aye, he said that, but he to whom flesh and spirit were much the same, may have meant that we should come together in the Underworld. Oh! why did you ever suffer the Prince to return to the Court at Tanis? Although I could not say it, it was my desire that he should bide with us at the pyramids. Then he might have fled safely with us to Babylon and by now, perchance, we should have been wed."

"Or perchance other things would have happened, Niece. If any knew the decrees of Heaven, that man was Roi, and he held that believing his honour to be at stake, the Prince, his embassy accomplished, must be allowed to follow his desire and make report to Apepi his father. So he departed to fulfil his mission, and since then matters have not gone so ill for you."

"I think that they have gone very ill," she said stubbornly.

"How so, Niece? We know through our spies that the Prince and the priest Temu escaped from Tanis and came to the pyramids where they lay hid a while. We know also that by the help of those high-born warrior brethren of our Order whom I deputed to the task, they escaped again from the pyramids and fled safely out of Egypt. It seems that they were followed and that there was fighting in which it well may be that those brethren, or some of them, lost their lives, as they were sworn to do. If so, peace be to their gallant spirits. But of the death of the Prince, or even of Temu, there is no certain word, nor," he added slowly, "does a dream or voice tell me or any of us that he is dead."

"As it would have told Roi," interrupted Nefra.

"As mayhap it would have told Roi, and as mayhap Roi, being still living though elsewhere, would have told me who fill his office. Niece, be not so rough-tongued and ungrateful. Have not all things happened according to your desire? Has not the royal Ditanah, my father, given you a great army to set you on your throne? Has he not at your prayer, and, as I can tell you now, at mine made in secret, abandoned his policy of wedding you to his heir, Mir-bel, and sent that prince far from Babylon to where he cannot molest you? Has he not—though this has been hid from you—set me in command of that army, that it may be handled according to your desire and mine, putting trust in me that when its work is done, I will lay down my generalship and from a mighty prince of war once more become a priest, I, who were I evil-hearted might use it to set the crown upon my head?"

"It seems that he has done all these things, Uncle, but what of them if Khian is dead? Then I seek no throne; then I seek nothing but a grave. Nay, first I seek vengeance. I tell you that of Apepi and his Shepherds I will not leave one living, of his cities not one stone shall remain upon another."

"Kind words from a Sister of the Dawn, and from her one of whose titles is Uniter of Lands—not their destroyer!" exclaimed Tau, shrugging his shoulders, and adding, "O Child, do you not understand that all life is a trial and that as we pass the trials, so we shall be rewarded or condemned? You are mad with fear for one whom you love, and therefore I do not blame you overmuch, though I think that you will live to grieve over those fierce threats."

"You are right. I am mad, and being mad, I will cause others to drink of my cup of fear and sorrows, that cup in which they have mixed the wine. Send Ru to me, my Uncle, that although I be woman he may teach me how to fight. And bid those Babylonian smiths come measure me for armour of the best."

Then Tau departed, smiling. Still he sent Ru and with him came the royal armourer.

So it happened that soon, had there been any to look over the wall of a certain courtyard of the palace, a strange sight might have been seen of a lissom maid clad in silver mail cutting and thrusting at a huge black giant, who often enough cried out beneath the smart of her blows, and once, stung beyond endurance, smote her so shrewdly on the helm with the flat of a wooden sword that she fell headlong to the ground, only to spring up again, while he stood dismayed, and deal him such a thrust beneath the breast bone, that his breath left him and he did likewise. Yes, there he lay, grunting out between his gasps:

"The gods help Apepi if this lion's whelp gets him in her claws!" while she bade him be silent because by all the laws of swordsmanship he was dead.

At other times she would practise shooting with a bow, an art in which she had no small skill, or when she wearied of this, at the driving of chariots in the private circus of the palace, taking with her one of the slave women, a bold, desert-bred girl, for passenger, because Ru was too heavy and Kemmah said that she was mad and refused to come.

"So you thought when I began to climb the pyramids, yet they served me my turn, Nurse," she answered, and went on driving more furiously than ever woman drove before.

Now when her grandsire, the old King Ditanah, heard of these things, he was amazed, and caused himself to be hidden in places whence he could watch her secretly at her warlike exercises. Having done so and listened to the tale of her conquest of the pyramids, he sent for Tau and said to him with a curious smile upon his puckered face:

"I think, Son Abeshu, that I should have given the command of my great army, not to you, who, if once a great warrior, have become a priest, but to this granddaughter of mine who, if once a priestess, has become a goddess of war."

"Nay, Sire," answered Tau, "for if you gave her that army, you would never get it back again. Every man in it would learn to love her and she would use it to conquer the world."

"Well, why not?" asked Ditanah, and hobbled away, thinking in his heart that if it had truly pleased the gods to take the Prince Khian to their bosom, so that Mir-bel might be recalled to Court, his tears would be hard to weep. For with such a beauteous and royal-hearted lady for its queen and that of Egypt, surely the glory of Babylon would fill earth and Heaven. Indeed—was it too late? Then he remembered that on this matter he had passed his royal word, sighed, and hobbled on.

****

These martial exercises served Nefra in two ways: they gave her back her health which she had begun to lose in the soft life of the Babylonian palace and they held her mind from brooding upon its fears—that is, while she was engaged in them. Yet at night these returned to her, nor indeed were they ever quite absent from her thoughts. She importuned Tau, and even her grandsire the King, who caused search to be made all along the Egyptian frontier of his empire. Messages came back from the searchers that no traces of fugitives could be found. But among them was another message, namely, that certain hills could not be approached because they were watched by horsemen of the army of Apepi. Inquiry was made as to these hills, and it was found that in a camp among them were stationed a company of Babylonian troops from which no reports had been received of late. Therefore, as often happened in so vast an empire, for a while this outpost had been forgotten by that general in whose command it lay, or if remembered at all, it was supposed to have been overwhelmed by rebellious, desert- dwelling tribes.

When Tau heard this news he went to the King his father and gained leave from him to send a hundred picked horsemen to disperse the outposts of Apepi and search those hills; also he set spies to work. But of this business he said nothing to Nefra, fearing lest he should fill her with false hope.

****

At length the vast army that had been gathered in the military camps upon the banks of the Euphrates beyond the walls of Babylon was ready to advance, two hundred thousand foot-soldiers and horse-men, a thousand or more of chariots, countless camp followers, and a multitude of camels and asses bearing provisions, besides those which were already stacked at the water holes along the line of march.

Then came Nefra's farewell to Babylon. In state, wearing the crown of Egypt, she visited the Sepulchre of Kings and in its temple laid offerings upon her mother's grave. This duty done, at the Court in the great hall of the palace she bade farewell to her grandsire, Ditanah the Great King, who blessed her, wished her well, and even wept a little at parting from her whom he could never hope to see again; also because he was too old to accompany his son upon this war. With Tau also, now clad in the armour of a General and Prince of Babylon, and looking like one who had never felt the rubbing of a monk's robe, he conversed apart, saying sadly:

"Strange lots are ours, beloved son. Many years ago we were dear to each other. Then we quarrelled, more through my fault than yours, for in those days my heart was hard, and you went your way to become a priest of some pure and gentle faith, and your heirship was given to another. Now for a little hour you are once more a Prince and a General commanding a great host, who yet purpose, if you live, to lay down these ranks and titles and, your mission ended, again to seek some desert cell and wear out your days in prayer. And, I the King of Kings, your father, remain here awaiting death that soon must overtake me, and oh! I wonder, Son Abeshu, which of us has chosen the better lot and done more righteously in the eyes of God. Yes, I wonder much from whom all these pomps and glories flee away like shadows."

"There is a great taskmaster, Sire," answered Tau, "who portions out to each of us his place and labours. Man does not choose his lot; it is chosen for him, to work for good or ill within its appointed round. Such at least is the teaching of my faith, believing which I seek no throne or power, but am content to build on that foundation as truly as I may. So let it be with you, my royal Father."

"Aye, Son, so let it be, since so it must be."

Then very tenderly they bade each other farewell and parted to meet no more upon the earth, since when that army returned to Babylon another King of Kings was seated on the throne.

So by proclamation Babylon declared war upon the Shepherds, who long before had learned that this storm was about to burst upon them and were making ready to meet it as best they might.

For very many days the great army marched across the plains and deserts, as the progress of so vast a host was slow, till at length it drew near to the borders of Egypt. Then it was that Tau heard from his spies and skirmishers that Apepi with all his strength, a mighty power, had built a line of forts upon his boundary and in front of these was preparing to give battle to the Babylonians. These tidings he took to Nefra who sat in her chariot armed in glittering mail like some young war goddess, surrounded by a bodyguard under the command of Ru.

"It is well," she said indifferently. "The sooner we fight the sooner it will be over and the sooner I shall be avenged upon the Shepherds of the blood of him whom I have lost." For having received no tidings of Khian, now she had become almost sure that he was dead.

"Do not run to meet evil, Niece," said Tau sadly. "Is there not enough of it at hand that you must go to seek out more? Have I not told you that I believe the Prince to be alive?"

"Then where is he, Uncle? How comes it that you under whose command is all the might of Babylon cannot spare some few thousands to seek him out?"

"Perchance I am seeking, Niece," Tau answered gently.

As he spoke a slave ran up, saying:

"Letters from the King of Kings! Letters from Babylon!" and having touched his forehead with the roll, he gave it to Tau who opened and read. Within was another roll, a little crumpled roll such as might have been hidden in a headdress or a shoe.

Tau glanced at the contents of this second roll and gave it to Nefra.

"A writing for you, Niece," he said quietly.

Seizing it, she read. It was brief and ran thus:

"Again, O Lady, a certain one whose name you may guess writes to say that save for a hurt to his leg which cripples him he is well in health. This he does because he has learned that the enemies who surround the place where he lies may have cut off former messengers. Should he who bears this come safely to you at Babylon or elsewhere, he will tell you all. More I dare not write.

"Signed with the sign of the Dawn which you yourself taught me how to shape."

Nefra finished reading, then fell rather than leapt from the chariot into the arms of Tau.

"He lives!" she gasped. "Or he lived. Where is the messenger?"

As she spoke the words a guard appeared escorting an officer who was travel-stained and weary.

"One who craves audience with you, Prince Abeshu, and at once," said the leader of the guard.

Tau looked at the officer and knew him again. It was he whom the King had sent from Babylon to search for the missing outpost.

"Your report," he said, and waited with fear in his heart.

"Prince," answered the man, saluting, "we won through to the outpost and found all well there, since it is so strongly placed that the Shepherd skirmishers have not dared attack. Also we found those travellers who were missing."

Again Nefra paled and leaned against the chariot, for she could not speak.

"What of them?" asked Tau.

"Prince, the priest is well. Four brethren who travelled with them were slain one by one in a certain pass; they died nobly defending those in their charge. The lord whose name is not spoken, who escaped with the priest, is still sick, that is, he is wounded in the left knee and the wound runs. He cannot walk, and though now it is believed that his leg will be saved, always he must be lame, for the knee is stiff."

"Did you see him?" asked Tau.

"Yes, Prince, I and another of my company saw him. While the rest of us, pretending to retreat, drew off the Shepherds horsemen, we two won our way to the camp which is on a plain surrounded by hills, not to be reached except through two passes, one to the west and one to the east. There we found the garrison, well though weary, for of food they have enough, also the priest and the other traveller who is hurt. These told us how they came to the place and of the death of their four guides, which is a great story."

"Then repeat it afterwards," said Tau. "It seems that you escaped. Why did you not bring these travellers with you?"

"Prince, how could the two of us carry a man who cannot walk, down a mountain path, even with the help of the priest? Moreover, if we could have brought him to the plain, it was full of enemies all mounted on good horses through whom it would scarcely have been possible to bear him safely, while the garrison had received no orders to attempt to leave its post. Therefore it was determined that he should remain where he is safe enough, until a sufficient force could be sent to bring him away."

Then the captain went on to tell how he and his companion had rejoined their men at night and fought their way through the horsemen of Apepi who watched the stronghold, though with loss; how also they had learned from some desert wanderers that the army of the Great King was marching upon Egypt by a road that ran not more than thirty leagues from where they were, and how therefore they had ridden for the army, instead of returning to report at Babylon.

"You have done wisely," said Tau. "Had you attempted to bring that wounded lord with you, doubtless he would have been killed or captured."

Then he went away to give certain orders, leaving the officer with Nefra, who had many questions to put to him.

When Tau returned an hour later Nefra was still questioning him. Tau looked at them and asked:

"Friend, how long is it since you slept?"

"Four nights, Prince," answered the officer.

"And how long is it since you and your companions ate?"

"Forty-eight hours, Prince. Indeed, if we might crave a cup of water and a bite of bread, who have ridden hard and done some fighting——"

"These await you, Captain, when it pleases her Majesty of Egypt to dismiss you."

Then Nefra reddened and turned away ashamed. When the men had gone to eat and rest, humbly enough she asked Tau what was his plan.

"My plan is, Niece, to send five thousand mounted men, though we can ill spare them, to clear the desert between this place and the stronghold where he who was named the Scribe Rasa lies wounded— *not* dead, as you feared, Niece, and to bring him with our brother Temu and the garrison of the camp to join the army on its march which, travelling in a chariot or a litter, he should do within some six days."

"A good plan," said Nefra, clapping her hands. "I will go with the five thousand and in command of them. Kemmah can accompany me."

"No, Niece, you shall not go. You stay here with the army."

"Shall not! Shall not!" exclaimed Nefra, biting her lip as was her fashion when crossed. "Why?"

"For many reasons, Niece, of which the first is that it would not be safe. We cannot tell how many troops Apepi has between here and that stronghold, but we know he would risk much to capture his son now that the great war has begun; also the Lady Kemmah could not bear such a journey."

"If it is not safe for me who am sound and well, neither is it safe for Khian who is wounded, and if things be thus then let the whole army turn and march to the stronghold."

"It cannot be, Niece. This army is a trust placed in my hands and its business is to push on and give battle to Apepi, not to wander away into the desert where perhaps it may be overcome by thirst or other disasters."

"Cannot be! I say it must be, my Uncle, I, the Queen of Egypt, desire it; it is an order."

Tau looked at her in his calm fashion and answered:

"This army is under my command, not yours, Niece, and having put on armour the Queen of Egypt is but one officer among thousands," and he touched her shining mail. "Therefore I must pray even the Queen of Egypt to obey me. Or if that is not enough, I must pray Nefra, a Sister of the Dawn, to accept the word of the Prophet of the Dawn without question, as she is sworn to do. The safety of the Queen of Egypt is much, as is the safety of the Prince Khian. But the safety and the triumph of the great host of the King of Kings are more."

Nefra heard and was about to answer furiously, for her high spirit was aflame. Yet there was that on the strong face and in the quiet eyes of Tau that stilled her words before they were uttered. She looked at him a while, then burst into tears and, turning, departed to her tent.

****

Next morning at the dawn the five thousand horsemen with certain chariots, guided by that officer and others who had brought tidings, departed to rescue Khian and his companions from the stronghold where he was imprisoned.

CHAPTER 21

Traitor or Hero

The Babylonian host marched on and came in safety to the borders of Egypt, the mightiest host perhaps that ever had invaded the Land of Nile. There it encamped, protected in front by water, to rest and prepare before it attacked Apepi encamped with all his strength some three leagues away around the forts that he had built. The captains of the Shepherds, riding out, saw with their own eyes how terrible and numberless, how well-ordered also, was the army of the King of Kings with its horsemen, its chariots, its camelry, its footmen, and its archers that seemed to stretch for miles; no Eastern mob but disciplined and trained to war. They saw and trembled, and returning, made report to Apepi at his Council.

"Let Pharaoh hearken!" they said. "For every man we muster, the Babylonians have two under the command of the Prince Abeshu who is reported to be a great general, though some say that he was once a priest and a magician. The spies tell also that with them marches the Princess Nefra, daughter of Kheperra, she who slipped through Pharaoh's fingers and is affianced to Pharaoh's son, who also slipped through his fingers and, if he lives, is hidden we know not where, unless he, too, be with the Babylonians. It is impossible that Pharaoh can stand against such a host as this, which will overrun the land like locusts and devour us like corn."

Apepi heard and rage took hold of him, so that he gnawed at his beard. Suddenly he turned to Anath, the old Vizier, saying:

"You have heard what these cravens say. Now do you give me your counsel, you who are cunning as a jackal that has often escaped the trap. What shall I do?"

Anath turned aside and spoke with certain other of his fellow councillors. Then he came and bowed before Apepi and said:

"Life! Blood! Strength! O Pharaoh! Such wisdom as the gods have

211

given us bids us urge Pharaoh, as do the diviners who have consulted with their spirits, not to join battle but to make peace with Babylon before it is too late."

"Is it so?" asked Apepi. "What terms then can I offer to the King of Babylon, who comes to seize Egypt and add it to his empire?"

"We think, Pharaoh," answered Anath, "that Ditanah does not desire to take Egypt. We have heard from those who serve Pharaoh in secret at Babylon, that Ditanah is bewitched by Nefra the Beautiful. It seems that when those wizards of the Dawn, through help of their magic arts, escaped to Babylon, they took with them the body of the Queen Rima, the widow of King Kheperra. The tale runs that the coffin of Queen Rima was opened before the King of Kings, and that at the bidding of the Princess Nefra and of the head wizards of the Dawn, the body of Rima or the ghost of Rima spoke to Ditanah who begat it, bidding him to attack Egypt or bear the curse of the dead. It bade him also to give Nefra in marriage, not to his grandson and heir, Mir-bel, but to the son of your Majesty, the Prince Khian, to whom she became affianced yonder by the pyramids, and to send a great army to avenge the death of her husband, Kheperra, and her own wrongs by casting your Majesty from the throne and setting the Princess Nefra and the Prince Khian in your place. Moreover, the royal Rima, or her spirit, said to Ditanah, King of Kings, that if he neglected to do her bidding, he and his country should be everlastingly accursed, but if he obeyed, her blessings should come upon them. Therefore because of the words of dead Rima, his daughter, and because of the spells laid upon him by the Princess Nefra and the wizards of the Dawn, Ditanah has sent this army against your Majesty to fulfil the commands of Rima upon you and upon the people of the Shepherds."

"What then must I do to turn aside the wrath of this Babylonian?" asked Apepi of the Vizier, glaring at him.

"That which the King of Kings demands, or so it seems, O Pharaoh—wed the Prince Khian, if he still lives and can be found, to the royal Nefra and give up to them the Crowns of the Upper and the Lower Lands."

"Is this your counsel, Vizier?"

"Who am I and who are we that we should dare to show a path to be trodden by the feet of Pharaoh?" asked Anath, cringing before his master. "Yet, if he takes another and these captains are right, perchance soon there will be a new Pharaoh, and if the Prince Khian be dead, as some believe, the People of the Shepherds will be driven from the Nile back into the desert whence they came centuries ago—and the King of Kings, or the Princess Nefra under him, will rule Egypt."

Now Apepi leapt to his feet roaring with rage and with the wand-like sceptre that he carried smote Anath on the head so hard that the blood came and the Vizier fell to his knees.

"Dog!" he cried, "speak more such words and you shall die a traitor's death beneath the whips. Long have I suspected that you were in the pay of Babylon and now I grow sure of it. So I am to surrender my throne and take Ditanah for my lord, and should he still live, give the woman whom I had chosen for my wife to be the queen of the son who has betrayed me. First will I see Egypt devoured by fire and sword and perish with her. Out of my sight, you white-hearted cur!"

Anath waited for no more. Yet when he turned at the doorway to make the customary obeisance, though Apepi could not see it in the shadow, there was a very evil look upon his face.

"Struck!" he murmured to himself. "I the great officer, I, the Vizier, struck before the Council and the servants! Well, if Apepi has a staff I have a sword. Now come on, Babylon! I must to my work. Oh! Khian, where are you?"

****

Apepi, the Pharaoh of the North, dismissed his councillors and his generals and sat in the chamber of the fort that he had built, brooding and alone. Although often he was possessed by that devil of rage who sleeps so lightly in the breasts of tyrants, also by other passions, he was a far-seeing statesman and a good general, having inherited from his forefathers the gifts by help of which they had conquered Egypt. Thus he knew that Anath, the old Vizier, the clearest and most cunning thinker in the land, was right when he told him that he could not stand against all the strength of Babylon, drilled and martialled as never it had been before, and marching under the guidance of those wizards of the Dawn who had escaped him, leaving behind him their high priest to lay upon him ere he died the curse of the oath-breaker and the seeker of innocent blood. Yet for telling him this truth he had offered public insult to Anath, smiting him as he would a slave, such insult as the old noble and officer in whose veins, it was said, ran the pure blood of Egypt, never would forget.

Would it not be better, then, to follow the blow on the head with a thrust to the heart and to have done with Anath? Nay, it was not safe; he was too powerful, he had too many in his pay. They might rise against him, now when all complained at being forced into a war they hated; they might destroy him as they believed he had destroyed his son, Prince Khian, whom they loved. He must send for Anath and crave pardon for what he had done when beside himself with rage and doubt, promising him great atonement and more honours, and biding his time to balance their account.

Yet could he accept this Anath's counsel, and to save his life and the shattering of the Shepherd's power, bow his neck beneath the yoke of Babylon? What did it mean? That he must abandon his throne and in favour of Khian if he still lived, of Khian, who had stolen from him the woman upon whose beauty he had set his heart, and sent her to call up the Babylonian hordes against him, his king and father. Or, if Khian were dead, then this Nefra, Queen of the South and indeed of all Egypt by right of blood, would take that throne as the vassal of Babylon and doubtless wed its heir. Therefore what could he gain by surrender? One thing only—to live on in exile as a private man, eating out his heart with memories of the glories of the past and watching the Egyptians and their great ally stamp upon the Shepherd race.

It was not to be borne. If he must fall, it should be fighting as his forefathers would have done. How could he succeed against so mighty a foe? Not in a set battle; there they would overwhelm him, or if he kept to the walls of his forts, surround them and sweep on to capture Egypt. Yet generalship and craft might still give him victory. He had it; he would send all his best horsemen, twenty thousand or more of them of the old fighting Shepherd blood, to make a circuit in the desert and fall upon the rear of the Babylonians as they advanced to give battle, which doubtless according to their custom they would do while it was still dark; in order that they might attack in the uncertain light of dawn. By some such unexpected thrust their array might be confused and broken, so that he would have to deal not with an army, but with a mob. At least since no other offered, the plan should be tried.

****

The five thousand despatched by Tau came safely to the stronghold in the hills, and reported themselves and their mission to the captain of the outpost, and to his wounded guest whom all knew to be the Prince Khian, though none called him by that name. Khian heard their tale and grew faint with joy when he learned that the great army of Babylon was near to him and that with it, safe and sound, was Nefra his beloved, as a writing in her own hand told him. Sad and heavy had been his long confinement in this place, crippled as he was, but now at length the night of fear and waiting had passed away and there in front of him burned the dawn of joy.

Until the following morning the five thousand rested themselves and their horses; then, taking with them the garrison of the outpost who were glad enough to bid it good-bye, they started to rejoin the Babylonian army that they had planned to meet at a certain spot on the frontier of Egypt. In the centre of their array, in a chariot because he could not ride, went Khian, followed by Temu in another chariot because he would not ride, having sworn an oath, unless Fate forced him, never to mount another horse.

So they passed on safely across the desert, for Apepi's skirmishers who had hemmed them in for so long had vanished away. They could not travel fast because of the soldiers of the garrison who must march on foot; indeed their progress was so slow that Khian, who was on fire to rejoin Nefra, wished to gallop on to the Babylonian army escorted only by a few horsemen. But this the officer in command of the five thousand would not suffer, having been strictly charged by Tau, who foresaw that such a thing might happen, to keep him who was called the Scribe Rasa safe in the heart of his force. In vain did Khian plead. Those, said the officer, were his orders and he must obey them.

On the third afternoon of their march, they learned from desert men that they drew near to the Babylonian host which was encamped over against the forts that Apepi had built. As it was still too far away to be reached that night and those on foot were very weary, its general halted the five thousand to eat and rest at a place where there was water, giving orders that the force was to march again at midnight by the light of the setting moon, which, if all went well, should bring them to the army shortly after dawn.

This plan was carried out. At midnight they broke camp and went forward through the hot desert air by the light of the half moon. When they had marched for about two hours Temu caused his chariot to be brought alongside that of Khian, and though the Prince was somewhat silent, talked on to him after his fashion, for none guessed that on the farther side of a certain rise of ground the five and twenty thousand horsemen whom Apepi had despatched to fall upon the flank of the Babylonians were creeping towards them purposing to attack the camp of the great army at the first break of dawn. Why should it be guessed, seeing that outposts rode ahead of them to give warning of any danger? How could they know that those outposts had been surrounded and captured or killed, when as they thought

215

they were riding into the fringe of the host of Babylon, thus giving the Shepherds warning of the approach of foes?

"Brother," said Temu, "during all this while you have been very impatient, complaining of your wound which will get quite well in time, though it may leave you stiff-legged and lame for life, complaining because you were kept yonder in the hills, instead of thanking the gods that you ever reached them safely by the help of those rough-tongued but courageous Arab brethren who gave themselves fanciful names, for which faults as your elder in our Order I have often reproved you, saying that like myself you should have faith. Now you see the end of it, namely, that faith has triumphed as it always does. Within an hour or two we shall reach the mighty host of Babylon and make obeisance to Tau, the Prophet of the Dawn. All our troubles are ended, or rather all your troubles, since because of faith *I* never doubted but that they would melt away——"

At this moment Temu himself melted away, for a javelin or an arrow pierced his charioteer through the heart so that the man fell dead on the flanks of the horses, causing them to start forward at full gallop in their fright, and charging through the ranks to vanish at speed into the desert, while Temu clung to the chariot rail and grasped wildly at the reins. The horses were good horses, being indeed two of those that had borne them on their gallop from the water to the hills, now fat and strong again. They rushed on up the rise; they came among the Shepherd troops where the line was thin, they broke through it unharmed, being scarcely seen in the dim light before they were gone. They galloped on across the sands, smelling other horses ahead of them, or perchance it was water that they smelt. At least they rushed on while Temu, flung to the bottom of the chariot, dragged at the reins in vain. That is, he dragged once or twice, then let them be, muttering:

"Faith! Have faith! These accursed beasts must go where Fate drives them, and I see no more soldiers."

Presently, however, he saw plenty, for now the chariot, heedless of the challenges of the sentries, was rushing down the central avenue of the Babylonian camp. At length the feet of one of the horses became entangled in the ropes of a tent, so that it fell, bringing down its companion with it, and Temu rolled on to the ground in front of a general who was giving orders to some officer.

"Who is this?" asked the General testily, "and what does that chariot here? Take it away."

Then Temu, knowing the voice, sat up and said:

"O Holy Prophet, as I understand that you are now that Roi is dead, O Father Tau, that is, if a Prophet and Father of the Dawn can be clad in armour which is against all the rules, I am Temu, a priest of your Brotherhood, as you may remember, for it was you who sent me on a certain business to the Court of Apepi, King of the North, since which time I have suffered many things."

"I remember you, Brother," said Tau. "But whence come you in this chariot, and why?"

"I do not know, Prophet. One moment I was talking to him who is called the Scribe Rasa, with whom I have shared many adventures, but who, I think, has another name, and the next my charioteer pitched forward with a missile through his breast, and those mad brutes of horses on which he fell were dragging me away whither I knew not. All I know is that we passed through a host clad in such armour as the Shepherds use, for the moonlight shone upon it and upon Apepi's banners, which I knew well, for I saw enough of them at Tanis. Then the horses, directed of Heaven, came on here. And that is all the story."

"The Scribe Rasa!" exclaimed a woman's voice, that of Nefra who, seeing the fall of the horses, had come from her tent, accompanied by Ru, to learn its cause. "Where did you leave the Scribe Rasa, Priest?"

"Cease from questions, Niece," broke in Tau. "Can you not understand that the force we sent some days ago to rescue a certain garrison has been ambushed and that by some accident this brother has escaped to bring us tidings. Or perchance," he added, as a thought struck him, "Apepi's army has moved from its defences to attack us from the south presently when the sun rises."

Then he gave certain orders. Trumpets blew, captains ran up, men by the thousand, still yawning, took their appointed places; all the awakened camp burst into active martial life.

Meanwhile, not so very far away, a desperate battle raged. The five and twenty thousand of the Shepherds, attackers who thought themselves attacked, hurled themselves upon the five thousand Babylonians who had marched into their midst. The Babylonians, being alert and well officered, strove to cut a path through the Shepherds, aye, and did so, losing many men as they struggled forward. Squadrons rushed on them, dimly seen in the moonlight, and were beaten back. There was charge and counter-charge. Horses screamed, men fell and groaned out their lives.

The moon grew dark, but still the battle went on in the twilight that precedes the dawn, when it was difficult to distinguish friend from foe. The light of day began to gather and by it the captain of the Babylonians saw that he could advance no more. Nor could he fly, for the cloud of Apepi's Horse was all about him. Therefore he made a square of those who remained to him, perhaps two thousand or more sound men and many wounded, and gave orders that none must surrender, since this was a fight to the death for the honour of Babylon.

When Apepi's captains in the gathering light perceived with how small a body they had to do, they were dismayed who thought that all this while they had been attacking the flank of the Babylonian host in the darkness. And now the dawn had come and their opportunity was gone; they had failed in their mission and how could they face Apepi with such a tale? In the fighting they had seized prisoners, some of them wounded. Those men they questioned. Under threat of death by torment, or with beatings, from some of these they drew the truth that this was but a force of Babylonian skirmishers sent to relieve an outpost which they were bringing back with them to the army.

"Who, then, is the man that sits in a chariot among the horsemen?" asked Apepi's captain.

The prisoners answered that they did not know, whereon he ordered them to be flogged a while, and then repeated his question. Thus he learned that this lord in the chariot was none other than Khian the Prince whom he himself had been ordered to capture when he was escaping from Egypt, for though the prisoners gave only the name of Rasa the Scribe, well he knew that Rasa and Khian were the same man.

Then that captain saw light in the midst of a great darkness. He had failed, it was true; he had not fallen upon the flank of the army of Babylon at this hour of dawn, or thrown it into confusion and panic, as he had hoped to do, but instead had become engaged with a petty force of which the destruction would help Apepi not at all. But now he learned that with that force was one whose capture would mean as much, or more, to Apepi as a great slaughter of the Babylonians. Instantly he made up his mind; he would not try to attack the army of the great King; it was too late. No, he would destroy these horsemen and take the Prince Khian, living or dead, as an offering to Apepi, hoping thus to assuage his wrath.

Instantly he gave orders and the attack began. Being mounted, neither side had bows and now javelins were few. Therefore the fray must be fought out with swords. The Babylonians had picketed their horses in the centre of the square or given them to the wounded there to hold, turning themselves into foot-soldiers. Moreover, by command of their general, with hands and stones and cooking vessels they were heaping the desert sands into a bank which, with two thousand men or more labouring at it for their lives, rose as though by magic, for the sand was soft and easy to handle. At this bank the Shepherds charged from every side. But the Babylonian square, set on the crest of a desert sand wave, was small, for its general had drawn up his men three deep, each line standing behind the other. Therefore only a few of the clouds of Apepi's horsemen could come at them at once, and at these the Babylonians stabbed with their swords, or cut at the horse's legs as they scrambled up the sand slopes, laming them, or causing them to scream in agony and rush away.

Soon Apepi's captain saw that victory would be slow, which fitted his plans but ill. Every moment he was in fear lest the outposts of the great army should discover what was passing not so very far away and send out a mighty force to destroy him. He feared also that the wounded man in the chariot whom he guessed to be the Prince Khian might be killed in the fighting, whereas he desired to take him living to Apepi. Lastly he feared that even if he were not attacked, soon he and his horsemen would be cut off from Egypt and driven back into the desert, to perish there of thirst and hunger. Therefore, ceasing from his onslaught, he sent officers under a flag of truce to the Babylonian general, charged to deliver this message:

"Your case is desperate since I outnumber you ten to one. Surrender and in the name of Apepi I promise you your lives. Fight on and I will destroy you all."

The Babylonian heard, but being a crafty man, would give no immediate answer, for he, too, hoped that news of their plight would reach the great army either through messengers whom he had despatched when they were first attacked, or otherwise. Therefore desiring to gain time he replied that he must take counsel with his officers and presently would let their mind be known. He went to the centre of the square and coming to Khian, told him all.

"Now what shall we do?" he asked. "If we continue the fight, we must soon be overwhelmed. Yet surrender we cannot for the honour of Babylon; indeed, first will I fall upon my sword."

"It seems that you have answered your own question, General," replied Khian, smiling. "Yet here is my poor counsel. Offer to give me up, for you know well who I am and it is whom they seek. I think that if you do this, that captain will let the rest of you go free."

Now even in his sore strait that general laughed aloud, saying:

"Have you bethought you, Prince, for since you have declared yourself I call you what you are, how I should be greeted by the Prince Abeshu, also named the Lord Tau, who commands the army of the Great King, and by a certain lady who marches with that army, if I return to tell them such a tale? Rather would I die, Prince, with honour upon the field, than shamed before all the host of Babylon. No, I have another plan. I will parley with these Shepherds as one who bargains, asking for the promise of safety in writing, and while I do so all must creep to their horses, taking the lightly wounded behind them and leaving the rest to fate. Then suddenly we will charge upon the Shepherds and, now that we have light, cut our way through or perish."

"So be it," said Khian, but in his heart were thoughts that his lips did not utter. He knew that such a charge made by weary men upon wearied horses could not succeed; that if it were attempted all who remained alive of the Babylonian horsemen would perish, together with those on foot, among them his hosts of the mountain garrison, and that the wounded would be slaughtered where they lay. He was sure also that what the Shepherd captain wanted was himself, not the lives of more Babylonian horsemen, whose slaying or escape could make no difference to the issue of the war, and that if he could secure the great prize, he would turn and ride for Egypt. Therefore certainly it was laid upon him to offer up himself as a sacrifice. He shivered at the thought, knowing that this meant death, perhaps death by torture, at the hands of Apepi, and what was worse, that never more after all that he had suffered could he hope to look upon the face of Nefra beneath the sun. Oh! he must choose, and choose at once.

Khian cast down his eyes and with all his soul prayed to that Spirit whom he had learned to worship, that he might find guidance in his agony. Lo! it seemed to come. It seemed as though there amidst the stamp and neighs of horses, the groans of the wounded, the orders of officers who, having received the General's word, already were making preparation for that last wild rush for life, he heard the quiet, well-remembered voice of Roi, saying:

"My son, follow after duty, even down the road of sacrifice, and leave the rest to God."

Khian hesitated no longer. He was alone in the chariot, for its driver had descended to give the horses the last of the forage they had carried with them and a sup of water that remained, and stood at a distance watching them finish their food as best they could, for the bits in their mouths hampered them. He seized the reins, he smote the stallions with the whip, and the beasts sprang forward.

Now they had come to the low bank of sand and were scrambling over it, dragging the light war chariot after them. Some fifty paces away and as many perhaps from the first of Apepi's horsemen stood the General of the Babylonians and one officer talking to the Captain of the Shepherds, also accompanied by one officer, a man whom he knew well enough for they had served together in the Syrian wars. They had turned and did not see him coming or hear the chariot wheels on the soft sand. Apepi's captain had grown angry and cried in a loud voice:

"Hear my last offer. Give up to me the Prince Khian who is with you, and you and your soldiers may go free. Refuse, and I will kill you every one and take him, living or dead, to his father, Apepi the Pharaoh. Answer. I speak no more."

"*I* will answer," said Khian from the chariot, whereon they turned in amaze and stared. "I am the Prince Khian, and you, Friend, know me well. I, too, know you for a man of honour and accept your promise to let these Babylonians go their way unharmed, taking their wounded with them, and in payment I surrender myself to you. Is it sworn?"

"It is sworn, Prince," said the Captain, saluting. "Yet remember that Apepi is very wrath with your Highness," he added slowly, as though in warning.

"I remember," answered Khian. Then he turned to the Babylonian General, who all this while had stood like one transfixed, and said: "Say to the Lord Tau and to the Lady of Egypt that I have gone where my duty calls me and that if it be decreed that we should meet no more, I trust that they will not think ill of me, seeing that what seems false often is the truth and that sometimes ill deeds are done for good ends. For the rest, let them judge as they will of me, who follow my own light."

"Lord," exclaimed the General like one who wakes from sleep, "surely you do not desert us for the Shepherds?"

"Am I not a Shepherd?" asked Khian, smiling strangely. "Farewell, Friend. Good fortune go with you and your company, no drop of whose blood shall be shed for me."

Then he called to the horses and they went forward while the General wrung his hands and muttered the names of strange Babylonian gods.

"I do not understand your Highness," said Apepi's captain as he walked by the chariot back towards his horsemen, "which is not strange, since always you were different from other men, and I am wondering whether those Babylonians will write you down as a traitor or as a hero. Meanwhile, I who know you to be honest, ask your promise that even if you see opportunity you will not escape to them lest I should be forced to kill you."

"It is yours, Friend. Henceforth, like a certain Temu, I walk by faith, though whither faith has led him this day I do not know, who last saw him vanishing into the heart of your host."

"Mad!" muttered the Captain. "Still if he has lost his wits, he will keep his word, and that may save my head."

CHAPTER 22

Khian Returns to Tanis

Swiftly the Shepherd horsemen galloped back towards Apepi's forts across the border line of Egypt, leaving their wounded to follow after them as best they might or perish, and in the centre of their array, surrounded by a guard, raced the chariot of Khian. Their captain knew there was no time to lose, for soon those Babylonians whom he had spared would be at the camp of the Great King—and then———! What he did not know was that two hours before Temu had reached that camp and that already a mounted army was sweeping down to cut him off.

Far away in the desert appeared a cloud of dust. It grew nearer and more near, and now through the dust shone helms and spears and burnished chariots. Then the Shepherds knew the worst. Their path was blocked, Babylon was upon them! Flight was impossible. Their case now was that of the five thousand whom they had surprised not twelve hours before, and they must charge as these had done, and with as little hope of victory.

They drew together; they lined up their squadrons to the shape of a wedge, skilfully enough, as Khian noted, and rushed forward bearing somewhat to the right, that they might strike the Babylonian line where it was thinnest. The two armies drew near together, some twenty thousand of the Shepherds against fifty thousand of their foes who were massed in dense squadrons divided by companies of chariots. A roar of triumph went up from the Babylonians, but the doomed Shepherds were silent.

Apepi's captain appeared by the chariot of Khian.

"Prince," he cried as he galloped, "the gods are against me and I think that our end is near. Yet I trust to you to remember your oath, upon faith of which I spared your company, and to make no effort to escape. If you are captured, it is so decreed, but while you are able, I repeat I trust to you to head straight for the boundary which is near, and to surrender yourself to Apepi or his troops. Do I trust in vain?"

"My honour has never yet been doubted," Khian called back.

Then that captain saluted with his sword and, spurring his horse, vanished away.

With a shock and a sound like thunder the hordes of horsemen met. Deep into the Babylonian array cut the Shepherd wedge, throwing men and steeds to either side of it, as a gale-driven ship throws waves of the sea. Yet slowly Apepi's squadrons lost their speed as more and more of the Babylonians poured upon their flank. The point of the wedge, passing through the first group, became engaged with fresh squadrons beyond, that escorted a company of chariots which had raced in front to cut them off.

The fighting grew desperate. Slowly those before him were killed, scattered, or trodden down, so that Khian found his chariot in the forefront of the battle. At a little distance he perceived a throng of the Shepherds, some of them dismounted, attacking a few of the Babylonians who were gathered round a splendid chariot that had outraced the rest, whereof the wounded horses were struggling on the ground. In this chariot, sword in hand, was one clad in mail that seemed to be fashioned of silver and gold, whom he took to be a beautiful youth, doubtless some princeling of the royal House of Babylon sent out to look upon the face of war, while on that side of it on which the Shepherds, six or eight of them, pressed their attack, stood a black-faced giant hung about with plates of brazen armour that clanked as he swung his great axe aloft and brought it crashing down upon those within its reach. One glance told Khian that this was the mighty Ethiopian, Ru himself! Then with a sick heart he understood the figure in the chariot was no noble Babylonian youth but none other than Nefra, his betrothed.

Oh! she was sore beset. Horsemen were coming to her aid, but the nearest of them were still a full bow-shot away, for in her fierce folly she had outdriven them all. Ru smote and smote, but he could not be everywhere, and while some drew him to the rear of the chariot which they were striving to enter from behind, others, five or six of them, ran together at its side, purposing to rush forward and kill or drag away her who stood therein. It was as if they knew that this was a prize indeed, one for whose sake all must be risked, and as he came nearer, Khian perceived how they knew, for now he saw that about her silver helm she wore the snake-headed coronet, the royal *uraeus* with the sparkling eyes that proclaimed her Egypt's queen. The men gathered, watching Ru as with savage war cries he beat down foe after foe, and waiting their chance to spring upon their prey and pierce her through or capture her.

Khian thought for a moment.

"I swore not to escape, but never that I would not fight upon my way to doom," he said to himself and pulled at the reins, turning the rushing horses straight upon that knot of men. As he came the first of them leapt at Nefra. She smote with her sword and the blow fell upon his thick headdress. He shot out his long arms, for he was a great fellow, and gripped her round the middle, dragging her to him. The others stood waiting to seize her as she fell to the ground and carry her off if they could, or kill her if they could not. So eagerly did they watch that they never saw or heard the white-horsed war chariot thunder down upon them from where they knew there were no foes. Khian called to the stallions, beasts trained to war, and turning neither to left nor right they rushed on. They smote those men and down they went beneath the hoofs and wheels. Only one remained standing, he who dragged Nefra from the chariot. In Khian's hand was a spear. He hurled it as he passed and it pierced that man through and through, so that, loosing his grip of Nefra, he fell to the ground and died.

Now Ru had seen and was rushing back. Nefra, freed, stared at her deliverer—and knew him.

"Khian!" she cried. "Khian! Come to me."

Ru knew him also and shouted:

"Halt, Lord Rasa!"

But Khian only shook his head and galloped on.

Then the Babylonian deliverers came up as a flood comes along a dry river bed and covered all. But already Khian was far off with the remnant of the Shepherd Horse.

****

The battle rolled away. Of the twenty thousand Shepherds or more but some few hundreds escaped; the rest were cut or hunted down before they reached the border line of Egypt. But among those who came unharmed to the army of Apepi was the Prince Khian, for through all that fray it was as though some god protected him and the horses that drew his chariot. On he drove till he saw where a general's standard flew. Then he halted the bloodstained, weary beasts and called aloud:

"I am the Prince Khian. Come, bear me hence for I am hurt and cannot walk."

The officers who heard him saluted and their men cheered, for they thought that the Prince Khian whom they loved and who had been their comrade in the Syrian wars had escaped from the Babylonians that he might fight against them with his own people. Tenderly they lifted him from the chariot and gave him wine and food, the best they had, then placed him in a litter such as they used for wounded men and bore him to the royal encampment in and around the new-built forts. Over these forts flew Pharaoh's banners, yet when they came to them they found confusion and open gates. Pharaoh, heralds announced, had been called back to Tanis, leaving orders to his armies to follow after him, that they might re-form there to protect the great city and Egypt.

Now when the captains heard these commands they stared at each other and murmured. But Khian, looking back across the frontier line, learned their reason. Yonder the sands were black with all the ordered hosts of Babylon. On they came, foot and horse and chariots, a mighty flood of men, before the shock of whose onslaught the army of the Shepherds must have broken and gone down. Therefore it was that when he learned that his flank attack had miscarried and saw all the might of Babylon sweeping down upon him, Apepi had fled to Tanis, leaving his troops to follow as best they could.

Understanding at last how matters stood, some of the chief officers came to Khian and prayed him to take command of the army, by right of his rank and repute in war. But he smiled and remained silent, as they thought because he was sick and could not stand upon his feet. While they still pressed him there came that captain to whom he had sworn the oath and who, like himself, had escaped the slaughter of Apepi's horsemen. Calling them aside he told his comrades of how he had captured the Prince among the Babylonians, and the rest. Then they pressed Khian no more, though had he chosen to put another colour on the tale perhaps they would still have listened. Or had he offered to go to the Babylonians and pray the clemency of the Queen of Egypt and of the Prince Abeshu their General, for Pharaoh's army, perhaps they would also have listened. But as he did neither of these things, they yoked fresh horses to his chariot and setting him in it, took him with them in their flight to Tanis.

Thus it came about that when the Babylonians poured up to the camp of the Shepherds to give them battle, save for some sick and wounded men, they found them gone. Learning the truth from these men, who by Tau's command were spared and cared for, also that the Prince Khian had come in safety to the camp and been welcomed there and, as some said, was now in command of the retreating army, at once they started in pursuit.

At their first bivouac Tau, with some of the generals under him, waited upon Nefra, there being present also Ru, Temu the priest, and the Lady Kemmah. By the wish of Tau, Nefra and Ru told all the tale of their meeting with Khian in the battle of the horsemen and of how he had driven his horses over those who attacked Nefra, thrust his spear through him who was dragging her from the chariot, and then, when they called to him to stay with them, had shaken his head and fled away, making no attempt to check the horses, as he might have done, thereby escaping from the Shepherds if he were their captive.

Now when he had heard this strange tale, Tau asked those present to interpret it. The Babylonian Generals, one and all, answered that either this Prince was mad, or evidently he was a traitor. It was clear, they said, that otherwise he would have escaped when he had opportunity, and it was also clear that being a Shepherd and the son of their King, he had followed his heart back to the Shepherds and to his father. Kemmah, who spoke next, held that certainly he was mad, for how, she asked, could a sane man fly away from the loveliest woman in the world, to whom he was affianced, and one who was a queen as well?—Unless, indeed, she added as an afterthought, since they parted he had met one yet lovelier, words at which Nefra sharply bid her be silent.

Then Temu, who had been the Prince's companion in his captivities and flights, was called upon. But all he could do was to mutter, "Faith! Have faith!" adding that in this matter it was easy because he could not believe that any one who had once tasted of the palace dungeon at Tanis or of the tomb chamber in the dark of the pyramid could wish to return to either of them again. Then he began to set out the tale of their escapes and of all that he had suffered on horseback and in the chariot, until an officer pulled him back to his seat.

Then spoke Nefra, asking angrily of the Babylonian Generals:

"Have you ever known, Lords, of a man who wished to play the traitor, who began his treachery by killing sundry of those to whom he had sold himself? Do you not understand that if this Prince wished to be rid of me in order that in future he might lay an undisputed claim to the double throne of Egypt, all he needed to do was to pass on and leave those Shepherd knaves to kill me as—Ru, after his fashion, being elsewhere when he was wanted—doubtless they would have done. Yet he drives his chariot over four of them and pierces the fifth through with his spear. Then—the gods alone know why, though I doubt not for some good reason, other than that advanced by the

Lady Kemmah," she added acidly, "he departs, shaking his head, and so swiftly that he could not be caught, as yonder priest says, to taste once more of Apepi's dungeons, or"—here her voice grew faint and her eyes filled with tears—"of worse things."

When they had finished Tau said:

"All who know the Prince Khian have learned that in some ways he is different from most men, and it is probable that among those differences the truth may be found. Indeed I think that I have discovered it, but if so, as we have talked enough, I will keep it to myself until I know whether I be right or wrong. Meanwhile, I would ask you all to listen to the prayer of our brother, Temu, and have faith, such as that which her Majesty of Egypt showed when she rushed forth alone into battle against the commands of those set over her, and now again shows in him who preserved her from death."

Then he rose and departed from the tent, leaving Nefra abashed and yet indignant.

****

Those who remained of the army of the Frontier came at length to Tanis which was strongly held by Apepi's second army of reserve. They were not many, for the Babylonian pursuit had been sharp and captured thousands. Moreover, when in this way or in that it became known that none of these were put to the sword or set aside to be sold as slaves, but that all asked of them was that they should take an oath of fealty to Queen Nefra of Egypt and serve under her banner, other thousands grew weary of that rapid march and lagged behind until they were overtaken by the Babylonian pickets.

Among the faithful that at length straggled through its gates, however, were the Prince Khian and that captain to whom he had surrendered and sworn a certain oath. Together these two, between whom there was now a bond of lasting friendship, were brought to the palace and to the wonder of Khian placed in the apartments that had been his own when he was Prince and heir apparent of the North. Here slaves waited upon him, his own slaves, and doctors came to treat his knee, now much inflamed and swollen with so long and rough a journey. Yet, as Khian noted, with all of these were mingled spies and guards: spies to watch and note every spoken word and guards to frustrate any effort at escape. In short, he was now as close a prisoner as he had been in that dungeon whence he escaped with Temu.

There in his own place Khian, who had been brought to it at dawn, rested till the third hour after sunset, sleeping the most of this

228

time, save when he bathed and ate, for he was very weary. At length came an officer and soldiers with a litter to bear him into the presence of Apepi, his father. At the head of this company was Anath the Vizier who, as Khian noted, had grown thinner and more grey and whose quick black eyes darted from place to place as though everywhere he expected to see a murderer, and following after him a sharp-faced scribe whom Khian took to be a spy.

Anath bowed a greeting nicely judged, neither too scanty nor too full, saying:

"Welcome home, Prince, after long travels and many adventures. Pharaoh needs your presence. Be pleased to accompany me."

Then he was set in his litter borne by eight soldiers, at the side of which walked Anath, while the captain followed after. In turning the corner of one of the passages the long litter tilted and Anath put out his hands to steady it, or to save himself from being pressed against the wall, while the spy for a moment was left out of sight and hearing on the farther side of a corner. Swiftly Anath whispered into Khian's ear:

"The danger is great. Yet be calm and keep courage, for you have friends, ready even to die for you, of whom I am the first."

Then the spy appeared and Anath straightened himself and was silent.

They came into the presence of Pharaoh who sat in a low chair clad in mail with a sword in his hand. The litter was set down and its bearers helped Khian to a seat that was placed opposite to that of Pharaoh.

"You seem to have taken some hurt, Son," said Apepi in a cold voice. "Who gave it to you?"

"One of your Majesty's soldiers during a fray in a pass of certain hills, who overtook me when I was flying from Egypt a while ago, Pharaoh."

"Oh! I heard some such tale. But why were you flying from Egypt?"

"To save myself and to win another, Pharaoh."

"Yes, again I remember. The one who have done so far, though with damage; the other you have not done and shall never do," Apepi said slowly. Then he looked at the captain, who accompanied Khian, and asked:

"Are you that man whom I sent in command of some five and twenty thousand horse to fall upon the flank of the Babylonians? If so, tell me why you failed in your task?"

In brief, soldierlike words the captain told him all the story: how he had met the body of Babylonian Horse during the night and become engaged with them; how in the end Khian had bought the lives of those of them who remained by his surrender of himself; how they

229

had fallen in with the great force of mounted Babylonians and chariots which in the end destroyed them nearly all; how the Prince Khian had kept his word when he might have escaped, and thus was now a prisoner at Tanis, and the rest.

Apepi listened till he had finished and said:

"Enough, man. You have failed and by your failure have brought me to the gates of ruin. My army is dispersed and the Babylonians, under the command of one of the accursed wizards of the Dawn, sweep down on Tanis to capture it, after which they purpose to seize all Egypt and set this girl Nefra as their puppet on its throne. All these things have happened because you failed in the task I laid upon you and instead of falling upon the Babylonian flank, were trapped and wasted your strength and time in a petty fight with some few thousand men. For such as you there is no more place upon the earth. Get you down to the Underworld and there learn generalship, if you may."

Then he made a sign whereon certain armed slaves ran forward. The captain, answering nothing to Apepi, turned to Khian and saluted him, saying:

"Now, Prince, I am sorry that I did not loose you from your oath and bid you escape while you could. For if I am treated thus, what chance is there for you? Well, I go to make report of these matters to Osiris who, I have been told, is a just god and an avenger of innocent blood. Farewell."

Before Khian could answer the slaves seized the man and dragged him behind a curtain, whence presently one of them reappeared holding up a human head to tell Pharaoh that his will was done. At this sight for the first time Khian hated his father and hoped in his heart that Apepi himself might be overtaken by the fate which he had brought upon a loyal servant who had done his best.

Now father and son were left alone and stared at each other in silence. At length Khian spoke.

"If it be the will of your Majesty that I should follow on the path that has been trodden by yonder victim, I pray that it may be soon, since I am weary and would sleep."

Apepi laughed cruelly and answered:

"All in good time, but not yet, I think. Do you not understand, Son, that you are the only arrow left in my quiver? It seems that by aid of the arts of these wizards of the Dawn you have bewitched this royal Egyptian in such fashion that she dotes on you, she, the chosen of your father, from whom you stole her. Now how do you think it will please her when she appears before the walls of Tanis with the Babylonians, as doubtless she will do to-morrow with the light, if she saw you, her darling, set upon the eastern gate and there about to die as that fool died or in worse fashion?"

"I do not know," answered Khian, "but I think that if such a thing chanced, very soon Tanis would be given to fire and all that breathe within its walls would also die, and with them one—who does not wish to die."

"You are right, my Son," mocked Apepi. "An angry woman with a hundred thousand men behind her might commit such crimes upon the helpless. Therefore I propose to keep your head upon your shoulders, at least for the present. This is my plan—tell me if you do not think it good. You shall appear upon the gateway and heralds shall announce, or perhaps this would best be done by messenger, that you are about to suffer death for treason in the presence of Pharaoh and his Court, or as many of them as can find standing room upon that gateway. It will be announced, however, that Pharaoh, out of his great pity and love, will spare you upon certain terms. Can you perhaps guess those terms?"

"No," answered Khian hoarsely.

"I think you lie; I think you know them well enough. Still, Son, I will repeat them to you, that you may never say you have not been fairly dealt with. They are short and simple. First, that having surrendered all its treasure and some trappings such as horses and chariots and signed a perpetual peace with us, the Shepherds, the Babylonian army retreats whence it came.

"Secondly, that the Princess Nefra gives up herself to me, that in the presence of both armies and of the holy gods the priests may declare her my wife and queen, who brings to me as her dower all the rights and inheritances that are hers by blood in Egypt."

"Never will she consent," said Khian.

"Of course, Son, that is the danger, since no one can tell what a woman will or will not do. But do you not think that if such should chance to be her mind and that she should determine that you must be sacrificed to what she holds her duty, you who otherwise would be set free among the Babylonians, the sight of a little torture and the sound of your groans might work the needful change? There are some clever blacks in this place and by the way, that knee of yours is still swollen and painful, is it not? They might begin there. Hot irons—yes, hot irons!"

Khian looked at him and said in a low voice:

"Do your worst, devil who begat me, if indeed I am your son, which now is hard to believe. You speak of the priests of the Dawn as wizards. Know that I am a priest of the Dawn who share their wizardry or their wisdom, and it tells me that all your plots will fail and that your wickedness will fall back upon your own head."

"Ah! does it? I understand your scheme. You think that you will kill yourself. Well, this shall not happen, for be sure that you shall be too well watched. Nor will you escape from the palace for the second time. Good-night, Son. Rest while you may, for I fear that it will be necessary to awake you early."

CHAPTER 23

The Queen of the Dawn

Before the hour of dawn Khian was carried up the pylon stairs to the top of the eastern gate of Tanis. It was a large flat place where fifty or more might stand with comfort, and being lame he was seated in a chair upon its eastern edge. Ra the Sun arose and showed him all. Beneath him was a wide moat filled with water from the Nile, but the bridge which spanned it had been hoisted up by the aid of ropes and pulleys and was made fast to the gateway pillars.

Beyond the moat and almost at its edge, for in their overwhelming might they seemed to fear nothing from their broken foes, appeared the heart of the host of Babylon, whereof the wings already encircled the city of Tanis, cutting off the escape of those who were within its walls. A little way back from the edge of this moat, though out of the reach of arrows, pavilions were pitched, over which, side by side, flew the royal ensigns of Egypt and Babylon, showing to Khian that there rested Nefra and the Prince Abeshu who was also called the Lord Tau. For the rest the walls on either flank of the gateway were garrisoned by Shepherd troops who seemed restless and ill at ease, while on its top, attended by Anath and other councillors, sat Pharaoh Apepi gorgeously attired and wearing the double crown of the Upper and the Lower Lands.

Trumpets blew and guards gathered about the royal pavilions, after which there was silence. On the farther side of the moat behind the outposts, the ordered ranks of the marshalled Babylonian soldiers stood staring up at the gateway crest; wall upon wall of white faces, every one, as it seemed to Khian, turned towards himself. Presently a messenger bearing a white flag appeared crossing the moat upon a boat and from its farther bank was escorted through the lines to the pavilions where flew the standards of Babylon and Egypt and there handed a letter to the captain of the General's guard who entered and delivered it to Tau. Tau opened it and read, then said to Nefra who stood beside him, large-eyed and haggard-faced:

"These are the terms of Apepi: That having given up all its treasure and signed a treaty of perpetual peace, the Babylonian army must march back to Babylon."

"What else, my Uncle?"

"That you, the Queen of Egypt, surrender your person forthwith to Apepi and with due ceremony be wed to him in front of the gateway and in sight of the people of the Shepherds and of the armies of Babylon."

"What else, my Uncle?"

"That if these terms be refused, then the Prince Khian will be tormented before our eyes until they are accepted or until life leaves him. Now what answer, Niece and Queen?"

Nefra's face grew ashen. She bowed her head until it touched her knees and rocked her body to and fro; then she straightened herself and asked:

"What would Khian wish that I should do? I know! I know! He would wish that I should defy Apepi, leaving his fate in the hand of God."

"Have faith! Have faith!" muttered Temu who was seated behind her with papyrus on his knee.

"Aye, Brother," went on Nefra, "I have faith, and if it fails me, well, there is always death behind and in death I shall find Khian. Shall I of the ancient blood, his sworn betrothed, come to him beyond the grave, defiled, the woman of that dog of an old Shepherd king? Never! Shall Babylon, my great ally, bow herself before these runaways who did not dare to await the battle? Never! Let Khian die if die he must, and let me die with him. But if so, not one man shall be left living in Tanis, and not one man of Shepherd blood throughout the North. Write it down, Temu, as the Prince Abeshu shall tell you, and let the messenger take it back to that cruel crossbred cur Apepi, and let heralds call it out to those who stand upon the gateway and the walls, while the captains bid the attack begin at every other mouth of Tanis."

Tau heard and smiled in his slow, secret way. Then to officers mounted on swift horses he issued certain orders on receipt of which presently thousands of men began to move to the onslaught upon the great city. This done, he turned to Temu and other scribes, saying to them the words that they should write. Also he summoned heralds and caused them to learn those words by heart and depart to shout them out at very gate.

At length all was ready, and the messenger, having received the roll, departed to the moat escorted by Ru, who gave him another message on his own account. It was:

"Tell that Sheep herder who calls himself a king, and tell all his councillors and the captains who remain to him, that if a finger is lifted against the Prince Khian, presently I, the Ethiopian Ru, will twist out their tongues and drive in their eyes with my own fingers, and afterwards cast them into the desert to starve. Aye, and yours also, Messenger, if you fail to report this my message so that I can hear you from this shore of the moat."

Now the messenger looked up at the giant Nubian who glared down at him grinding his great white teeth and swore that he would do his bidding. Then he entered his little boat and, crossing the water, was admitted by a tiny door in the gateway tower, so that presently he appeared upon its crest and handed the writing to Apepi. Moreover, as he had sworn to do, he repeated the message of Ru in a loud voice, the words of which seemed to please those upon the gateway little, for they gathered into knots debating them fearfully. Heralds also called out that which had been written in the roll, so that all upon the wall might learn and understand.

Khian, bound upon the edge of the gateway so that if spears were thrown or arrows shot these might pierce him first, heard the proclamation and was glad, because now he knew that not for his life's sake would Nefra be shamed. Yet he turned his head and spoke over his shoulder to Apepi who stood behind him, and to Anath and the other councillors, saying:

"Pharaoh and Lords, what the Prince Abeshu and the royal Nefra have sworn most certainly they will do. Torture and kill me before their eyes if you desire, but be sure that it will not change their purpose, for not with my poor life can you buy their honour. For myself I fear not death, but I ask of you—is it your will to follow me, every one of you, and to give all the people of Tanis and the nation of the Shepherds to the sword? If you spare me and set me free, you and they will be spared. If you lift a hand against me, you and they will die. I have spoken; do what you will."

Now, although because of his bonds he could not see what passed, Khian heard tumult behind him. He heard Anath the Vizier and other councillors praying Pharaoh to forego his purpose because their case and the case of the whole city was desperate, beleaguered as they were by the countless hosts of Babylon, and it seemed mad to die that Pharaoh might satisfy his hate upon the Prince his son. Moreover, crowds from the city who had also heard the proclamation were rushing into the open space behind the gate, sweeping aside the soldiers by whom it was guarded, and shouting such words as:

"Pharaoh! Spare the Prince Khian! Must we all die because you would torment and murder him who was born of you?"

Then above the tumult Anath spoke again, saying in a high cold voice, like one who threatens rather than prays:

"Pharaoh, this is a very evil business. The Prince is beloved in Tanis and it is not well for kings to kill those whom the people love when the enemy is at their gates."

Now Apepi answered, hissing like one mad with rage:

"Be silent, Anath and the rest of you, or as I serve this traitor, so shall you be served. Slaves, to your task!"

Behind Khian arose guttural murmurings. It seemed to him that the black tormentors shrank from their office. Again the furious Pharaoh commanded, but still they hung back. Then came the sound of a blow and groans and Khian knew that he had cut one of them down and guessed that the others would no longer dare to resist his will. On the farther side of the moat he saw Ru the giant marching to and fro like a caged lion and shaking his great axe. Beyond him now were ranged a company of archers, their arrows set upon the strings, waiting the word to loose, while behind the archers he perceived Tau, and leaning on him Nefra clad in her glittering mail. Then he lifted up his voice and cried:

"Ru! Hear me—Khian. Bid the archers shoot, for thus would I die, rather than in torment."

He could say no more for Apepi, stepping forward, struck him heavily upon the face and bade the torturers gag him, a sight at which the army of Babylon groaned, as did the inhabitants of Tanis who now packed the Place of the Gateway in thousands. Ru roared out a curse that sounded like the bellow of a wounded bull, then turning, repeated Khian's words to the archers who lifted their bows and looked to Tau for the order to shoot. But Tau gave no order, only motioned to them to hold their hands, while Nefra sank to her knees as though she swooned.

Khian became aware of black hands tearing at his garments, then there was a smell of fire and an agony darted through him. The slow sacrifice was begun! He shut his eyes, making his soul ready to depart.

There was a sound behind him, a very strange sound of wrestling and blows. He opened his eyes and looked. Past him, staggering backwards, went the form of Pharaoh, and in his breast was fixed a knife.

At the edge of the gateway platform he stopped, clinging to the seat in which Khian was bound.

"Dog!" he gasped, "Dog of a Vizier! I have spared you too long; it should have been done last night. But I waited——"

"Aye," answered the voice of Anath, "you over-shot yourself, Pharaoh, and gave the dog time to bite. Away with you to Set, son-murderer."

A withered form, that of Anath, leapt forward, its black eyes gleaming in the yellow wrinkled face, a thin arm smote with the tormentor's hearted iron at the hands that gripped the seat, crushing and burning them. Apepi loosed his hold and with a cry fell backwards into the moat beneath.

Ru saw him fall and leaped into the water, swimming with great strokes. As the Pharaoh rose he seized him with his mighty hands and dragged him to the bank where he broke him like a stick, then cast him to the shore.

"Pharaoh Apepi is dead!" piped the thin voice of Anath, "but Pharaoh Khian lives! Life! Blood! Strength! Pharaoh! Pharaoh! Pharaoh!"

So he cried as he hacked at Khian's bonds and dragged away the gag, and all the multitude beneath took up the ancient greeting, shouting:

"Life! Blood! Strength! Pharaoh! Pharaoh! Pharaoh!"

****

It was evening. Khian lay upon a couch in the royal pavilion of the Babylonians, whither by his own command he had been brought, since as yet Nefra could not enter the city. The Lady Kemmah and a leech bathed his bruised face and bandaged his swollen knee, while Nefra, who stood near, shivered at the sight of a long red burn upon his flesh made by the touch of hot iron.

Then suddenly a question burst from her:

"Tell me, Khian, why did you fly away from me in the battle, when you might have escaped and spared us all this agony?"

"Did not some two thousand sound men and with them very many wounded rejoin this army upon that day, Lady," asked Khian, "being the survivors of the force which was sent to rescue me and the garrison of the mountain stronghold?"

"They did, and were questioned, but knew nothing except that you drove out your chariot and surrendered yourself to the Shepherds, after which the attack upon them ceased."

"Then do you not understand that sometimes it is right that one man should offer himself up for many?"

"Yes," answered Nefra, colouring, "I understand now—that you are even nobler than I thought. Yet, when you could have escaped, why did you fly away, as I saw you do?"

"Ask the Prophet Tau," replied Khian wearily.

"Why did Khian fly away, my Uncle? Tell me if you know, since he will not."

"Does not the oath sworn of those who enter into the fellowship of the Dawn demand that they shall never break a promise, Niece? Perchance our brother here had vowed to deliver himself up in Egypt, and did so, even when he might have stayed at your side. So at least I have believed from the first."

"Is that so, Khian?"

"It is so, Nefra. With this oath I bought the lives of those men. Would you have had me break it even to win my own—and you?"

"I cannot say, but oh! Khian, you are noble, who did this knowing that if you died, all my life I should have been ignorant *why* you died, seeming to desert me."

"Not so, Nefra, since Tau knew and would have told you at his own time."

"How did you know that which was hid from me, my Uncle?"

"My office has its secrets, Niece. Enough that I knew, as I knew also that it would never be necessary for me set out the truth to you."

"So you let me suffer all these things when there was no need, my Uncle!" exclaimed Nefra angrily.

"Perhaps, Niece, and to your own good. Why should you alone escape from suffering which is the medicine of the soul, you, who if you be the Queen of Egypt, are, as I would pray you to remember, first and foremost a sister of the Dawn and the servant of its laws? Be humble, Sister. Sacrifice your self-will. Learn to obey if you would command, and seek, not self-will or glory but the light. For so, when these little storms have rolled away, you shall find the eternal calm."

"Faith! Have faith!" muttered Temu who stood behind.

"Aye," went on Tau, "have faith and humility, for by faith we climb and in humility we serve—not ourselves but others, which is the only true service. I say these things to you now even in the hour of your joy, for soon we must part, I to my hermitage and you to your throne, and then who can reprove the Pharaoh on the throne?"

"You could and will, I am sure, my Uncle," Nefra answered, tossing her head.

Then suddenly her mood changed and, turning, she threw her arms about him and kissed him on the brow, saying:

"Oh! my most beloved Uncle, what is there that I do not owe to you? When I was a babe you saved me and my mother from the hands of those traitorous Theban nobles, with whom soon I hope to talk if they be still alive."

"I think that the Lady Kemmah and Ru here had something to do with that, Niece."

"Yes, yet they did but fulfil their offices, whereas you travelled up Nile to rescue us."

"Fulfilling *my* orders, Niece."

"Then you brought us to the pyramids and there you watched over my childhood, teaching me all the little that I know. Afterwards it was you who led me to Babylon and in secret worked upon the heart of the Great King, so that, as though at my prayers, he abandoned his plan of wedding me to Mir-bel and gave me this great army that has brought us victory and peace."

"God, for His own purposes, changed the heart of my father, Di-tanah, on that matter, not I, Niece."

"Afterwards," she continued, taking no heed of his words, "you comforted me in a hundred ways; also it was you who held me back from accompanying the five thousand to the mountain stronghold which, had I done so, would have brought me to death or shame. Oh! and I know not what besides. And how have I paid you back? Often enough with pride and angry words and rebellion against your commands; aye, and disbelief when you told me that if I found patience all would work for my good and that of Khian, whom I believed dead, even when you bade me hope on. Yet," she added in another voice, "if I behaved thus, it was your fault, not mine, for who was it that spoiled me in my youth, giving me my way when I should have been taught obedience?"

"The holy Roi, I think; also the Lady Kemmah," answered Tau with his quiet smile.

At this moment guards challenged without. Then the curtain of the pavilion was drawn and, heralded by Ru, there entered the old Vizier Anath and with him others of the councillors and captains of the Shepherds.

Anath and his company prostrated themselves thrice, to Nefra, to Khian, and to the Prince Abeshu, the General of the armies of Babylon.

"Queen and Princess," he said, "on behalf of all the Shepherds we come to surrender to you the city of Tanis and to pray your clemency for those who have fought against you and for every one who breathes within its walls. Is it granted?"

"Be my mouth and answer," said Nefra to Tau. "Your mind is my mind and by your words I will be bound, as I think will his Highness, the Prince Khian, who is still too sick for ceremonies."

"It is granted," said Tau. "To those who will be loyal to Nefra, Queen of Egypt, and to Khian, Prince of the North, whom she purposes to take as husband, all is forgiven. To-morrow we enter Tanis and proclaim the great peace."

"We hear and thank you, Queen and Princess," said Anath. "Now I have a word to say to the Prince Khian, I who come before him with the blood of Pharaoh on my hands, for which deed I crave pardon. Let the Prince hearken. When the Prince was cast into yonder prison, it was I who saved him with the help of yonder Brother of the Dawn and a certain jailer. Being suspected of this deed by Pharaoh I was disgraced and myself imprisoned. Therefore I could not rescue him when he was shut up in the pyramid or prevent his pursuit to the mountain outpost of the Babylonians where he took refuge. Afterwards I regained power because Pharaoh knew that I alone might perchance save him from the fangs of the Lion of Babylon. When the great host poured down upon Egypt I counselled Pharaoh to surrender and, if the Prince still lived, proclaim a marriage between his son, Khian and the royal Nefra. For answer he struck me like a dog—see, here are the marks"—and he touched his head. "Afterwards Pharaoh fled, his attack having failed, and the Prince Khian, through his own nobleness, fell into his power. I pleaded for his life in vain, both in the palace and on the gateway, but Pharaoh was mad with jealousy and hate and would have put the Prince to death by torment before the very eyes of the royal Nefra and of the host of Babylon. Then, before it was too late, I smote, and saved the Prince and the people of the Shepherds. Have I pardon for this deed?"

Now Tau went to where Khian lay upon his couch and talked with him apart. Presently he returned and said:

"Anath, what you did must be done. To-morrow make sacrifice in the temple of your gods and receive the forgiveness of your gods for the shedding of royal blood to save other royal blood and the lives of tens of thousands who are innocent. Then appear before us in the palace of Tanis that there may be given back to you the wand and chain of office of Vizier of the Upper and the Lower Lands. The word is spoken. Record it, Scribe Temu. Anath, withdraw!"

****

Thirty days had passed. Tau handed over the command of the

host of Babylon to the general next in rank to him at a great ceremony, and putting off his mail and royal emblems, had donned the white robe of the Prophet of the Dawn and returned to the Temple of the Pyramid, leaving Temu behind him because such was the will of Nefra and Khian. Save for a force of ten thousand picked men who remained to guard the grand-daughter of the Great King until all was accomplished, that army had marched for Babylon. There were ceremonies at which all who served his father, now known as "Apepi the Accursed," swore fealty to Khian his son, but at these Nefra was not present, nor as yet had there been any coronation, for indeed none knew whether Khian of the North or Nefra of the South ruled over Egypt. Some grumbled that this should be so, but others glanced at the encampment of the ten thousand Babylonian guards and bade them be silent.

Khian recovered but slowly. With skilful tending his leg healed indeed, though now he knew that all his life he must be lame, but the sufferings which he had undergone had left him shaken in both mind and body. First there was the palace dungeon, then the long confinement in the bowels of the pyramid, then the flight from the pursuers to the Babylonian outpost; also the wound that would not heal, while for moons he must lie upon his back among strangers whose tongue as yet he did not speak, companioned only by Temu with his prayers and maxims, and ignorant of the fate of Nefra.

Afterwards followed the wild joy of the knowledge that she lived and was near, the rescue by the five thousand, the desperate battle in the desert, the surrender and the sacrifice, the sight of Nefra in the second battle, and her abandonment for honour's sake, knowing that she would not understand; the coming to Egypt and to Tanis, the meeting with his father Apepi; the pain of the hot iron and the agony of suspense upon the pylon top while Nefra watched below. All these events, young and strong though he was, had broken his body and eaten into his spirit, so that he must rest and keep himself apart by day, while at night, when at last sleep found him, he was visited by evil dreams and tremors, so that at length it was said throughout the city that soon the Pharaoh to be would join his forefathers in their burial place.

Anath came to him with reports of affairs, to which he listened patiently, saying little. Temu read to him from ancient rolls, or offered up the prayers of the Order of the Dawn at his side, and talked of faith. Ru visited him also and spoke of battle or of the wonders of Babylon, and how Nefra there had learned the arts of war, a tale at which he laughed a little. Lastly, from time to time, accompanied by Kemmah who stood far off gazing through the window- place, came Nefra herself and spoke softly of love and marriage when he should be well again.

Still he did not grow well, so having talked with Tau by messenger, Nefra took another counsel. Telling Khian that Tanis in the low land was too hot for him, she set him in a ship and travelled with him slowly up the Nile, till at last the pyramids appeared. At the first sight of these pyramids Khian's manner changed; he became alert and eager as he used to be, even gay, talking to her of all that had befallen him among them. Rejoicing at this change, that evening she caused him to be borne ashore to a camp that had been set in the midst of the palm grove where first she had found him sleeping and whence, after Ru had taken his goods, disguised as a messenger, she had conducted him to the secret home of the Brotherhood.

Here that night Khian slept better than he had done since, many months before, wearing Nefra's betrothal ring upon his finger, he had left this spot to return to Tanis and make report of his mission to Apepi.

On the following morning, while it was still quite dark, Ru entered his tent and assisted him to rise. Then he set him in a litter in which Khian, asking no questions, was borne across the sands till they came to a great shape outlined against the starry sky, which he knew to be that of the Sphinx. Here he descended from the litter, which departed, leaving him alone.

At length the dawn began to break and in its tender light he saw that he was not alone, for by his side, wrapped in a grey cloak, stood a hooded figure that might have been that of a lad or a slender woman.

By the gods! he knew this figure: it was that of the "Young Person" who—oh! years and years ago—had guided him from the palm grove to the Sphinx and there had tied a bandage about his eyes. The height was the same, the very cloak and hood seemed to be the same.

"So, Young Person," he said, "you still ply your business of guiding travellers across the sands."

"That is so, Scribe Rasa," answered the figure in a gruff voice.

"And do you still steal their packages—or hide them? My litter I think has gone."

"I still take that which I desire, Scribe Rasa, who must live and be happy if I can."

"And do you still blindfold messengers?"

"Yes, Scribe Rasa, when it is necessary to hide secrets from them. Indeed, be pleased to suffer that I do so to you for the second time, and bide here a while alone."

"I obey," he answered, laughing, "for although you may not know it, Young Person, since first we met I have suffered many things and learned one great lesson from them, also from the lips of a certain Temu, namely, to have faith. Therefore blind on and I will submit as gently as though I were sure that when sight is given back to my eyes they would behold a vision of heaven come to earth. See, I kneel, or rather stoop, for kneel I cannot."

The grey-cloaked figure bent over him, the silken kerchief once more was bound upon his brow—oh! how well he remembered its soft substance and its odour! Then, leaning on his guide's shoulder, he limped a little distance till the feigned voice bade him be seated upon a bank of sand and wait.

Presently voices, men's voices, prayed him to rise. He did so with their help, and those men supported him down passages in which their footsteps echoed, to some chamber where they clothed him in new garments and set a headdress on his brow, what headdress or what garments he did not know, and when he asked they would not answer.

Again he was helped forth, as he thought into a large place where whisperings ran as though from a gathered multitude. Someone bade him to be seated and he sank on to a cushioned chair and waited.

Far away a voice cried:

"Ra is risen!" and from all round him rose a sound of singing.

He knew the sound. It was that of the ancient chant with which on days of festival the Brotherhood of the Dawn greeted the rising of the sun. It died away; there was deep silence; he heard a rustling as of robes. Then suddenly and in unison from a hundred throats there rose a great cry of:

"The Queen of the Dawn! Hail! Queen of the Dawn! Hail, Light-Bringer! Hail Life-Giver! Hail, Consecrated Sister! Hail, Heaven-appointed Uniter of the riven Lands!"

Khian could bear no more. He snatched at the bandage about his eyes. Perhaps it had been loosened, at least it fell. Lo! there before him stood Nefra glittering in the rays of the risen sun, wearing the robes of Egypt's queen and crowned with Egypt's crown, a living loveliness; a glory to behold.

For a moment she stood thus while the shoutings echoed from the vaulted roof of the great temple hall. She lifted her sceptre and there was silence. Then she turned and came to him who, he found, was seated on a throne. To Kemmah and to Ru she gave the sceptre and her regal symbols. From her head she lifted the double crown and set it on his brow. She kneeled and did him homage; yes, with her lips she touched his hand.

"Egypt's Queen greets Egypt's King!" she said.

Khian stared at her, astonished. Then, though of a sudden pain and weakness struck him once more, he struggled from the throne, purposing to offer it to her. But she shook her head and would none of it. Supporting him with her strong young arm, she led him to where stood Tau the Prophet in front of the gathered Councillors of the Dawn. Tau joined their hands. In the presence of the Brotherhood, living and dead, and in the name of that Spirit whom they worshipped, he blessed them, giving them to each other, uniting them to all eternity, on earth and beyond the earth.

So it was finished.

****

Nefra and Khian stood together gazing by the light of the moon at the mighty mass of the Pyramid of Ur.

"Our holiday is done, Wife," he said, "and to-morrow, ceasing to be but a Brother and a Sister of the Dawn, we must become the rulers of Egypt united at last from the Cataracts to the sea. Strange has been our lot since first side by side we looked upon yonder pyramid. Yet, Beloved, I think that the Strength which preserved us through so many perils and now, from sickness and the gates of death has brought me with joy to those of health, will be with us in the years to come."

"So Roi the holy prophesied, and in him, if in any man, lived the spirit of Truth, Husband. At least, thanking the gods for what they have given us, let us go straight forward in humility, remembering that though we be King and Queen of Egypt, first and foremost we remain Brother and Sister of the Dawn, sworn to its holy faith and to the service of mankind."

At that moment this royal pair heard a sound behind them and, turning, beheld the lean and withered Sheik of the Pyramids.

"Would your Majesties wish to ascend?" he said, bowing and pointing to the mass of Ur. "The moon is very clear and there is no wind; also I desire to show Pharaoh the spot whence those accursed cliff-climbers rolled to their doom on the day of his escape."

"Nay, Captain," answered Khian, "of Ur I have had enough who am lamed for life. Henceforth be you its king."

"And its spirit also," added Nefra, "for no more may I stand upon the crests of pyramids who am doomed to a dizzier pinnacle of power. Farewell, you gallant man. Our thanks be yours with all you seek and we can give."

Then Khian and Nefra turned and, hand clasped in hand, wandered back to where Ru and Kemmah waited with the escort to accompany them to the vessel that made ready to sail with the night wind.

******

"Now," said Kemmah the white-haired to Ru the mighty Ethiop, "now I understand the meaning of the vision that I saw when yonder Queen was born, and why the goddesses of Egypt gave to her the name of Uniter of Lands."

"Yes," answered Ru, "and I understand why the gods of Ethiopia gave me a good axe and the strength to use it well on a certain Theban stairway."

Moon of Israel

Author's Note

This book suggests that the real Pharaoh of the Exodus was not Meneptah or Merenptah, son of Rameses the Great, but the mysterious usurper, Amenmeses, who for a year or two occupied the throne between the death of Meneptah and the accession of his son the heir-apparent, the gentle-natured Seti II.

Of the fate of Amenmeses history says nothing; he may well have perished in the Red Sea or rather the Sea of Reeds, for, unlike those of Meneptah and the second Seti, his body has not been found.

Students of Egyptology will be familiar with the writings of the scribe and novelist Anana, or Ana as he is here called.

****

It was the Author's hope to dedicate this story to Sir Gaston Maspero, K.C.M.G., Director of the Cairo Museum, with whom on several occasions he discussed its plot some years ago. Unhappily, however, weighed down by one of the bereavements of the war, this great Egyptologist died in the interval between its writing and its publication. Still, since Lady Maspero informs him that such is the wish of his family, he adds the dedication which he had proposed to offer to that eminent writer and student of the past.

Dear Sir Gaston Maspero,

When you assured me as to a romance of mine concerning ancient Egypt, that it was so full of the "inner spirit of the old Egyptians" that, after kindred efforts of your own and a lifetime of study, you could not conceive how it had been possible for it to spring from the brain of a modern man, I thought your verdict, coming from such a judge, one of the greatest compliments that ever I received. It is this opinion of yours indeed which induces me to offer you another tale of a like complexion. Especially am I encouraged thereto by a certain conversation between us in Cairo, while we gazed at the majestic countenance of the Pharaoh Meneptah, for then it was, as you may recall, that you said you thought the plan of this book probable and that it commended itself to your knowledge of those dim days.

With gratitude for your help and kindness and the sincerest homage to your accumulated lore concerning the most mysterious of all the perished peoples of the earth,
Believe me to remain
Your true admirer,
H. Rider Haggard

Chapter 1

Scribe Ana Comes to Tanis

This is the story of me, Ana the scribe, son of Meri, and of certain of the days that I have spent upon the earth. These things I have written down now that I am very old in the reign of Rameses, the third of that name, when Egypt is once more strong and as she was in the ancient time. I have written them before death takes me, that they may be buried with me in death, for as my spirit shall arise in the hour of resurrection, so also these my words may arise in their hour and tell to those who shall come after me upon the earth of what I knew upon the earth. Let it be as Those in heaven shall decree. At least I write and what I write is true.

I tell of his divine Majesty whom I loved and love as my own soul, Seti Meneptah the second, whose day of birth was my day of birth, the Hawk who has flown to heaven before me; of Userti the Proud, his queen, she who afterwards married his divine Majesty, Saptah, whom I saw laid in her tomb at Thebes. I tell of Merapi, who was named Moon of Israel, and of her people, the Hebrews, who dwelt for long in Egypt and departed thence, having paid us back in loss and shame for all the good and ill we gave them. I tell of the war between the gods of Egypt and the god of Israel, and of much that befell therein.

Also I, the King's Companion, the great scribe, the beloved of the Pharaohs who have lived beneath the sun with me, tell of other men and matters. Behold! is it not written in this roll? Read, ye who shall find in the days unborn, if your gods have given you skill. Read, O children of the future, and learn the secrets of that past which to you is so far away and yet in truth so near.

****

As it chanced, although the Prince Seti and I were born upon the

251

same day and therefore, like the other mothers of gentle rank whose children saw the light upon that day, my mother received Pharaoh's gift and I received the title of Royal Twin in Ra, never did I set eyes upon the divine Prince Seti until the thirtieth birthday of both of us. All of which happened thus.

In those days the great Pharaoh, Rameses the second, and after him his son Meneptah who succeeded when he was already old, since the mighty Rameses was taken to Osiris after he had counted one hundred risings of the Nile, dwelt for the most part at the city of Tanis in the desert, whereas I dwelt with my parents at the ancient, white-walled city of Memphis on the Nile. At times Meneptah and his court visited Memphis, as also they visited Thebes, where this king lies in his royal tomb to-day. But save on one occasion, the young Prince Seti, the heir-apparent, the Hope of Egypt, came not with them, because his mother, Asnefert, did not favour Memphis, where some trouble had befallen her in youth—they say it was a love matter that cost the lover his life and her a sore heart—and Seti stayed with his mother who would not suffer him out of sight of her eyes.

Once he came indeed when he was fifteen years of age, to be proclaimed to the people as son of his father, as Son of the Sun, as the future wearer of the Double Crown, and then we, his twins in Ra—there were nineteen of us who were gently born—were called by name to meet him and to kiss his royal feet. I made ready to go in a fine new robe embroidered in purple with the name of Seti and my own. But on that very morning by the gift of some evil god I was smitten with spots all over my face and body, a common sickness that affects the young. So it happened that I did not see the Prince, for before I was well again he had left Memphis.

Now my father Meri was a scribe of the great temple of Ptah, and I was brought up to his trade in the school of the temple, where I copied many rolls and also wrote out Books of the Dead which I adorned with paintings. Indeed, in this business I became so clever that, after my father went blind some years before his death, I earned enough to keep him, and my sisters also until they married. Mother I had none, for she was gathered to Osiris while I was still very little. So life went on from year to year, but in my heart I hated my lot. While I was still a boy there rose up in me a desire—not to copy what others had written, but to write what others should copy. I became a dreamer of dreams. Walking at night beneath the palm-trees upon the banks of the Nile I watched the moon shining upon the waters, and in its rays I seemed to see many beautiful things.

Pictures appeared there which were different from any that I saw in the world of men, although in them were men and women and even gods.

Of these pictures I made stories in my heart and at last, although that was not for some years, I began to write these stories down in my spare hours. My sisters found me doing so and told my father, who scolded me for such foolishness which he said would never furnish me with bread and beer. But still I wrote on in secret by the light of the lamp in my chamber at night. Then my sisters married, and one day my father died suddenly while he was reciting prayers in the temple. I caused him to be embalmed in the best fashion and buried with honour in the tomb he had made ready for himself, although to pay the costs I was obliged to copy Books of the Dead for nearly two years, working so hard that I found no time for the writing of stories.

When at length I was free from debt I met a maiden from Thebes with a beautiful face that always seemed to smile, and she took my heart from my breast into her own. In the end, after I returned from fighting in the war against the Nine Bow Barbarians, to which I was summoned like other men, I married her. As for her name, let it be, I will not think of it even to myself. We had one child, a little girl which died within two years of her birth, and then I learned what sorrow can mean to man. At first my wife was sad, but her grief departed with time and she smiled again as she used to do. Only she said that she would bear no more children for the gods to take. Having little to do she began to go about the city and make friends whom I did not know, for of these, being a beautiful woman, she found many. The end of it was that she departed back to Thebes with a soldier whom I had never seen, for I was always working at home thinking of the babe who was dead and how happiness is a bird that no man can snare, though sometimes, of its own will, it flies in at his window-place.

It was after this that my hair went white before I had counted thirty years.

Now, as I had none to work for and my wants were few and simple, I found more time for the writing of stories which, for the most part, were somewhat sad. One of these stories a fellow scribe borrowed from me and read aloud to a company, whom it pleased so much that there were many who asked leave to copy it and publish it abroad. So by degrees I became known as a teller of tales, which tales I caused to be copied and sold, though out of them I made but little. Still my fame grew till on a day I received a message from the Prince Seti, my twin in Ra, saying that he had read certain of my writings which pleased him much and that it was his wish to look upon my face. I thanked him humbly by the messenger and answered that I would travel to Tanis and wait upon his Highness. First, however, I finished the longest story which I had yet written. It was called the Tale of Two Brothers, and told how the faithless wife of one of them brought trouble on the other, so that he was killed. Of how, also, the just gods brought him to life again, and many other matters. This story I dedicated to his Highness, the Prince Seti, and with it in the bosom of my robe I travelled to Tanis, having hidden about me a sum of gold that I had saved.

So I came to Tanis at the beginning of winter and, walking to the palace of the Prince, boldly demanded an audience. But now my troubles began, for the guards and watchmen thrust me from the doors. In the end I bribed them and was admitted to the antechambers, where were merchants, jugglers, dancing-women, officers, and many others, all of them, it seemed, waiting to see the Prince; folk who, having nothing to do, pleased themselves by making mock of me, a stranger. When I had mixed with them for several days, I gained their friendship by telling to them one of my stories, after which I was always welcome among them. Still I could come no nearer to the Prince, and as my store of money was beginning to run low, I bethought me that I would return to Memphis.

One day, however, a long-bearded old man, with a gold-tipped wand of office, who had a bull's head embroidered on his robe, stopped in front of me and, calling me a white-headed crow, asked me what I was doing hopping day by day about the chambers of the palace. I told him my name and business and he told me his, which it seemed was Pambasa, one of the Prince's chamberlains. When I asked him to take me to the Prince, he laughed in my face and said darkly that the road to his Highness's presence was paved with gold. I understood what he meant and gave him a gift which he took as readily as a cock picks corn, saying that he would speak of me to his master and that I must come back again.

I came thrice and each time that old cock picked more corn. At last I grew enraged and, forgetting where I was, began to shout at him and call him a thief, so that folks gathered round to listen. This seemed to frighten him. At first he looked towards the door as though to summon the guard to thrust me out; then changed his mind, and in a grumbling voice bade me follow him. We went down long passages, past soldiers who stood at watch in them still as mummies in their coffins, till at length we came to some broidered curtains. Here Pambasa whispered to me to wait, and passed through the curtains which he left not quite closed, so that I could see the room beyond and hear all that took place there.

It was a small room like to that of any scribe, for on the tables were palettes, pens of reed, ink in alabaster vases, and sheets of papyrus pinned upon boards. The walls were painted, not as I was wont to paint the Books of the Dead, but after the fashion of an earlier time, such as I have seen in certain ancient tombs, with pictures of wild fowl rising from the swamps and of trees and plants as they grow. Against the walls hung racks in which were papyrus rolls, and on the hearth burned a fire of cedar-wood.

By this fire stood the Prince, whom I knew from his statues. His years appeared fewer than mine although we were born upon the same day, and he was tall and thin, very fair also for one of our people, perhaps because of the Syrian blood that ran in his veins. His hair was straight and brown like to that of northern folk who come to trade in the markets of Egypt, and his eyes were grey rather than black, set beneath somewhat prominent brows such as those of his father, Meneptah. His face was sweet as a woman's, but made curious by certain wrinkles which ran from the corners of the eyes towards the ears. I think that these came from the bending of the brow in thought, but others say that they were inherited from an ancestress on the female side. Bakenkhonsu my friend, the old prophet who served under the first Seti and died but the other day, having lived a hundred and twenty years, told me that he knew her before she was married, and that she and her descendant, Seti, might have been twins.

In his hand the Prince held an open roll, a very ancient writing as I, who am skilled in such matters that have to do with my trade, knew from its appearance. Lifting his eyes suddenly from the study of this roll, he saw the chamberlain standing before him.

"You came at a good time, Pambasa," he said in a voice that was very soft and pleasant, and yet most manlike. "You are old and doubtless wise. Say, are you wise, Pambasa?"

"Yes, your Highness. I am wise like your Highness's uncle, Khaemuas the mighty magician, whose sandals I used to clean when I was young."

"Is it so? Then why are you so careful to hide your wisdom which should be open like a flower for us poor bees to suck at? Well, I am glad to learn that you are wise, for in this book of magic that I have been reading I find problems worthy of Khaemuas the departed, whom I only remember as a brooding, black-browed man much like my cousin, Amenmeses his son—save that no one can call Amenmeses wise."

"Why is your Highness glad?"

"Because you, being by your own account his equal, can now interpret the matter as Khaemuas would have done. You know, Pambasa, that had he lived he would have been Pharaoh in place of my father. He died too soon, however, which proves to me that there was something in this tale of his wisdom, since no really wise man would ever wish to be Pharaoh of Egypt."

Pambasa stared with his mouth open.

"Not wish to be Pharaoh!" he began—

"Now, Pambasa the Wise," went on the Prince as though he had not heard him. "Listen. This old book gives a charm 'to empty the heart of its weariness,' that it says is the oldest and most common sickness in the world from which only kittens, some children, and mad people are free. It appears that the cure for this sickness, so says the book, is to stand on the top of the pyramid of Khufu at midnight at that moment when the moon is largest in the whole year, and drink from the cup of dreams, reciting meanwhile a spell written here at length in language which I cannot read."

"There is no virtue in spells, Prince, if anyone can read them."

"And no use, it would seem, if they can be read by none."

"Moreover, how can any one climb the pyramid of Khufu, which is covered with polished marble, even in the day let alone at midnight, your Highness, and there drink of the cup of dreams?"

"I do not know, Pambasa. All I know is that I weary of this foolishness, and of the world. Tell me of something that will lighten my heart, for it is heavy."

"There are jugglers without, Prince, one of whom says he can throw a rope into the air and climb up it until he vanishes into heaven."

"When he has done it in your sight, Pambasa, bring him to me, but not before. Death is the only rope by which we climb to heaven—or be lowered into hell. For remember there is a god called Set, after whom, like my great-grandfather, I am named by the way—the priests alone know why—as well as one called Osiris."

"Then there are the dancers, Prince, and among them some very finely made girls, for I saw them bathing in the palace lake, such as would have delighted the heart of your grandfather, the great Rameses."

"They do not delight my heart who want no naked women prancing here. Try again, Pambasa."

"I can think of nothing else, Prince. Yet, stay. There is a scribe without named Ana, a thin, sharp-nosed man who says he is your Highness's twin in Ra."

"Ana!" said the Prince. "He of Memphis who writes stories? Why did you not say so before, you old fool? Let him enter at once, at once."

Now hearing this I, Ana, walked through the curtains and prostrated myself, saying,

"I am that scribe, O Royal Son of the Sun."

"How dare you enter the Prince's presence without being bidden——" began Pambasa, but Seti broke in with a stern voice, saying,

"And how dare you, Pambasa, keep this learned man waiting at my door like a dog? Rise, Ana, and cease from giving me titles, for we are not at Court. Tell me, how long have you been in Tanis?"

"Many days, O Prince," I answered, "seeking your presence and in vain."

"And how did you win it at last?"

"By payment, O Prince," I answered innocently, "as it seems is usual. The doorkeepers——"

"I understand," said Seti, "the doorkeepers! Pambasa, you will ascertain what amount this learned scribe has disbursed to 'the doorkeepers' and refund him double. Begone now and see to the matter."

So Pambasa went, casting a piteous look at me out of the corner of his eye.

"Tell me," said Seti when he was gone, "you who must be wise in your fashion, why does a Court always breed thieves?"

"I suppose for the same reason, O Prince, that a dog's back breeds fleas. Fleas must live, and there is the dog."

"True," he answered, "and these palace fleas are not paid enough. If ever I have power I will see to it. They shall be fewer but better fed. Now, Ana, be seated. I know you though you do not know me, and already I have learned to love you through your writings. Tell me of yourself."

So I told him all my simple tale, to which he listened without a word, and then asked me why I had come to see him. I replied that it was because he had sent for me, which he had forgotten; also because I brought him a story that I had dared to dedicate to him. Then I laid the roll before him on the table.

"I am honoured," he said in a pleased voice, "I am greatly honoured. If I like it well, your story shall go to the tomb with me for my Ka to read and re-read until the day of resurrection, though first I will study it in the flesh. Do you know this city of Tanis, Ana?"

I answered that I knew little of it, who had spent my time here haunting the doors of his Highness.

"Then with your leave I will be your guide through it this night, and afterwards we will sup and talk."

I bowed and he clapped his hands, whereon a servant appeared, not Pambasa, but another.

"Bring two cloaks," said the Prince, "I go abroad with the scribe, Ana. Let a guard of four Nubians, no more, follow us, but at a distance and disguised. Let them wait at the private entrance."

The man bowed and departed swiftly.

Almost immediately a black slave appeared with two long hooded cloaks, such as camel-drivers wear, which he helped us to put on. Then, taking a lamp, he led us from the room through a doorway opposite to that by which I had entered, down passages and a narrow stair that ended in a courtyard. Crossing this we came to a wall, great and thick, in which were double doors sheathed with copper that opened mysteriously at our approach. Outside of these doors stood four tall men, also wrapped in cloaks, who seemed to take no note of us. Still, looking back when we had gone a little way, I observed that they were following us, as though by chance.

How fine a thing, thought I to myself, it is to be a Prince who by lifting a finger can thus command service at any moment of the day or night.

Just at that moment Seti said to me:

"See, Ana, how sad a thing it is to be a Prince, who cannot even stir abroad without notice to his household and commanding the service of a secret guard to spy upon his every action, and doubtless to make report thereof to the police of Pharaoh."

There are two faces to everything, thought I to myself again.

CHAPTER 2

The Breaking of the Cup

We walked down a broad street bordered by trees, beyond which were lime-washed, flat-roofed houses built of sun-dried brick, standing, each of them, in its own garden, till at length we came to the great market-place just as the full moon rose above the palm-trees, making the world almost as light as day. Tanis, or Rameses as it is also called, was a very fine city then, if only half the size of Memphis, though now that the Court has left it I hear it is much deserted. About this market-place stood great temples of the gods, with pylons and avenues of sphinxes, also that wonder of the world, the colossal statue of the second Rameses, while to the north upon a mound was the glorious palace of Pharaoh. Other palaces there were also, inhabited by the nobles and officers of the Court, and between them ran long streets where dwelt the citizens, ending, some of them, on that branch of the Nile by which the ancient city stood.

Seti halted to gaze at these wondrous buildings.

"They are very old," he said, "but most of them, like the walls and those temples of Amon and Ptah, have been rebuilt in the time of my grandfather or since his day by the labour of Israelitish slaves who dwell yonder in the rich land of Goshen."

"They must have cost much gold," I answered.

"The Kings of Egypt do not pay their slaves," remarked the Prince shortly.

Then we went on and mingled with the thousands of the people who were wandering to and fro seeking rest after the business of the day. Here on the frontier of Egypt were gathered folk of every race; Bedouins from the desert, Syrians from beyond the Red Sea, merchants from the rich Isle of Chittim, travellers from the coast, and traders from the land of Punt and from the unknown countries of the north. All were talking, laughing and making merry, save some who gathered in circles to listen to a teller of tales or wandering musicians, or to watch women who danced half naked for gifts.

Now and again the crowd would part to let pass the chariot of some noble or lady before which went running footmen who shouted, "Make way, Make way!" and laid about them with their long wands. Then came a procession of white-robed priests of Isis travelling by moonlight as was fitting for the servants of the Lady of the Moon, and bearing aloft the holy image of the goddess before which all men bowed and for a little while were silent. After this followed the corpse of some great one newly dead, preceded by a troop of hired mourners who rent the air with their lamentations as they conducted it to the quarter of the embalmers. Lastly, from out of one of the side streets emerged a gang of several hundred hook-nosed and bearded men, among whom were a few women, loosely roped together and escorted by a company of armed guards.

"Who are these?" I asked, for I had never seen their like.

"Slaves of the people of Israel who return from their labour at the digging of the new canal which is to run to the Red Sea," answered the Prince.

We stood still to watch them go by, and I noted how proudly their eyes flashed and how fierce was their bearing although they were but men in bonds, very weary too and stained by toil in mud and water. Presently this happened. A white-bearded man lagged behind, dragging on the line and checking the march. Thereupon an overseer ran up and flogged him with a cruel whip cut from the hide of the sea-horse. The man turned and, lifting a wooden spade that he carried, struck the overseer such a blow that he cracked his skull so that he fell down dead. Other overseers rushed at the Hebrew, as these Israelites were called, and beat him till he also fell. Then a soldier appeared and, seeing what had happened, drew his bronze sword. From among the throng sprang out a girl, young and very lovely although she was but roughly clad.

Since then I have seen Merapi, Moon of Israel, as she was called, clad in the proud raiment of a queen, and once even of a goddess, but never, I think, did she look more beauteous than in this hour of her slavery. Her large eyes, neither blue nor black, caught the light of the moon and were aswim with tears. Her plenteous bronze-hued hair flowed in great curls over the snow-white bosom that her rough robe revealed. Her delicate hands were lifted as though to ward off the blows which fell upon him whom she sought to protect. Her tall and slender shape stood out against a flare of light which burned upon some market stall. She was beauteous exceedingly, so beauteous that my heart stood still at the sight of her, yes, mine that for some years had held no thought of woman save such as were black and evil.

She cried aloud. Standing over the fallen man she appealed to the soldier for mercy. Then, seeing that there was none to hope for from him, she cast her great eyes around until they fell upon the Prince Seti.

"Oh! Sir," she wailed, "you have a noble air. Will you stand by and see my father murdered for no fault?"

"Drag her off, or I smite through her," shouted the captain, for now she had thrown herself down upon the fallen Israelite. The overseers obeyed, tearing her away.

"Hold, butcher!" cried the Prince.

"Who are you, dog, that dare to teach Pharaoh's officer his duty?" answered the captain, smiting the Prince in the face with his left hand.

Then swiftly he struck downwards and I saw the bronze sword pass through the body of the Israelite who quivered and lay still. It was all done in an instant, and on the silence that followed rang out the sound of a woman's wail. For a moment Seti choked—with rage, I think. Then he spoke a single word—"Guards!"

The four Nubians, who, as ordered, had kept at a distance, burst through the gathered throng. Ere they reached us I, who till now had stood amazed, sprang at the captain and gripped him by the throat. He struck at me with his bloody sword, but the blow, falling on my long cloak, only bruised me on the left thigh. Then I, who was strong in those days, grappled with him and we rolled together on the ground.

After this there was great tumult. The Hebrew slaves burst their rope and flung themselves upon the soldiers like dogs upon a jackal, battering them with their bare fists. The soldiers defended themselves with swords; the overseers plied their hide whips; women screamed, men shouted. The captain whom I had seized began to get the better of me; at least I saw his sword flash above me and thought that all was over. Doubtless it would have been, had not Seti himself dragged the man backwards and thus given the four Nubian guards time to seize him. Next I heard the Prince cry out in a ringing voice:

"Hold! It is Seti, the son of Pharaoh, the Governor of Tanis, with whom you have to do. See," and he threw back the hood of his cloak so that the moon shone upon his face.

Instantly there was a great quiet. Now, first one and then another as the truth sunk into them, men began to fall upon their knees, and I heard one say in an awed voice:

"The royal Son, the Prince of Egypt struck in the face by a soldier! Blood must pay for it."

"How is that officer named?" asked Seti, pointing to the man who had killed the Israelite and well-nigh killed me.

Someone answered that he was named Khuaka.

"Bring him to the steps of the temple of Amon," said Seti to the Nubians who held him fast. "Follow me, friend Ana, if you have the strength. Nay, lean upon my shoulder."

So resting upon the shoulder of the Prince, for I was bruised and breathless, I walked with him a hundred paces or more to the steps of the great temple where we climbed to the platform at the head of the stairs. After us came the prisoner, and after him all the multitude, a very great number who stood upon the steps and on the flat ground beyond. The Prince, who was very white and quiet, sat himself down upon the low granite base of a tall obelisk which stood in front of the temple pylon, and said:

"As Governor of Tanis, the City of Rameses, with power of life and death at all hours and in all places, I declare my Court open."

"The Royal Court is open!" cried the multitude in the accustomed form.

"This is the case," said the Prince. "Yonder man who is named Khuaka, by his dress a captain of Pharaoh's army, is charged with the murder of a certain Hebrew, and with the attempted murder of Ana the scribe. Let witnesses be called. Bring the body of the dead man and lay it here before me. Bring the woman who strove to protect him, that she may speak."

The body was brought and laid upon the platform, its wide eyes staring up at the moon. Then soldiers who had gathered thrust forward the weeping girl.

"Cease from tears," said Seti, "and swear by Kephera the creator, and by Maat the goddess of truth and law, to speak nothing but the truth."

The girl looked up and said in a rich low voice that in some way reminded me of honey being poured from a jar, perhaps because it was thick with strangled sobs:

"O Royal Son of Egypt, I cannot swear by those gods who am a daughter of Israel."

The Prince looked at her attentively and asked:

"By what god then can you swear, O Daughter of Israel?"

"By Jahveh, O Prince, whom we hold to be the one and only God, the Maker of the world and all that is therein."

"Then perhaps his other name is Kephera," said the Prince with a little smile. "But have it as you will. Swear, then, by your god Jahveh."

Then she lifted both her hands above her head and said:

"I, Merapi, daughter of Nathan of the tribe of Levi of the people of Israel, swear that I will speak the truth and all the truth in the name of Jahveh, the God of Israel."

"Tell us what you know of the matter of the death of this man, O Merapi."

"Nothing that you do not know yourself, O Prince. He who lies there," and she swept her hand towards the corpse, turning her eyes away, "was my father, an elder of Israel. The captain Khuaka came when the corn was young to the Land of Goshen to choose those who should work for Pharaoh. He wished to take me into his house. My father refused because from my childhood I had been affianced to a man of Israel; also because it is not lawful under the law for our people to intermarry with your people. Then the captain Khuaka seized my father, although he was of high rank and beyond the age to work for Pharaoh, and he was taken away, as I think, because he would not suffer me to wed Khuaka. A while later I dreamed that my father was sick. Thrice I dreamed it and ran away to Tanis to visit him. But this morning I found him and, O Prince, you know the rest."

"Is there no more?" asked Seti.

The girl hesitated, then answered:

"Only this, O Prince. This man saw me with my father giving him food, for he was weak and overcome with the toil of digging the mud in the heat of the sun, he who being a noble of our people knew nothing of such labour from his youth. In my presence Khuaka asked my father if now he would give me to him. My father answered that sooner would he see me kissed by snakes and devoured by crocodiles. 'I hear you,' answered Khuaka. 'Learn, now, slave Nathan, before to-morrow's sun arises, you shall be kissed by swords and devoured by crocodiles or jackals.' 'So be it,' said my father, 'but learn, O Khuaka, that if so, it is revealed to me who am a priest and a prophet of Jahveh, that before to-morrow's sun you also shall be kissed by swords and of the rest we will talk at the foot of Jahveh's throne.'

"Afterwards, as you know, Prince, the overseer flogged my father as I heard Khuaka order him to do if he lagged through weariness, and then Khuaka killed him because my father in his madness struck the overseer with a mattock. I have no more to say, save that I pray that I may be sent back to my own people there to mourn my father according to our custom."

"To whom would you be sent? Your mother?"

"Nay, O Prince, my mother, a lady of Syria, is dead. I will go to my uncle, Jabez the Levite."

"Stand aside," said Seti. "The matter shall be seen to later. Appear, O Ana the Scribe. Swear the oath and tell us what you have seen of this man's death, since two witnesses are needful."

So I swore and repeated all this story that I have written down.

"Now, Khuaka," said the Prince when I had finished, "have you aught to say?"

"Only this, O Royal One," answered the captain throwing himself upon his knees, "that I struck you by accident, not knowing that the person of your Highness was hidden in that long cloak. For this deed it is true that I am worthy of death, but I pray you to pardon me because I knew not what I did. The rest is nothing, since I only slew a mutinous slave of the Israelites, as such are slain every day."

"Tell me, O Khuaka, who are being tried for this man's death and not for the striking of one of royal blood by chance, under which law it is lawful for you to kill an Israelite without trial before the appointed officers of Pharaoh."

"I am not learned. I do not know the law, O Prince. All that this woman said is false."

"At least it is not false that yonder man lies dead and that you slew him, as you yourself admit. Learn now, and let all Egypt learn, that even an Israelite may not be murdered for no offence save that of weariness and of paying back unearned blow with blow. Your blood shall answer for his blood. Soldiers! Strike off his head."

The Nubians leapt upon him, and when I looked again Khuaka's headless corpse lay by the corpse of the Hebrew Nathan and their blood was mingled upon the steps of the temple.

"The business of the Court is finished," said the Prince. "Officers, see that this woman is escorted to her own people, and with her the body of her father for burial. See, too, upon your lives that no insult or harm is done to her. Scribe Ana, accompany me hence to my house where I would speak with you. Let guards precede and follow me."

He rose and all the people bowed. As he turned to go the lady Merapi stepped forward, and falling upon her knees, said:

"O most just Prince, now and ever I am your servant."

Then we set out, and as we left the market-place on our way to the palace of the Prince, I heard a tumult of voices behind us, some in praise and some in blame of what had been done. We walked on in silence broken only by the measured tramp of the guards. Presently the moon passed behind a cloud and the world was dark. Then from the edge of the cloud sprang out a ray of light that lay straight and narrow above us on the heavens. Seti studied it a while and said:

"Tell me, O Ana, of what does that moonbeam put you in mind?"

"Of a sword, O Prince," I answered, "stretched out over Egypt and held in the black hand of some mighty god or spirit. See, there is the blade from which fall little clouds like drops of blood, there is the hilt of gold, and look! there beneath is the face of the god. Fire streams from his eyebrows and his brow is black and awful. I am afraid, though what I fear I know not."

"You have a poet's mind, Ana. Still, what you see I see and of this I am sure, that some sword of vengeance is indeed stretched out over Egypt because of its evil doings, whereof this light may be the symbol. Behold! it seems to fall upon the temples of the gods and the palace of Pharaoh, and to cleave them. Now it is gone and the night is as nights were from the beginning of the world. Come to my chamber and let us eat. I am weary, I need food and wine, as you must after struggling with that lustful murderer whom I have sent to his own place."

The guards saluted and were dismissed. We mounted to the Prince's private chambers, in one of which his servants clad me in fine linen robes after a skilled physician of the household had doctored the bruises upon my thigh over which he tied a bandage spread with balm. Then I was led to a small dining-hall, where I found the Prince waiting for me as though I were some honoured guest and not a poor scribe who had wondered hence from Memphis with my wares. He caused me to sit down at his right hand and even drew up the chair for me himself, whereat I felt abashed. To this day I remember that leather-seated chair. The arms of it ended in ivory sphinxes and on its back of black wood in an oval was inlaid the name of the great Rameses, to whom indeed it had once belonged. Dishes were handed to us—only two of them and those quite simple, for Seti was no great eater—by a young Nubian slave of a very merry face, and with them wine more delicious than any I had ever tasted.

We ate and drank and the Prince talked to me of my business as a scribe and of the making of tales, which seemed to interest him very much. Indeed one might have thought that he was a pupil in the schools and I the teacher, so humbly and with such care did he weigh everything that I said about my art. Of matters of state or of the dreadful scene of blood through which we had just passed he spoke no word. At the end, however, after a little pause during which he held up a cup of alabaster as thin as an eggshell, studying the light playing through it on the rich red wine within, he said to me:

"Friend Ana, we have passed a stirring hour together, the first perhaps of many, or mayhap the last. Also we were born upon the same day and therefore, unless the astrologers lie, as do other men—and women—beneath the same star. Lastly, if I may say it, I like you well, though I know not how you like me, and when you are in the room with me I feel at ease, which is strange, for I know of no other with whom it is so.

"Now by a chance only this morning I found in some old records which I was studying, that the heir to the throne of Egypt a thousand years ago, had, and therefore, as nothing ever changes in Egypt, still has, a right to a private librarian for which the State, that is, the toilers of the land, must pay as in the end they pay for all. Some dynasties have gone by, it seems, since there was such a librarian, I think because most of the heirs to the throne could not, or did not, read. Also by chance I mentioned the matter to the Vizier Nehesi who grudges me every ounce of gold I spend, as though it were one taken out of his own pouch, which perhaps it is. He answered with that crooked smile of his:

"'Since I know well, Prince, that there is no scribe in Egypt whom you would suffer about you for a single month, I will set the cost of a librarian at the figure at which it stood in the Eleventh Dynasty upon the roll of your Highness's household and defray it from the Royal Treasury until he is discharged.'

"Therefore, Scribe Ana, I offer you this post for one month; that is all for which I can promise you will be paid whatever it may be, for I forget the sum."

"I thank you, O Prince," I exclaimed.

"Do not thank me. Indeed if you are wise you will refuse. You have met Pambasa. Well, Nehesi is Pambasa multiplied by ten, a rogue, a thief, a bully, and one who has Pharaoh's ear. He will make your life a torment to you and clip every ring of gold that at length you wring out of his grip. Moreover the place is wearisome, and I am fanciful and often ill-humoured. Do not thank me, I say. Refuse; return to Memphis and write stories. Shun courts and their plottings. Pharaoh himself is but a face and a puppet through which other voices talk and other eyes shine, and the sceptre which he wields is pulled by strings. And if this is so with Pharaoh, what is the case with his son? Then there are the women, Ana. They will make love to you, Ana, they even do so to me, and I think you told me that you know something of women. Do not accept, go back to Memphis. I will send you some old manuscripts to copy and pay you whatever it is Nehesi allows for the librarian."

"Yet I accept, O Prince. As for Nehesi I fear him not at all, since at the worst I can write a story about him at which the world will laugh, and rather than that he will pay me my salary."

"You have more wisdom than I thought, Ana. It never came into my mind to put Nehesi in a story, though it is true I tell tales about him which is much the same thing."

He bend forward, leaning his head upon his hand, and ceasing from his bantering tone, looked me in the eyes and asked:

"Why do you accept? Let me think now. It is not because you care for wealth if that is to be won here; nor for the pomp and show of courts; nor for the company of the great who really are so small. For all these things you, Ana, have no craving if I read your heart aright, you who are an artist, nothing less and nothing more. Tell me, then, why will you, a free man who can earn your living, linger round a throne and set your neck beneath the heel of princes to be crushed into the common mould of servitors and King's Companions and Bearers of the Footstool?"

"I will tell you, Prince. First, because thrones make history, as history makes thrones, and I think that great events are on foot in Egypt in which I would have my share. Secondly, because the gods bring gifts to men only once or twice in their lives and to refuse them is to offend the gods who gave them those lives to use to ends of which we know nothing. And thirdly"—here I hesitated.

"And thirdly—out with the thirdly for, doubtless, it is the real reason."

"And thirdly, O Prince—well, the word sounds strangely upon a man's lips—but thirdly because I love you. From the moment that my eyes fell upon your face I loved you as I never loved any other man—not even my father. I know not why. Certainly it is not because you are a prince."

When he heard these words Seti sat brooding and so silent that, fearing lest I, a humble scribe, had been too bold, I added hastily:

"Let your Highness pardon his servant for his presumptuous words. It was his servant's heart that spoke and not his lips."

He lifted his hand and I stopped.

"Ana, my twin in Ra," he said, "do you know that I never had a friend?"

"A prince who has no friend!"

"Never, none. Now I begin to think that I have found one. The thought is strange and warms me. Do you know also that when my eyes fell upon your face I loved you also, the gods know why. It was as though I had found one who was dear to me thousands of years ago but whom I had lost and forgotten. Perhaps this is but foolishness, or perhaps here we have the shadow of something great and beautiful which dwells elsewhere, in the place we call the Kingdom of Osiris, beyond the grave, Ana."

"Such thoughts have come to me at times, Prince. I mean that all we see is shadow; that we ourselves are shadows and that the realities who cast them live in a different home which is lit by some spirit sun that never sets."

The Prince nodded his head and again was silent for a while. Then he took his beautiful alabaster cup, and pouring wine into it, he drank a little and passed the cup to me.

"Drink also, Ana," he said, "and pledge me as I pledge you, in token that by decree of the Creator who made the hearts of men, henceforward our two hearts are as the same heart through good and ill, through triumph and defeat, till death takes one of us. Henceforward, Ana, unless you show yourself unworthy, I hide no thought from you."

Flushing with joy I took the cup, saying:

"I add to your words, O Prince. We are one, not for this life alone but for all the lives to be. Death, O Prince, is, I think, but a single step in the pylon stair which leads at last to that dizzy height whence we see the face of God and hear his voice tell us what and why we are."

Then I pledged him, and drank, bowing, and he bowed back to me.

"What shall we do with the cup, Ana, the sacred cup that has held this rich heart-wine? Shall I keep it? No, it no longer belongs to me. Shall I give it to you? No, it can never be yours alone. See, we will break the priceless thing."

Seizing it by its stem with all his strength he struck the cup upon the table. Then what seemed to be to me a marvel happened, for instead of shattering as I thought it surely would, it split in two from rim to foot. Whether this was by chance, or whether the artist who fashioned it in some bygone generation had worked the two halves separately and cunningly cemented them together, to this hour I do not know. At least so it befell.

"This is fortunate, Ana," said the Prince, laughing a little in his light way. "Now take you the half that lies nearest to you and I will take mine. If you die first I will lay my half upon your breast, and if I die first you shall do the same by me, or if the priests forbid it because I am royal and may not be profaned, cast the thing into my tomb. What should we have done had the alabaster shattered into fragments, Ana, and what omen should we have read in them?"

"Why ask, O Prince, seeing that it has befallen otherwise?"

Then I took my half, laid it against my forehead and hid it in the bosom of my robe, and as I did, so did Seti.

So in this strange fashion the royal Seti and I sealed the holy compact of our brotherhood, as I think not for the first time or the last.

CHAPTER 3

Userti

Seti rose, stretching out his arms.

"That is finished," he said, "as everything finishes, and for once I am sorry. Now what next? Sleep, I suppose, in which all ends, or perhaps you would say all begins."

As he spoke the curtains at the end of the room were drawn and between them appeared the chamberlain, Pambasa, holding his gold-tipped wand ceremoniously before him.

"What is it now, man?" asked Seti. "Can I not even sup in peace? Stay, before you answer tell me, do things end or begin in sleep? The learned Ana and I differ on the matter and would hear your wisdom. Bear in mind, Pambasa, that before we are born we must have slept, since of that time we remember nothing, and after we are dead we certainly seem to sleep, as any who have looked on mummies know. Now answer."

The chamberlain stared at the wine flask on the table as though he suspected his master of having drunk too much. Then in a hard official voice he said:

"She comes! She comes! She comes, offering greetings and adoration to the Royal Son of Ra."

"Does she indeed?" asked Seti. "If so, why say it three times? And who comes?"

"The high Princess, the heiress of Egypt, the daughter of Pharaoh, your Highness's royal half-sister, the great lady Userti."

"Let her enter then. Ana, stand you behind me. If you grow weary and I give leave you can depart; the slaves will show you your sleeping-place."

Pambasa went, and presently through the curtain appeared a royal-looking lady splendidly apparelled. She was accompanied by four waiting women who fell back on the threshold and were no more

270

seen. The Prince stepped forward, took both her hands in his and kissed her on the brow, then drew back again, after which they stood a moment looking at each other. While they remained thus I studied her who was known throughout the land as the "Beautiful Royal Daughter," but whom till now I had never seen. In truth I did not think her beautiful, although even had she been clad in a peasant's robe I should have been sure that she was royal. Her face was too hard for beauty and her black eyes, with a tinge of grey in them, were too small. Also her nose was too sharp and her lips were too thin. Indeed, had it not been for the delicately and finely-shaped woman's form beneath, I might have thought that a prince and not a princess stood before me. For the rest in most ways she resembled her half-brother Seti, though her countenance lacked the kindliness of his; or rather both of them resembled their father, Meneptah.

"Greeting, Sister," he said, eyeing her with a smile in which I caught a gleam of mockery. "Purple-bordered robes, emerald necklace and enamelled crown of gold, rings and pectoral, everything except a sceptre—why are you so royally arrayed to visit one so humble as your loving brother? You come like sunlight into the darkness of the hermit's cell and dazzle the poor hermit, or rather hermits," and he pointed to me.

"Cease your jests, Seti," she replied in a full, strong voice. "I wear these ornaments because they please me. Also I have supped with our father, and those who sit at Pharaoh's table must be suitably arrayed, though I have noted that sometimes you think otherwise."

"Indeed. I trust that the good god, our divine parent, is well to-night as you leave him so early."

"I leave him because he sent me with a message to you." She paused, looking at me sharply, then asked, "Who is that man? I do not know him."

"It is your misfortune, Userti, but one which can be mended. He is named Ana the Scribe, who writes strange stories of great interest which you would do well to read who dwell too much upon the outside of life. He is from Memphis and his father's name was—I forget what. Ana, what was your father's name?"

"One too humble for royal ears, Prince," I answered, "but my grandfather was Pentaur the poet who wrote of the deeds of the mighty Rameses."

"Is it so? Why did you not tell me that before? The descent should earn you a pension from the Court if you can extract it from Nehesi. Well, Userti, his grandfather's name was Pentaur whose immortal verses you have doubtless read upon temple walls, where our grandfather was careful to publish them."

"I have—to my sorrow—and thought them poor, boastful stuff," she answered coldly.

"To be honest, if Ana will forgive me, so do I. I can assure you that his stories are a great improvement on them. Friend Ana, this is my sister, Userti, my father's daughter though our mothers were not the same."

"I pray you, Seti, to be so good as to give me my rightful titles in speaking of me to scribes and other of your servants."

"Your pardon, Userti. This, Ana, is the first Lady of Egypt, the Royal Heiress, the Princess of the Two Lands, the High-priestess of Amon, the Cherished of the Gods, the half-sister of the Heir-apparent, the Daughter of Hathor, the Lotus Bloom of Love, the Queen to be of—Userti, whose queen will you be? Have you made up your mind? For myself I know no one worthy of so much beauty, excellence, learning and—what shall I add—sweetness, yes, sweetness."

"Seti," she said stamping her foot, "if it pleases you to make a mock of me before a stranger, I suppose that I must submit. Send him away, I would speak with you."

"Make a mock of you! Oh! mine is a hard fate. When truth gushes from the well of my heart, I am told I mock, and when I mock, all say—he speaks truth. Be seated, Sister, and talk on freely. This Ana is my sworn friend who saved my life but now, for which deed perhaps he should be my enemy. His memory is excellent also and he will remember what you say and write it down afterwards, whereas I might forget. Therefore, with your leave, I will ask him to stay here."

"My Prince," I broke in, "I pray you suffer me to go."

"My Secretary," he answered with a note of command in his voice, "I pray you to remain where you are."

So I sat myself on the ground after the fashion of a scribe, having no choice, and the Princess sat herself on a couch at the end of the table, but Seti remained standing. Then the Princess said:

"Since it is your will, Brother, that I should talk secrets into other ears than yours, I obey you. Still"—here she looked at me wrathfully—"let the tongue be careful that it does not repeat what the ears have heard, lest there should be neither ears nor tongue. My Brother, it has been reported to Pharaoh, while we ate together, that there is tumult in this town. It has been reported to him that because of a trouble about some base Israelite you caused one of his officers to be beheaded, after which there came a riot which still rages."

"Strange that truth should have come to the ears of Pharaoh so quickly. Now, my Sister, if he had heard it three moons hence I could have believed you—almost."

"Then you did behead the officer?"

"Yes, I beheaded him about two hours ago."

"Pharaoh will demand an account of the matter."

"Pharaoh," answered Seti lifting his eyes, "has no power to question the justice of the Governor of Tanis in the north."

"You are in error, Seti. Pharaoh has all power."

"Nay, Sister, Pharaoh is but one man among millions of other men, and though he speaks it is their spirit which bends his tongue, while above that spirit is a great greater spirit who decrees what they shall think to ends of which we know nothing."

"I do not understand, Seti."

"I never thought you would, Userti, but when you have leisure, ask Ana here to explain the matter to you. I am sure that *he* understands."

"Oh! I have borne enough," exclaimed Userti rising. "Hearken to the command of Pharaoh, Prince Seti. It is that you wait upon him to-morrow in full council, at an hour before noon, there to talk with him of this question of the Israelitish slaves and the officer whom it has pleased you to kill. I came to speak other words to you also, but as they were for your private ear, these can bide a more fitting opportunity. Farewell, my Brother."

"What, are you going so soon, Sister? I wished to tell you the story about those Israelites, and especially of the maid whose name is— what was her name, Ana?"

"Merapi, Moon of Israel, Prince," I added with a groan.

"About the maid called Merapi, Moon of Israel, I think the sweetest that ever I have looked upon, whose father the dead captain murdered in my sight."

"So there is a woman in the business? Well, I guessed it."

"In what business is there not a woman, Userti, even in that of a message from Pharaoh. Pambasa, Pambasa, escort the Princess and summon her servants, women everyone of them, unless my senses mock me. Good-night to you, O Sister and Lady of the Two Lands, and forgive me—that coronet of yours is somewhat awry."

At last she was gone and I rose, wiping my brow with a corner of my robe, and looking at the Prince who stood before the fire laughing softly.

"Make a note of all this talk, Ana," he said; "there is more in it than meets the ear."

273

"I need no note, Prince," I answered; "every word is burnt upon my mind as a hot iron burns a tablet of wood. With reason too, since now her Highness will hate me for all her life."

"Much better so, Ana, than that she should pretend to love you, which she never would have done while you are my friend. Women oftimes respect those whom they hate and even will advance them because of policy, but let those whom they pretend to love beware. The time may come when you will yet be Userti's most trusted councillor."

Now here I, Ana the Scribe, will state that in after days, when this same queen was the wife of Pharaoh Saptah, I did, as it chanced, become her most trusted councillor. Moreover, in those times, yes, and even in the hour of her death, she swore from the moment her eyes first fell on me she had known me to be true-hearted and held me in esteem as no self-seeker. More, I think she believed what she said, having forgotten that once she looked upon me as her enemy. This indeed I never was, who always held her in high regard and honour as a great lady who loved her country, though one who sometimes was not wise. But as I could not foresee these things on that night of long ago, I only stared at the Prince and said:

"Oh! why did you not allow me to depart as your Highness said I might at the beginning? Soon or late my head will pay the price of this night's work."

"Then she must take mine with it. Listen, Ana. I kept you here, not to vex the Princess or you, but for a good reason. You know that it is the custom of the royal dynasties of Egypt for kings, or those who will be kings, to wed their near kin in order that the blood may remain the purer."

"Yes, Prince, and not only among those who are royal. Still, I think it an evil custom."

"As I do, since the race wherein it is practised grows ever weaker in body and in mind; which is why, perhaps, my father is not what his father was and I am not what my father is."

"Also, Prince, it is hard to mingle the love of the sister and of the wife."

"Very hard, Ana; so hard that when it is attempted both are apt to vanish. Well, our mothers having been true royal wives, though hers died before mine was wedded by my father, Pharaoh desires that I should marry my half-sister, Userti, and what is worse, she desires it also. Moreover, the people, who fear trouble ahead in Egypt if we, who alone are left of the true royal race born of queens, remain apart and she takes another lord, or I take another wife, demand that it should be brought about, since they believe that whoever calls Userti the Strong his spouse will one day rule the land."

"Why does the Princess wish it—that she may be a queen?"

"Yes, Ana, though were she to wed my cousin, Amenmeses, the son of Pharaoh's elder brother Khaemuas, she might still be a queen, if I chose to stand aside as I would not be loth to do."

"Would Egypt suffer this, Prince?"

"I do not know, nor does it matter since she hates Amenmeses, who is strong-willed and ambitious, and will have none of him. Also he is already married."

"Is there no other royal one whom she might take, Prince?"

"None. Moreover she wishes me alone."

"Why, Prince?"

"Because of ancient custom which she worships. Also because she knows me well and in her fashion is fond of me, whom she believes to be a gentle-minded dreamer that she can rule. Lastly, because I am the lawful heir to the Crown and without me to share it, she thinks that she would never be safe upon the Throne, especially if I should marry some other woman, of whom she would be jealous. It is the Throne she desires and would wed, not the Prince Seti, her half-brother, whom she takes with it to be in name her husband, as Pharaoh commands that she should do. Love plays no part in Userti's breast, Ana, which makes her the more dangerous, since what she seeks with a cold heart of policy, that she will surely find."

"Then it would seem, Prince, that the cage is built about you. After all it is a very splendid cage and made of gold."

"Yes, Ana, yet not one in which I would live. Still, except by death how can I escape from the threefold chain of the will of Pharaoh, of Egypt, and of Userti? Oh!" he went on in a new voice, one that had in it both sorrow and passion, "this is a matter in which I would have chosen for myself who in all others must be a servant. And I may not choose!"

"Is there perchance some other lady, Prince?"

"None! By Hathor, none—at least I think not. Yet I would have been free to search for such a one and take her when I found her, if she were but a fisher-girl."

"The Kings of Egypt can have large households, Prince."

"I know it. Are there not still scores whom I should call aunt and uncle? I think that my grandsire, Rameses, blessed Egypt with quite three hundred children, and in so doing in a way was wise, since thus he might be sure that, while the world endures, in it will flow some the blood that once was his."

"Yet in life or death how will that help him, Prince? Some must beget the multitudes of the earth, what does it matter who these may have been?"

"Nothing at all, Ana, since by good or evil fortune they are born. Therefore, why talk of large households? Though, like any man who can pay for it, Pharaoh may have a large household, I seek a queen who shall reign in my heart as well as on my throne, not a 'large household,' Ana. Oh! I am weary. Pambasa, come hither and conduct my secretary, Ana, to the empty room that is next to my own, the painted chamber which looks toward the north, and bid my slaves attend to all his wants as they would to mine."

****

"Why did you tell me you were a scribe, my lord Ana?" asked Pambasa, as he led me to my beautiful sleeping-place.

"Because that is my trade, Chamberlain."

He looked at me, shaking his great head till the long white beard waved across his breast like a temple banner in the faint evening breeze, and answered:

"You are no scribe, you are a magician who can win the love and favour of his Highness in an hour which others cannot do between two risings of the Nile. Had you said so at once, you would have been differently treated yonder in the hall of waiting. Forgive me therefore what I did in ignorance, and, my lord, I pray it may please you not to melt away in the night, lest my feet should answer for it beneath the sticks."

It was the fourth hour from sunrise of the following day that, for the first time in my life I found myself in the Court of Pharaoh standing with other members of his household in the train of his Highness, the Prince Seti. It was a very great place, for Pharaoh sat in the judgment hall, whereof the roof is upheld by round and sculptured columns, between which were set statues of Pharaohs who had been. Save at the throne end of the hall, where the light flowed down through clerestories, the vast chamber was dim almost to darkness; at least so it seemed to me entering there out of the brilliant sunshine. Through this gloom many folk moved like shadows; captains, nobles, and state officers who had been summoned to the Court, and among them white-robed and shaven priests. Also there were others of whom I took no count, such as Arab headmen from the desert, traders with jewels and other wares to sell, farmers and even peasants with petitions to present, lawyers and their clients, and I know not who besides, through which of all these none were suffered to advance beyond a certain mark where the light began to fall. Speaking in whispers all of these folk flitted to and fro like bats in a tomb.

We waited between two Hathor-headed pillars in one of the vestibules of the hall, the Prince Seti, who was clad in purple-broidered garments and wore upon his brow a fillet of gold from which rose the *uraeus* or hooded snake, also of gold, that royal ones alone might wear, leaning against the base of a statue, while the rest of us stood silent behind him. For a time he was silent also, as a man might be whose thoughts were otherwhere. At length he turned and said to me:

"This is weary work. Would I had asked you to bring that new tale of yours, Scribe Ana, that we might have read it together."

"Shall I tell you the plot of it, Prince?"

"Yes. I mean, not now, lest I should forget my manners listening to you. Look," and he pointed to a dark-browed, fierce-eyed man of middle age who passed up the hall as though he did not see us, "there goes my cousin, Amenmeses. You know him, do you not?"

I shook my head.

"Then tell me what you think of him, at once before the first judgment fades."

"I think he is a royal-looking lord, obstinate in mind and strong in body, handsome too in his way."

"All can see that, Ana. What else?"

"I think," I said in a low voice so that none might overhear, "that his heart is as black as his brow; that he has grown wicked with jealousy and hate and will do you evil."

"Can a man grow wicked, Ana? Is he not as he was born till the end? I do not know, nor do you. Still you are right, he is jealous and will do me evil if it brings him good. But tell me, which of us will triumph at the last?"

While I hesitated what to answer I became aware that someone had joined us. Looking round I perceived a very ancient man clad in a white robe. He was broad-faced and bald-headed, and his eyes burned beneath his shaggy eyebrows like two coals in ashes. He supported himself on a staff of cedar-wood, gripping it with both hands that for thinness were like to those of a mummy. For a while he considered us both as though he were reading our souls, then said in a full and jovial voice:

"Greeting, Prince."

Seti turned, looked at him, and answered:

"Greeting, Bakenkhonsu. How comes it that you are still alive? When we parted at Thebes I made sure——"

"That on your return you would find me in my tomb. Not so, Prince, it is I who shall live to look upon you in your tomb, yes, and on others who are yet to sit in the seat of Pharaoh. Why not? Ho! ho! Why not, seeing that I am but a hundred and seven, I who remember the first Rameses and have played with his grandson, your grandsire, as a boy? Why should I not live, Prince, to nurse your grandson—if the gods should grant you one who as yet have neither wife nor child?"

"Because you will get tired of life, Bakenkhonsu, as I am already, and the gods will not be able to spare you much longer."

"The gods can endure yet a while without me, Prince, when so many are flocking to their table. Indeed it is their desire that one good priest should be left in Egypt. Ki the Magician told me so only this morning. He had it straight from Heaven in a dream last night."

"Why have you been to visit Ki?" asked Seti, looking at him sharply. "I should have thought that being both of a trade you would have hated each other."

"Not so, Prince. On the contrary we add up each other's account; I mean, check and interpret each other's visions, with which we are both of us much troubled just now. Is that young man a scribe from Memphis?"

"Yes, and my friend. His grandsire was Pentaur the poet."

"Indeed. I knew Pentaur well. Often has he read me to sleep with his long poems, rank stuff that grew like coarse grass upon a deep but half-drained soil. Are you sure, young man, that Pentaur was your grandfather? You are not like him. Quite a different kind of herbage, and you know that it is a matter upon which we must take a woman's word."

Seti burst out laughing and I looked at the old priest angrily, though now that I came to think of it my father always said that his mother was one of the biggest liars in Egypt.

"Well, let it be," went on Bakenkhonsu, "till we find out the truth before Thoth. Ki was speaking of you, young man. I did not pay much attention to him, but it was something about a sudden vow of friendship between you and the Prince here. There was a cup in the story too, an alabaster cup that seemed familiar to me. Ki said it was broken."

Seti started and I began angrily:

"What do you know of that cup? Where were you hid, O Priest?"

"Oh, in your souls, I suppose," he answered dreamily, "or rather Ki was. But I know nothing, and am not curious. If you had broken the cup with a woman now, it would have been more interesting, even

278

to an old man. Be so good as to answer the Prince's question as to whether he or his cousin Amenmeses will triumph at the last, for on that matter both Ki and I are curious."

"Am I a seer," I began again still more angrily, "that I should read the future?"

"I think so, a little, but that is what I want to find out."

He hobbled towards me, laid one of his claw-like hands upon my arm, and said in a new voice of command:

"Look now upon that throne and tell me what you see there."

I obeyed him because I must, staring up the hall at the empty throne. At first I saw nothing. Then figures seemed to flit around it. From among these figures emerged the shape of the Count Amenmeses. He sat upon the throne, looking about him proudly, and I noted that he was no longer clad as a prince but as Pharaoh himself. Presently hook-nosed men appeared who dragged him from his seat. He fell, as I thought, into water, for it seemed to splash up above him. Next Seti the Prince appeared to mount the throne, led thither by a woman, of whom I could only see the back. I saw him distinctly wearing the double crown and holding a sceptre in his hand. He also melted away and others came whom I did not know, though I thought that one of them was like to the Princess Userti.

Now all were gone and I was telling Bakenkhonsu everything I had witnessed like a man who speaks in his sleep, not by his own will. Suddenly I woke up and laughed at my own foolishness. But the other two did not laugh; they regarded me very gravely.

"I thought that you were something of a seer," said the old priest, "or rather Ki thought it. I could not quite believe Ki, because he said that the young person whom I should find with the Prince here this morning would be one who loved him with all the heart, and it is only a woman who loves with all the heart, is it not? Or so the world believes. Well, I will talk the matter over with Ki. Hush! Pharaoh comes."

As he spoke from far away rose a cry of—*"Life! Blood! Strength! Pharaoh! Pharaoh! Pharaoh!"*

CHAPTER 4

The Court of Betrothal

"Life! Blood! Strength!" echoed everyone in the great hall, falling to their knees and bending their foreheads to the ground. Even the Prince and the aged Bakenkhonsu prostrated themselves thus as though before the presence of a god. And, indeed, Pharaoh Meneptah, passing through the patch of sunlight at the head of the hall, wearing the double crown upon his head and arrayed in royal robes and ornaments, looked like a god, no less, as the multitude of the people of Egypt held him to be. He was an old man with the face of one worn by years and care, but from his person majesty seemed to flow.

With him, walking a step or two behind, went Nehesi his Vizier, a shrivelled, parchment-faced officer whose cunning eyes rolled about the place, and Roi the High-priest, and Hora the Chamberlain of the Table, and Meranu the Washer of the King's Hands, and Yuy the private scribe, and many others whom Bakenkhonsu named to me as they appeared. Then there were fan-bearers and a gorgeous band of lords who were called King's Companions and Head Butlers and I know not who besides, and after these guards with spears and helms that shone like god, and black swordsmen from the southern land of Kesh.

But one woman accompanied his Majesty, walking alone immediately behind him in front of the Vizier and the High-priest. She was the Royal Daughter, the Princess Userti, who looked, I thought, prouder and more splendid than any there, though somewhat pale and anxious.

Pharaoh came to the steps of the throne. The Vizier and the High-priest advanced to help him up the steps, for he was feeble with age. He waved them aside, and beckoning to his daughter, rested his hand upon her shoulder and by her aid mounted the throne. I thought that there was meaning in this; it was as though he would show to all the assembly that this princess was the prop of Egypt.

For a little while he stood still and Userti sat herself down on the topmost step, resting her chin upon her jewelled hand. There he stood searching the place with his eyes. He lifted his sceptre and all rose, hundreds and hundreds of them throughout the hall, their garments rustling as they rose like leaves in a sudden wind. He seated himself and once more from every throat went up the regal salutation that was the king's alone, of—

"Life! Blood! Strength! Pharaoh! Pharaoh! Pharaoh!"

In the silence that followed I heard him say, to the Princess, I think:

"Amenmeses I see, and others of our kin, but where is my son Seti, the Prince of Egypt?"

"Watching us no doubt from some vestibule. My brother loves not ceremonials," answered Userti.

Then, with a little sigh, Seti stepped forward, followed by Bak-enkhonsu and myself, and at a distance by other members of his household. As he marched up the long hall all drew to this side or that, saluting him with low bows. Arriving in front of the throne he bent till his knee touched the ground, saying:

"I give greeting, O King and Father."

"I give greeting, O Prince and Son. Be seated," answered Meneptah.

Seti seated himself in a chair that had been made ready for him at the foot of the throne, and on its right, and in another chair to the left, but set farther from the steps, Amenmeses seated himself also. At a motion from the Prince I took my stand behind his chair.

The formal business of the Court began. At the beckoning of an usher people of all sorts appeared singly and handed in petitions written on rolled-up papyri, which the Vizier Nehesi took and threw into a leathern sack that was held open by a black slave. In some cases an answer to his petition, whereof this was only the formal delivery, was handed back to the suppliant, who touched his brow with the roll that perhaps meant everything to him, and bowed himself away to learn his fate. Then appeared sheiks of the desert tribes, and captains from fortresses in Syria, and traders who had been harmed by enemies, and even peasants who had suffered violence from officers, each to make his prayer. Of all of these supplications the scribes took notes, while to some the Vizier and councillors made answer. But as yet Pharaoh said nothing. There he sat silent on his splendid throne of ivory and gold, like a god of stone above the altar, staring down the long hall and through the open doors as though he would read the secrets of the skies beyond.

"I told you that courts were wearisome, friend Ana," whispered the Prince to me without turning his head. "Do you not already begin to wish that you were back writing tales at Memphis?"

Before I could answer some movement in the throng at the end of the hall drew the eyes of the Prince and of all of us. I looked, and saw advancing towards the throne a tall, bearded man already old, although his black hair was but grizzled with grey. He was arrayed in a white linen robe, over which hung a woollen cloak such as shepherds wear, and he carried in his hand a long thornwood staff. His face was splendid and very handsome, and his black eyes flashed like fire. He walked forward slowly, looking neither to the left nor the right, and the throng made way for him as though he were a prince. Indeed, I thought that they showed more fear of him than of any prince, since they shrank from him as he came. Nor was he alone, for after him walked another man who was very like to him, but as I judged, still older, for his beard, which hung down to his middle, was snow-white as was the hair on his head. He also was dressed in a sheepskin cloak and carried a staff in his hand. Now a whisper rose among the people and the whisper said:

"The prophets of the men of Israel! The prophets of the men of Israel!"

The two stood before the throne and looked at Pharaoh, making no obeisance. Pharaoh looked at them and was silent. For a long space they stood thus in the midst of a great quiet, but Pharaoh would not speak, and none of his officers seemed to dare to open their mouths. At length the first of the prophets spoke in a clear, cold voice as some conqueror might do.

"You know me, Pharaoh, and my errand."

"I know you," answered Pharaoh slowly, "as well I may, seeing that we played together when we were little. You are that Hebrew whom my sister, she who sleeps in Osiris, took to be as a son to her, giving to you a name that means 'drawn forth' because she drew you forth as an infant from among the reeds of Nile. Aye, I know you and your brother also, but your errand I know not."

"This is my errand, Pharaoh, or rather the errand of Jahveh, God of Israel, for whom I speak. Have you not heard it before? It is that you should let his people go to do sacrifice to him in the wilderness."

"Who is Jahveh? I know not Jahveh who serve Amon and the gods of Egypt, and why should I let your people go?"

"Jahveh is the God of Israel, the great God of all gods whose power you shall learn if you will not hearken, Pharaoh. As for why you should let the people go, ask it of the Prince your son who sits yonder. Ask him of what he saw in the streets of this city but last night, and of a certain judgment that he passed upon one of the officers of Pharaoh.

Or if he will not tell you, learn it from the lips of the maiden who is named Merapi, Moon of Israel, the daughter of Nathan the Levite. Stand forward, Merapi, daughter of Nathan."

Then from the throng at the back of the hall came forward Merapi, clad in a white robe and with a black veil thrown about her head in token of mourning, but not so as to hide her face. Up the hall she glided and made obeisance to Pharaoh, as she did so, casting one swift look at Seti where he sat. Then she stood still, looking, as I thought, wonderfully beautiful in that simple robe of white and the evil of black.

"Speak, woman," said Pharaoh.

She obeyed, telling all the tale in her low and honeyed voice, nor did any seem to think it long or wearisome. At length she ended, and Pharaoh said:

"Say, Seti my son, is this truth?"

"It is truth, O my Father. By virtue of my powers as Governor of this city I caused the captain Khuaka to be put to death for the crime of murder done by him before my eyes in the streets of the city."

"Perchance you did right and perchance you did wrong, Son Seti. At least you are the best judge, and because he struck your royal person, this Khuaka deserved to die."

Again he was silent for a while staring through the open doors at the sky beyond. Then he said:

"What would ye more, Prophets of Jahveh? Justice has been done upon my officer who slew the man of your people. A life has been taken for a life according to the strict letter of the law. The matter is finished. Unless you have aught to say, get you gone."

"By the command of the Lord our God," answered the prophet, "we have this to say to you, O Pharaoh. Lift the heavy yoke from off the neck of the people of Israel. Bid that they cease from the labour of the making of bricks to build your walls and cities."

"And if I refuse, what then?"

"Then the curse of Jahveh shall be on you, Pharaoh, and with plague upon plague shall he smite this land of Egypt."

Now a sudden rage seized Meneptah.

"What!" he cried. "Do you dare to threaten me in my own palace, and would ye cause all the multitude of the people of Israel who have grown fat in the land to cease from their labours? Hearken, my servants, and, scribes, write down my decree. Go ye to the country of Goshen and say to the Israelites that the bricks they made they shall make as aforetime and more work shall they do than aforetime in the days of my father, Rameses. Only no more straw shall be given to them for the making of the bricks. Because they are idle, let them go forth and gather the straw themselves; let them gather it from the face of the fields."

There was silence for a while. Then with one voice both the prophets spoke, pointing with their wands to Pharaoh:

"In the Name of the Lord God we curse you, Pharaoh, who soon shall die and make answer for this sin. The people of Egypt we curse also. Ruin shall be their portion; death shall be their bread and blood shall they drink in a great darkness. Moreover, at the last Pharaoh shall let the people go."

Then, waiting no answer, they turned and strode away side by side, nor did any man hinder them in their goings. Again there was silence in the hall, the silence of fear, for these were awful words that the prophets had spoken. Pharaoh knew it, for his chin sank upon his breast and his face that had been red with rage turned white. Userti hid her eyes with her hand as though to shut out some evil vision, and even Seti seemed ill at ease as though that awful curse had found a home within his heart.

At a motion of Pharaoh's hand the Vizier Nehesi struck the ground thrice with his wand of office and pointed to the door, thus giving the accustomed sign that the Court was finished, whereon all the people turned and went away with bent heads speaking no words one to another. Presently the great hall was emptied save for the officers and guards and those who attended upon Pharaoh. When everyone had gone Seti the Prince rose and bowed before the throne.

"O Pharaoh," he said, "be pleased to hearken. We have heard very evil words spoken by these Hebrew men, words that threaten your divine life, O Pharaoh, and call down a curse upon the Upper and the Lower Land. Pharaoh, these people of Israel hold that they suffer wrong and are oppressed. Now give me, your son, a writing under your hand and seal, by virtue of which I shall have power to go down to the Land of Goshen and inquire of this matter, and afterwards make report of the truth to you. Then, if it seems to you that the People of Israel are unjustly dealt by, you may lighten their burden and bring the curse of their prophets to nothing. But if it seems to you that the tales they tell are idle then your words shall stand."

Now, listening, I, Ana, thought that Pharaoh would once more be angry. But it was not so, for when he spoke again it was in the voice of one who is crushed by grief or weariness.

"Have your will, Son," he said. "Only take with you a great guard of soldiers lest these hook-nosed dogs should do you mischief. I trust them not, who, like the Hyksos whose blood runs in many of them, were ever the foes of Egypt. Did they not conspire with the Ninebow Barbarians whom I crushed in the great battle, and do they not now threaten us in the name of their outland god? Still, let the writing be prepared and I will seal it. And stay. I think, Seti, that you, who were ever gentle-natured, have somewhat too soft a heart towards these shepherd slaves. Therefore I will not send you alone. Amenmeses your cousin shall go with you, but under your command. It is spoken."

"Life! Blood! Strength!" said both Seti and Amenmeses, thus acknowledging the king's command.

Now I thought that all was finished. But it was not so, for presently Pharaoh said:

"Let the guards withdraw to the end of the hall and with them the servants. Let the King's councillors and the officers of the household remain."

Instantly all saluted and withdrew out of hearing. I, too, made ready to go, but the Prince said to me:

"Stay, that you may take note of what passes."

Pharaoh, watching, saw if he did not hear.

"Who is that man, Son?" he asked.

"He is Ana my private scribe and librarian, O Pharaoh, whom I trust. It was he who saved me from harm but last night."

"You say it, Son. Let him remain in attendance on you, knowing that if he betrays our council he dies."

Userti looked up frowning as though she were about to speak. If so, she changed her mind and was silent, perhaps because Pharaoh's word once spoken could not be altered. Bakenkhonsu remained also as a Councillor of the King according to his right.

When all had gone Pharaoh, who had been brooding, lifted his head and spoke slowly but in the voice of one who gives a judgment that may not be questioned, saying:

"Prince Seti, you are my only son born of Queen Ast-Nefert, royal Sister, royal Mother, who sleeps in the bosom of Osiris. It is true that you are not my first-born son, since the Count Ramessu"—here he pointed to a stout mild-faced man of pleasing, rather foolish appearance—"is your elder by two years. But, as he knows well, his mother, who is still with us, is a Syrian by birth and of no royal blood, and therefore he can never sit upon the throne of Egypt. Is it not so, my son Ramessu?"

"It is so, O Pharaoh," answered the Count in a pleasant voice, "not do I seek ever to sit upon that throne, who am well content with the offices and wealth that Pharaoh has been pleased to confer upon me, his first-born."

"Let the words of the Count Ramessu be written down," said Pharaoh, "and placed in the temple of Ptah of this city, and in the temples of Ptah at Memphis and of Amon at Thebes, that hereafter they may never be questioned."

The scribes in attendance wrote down the words and, at a sign from the Prince Seti, I also wrote them down, setting the papyrus I had with me on my knee. When this was finished Pharaoh went on.

"Therefore, O Prince Seti, you are the heir of Egypt and perhaps, as those Hebrew prophets said, will ere long be called upon to sit in my place on its throne."

"May the King live for ever!" exclaimed Seti, "for well he knows that I do not seek his crown and dignities."

"I do know it well, my son; so well that I wish you thought more of that crown and those dignities which, if the gods will, must come to you. If they will it not, next in the order of succession stands your cousin, the Count Amenmeses, who is also of royal blood both on his father's and his mother's side, and after him I know not who, unless it be my daughter and your half-sister, the royal Princess Userti, Lady of Egypt."

Now Userti spoke, very earnestly, saying:

"O Pharaoh, surely my right in the succession, according to ancient precedent, precedes that of my cousin, the Count Amenmeses."

Amenmeses was about to answer, but Pharaoh lifted his hand and he was silent.

"It is matter for those learned in such lore to discuss," Meneptah replied in a somewhat hesitating voice. "I pray the gods that it may never be needful that this high question should be considered in the Council. Nevertheless, let the words of the royal Princess be written down. Now, Prince Seti," he went on when this had been done, "you are still unmarried, and if you have children they are not royal."

"I have none, O Pharaoh," said Seti.

"Is it so?" answered Meneptah indifferently. "The Count Amenmeses has children I know, for I have seen them, but by his wife Unuri, who also is of the royal line, he has none."

Here I heard Amenmeses mutter, "Being my aunt that is not strange," a saying at which Seti smiled.

"My daughter, the Princess, is also unmarried. So it seems that the fountain of the royal blood is running dry——"

"Now it is coming," whispered Seti below his breath so that only I could hear.

"Therefore," continued Pharaoh, "as you know, Prince Seti, for the royal Princess of Egypt by my command went to speak to you of this matter last night, I make a decree——"

"Pardon, O Pharaoh," interrupted the Prince, "my sister spoke to me of no decree last night, save that I should attend at the court here to-day."

"Because I could not, Seti, seeing that another was present with you whom you refused to dismiss," and she let her eyes rest on me.

"It matters not," said Pharaoh, "since now I will utter it with my own lips which perhaps is better. It is my will, Prince, that you forthwith wed the royal Princess Userti, that children of the true blood of the Ramessides may be born. Hear and obey."

Now Userti shifted her eyes from me to Seti, watching him very closely. Seated at his side upon the ground with my writing roll spread across my knee, I, too, watched him closely, and noted that his lips turned white and his face grew fixed and strange.

"I hear the command of Pharaoh," he said in a low voice making obeisance, and hesitated.

"Have you aught to add?" asked Meneptah sharply.

"Only, O Pharaoh, that though this would be a marriage decreed for reasons of the State, still there is a lady who must be given in marriage, and she my half-sister who heretofore has only loved me as a relative. Therefore, I would know from her lips if it is her will to take me as a husband."

Now all looked at Userti who replied in a cold voice:

"In this matter, Prince, as in all others I have no will but that of Pharaoh."

"You have heard," interrupted Meneptah impatiently, "and as in our House it has always been the custom for kin to marry kin, why should it not be her will? Also, who else should she marry? Amenmeses is already wed. There remains only Saptah his brother who is younger than herself——"

"So am I," murmured Seti, "by two long years," but happily Userti did not hear him.

"Nay, my father," she said with decision, "never will I take a deformed man to husband."

Now from the shadow on the further side of the throne, where I could not see him, there hobbled forward a young noble, short in stature, light-haired like Seti, and with a sharp, clever face which put me in mind of that of a jackal (indeed for this reason he was named Thoth by the common people, after the jackal-headed god). He was very angry, for his cheeks were flushed and his small eyes flashed.

"Must I listen, Pharaoh," he said in a little voice, "while my cousin the Royal Princess reproaches me in public for my lame foot, which I have because my nurse let me fall when I was still in arms?"

"Then his nurse let his grandfather fall also, for he too was club-footed, as I who have seen him naked in his cradle can bear witness," whispered old Bakenkhonsu.

"It seems so, Count Saptah, unless you stop your ears," replied Pharaoh.

"She says she will not marry me," went on Saptah, "me who from childhood have been a slave to her and to no other woman."

"Not by my wish, Saptah. Indeed, I pray you to go and be a slave to any woman whom you will," exclaimed Userti.

"But I say," continued Saptah, "that one day she shall marry me, for the Prince Seti will not live for ever."

"How do you know that, Cousin?" asked Seti. "The High-priest here will tell you a different story."

Now certain of those present turned their heads away to hide the smile upon their faces. Yet on this day some god spoke with Saptah's voice making him a prophet, since in a year to come she did marry him, in order that she might stay upon the throne at a time of trouble when Egypt would not suffer that a woman should have sole rule over the land.

But Pharaoh did not smile like the courtiers; indeed he grew angry.

"Peace, Saptah!" he said. "Who are you that wrangle before me, talking of the death of kings and saying that you will wed the Royal princess? One more such word and you shall be driven into banishment. Hearken now. Almost am I minded to declare my daughter, the Royal Princess, sole heiress to the throne, seeing that in her there is more strength and wisdom than in any other of our House."

"If such be Pharaoh's will, let Pharaoh's will be done," said Seti most humbly. "Well I know my own unworthiness to fill so high a station, and by all the gods I swear that my beloved sister will find no more faithful subject than myself."

"You mean, Seti," interrupted Userti, "that rather than marry me you would abandon your right to the double crown. Truly I am honoured. Seti, whether you reign or I, I will not marry you."

"What words are these I hear?" cried Meneptah. "Is there indeed one in this land of Egypt who dares to say that Pharaoh's decree shall be disobeyed? Write it down, Scribes, and you, O Officers, let it be proclaimed from Thebes to the sea, that on the third day from now at the hour of noon in the temple of Hathor in this city, the Prince, the Royal Heir, Seti Meneptah, Beloved of Ra, will wed the Royal Princess of Egypt, Lily of Love, Beloved of Hathor, Userti, Daughter of me, the god."

"Life! Blood! Strength!" called all the Court.

Then, guided by some high officer, the Prince Seti was led before the throne and the Princess Userti was set beside him, or rather facing him. According to the ancient custom a great gold cup was brought and filled with red wine, to me it looked like blood. Userti took the cup and, kneeling, gave it to the Prince, who drank and gave it back to her that she might also drink in solemn token of their betrothal. Is not the scene graven on the broad bracelets of gold which in after days Seti wore when he sat upon the throne, those same bracelets that at a future time I with my own hands clasped about the wrists of dead Userti?

Then he stretched out his hand which she touched with her lips, and bending down he kissed her on the brow. Lastly, Pharaoh, descending to the lowest step of the throne, laid his sceptre, first upon the head of the Prince, and next upon that of the Princess, blessing them both in the name of himself, of his Ka or Double, and of the spirits and Kas of all their forefathers, kings and queens of Egypt, thus appointing them to come after him when he had been gathered to the bosom of the gods.

These things done, he departed in state, surrounded by his court, preceded and followed by his guards and leaning on the arm of the Princess Userti, whom he loved better than anyone in the world.

A while later I stood alone with the Prince in his private chamber, where I had first seen him.

"That is finished," he said in a cheerful voice, "and I tell you, Ana, that I feel quite, quite happy. Have you ever shivered upon the bank of a river of a winter morning, fearing to enter, and yet, when you did enter, have you not been pleased to find that the icy water refreshed you and made you not cold but hot?"

"Yes, Prince. It is when one comes out of the water, if the wind blows and no sun shines, that one feels colder than before."

"True, Ana, and therefore one must not come out. One should stop there till one—drowns or is eaten by a crocodile. But, say, did I do it well?"

"Old Bakenkhonsu told me, Prince, that he had been present at many royal betrothals, I think he said eleven, and had never seen one conducted with more grace. He added that the way in which you kissed the brow of her Highness was perfect, as was all your demeanour after the first argument."

"And so it would remain, Ana, if I were never called upon to do more than kiss her brow, to which I have been accustomed from boyhood. Oh! Ana, Ana," he added in a kind of cry, "already you are becoming a courtier like the rest of them, a courtier who cannot speak the truth. Well, nor can I, so why should I blame you? Tell me again all about your marriage, Ana, of how it began and how it ended."

CHAPTER 5

The Prophecy

Whether or no the Prince Seti saw Userti again before the hour of his marriage with her I cannot say, because he never told me. Indeed I was not present at the marriage, for the reason that I had been granted leave to return to Memphis, there to settle my affairs and sell my house on entering upon my appointment as private scribe to his Highness. Thus it came about that fourteen full days went by from that of the holding of the Court of Betrothal before I found myself standing once more at the gate of the Prince's palace, attended by a servant who led an ass on which were laden all my manuscripts and certain possessions that had descended to me from my ancestors with the title-deeds of their tombs. Different indeed was my reception on this my second coming. Even as I reached the steps the old chamberlain Pambasa appeared, running down them so fast that his white robes and beard streamed upon the air.

"Greeting, most learned scribe, most honourable Ana," he panted. "Glad indeed am I to see you, since very hour his Highness asks if you have returned, and blames me because you have not come. Verily I believe that if you had stayed upon the road another day I should have been sent to look for you, who have had sharp words said to me because I did not arrange that you should be accompanied by a guard, as though the Vizier Nehesi would have paid the costs of a guard without the direct order of Pharaoh. O most excellent Ana, give me of the charm which you have doubtless used to win the love of our royal master, and I will pay you well for it who find it easier to earn his wrath."

"I will, Pambasa. Here it is—write better stories than I do instead of telling them, and he will love you more than he does me. But say— how went the marriage? I have heard upon the way that it was very splendid."

"Splendid! Oh! it was ten times more than splendid. It was as though the god Osiris were once more wed to the goddess Isis in the very halls of heaven. Indeed his Highness, the bridegroom, was dressed as a god, yes, he wore the robes and the holy ornaments of Amon. And the procession! And the feast that Pharaoh gave! I tell you that the Prince was so overcome with joy and all this weight of glory that, before it was over, looking at him I saw that his eyes were closed, being dazzled by the gleam of gold and jewels and the loveliness of his royal bride. He told me that it was so himself, fearing perhaps lest I should have thought that he was asleep. Then there were the presents, something to everyone of us according to his degree. I got—well it matters not. And, learned Ana, I did not forget you. Knowing well that everything would be gone before you returned I spoke your name in the ear of his Highness, offering to keep your gift."

"Indeed, Pambasa, and what did he say?"

"He said that he was keeping it himself. When I stared wondering what it might be, for I saw nothing on him, he added, 'It is here,' and touched the private signet guard that he has always worn, an ancient ring of gold, but of no great value I should say, with 'Beloved of Thoth and of the King' cut upon it. It seems that he must take it off to make room for another and much finer ring which her Highness has given him."

Now, by this time, the ass having been unloaded by the slaves and led away, we had passed through the hall where many were idling as ever, and were come to the private apartments of the palace.

"This way," said Pambasa. "The orders are that I am to take you to the Prince wherever he may be, and just now he is seated in the great apartment with her Highness, where they have been receiving homage and deputations from distant cities. The last left about half an hour ago."

"First I will prepare myself, worthy Pambasa," I began.

"No, no, the orders are instant, I dare not disobey them. Enter," and with a courtly flourish he drew a rich curtain.

"By Amon," exclaimed a weary voice which I knew as that of the Prince, "here come more councillors or priests. Prepare, my sister, prepare!"

"I pray you, Seti," answered another voice, that of Userti, "to learn to call me by my right name, which is no longer sister. Nor, indeed, am I your full sister."

"I crave your pardon," said Seti. "Prepare, Royal Wife, prepare!"

By now the curtain was fully drawn and I stood, travel-stained, forlorn and, to tell the truth, trembling a little, for I feared her Highness, in the doorway, hesitating to pass the threshold. Beyond was a splendid chamber full of light, in the centre of which upon a carven and golden chair, one of two that were set there, sat her Highness magnificently apparelled, faultlessly beautiful and calm. She was engaged in studying a painted roll, left no doubt by the last deputation, for others similar to it were laid neatly side by side upon a table.

The second chair was empty, for the Prince was walking restlessly up and down the chamber, his ceremonial robe somewhat disarrayed and the *uraeus* circlet of gold which he wore, tilted back upon his head, because of his habit of running his fingers through his brown hair. As I still stood in the dark shadow, for Pambasa had left me, and thus remained unseen, the talk went on.

"I am prepared, Husband. Pardon me, it is you who look otherwise. Why would you dismiss the scribes and the household before the ceremony was ended?"

"Because they wearied me," said Seti, "with their continual bowing and praising and formalities."

"In which I saw nothing unusual. Now they must be recalled."

"Let whoever it is enter," he exclaimed.

Then I stepped forward into the light, prostrating myself.

"Why," he cried, "it is Ana returned from Memphis! Draw near, Ana, and a thousand welcomes to you. Do you know I thought that you were another high-priest, or governor of some Nome of which I had never heard."

"Ana! Who is Ana?" asked the Princess. "Oh! I remember that scribe———. Well, it is plain that he has returned from Memphis," and she eyed my dusty robe.

"Royal One," I murmured abashed, "do not blame me that I enter your presence thus. Pambasa led me here against my will by the direct order of the Prince."

"Is it so? Say, Seti, does this man bring tidings of import from Memphis that you needed his presence in such haste?"

"Yes, Userti, at least I think so. You have the writings safe, have you not, Ana?"

"Quite safe, your Highness," I answered, though I knew not of what writings he spoke, unless they were the manuscripts of my stories.

"Then, my Lord, I will leave you to talk of the tidings from Memphis and these writings," said the Princess.

"Yes, yes. We must talk of them, Userti. Also of the journey to the land of Goshen on which Ana starts with me to-morrow."

"To-morrow! Why this morning you told me it was fixed for three days hence."

"Did I, Sister—I mean Wife? If so, it was because I was not sure whether Ana, who is to be my chariot companion, would be back."

"A scribe your chariot companion! Surely it would be more fitting that your cousin Amenmeses———"

"To Set with Amenmeses!" he exclaimed. "You know well, Userti, that the man is hateful to me with his cunning yet empty talk."

"Indeed! I grieve to hear it, for when you hate you show it, and Amenmeses may be a bad enemy. Then if not our cousin Amenmeses who is not hateful to me, there is Saptah."

"I thank you; I will not travel in a cage with a jackal."

"Jackal! I do not love Saptah, but one of the royal blood of Egypt a jackal! Then there is Nehesi the Vizier, or the General of the escort whose name I forget."

"Do you think, Userti, that I wish to talk about state economies with that old money-sack, or to listen to boastings of deeds he never did in war from a half-bred Nubian butcher?"

"I do not know, Husband. Yet of what will you talk with this Ana? Of poems, I suppose, and silliness. Or will it be perchance of Merapi, Moon of Israel, whom I gather both of you think so beautiful. Well, have your way. You tell me that I am not to accompany you upon this journey, I your new-made wife, and now I find that it is because you wish my place to be filled by a writer of tales whom you picked up the other day—your 'twin in Ra' forsooth! Fare you well, my Lord," and she rose from her seat, gathering up her robes with both hands.

Then Seti grew angry.

"Userti," he said, stamping upon the floor, "you should not use such words. You know well that I do not take you with me because there may be danger yonder among the Hebrews. Moreover, it is not Pharaoh's wish."

She turned and answered with cold courtesy:

"Then I crave your pardon and thank you for your kind thought for the safety of my person. I knew not this mission was so dangerous. Be careful, Seti, that the scribe Ana comes to no harm."

So saying she bowed and vanished through the curtains.

"Ana," said Seti, "tell me, for I never was quick at figures, how many minutes is it from now till the fourth hour to-morrow morning when I shall order my chariot to be ready? Also, do you know whether it is possible to travel from Goshen across the marshes and to return by Syria? Or, failing that, to travel across the desert to Thebes and sail down the Nile in the spring?"

"Oh! my Prince, my Prince," I said, "I pray you to dismiss me. Let me go anywhere out of the reach of her Highness's tongue."

"It is strange how alike we think upon every matter, Ana, even of Merapi and the tongues of royal ladies. Hearken to my command. You are not to go. If it is a question of going, there are others who will go first. Moreover, you cannot go, but must stay and bear your burdens as I bear mine. Remember the broken cup, Ana."

"I remember, my Prince, but sooner would I be scourged with rods than by such words as those to which I must listen."

Yet that very night, when I had left the Prince, I was destined to hear more pleasant words from this same changeful, or perchance politic, royal lady. She sent for me and I went, much afraid. I found her in a small chamber alone, save for one old lady of honour who sat the end of the room and appeared to be deaf, which perhaps was why she was chosen. Userti bade me be seated before her very courteously, and spoke to me thus, whether because of some talk she had held with the Prince or not, I do not know.

"Scribe Ana, I ask your pardon if, being vexed and wearied, I said to you and of you to-day what I now wish I had left unsaid. I know well that you, being of the gentle blood of Egypt, will make no report of what you heard outside these walls."

"May my tongue be cut out first," I answered.

"It seems, Scribe Ana, that my lord the Prince has taken a great love of you. How or why this came about so suddenly, you being a man, I do not understand, but I am sure that as it is so, it must be because there is much in you to love, since never did I know the Prince to show deep regard for one who was not most honourable and worthy. Now things being so, it is plain that you will become the favourite of his Highness, a man who does not change his mind in such matters, and that he will tell you all his secret thoughts, perhaps some that he hides from the Councillors of State, or even from me. In short you will grow into a power in the land and perhaps one day be the greatest in it—after Pharaoh—although you may still seem to be but a private scribe.

"I do not pretend to you that I should have wished this to be so, who would rather that my husband had but one real councillor—myself. Yet seeing that it is so, I bow my head, hoping that it may be decreed for the best. If ever any jealousy should overcome me in this matter and I should speak sharply to you, as I did to-day, I ask your pardon in advance for that which has not happened, as I have asked it for that which has happened. I pray of you, Scribe Ana, that you will do your best to influence the mind of the Prince for good, since he is easily led by any whom he loves. I pray you also being quick and thoughtful, as I see you are, that you will make a study of statecraft, and of the policies of our Royal House, coming to me, if it be needful, for instruction therein, so that you may be able to guide the feet of the Prince aright, should he turn to you for counsel."

"All of this I will do, your Highness, if by any chance it lies in my power, though who am I that I should hope to make a path for the feet of kings? Moreover, I would add this, although he is so gentle-natured, I think that in the end the Prince is one who will always choose his own path."

"It may be so Ana. At the least I thank you. I pray you to be sure also that in me you will always have a friend and not an enemy, although at times the quickness of my nature, which has never been controlled, may lead you to think otherwise. Now I will say one more thing that shall be secret between us. I know that the Prince loves me as a friend and relative rather than as a wife, and that he would not have sought this marriage of himself, as is perhaps natural. I know, too, that other women will come into his life, though these may be fewer than in the case of most kings, because he is more hard to please. Of such I cannot complain, as this is according to the customs of our country. I fear only one thing—namely that some woman, ceasing to be his toy, may take Seti's heart and make him altogether hers. In this matter, Scribe Ana, as in others I ask your help, since I would be queen of Egypt in all ways, not in name only."

"Your Highness, how can I say to the Prince—'So much shall you love this or that woman and no more?' Moreover, why do you fear that which has not and may never come about?"

"I do not know how you can say such a thing, Scribe, still I ask you to say it if you can. As to why I fear, it is because I seem to feel the near shadow of some woman lying cold upon me and building a wall of blackness between his Highness and myself."

"It is but a dream, Princess."

"Mayhap. I hope so. Yet I think otherwise. Oh! Ana, cannot you, who study the hearts of men and women, understand my case? I have married where I can never hope to be loved as other women are, I who am a wife, yet not a wife. I read your thought; it is—why then did you marry? Since I have told you so much I will tell you that also. First, it is because the Prince is different to other men and in his own fashion above them, yes, far above any with whom I could have wed as royal heiress of Egypt. Secondly, because being cut off from love, what remains to me but ambition? At least I would be a great queen, as was Hatshepu in her day, and lift my country out of the many troubles in which it is sunk and write my name large upon the books of history, which I could only do by taking Pharaoh's heir to husband, as is my duty."

She brooded a while, then added, "Now I have shown you all my thought. Whether I have been wise to do so the gods know alone and time will tell me."

"Princess," I said, "I thank you for trusting me and I will help you if I may. Yet I am troubled. I, a humble man if of good blood, who a little while ago was but a scribe and a student, a dreamer who had known trouble also, have suddenly by chance, or some divine decree, been lifted high in the favour of the heir of Egypt, and it would seem have even won your trust. Now I wonder how I shall bear myself in this new place which in truth I never sought."

"I do not know, who find the present and its troubles enough to carry. But, doubtless, the decree of which you speak that set you there has also written down what will be the end of all. Meanwhile, I have a gift for you. Say, Scribe, have you ever handled any weapon besides a pen?"

"Yes, your Highness, as a lad I was skilled in sword play. Moreover, though I do not love war and bloodshed, some years ago I fought in the great battle between the Ninebow Barbarians, when Pharaoh called upon the young men of Memphis to do their part. With my own hands I slew two in fair fight, though one nearly brought me to my end," and I pointed to a scar which showed red through my grey hair where a spear had bitten deep.

"It is well, or so I think, who love soldiers better than stainers of papyrus pith."

Then, going to a painted chest of reeds, she took from it a wonderful shirt of mail fashioned of bronze rings, and a short sword also of bronze, having a golden hilt of which the end was shaped to the likeness of the head of a lion, and with her own hands gave them to me, saying:

"These are spoils that my grandsire, the great Rameses, took in his youth from a prince of the Khitah, whom he smote with his own hands in Syria in that battle whereof your grandfather made the poem. Wear the shirt, which no spear will pierce, beneath your robe and gird the sword about you when you go down yonder among the Israelites, whom I do not trust. I have given a like coat to the Prince. Let it be your duty to see that it is upon his sacred person day and night. Let it be your duty also, if need arises, with this sword to defend him to the death. Farewell."

"May all the gods reject me from the Fields of the Blessed if I fail in this trust," I answered, and departed wondering, to seek sleep which, as it chanced, I was not to find for a while.

For as I went down the corridor, led by one of the ladies of the household, whom should I find waiting at the end of it but old Pambasa to inform me with many bows that the Prince needed my presence. I asked how that could be seeing he had dismissed me for the night. He replied that he did not know, but he was commanded to conduct me to the private chamber, the same room in which I had first seen his Highness. Thither I went and found him warming himself at the fire, for the night was cold. Looking up he bade Pambasa admit those who were waiting, then noting the shirt of mail and the sword I carried in my hand, said:

"You have been with the Princess, have you not, and she must have had much to say to you for your talk was long? Well, I think I can guess its purport who from a child have known her mind. She told you to watch me well, body and heart and all that comes from the heart—oh! and much else. Also she gave you that Syrian gear to wear among the Hebrews as she has given the like to me, being of a careful mind which foresees everything. Now, hearken, Ana; I grieve to keep you from your rest, who must be weary both with talk and travel. But old Bakenkhonsu, whom you know, waits without, and with him Ki the great magician, whom I think you have not seen. He is a man of wonderful lore and in some ways not altogether human. At least he does strange feats of magic, and at times both the past and the future seem to be open to his sight, though as we know neither the one nor the other, who can tell whether he reads them truly. Doubtless he has, or thinks he has, some message to me from the heavens, which I thought you might wish to hear."

"I wish it much, Prince, if I am worthy, and you will protect me from the anger of this magician whom I fear."

"Anger sometimes turns to trust, Ana. Did you not find it so just now in the case of her Highness, as I told you might very well happen? Hush! They come. Be seated and prepare your tablets to make record of what they say."

The curtains were drawn and through them came the aged Bakenkhonsu leaning upon his staff, and with him another man, Ki himself, clad in a white robe and having his head shaven, for he was an hereditary priest of Amon of Thebes and an initiate of Isis, Mother of Mysteries. Also his office was that of Kherheb, or chief magician of Egypt. At first sight there was nothing strange about this man. Indeed, he might well have been a middle-aged merchant by his looks; in body he was short and stout; in face fat and smiling. But in this jovial countenance were set two very strange eyes, grey-hued rather than black. While the rest of the face seemed to smile these eyes looked straight into nothingness as do those of a statue. Indeed they were like to the eyes or rather the eye-places of a stone statue, so deeply were they set into the head. For my part I can only say I thought them awful, and by their look judged that whatever Ki might be he was no cheat.

This strange pair bowed to the Prince and seated themselves at a sign from him, Bakenkhonsu upon a stool because he found it difficult to rise, and Ki, who was younger, scribe fashion on the ground.

"What did I tell you, Bakenkhonsu?" said Ki in a full, rich voice, ending the words with a curious chuckle.

"You told me, Magician, that we should find the Prince in this chamber of which you described every detail to me as I see it now, although neither of us have entered it before. You said also that seated therein on the ground would be the scribe Ana, whom I know but you do not, having in his hands waxen tablets and a stylus and by him a coat of curious mail and a lion-hilted sword."

"That is strange," interrupted the Prince, "but forgive me, Bakenkhonsu sees these things. If you, O Ki, would tell us what is written upon Ana's tablets which neither of you can see, it would be stranger still, that is if anything is written."

Ki smiled and stared upwards at the ceiling. Presently he said:

"The scribe Ana uses a shorthand of his own that is not easy to decipher. Yet I see written on the tablets the price he obtained for some house in a city that is not named—it is so much. Also I see the sums he disbursed for himself, a servant, and the food of an ass at two inns where he stopped upon a journey. They are so much and so much. Also there is a list of papyrus rolls and the words, 'blue cloak,' and then an erasure."

"Is that right, Ana?" asked the Prince.

"Quite right," I answered with awe, "only the words 'blue cloak,' which it is true I wrote upon the tablet, have also been erased."

Ki chuckled and turned his eyes from the ceiling to my face.

"Would your Highness wish me to tell you anything of what is written upon the tablets of this scribe's memory as well as upon those of wax which he holds in his hand? They are easier to decipher than the others and I see on them many things of interest. For instance, secret words that seem to have been said to him by some Great One within an hour, matters of high policy, I think. For instance, a certain saying, I think of your Highness's, as to shivering upon the edge of water on a cold day, which when entered produced heat, and the answer thereto. For instance, words that were spoken in this palace when an alabaster cup was broke. By the way, Scribe, that was a very good place you chose in which to hide one half of the cup in the false bottom of a chest in your chamber, a chest that is fastened with a cord and sealed with a scarab of the time of the second Rameses. I think that the other half of the cup is somewhat nearer at hand," and turning, he stared at the wall where I could see nothing save slabs of alabaster.

Now I sat open-mouthed, for how could this man know these things, and the Prince laughed outright, saying:

"Ana, I begin to think you keep your counsel ill. At least I should think so, were it not that you have had no time to tell what the Princess yonder may have said to you, and can scarcely know the trick of the sliding panel in that wall which I have never shown to you."

Ki chuckled again and a smile grew on old Bakenkhonsu's broad and wrinkled face.

"O Prince," I began, "I swear to you that never has one word passed my lips of aught——"

"I know it, friend," broke in the Prince, "but it seems there are some who do not wait for words but can read the Book of Thought. Therefore it is not well to meet them too often, since all have thoughts that should be known only to them and God. Magician, what is your business with me? Speak on as though we were alone."

"This, Prince. You go upon a journey among the Hebrews, as all have heard. Now, Bakenkhonsu and I, also two seers of my College, seeing that we all love you and that your welfare is much to Egypt, have separately sought out the future as regards the issue of this journey. Although what we have learned differs in some matters, on others it is the same. Therefore we thought it our duty to tell you what we have learned."

"Say on, Kherheb."

"First, then, that your Highness's life will be in danger."

"Life is always in danger, Ki. Shall I lose it? If so, do not fear to tell me."

"We do not know, but we think not, because of the rest that is revealed to us. We learn that it is not your body only that will be in danger. Upon this journey you will see a woman whom you will come to love. This woman will, we think, bring you much sorrow and also much joy."

"Then perhaps the journey is worth making, Ki, since many travel far before they find aught they can love. Tell me, have I met this woman?"

"There we are troubled, Prince, for it would seem—unless we are deceived—that you have met her often and often; that you have known her for thousands of years, as you have known that man at your side for thousands of years."

Seti's face grew very interested.

"What do you mean, Magician?" he asked, eyeing him keenly. "How can I who am still young have known a woman and a man for thousands of years?"

Ki considered him with his strange eyes, and answered:

"You have many titles, Prince. Is not one of them 'Lord of Rebirths,' and if so, how did you get it and what does it mean?"

"It is. What it means I do not know, but it was given to me because of some dream that my mother had the night before I was born. Do *you* tell *me* what it means, since you seem to know so much."

"I cannot, Prince. The secret is not one that has been shown to me. Yet there was an aged man, a magician like myself from whom I learned much in my youth—Bakenkhonsu knew him well—who made a study of this matter. He told me he was sure, because it had been revealed to him, that men do not live once only and then depart hence for ever. He said that they live many times and in many shapes, though not always on this world, and that between each life there is a wall of darkness."

"If so, of what use are lives which we do not remember after death has shut the door of each of them?"

"The doors may open again at last, Prince, and show us all the chambers through which our feet have wandered from the beginning."

"Our religion teaches us, Ki, that after death we live eternally elsewhere in our own bodies, which we find again on the day of resurrection. Now eternity, having no end, can have no beginning; it is a circle. Therefore if the one be true, namely that we live on, it would seem that the other must be true, namely that we have always lived."

"That is well reasoned, Prince. In the early days, before the priests froze the thought of man into blocks of stone and built of them shrines to a thousand gods, many held that this reasoning was true, as then they held that there was but one god."

"As do these Israelites whom I go to visit. What say you of their god, Ki?"

"That *he* is the same as our gods, Prince. To men's eyes God has many faces, and each swears that the one he sees is the only true god. Yet they are wrong, for all are true."

"Or perchance false, Ki, unless even falsehood is a part of truth. Well, you have told me of two dangers, one to my body and one to my heart. Has any other been revealed to your wisdom?"

"Yes, Prince. The third is that this journey may in the end cost you your throne."

"If I die certainly it will cost me my throne."

"No, Prince, if you live."

"Even so, Ki, I think that I could endure life seated more humbly than on a throne, though whether her Highness could endure it is another matter. Then you say that if I go upon this journey another will be Pharaoh in my place."

"We do not say that, Prince. It is true that our arts have shown us another filling your place in a time of wizardry and wonders and of the death of thousands. Yet when we look again we see not that other but you once more filling your own place."

Here I, Ana, bethought me of my vision in Pharaoh's hall.

"The matter is even worse than I thought, Ki, since having once left the crown behind me, I think that I should have no wish to wear it any more," said Seti. "Who shows you all these things, and how?"

"Our *Kas*, which are our secret selves, show them to us, Prince, and in many ways. Sometimes it is by dreams or visions, sometimes by pictures on water, sometimes by writings in the desert sand. In all these fashions, and by others, our *Kas*, drawing from the infinite well of wisdom that is hidden in the being of every man, give us glimpses of the truth, as they give us who are instructed power to work marvels."

"Of the truth. Then these things you tell me are true?"

"We believe so, Prince."

"Then being true must happen. So what is the use of your warning me against what must happen? There cannot be two truths. What would you have me do? Not go upon this journey? Why have you told me that I must not go, since if I did not go the truth would become a lie, which it cannot? You say it is fated that I should go and because I go such and such things will come about. And yet you tell me not to go, for that is what you mean. Oh! Kherheb Ki and Bakenkhonsu, doubtless you are great magicians and strong in wisdom, but there are greater than you who rule the world, and there is a wisdom to which yours is but as a drop of water to the Nile. I thank you for your warnings, but to-morrow I go down to the land of Goshen to fulfil the commands of Pharaoh. If I come back again we will talk more of these matters here upon the earth. If I do not come back, perchance we will talk of them elsewhere. Farewell."

CHAPTER 6

The Land of Goshen

The Prince Seti and all his train, a very great company, came in safety to the land of Goshen, I, Ana, travelling with him in his chariot. It was then as now a rich land, quite flat after the last line of desert hills through which we travelled by a narrow, tortuous path. Everywhere it was watered by canals, between which lay the grain fields wherein the seed had just been sown. Also there were other fields of green fodder whereon were tethered beasts by the hundred, and beyond these, upon the drier soil, grazed flocks of sheep. The town Goshen, if so it could be called, was but a poor place, numbers of mud huts, no more, in the centre of which stood a building, also of mud, with two brick pillars in front of it, that we were told was the temple of this people, into the inner parts of which none might enter save their High-priest. I laughed at the sight of it, but the Prince reproved me, saying that I should not judge the spirit by the body, or of the god by his house.

We camped outside this town and soon learned that the people who dwelt in it or elsewhere in other towns must be numbered by the ten thousand, for more of them than I could count wandered round the camp to look at us. The men were fierce-eyed and hook-nosed; the young women well-shaped and pleasant to behold; the older women for the most part stout and somewhat unwieldy, and the children very beautiful. All were roughly clad in robes of loosely-woven, dark-coloured cloth, beneath which the women wore garments of white linen. Notwithstanding the wealth we saw about us in corn and cattle, their ornaments seemed to be few, or perhaps these were hidden from our sight.

It was easy to see that they hated us Egyptians, and even dared to despise us. Hate shone in their glittering eyes, and I heard them calling us the 'idol-worshippers' one to the other, and asking where was our god, the Bull, for being ignorant they thought that we worshipped

Apis (as mayhap some of the common people do) instead of looking upon the sacred beast as a symbol of the powers of Nature. Indeed they did more, for on the first night after our coming they slaughtered a bull marked much as Apis is, and in the morning we found it lying near the gate of the camp, and pinned to its hide with sharp thorns great numbers of the scarabaeus beetle still living. For again they did not know that among us Egyptians this beetle is no god but an emblem of the Creator, because it rolls a ball of mud between its feet and sets therein its eggs to hatch, as the Creator rolls the world that seems to be round, and causes it to produce life.

Now all were angry at these insults except the Prince, who laughed and said that he thought the jest coarse but clever. But worse was to happen. It seems that a soldier with wine in him had done insult to a Hebrew maiden who came alone to draw water at a canal. The news spread among the people and some thousands of them rushed to the camp, shouting and demanding vengence in so threatening a manner that it was necessary to form up the regiments of guards.

The Prince being summoned commanded that the girl and her kin should be admitted and state their case. She came, weeping and wailing and tearing her garments, throwing dust on her head also, though it appeared that she had taken no great harm from the soldier from whom she ran away. The Prince bade her point out the man if she could see him, and she showed us one of the bodyguard of the Count Amenmeses, whose face was scratched as though by a woman's nails. On being questioned he said he could remember little of the matter, but confessed that he had seen the maiden by the canal at moonrise and jested with her.

The kin of this girl clamoured that he should be killed, because he had offered insult to a high-born lady of Israel. This Seti refused, saying that the offence was not one of death, but that he would order him to be publicly beaten. Thereupon Amenmeses, who was fond of the soldier, a good man enough when not in his cups, sprang up in a rage, saying that no servant of his should be touched because he had offered to caress some light Israelitish woman who had no business to be wandering about alone at night. He added that if the man were flogged he and all those under his command would leave the camp and march back to make report to Pharaoh.

Now the Prince, having consulted with the councillors, told the woman and her kin that as Pharaoh had been appealed to, he must judge of the matter, and commanded them to appear at his court within a month and state their case against the soldier. They went away very ill-satisfied, saying that Amenmeses had insulted their daughter even more than his servant had done. The end of this matter was that on the following night this soldier was discovered dead, pierced through and through with knife thrusts. The girl, her parents and brethren could not be found, having fled away into the desert, nor was there any evidence to show by whom the soldier had been murdered. Therefore nothing could be done in the business except bury the victim.

On the following morning the Inquiry began with due ceremony, the Prince Seti and the Count Amenmeses taking their seats at the head of a large pavilion with the councillors behind them and the scribes, among whom I was, seated at their feet. Then we learned that the two prophets whom I had seen at Pharaoh's court were not in the land of Goshen, having left before we arrived "to sacrifice to God in the wilderness," nor did any know when they would return. Other elders and priests, however, appeared and began to set out their case, which they did at great length and in a fierce and turbulent fashion, speaking often all of them at once, thus making it difficult for the interpreters to render their words, since they pretended that they did not know the Egyptian tongue.

Moreover they told their story from the very beginning, when they had entered Egypt hundreds of years before and were succoured by the vizier of the Pharaoh of that day, one Yusuf, a powerful and clever man of their race who stored corn in a time of famine and low Niles. This Pharaoh was of the Hyksos people, one of the Shepherd kings whom we Egyptians hated and after many wars drove out of Khem. Under these Shepherd kings, being joined by many of their own blood, the Israelites grew rich and powerful, so that the Pharaohs who came after and who loved them not, began to fear them.

This was as far as the story was taken on the first day.

On the second day began the tale of their oppression, under which, however, they still multiplied like gnats upon the Nile, and grew so strong and numerous that at length the great Rameses did a wicked thing, ordering that their male children should be put to death. This order was never carried out, because his daughter, she who found Moses among the reeds of the river, pleaded for them.

At this point the Prince, wearied with the noise and heat in that crowded place, broke off the sitting until the morrow. Commanding me to accompany him, he ordered a chariot, not his own, to be made ready, and, although I prayed him not to do so, set out unguarded save for myself and the charioteer, saying that he would see how these people laboured with his own eyes.

Taking a Hebrew lad to run before the horses as our guide, we drove to the banks of a canal where the Israelites made bricks of mud which, after drying in the sun, were laden into boats that waited for them on the canal and taken away to other parts of Egypt to be used on Pharaoh's works. Thousands of men were engaged upon this labour, toiling in gangs under the command of Egyptian overseers who kept count of the bricks, cutting their number upon tally sticks, or sometimes writing them upon sherds. These overseers were brutal fellows, for the most part of the low class, who used vile language to the slaves. Nor were they content with words. Noting a crowd gathered at one place and hearing cries, we went to see what passed. Here we found a lad stretched upon the ground being cruelly beaten with hide whips, so that the blood ran down him. At a sign from the Prince I asked what he had done and was told roughly, for the overseers and their guards did not know who we were, that during the past six days he had only made half of his allotted tale of bricks.

"Loose him," said the Prince quietly.

"Who are you that give me orders?" asked the head overseer, who was helping to hold the lad while the guards flogged him. "Begone, lest I serve you as I serve this idle fellow."

Seti looked at him, and as he looked his lips turned white.

"Tell him," he said to me.

"You dog!" I gasped. "Do you know who it is to whom you dare to speak thus?"

"No, nor care. Lay on, guard."

The Prince, whose robes were hidden by a wide-sleeved cloak of common stuff and make, threw the cloak open revealing beneath it the pectoral he had worn in the Court, a beautiful thing of gold whereon were inscribed his royal names and titles in black and red enamel. Also he held up his right hand on which was a signet of Pharaoh's that he wore as his commissioner. The men stared, then one of them who was more learned than the rest cried:

"By the gods! this is his Highness the Prince of Egypt!" at which words all of them fell upon their faces.

"Rise," said Seti to the lad who looked at him, forgetting his pain in his wonderment, "and tell me why you have not delivered your tale of bricks."

"Sir," sobbed the boy in bad Egyptian, "for two reasons. First, because I am a cripple, see," and he held up his left arm which was withered and thin as a mummy's, "and therefore cannot work quickly. Secondly, because my mother, whose only child I am, is a widow and lies sick in bed, so that there are no women or children in our home who can go out to gather straw for me, as Pharaoh has commanded that we should do. Therefore I must spend many hours in searching for straw, since I have no means wherewith to pay others to do this for me."

"Ana," said the Prince, "write down this youth's name with the place of his abode, and if his tale prove true, see that his wants and those of his mother are relieved before we depart from Goshen. Write down also the names of this overseer and his fellows and command them to report themselves at my camp to-morrow at sunrise, when their case shall be considered. Say to the lad also that, being one afflicted by the gods, Pharaoh frees him from the making of bricks and all other labour of the State."

Now while I did these things the overseer and his companions beat their heads upon the ground and prayed for mercy, being cowards as the cruel always are. His Highness answered them never a word, but only looked at them with cold eyes, and I noted that his face which was so kind had grown terrible. So those men thought also, for that night they ran away to Syria, leaving their families and all their goods behind them, nor were they ever seen again in Egypt.

When I had finished writing the Prince turned and, walking to where the chariot waited, bade the driver cross the canal by a bridge there was here. We drove on a while in silence, following a track which ran between the cultivated land and the desert. At length I pointed to the sinking sun and asked if it were not time to return.

"Why?" replied the Prince. "The sun dies, but there rises the full moon to give us light, and what have we to fear with swords at our sides and her Highness Userti's mail beneath our robes? Oh! Ana, I am weary of men with their cruelties and shouts and strugglings, and I find this wilderness a place of rest, for in it I seem to draw nearer to my own soul and the Heaven whence it came, or so I hope."

"Your Highness is fortunate to have a soul to which he cares to draw near; it is not so with all of us;" I answered laughing, for I sought to change the current of his thoughts by provoking argument of a sort that he loved.

Just then, however, the horses, which were not of the best, came to a halt on a slope of heavy sand. Nor would Seti allow the driver to flog them, but commanded him to let them rest a space. While they did so we descended from the chariot and walked up the desert rise, he leaning on my arm. As we reached its crest we heard sobs and a soft voice speaking on the further side. Who it was that spoke and sobbed we could not see, because of a line of tamarisk shrubs which once had been a fence.

"More cruelty, or at least more sorrow," whispered Seti. "Let us look."

So we crept to the tamarisks, and peeping through their feathery tops, saw a very sweet sight in the pure rays of that desert moon. There, not five paces away, stood a woman clad in white, young and shapely in form. Her face we could not see because it was turned from us, also the long dark hair which streamed about her shoulders hid it. She was praying aloud, speaking now in Hebrew, of which both of us knew something, and now in Egyptian, as does one who is accustomed to think in either tongue, and stopping from time to time to sob.

"O God of my people," she said, "send me succour and bring me safe home, that Thy child may not be left alone in the wilderness to become the prey of wild beasts, or of men who are worse than beasts."

Then she sobbed, knelt down on a great bundle which I saw was stubble straw, and again began to pray. This time it was in Egyptian, as though she feared lest the Hebrew should be overheard and understood.

"O God," she said, "O God of my fathers, help my poor heart, help my poor heart!"

We were about to withdraw, or rather to ask her what she ailed, when suddenly she turned her head, so that the light fell full upon her face. So lovely was it that I caught my breath and the Prince at my side started. Indeed it was more than lovely, for as a lamp shines through an alabaster vase or a shell of pearl so did the spirit within this woman shine through her tear-stained face, making it mysterious as the night. Then I understood, perhaps for the first time, that it is the spirit which gives true beauty both to maid and man and not the flesh. The white vase of alabaster, however shapely, is still a vase alone; it is the hidden lamp within that graces it with the glory of a star. And those eyes, those large, dreaming eyes aswim with tears and hued like richest lapis-lazuli, oh! what man could look on them and not be stirred?

"Merapi!" I whispered.

"Moon of Israel!" murmured Seti, "filled with the moon, lovely as the moon, mystic as the moon and worshipping the moon, her mother."

"She is in trouble; let us help her," I said.

"Nay, wait a while, Ana, for never again shall you and I see such a sight as this."

Low as we spoke beneath our breath, I think the lady heard us. At least her face changed and grew frightened. Hastily she rose, lifted the great bundle of straw upon which she had been kneeling and placed it on her head. She ran a few steps, then stumbled and sank down with a little moan of pain. In an instant we were at her side. She stared at us affrighted, for who we were she could not see because of the wide hoods of our common cloaks that made us look like midnight thieves, or slave-dealing Bedouin.

"Oh! Sirs," she babbled, "harm me not. I have nothing of value on me save this amulet."

"Who are you and what do you here?" asked the Prince disguising his voice.

"Sirs, I am Merapi, the daughter of Nathan the Levite, he whom the accursed Egyptian captain, Khuaka, murdered at Tanis."

"How do you dare to call the Egyptians accursed?" asked Seti in tones made gruff to hide his laughter.

"Oh! Sirs, because they are—I mean because I thought you were Arabs who hate them, as we do. At least this Egyptian was accursed, for the high Prince Seti, Pharaoh's heir, caused him to be beheaded for that crime."

"And do you hate the high Prince Seti, Pharaoh's heir, and call him accursed?"

She hesitated, then in a doubtful voice said:

"No, I do not hate him."

"Why not, seeing that you hate the Egyptians of whom he is one of the first and therefore twice worthy of hatred, being the son of your oppressor, Pharaoh?"

"Because, although I have tried my best, I cannot. Also," she added with the joy of one who has found a good reason, "he avenged my father."

"This is no cause, girl, seeing that he only did what the law forced him to do. They say that this dog of a Pharaoh's son is here in Goshen upon some mission. Is it true, and have you seen him? Answer, for we of the desert folk desire to know."

"I believe it is true, Sir, but I have not seen him."

"Why not, if he is here?"

"Because I do not wish to, Sir. Why should a daughter of Israel desire to look upon the face of a prince of Egypt?"

"In truth I do not know," replied Seti forgetting his feigned voice. Then, seeing that she glanced at him sharply, he added in gruff tones:

"Brother, either this woman lies or she is none other than the maid they call Moon of Israel who dwells with old Jabez the Levite, her uncle. What think you?"

"I think, Brother, that she lies, and for three reasons," I answered, falling into the jest. "First, she is too fair to be of the black Hebrew blood."

"Oh! Sir," moaned Merapi, "my mother was a Syrian lady of the mountains, with a skin as white as milk, and eyes blue as the heavens."

"Secondly," I went on without heeding her, "if the great Prince Seti is really in Goshen and she dwells there, it is unnatural that she should not have gone to look upon him. Being a woman only two things would have kept her away, one—that she feared and hated him, which she denies, and the other—that she liked him too well, and, being prudent, thought it wisest not to look upon him more."

When she heard the first of these words, Merapi glanced up with her lips parted as though to answer. Instead, she dropped her eyes and suddenly seemed to choke, while even in the moonlight I saw the red blood pour to her brow and along her white arms.

"Sir," she gasped, "why should you affront me? I swear that never till this moment did I think such a thing. Surely it would be treason."

"Without doubt," interrupted Seti, "yet one of a sort that kings might pardon."

"Thirdly," I went on as though I had heard neither of them, "if this girl were what she declares, she would not be wandering alone in the desert at night, seeing that I have heard among the Arabs that Merapi, daughter of Nathan the Levite, is a lady of no mean blood among the Hebrews and that her family has wealth. Still, however much she lies, we can see for ourselves that she is beautiful."

"Yes, Brother, in that we are fortunate, since without doubt she will sell for a high price among the slave traders beyond the desert."

"Oh! Sir," cried Merapi seizing the hem of his robe, "surely you who I feel, I know not why, are no evil thief, you who have a mother and, perchance, sisters, would not doom a maiden to such a fate. Misjudge me not because I am alone. Pharaoh has commanded that we must find straw for the making of bricks. This morning I came far to search for it on behalf of a neighbour whose wife is ill in childbed. But towards sundown I slipped and cut myself upon the edge of a sharp stone. See," and holding up her foot she showed a wound beneath the instep from which the blood still dropped, a sight that moved both of us not a little, "and now I cannot walk and carry this heavy straw which I have been at such pains to gather."

"Perchance she speaks truth, Brother," said the Prince, "and if we took her home we might earn no small reward from Jabez the Levite. But first tell me, Maiden, what was that prayer which you made to the moon, that Hathor should help your heart?"

"Sir," she answered, "only the idolatrous Egyptians pray to Hathor, the Lady of Love."

"I thought that all the world prayed to the Lady of Love, Maiden. But what of the prayer? Is there some man whom you desire?"

"None," she answered angrily.

"Then why does your heart need so much help that you ask it of the air? Is there perchance someone whom you do *not* desire?"

She hung her head and made no answer.

"Come, Brother," said the Prince, "this lady is weary of us, and I think that if she were a true woman she would answer our questions more readily. Let us go and leave her. As she cannot walk we can take her later if we wish."

"Sirs," she said, "I am glad that you are going, since the hyenas will be safer company than two men who can threaten to sell a helpless woman into slavery. Yet as we part to meet no more I will answer your question. In the prayer to which you were not ashamed to listen I did not pray for any lover, I prayed to be rid of one."

"Now, Ana," said the Prince bursting into laughter and throwing back his dark cloak, "do you discover the name of that unhappy man of whom the lady Merapi wishes to be rid, for I dare not."

She gazed into his face and uttered a little cry.

"Ah!" she said, "I thought I knew the voice again when once you forget your part. Prince Seti, does your Highness think that this was a kind jest to practise upon one alone and in fear?"

"Lady Merapi," he answered smiling, "be not wroth, for at least it was a good one and you have told us nothing that we did not know. You may remember that at Tanis you said that you were affianced and there was that in your voice——. Suffer me now to tend this wound of yours."

Then he knelt down, tore a strip from his ceremonial robe of fine linen, and began to bind up her foot, not unskilfully, being a man full of strange and unexpected knowledge. As he worked at the task, watching them, I saw their eyes meet, saw too that rich flood of colour creep once more to Merapi's brow. Then I began to think it unseemly that the Prince of Egypt should play the leech to a woman's hurts, and to wonder why he had not left that humble task to me.

Presently the bandaging was done and made fast with a royal scarabaeus mounted on a pin of gold, which the Prince wore in his garments. On it was cut the *uraeus* crown and beneath it were the signs which read "Lord of the Lower and the Upper Land," being Pharaoh's style and title.

"See now, Lady," he said, "you have Egypt beneath your foot," and when she asked him what he meant, he read her the writing upon the jewel, whereat for the third time she coloured to the eyes. Then he lifted her up, instructing her to rest her weight upon his shoulder, saying he feared lest the scarab, which he valued, should be broken.

Thus we started, I bearing the bundle of straw behind as he bade me, since, he said, having been gathered with such toil, it must not be lost. On reaching the chariot, where we found the guide gone and the driver asleep, he sat her in it upon his cloak, and wrapped her in mine which he borrowed, saying I should not need it who must carry the straw. Then he mounted also and they drove away at a foot's pace. As I walked after the chariot with the straw that fell about my ears, I heard nothing of their further talk, if indeed they talked at all which, the driver being present, perhaps they did not. Nor in truth did I listen who was engaged in thought as to the hard lot of these poor Hebrews, who must collect this dirty stuff and bear it so far, made heavy as it was by the clay that clung about the roots.

Even now, as it chanced, we did not reach Goshen without further trouble. Just as we had crossed the bridge over the canal I, toiling behind, saw in the clear moonlight a young man running towards us. He was a Hebrew, tall, well-made and very handsome in his fashion. His eyes were dark and fierce, his nose was hooked, his teeth where regular and white, and his long, black hair hung down in a mass upon his shoulders. He held a wooden staff in his hand and a naked knife was girded about his middle. Seeing the chariot he halted and peered at it, then asked in Hebrew if those who travelled had seen aught of a young Israelitish lady who was lost.

"If you seek me, Laban, I am here," replied Merapi, speaking from the shadow of the cloak.

"What do you there alone with an Egyptian, Merapi?" he said fiercely.

What followed I do not know for they spoke so quickly in their unfamiliar tongue that I could not understand them. At length Merapi turned to the Prince, saying:

"Lord, this is Laban my affianced, who commands me to descend from the chariot and accompany him as best I can."

"And I, Lady, command you to stay in it. Laban your affianced can accompany us."

Now at this Laban grew angry, as I could see he was prone to do, and stretched out his hand as though to push Seti aside and seize Merapi.

"Have a care, man," said the Prince, while I, throwing down the straw, drew my sword and sprang between them, crying:

"Slave, would you lay hands upon the Prince of Egypt?"

"Prince of Egypt!" he said, drawing back astonished, then added sullenly, "Well what does the Prince of Egypt with my affianced?"

"He helps her who is hurt to her home, having found her helpless in the desert with this accursed straw," I answered.

"Forward, driver," said the Prince, and Merapi added, "Peace, Laban, and bear the straw which his Highness's companion has carried such a weary way."

He hesitated a moment, then snatched up the bundle and set it on his head.

As we walked side by side, his evil temper seemed to get the better of him. Without ceasing, he grumbled because Merapi was alone in the chariot with an Egyptian. At length I could bear it no longer.

"Be silent, fellow," I said. "Least of all men should you complain of what his Highness does, seeing that already he has avenged the killing of this lady's father, and now has saved her from lying out all night among the wild beasts and men of the wilderness."

"Of the first I have heard more than enough," he answered, "and of the second doubtless I shall hear more than enough also. Ever since my affianced met this prince, she has looked on me with different eyes and spoken to me with another voice. Yes, and when I press for marriage, she says it cannot be for a long while yet, because she is mourning for her father; her father forsooth, whom she never forgave because he betrothed her to me according to the custom of our people."

"Perhaps she loves some other man?" I queried, wishing to learn all I could about this lady.

"She loves no man, or did not a while ago. She loves herself alone."

"One with so much beauty may look high in marriage."

"High!" he replied furiously. "How can she look higher than myself who am a lord of the line of Judah, and therefore greater far than an upstart prince or any other Egyptian, were he Pharaoh himself?"

"Surely you must be trumpeter to your tribe," I mocked, for my temper was rising.

"Why?" he asked. "Are not the Hebrews greater than the Egyptians, as those oppressors soon shall learn, and is not a lord of Israel more than any idol-worshipper among your people?"

I looked at the man clad in mean garments and foul from his labour in the brickfield, marvelling at his insolence. There was no doubt but that he believed what he said; I could see it in his proud eye and bearing. He thought that his tribe was of more import in the world than our great and ancient nation, and that he, an unknown youth, equalled or surpassed Pharaoh himself. Then, being enraged by these insults, I answered:

314

"You say so, but let us put it to the proof. I am but a scribe, yet I have seen war. Linger a little that we may learn whether a lord of Israel is better than a scribe of Egypt."

"Gladly would I chastise you, Writer," he answered, "did I not see your plot. You wish to delay me here, and perhaps to murder me by some foul means, while your master basks in the smiles of the Moon of Israel. Therefore I will not stay, but another time it shall be as you wish, and perhaps ere long."

Now I think that I should have struck him in the face, though I am not one of those who love brawling. But at this moment there appeared a company of Egyptian horse led by none other than the Count Amenmeses. Seeing the Prince in the Chariot, they halted and gave the salute. Amenmeses leapt to the ground.

"We are come out to search for your Highness," he said, "fearing lest some hurt had befallen you."

"I thank you, Cousin," answered the Prince, "but the hurt has befallen another, not me."

"That is well, your Highness," said the Count, studying Merapi with a smile. "Where is the lady wounded? Not in the breast, I trust."

"No, Cousin, in the foot, which is why she travels with me in this chariot."

"Your Highness was ever kind to the unfortunate. I pray you let me take your place, or suffer me to set this girl upon a horse."

"Drive on," said Seti.

So, escorted by the soldiers, whom I heard making jests to each other about the Prince and the lady, as I think did the Hebrew Laban also, for he glared about him and ground his teeth, we came at last to the town. Here, guided by Merapi, the chariot was halted at the house of Jabez her uncle, a white-bearded old Hebrew with a cunning eye, who rushed from the door of his mud-roofed dwelling crying he had done no harm that soldiers should come to take him.

"It is not you whom the Egyptians wish to capture, it is your niece and my betrothed," shouted Laban, whereat the soldiers laughed, as did some women who had gathered round. Meanwhile the Prince was helping Merapi to descend out of the chariot, from which indeed he lifted her. The sight seemed to madden Laban, who rushed forward to tear her from his arms, and in the attempt jostled his Highness. The captain of the soldiers—he was an officer of Pharaoh's bodyguard—lifted his sword in a fury and struck Laban such a blow upon the head with the flat of the blade that he fell upon his face and lay there groaning.

"Away with that Hebrew dog and scourge him!" cried the captain. "Is the royal blood of Egypt to be handled by such as he?"

Soldiers sprang forward to do his bidding, but Seti said quietly:

"Let the fellow be, friends; he lacks manners, that is all. Is he hurt?"

As he spoke Laban leapt to his feet and, fearing worse things, fled away with a curse and a glare of hate at the Prince.

"Farewell, Lady," said Seti. "I wish you a quick recovery."

"I thank your Highness," she answered, looking about her confusedly. "Be pleased to wait a little while that I may return to you your jewel."

"Nay, keep it, Lady, and if ever you are in need or trouble of any sort, send it to me who know it well and you shall not lack succour."

She glanced at him and burst into tears.

"Why do you weep?" he asked.

"Oh! your Highness, because I fear that trouble is near at hand. My affianced, Laban, has a revengeful heart. Help me to the house, my uncle."

"Listen, Hebrew," said Seti, raising his voice; "if aught that is evil befalls this niece of yours, or if she is forced to walk whither she would not go, sorrow shall be your portion and that of all with whom you have to do. Do you hear?"

"O my Lord, I hear, I hear. Fear nothing. She shall be guarded carefully as—as she will doubtless guard that trinket on her foot."

****

"Ana," said the Prince to me that night, when I was talking with him before he went to rest, "I know not why, but I fear that man Laban; he has an evil eye."

"I too think it would have been better if your Highness had left him to be dealt with by the soldiers, after which there would have been nothing to fear from him in this world."

"Well, I did not, so there's an end. Ana, she is a fair woman and a sweet."

"The fairest and the sweetest that ever I saw, my Prince."

"Be careful, Ana. I pray you be careful, lest you should fall in love with one who is already affianced."

I only looked at him in answer, and as I looked I bethought me of the words of Ki the Magician. So, I think, did the Prince; at least he laughed not unhappily and turned away.

For my part I rested ill that night, and when at last I slept, it was to dream of Merapi making her prayer in the rays of the moon.

CHAPTER 7

The Ambush

Eight full days went by before we left the land of Goshen. The story that the Israelites had to tell was long, sad also. Moreover, they gave evidence as to many cruel things that they had suffered, and when this was finished the testimony of the guards and others must be called, all of which it was necessary to write down. Lastly, the Prince seemed to be in no hurry to be gone, as he said because he hoped that the two prophets would return from the wilderness, which they never did. During all this time Seti saw no more of Merapi, nor indeed did he speak of her, even when the Count Amenmeses jested him as to his chariot companion and asked him if he had driven again in the desert by moonlight.

I, however, saw her once. When I was wandering in the town one day towards sunset, I met her walking with her uncle Jabez upon one side and her lover, Laban, on the other, like a prisoner between two guards. I thought she looked unhappy, but her foot seemed to be well again; at least she moved without limping.

I stopped to salute her, but Laban scowled and hurried her away. Jabez stayed behind and fell into talk with me. He told me that she was recovered of her hurt, but that there had been trouble between her and Laban because of all that happened on that evening when she came by it, ending in his encounter with the captain.

"This young man seems to be of a jealous nature," I said, "one who will make a harsh husband for any woman."

"Yes, learned scribe, jealousy has been his curse from youth as it is with so many of our people, and I thank God that I am not the woman whom he is to marry."

"Why, then, do you suffer her to marry him, Jabez?"

"Because her father affianced her to this lion's whelp when she was scarce more than a child, and among us that is a bond hard to break.

For my own part," he added, dropping his voice, and glancing round with shifting eyes, "I should like to see my niece in some different place to that of the wife of Laban. With her great beauty and wit, she might become anything—anything if she had opportunity. But under our laws, even if Laban died, as might happen to so violent a man, she could wed no one who is not a Hebrew."

"I thought she told us that her mother was a Syrian."

"That is so, Scribe Ana. She was a beautiful captive of war whom Nathan came to love and made his wife, and the daughter takes after her. Still she is Hebrew and of the Hebrew faith and congregation. Had it not been so, she might have shone like a star, nay, like the very moon after which she is named, perhaps in the court of Pharaoh himself."

"As the great queen Taia did, she who changed the religion of Egypt to the worship of one god in a bygone generation," I suggested.

"I have heard of her, Scribe Ana. She was a wondrous woman, beautiful too by her statues. Would that you Egyptians could find such another to turn your hearts to a purer faith and to soften them towards us poor aliens. When does his Highness leave the land of Goshen?"

"At sunrise on the third day from this."

"Provision will be needed for the journey, much provision for so large a train. I deal in sheep and other foodstuffs, Scribe Ana."

"I will mention the matter to his Highness and to the Vizier, Jabez."

"I thank you, Scribe, and will in waiting at the camp to-morrow morning. See, Laban returns with Merapi. One word, let his Highness beware of Laban. He is very revengeful and has not forgotten that sword-blow on the head."

"Let Laban be careful," I answered. "Had it not been for his Highness the soldiers would have killed him the other night because he dared to offer affront to the royal blood. A second time he will not escape. Moreover, Pharaoh would avenge aught he did upon the people of Israel."

"I understand. It would be sad if Laban were killed, very sad. But the people of Israel have One who can protect them even against Pharaoh and all his hosts. Farewell, learned Scribe. If ever I come to Tanis, with your leave we will talk more together."

That night I told the Prince all that had passed. He listened, and said:

"I grieve for the lady Merapi, for hers is like to be a hard fate. Yet," he added laughing, "perhaps it is as well for you, friend, that you should see no more of her who is sure to bring trouble wherever she goes. That woman has a face which haunts the mind, as the Ka haunts the tomb, and for my part I do not wish to look upon it again."

"I am glad to hear it, Prince, and for my part, I have done with women, however sweet. I will tell this Jabez that the provisions for the journey will be bought elsewhere."

"Nay, buy them from him, and if Nehesi grumbles at the price, pay it on my account. The way to a Hebrew's heart is through his treasure bags. If Jabez is well treated, it may make him kinder to his niece, of whom I shall always have a pleasant memory, for which I am grateful among this sour folk who hate us, and with reason."

So the sheep and all the foodstuffs for the journey were bought from Jabez at his own price, for which he thanked me much, and on the third day we started. At the last moment the Prince, whose mood seemed to be perverse that evening, refused to travel with the host upon the morrow because of the noise and dust. In vain did the Count Amenmeses reason with him, and Nehesi and the great officers implore him almost on their knees, saying that they must answer for his safety to Pharaoh and the Princess Userti. He bade them begone, replying that he would join them at their camp on the following night. I also prayed him to listen, but he told me sharply that what he said he had said, and that he and I would journey in his chariot alone, with two armed runners and no more, adding that if I thought there was danger I could go forward with the troops. Then I bit my lip and was silent, whereon, seeing that he had hurt me, he turned and craved my pardon humbly enough as his kind heart taught him to do.

"I can bear no more of Amenmeses and those officers," he said, "and I love to be in the desert alone. Last time we journeyed there we met with adventures that were pleasant, Ana, and at Tanis doubtless I shall find others that are not pleasant. Admit that Hebrew priest who is waiting to instruct me in the mysteries of his faith which I desire to understand."

So I bowed and left him to make report that I had failed to shake his will. Taking the risk of his wrath, however, I did this—for had I not sworn to the Princess that I would protect him? In place of the runners I chose two of the best and bravest soldiers to play their part. Moreover, I instructed that captain who smote down Laban to hide away with a score of picked men and enough chariots to carry them, and to follow after the Prince, keeping just out of sight.

So on the morrow the troops, nobles, and officers went on at daybreak, together with the baggage carriers; nor did we follow them till many hours had gone by. Some of this time the Prince spent in driving about the town, taking note of the condition of the people. These, as I saw, looked on us sullenly enough, more so than before, I thought, perhaps because we were unguarded. Indeed, turning round I caught sight of a man shaking his fist and of an old hag spitting after us, and wished that we were out of the land of Goshen. But when I reported it to the Prince he only laughed and took no heed.

"All can see that they hate us Egyptians," he said. "Well, let it be our task to try to turn their hate to love."

"That you will never do, Prince, it is too deep-rooted in their hearts; for generations they have drunk it in with their mother's milk. Moreover, this is a war of the gods of Egypt and of Israel, and men must go where their gods drive them."

"Do you think so, Ana? Then are men nothing but dust blown by the winds of heaven, blown from the darkness that is before the dawn to be gathered at last and for ever into the darkness of the grave of night?"

He brooded a while, then went on.

"Yet if I were Pharaoh I would let these people go, for without doubt their god has much power and I tell you that I fear them."

"Why will he not let them go?" I asked. "They are a weakness, not a strength to Egypt, as was shown at the time of the invasion of the Barbarians with whom they sided. Moreover, the value of this rich land of theirs, which they cannot take with them, is greater than that of all their labour."

"I do not know, friend. The matter is one upon which my father keeps his own counsel, even from the Princess Userti. Perhaps it is because he will not change the policy of his father, Rameses; perhaps because he is stiff-necked to those who cross his will. Or it may be that he is held in this path by a madness sent of some god to bring loss and shame on Egypt."

"Then, Prince, all the priests and nobles are mad also, from Count Amenmeses down."

"Where Pharaoh leads priests and nobles follow. The question is, who leads Pharaoh? Here is the temple of these Hebrews; let us enter."

So we descended from the chariot, where, for my part, I would have remained, and walked through the gateway in the surrounding mud wall into the outer court of the temple, which on this the holy seventh day of the Hebrews was full of praying women, who feigned not to see us yet watched us out of the corners of their eyes. Passing through them we came to a doorway, by which we entered another court that was roofed over. Here were many men who murmured as we appeared. They were engaged in listening to a preacher in a white robe, who wore a strange shaped cap and some ornaments on his breast. I knew the man; he was the priest Kohath who had instructed the Prince in so much of the mysteries of the Hebrew faith as he chose to reveal. On seeing us he ceased suddenly in his discourse, uttered some hasty blessing and advanced to greet us.

I waited behind the Prince, thinking it well to watch his back among all those fierce men, and did not hear what the priest said to him, as he whispered in that holy place. Kohath led him forward, to free him from the throng, I thought, till they came to the head of the little temple that was marked by some steps, above which hung a thick and heavy curtain. The Prince, walking on, did not see the lowest of these steps in the gloom, which was deep. His foot caught on it; he fell forward, and to save himself grasped at the curtain where the two halves of it met, and dragged it open, revealing a chamber plain and small beyond, in which was an altar. That was all I had time to see, for next instant a roar of rage rent the air and knives flashed in the gloom.

"The Egyptian defiles the tabernacle!" shouted one. "Drag him out and kill him!" screamed another.

"Friends," said Seti, turning as they surged towards him, "if I have done aught wrong it was by chance——"

He could add no more, seeing that they were on him, or rather on me who had leapt in front of him. Already they had grasped my robes and my hand was on my sword-hilt, when the priest Kohath cried out:

"Men of Israel, are you mad? Would you bring Pharaoh's vengeance on us?"

They halted a little and their spokesman shouted:

"We defy Pharaoh! Our God will protect us from Pharaoh. Drag him forth and kill him beyond the wall!"

Again they began to move, when a man, in whom I recognized Jabez, the uncle of Merapi, called aloud:

"Cease! If this Prince of Egypt has done insult to Jahveh by will and not by chance, it is certain that he will avenge himself upon him. Shall men take the judgment of God into their own hands? Stand back and wait awhile. If Jahveh is affronted, the Egyptian will fall dead. If he does not fall dead, let him pass hence unharmed, for such is Jahveh's will. Stand back, I say, while I count threescore."

They withdrew a space and slowly Jabez began to count.

Although at that time I knew nothing of the power of the god of Israel, I will say that I was filled with fear as one by one he counted, pausing at each ten. The scene was very strange. There by the steps stood the Prince against the background of the curtain, his arms folded and a little smile of wonder mixed with contempt upon his face, but not a sign of fear. On one side of him was I, who knew well that I should share his fate whatever it might be, and indeed desired no other; and on the other the priest Kohath, whose hands shook and whose eyes started from his head. In front of us old Jabez counted, watching the fierce-faced congregation that in a dead silence waited for the issue. The count went on. Thirty. Forty. Fifty— oh! it seemed an age.

At length sixty fell from his lips. He waited a while and all watched the Prince, not doubting but that he would fall dead. But instead he turned to Kohath and asked quietly if this ordeal was now finished, as he desired to make an offering to the temple, which he had been invited to visit, and begone.

"Our God has given his answer," said Jabez. "Accept it, men of Israel. What this Prince did he did by chance, not of design."

They turned and went without a word, and after I had laid the offering, no mean one, in the appointed place, we followed them.

"It would seem that yours is no gentle god," said the Prince to Kohath, when at length we were outside the temple.

"At least he is just, your Highness. Had it been otherwise, you who had violated his sanctuary, although by chance, would ere now be dead."

"Then you hold, Priest, that Jahveh has power to slay us when he is angry?"

"Without a doubt, your Highness—as, if our Prophets speak truth, I think that Egypt will learn ere all be done," he added grimly.

Seti looked at him and answered:

"It may be so, but all gods, or their priests, claim the power to torment and slay those who worship other gods. It is not only women who are jealous, Kohath, or so it seems. Yet I think that you do your god injustice, seeing that even if this strength is his, he proved more merciful than his worshippers who knew well that I only grasped the veil to save myself from falling. If ever I visit your temple again it shall be in the company of those who can match might against might, whether of the spirit or the sword. Farewell."

So we reached the chariot, near to which stood Jabez, he who had saved us.

"Prince," he whispered, glancing at the crowd who lingered not far away, silent and glowering, "I pray you leave this land swiftly for here your life is not safe. I know it was by chance, but you have defiled the sanctuary and seen that upon which eyes may not look save those of the highest priests, an offence no Israelite can forgive."

"And you, or your people, Jabez, would have defiled this sanctuary of my life, spilling my heart's blood and *not* by chance. Surely you are a strange folk who seek to make an enemy of one who has tried to be your friend."

"I do not seek it," exclaimed Jabez. "I would that we might have Pharaoh's mouth and ear who soon will himself be Pharaoh upon our side. O Prince of Egypt, be not wroth with all the children of Israel because their wrongs have made some few of them stubborn and hard-hearted. Begone now, and of your goodness remember my words."

"I will remember," said Seti, signing to the charioteer to drive on.

Yet still the Prince lingered in the town, saying that he feared nothing and would learn all he could of this people and their ways that he might report the better of them to Pharaoh. For my part I believed that there was one face which he wished to see again before he left, but of this I thought it wise to say nothing.

At length about midday we did depart, and drove eastwards on the track of Amenmeses and our company. All the afternoon we drove thus, preceded by the two soldiers disguised as runners and followed, as a distant cloud of dust told me, by the captain and his chariots, whom I had secretly commanded to keep us in sight.

Towards evening we came to the pass in the story hills which bounded the land of Goshen. Here Seti descended from the chariot, and we climbed, accompanied by the two soldiers whom I signed to follow us, to the crest of one of these hills that was strewn with huge boulders and lined with ridges of sandstone, between which gullies had been cut by the winds of thousands of years.

Leaning against one of these ridges we looked back upon a wondrous sight. Far away across the fertile plain appeared the town that we had left, and behind it the sun sank. It would seem as though some storm had broken there, although the firmament above us was clear and blue. At least in front of the town two huge pillars of cloud stretched from earth to heaven like the columns of some mighty gateway. One of these pillars was as though it were made of black marble, and the other like to molten gold. Between them ran a road of light ending in a glory, and in the midst of the glory the round ball of Ra, the Sun, burned like the eye of God. The spectacle was as awesome as it was splendid.

"Have you ever seen such a sky in Egypt, Prince?" I asked.

"Never," he answered, and although he spoke low, in that great stillness his voice sounded loud to me.

For a while longer we watched, till suddenly the sun sank, and only the glory about it and above remained, which took shapes like to the palaces and temples of a city in the heavens, a far city that no mortal could reach except in dreams.

"I know not why, Ana," said Seti, "but for the first time since I was a man I feel afraid. It seems to me that there are omens in the sky and I cannot read them. Would that Ki were here to tell us what is signified by the pillar of blackness to the right and the pillar of fire to the left, and what god has his home in the city of glory behind, and how man's feet may walk along the shining road which leads to its pylon gates. I tell you that I am afraid; it is as though Death were very near to me and all his wonders open to my mortal sight."

"I too am afraid," I whispered. "Look! The pillars move. That of fire goes before; that of black cloud follows after, and between them I seem to see a countless multitude marching in unending companies. See how the light glitters on their spears! Surely the god of the Hebrews is afoot."

"He, or some other god, or no god at all, who knows? Come, Ana, let us be going if we would reach that camp ere dark."

So we descended from the ridge, and re-entering the chariot, drove on towards the neck of the pass. Now this neck was very narrow, not more than four paces wide for a certain distance, and, on either side of the roadway were tumbled sandstone boulders, between which grew desert plants, and gullies that had been cut by storm-water, while beyond these rose the sides of the mountain. Here the horses went at a walk towards a turn in the path, at which point the land began to fall again.

When we were about half a spear's throw from this turn of a sudden I heard a sound and, glancing to the right, perceived a woman leaping down the hillside towards us. The charioteer saw also and halted the horses, and the two runner guards turned and drew their swords. In less than half a minute the woman had reached us, coming out of the shadow so that the light fell upon her face.

"Merapi!" exclaimed the Prince and I, speaking as though with one breath.

Merapi it was indeed, but in evil case. Her long hair had broken loose and fell about her, the cloak she wore was torn, and there were blood and foam upon her lips. She stood gasping, since speak she could not for breathlessness, supporting herself with one hand upon the side of the chariot and with the other pointing to the bend in the road. At last a word came, one only. It was:

"Murder!"

"She means that she is going to be murdered," said the Prince to me.

"No," she panted, "you—you! The Hebrews. Go back!"

"Turn the horses!" I cried to the charioteer.

He began to obey helped by the two guards, but because of the narrowness of the road and the steepness of the banks this was not easy. Indeed they were but half round in such fashion that they blocked the pathway from side to side, when a wild yell of 'Jahveh' broke upon our ears, and from round the bend, a few paces away, rushed a horde of fierce, hook-nosed men, brandishing knives and swords. Scarcely was there time for us to leap behind the shelter of the chariot and make ready, when they were on us.

"Hearken," I said to the charioteer as they came, "run as you never ran before, and bring up the guard behind!"

He sprang away like an arrow.

"Get back, Lady," cried Seti. "This is no woman's work, and see here comes Laban to seek you," and he pointed with his sword at the leader of the murderers.

She obeyed, staggering a few paces to a stone at the roadside, behind which she crouched. Afterwards she told me that she had no strength to go further, and indeed no will, since if we were killed, it were better that she who had warned us should be killed also.

Now they had reached us, the whole flood of them, thirty or forty men. The first who came stabbed the frightened horses, and down they went against the bank, struggling. On the chariot leapt the Hebrews, seeking to come at us, and we met them as best we might, tearing off our cloaks and throwing them over our left arms to serve as shields.

Oh! what a fight was that. In the open, or had we not been prepared, we must have been slain at once, but, as it was, the place and the barrier of the chariot gave us some advantage. So narrow was the roadway, the walls of which were here too steep to climb, that not more than four of the Hebrews could strike at us at once, which four must first surmount the chariot or the still living horses.

But we also were four, and thanks to Userti, two of us were clad in mail beneath our robes—four strong men fighting for their lives. Against us came four of the Hebrews. One leapt from the chariot straight at Seti, who received him upon the point of his iron sword, whereof I heard the hilt ring against his breast-bone, that same famous iron sword which to-day lies buried with him in his grave.

Down he came dead, throwing the Prince to the ground by the weight of his body. The Hebrew who attacked me caught his foot on the chariot pole and fell forward, so I killed him easily with a blow upon the head, which gave me time to drag the Prince to his feet again before another followed. The two guards also, sturdy fighters both of them, killed or mortally wounded their men. But others were pressing behind so thick and fast that I could keep no count of all that happened afterwards.

Presently I saw one of the guards fall, slain by Laban. A stab on the breast sent me reeling backwards; had it not been for that mail I was sped. The other guard killed him who would have killed me, and then himself was killed by two who came on him at once.

Now only the Prince and I were left, fighting back to back. He closed with one man, a very great fellow, and wounded him on the hand, so that he dropped his sword. This man gripped him round the middle and they rolled together on the ground. Laban appeared and stabbed the Prince in the back, but the curved knife he was using snapped on the Syrian mail. I struck at Laban and wounded him on the head, dazing him so that he staggered back and seemed to fall over the chariot. Then others rushed at me, and but for Userti's armour three times at least I must have died. Fighting madly, I staggered against the rock, and whilst waiting for a new onset, saw that Seti, hurt by Laban's thrust, was now beneath the great Hebrew who had him by the throat, and was choking the life out of him.

I saw something else also—a woman holding a sword with both hands and stabbing downward, after which the grip of the Hebrew loosened from Seti's throat.

"Traitress!" cried one, and struck at her, so that she reeled back hurt. Then when all seemed finished, and beneath the rain of blows my senses were failing, I heard the thunder of horses' hoofs and the shout of *"Egypt! Egypt!"* from the throats of soldiers. The flash of bronze caught my dazed eyes, and with the roar of battle in my ears I seemed to fall asleep just as the light of day departed.

CHAPTER 8

Seti Counsels Pharaoh

Dream upon dream. Dreams of voices, dreams of faces, dreams of sunlight and of moonlight and of myself being borne forward, always forward; dreams of shouting crowds, and, above all, dreams of Merapi's eyes looking down on me like two watching stars from heaven. Then at last the awakening, and with it throbs of pain and qualms of sickness.

At first I thought that I was dead and lying in a tomb. Then by degrees I saw that I was in no tomb but in a darkened room that was familiar to me, my own room in Seti's palace at Tanis. It must be so, for there, near to the bed on which I lay, was my own chest filled with the manuscripts that I had brought from Memphis. I tried to lift my left hand, but could not, and looking down saw that the arm was bandaged like to that of a mummy, which made me think again that I must be dead, if the dead could suffer so much pain. I closed my eyes and thought or slept a while.

As I lay thus I heard voices. One of them seemed to be that of a physician, who said, "Yes, he will live and ere long recover. The blow upon the head which has made him senseless for so many days was the worst of his wounds, but the bone was but bruised, not shattered or driven in upon the brain. The flesh cuts on his arms are healing well, and the mail he wore protected his vitals from being pierced."

"I am glad, physician," answered a voice that I knew to be that of Userti, "since without a doubt, had it not been for Ana, his Highness would have perished. It is strange that one whom I thought to be nothing but a dreaming scribe should have shown himself so brave a warrior. The Prince says that this Ana killed three of those dogs with his own hands, and wounded others."

"It was well done, your Highness," answered the physician, "but still better was his forethought in providing a rear-guard and in despatching the charioteer to call it up. It seems to have been the Hebrew lady who really saved the life of his Highness, when, forgetting her sex, she stabbed the murderer who had him by the throat."

"That is the Prince's tale, or so I understand," she answered coldly. "Yet it seems strange that a weak and worn-out girl could have pierced a giant through from back to breast."

"At least she warned him of the ambush, your Highness."

"So they say. Perhaps Ana here will soon tell us the truth about these matters. Tend him well, physician, and you shall not lack for your reward."

Then they went away, still talking, and I lay quiet, filled with thankfulness and wonder, for now everything came back to me.

A while later, as I lay with my eyes still shut, for even that low light seemed to hurt them, I became aware of a woman's soft step stealing round my bed and of a fragrance such as comes from a woman's robes and hair. I looked and saw Merapi's star-like eyes gazing down on me just as I had seen them in my dreams.

"Greeting, Moon of Israel," I said. "Of a truth we meet again in strange case."

"Oh!" she whispered, "are you awake at last? I thank God, Scribe Ana, who for three days thought that you must die."

"As, had it not been for you, Lady, surely I should have done—I and another. Now it seems that all three of us will live."

"Would that but two lived, the Prince and you, Ana. Would that *I* had died," she answered, sighing heavily.

"Why?"

"Cannot you guess? Because I am outcast who has betrayed my people. Because their blood flows between me and them. For I killed that man, and he was my own kinsman, for the sake of an Egyptian—I mean, Egyptians. Therefore the curse of Jahveh is on me, and as my kinsman died doubtless I shall die in a day to come, and afterwards—what?"

"Afterwards peace and great reward, if there be justice in earth or heaven, O most noble among women."

"Would that I could think so! Hush, I hear steps. Drink this; I am the chief of your nurses, Scribe Ana, an honourable post, since to-day all Egypt loves and praises you."

"Surely it is you, lady Merapi, whom all Egypt should love and praise," I answered.

Then the Prince Seti entered. I strove to salute him by lifting my less injured arm, but he caught my hand and pressed it tenderly.

"Hail to you, beloved of Menthu, god of war," he said, with his pleasant laugh. "I thought I had hired a scribe, and lo! in this scribe I find a soldier who might be an army's boast."

At this moment he caught sight of Merapi, who had moved back into the shadow.

"Hail to you also, Moon of Israel," he said bowing. "If I name Ana here a warrior of the best, what name can both of us find for you to whom we owe our lives? Nay, look not down, but answer."

"Prince of Egypt," she replied confusedly, "I did but little. The plot came to my ears through Jabez my uncle, and I fled away and, knowing the short paths from childhood, was just in time. Had I stayed to think perchance I should not have dared."

"And what of the rest, Lady? What of the Hebrew who was choking me and of a certain sword thrust that loosed his hands for ever?"

"Of that, your Highness, I can recall nothing, or very little," then, doubtless remembering what she had just said to me, she made obeisance and passed from the chamber.

"She can tell falsehoods as sweetly as she does all else," said Seti, when he had watched her go. "Oh! what a woman have we here, Ana. Perfect in beauty, perfect in courage, perfect in mind. Where are her faults, I wonder? Let it be your part to search them out, since I find none."

"Ask them of Ki, O Prince. He is a very great magician, so great that perhaps his art may even avail to discover what a woman seeks to hide. Also you may remember that he gave you certain warnings before we journeyed to Goshen."

"Yes—he told me that my life would be in danger, as certainly it was. There he was right. He told me also that I should see a woman whom I should come to love. There he was wrong. I have seen no such woman. Oh! I know well what is passing in your mind. Because I hold the lady Merapi to be beautiful and brave, you think that I love her. But it is not so. I love no woman, except, of course, her Highness. Ana, you judge me by yourself."

"Ki said 'come to love,' Prince. There is yet time."

"Not so, Ana. If one loves, one loves at once. Soon I shall be old and she will be fat and ugly, and how can one love then? Get well quickly, Ana, for I wish you to help me with my report to Pharaoh. I shall tell him that I think these Israelites are much oppressed and that he should make them amends and let them go."

"What will Pharaoh say to that after they have just tried to kill his heir?"

"I think Pharaoh will be angry, and so will the people of Egypt, who do not reason well. He will not see that, believing what they do,

Laban and his band were right to try to kill me who, however unwittingly, desecrated the sanctuary of their god. Had they done otherwise they would have been no good Hebrews, and for my part I cannot bear them malice. Yet all Egypt is afire about this business and cries out that the Israelites should be destroyed."

"It seems to me, Prince, that whatever may be the case with Ki's second prophecy, his third is in the way of fulfilment—namely that this journey to Goshen may cause you to risk your throne."

He shrugged his shoulders and answered:

"Not even for that, Ana, will I say to Pharaoh what is not in my mind. But let that matter be till you are stronger."

"What chanced at the end of the fight, Prince, and how came I here?"

"The guard killed most of the Hebrews who remained alive. Some few fled and escaped in the darkness, among them Laban their leader, although you had wounded him, and six were taken alive. They await their trial. I was but little hurt and you, whom we thought dead, were but senseless, and senseless or wandering you have remained till this hour. We carried you in a litter, and here you have been these three days."

"And the lady Merapi?"

"We set her in a chariot and brought her to the city, since had we left her she would certainly have been murdered by her people. When Pharaoh heard what she had done, as I did not think it well that she should dwell here, he gave her the small house in this garden that she might be guarded, and with it slave women to attend upon her. So there she dwells, having the freedom of the palace, and all the while has filled the office of your nurse."

At this moment I grew faint and shut my eyes. When I opened them again, the Prince had gone. Six more days went by before I was allowed to leave my bed, and during this time I saw much of Merapi. She was very sad and lived in fear of being killed by the Hebrews. Also she was troubled in her heart because she thought she had betrayed her faith and people. "At least you are rid of Laban," I said.

"Never shall I be rid of him while we both live," she answered. "I belong to him and he will not loose my bond, because his heart is set on me."

"And is your heart set on him?" I asked.

Her beautiful eyes filled with tears.

"A woman may not have a heart. Oh! Ana, I am unhappy," she answered, and went away.

Also I saw others. The Princess came to visit me. She thanked me much because I had fulfilled my promise to her and guarded the Prince. Moreover she brought me a gift of gold from Pharaoh, and other gifts of fine raiment from herself. She questioned me closely about Merapi, of whom I could see she was already jealous, and was glad when she learned that she was affianced to a Hebrew. Old Bakenkhonsu came too, and asked me many things about the Prince, the Hebrews and Merapi, especially Merapi, of whose deeds, he said, all Egypt was talking, questions that I answered as best I could.

"Here we have that woman of whom Ki told us," he said, "she who shall bring so much joy and so much sorrow to the Prince of Egypt."

"Why so?" I asked. "He has not taken her into his house, nor do I think that he means to do so."

"Yet he will, Ana, whether he means it or not. For his sake she betrayed her people, which among the Israelites is a deadly crime. Twice she saved his life, once by warning him of the ambush, and again by stabbing with her own hands one of her kinsmen who was murdering him. Is it not so? Tell me; you were there."

"It is so, but what then?"

"This: that whatever she may say, she loves him; unless indeed, it is you whom she loves," and he looked at me shrewdly.

"When a woman has a prince, and such a prince to her hand, would she trouble herself to set snares to catch a scribe?" I asked, with some bitterness.

"Oho!" he said, with one of his great laughs, "so things stand thus, do they? Well, I thought it, but, friend Ana, be warned in time. Do not try to conjure down the Moon to be your household lamp lest she should set, and the Sun, her lord, should grow wroth and burn you up. Well, she loves him, and therefore soon or late she will make him love her, being what she is."

"How, Bakenkhonsu?"

"With most men, Ana, it would be simple. A sigh, some half-hidden tears at the right moment, and the thing is done, as I have known it done a thousand times. But this prince being what he is, it may be otherwise. She may show him that her name is gone from him; that because of him she is hated by her people, and rejected by her god, and thus stir his pity, which is Love's own sister. Or mayhap, being also, as I am told, wise, she will give him counsel as to all these matters of the Israelites, and thus creep into his heart under the guise of friendship, and then her sweetness and her beauty will do the rest in Nature's way. At least by this road or by that, upstream or downstream, thither she will come."

"If so, what of it? It is the custom of the kings of Egypt to have more wives than one."

"This, Ana; Seti, I think, is a man who in truth will have but one, and that one will be this Hebrew. Yes, a Hebrew woman will rule Egypt, and turn him to the worship of her god, for never will she worship ours. Indeed, when they see that she is lost to them, her people will use her thus. Or perchance her god himself will use her to fulfil his purpose, as already he may have used her."

"And afterwards, Bakenkhonsu?"

"Afterwards—who knows? I am not a magician, at least not one of any account, ask it of Ki. But I am very, very old and I have watched the world, and I tell you that these things will happen, unless——" and he paused.

"Unless what?"

He dropped his voice.

"Unless Userti is bolder than I think, and kills her first or, better still, procures some Hebrew to kill her—say, that cast-off lover of hers. If you would be a friend to Pharaoh and to Egypt, you might whisper it in her ear, Ana."

"Never!" I answered angrily.

"I did not think you would, Ana, who also struggle in this net of moonbeams that is stronger and more real than any twisted out of palm or flax. Well, nor will I, who in my age love to watch such human sport and, being so near to them, fear to thwart the schemes of gods. Let this scroll unroll itself as it will, and when it is open, read it, Ana, and remember what I said to you this day. It will be a pretty tale, written at the end with blood for ink. Oho! O-ho-ho!" and, laughing, he hobbled from the room, leaving me frightened.

Moreover the Prince visited me every day, and even before I left my bed began to dictate to me his report to Pharaoh, since he would employ no other scribe. The substance of it was what he had foreshadowed, namely that the people of Israel, having suffered much for generations at the hands of the Egyptians, should now be allowed to depart as their prophets demanded, and go whither they would unharmed. Of the attack upon us in the pass he made light, saying it was the evil work of a few zealots wrought on by fancied insult to their god, a deed for which the whole people should not be called upon to suffer. The last words of the report were:

"Remember, O Pharaoh, I pray thee, that Amon, god of the Egyptians, and Jahveh, the god of the Israelites, cannot rule together in the same land. If both abide in Egypt there will be a war of the gods wherein mortals may be ground to dust. Therefore, I pray thee, let Israel go."

After I had risen and was recovered, I copied out this report in my fairest writing, refusing to tell any of its purport, although all asked, among them the Vizier Nehesi, who offered me a bribe to disclose its secret. This came to the ears of Seti, I know not how, and he was much pleased with me about the matter, saying he rejoiced to find that there was one scribe in Egypt who could not be bought. Userti also questioned me, and when I refused to answer, strange to say, was not angry, because, she declared, I only did my duty.

At last the roll was finished and sealed, and the Prince with his own hand, but without speaking, laid it on the knees of Pharaoh at a public Court, for this he would trust no one else to do. Amenmeses also brought up his report, as did Nehesi the Vizier, and the Captain of the guard which saved us from death. Eight days later the Prince was summoned to a great Council of State, as were all others of the royal House, together with the high officers. I too received a summons, as one who had been concerned in these matters.

The Prince, accompanied by the Princess, drove to the palace in Pharaoh's golden chariot, drawn by two milk-white horses of the blood of those famous steeds that had saved the life of the great Rameses in the Syrian war. All down the streets, that were filled with thousands of the people, they were received with shouts of welcome.

"See," said the old councillor Bakenkhonsu, who was my companion in a second chariot, "Egypt is proud and glad. It thought that its Prince was but a dreamer of dreams. But now it has heard the tale of the ambush in the pass and learned that he is a man of war, a warrior who can fight with the best. Therefore it loves him and rejoices."

"Then, by the same rule, Bakenkhonsu, a butcher should be more great than the wisest of scribes."

"So he is, Ana, especially if the butcher be one of men. The writer creates, but the slayer kills, and in a world ruled of death he who kills has more honour than he who creates. Hearken, now they are shouting out your name. Is that because you are the author of certain writings? I tell you, No. It is because you killed three men yonder in the pass. If you would become famous and beloved, Ana, cease from the writing of books and take to the cutting of throats."

"Yet the writer still lives when he is dead."

"Oho!" laughed Bakenkhonsu, "you are even more foolish than I thought. How is a man advantaged by what happens when he is dead? Why, to-day that blind beggar whining on the temple steps means more to Egypt than all the mummies of all the Pharaohs, unless they can be robbed. Take what life can give you, Ana, and do not trouble about the offerings which are laid in the tombs for time to crumble."

"That is a mean faith, Bakenkhonsu."

"Very mean, Ana, like all else that we can taste and handle. A mean faith suited to mean hearts, among whom should be reckoned all save one in every thousand. Yet, if you would prosper, follow it, and when you are dead I will come and laugh upon your grave, and say, 'Here lies one of whom I had hoped higher things, as I hope them of your master.'"

"And not in vain, Bakenkhonsu, whatever may happen to the servant."

"That we shall learn, and ere long, I think. I wonder who will ride at his side before the next Nile flood. By then, perchance, he will have changed Pharaoh's golden chariot for an ox-cart, and you will goad the oxen and talk to him of the stars—or, mayhap of the moon. Well, you might both be happier thus, and she of the moon is a jealous goddess who loves worship. Oho-ho! Here are the palace steps. Help me to descend, Priest of the Lady of the Moon."

We entered the palace and were led through the great hall to a smaller chamber where Pharaoh, who did not wear his robes of state, awaited us, seated in a cedar chair. Glancing at him I saw that his face was stern and troubled; also it seemed to me that he had grown older. The Prince and Princess made obeisance to him, as did we lesser folk, but he took no heed. When all were present and the doors had been shut, Pharaoh said:

"I have read your report, Son Seti, concerning your visit to the Israelites, and all that chanced to you; and also the reports of you, nephew Amenmeses, and of you, Officers, who accompanied the Prince of Egypt. Before I speak of them, let the Scribe Ana, who was the chariot companion of his Highness when the Hebrews attacked him, stand forward and tell me all that passed."

So I advanced, and with bowed head repeated that tale, only leaving out so far as was possible any mention of myself. When I had finished, Pharaoh said:

"He who speaks but half the truth is sometimes more mischievous than a liar. Did you then sit in the chariot, Scribe, doing nothing while the Prince battled for his life? Or did you run away? Speak, Seti, and say what part this man played for good or ill."

Then the Prince told of my share in the fight, with words that brought the blood to my brow. He told also how that it was I who,

334

taking the risk of his wrath, had ordered the guard of twenty men to follow us unseen, had disguised two seasoned soldiers as chariot runners, and had thought to send back the driver to summon help at the commencement of the fray; how I had been hurt also, and was but lately recovered. When he had finished, Pharaoh said:

"That this story is true I know from others. Scribe, you have done well. But for you to-day his Highness would lie upon the table of the embalmers, as indeed for his folly he deserves to do, and Egypt would mourn from Thebes to the mouths of Nile. Come hither."

I came with trembling steps, and knelt before his Majesty. Around his neck hung a beauteous chain of wrought gold. He took it, and cast it over my head, saying:

"Because you have shown yourself both brave and wise, with this gold I give you the title of Councillor and King's Companion, and the right to inscribe the same upon your funeral stele. Let it be noted. Retire, Scribe Ana, Councillor and King's Companion."

So I withdrew confused, and as I passed Seti, he whispered in my ear:

"I pray you, my lord, do not cease to be Prince's Companion, because you have become that of the King."

Then Pharaoh ordered that the Captain of the guard should be advanced in rank, and that gifts should be given to each of the soldiers, and provision be made for the children of those who had been killed, with double allowance to the families of the two men whom I had disguised as runners.

This done, once more Pharaoh spoke, slowly and with much meaning, having first ordered that all attendants and guards should leave the chamber. I was about to go also, but old Bakenkhonsu caught me by the robe, saying that in my new rank of Councillor I had the right to remain.

"Prince Seti," he said, "after all that I have heard, I find this report of yours strange reading. Moreover, the tenor of it is different indeed to that of those of the Count Amenmeses and the officers. You counsel me to let these Israelites go where they will, because of certain hardships that they have suffered in the past, which hardships, however, have left them many and rich. That counsel I am not minded to take. Rather am I minded to send an army to the land of Goshen with orders to despatch this people, who conspired to murder the Prince of Egypt, through the Gateway of the West, there to worship their god in heaven or in hell. Aye, to slay them all from the greybeard down to the suckling at the breast."

"I hear Pharaoh," said Seti, quietly.

"Such is my will," went on Meneptah, "and those who accompanied you upon your business, and all my councillors think as I do, for truly Egypt cannot bear so hideous a treason. Yet, according to our law and custom it is needful, before such great acts of war and policy are undertaken, that he who stands next to the throne, and is destined to fill it, should give consent thereto. Do you consent, Prince of Egypt?"

"I do not consent, Pharaoh. I think it would be a wicked deed that tens of thousands should be massacred for the reason that a few fools waylaid a man who chanced to be of royal blood, because by inadvertence, he had desecrated their sanctuary."

Now I saw that this answer made Pharaoh wroth, for never before had his will been crossed in such a fashion. Still he controlled himself, and asked:

"Do you then consent, Prince, to a gentler sentence, namely that the Hebrew people should be broken up; that the more dangerous of them should be sent to labour in the desert mines and quarries, and the rest distributed throughout Egypt, there to live as slaves?"

"I do not consent, Pharaoh. My poor counsel is written in yonder roll and cannot be changed."

Meneptah's eyes flashed, but again he controlled himself, and asked:

"If you should come to fill this place of mine, Prince Seti, tell us, here assembled, what policy will you pursue towards these Hebrews?"

"That policy, O Pharaoh, which I have counselled in the roll. If ever I fill the throne, I shall let them go whither they will, taking their goods with them."

Now all those present stared at him and murmured. But Pharaoh rose, shaking with wrath. Seizing his robe where it was fastened at the breast, he rent it, and cried in a terrible voice:

"Hear him, ye gods of Egypt! Hear this son of mine who defies me to my face and would set your necks beneath the heel of a stranger god. Prince Seti, in the presence of these royal ones, and these my councillors, I——"

He said no more, for the Princess Userti, who till now had remained silent, ran to him, and throwing her arms about him, began to whisper in his ear. He hearkened to her, then sat himself down, and spoke again:

"The Princess brings it to my mind that this is a great matter, one not to be dealt with hastily. It may happen that when the Prince has taken counsel with her, and with his own heart, and perchance has sought the wisdom of the gods, he will change the words which have passed his lips. I command you, Prince, to wait upon me here at this same hour on the third day from this. Meanwhile, I command all present, upon pain of death, to say nothing of what has passed within these walls."

"I hear Pharaoh," said the Prince, bowing.

Meneptah rose to show that the Council was discharged, when the Vizier Nehesi approached him, and asked:

"What of the Hebrew prisoners, O Pharaoh, those murderers who were captured in the pass?"

"Their guilt is proved. Let them be beaten with rods till they die, and if they have wives or children, let them be seized and sold as slaves."

"Pharaoh's will be done!" said the Vizier.

CHAPTER 9

The Smiting of Amon

That evening I sat ill at ease in my work-chamber in Seti's palace, making pretence to write, I who felt that great evils threatened my lord the Prince, and knew not what to do to turn them from him. The door opened, and old Pambasa the chamberlain appeared and addressed me by my new titles, saying that the Hebrew lady Merapi, who had been my nurse in sickness, wished to speak with me. Presently she came and stood before me.

"Scribe Ana," she said, "I have but just seen my uncle Jabez, who has come, or been sent, with a message to me," and she hesitated.

"Why was he sent, Lady? To bring you news of Laban?"

"Not so. Laban has fled away and none know where he is, and Jabez has only escaped much trouble as the uncle of a traitress by undertaking this mission."

"What is the mission?"

"To pray me, if I would save myself from death and the vengeance of God, to work upon the heart of his Highness, which I know not how to do——"

"Yet I think you might find means, Merapi."

"——save through you, his friend and counsellor," she went on, turning away her face. "Jabez has learned that it is in the mind of Pharaoh utterly to destroy the people of Israel."

"How does he know that, Merapi?"

"I cannot say, but I think all the Hebrews know. I knew it myself though none had told me. He has learned also that this cannot be done under the law of Egypt unless the Prince who is heir to the throne and of full age consents. Now I am come to pray you to pray the Prince not to consent."

"Why not pray to the Prince yourself, Merapi——" I began, when from the shadows behind me I heard the voice of Seti, who had entered by the private door bearing some writings in his hand, saying:

"And what prayer has the lady Merapi to make to me? Nay, rise and speak, Moon of Israel."

"O Prince," she pleaded, "my prayer is that you will save the Hebrews from death by the sword, as you alone have the power to do."

At this moment the doors opened and in swept the royal Userti.

"What does this woman here?" she asked.

"I think that she came to see Ana, wife, as I did, and as doubtless you do. Also being here she prays me to save her people from the sword."

"And I pray you, husband, to give her people to the sword, which they have earned, who would have murdered you."

"And been paid, everyone of them, Userti, unless some still linger beneath the rods," he added with a shudder. "The rest are innocent—why should they die?"

"Because your throne hangs upon it, Seti. I say that if you continue to thwart the will of Pharaoh, as by the law of Egypt you can do, he will disinherit you and set your cousin Amenmeses in your place, as by the law of Egypt he can do."

"I thought it, Userti. Yet why should I turn my back upon the right over a matter of my private fortunes? The question is—is it the right?"

She stared at him in amazement, she who never understood Seti and could not dream that he would throw away the greatest throne in all the world to save a subject people, merely because he thought that they should not die. Still, warned by some instinct, she left the first question unanswered, dealing only with the second.

"It is the right," she said, "for many reasons whereof I need give but one, for in it lie all the others. The gods of Egypt are the true gods whom we must serve and obey, or perish here and hereafter. The god of the Israelites is a false god and those who worship him are heretics and by their heresy under sentence of death. Therefore it is most right that those whom the true gods have condemned should die by the swords of their servants."

"That is well argued, Userti, and if it be so, mayhap my mind will become as yours in this matter, so that I shall no longer stand between Pharaoh and his desire. But is it so? There's the problem. I will not ask you why you say that the gods of the Egyptians are the true gods, because I know what you would answer, or rather that you could give no answer. But I will ask this lady whether her god is a false god, and if she replies that he is not, I will ask her to prove this to me if she can. If she is able to prove it, then I think that what I said to Pharaoh to-day I shall repeat three days hence. If she is not able to prove it, then I shall consider very earnestly of the matter. Answer now, Moon of Israel, remembering that many thousands of lives may hang on what you say."

"O your Highness," began Merapi. Then she paused, clasped her hands and looked upwards. I think that she was praying, for her lips moved. As she stood thus I saw, and I think Seti saw also, a very wonderful light grow on her face and gather in her eyes, a kind of divine fire of inspiration and resolve.

"How can I, a poor Hebrew maiden, prove to your Highness that my God is the true God and that the gods of Egypt are false gods? I know not, and yet, is there any one god among all the many whom you worship, whom you are prepared to set up against him?"

"Of a surety, Israelite," answered Userti. "There is Amon-Ra, Father of the gods, of whom all other gods have their being, and from whom they draw their strength. Yonder his statue sits in the sanctuary of his ancient temple. Let your god stir him from his place! But what will you bring forward against the majesty of Amon-Ra?"

"My God has no statues, Princess, and his place is in the hearts of men, or so I have been taught by his prophets. I have nothing to bring forward in this war save that which must be offered in all wars—my life."

"What do you mean?" asked Seti, astounded.

"I mean that I, unfriended and alone, will enter the presence of Amon-Ra in his chosen sanctuary, and in the name of my God will challenge him to kill me, if he can."

We stared at her, and Userti exclaimed:

"If he can! Hearken now to this blasphemer, and do you, Seti, accept her challenge as hereditary high-priest of the god Amon? Let her life pay forfeit for her sacrilege."

"And if the great god Amon cannot, or does not deign to kill you, Lady, how will that prove that your god is greater than he?" asked the Prince. "Perhaps he might smile and in his pity, let the insult pass, as your god did by me."

"Thus it shall be proved, your Highness. If naught happens to me, or if I am protected from anything that does happen, then I will dare to call upon my god to work a sign and a wonder, and to humble Amon-Ra before your eyes."

"And if your god should also smile and let the matter pass, Lady, as he did by me the other day when his priests called upon him, what shall we have learned as to his strength, or as to that of Amon-Ra?"

"O Prince, you will have learned nothing. Yet if I escape from the wrath of Amon and my God is deaf to my prayer, then I am ready to be delivered over into the hands of the priests of Amon that they may avenge my sacrilege upon me."

"There speaks a great heart," said Seti; "yet I am not minded that this lady should set her life upon such an issue. I do not believe that either the high-god of Egypt or the god of the Israelites will stir, but I am quite sure that the priests of Amon will avenge the sacrilege, and that cruelly enough. The dice are loaded against you, Lady. You shall not prove your faith with blood."

"Why not?" asked Userti. "What is this girl to you, Seti, that you should stand between her and the fruit of her wickedness, you who at least in name are the high-priest of the god whom she blasphemes and who wear his robes at temple feasts? She believes in her god, leave it to her god to help her as she has dared to say he will."

"You believe in Amon, Userti. Are you prepared to stake your life against hers in this contest?"

"I am not so mad and vain, Seti, as to believe that the god of all the world will descend from heaven to save me at my prayer, as this impious girl pretends that she believes."

"You refuse. Then, Ana, what say you, who are a loyal worshipper of Amon?"

"I say, O Prince, that it would be presumptuous of me to take precedence of his high-priest in such a matter."

Seti smiled and answered:

"And the high-priest says that it would be presumptuous of him to push so far the prerogative of a high office which he never sought."

"Your Highness," broke in Merapi in her honeyed, pleading voice, "I pray you to be gracious to me, and to suffer me to make this trial, which I have sought, I know not why. Words such as I have spoken cannot be recalled. Already they are registered in the books of Eternity, and soon or late, in this way or in that, must be fulfilled. My life is staked, and I desire to learn at once if it be forfeit."

Now even Userti looked on her with admiration, but answered only:

"Of a truth, Israelite, I trust that this courage will not forsake you when you are handed over to the mercies of Ki, the Sacrificer of Amon, and the priests, in the vaults of the temple you would profane."

"I also trust that it will not, your Highness, if such should be my fate. Your word, Prince of Egypt."

Seti looked at her standing before him so calmly with bowed head, and hands crossed upon her breast. Then he looked at Userti, who wore a mocking smile upon her face. She read the meaning of that smile as I did. It was that she did not believe that he would allow this beautiful woman, who had saved his life, to risk her life for the sake of any or all the powers of heaven or hell. For a little while he walked to and fro about the chamber, then he stopped and said suddenly addressing, not Merapi, but Userti:

"Have your will, remembering that if this brave woman fails and dies, her blood is on your hands, and that if she triumphs and lives, I shall hold her to be one of the noblest of her sex, and shall make study of all this matter of religion. Moon of Israel, as titular high-priest of Amon-Ra, I accept your challenge on behalf of the god, though whether he will take note of it I do not know. The trial shall be made to-morrow night in the sanctuary of the temple, at an hour that will be communicated to you. I shall be present to make sure that you meet with justice, as will some others. Register my commands, Scribe Ana, and let the head-priest of Amon, Roi, and the sacrificer to Amon, Ki the Magician, be summoned, that I may speak with them. Farewell, Lady."

She went, but at the door turned and said:

"I thank you, Prince, on my own behalf, and on that of my people. Whatever chances, I beseech you do not forget the prayer that I have made to you to save them, being innocent, from the sword. Now I ask that I may be left quite alone till I am summoned to the temple, who must make such preparation as I can to meet my fate, whatever it may be."

Userti departed also without a word.

"Oh! friend, what have I done?" said Seti. "Are there any gods? Tell me, are there any gods?"

"Perhaps we shall learn to-morrow night, Prince," I answered. "At least Merapi thinks that there is a god, and doubtless has been commanded to put her faith to proof. This, as I believe, was the real message that Jabez her uncle has brought to her."

****

It was the hour before the dawn, just when the night is darkest. We stood in the sanctuary of the ancient temple of Amon-Ra, that was lit with many lamps. It was an awful place. On either side the great columns towered to the massive roof. At the head of the sanctuary sat the statue of Amon-Ra, thrice the size of a man. On his brow, rising from the crown, were two tall feathers of stone, and in his hands he held the Scourge of Rule and the symbols of Power and Everlastingness. The lamplight flickered upon his stern and terrible face staring towards the east. To his right was the statue of Mut, the Mother of all things. On her head was the double crown of Egypt and the *uraeus* crest, and in her hand the looped cross, the sign of Life eternal. To his left sat Khonsu, the hawk-headed god of the moon. On his head was the crescent of the young moon carrying the disc of the full moon; in his right hand he also held the looped cross, the sign of Life eternal, and in his left the Staff of Strength. Such was this mighty triad, but of these the greatest was Amon-Ra, to whom the shrine was dedicated. Fearful they stood towering above us against the background of blackness.

Gathered there were Seti the Prince, clothed in a priest's white robe, and wearing a linen headdress, but no ornaments, and Userti the Princess, high-priestess of Hathor, Lady of the West, Goddess of Love and Nature. She wore Hathor's vulture headdress, and on it the disc of the moon fashioned of silver. Also were present Roi the head-priest, clad in his sacerdotal robes, an old and wizened man with a strong, fierce face, Ki the Sacrificer and Magician, Bakenkhonsu the ancient, myself, and a company of the priests of Amon-Ra, Mut, and Khonsu. From behind the statues came the sound of solemn singing, though who sang we could not see.

Presently from out of the darkness that lay beyond the lamps appeared a woman, led by two priestesses and wrapped in a long cloak. They brought her to an open place in front of the statue of Amon, took from her the cloak and departed, glancing back at her with eyes of hate and fear. There before us stood Merapi, clad in white, with a simple wimple about her head made fast beneath her chin with that scarabaeus clasp which Seti had given to her in the city of Goshen, one spot of brightest blue amid a cloud of white. She looked neither to right nor left of her. Once only she glanced at the towering statue of the god that frowned above, then with a little shiver, fixed her eyes upon the pattern of the floor.

"What does she look like?" whispered Bakenkhonsu to me.

"A corpse made ready for the embalmers," I answered.

He shook his great head.

"Then a bride made ready for her husband."

Again he shook his head.

"Then a priestess about to read from the roll of Mysteries."

"Now you have it, Ana, and to understand what she reads, which few priestesses ever do. Also all three answers were right, for in this woman I seem to see doom that is Death, life that is Love, and spirit that is Power. She has a soul which both Heaven and Earth have kissed."

"Aye, but which of them will claim her in the end?"

"That we may learn before the dawn, Ana. Hush! the fight begins."

The head-priest, Roi, advanced and, standing before the god, sprinkled his feet with water and with perfume. Then he stretched out his hands, whereon all present prostrated themselves, save Merapi only, who stood alone in that great place like the survivor of a battle.

"Hail to thee, Amon-Ra," he began, "Lord of Heaven, Establisher of all things, Maker of the gods, who unrolled the skies and built the foundations of the Earth. O god of gods, appears before thee this woman Merapi, daughter of Nathan, a child of the Hebrew race that owns thee not. This woman blasphemes thy might; this woman defies thee; this woman sets up her god above thee. Is it not so, woman?"

"It is so," answered Merapi in a low voice.

"Thus does she defy thee, thou Only One of many Forms, saying 'if the god Amon of the Egyptians be a greater god than my god, let him snatch me out of the arms of my god and here in this the shrine of Amon take the breath from out my lips and leave me a thing of clay.' Are these thy words, O woman?"

"They are my words," she said in the same low voice, and oh! I shivered as I heard.

The priest went on.

"O Lord of Time, Lord of Life, Lord of Spirits and the Divinities of Heaven, Lord of Terror, come forth now in thy majesty and smite this blasphemer to the dust."

Roi withdrew and Seti stood forward.

"Know, O god Amon," he said, addressing the statue as though he wee speaking to a living man, "from the lips of me, thy high-priest, by birth the Prince and Heir of Egypt, that great things hang upon this matter here in the Land of Egypt, mayhap even who shall sit upon the throne that thou givest to its kings. This woman of Israel dares thee to thy face, saying that there is a greater god than thou art and that thou canst not harm her through the buckler of his strength. She says, moreover, that she will call upon her god to work a sign and a wonder upon thee. Lastly, she says that if thou dost not harm her and if her god works no sign upon thee, then she is ready to be handed over to thy priests and die the death of a blasphemer. Thy honour is set against her life, O great God of Egypt, and we, thy worshippers, watch to see the balance turn."

"Well and justly put," muttered Bakenkhonsu to me. "Now if Amon fails us, what will you think of Amon, Ana?"

"I shall learn the high-priest's mind and think what the high-priest thinks," I answered darkly, though in my heart I was terribly afraid for Merapi, and, to speak truth, for myself also, because of the doubts which arose in me and would not be quenched.

Seti withdrew, taking his stand by Userti, and Ki stood forward and said:

"O Amon, I thy Sacrificer, I thy Magician, to whom thou givest power, I the priest and servant of Isis, Mother of Mysteries, Queen of the company of the gods, call upon thee. She who stands before thee is but a Hebrew woman. Yet, as thou knowest well, O Father, in this house she is more than woman, inasmuch as she is the Voice and Sword of thine enemy, Jahveh, god of the Israelites. She thinks, mayhap, that she has come here of her own will, but thou knowest, Father Amon, as I know, that she is sent by the great prophets of her people, those magicians who guide her soul with spells to work thee evil and to set thee, Amon, beneath the heel of Jahveh. The stake seems small, the life of this one maid, no more; yet it is very great. This is the stake, O Father: Shall Amon rule the world, or Jahveh. If thou fallest to-night, thou fallest for ever; if thou dost triumph to-night, thou dost triumph for ever. In yonder shape of stone hides thy spirit; in yonder shape of woman's flesh hides the spirit of thy foe. Smite her, O Amon, smite her to small dust; let not the strength that is in her prevail against thy strength, lest thy name should be defiled and sorrows and loss should come upon the land which is thy throne; lest, too, the wizards of the Israelites should overcome us thy servants. Thus prayeth Ki thy magician, on whose soul it has pleased thee to pour strength and wisdom."

Then followed a great silence.

Watching the statue of the god, presently I thought that it moved, and as I could see by the stir among them, so did the others. I thought that its stone eyes rolled, I thought that it lifted the Scourge of Power in its granite hand, though whether these things were done by some spirit or by some priest, or by the magic of Ki, I do not know. At the least, a great wind began to blow about the temple, stirring our robes and causing the lamps to flicker. Only the robes of Merapi did not stir. Yet she saw what I could not see, for suddenly her eyes grew frightened.

"The god is awake," whispered Bakenkhonsu. "Now good-bye to your fair Israelite. See, the Prince trembles, Ki smiles, and the face of Userti glows with triumph."

As he spoke the blue scarabaeus was snatched from Merapi's breast as though by a hand. It fell to the floor as did her wimple, so that now she appeared with her rich hair flowing down her robe. Then the eyes of the statue seemed to cease to roll, the wind ceased to blow, and again there was silence.

Merapi stooped, lifted the wimple, replaced it on her head, found the scarabaeus clasp, and very quietly, as a woman who was tiring herself might do, made it fast in its place again, a sight at which I heard Userti gasp.

For a long while we waited. Watching the faces of the congregation, I saw amazement and doubt on those of the priests, rage on that of Ki, and on Seti's the flicker of a little smile. Merapi's eyes were closed as though she were asleep. At length she opened them, and turning her head towards the Prince said:

"O high-priest of Amon-Ra, has your god worked his will on me, or must I wait longer before I call upon my God?"

"Do what you will or can, woman, and make an end, for almost it is the moment of dawn when the temple worship opens."

Then Merapi clasped her hands, and looking upwards, prayed aloud very sweetly and simply, saying:

"O God of my fathers, trusting in Thee, I, a poor maid of Thy people Israel, have set the life Thou gavest me in Thy Hand. If, as I believe, Thou art the God of gods, I pray Thee show a sign and a wonder upon this god of the Egyptians, and thereby declare Thine Honour and keep my breath within my breast. If it pleases Thee not, then let me die, as doubtless for my many sins I deserve to do. O God of my fathers, I have made my prayer. Hear it or reject it according to Thy Will."

So she ended, and listening to her, I felt the tears rising in my eyes, because she was so much alone, and I feared that this god of hers would never come to save her from the torments of the priests. Seti also turned his head away, and stared down the sanctuary at the sky over the open court where the lights of dawn were gathering.

Once more there was silence. Then again that wind blew, very strongly, extinguishing the lamps, and, as it seemed to me, whirling away Merapi from where she was, so that now she stood to one side of the statue. The sanctuary was filled with gloom, till presently the first rays of the rising sun struck upon the roof. They fell down, down, as minute followed minute, till at length they rested like a sword of flame upon the statue of Amon-Ra. Once more that statue seemed to move. I thought that it lifted its stone arms to protect its head. Then in a moment with a rending noise, its mighty mass burst asunder, and fell in small dust about the throne, almost hiding it from sight.

"Behold my God has answered me, the most humble of His servants," said Merapi in the same sweet and gentle voice. "Behold the sign and the wonder!"

"Witch!" screamed the head-priest Roi, and fled away, followed by his fellows.

"Sorceress!" hissed Userti, and fled also, as did all the others, save the Prince, Bakenkhonsu, I Ana, and Ki the Magician.

We stood amazed, and while we did so, Ki turned to Merapi and spoke. His face was terrible with fear and fury, and his eyes shone like lamps. Although he did but whisper, I who was nearest to them heard all that was said, which the others could not do.

"Your magic is good, Israelite," he muttered, "so good that it has overcome mine here in the temple where I serve."

"I have no magic," she answered very low. "I obeyed a command, no more."

He laughed bitterly, and asked:

"Should two of a trade waste time on foolishness? Listen now. Teach me your secrets, and I will teach you mine, and together we will drive Egypt like a chariot."

"I have no secrets, I have only faith," said Merapi again.

"Woman," he went on, "woman or devil, will you take me for friend or foe? Here I have been shamed, since it was to me and not to their gods that the priests trusted to destroy you. Yet I can still forgive. Choose now, knowing that as my friendship will lead you to rule, to life and splendour, so my hate will drive you to shame and death."

"You are beside yourself, and know not what you say. I tell you that I have no magic to give or to withhold," she answered, as one who did not understand or was indifferent, and turned away from him.

Thereon he muttered some curse which I could not catch, bowed to the heap of dust that had been the statue of the god, and vanished away among the pillars of the sanctuary.

"Oho-ho!" laughed Bakenkhonsu. "Not in vain have I lived to be so very old, for now it seems we have a new god in Egypt, and there stands his prophetess."

Merapi came to the prince.

"O high-priest of Amon," she said, "does it please you to let me go, for I am very weary?"

CHAPTER 10

The Death of Pharaoh

It was the appointed day and hour. By command of the Prince I drove with him to the palace of Pharaoh, whither her Highness the Princess refused to be his companion, and for the first time we talked together of that which had passed in the temple.

"Have you seen the lady Merapi?" he asked of me.

I answered No, as I was told that she was sick within her house and lay abed suffering from weariness, or I knew not what.

"She does well to keep there," said Seti, "I think that if she came out those priests would murder her if they could. Also there are others," and he glanced back at the chariot that bore Userti in state. "Say, Ana, can you interpret all this matter?"

"Not I, Prince. I thought that perhaps your Highness, the high-priest of Anon, could give me light."

"The high-priest of Amon wanders in thick darkness. Ki and the rest swear that this Israelite is a sorceress who has outmatched their magic, but to me it seems more simple to believe that what she says is true; that her god is greater than Amon."

"And if this be true, Prince, what are we to do who are sworn to the gods of Egypt?"

"Bow our heads and fall with them, I suppose, Ana, since honour will not suffer us to desert them."

"Even if they be false, Prince?"

"I do not think that they are false, Ana, though mayhap they be less true. At least they are the gods of the Egyptians and we are Egyptians." He paused and glanced at the crowded streets, then added, "See, when I passed this way three days ago I was received with shouts of welcome by the people. Now they are silent, every one."

"Perhaps they have heard of what passed in the temple."

"Doubtless, but it is not that which troubles them who think that the gods can guard themselves. They have heard also that I would be-friend the Hebrews whom they hate, and therefore they begin to hate me. Why should I complain when Pharaoh shows them the way?"

"Prince," I whispered, "what will you say to Pharaoh?"

"That depends on what Pharaoh says to me. Ana, if I will not desert our gods because they seem to be the weaker, though it should prove to my advantage, do you think that I would desert these He-brews because they seem to be weaker, even to gain a throne?"

"There greatness speaks," I murmured, and as we descended from the chariot he thanked me with a look.

We passed through the great hall to that same chamber where Pharaoh had given me the chain of gold. Already he was there seat-ed at the head of the chamber and wearing on his head the double crown. About him were gathered all those of royal blood and the great officers of state. We made our obeisances, but of these he seemed to take no note. His eyes were almost closed, and to me he looked like a man who is very ill. The Princess Userti entered after us and to her he spoke some words of welcome, giving her his hand to kiss. Then he ordered the doors to be closed. As he did so, an officer of the house-hold entered and said that a messenger had come from the Hebrews who desired speech with Pharaoh.

"Let him enter," said Meneptah, and presently he appeared.

He was a wild-eyed man of middle age, with long hair that fell over his sheepskin robe. To me he looked like a soothsayer. He stood before Pharaoh, making no salutation.

"Deliver your message and be gone," said Nehesi the Vizier.

"These are the words of the Fathers of Israel, spoken by my lips," cried the man in a voice that rang all round the vaulted chamber. "It has come to our ears, O Pharaoh, that the woman Merapi, daughter of Nathan, who has refuged in your city, she who is named Moon of Israel, has shown herself to be a prophetess of power, one to whom our God has given strength, in that, standing alone amidst the priests and magicians of Amon of the Egyptians, she took no harm from their sorceries and was able with the sword of prayer to smite the idol of Amon to the dust. We demand that this prophetess be restored to us, making oath on our part that she shall be given over safely to her betrothed husband and that no harm shall come to her for any crimes or treasons she may have committed against her people."

"As to this matter," replied Pharaoh quietly, "make your prayer to the Prince of Egypt, in whose household I understand the woman dwells. If it pleases him to surrender her who, I take it, is a witch or a cunning worker of tricks, to her betrothed and her kindred, let him do so. It is not for Pharaoh to judge of the fate of private slaves."

The man wheeled round and addressed Seti, saying:

"You have heard, Son of the King. Will you deliver up this woman?"

"Neither do I promise to deliver her up nor not to deliver her up," answered Seti, "since the lady Merapi is no member of my household, nor have I any authority over her. She who saved my life dwells within my walls for safety's sake. If it pleases her to go, she can go; if it pleases her to remain, she can remain. When this Court is finished I give you safe-conduct to appear and in my presence learn her pleasure from her lips."

"You have your answer; now be gone," said Nehesi.

"Nay," cried the man, "I have more words to speak. Thus say the Fathers of Israel: We know the black counsel of your heart, O Pharaoh. It has been revealed to us that it is in your mind to put the Hebrews to the sword, as it is in the mind of the Prince of Egypt to save them from the sword. Change that mind of yours, O Pharaoh, and swiftly, lest death fall upon you from heaven above."

"Cease!" thundered Meneptah in a voice that stilled the murmurs of the court. "Dog of a Hebrew, do you dare to threaten Pharaoh on his own throne? I tell you that were you not a messenger, and therefore according to our ancient law safe till the sun sets, you should be hewn limb from limb. Away with him, and if he is found in this city after nightfall let him be slain!"

Then certain of the councillors sprang upon the man and thrust him forth roughly. At the door he wrenched himself free and shouted:

"Think upon my words, Pharaoh, before this sun has set. And you, great ones of Egypt, think on them also before it appears again."

They drove him out with blows and the doors were shut. Once more Meneptah began to speak, saying:

"Now that this brawler is gone, what have you to say to me, Prince of Egypt? Do you still give me the counsel that you wrote in the roll? Do you still refuse, as heir of the Throne, to assent to my decree that these accursed Hebrews be destroyed with the sword of my justice?"

Now all turned their eyes on Seti, who thought a while, and answered:

"Let Pharaoh pardon me, but the counsel that I gave I still give; the assent that I refused I still refuse, because my heart tells me that so it is right to do, and so I think will Egypt be saved from many troubles."

When the scribes had finished writing down these words Pharaoh asked again:

"Prince of Egypt, if in a day to come you should fill my place, is it still your intent to let this people of the Hebrews go unharmed, taking with them the wealth that they have gathered here?"

"Let Pharaoh pardon me, that is still my intent."

Now at these fateful words there arose a sigh of astonishment from all that heard them. Before it had died away Pharaoh had turned to Userti and was asking:

"Are these your counsel, your will, and your intent also, O Princess of Egypt?"

"Let Pharaoh hear me," answered Userti in a cold, clear voice, "they are not. In this great matter my lord the Prince walks one road and I walk another. My counsel, will, and intent are those of Pharaoh."

"Seti my son," said Meneptah, more kindly than I had ever heard him speak before, "for the last time, not as your king but as your father, I pray you to consider. Remembering that as it lies in your power, being of full age and having been joined with me in many matters of government, to refuse your assent to a great act of state, so it lies in my power with the assent of the high-priests and of my ministers to remove you from my path. Seti, I can disinherit you and set another in your place, and if you persist, that and no less I shall do. Consider, therefore, my son."

In the midst of an intense silence Seti answered:

"I have considered, O my Father, and whatever be the cost to me I cannot go back upon my words."

Then Pharaoh rose and cried:

"Take note all you assembled here, and let it be proclaimed to the people of Egypt without the gates, that they take note also, that I depose Seti my son from his place as Prince of Egypt and declare that he is removed from the succession to the double Crown. Take note that my daughter Userti, Princess of Egypt, wife of the Prince Seti, I do not depose. Whatever rights and heritages are hers as heiress of Egypt let those rights and heritages remain to her, and if a child be born of her and Prince Seti, who lives, let that child be heir to the Throne of Egypt. Take note that, if no such child is born or until it is born, I name my nephew, the count Amenmeses, son of by brother Khaemuas, now gathered to Osiris, to fill the Throne of Egypt when I am no more. Come hither, Count Amenmeses."

He advanced and stood before him. Then Pharaoh lifted from his head the double crown he wore and for a moment set it on the brow of Amenmeses, saying as he replaced it on his own head:

"By this act and token do I name and constitute you, Amenmeses, to be Royal Prince of Egypt in place of my son, Prince Seti, deposed. Withdraw, Royal Prince of Egypt. I have spoken."

"Life! Blood! Strength!" cried all the company bowing before Pharaoh, all save the Prince Seti who neither bowed nor stirred. Only he cried:

"And I have heard. Will Pharaoh be pleased to declare whether with my royal heritage he takes my life? If so, let it be here and now. My cousin Amenmeses wears a sword."

"Nay, Son," answered Meneptah sadly, "your life is left to you and with it all your private rank and your possessions whatsoever and wherever they may be."

"Let Pharaoh's will be done," replied Seti indifferently, "in this as in all things. Pharaoh spares my life until such time as Amenmeses his successor shall fill his place, when it shall be taken."

Meneptah started; this thought was new to him.

"Stand forth, Amenmeses," he cried, "and swear now the threefold oath that may not be broken. Swear by Amon, by Ptah, and by Osiris, god of death, that never will you attempt to harm the Prince Seti, your cousin, either in body or in such state and prerogative as remain to him. Let Roi, the head-priest of Amon, administer the oath now before us all."

So Roi spoke the oath in the ancient form, which was terrible even to hear, and Amenmeses, unwillingly enough as I thought, repeated it after him, adding however these words at the end, "All these things I swear and all these penalties in this world and the world to be I invoke upon my head, provided only that when the time comes the Prince Seti leaves me in peace upon the throne to which it has pleased Pharaoh to decree to me."

Now some there murmured that this was not enough, since in their hearts there were few who did not love Seti and grieve to see him thus stripped of his royal heritage because his judgment differed from that of Pharaoh over a matter of State policy. But Seti only laughed and said scornfully:

"Let be, for of what value are such oaths? Pharaoh on the throne is above all oaths who must make answer to the gods only and from the hearts of some the gods are far away. Let Amenmeses not fear that I shall quarrel with him over this matter of a crown, I who in truth have never longed for the pomp and cares of royalty and who, deprived of these, still possess all that I can desire. I go my way henceforward as one of many, a noble of Egypt—no more, and if in a day to come it pleases the Pharaoh to be to shorten my wanderings, I am not sure that even then I shall grieve so very much, who am content to accept the judgment of the gods, as in the end he must do also. Yet, Pharaoh my father, before we part I ask leave to speak the thoughts that rise in me."

"Say on," muttered Meneptah.

"Pharaoh, having your leave, I tell you that I think you have done a very evil work this day, one that is unpleasing to those Powers which rule the world, whoever and whatsoever they may be, one too that will bring upon Egypt sorrows countless as the sand. I believe that these Hebrews whom you unjustly seek to slay worship a god as great or greater than our own, and that they and he will triumph over Egypt. I believe also that the mighty heritage which you have taken from me will bring neither joy nor honour to him by whom it has been received."

Here Amenmeses started forward, but Meneptah held up his hand, and he was silent.

"I believe, Pharaoh—alas! that I must say it—that your days on earth are few and that for the last time we look on each other living. Farewell, Pharaoh my father, whom still I love mayhap more in this hour of parting than ever I did before. Farewell, Amenmeses, Prince of Egypt. Take from me this ornament which henceforth should be worn by you only," and lifting from his headdress that royal circlet which marks the heir to the throne, he held it to Amenmeses, who took it and, with a smile of triumph, set it on his brow.

"Farewell, Lords and Councillors; it is my hope that in yonder prince you will find a master more to your liking that ever I could have been. Come, Ana, my friend, if it still pleases you to cling to me for a little while, now that I have nothing left to give."

For a few moments he stood still looking very earnestly at his father, who looked back at him with tears in his deep-set, faded eyes.

Then, though whether this was by chance I cannot say, taking no note of the Princess Userti, who gazed at him perplexed and wrathful, Seti drew himself up and cried in the ancient form:

"Life! Blood! Strength! Pharaoh! Pharaoh! Pharaoh!" and bowed almost to the ground.

Meneptah heard. Muttering beneath his breath, "Oh! Seti, my son, my most beloved son!" he stretched out his arms as though to call him back or perhaps to clasp him. As he did so I saw his face change. Next instant he fell forward to the ground and lay there still. All the company stood struck with horror, only the royal physician ran to him, while Roi and others who were priests began to mutter prayers.

"Has the good god been gathered to Osiris?" asked Amenmeses presently in a hoarse voice, "because if it be so, I am Pharaoh."

"Nay, Amenmeses," exclaimed Userti, "the decrees have not yet been sealed or promulgated. They have neither strength nor weight."

Before he could answer the physician cried:

"Peace! Pharaoh still lives, his heart beats. This is but a fit which may pass. Begone, every one, he must have quiet."

So we went, but first Seti knelt down and kissed his father on the brow.

****

An hour later the Princess Userti broke into the room of his palace where the Prince and I were talking.

"Seti," she said, "Pharaoh still lives, but the physicians say he will be dead by dawn. There is yet time. Here I have a writing, sealed with his signet and witnessed, wherein he recalls all that he decreed in the Court to-day, and declares you, his son, to be the true and only heir of the throne of Egypt."

"Is it so, wife? Tell me now how did a dying man in a swoon command and seal this writing?" and he touched the scroll she held in her hand.

"He recovered for a little while; Nehesi will tell you how," she replied, looking him in the face with cold eyes. Then before he could speak, she added, "Waste no more breath in questions, but act and at once. The General of the guards waits below; he is your faithful servant. Through him I have promised a gift to every soldier on the day that you are crowned. Nehesi and most of the officers are on our side. Only the priests are against us because of that Hebrew witch whom you shelter, and of her tribe whom you befriend; but they have not had time to stir up the people nor will they attempt revolt. Act, Seti, act, for none will move without your express command. Moreover, no question will be raised afterwards, since from Thebes to the sea and throughout the world you are known to be the heir of Egypt."

"What would you have me do, wife?" asked Seti, when she paused for lack of breath.

"Cannot you guess? Must I put statecraft into your head as well as a sword into your hand? Why that scribe of yours, who follows your heels like a favoured dog, would be more apt a pupil. Hearken then. Amenmeses has sent out to gather strength, but as yet there are not fifty men about him whom he can trust." She leant forward and whispered fiercely, "Kill the traitor, Amenmeses—all will hold it a right-eous act, and the General waits your word. Shall I summon him?"

"I think not," answered Seti. "Because Pharaoh, as he has a right to do, is pleased to name a certain man of royal blood to succeed him, how does this make that man a traitor to Pharaoh who still lives? But, traitor or none, I will not murder my cousin Amenmeses."

"Then he will murder you."

"Maybe. That is a matter between him and the gods which I leave them to settle. The oath he swore to-day is not one to be lightly bro-ken. But whether he breaks it or not, I also swore an oath, at least in my heart, namely that I would not attempt to dispute the will of Pharaoh whom, after all, I love as my father and honour as my king, Pharaoh who still lives and may, as I hope, recover. What should I say to him if he recovered or, at the worst, when at last we meet elsewhere?"

"Pharaoh never will recover; I have spoken to the physician and he told me so. Already they pierce his skull to let out the evil spirit of sickness, after which none of our family have lived for very long."

"Because, as I hold, thereby, whatever priests and physicians may say, they let in the good spirit of death. Ana, I pray you if I——"

"Man," she broke in, striking her hand upon the table by which she stood, "do you understand that while you muse and moralise your crown is passing from you?"

"It has already passed, Lady. Did you not see me give it to Amen-meses?"

"Do you understand that you who should be the greatest king in all the world, in some few hours if indeed you are allowed to live, will be nothing but a private citizen of Egypt, one at whom the very beg-gars may spit and take no harm?"

"Surely, Wife. Moreover, there is little virtue in what I do, since on the whole I prefer that prospect and am willing to take the risk of being hurried from an evil world. Hearken," he added, with a change of tone and gesture. "You think me a fool and a weakling; a dreamer also, you, the clear-eyed, hard-brained stateswoman who look to the glittering gain of the moment for which you are ready to pay in blood, and guess nothing of what lies beyond. I am none of these things, except, perchance, the last. I am only a man who strives to be just and to do right, as right seems to me, and if I dream, it is of good, not evil, as I understand good and evil. You are sure that this dreaming of mine will lead me to worldly loss and shame. Even of that *I* am not sure. The thought comes to me that it may lead me to those very baubles on which you set your heart, but by a path strewn with spices and with flowers, not by one paved with the bones of men and reeking with their gore. Crowns that are bought with the promise of blood and held with cruelty are apt to be lost in blood, Userti."

She waved her hand. "I pray you keep the rest, Seti, till I have more time to listen. Moreover if I need prophecies, I think it better to turn to Ki and those who make them their life-study. For me this is a day of deeds, not dreams, and since you refuse my help, and behave as a sick girl lost in fancies, I must see to myself. As while you live I cannot reign alone or wage war in my own name only, I go to make terms with Amenmeses, who will pay me high for peace."

"You go—and do you return, Userti?"

She drew herself to her full height, looking very royal, and answered slowly:

"I do not return. I, the Princess of Egypt, cannot live as the wife of a common man who falls from a throne to set himself upon the earth, and smears his own brow with mud for a *uraeus* crown. When your prophecies come true, Seti, and you crawl from your dust, then perhaps we may speak again."

"Aye, Userti, but the question is, what shall we say?"

"Meanwhile," she added, as she turned, "I leave you to your chosen counsellors—yonder scribe, whom foolishness, not wisdom, has whitened before his time, and perchance the Hebrew sorceress, who can give you moonbeams to drink from those false lips of hers. Farewell, Seti, once a prince and my husband."

"Farewell, Userti, who, I fear, must still remain my sister."

Then he watched her go, and turning to me, said:

"To-day, Ana, I have lost both a crown and a wife, yet strange to tell I do not know which of these calamities grieves me least. Yet it is time that fortune turned. Or mayhap all the evils are not done. Would you not go also, Ana? Although she gibes at you in her anger, the Princess thinks well of you, and would keep you in her service. Remember, whoever falls in Egypt, she will be great till the last."

"Oh! Prince," I answered, "have I not borne enough to-day that you must add insult to my load, you with whom I broke the cup and swore the oath?"

"What!" he laughed. "Is there one in Egypt who remembers oaths to his own loss? I thank you, Ana," and taking my hand he pressed it.

At that moment the door opened, and old Pambasa entered, saying:

"The Hebrew woman, Merapi, would see you; also two Hebrew men."

"Admit them," said Seti. "Note, Ana, how yonder old time-server turns his face from the setting sun. This morning even it would have been 'to see your Highness,' uttered with bows so low that his beard swept the floor. Now it is 'to see you' and not so much as an inclination of the head in common courtesy. This, moreover, from one who has robbed me year by year and grown fat on bribes. It is the first of many bitter lessons, or rather the second—that of her Highness was the first; I pray that I may learn them with humility."

While he mused thus and, having no comfort to offer, I listened sad at heart, Merapi entered, and a moment after her the wide-eyed messenger whom we had seen in Pharaoh's Court, and her uncle Jabez the cunning merchant. She bowed low to Seti, and smiled at me. Then the other two appeared, and with small salutation the messenger began to speak.

"You know my demand, Prince," he said. "It is that this woman should be returned to her people. Jabez, her uncle, will lead her away."

"And you know my answer, Israelite," answered Seti. "It is that I have no power over the coming or the going of the lady Merapi, or at least wish to claim none. Address yourself to her."

"What is it you wish with me, Priest?" asked Merapi quickly.

"That you should return to the town of Goshen, daughter of Nathan. Have you no ears to hear?"

"I hear, but if I return, what will you of me?"

"That you who have proved yourself a prophetess by your deeds in yonder temple should dedicate your powers to the service of your people, receiving in return full forgiveness for the evils you have wrought against them, which we swear to you in the name of God."

"I am no prophetess, and I have wrought no evils against my people, Priest. I have only saved them from the evil of murdering one who has shown himself their friend, even as I hear to the laying down of his crown for their sake."

"That is for the Fathers of Israel and not for you to judge, woman. Your answer?"

"It is neither for them nor for me, but for God only." She paused, then added, "Is this all you ask of me?"

"It is all the Fathers ask, but Laban asks his affianced wife."

"And am I to be given in marriage to—this assassin?"

"Without doubt you are to be given to this brave soldier, being already his."

"And if I refuse?"

"Then, Daughter of Nathan, it is my part to curse you in the name of God, and to declare you cut off and outcast from the people of

God. It is my part to announce to you further that your life is forfeit, and that any Hebrew may kill you when and how he can, and take no blame."

Merapi paled a little, then turning to Jabez, asked:

"You have heard, my uncle. What say you?"

Jabez looked round shiftily, and said in his unctuous voice:

"My niece, surely you must obey the commands of the Elders of Israel who speak the will of Heaven, as you obeyed them when you matched yourself against the might of Amon."

"You gave me a different counsel yesterday, my uncle. Then you said I had better bide where I was."

The messenger turned and glared at him.

"There is a great difference between yesterday and to-day," went on Jabez hurriedly. "Yesterday you were protected by one who would soon be Pharaoh, and might have been able to move his mind in favour of your folk. To-day his greatness is stripped from him, and his will has no more weight in Egypt. A dead lion is not to be feared, my niece."

Seti smiled at this insult, but Merapi's face, like my own, grew red, as though with anger.

"Sleeping lions have been taken for dead ere now, my uncle, as those who would spurn them have discovered to their cost. Prince Seti, have you no word to help me in this strait?"

"What is the strait, Lady? If you wish to go to your people and—to Laban, who, I understand, is recovered from his hurts, there is naught between you and me save my gratitude to you which gives me the right to say you shall not go. If, however, you wish to stay, then perhaps I am still not so powerless to shield or smite as this worthy Jabez thinks, who still remain the greatest lord in Egypt and one with those that love him. Therefore should you desire to remain, I think that you may do so unmolested of any, and least of all by that friend in whose shadow it pleases you to sojourn."

"Those are very gentle words," murmured Merapi, "words that few would speak to a maid from whom naught is asked and who has naught to give."

"A truce to this talk," snarled the messenger. "Do you obey or do you rebel? Your answer."

She turned and looked him full in the face, saying:

"I do not return to Goshen and to Laban, of whose sword I have seen enough."

"Mayhap you will see more of it before all is done. For the last time, think ere the curse of your God and your people falls upon you, and after it, death. For fall I say it shall, I, who, as Pharaoh knows today, am no false prophet, and as that Prince knows also."

"I do not think that my God, who sees the hearts of those that he has made, will avenge himself upon a woman because she refuses to be wedded to a murderer whom of her own will she never chose, which, Priest, is the fate you offer me. Therefore I am content to leave judgment in the hands of the great Judge of all. For the rest I defy you and your commands. If I must be slaughtered, let me die, but at least let me die mistress of myself and free, who am no man's love, or wife, or slave."

"Well spoken!" whispered Seti to me.

Then this priest became terrible. Waving his arms and rolling his wild eyes, he poured out some hideous curse upon the head of this poor maid, much of which, as it was spoken rapidly in an ancient form of Hebrew, we did not understand. He cursed her living, dying, and after death. He cursed her in her love and hate, wedded or alone. He cursed her in child-bearing or in barrenness, and he cursed her children after her to all generations. Lastly, he declared her cut off from and rejected by the god she worshipped, and sentenced her to death at the hands of any who could slay her. So horrible was that curse that she shrank away from him, while Jabez crouched about the ground hiding his eyes with his hands, and even I felt my blood turn cold.

At length he paused, foaming at the lips. Then, suddenly, shouting, "After judgment, doom!" he drew a knife from his robe and sprang at her.

She fled behind us. He followed, but Seti, crying, "Ah, I thought it," leapt between them, as he did so drawing the iron sword which he wore with his ceremonial dress. At him he sprang and the next thing I saw was the red point of the sword standing out beyond the priest's shoulders.

Down he fell, babbling:

"Is this how you show your love for Israel, Prince?"

"It is how I show my hate of murderers," answered Seti.

Then the man died.

"Oh!" cried Merapi wringing her hands, "once more I have caused Hebrew blood to flow and now all this curse will fall on me."

"Nay, on me, Lady, if there is anything in curses, which I doubt, for this deed was mine, and at the worst yonder mad brute's knife did not fall on you."

"Yes, life is left if only for a little while. Had it not been for you, Prince, by now, I——" and she shuddered.

"And had it not been for you, Moon of Israel, by now I——" and he smiled, adding, "Surely Fate weaves a strange web round you and me. First you save me from the sword; then I save you. I think, Lady, that in the end we ought to die together and give Ana here stuff for the best of all his stories. Friend Jabez," he went on to the Israelite who was still crouching in the corner with the eyes starting from his head, "get you back to your gentle-hearted people and make it clear to them why the lady Merapi cannot companion you, taking with you that carrion to prove your tale. Tell them that if they send more men to molest your niece a like fate awaits them, but that now as before I do not turn my back upon them because of the deeds of a few mad-men or evil-doers, as I have given them proof to-day. Ana, make ready, since soon I leave for Memphis. See that the Lady Merapi, who will travel alone, has fit escort for her journey, that is if it pleases her to depart from Tanis."

CHAPTER 11

The Crowning of Amenmeses

Now, notwithstanding all the woes that fell on Egypt and a certain secret sorrow of my own, began the happiest of the days which the gods have given me. We went to Mennefer or Memphis, the white-walled city where I was born, the city that I loved. Now no longer did I dwell in a little house near to the enclosure of the temple of Ptah, which is vaster and more splendid than all those of Thebes or Tanis. My home was in the beautiful palace of Seti, which he had inherited from his mother, the Great Royal Wife. It stood, and indeed still stands, on a piled-up mound without the walls near to the temple of the goddess Neit, who always has her habitation to the north of the wall, why I do not know, because even her priests cannot tell me. In front of this palace, facing to the north, is a great portico, whereof the roof is borne upon palm-headed, painted columns whence may be seen the most lovely prospect in Egypt. First the gardens, then the palm-groves, then the cultivated land, then the broad and gentle Nile and, far away, the desert.

Here, then, we dwelt, keeping small state and almost unguarded, but in wealth and comfort, spending our time in the library of the palace, or in those of the temples, and when we wearied of work, in the lovely gardens or, perchance, sailing upon the bosom of the Nile. The lady Merapi dwelt there also, but in a separate wing of the palace, with certain slaves and servants whom Seti had given to her. Sometimes we met her in the gardens, where it pleased her to walk at the same hours that we did, namely before the sun grew hot, or in the cool of the evening, and now and again when the moon shone at night. Then the three of us would talk together, for Seti never sought her company alone or within walls.

Those talks were very pleasant. Moreover they grew more frequent as time went on, since Merapi had a thirst for learning, and the Prince would bring her rolls to read in a little summer-house there was. Here we would sit, or if the heat was great, outside beneath the shadow of two spreading trees that stretched above the roof of the little pleasure-house, while Seti discoursed of the contents of the rolls and instructed her in the secrets of our writing. Sometimes, too, I read them stories of my making, to which it pleased them both to listen, or so they said, and I, in my vanity, believed. Also we would talk of the mystery and the wonder of the world and of the Hebrews and their fate, or of what passed in Egypt and the neighbouring lands.

Nor was Merapi altogether lonesome, seeing that there dwelt in Memphis certain ladies who had Hebrew blood in their veins, or were born of the Israelites and had married Egyptians against their law. Among these she made friends, and together they worshipped in their own fashion with none to say them nay, since here no priests were allowed to trouble them.

For our part we held intercourse with as many as we pleased, since few forgot that Seti was by blood the Prince of Egypt, that is, a man almost half divine, and all were eager to visit him. Also he was much beloved for his own sake and more particularly by the poor, whose wants it was his delight to relieve to the full limit of his wealth. Thus it came about that whenever he went abroad, although against his will, he was received with honours and homage that were almost royal, for though Pharaoh could rob him of the Crown he could not empty his veins of the blood of kings.

It was on this account that I feared for his safety, since I was sure that through his spies Amenmeses knew all and would grow jealous of a dethroned prince who was still so much adored by those over whom of right he should have ruled. I told Seti of my doubts and that when he travelled the streets he should be guarded by armed men. But he only laughed and answered that, as the Hebrews had failed to kill him, he did not think that any others would succeed. Moreover he believed there were no Egyptians in the land who would lift a sword against him, or put poison in his drink, whoever bade them. Also he added these words:

"The best way to escape death is to have no fear of death, for then Osiris shuns us."

****

Now I must tell of the happenings at Tanis. Pharaoh Meneptah lingered but a few hours and never found his mind again before his spirit flew to Heaven. Then there was great mourning in the land, for, if he was not loved, Meneptah was honoured and feared. Only among the Israelites there was open rejoicing, because he had been their enemy and their prophets had foretold that death was near to him. They gave it out that he had been smitten of their God, which caused the Egyptians to hate them more than ever. There was doubt, too, and bewilderment in Egypt, for though his proclamation disinheriting the Prince Seti had been published abroad, the people, and especially those who dwelt in the south, could not understand why this should have been done over a matter of the shepherd slaves who dwelt in Goshen. Indeed, had the Prince but held up his hand, tens of thousands would have rallied to his standard. Yet this he refused to do, which astonished all the world, who thought it marvellous that any man should refuse a throne which would have lifted him almost to the level of the gods. Indeed, to avoid their importunities he had set out at once for Memphis, and there remained hidden away during the period of mourning for his father. So it came about that Amenmeses succeeded with none to say him nay, since without her husband Userti could not or would not act.

After the days of embalmment were accomplished the body of Pharaoh Meneptah was carried up the Nile to be laid in his eternal house, the splendid tomb that he had made ready for himself in the Valley of Dead Kings at Thebes. To this great ceremony the Prince Seti was not bidden, lest, as Bakenkhonsu told me afterwards, his presence should cause some rising in his favour, with or without his will. For this reason also the dead god, as he was named, was not suffered to rest at Memphis on his last journey up the Nile. Disguised as a man of the people the Prince watched his father's body pass in the funeral barge guarded by shaven, white-robed priests, the centre of a splendid procession. In front went other barges filled with soldiers and officers of state, behind came the new Pharaoh and all the great ones of Egypt, while the sounds of lamentation floated far over the face of the waters. They appeared, they passed, they disappeared, and when they had vanished Seti wept a little, for in his own fashion he loved his father.

"Of what use is it to be a king and named half-divine, Ana," he said to me, "seeing that the end of such gods as these is the same as that of the beggar at the gate?"

"This, Prince," I answered, "that a king can do more good than a beggar while the breath is in his nostrils, and leave behind him a great example to others."

"Or more harm, Ana. Also the beggar can leave a great example, that of patience in affliction. Still, if I were sure that I should do nothing but good, then perhaps I would be a king. But I have noted that those who desire to do the most good often work the greatest harm."

"Which, if followed out, would be an argument for wishing to do evil, Prince."

"Not so," he answered, "because good triumphs at the last. For good is truth and truth rules earth and heaven."

"Then it is clear, Prince, that you should seek to be a king."

"I will remember the argument, Ana, if ever time brings me an opportunity unstained by blood," he answered.

When the obsequies of Pharaoh were finished, Amenmeses returned to Tanis, and there was crowned as Pharaoh. I attended this great ceremony, bearing coronation gifts of certain royal ornaments which the Prince sent to Pharaoh, saying it was not fit that he, as a private person, should wear them any longer. These I presented to Pharaoh, who took them doubtfully, declaring that he did not understand the Prince Seti's mind and actions.

"They hide no snare, O Pharaoh," I said. "As you rejoice in the glory that the gods have sent you, so the Prince my master rejoices in the rest and peace which the gods have given him, asking no more."

"It may be so, Scribe, but I find this so strange a thing, that sometimes I fear lest the rich flowers of this glory of mine should hide some deadly snake, whereof the Prince knows, if he did not set it there."

"I cannot say, O Pharaoh, but without doubt, although he could work no guile, the Prince is not as are other men. His mind is both wide and deep."

"Too deep for me," muttered Amenmeses. "Nevertheless, say to my royal cousin that I thank him for his gifts, especially as some of them were worn, when he was heir to Egypt, by my father Khaemuas, who I would had left me his wisdom as well as his blood. Say to him also that while he refrains from working me harm upon the throne, as I know he has done up to the present, he may be sure that I will work him none in the station which he has chosen."

Also I saw the Princess Userti who questioned me closely concerning her lord. I told her everything, keeping naught back. She listened and asked:

"What of that Hebrew woman, Moon of Israel? Without doubt she fills my place."

"Not so, Princess," I answered. "The Prince lives alone. Neither she nor any other woman fills your place. She is a friend to him, no more."

"A friend! Well, at least we know the end of such friendships. Oh! surely the Prince must be stricken with madness from the gods!"

"It may be so, your Highness, but I think that if the gods smote more men with such madness, the world would be better than it is."

"The world is the world, and the business of those who are born to greatness is to rule it as it is, not to hide away amongst books and flowers, and to talk folly with a beautiful outland woman, and a scribe however learned," she answered bitterly, adding, "Oh! if the Prince is not mad, certainly he drives others to madness, and me, his spouse, among them. That throne is his, his; yet he suffers a cross-grained dolt to take his place, and sends him gifts and blessings."

"I think your Highness should wait till the end of the story before you judge of it."

She looked at me sharply, and asked:

"Why do you say that? Is the Prince no fool after all? Do he and you, who both seem to be so simple, perchance play a great and hidden game, as I have known men feign folly in order to do with safety? Or has that witch of an Israelite some secret knowledge in which she instructs you, such as a woman who can shatter the statue of Amon to fine dust might well possess? You make believe not to know, which means that you will not answer. Oh! Scribe Ana, if only it were safe, I think I could find a way to wring the truth out of you, although you do pretend to be but a babe for innocence."

"It pleases your Highness to threaten and without cause."

"No," she answered, changing her voice and manner, "I do not threaten; it is only the madness that I have caught from Seti. Would you not be mad if you knew that another woman was to be crowned to-morrow in your place, because—because——" and she began to weep, which frightened me more than all her rough words.

Presently she dried her tears, and said:

"Say to my lord that I rejoice to hear that he is well and send him greetings, but that never of my own wish will I look upon his living face again unless indeed he takes another counsel, and sets himself to win that which is his own. Say to him that though he has so little care for me, and pays no heed to my desires, still I watch over his welfare and his safety, as best I may."

"His safety, Princess! Pharaoh assured me not an hour ago that he had naught to fear, as indeed he fears naught."

"Oh! which of you is the more foolish," she exclaimed stamping her foot, "the man or his master? You believe that the Prince has naught to fear because that usurper tells you so, and he believes it—

well, because he fears naught. For a little while he may sleep in peace. But let him wait until troubles of this sort or of that arise in Egypt and, understanding that the gods send them on account of the great wickedness that my father wrought when death had him by the throat and his mind was clouded, the people begin to turn their eyes towards their lawful king. Then the usurper will grow jealous, and if he has his way, the Prince will sleep in peace—for ever. If his throat remains uncut, it will be for one reason only, that I hold back the murderer's hand. Farewell, I can talk no more, for I say to you that my brain is afire—and to-morrow he should have been crowned, and I with him," and she swept away, royal as ever, leaving me wondering what she meant when she spoke of troubles arising in Egypt, or if the words were but uttered at hazard.

Afterwards Bakenkhonsu and I supped together at the college of the temple of Ptah, of which because of his age he was called the father, when I heard more of this matter.

"Ana," he said, "I tell you that such gloom hangs over Egypt as I have never known even when it was thought that the Ninebow Barbarians would conquer and enslave the land. Amenmeses will be the fifth Pharaoh whom I have seen crowned, the first of them when I was but a little child hanging to my mother's robe, and not once have I known such joylessness."

"That may be because the crown passes to one who should not wear it, Bakenkhonsu."

He shook his head. "Not altogether. I think this darkness comes from the heavens as light does. Men are afraid they know not of what."

"The Israelites," I suggested.

"Now you are near to it, Ana, for doubtless they have much to do with the matter. Had it not been for them Seti and not Amenmeses would be crowned to-morrow. Also the tale of the marvel which the beautiful Hebrew woman wrought in the temple yonder has got abroad and is taken as an omen. Did I tell you that six days gone a fine new statue of the god was consecrated there and on the following morning was found lying on its side, or rather with its head resting on the breast of Mut?"

"If so, Merapi is blameless, because she has gone away from this city."

"Of course she has gone away, for has not Seti gone also? But I think she left something behind her. However that may be, even our new divine lord is afraid. He dreams ill, Ana," he added, dropping his voice, "so ill that he has called in Ki, the Kherheb,[1] to interpret his visions."

---

1. "Kherheb" was the title of the chief official magician in ancient Egypt.

"And what said Ki?"

"Ki could say nothing or, rather, that the only answer vouchsafed to him and his company, when they made inquiry of their Kas, was that this god's reign would be very short and that it and his life would end together."

"Which perhaps did not please the god Amenmeses, Bakenkhonsu?"

"Which did not please the god at all. He threatened Ki. It is a foolish thing to threaten a great magician, Ana, as the Kherheb Ki, himself indeed told him, looking him in the eyes. Then he prayed his pardon and asked who would succeed him on the throne, but Ki said he did not know, as a Kherheb who had been threatened could never remember anything, which indeed he never can—except to pay back the threatener."

"And did he know, Bakenkhonsu?"

By way of answer the old Councillor crumbled some bread fine upon the table, then with his finger traced among the crumbs the rough likeness of a jackal-headed god and of two feathers, after which with a swift movement he swept the crumbs onto the floor.

"Seti!" I whispered, reading the hieroglyphs of the Prince's name, and he nodded and laughed in his great fashion.

"Men come to their own sometimes, Ana, especially if they do not seek their own," he said. "But if so, much must happen first that is terrible. The new Pharaoh is not the only man who dreams, Ana. Of late years my sleep has been light and sometimes I dream, though I have no magic like to that of Ki."

"What did you dream?"

"I dreamed of a great multitude marching like locusts over Egypt. Before them went a column of fire in which were two hands. One of these held Amon by the throat and one held the new Pharaoh by the throat. After them came a column of cloud, and in it a shape like to that of an unwrapped mummy, a shape of death standing upon water that was full of countless dead."

Now I bethought me of the picture that the Prince and I had seen in the skies yonder in the land of Goshen, but of it I said nothing. Yet I think that Bakenkhonsu saw into my mind, for he asked:

"Do *you* never dream, Friend? You see visions that come true—Amenmeses on the throne, for instance. Do you not also dream at times? No? Well, then, the Prince? You look like men who might, and the time is ripe and pregnant. Oh! I remember. You are both of you dreaming, not of the pictures that pass across the terrible eyes of Ki, but of those that the moon reflects upon the waters of Memphis, the

Moon of Israel. Ana, be advised by me, put away the flesh and increase the spirit, for in it alone is happiness, whereof woman and all our joys are but earthly symbols, shadows thrown by that mortal cloud which lies between us and the Light Above. I see that you understand, because some of that light has struggled to your heart. Do you remember that you saw it shining in the hour when your little daughter died? Ah! I thought so. It was the gift she left you, a gift that will grow and grow in such a breast as yours, if only you will put away the flesh and make room for it, Ana. Man, do not weep—laugh as I do, Oho-ho! Give me my staff, and good-night. Forget not that we sit together at the crowning to-morrow, for you are a King's Companion and that rank once conferred is one which no new Pharaoh can take away. It is like the gift of the spirit, Ana, which is hard to win, but once won more eternal than the stars. Oh! why do I live so long who would bathe in it, as when a child I used to bathe in Nile?"

****

On the following day at the appointed hour I went to the great hall of the palace, that in which I had first seen Meneptah, and took my stand in the place allotted to me. It was somewhat far back, perhaps because it was not wished that I, who was known to be the private scribe of Seti, should remind Egypt of him by appearing where all could see me.

Great as was the hall the crowd filled it to its furthest corners. Moreover no common man was present there, but rather every noble and head-priest in Egypt, and with them their wives and daughters, so that all the dim courts shone with gold and precious gems set upon festal garments. While I was waiting old Bakenkhonsu hobbled towards me, the crowd making way for him, and I could see that there was laughter in his sunken eyes.

"We are ill-placed, Ana," he said. "Still if any of the many gods there are in Egypt should chance to rain fires on Pharaoh, we shall be the safer. Talking of gods," he went on in a whisper, "have you heard what happened an hour ago in the temple of Ptah of Tanis whence I have just come? Pharaoh and all the Blood-royal—save one—walked according to custom before the statue of the god which, as you know, should bow its head to show that he chooses and accepts the king. In front of Amenmeses went the Princess Userti, and as she passed the head of the god bowed, for I saw it, though all pretended that they did not see. Then came Pharaoh and stood waiting, but it would not bow, though the priests called in the old formula, 'The god greets the king.'

"At length he went on, looking as black as night, and others of the blood of Rameses followed in their order. Last of all limped Saptah and, behold! the god bowed again."

"How and why does it do these things?" I asked, "and at the wrong time?"

"Ask the priests, Ana, or Userti, or Saptah. Perhaps the divine neck has not been oiled of late, or too much oiled, or too little oiled, or prayers—or strings—may have gone wrong. Or Pharaoh may have been niggard in his gifts to that college of the great god of his House. Who am I that I should know the ways of gods? That in the temple where I served at Thebes fifty years ago did not pretend to bow or to trouble himself as to which of the royal race sat upon the throne. Hush! Here comes Pharaoh."

Then in a splendid procession, surrounded by princes, councillors, ladies, priests, and guards, Amenmeses and the Royal Wife, Urnure, a large woman who walked awkwardly, entered the hall, a glittering band. The high-priest, Roi, and the chancellor, Nehesi, received Pharaoh and led him to his throne. The multitude prostrated itself, trumpets blew and thrice the old salute of "Life! Blood! Strength! Pharaoh! Pharaoh! Pharaoh!" was cried aloud.

Amenmeses rose and bowed, and I saw that his heavy face was troubled and looked older. Then he swore some oath to gods and men which Roi dictated to him, and before all the company put on the double crown and the other emblems, and took in his hands the scourge and golden sickle. Next homage was paid. The Princess Userti came first and kissed Pharaoh's hand, but bent no knee. Indeed first she spoke with him a while. We could not hear what was said, but afterwards learned that she demanded that he should publicly repeat all the promises which her father Meneptah had made to her before him, confirming her in her place and rights. This in the end he did, though it seemed to me unwillingly enough.

So with many forms and ancient celebrations the ceremony went on, till all grew weary waiting for that time when Pharaoh should make his speech to the people. That speech, however, was never made, for presently, thrusting past us, I saw those two prophets of the Israelites who had visited Meneptah in this same hall. Men shrank from them, so that they walked straight up to the throne, nor did even the guards strive to bar their way. What they said there I could not hear, but I believe that they demanded that their people should be allowed to go to worship their god in their own fashion, and that Amenmeses refused as Meneptah had done.

Then one of them cast down a rod and it turned to a snake which hissed at Pharaoh, whereon the Kherheb Ki and his company also cast down rods that turned to snakes, though I could only hear the hissing. After this a great gloom fell upon the hall, so that men could not see each other's faces and everyone began to call aloud till the company broke up in confusion. Bakenkhonsu and I were borne together to the doorway by the pressure of the people, whence we were glad enough to see the sky again.

****

Thus ended the crowning of Amenmeses.

CHAPTER 12

The Message of Jabez

That night there were none who rejoiced in the streets of the city, and save in the palace and houses of those of the Court, none who feasted. I walked abroad in the market-place and noted the people going to and fro gloomily, or talking together in whispers. Presently a man whose face was hidden in a hood began to speak with me, saying that he had a message for my master, the Prince Seti. I answered that I took no messages from veiled strangers, whereon he threw back his hood, and I saw that it was Jabez, the uncle of Merapi. I asked him whether he had obeyed the Prince, and borne the body of that prophet back to Goshen and told the elders of the manner of the man's death.

"Yes," he answered, "nor were the Elders angry with the Prince over this matter. They said that their messenger had exceeded his authority, since they had never told him to curse Merapi, and much less attempt to kill her, and that the Prince did right to slay one who would have done murder before his royal eyes. Still they added that the curse, having once been spoken by this priest, would surely fall upon Merapi in this way or in that."

"What then should she do, Jabez?"

"I do not know, Scribe. If she returns to her people, perchance she will be absolved, but then she must surely marry Laban. It is for her to judge."

"And what would you do if you were in her place, Jabez?"

"I think that I should stay where I was, and make myself very dear to Seti, taking the chance that the curse may pass her by, since it was not lawfully decreed upon her. Whichever way she looks, trouble waits, and at the worst, a woman might wish to satisfy her heart before it falls, especially if that heart should happen to turn to one who will be Pharaoh."

"Why do you say 'who will be Pharaoh,' Jabez?" I asked, for we were standing in an empty place alone.

"That I may not tell you," he replied cunningly, "yet it will come about as I say. He who sits upon the throne is mad as Meneptah was mad, and will fight against a strength that is greater than his until it overwhelms him. In the Prince's heart alone does the light of wisdom shine. That which you saw to-day is only the first of many miracles, Scribe Ana. I can say no more."

"What then is your message, Jabez?"

"This: Because the Prince has striven to deal well with the people of Israel and for their sake has cast aside a crown, whatever may chance to others, let him fear nothing. No harm shall come to him, or to those about him, such as yourself, Scribe Ana, who also would deal justly by us. Yet it may happen that through my niece Merapi, on whose head the evil word has fallen, a great sorrow may come to both him and her.

"Therefore, perhaps, although setting this against that, she may be wise to stay in the house of Seti, he, on the balance, may be wise to turn her from his doors."

"What sorrow?" I asked, who grew bewildered with his dark talk, but there was no answer, for he had gone.

Near to my lodging another man met me, and the moonlight shining on his face showed me the terrible eyes of Ki.

"Scribe Ana," he said, "you leave for Memphis to-morrow at the dawn, and not two days hence as you purposed."

"How do you know that, Magician Ki?" I answered, for I had told my change of plan to none, not even to Bakenkhonsu, having indeed only determined upon it since Jabez left me.

"I know nothing, Ana, save that a faithful servant who has learned all you have learned to-day will hurry to make report of it to his master, especially if there is some other to whom he would also wish to make report, as Bakenkhonsu thinks."

"Bakenkhonsu talks too much, whatever he may think," I exclaimed testily.

"The aged grow garrulous. You were at the crowning to-day, were you not?"

"Yes, and if I saw aright from far away, those Hebrew prophets seemed to worst you at your own trade there, Kherheb, which must grieve you, as you were grieved in the temple when Amon fell."

"It does not grieve me, Ana. If I have powers, there may be others who have greater powers, as I learned in the temple of Amon. Why therefore should I feel ashamed?"

"Powers!" I replied with a laugh, for the strings of my mind seemed torn that night, "would not craft be a better word? How do you turn a stick into a snake, a thing which is impossible to man?"

"Craft might be a better word, since craft means knowledge as well as trickery. 'Impossible to man!' After what you saw a while ago in the temple of Amon, do you hold that there is anything impossible to man or woman? Perhaps you could do as much yourself."

"Why do you mock me, Ki? I study books, not snake-charming."

He looked at me in his calm fashion, as though he were reading, not my face, but the thoughts behind it. Then he looked at the cedar wand in his hand and gave it to me, saying:

"Study this, Ana, and tell me, what is it."

"Am I a child," I answered angrily, "that I should not know a priest's rod when I see one?"

"I think that you are something of a child, Ana," he murmured, all the while keeping those eyes of his fixed upon my face.

Then a horror came about. For the rod began to twist in my hand and when I stared at it, lo! it was a long, yellow snake which I held by the tail. I threw the reptile down with a scream, for it was turning its head as though to strike me, and there in the dust it twisted and writhed away from me and towards Ki. Yet an instant later it was only a stick of yellow cedar-wood, though between me and Ki there was a snake's track in the sand.

"It is somewhat shameless of you, Ana," said Ki, as he lifted the wand, "to reproach me with trickery while you yourself try to confound a poor juggler with such arts as these."

Then I know not what I said to him, save the end of it was that I supposed he would tell me next that I could fill a hall with darkness at noonday and cover a multitude with terror.

"Let us have done with jests," he said, "though these are well enough in their place. Will you take this rod again and point it to the moon? You refuse and you do well, for neither you nor I can cover up her face. Ana, because you are wise in your way and consort with one who is wiser, and were present in the temple when the statue of Amon was shattered by a certain witch who matched her strength against mine and conquered me, I, the great magician, have come to ask *you*—whence came that darkness in the hall to-day?"

"From God, I think," I answered in an awed whisper.

"So I think also, Ana. But tell me, or ask Merapi, Moon of Israel, to tell me—from what god? Oh! I say to you that a terrible power is afoot in this land and that the Prince Seti did well to refuse the throne of Egypt and to fly to Memphis. Repeat it to him, Ana."

Then he too was gone.

****

Now I returned in safety to Memphis and told all these tidings to the Prince, who listened to them eagerly. Once only was he greatly stirred; it was when I repeated to him the words of Userti, that never would she look upon his face again unless it pleased him to turn it towards the throne. On hearing this tears came into his eyes, and rising, he walked up and down the chamber.

"The fallen must not look for gentleness," he said, "and doubtless, Ana, you think it folly that I should grieve because I am thus deserted."

"Nay, Prince, for I too have been abandoned by a wife and the pain is unforgotten."

"It is not of the wife I think, Ana, since in truth her Highness is no wife to me. For whatever may be the ancient laws of Egypt, how could it happen otherwise, at any rate in my case and hers? It is of the sister. For though my mother was not hers, she and I were brought up together and in our way loved each other, though always it was her pleasure to lord it over me, as it was mine to submit and pay her back in jests. That is why she is so angry because now of a sudden I have thrown off her rule to follow my own will whereby she has lost the throne."

"It has always been the duty of the royal heiress of Egypt to marry the Pharaoh of Egypt, Prince, and having wed one who would be Pharaoh according to that duty, the blow cuts deep."

"Then she had best thrust aside that foolish wife of his and wed him who is Pharaoh. But that she will never do; Amenmeses she has always hated, so much that she loathed to be in the same place with him. Nor indeed would he wed her, who wishes to rule for himself, not through a woman whose title to the crown is better than his own. Well, she has put me away and there's an end. Henceforth I must go lonly, unless—unless——Continue your story, friend. It is kind of her in her greatness to promise to protect one so humble. I should remember that, although it is true that fallen heads sometimes rise again," he added bitterly.

"So at least Jabez thinks, Prince," and I told him how the Israelites were sure that he would be Pharaoh, whereat he laughed and said:

"Perhaps, for they are good prophets. For my part I neither know or care. Or maybe Jabez sees advantage in talking thus, for as you know he is a clever trader."

"I do not think so," I answered and stopped.

"Had Jabez more to say of any other matter, Ana? Of the lady Merapi, for instance?"

Now feeling it to be my duty, I told him every word that had passed between Jabez and myself, though somewhat shamefacedly.

"This Hebrew takes much for granted, Ana, even as to whom the Moon of Israel would wish to shine upon. Why, friend, it might be you whom she desires to touch with her light, or some youth in Goshen—not Laban—or no one."

"Me, Prince, me!" I exclaimed.

"Well, Ana, I am sure you would have it so. Be advised by me and ask her mind upon the matter. Look not so confused, man, for one who has been married you are too modest. Come tell me of this Crowning."

So glad enough to escape from the matter of Merapi, I spoke at length of all that had happened when Pharaoh Amenmeses took his seat upon the throne. When I described how the rod of the Hebrew prophet had been turned to a snake and how Ki and his company had done likewise, the Prince laughed and said that these were mere jugglers' tricks. But when I told of the darkness that had seemed to gather in the hall and of the gloom that filled the hearts of all men and of the awesome dream of Bakenkhonsu, also of the words of Ki after he had clouded my mind and played his jest upon me, he listened with much earnestness and answered:

"My mind is as Ki's in this matter. I too think that a terrible power is afoot in Egypt, one that has its home in the land of Goshen, and that I did well to refuse the throne. But from what god these fortunes come I do not know. Perhaps time will tell us. Meanwhile if there is aught in the prophesies of these Hebrews, as interpreted by Jabez, at least you and I may sleep in peace, which is more than will chance to Pharaoh on the throne that Userti covets. If so, this play will be worth the watching. You have done your mission well, Ana. Go rest you while I think over all that you have said."

****

It was evening and as the palace was very hot I went into the garden and making my way to that little pleasure-house where Seti and I were wont to study, I sat myself down there and, being weary, fell asleep. When I awoke from a dream about some woman who was weeping, night had fallen and the full moon shone in the sky, so that its rays fell on the garden before me.

Now in front of this little house, as I have said, grew trees that at this season of the year were covered with white and cup-like blossoms, and between these trees was a seat built up of sun-dried bricks. On this seat sat a woman whom I knew from her shape to be Merapi. Also she was sad, for although her head was bowed and her long hair hid her face I could hear her gentle sighs.

The sight of her moved me very much and I remembered what the Prince had said to me, telling me that I should do well to ask this lady whether she had any mind my way. Therefore if I did so, surely I could not be blamed. Yet I was certain that it was not to me that her heart turned, though to speak the truth, much I wished it otherwise. Who would look at the ibis in the swamp when the wide-winged eagle floated in heaven above?

An evil thought came into my mind, sent by Set. Suppose that this watcher's eyes were fixed upon the eagle, lord of the air. Suppose that she worshipped this eagle; that she loved it because its home was heaven, because to her it was the king of all the birds. And suppose one told her that if she lured it down to earth from the glorious safety of the skies, she would bring it to captivity or death at the hand of the snarer. Then would not that loving watcher say: "Let it go free and happy, however much I long to look upon it," and when it had sailed from sight, perhaps turn her eyes to the humble ibis in the mud?

Jabez had told me that if this woman and the Prince grew dear to each other she would bring great sorrow on his head. If I repeated his words to her, she who had faith in the prophecies of her people would certainly believe them. Moreover, whatever her heart might prompt, being so high-natured, never would she consent to do what might bring trouble on Seti's head, even if to refuse him should sink her soul in sorrow. Nor would she return to the Hebrews there to fall into the hands of one she hated. Then perhaps I——. Should I tell her? If Jabez had not meant that the matter must be brought to her ears, would he have spoken of it at all? In short was it not my duty to her, and perhaps also to the Prince who thereby might be saved from miseries to come, that is if this talk of future troubles were anything more than an idle story.

Such was the evil reasoning with which Set assailed my spirit. How I beat it down I do not know. Not by my own goodness, I am sure, since at the moment I was aflame with love for the sweet and beautiful lady who sat before me and in my foolishness would, I think, have given my life to kiss her hand. Not altogether for her sake either, since passion is very selfish. No, I believe it was because the love that I bore the Prince was more deep and real than that which I could feel for any woman, and I knew well that were she not in my sight no such treachery would have overcome my heart. For I was sure, although he had never said so to me, that Seti loved Merapi and above all earthly things desired her as his companion, while if once I spoke those words, whatever my own gain or loss and whatever her secret wish, that she would never be.

So I conquered, though the victory left me trembling like a child, and wishing that I had not been born to know the pangs of love denied. My reward was very swift, for just then Merapi unfastened a gem from the breast of her white robe and held it towards the moon, as though to study it. In an instant I knew it again. It was that royal scarab of lapis-lazuli with which in Goshen the Prince had made fast the bandage on her wounded food, which also had been snatched from her breast by some power on that night when the statue of Amon was shattered in the temple.

Long and earnestly she looked at it, then having glanced round to make sure she was alone, she pressed it to her lips and kissed it thrice with passion, muttering I know not what between the kisses. Now the scales fell from my eyes and I knew that she loved Seti, and oh! how I thanked my guardian god who had saved me from such useless shame.

I wiped the cold damp from my brow and was about to flee away, discovering myself with as few words as might be, when, looking up, I saw standing behind Merapi the figure of a man, who was watching her replace the ornament in her robe. While I hesitated a moment the man spoke and I knew the voice for that of Seti. Then again I thought of flight, but being somewhat timid by nature, feared to show myself until it was too late, thinking that afterward the Prince would make me the target of his wit. So I sat close and still, hearing and seeing all despite myself.

"What gem is that, Lady, which you admire and cherish so tenderly?" asked Seti in his slow voice that so often hid a hint of laughter.

She uttered a little scream and springing up, saw him.

"Oh! my lord," she exclaimed, "pardon your servant. I was sitting here in the cool, as you gave me leave to do, and the moon was so bright—that—I wished to be see if by it I could read the writing on this scarab."

Never before, thought I to myself, did I know one who read with her lips, though it is true that first she used her eyes.

"And could you, Lady? Will you suffer me to try?"

Very slowly and colouring, so that even the moonlight showed her blushes, she withdrew the ornament again and held it towards him.

"Surely this is familiar to me? Have I not seen it before?" he asked.

"Perhaps. I wore it that night in the temple, your Highness."

"You must not name me Highness, Lady. I have no longer any rank in Egypt."

"I know—because of—my people. Oh! it was noble."

"But about the scarabaeus——" he broke in, with a wave of his hand. "Surely it is the same with which the bandage was made fast upon your hurt—oh! years ago?"

"Yes, it is the same," she answered, looking down.

"I thought it. And when I gave it to you, I said some words that seemed to me well spoken at the time. What were they? I cannot remember. Have you also forgotten?"

"Yes—I mean—no. You said that now I had all Egypt beneath my foot, speaking of the royal cartouche upon the scarab."

"Ah! I recall. How true, and yet how false the jest, or prophecy."

"How can anything be both true and false, Prince?"

"That I could prove to you very easily, but it would take an hour or more, so it shall be for another time. This scarab is a poor thing, give it back to me and you shall have a better. Or would you choose this signet? As I am no longer Prince of Egypt it is useless to me."

"Keep the scarab, Prince. It is your own. But I will not take the ring because it is——"

"——useless to me, and you would not have that which is without value to the giver. Oh! I string words ill, but they were not what I meant."

"No, Prince, because your royal ring is too large for one so small."

"How can you tell until you have tried? Also that is a fault which might perhaps be mended."

Then he laughed, and she laughed also, but as yet she did not take the ring.

"Have you seen Ana?" he went on. "I believe he set out to search for you, in such a hurry indeed that he could scarcely finish his report to me."

"Did he say that?"

"No, he only looked it. So much so that I suggested he should seek you at once. He answered that he was going to rest after his long journey, or perhaps I said that he ought to do so. I forget, as often one does, on so beauteous a night when other thoughts seem nearer."

"Why did Ana wish to see me, Prince?"

"How can I tell? Why does a man who is still young—want to see a sweet and beautiful lady? Oh! I remember. He had met your uncle at Tanis who inquired as to your health. Perhaps that is why he wanted to see you."

"I do not wish to hear about my uncle at Tanis. He reminds me of too many things that give pain, and there are nights when one wishes to escape pain, which is sure to be found again on the morrow."

"Are you still of the same mind about returning to your people?" he asked, more earnestly.

"Surely. Oh! do not say that you will send me hence to——"

"Laban, Lady?"

"Laban amongst others. Remember, Prince, that I am one under a curse. If I return to Goshen, in this way or in that, soon I shall die."

"Ana says that your uncle Jabez declares that the mad fellow who tried to murder you had no authority to curse and much less to kill you. You must ask him to tell you all."

"Yet the curse will cling and crush me at the last. How can I, one lonely woman, stand against the might of the people of Israel and their priests?"

"Are you then lonely?"

"How can it be otherwise with an outcast, Prince?"

"No, it cannot be otherwise. I know it who am also an outcast."

"At least there is her Highness your wife, who doubtless will come to comfort you," she said, looking down.

"Her Highness will not come. If you had seen Ana, he would perhaps have told you that she has sworn not to look upon my face again, unless above it shines a crown."

"Oh! how can a woman be so cruel? Surely, Prince, such a stab must cut you to the heart," she exclaimed, with a little cry of pity.

"Her Highness is not only a woman; she is a Princess of Egypt which is different. For the rest it does cut me to the heart that my royal sister should have deserted me, for that which she loves better—power and pomp. But so it is, unless Ana dreams. It seems therefore that we are in the same case, both outcasts, you and I, is it not so?"

She made no answer but continued to look upon the ground, and he went on very slowly:

"A thought comes into my mind on which I would ask your judgment. If two who are forlorn came together they would be less forlorn by half, would they not?"

"It would seem so, Prince—that is if they remained forlorn at all. But I do not understand the riddle."

"Yet you have answered it. If you are lonely and I am lonely apart, we should, you say, be less lonely together."

"Prince," she murmured, shrinking away from him, "I spoke no such words."

"No, I spoke them for you. Hearken to me, Merapi. They think me a strange man in Egypt because I have held no woman dear, never having seen one whom I could hold dear." Here she looked at him searchingly, and he went on, "A while ago, before I visited your land of Goshen—Ana can tell you about the matter, for I think he wrote it down—Ki and old Bakenkhonsu came to see me. Now, as you know, Ki is without doubt a great magician, though it would seem not so great as some of your prophets. He told me that he and others had been searching out my future and that in Goshen I should find a woman whom it was fated I must love. He added that this woman would bring me much joy." Here Seti paused, doubtless remembering this was not all that Ki had said, or Jabez either. "Ki told me also," he went on slowly, "that I had already known this woman for thousands of years."

She started and a strange look came into her face.

"How can that be, Prince?"

"That is what I asked him and got no good answer. Still he said it, not only of the woman but of my friend Ana as well, which indeed would explain much, and it would appear that the other magicians said it also. Then I went to the land of Goshen and there I saw a woman——"

"For the first time, Prince?"

"No, for the third time."

Here she sank upon the bench and covered her eyes with her hands.

"——and loved her, and felt as though I had loved her for 'thousands of years.'"

"It is not true. You mock me, it is not true!" she whispered.

"It is true for if I did not know it then, I knew it afterwards, though never perhaps completely until to-day, when I learned that Userti had deserted me indeed. Moon of Israel, you are that woman. I will not tell you," he went on passionately, "that you are fairer than all other women, or sweeter, or more wise, though these things you seem to me. I will only tell you that I love you, yes, love you, whatever you may be. I cannot offer you the Throne of Egypt, even if the law would suffer it, but I can offer you the throne of this heart of mine. Now, Lady Merapi, what have you to say? Before you speak, remember that although you seem to be my prisoner here at Memphis, you have naught to fear from me. Whatever you may answer, such shelter and such friendship as I can give will be yours while I live, and never shall

I attempt to force myself upon you, however much it may pain me to pass you by. I know not the future. It may happen that I shall give you great place and power, it may happen that I shall give you nothing but poverty and exile, or even perhaps a share in my own death, but with either will go the worship of my body and my spirit. Now, speak."

She dropped her hands from her face, looking up at him, and there were tears shining in her beautiful eyes.

"It cannot be, Prince," she murmured.

"You mean you do not wish it to be?"

"I said that it cannot be. Such ties between an Egyptian and an Israelite are not lawful."

"Some in this city and elsewhere seem to find them so."

"And I am married, I mean perhaps I am married—at least in name."

"And I too am married, I mean——"

"That is different. Also there is another reason, the greatest of all, I am under a curse, and should bring you, not joy as Ki said, but sorrow, or, at the least, sorrow with the joy."

He looked at her searchingly.

"Has Ana——" he began, then continued, "if so what lives have you known that are not compounded of mingled joy and sorrow?"

"None. But the woe I should bring would outweigh the joy— to you. The curse of my God rests upon me and I cannot learn to worship yours. The curse of my people rests upon me, the law of my people divides me from you as with a sword, and should I draw close to you these will be increased upon my head, which matters not, but also upon yours," and she began to sob.

"Tell me," he said, taking her by the hand, "but one thing, and if the answer is No, I will trouble you no more. Is your heart mine?"

"It is," she sighed, "and has been ever since my eyes fell upon you yonder in the streets of Tanis. Oh! then a change came into me and I hated Laban, whom before I had only misliked. Moreover, I too felt that of which Ki spoke, as though I had known you for thousands of years. My heart is yours, my love is yours; all that makes me woman is yours, and never, never can turn from you to any other man. But still we must stay apart, for your sake, my Prince, for your sake."

"Then, were it not for me, you would be ready to run these hazards?"

"Surely! Am I not a woman who loves?"

"If that be so," he said with a little laugh, "being of full age and of an understanding which some have thought good, by your leave I think I will run them also. Oh! foolish woman, do you not understand that there is but one good thing in the world, one thing in which self and its miseries can be forgot, and that thing is love? Mayhap troubles will come. Well, let them come, for what do they matter if only the love or its memory remains, if once we have picked that beauteous flower and for an hour worn it on our breasts. You talk of the difference between the gods we worship and maybe it exists, but all gods send their gifts of love upon the earth, without which it would cease to be. Moreover, my faith teaches me more clearly perhaps than yours, that life does not end with death and therefore that love, being life's soul, must endure while it endures. Last of all, I think, as you think, that in some dim way there is truth in what the magicians said, and that long ago in the past we have been what once more we are about to be, and that the strength of this invisible tie has drawn us together out of the whole world and will bind us together long after the world is dead. It is not a matter of what we wish to do, Merapi, it is a matter of what Fate has decreed we shall do. Now, answer again."

But she made no answer, and when I looked up after a little moment she was in his arms and her lips were upon his lips.

****

Thus did Prince Seti of Egypt and Merapi, Moon of Israel, come together at Memphis in Egypt.

CHAPTER 13

The Red Nile

On the morrow of this night I found the Prince alone for a little while, and put him in mind of certain ancient manuscripts that he wished to read, which could only be consulted at Thebes where I might copy them; also of others that were said to be for sale there. He answered that they could wait, but I replied that the latter might find some other purchaser if I did not go at once.

"You are over fond of long journeys upon my business, Ana," he said. Then he considered me curiously for a while, and since he could read my mind, as indeed I could his, saw that I knew all, and added in a gentle voice:

"You should have done as I told you, and spoken first. If so, who knows———"

"You do, Prince," I answered, "you and another."

"Go, and the gods be with you, friend, but stay not too long copying those rolls, which any scribe can do. I think there is trouble at hand in Egypt, and I shall need you at my side. Another who holds you dear will need you also."

"I thank my lord and that other," I said, bowing, and went.

Moreover, while I was making some humble provision for my journey, I found that this was needless, since a slave came to tell me that the Prince's barge was waiting to sail with the wind. So in that barge I travelled to Thebes like a great noble, or a royal mummy being borne to burial. Only instead of wailing priests, until I sent them back to Memphis, musicians sat upon the prow, and when I willed, dancing girls came to amuse my leisure and, veiled in golden nets, to serve at my table.

So I journeyed as though I were the Prince himself, and as one who was known to have his ear was made much of by the governors of the Nomes, the chief men of the towns, and the high priests of the temples at every city where we moored. For, as I have said, although Amenmeses sat upon the throne, Seti still ruled in the hearts of the folk of Egypt. Moreover, as I sailed further up the Nile to districts where little was known of the Israelites, and the troubles they were bringing on the land, I found this to be so more and more. Why is it, the Great Ones would whisper in my ear, that his Highness the Prince Seti does not hold his father's place? Then I would tell them of the Hebrews, and they would laugh and say:

"Let the Prince unfurl his royal banner here, and we will show him what we think of the question of these Israelitish slaves. May not the Heir of Egypt form his own judgment on such a matter as to whether they should abide there in the north, or go away into that wilderness which they desire?"

To all of which, and much like it, I would only answer that their words should be reported. More I did not, and indeed did not dare to say, since everywhere I found that I was being followed and watched by the spies of Pharaoh.

At length I came to Thebes and took up my abode in a fine house that was the property of the Prince, which I found that a messenger had commanded should be made ready for me. It stood near by the entrance to the Avenue of Sphinxes, which leads to the greatest of all the Theban temples, where is that mighty columned hall built by the first Seti and his son, Rameses II, the Prince's grandfather.

Here, having entrance to the place, I would often wander at night, and in my spirit draw as near to heaven as ever it has been my lot to travel. Also, crossing the Nile to the western bank, I visited that desolate valley where the rulers of Egypt lie at rest. The tomb of Pharaoh Meneptah was still unsealed, and accompanied by a single priest with torches, I crept down its painted halls and looked upon the sarcophagus of him whom so lately I had seen seated in glory upon the throne, wondering, as I looked, how much or how little he knew of all that passed in Egypt to-day.

Moreover, I copied the papyri that I had come to seek, in which there was nothing worth preserving, and some of real value that I discovered in the ancient libraries of the temples, and purchased others. One of these indeed told a very strange tale that has given me much cause for thought, especially of late years now when all my friends are dead.

Thus I spent two months, and should have stayed longer had not messengers reached me from the Prince saying that he desired my return. Of these, one followed within three days of the other, and his words were:

"Think you, Scribe Ana, that because I am no more Prince of Egypt I am no longer to be obeyed? If so, bear in mind that the gods may decree that one day I shall grow taller than ever I was before, and then be sure that I will remember your disobedience, and make you shorter by a head. Come swiftly, my friend, for I grow lonely, and need a man to talk with."

To which I replied, that I returned as fast as the barge would carry me, being so heavily laden with the manuscripts that I had copied and purchased.

So I started, being, to tell truth, glad to get away, for this reason. Two nights before, when I was walking alone from the great temple of the house, a woman dressed in many colours appeared and accosted me as such lost ones do. I tried to shake her off, but she clung to me, and I saw that she had drunk more than enough of wine. Presently she asked, in a voice that I thought familiar, if I knew who was the officer that had come to Thebes on the business of some Royal One and abode in the dwelling that was known as House of the Prince. I answered that his name was Ana.

"Once I knew an Ana very well," she said, "but I left him."

"Why?" I asked, turning cold in my limbs, for although I could not see her face because of a hood she wore, now I began to be afraid.

"Because he was a poor fool," she answered, "no man at all, but one who was always thinking about writings and making them, and another came my way whom I liked better until he deserted me."

"And what happened to this Ana?" I asked.

"I do not know. I suppose he went on dreaming, or perhaps he took another wife; if so, I am sorry for her. Only, if by chance it is the same that has come to Thebes, he must be wealthy now, and I shall go and claim him and make him keep me well."

"Had you any children?" I asked.

"Only one, thank the gods, and that died—thank the gods again, for otherwise it might have lived to be such as I am," and she sobbed once in a hard fashion and then fell to her vile endearments.

As she did so, the hood slipped from her head and I saw that the face was that of my wife, still beauteous in a bold fashion, but grown dreadful with drink and sin. I trembled from head to foot, then said in the disguised voice that I had used to her.

"Woman, I know this Ana. He is dead and you were his ruin. Still, because I was his friend, take this and go reform your ways," and I drew from my robe and gave to her a bag containing no mean weight of gold.

She snatched it as a hawk snatches, and seeing its contents by the starlight, thanked me, saying:

"Surely Ana dead is worth more than Ana alive. Also it is well that he is dead, for he is gone where the child went, which he loved more than life, neglecting me for its sake and thereby making me what I am. Had he lived, too, being as I have said a fool, he would have had more ill-luck with women, whom he never understood. Farewell, friend of Ana, who have given me that which will enable me to find another husband," and laughing wildly she reeled off behind a sphinx and vanished into the darkness.

For this reason, then, I was glad to escape from Thebes. Moreover, that miserable one had hurt me sorely, making me sure of what I had only guessed, namely, that with women I was but a fool, so great a fool that then and there I swore by my guardian god that never would I look with love on one of them again, an oath which I have kept well whatever others I may have broken. Again she stabbed me through with the talk of our dead child, for it is true that when that sweet one took flight to Osiris my heart broke and in a fashion has never mended itself again. Lastly, I feared lest it might also be true that I had neglected the mother for the sake of this child which was the jewel of my worship, yes, and is, and thereby helped her on to shame. So much did this thought torment me that through an agent whom I trusted, who believed that I was but providing for one whom I had wronged, I caused enough to be paid to her to keep her in comfort.

She did marry again, a merchant about whom she had cast her toils, and in due course spent his wealth and brought him to ruin, after which he ran away from her. As for her, she died of her evil habits in the third year of the reign of Seti II. But, the gods be thanked she never knew that the private scribe of Pharaoh's chamber was that Ana who had been her husband. Here I will end her story.

Now as I was passing down the Nile with a heart more heavy than the great stone that served as anchor on the barge, we moored at dusk on the third night by the side of a vessel that was sailing up Nile with a strong northerly wind. On board this boat was an officer whom I had known at the Court of Pharaoh Meneptah, travelling to Thebes on duty. This man seemed so much afraid that I asked him if anything weighed upon his mind. Then he took me aside into a palm grove upon the bank, and seating himself on the pole whereby oxen turned a waterwheel, told me that strange things were passing at Tanis.

It seemed that the Hebrew prophets had once more appeared before Pharaoh, who since his accession had left the Israelites in peace, not attacking them with the sword as Meneptah had wished to do, it was thought through fear lest if he did so he should die as Meneptah died. As before, they had put up their prayer that the people of the Hebrews should be suffered to go to worship in the wilderness, and Pharaoh had refused them. Then when he went down to sail upon the river early in the morning of another day, they had met him and one of them struck the water with his rod, and it had turned to blood. Whereon Ki and Kherheb and his company also struck the water with their rods, and it turned to blood. That was six days ago, and now this officer swore to me that the blood was creeping up the Nile, a tale at which I laughed.

"Come then and see," he said, and led me back to his boat, where all the crew seemed as fearful as he was himself.

He took me forward to a great water jar that stood upon the prow and, behold! it seemed to be full of blood, and in it was a fish dead, and—stinking.

"This water," said he, "I drew from the Nile with my own hands, not five hours sail to the north. But now we have outsped the blood, which follows after us," and taking a lamp he held it over the prow of the boat and I saw that all its planks were splashed as though with blood.

"Be advised by me, learned scribe," he added, "and fill every jar and skin that you can gather with sweet water, lest to-morrow you and your company should go thirsty," and he laughed a very dreary laugh.

Then we parted without more words, for neither of us knew what to say, and about midnight he sailed on with the wind, taking his chance of grounding on the sandbanks in the darkness.

For my part I did as he bade me, though my rowers who had not spoken with his men, thought that I was mad to load up the barge with so much water.

At the first break of day I gave the order to start. Looking over the side of the barge it seemed to me as though the lights of dawn had fallen from the sky into the Nile whereof the water had become pink-hued. Moreover, this hue, which grew ever deeper, was travelling up stream, not down, against the course of nature, and could not therefore have been caused by red soil washed from the southern lands. The bargemen stared and muttered together. Then one of them, leaning over the side, scooped up water in the hollow of his hand and drew some into his mouth, only to spit it out again with a cry of fear.

"'Tis blood," he cried. "Blood! Osiris has been slain afresh, and his holy blood fills the banks of Nile."

So much were they afraid, indeed, that had I not forced them to hold to their course they would have turned and rowed up stream, or beached the boat and fled into the desert. But I cried to them to steer on northwards, for thus perhaps we should sooner be done with this horror, and they obeyed me. Ever as we went the hue of the water grew more red, almost to blackness, till at last it seemed as though we were travelling through a sea of gore in which dead fish floated by the thousand, or struggled dying on the surface. Also the stench was so dreadful that we must bind linen about our nostrils to strain the foetid air.

We came abreast of a town, and from its streets one great wail of terror rose to heaven. Men stood staring as though they were drunken, looking at their red arms which they had dipped in the stream, and women ran to and fro upon the bank, tearing their hair and robes, and crying out such words as—

"Wizard's work! Bewitched! Accursed! The gods have slain each other, and men too must die!" and so forth.

Also we saw peasants digging holes at a distance from the shore to see perchance if they might come to water that was sweet and wholesome. All day long we travelled thus through this horrible flood, while the spray driven by the strong north wind spotted our flesh and garments, till we were like butchers reeking from the shambles. Nor could we eat any food because of the stench from this spray, which made it to taste salt as does fresh blood, only we drank of the water which I had provided, and the rowers who had held me to be mad now named me the wisest of men; one who knew what would befall in the future.

At length towards evening we noted that the water was growing much less red with every hour that passed, which was another marvel, seeing that above us, upstream, it was the colour of jasper, whereon we paused from our rowing and, all defiled as we were, sang a hymn and gave thanks to Hapi, god of Nile, the Great, the Secret, the Hidden. Before sunset, indeed, the river was clean again, save that on the bank where we made fast for the night the stones and rushes were all stained, and the dead fish lay in thousands polluting the air. To escape the stench we climbed a cliff that here rose quite close to Nile, in which we saw the mouths of ancient tombs that long ago had been robbed and left empty, purposing to sleep in one of them.

A path worn by the feet of men ran to the largest of these tombs, whence, as we drew near, we heard the sound of wailing. Looking in, I saw a woman and some children crouched upon the floor of the tomb, their heads covered with dust who, when they perceived us, cried more loudly than before, though with harsh dry voices, think-ing no doubt that we were robbers or perhaps ghosts because of our bloodstained garments. Also there was another child, a little one, that did not cry, because it was dead. I asked the woman what passed, but even when she understood that we were only men who meant her no harm, she could not speak or do more than gasp "Water! Water!" We gave her and the children to drink from the jars which we had brought with us, which they did greedily, after which I drew her story from her.

She was the wife of a fisherman who made his home in this cave, and said that seven days before the Nile had turned to blood, so that they could not drink of it, and had no water save a little in a pot. Nor could they dig to find it, since here the ground was all rock. Nor could they escape, since when he saw the marvel, her husband in his fear had leapt from his boat and waded to land and the boat had floated away.

I asked where was her husband, and she pointed behind her. I went to look, and there found a man hanging by his neck from a rope that was fixed to the capital of a pillar in the tomb, quite dead and cold. Returning sick at heart, I inquired of her how this had come about. She answered that when he saw that all the fish had perished, taking away his living, and that thirst had killed his youngest child, he went mad, and creeping to the back of the tomb, without her knowledge hung himself with a net rope. It was a dreadful story.

Having given the widow of our food, we went to sleep in another tomb, not liking the company of those dead ones. Next morning at the dawn we took the woman and her children on board the barge, and rowed them three hours' journey to a town where she had a sister, whom she found. The dead man and the child we left there in the tomb, since my men would not defile themselves by touching them.

So, seeing much terror and misery on our journey, at last we came safe to Memphis. Leaving the boatmen to draw up the barge, I went to the palace, speaking with none, and was led at once to the Prince. I found him in a shaded chamber seated side by side with the lady Merapi, and holding her hand in such a fashion that they remind me of the life-sized Ka statues of a man and his wife, such as I have seen in the ancient tombs, cut when the sculptors knew how to fashion the perfect likenesses of men and women. This they no longer do to-day, I think because the priests have taught them that it is not lawful. He was talking to her in a low voice, while she listened, smiling sweetly as she ever did, but with eyes, fixed straight before her that were, as it seemed to me, filled with fear. I thought that she looked very beautiful with her hair outspread over her white robe, and held back from her temples by a little fillet of god. But as I looked, I rejoiced to find that my heart no longer yearned for her as it had upon that night when I had seen her seated beneath the trees without the pleasure-house. Now she was its friend, no more, and so she remained until all was finished, as both the Prince and she knew well enough.

When he saw me Seti sprang from his seat and came to greet me, as a man does the friend whom he loves. I kissed his hand, and going to Merapi, kissed hers also noting that on it now shone that ring which once she had rejected as too large.

"Tell me, Ana, all that has befallen you," he said in his pleasant, eager voice.

"Many things, Prince; one of them very strange and terrible," I answered.

"Strange and terrible things have happened here also," broke in Merapi, "and, alas! this is but the beginning of woes."

So saying, she rose, as though she could trust herself to speak no more, bowed first to her lord and then to me, and left the chamber.

I looked at the Prince and he answered the question in my eyes.

"Jabez has been here," he said, "and filled her heart with forebodings. If Pharaoh will not let the Israelites go, by Amon I wish he would let Jabez go to some place whence he never could return. But tell me, have you also met blood travelling against the stream of Nile? It would seem so," and he glanced at the rusty stains that no washing would remove from my garments.

I nodded and we talked together long and earnestly, but in the end were no wiser for all our talking. For neither of us knew how it came about that men by striking water with a rod could turn it into what seemed to be blood, as the Hebrew prophet and Ki both had done, or how that blood could travel up the Nile against the stream and everywhere endure for a space of seven days; yes, and spread too to all the canals in Egypt, so that men must dig holes for water and dig them fresh each day because the blood crept in and poisoned them. But both of us thought that this was the work of the gods, and most of all of that god whom the Hebrews worship.

"You remember, Ana," said the Prince, "the message which you brought to me from Jabez, namely that no harm should come to me because of these Israelites and their curses. Well, no harm has come as yet, except the harm of Jabez, for he came. On the day before the news of this blood plague reached us, Jabez appeared disguised as a merchant of Syrian stuffs, all of which he sold to me at three times their value. He obtained admission to the chambers of Merapi, where she is accustomed to see whom she wills, and under pretence of showing her his stuffs, spoke with her and, as I fear, told her what you and I were so careful to hide, that she would bring trouble on me. At the least she has never been quite the same since, and I have thought it wise to make her swear by an oath, which I know she will never break, that now we are one she will not attempt to separate herself from me while we both have life."

"Did he wish her to go away with him, Prince?"

"I do not know. She never told me so. Still I am sure that had he come with his evil talk before that day when you returned from Tanis, she would have gone. Now I hope that there are reasons that will keep her where she is."

"What then did he say, Prince?"

"Little beyond what he had already said to you, that great troubles were about to fall on Egypt. He added that he was sent to save me and mine from these troubles because I had been a friend to the Hebrews in so far as that was possible. Then he walked through this house and all round its gardens, as he went reciting something that was written on a roll, of which I could not understand the meaning, and now and again prostrating himself to pray to his god. Thus, where the canal enters the garden and where it leaves the garden he stayed to pray, as he did at the well whence drinking water is drawn. Moreover, led by Merapi, he visited all my cornlands and those where my cattle are herded, reciting and praying until the servants thought that he was mad. After this he returned with her and, as it chanced, I overheard their parting. She said to him:

"'The house you have blessed and it is safe; the fields you have blessed and they are safe; will you not bless me also, O my Uncle, and any that are born of me?'

"He answered, shaking his head, 'I have no command, my Niece, either to bless or to curse you, as did that fool whom the Prince slew. You have chosen your own path apart from your people. It may be well, or it may be ill, or perhaps both, and henceforth you must walk it alone to wherever it may lead. Farewell, for perhaps we shall meet no more.'

"Thus speaking they passed out of earshot, but I could see that still she pleaded and still he shook his head. In the end, however, she gave him an offering, of all that she had I think, though whether this went to the temple of the Hebrews or into his own pouch I know not. At least it seemed to soften him, for he kissed her on the brow tenderly enough and departed with the air of a happy merchant who has sold his wares. But of all that passed between them Merapi would tell me nothing. Nor did I tell her of what I had overheard."

"And then?"

"And then, Ana, came the story of the Hebrew prophet who made the water into blood, and of Ki and his disciples who did likewise. The latter I did not believe, because I said it would be more reasonable had Ki turned the blood back into water, instead of making more blood of which there was enough already."

"I think that magicians have no reason."

"Or can do mischief only, Ana. At any rate after the story came the blood itself and stayed with us seven whole days, leaving much sickness behind it because of the stench of the rotting fish. Now for the marvel—here about my house there was no blood, though above and below the canal was full of it. The water remained as it has always been and the fish swam in it as they have always done; also that of the well kept sweet and pure. When this came to be known thousands crowded to the place, clamouring for water; that is until they found that outside the gates it grew red in their vessels, after which, although some still came, they drank the water where they stood, which they must do quickly."

"And what tale do they tell of this in Memphis, Prince?" I asked astonished.

"Certain of them say that not Ki but I am the greatest magician in Egypt—never, Ana, was fame more lightly earned. And certain say that Merapi, of whose doings in the temple at Tanis some tale has reached them, is the real magician, she being an Israelite of the tribe of the Hebrew prophets. Hush! She returns."

CHAPTER 14

Ki Comes to Memphis

Now of all the terrors of which this turning of the water into blood was the beginning in Egypt, I, Ana, the scribe, will not write, for if I did so, never in my life-days should I, who am old, find time to finish the story of them. Over a period of many, many moons they came, one by one, till the land grew mad with want and woe. Always the tale was the same. The Hebrew prophets would visit Pharaoh at Tanis and demand that he should led their people go, threatening him with vengeance if he refused. Yet he did refuse, for some madness had hold of him, or perhaps the god of the Israelites laid an enchantment on him, why I know not.

Thus but a little while after the terror of blood came a plague of frogs that filled Egypt from north to south, and when these were taken away made the air to stink. This miracle Ki and his company worked also, sending the frogs into Goshen, where they plagued the Israelites. But however it came about, at Seti's palace at Memphis and on the land that he owned around it there were no frogs, or at least but few of them, although at night from the fields about the sound of their croaking went up like the sound of beaten drums.

Next came a plague of lice, and these Ki and his companions would have also called down upon the Hebrews, but they failed, and afterwards struggled no more against the magic of the Israelites. Then followed a plague of flies, so that the air was black with them and no food could be kept sweet. Only in Seti's palace there were no flies, and in the garden but a few. After this a terrible pest began among the cattle, whereof thousands died. But of Seti's great herd not one was even sick, nor, as we learned, was there a hoof the less in the land of Goshen.

This plague struck Egypt but a little while after Merapi had given birth to a son, a very beautiful child with his mother's eyes, that was named Seti after his father. Now the marvel of the escape of the Prince and his household and all that was his from these curses spread abroad and made much talk, so that many sent to inquire of it.

Among the first came old Bakenkhonsu with a message from Pharaoh, and a private one to myself from the Princess Userti, whose pride would not suffer her to ask aught of Seti. We could tell him nothing except what I have written, which at first he did not believe. Having satisfied himself, however, that the thing was true, he said that he had fallen sick and could not travel back to Tanis. Therefore he asked leave of the Prince to rest a while in his house, he who had been the friend of his father, his grandfather, and his great-grandfather. Seti laughed, as indeed did the cunning old man himself, and there with us Bakenkhonsu remained till the end, to our great joy, for he was the most pleasant of all companions and the most learned. As for his message, one of his servants took back the answer to Pharaoh and to Userti, with the news of his master's grievous sickness.

Some eight days or so later, as I stood one morning basking in the sun at that gate of the palace gardens which overlooks the temple of Ptah, idly watching the procession of priests passing through its courts and chanting as they went (for because of the many sicknesses at this time I left the palace but rarely), I saw a tall figure approaching me draped against the morning cold. The man drew near, and addressing me over the head of the guard, asked if he could see the lady Merapi. I answered No, as she was engaged in nursing her son.

"And in other things, I think," he said with meaning, in a voice that seemed familiar to me. "Well, can I see the Prince Seti?"

I answered No, he was also engaged.

"In nursing his own soul, studying the eyes of the lady Merapi, the smile of his infant, the wisdom of the scribe Ana, and the attributes of the hundred and one gods that are known to him, including that of Israel, I suppose," said the familiar voice, adding, "Then can I see this scribe Ana, who I understand, being lucky, holds himself learned."

Now, angered at the scoffing of this stranger (though all the time I felt that he was none), I answered that the scribe Ana was striving to mend his luck by the pursuit of the goddess of learning in his study.

"Let him pursue," mocked the stranger, "since she is the only woman that he is ever likely to catch. Yet it is true that once one caught him. If you are of his acquaintance ask him of his talk with her in the avenue of the Sphinxes outside the great temple at Thebes and of what it cost him in gold and tears."

Hearing this I put my hand to my forehead and rubbed my eyes, thinking that I must have fallen into a dream there in the sunshine. When I lifted it again all was the same as before. There stood the sentry, indifferent to that which had no interest for him; the cock that had moulted its tail still scratched in the dirt; the crested hoopoe still sat spreading its wings on the head of one of the two great statues of Rameses which watched the gate; a water-seller in the distance still cried his wares, but the stranger was gone. Then I knew that I had been dreaming and turned to go also, to find myself face to face with him.

"Man," I said, indignantly, "how in the name of Ptah and all his priests did you pass a sentry and through that gate without my seeing you?"

"Do not trouble yourself with a new problem when already you have so many to perplex you, friend Ana. Say, have you yet solved that of how a rod like this turned itself into a snake in your hand?" and he threw back his hood, revealing the shaved head and the glowing eyes of the Kherheb Ki.

"No, I have not," I answered, "and I thank you," for here he proffered me the staff, "but I will not try the trick again. Next time the beast might bite. Well, Ki, as you can pass in here without my leave, why do you ask it? In short, what do you want with me, now that those Hebrew prophets have put you on your back?"

"Hush, Ana. Never grow angry, it wastes strength, of which we have so little to spare, for you know, being so wise, or perhaps you do not know, that at birth the gods give us a certain store of it, and when that is used we die and have to go elsewhere to fetch more. At this rate your life will be short, Ana, for you squander it in emotions."

"What do you want?" I repeated, being too angry to dispute with him.

"I want to find an answer to the question you asked so roughly: Why the Hebrew prophets have, as you say, put me on my back?"

"Not being a magician, as you pretend you are, I can give you none, Ki."

"Never for one moment did I suppose that you could," he replied blandly, stretching out his hands, and leaving the staff which had fallen from them standing in front of him. (It was not till afterwards that I remembered that this accursed bit of wood stood there of itself without visible support, for it rested on the paving-stone of the gateway.) "But, as it chances, you have in this house the master, or rather the mistress of all magicians, as every Egyptian knows to-day, the lady Merapi, and I would see her."

"Why do you say she is a mistress of magicians?" I asked indignantly.

"Why does one bird know another of its own kind? Why does the water here remain pure, when all other water turns to blood? Why do not the frogs croak in Seti's halls, and why do the flies avoid his meat? Why, also, did the statue of Amon melt before her glance, while all my magic fell back from her breast like arrows from a shirt of mail? Those are the questions that Egypt asks, and I would have an answer to them from the beloved of Seti, or of the god Set, she who is named Moon of Israel."

"Then why not go seek it for yourself, Ki? To you, doubtless, it would be a small matter to take the form of a snake or a rat, or a bird, and creep or run or fly into the presence of Merapi."

"Mayhap it would not be difficult, Ana. Or, better still, I might visit her in her sleep, as I visited you on a certain night at Thebes, when you told me of a talk you had held with a woman in the avenue of the Sphinxes, and of what it cost you in gold and tears. But, as it chances, I wish to appear as a man and a friend, and to stay a while. Bakenkhonsu tells me that he finds life here at Memphis very pleasant, free too from the sicknesses which just now seem to be so common in Egypt; so why should not I do the same, Ana?"

I looked at his round, ripe face, on which was fixed a smile unchanging as that worn by the masks on mummy coffins, from which I think he must have copied it, and at the cold, deep eyes above, and shivered a little. To tell truth I feared this man, whom I felt to be in touch with presences and things that are not of our world, and thought it wisest to withstand him no more.

"That is a question which you had best put to my master Seti who owns this house. Come, I will lead you to him," I said.

So we went to the great portico of the palace, passing in and out through the painted pillars, towards my own apartments, whence I purposed to send a message to the Prince. As it chanced this was needless, since presently we saw him seated in a little bay out of reach of the sun. By his side was Merapi, and on a woven rug between them lay their sleeping infant, at whom both of them gazed adoringly.

"Strange that this mother's heart should hide more might than can be boasted by all the gods of Egypt. Strange that those mother's eyes can rive the ancient glory of Amon into dust!" Ki said to me in so low a voice that it almost seemed as though I heard his thought and not his words, which perhaps indeed I did.

Now we stood in front of these three, and the sun being behind us, for it was still early, the shadow of the cloaked Ki fell upon a babe and lay there. A hateful fancy came to me. It looked like the evil form of an embalmer bending over one new dead. The babe felt it, opened its large eyes and wailed. Merapi saw it, and snatched up her child. Seti too rose from his seat, exclaiming, "Who comes?"

Thereon, to my amazement, Ki prostrated himself and uttered the salutation which may only be given to the King of Egypt: "Life! Blood! Strength! Pharaoh! Pharaoh! Pharaoh!"

"Who dares utter those words to me?" said Seti. "Ana, what madman do you bring here?"

"May it please the Prince, *he* brought *me* here," I replied faintly.

"Fellow, tell me who bade you say such words, than which none were ever less welcome."

"Those whom I serve, Prince."

"And whom do you serve?"

"The gods of Egypt."

"Then, man, I think the gods must need your company. Pharaoh does not sit at Memphis, and were he to hear of them——"

"Pharaoh will never hear them, Prince, until he hears all things."

They stared at each other. Then, as I had done by the gate Seti rubbed his eyes, and said:

"Surely this is Ki. Why, then, did you look otherwise just now?"

"The gods can change the fashion of their messenger a thousand times in a flash, if so they will, O Prince."

Now Seti's anger passed, and turned to laughter.

"Ki, Ki," he said, "you should keep these tricks for Court. But, since you are in the mood, what salutation have you for this lady by my side?"

Ki considered her, till she who ever feared and hated him shrank before his gaze.

"Crown of Hathor, I greet you. Beloved of Isis, shine on perfect in the sky, shedding light and wisdom ere you set."

Now this saying puzzled me. Indeed, I did not fully understand it until Bakenkhonsu reminded me that Merapi's name was Moon of Israel, that Hathor, goddess of love, is crowned with the moon in all her statues, that Isis is the queen of mysteries and wisdom, and that Ki who thought Merapi perfect in love and beauty, also the greatest of all sorceresses, was likening her to these.

"Yes," I answered, "but what did he mean when he talked about her setting?"

"Does not the moon always set, and is it not sometimes eclipsed?" he asked shortly.

"So does the sun," I answered.

"True; so does the sun! You are growing wise, very wise indeed, friend Ana. Oho—ho!"

To return: When Seti heard these words, he laughed again, and said:

"I must think that saying over, but it is clear that you have a pretty turn for praise. Is it not so, Merapi, Crown of Hathor, and Holder of the wisdom of Isis?"

But Merapi, who, I think, understood more than either of us, turned pale, and shrank further away, but outwards into the sunshine.

"Well, Ki," went on Seti, "finish your greetings. What for the babe?"

Ki considered it also.

"Now that it is no longer in the shadow, I see that this shoot from the royal root of Pharaoh grows so fast and tall that my eyes cannot reach its crest. He is too high and great for greetings, Prince."

Then Merapi uttered a little cry, and bore the child away.

"She is afraid of magicians and their dark sayings," said Seti, looking after her with a troubled smile.

"That she should not be, Prince, seeing that she is the mistress of all our tribe."

"The lady Merapi a magician? Well, after a fashion, yes—where the hearts of men are concerned, do you not think so, Ana? But be more plain, Ki. It is still early, and I love riddles best at night."

"What other could have shattered the strong and holy house where the majesty of Amon dwells on earth? Not even those prophets of the Hebrews as I think. What other could fence this garden round against the curses that have fallen upon Egypt?" asked Ki earnestly, for now all his mocking manner had departed.

"I do not think she does these things, Ki. I think some Power does them through her, and I know that she dared to face Amon in his temple because she was bidden so to do by the priests of her people."

"Prince," he answered with a short laugh, "a while ago I sent you a message by Ana, which perhaps other thoughts may have driven from his memory. It was as to the nature of that Power of which you speak. In that message I said that you were wise, but now I perceive that you lack wisdom like the rest of us, for if you had it, you would know that the tool which carves is not the guiding hand, and the lightning which smites is not the sending strength. So with this fair love of yours, and so with me and all that work marvels. We do not the things we seem to do, who are but the tool and the lightning. What I would know is who or what guides her hand and gives her the might to shield or to destroy."

"The question is wide, Ki, or so it seems to me who, as you say, have little wisdom, and whoever can answer it holds the key of knowledge. Your magic is but a small thing which seems great because so few can handle it. What miracle is it that makes the flower to grow, the child to be born, the Nile to rise, and the sun and stars to shine in heaven? What causes man to be half a beast and half a god and to grow downward to the beast or upward to the god—or both? What is faith and what is unbelief? Who made these things, through them to declare the purposes of life, of death, and of eternity? You shake your head, you do not know; how then can I know who, as you point out, am but foolish? Go get your answer from the lady Merapi's self, only mayhap you will find your questions countered."

"I'll take my chance. Thanks to Merapi's lord! A boon, O Prince, since you will not suffer that other name which comes easiest to the lips of one to whom the Present and the Future are sometimes much alike."

Seti looked at him keenly, and for the first time with a tinge of fear in his eyes.

"Leave the Future to itself, Ki," he exclaimed. "Whatever may be the mind of Egypt, just now I hold the Present enough for me," and he glanced first at the chair in which Merapi had been seated and then at the cloth upon which his son had lain.

"I take back my words. The Prince is wiser than I thought. Magicians know the future because at times it rushes down upon them and they must. It is that which makes them lonely, since what they know they cannot say. But only fools will seek it."

"Yet now and again they lift a corner of the veil, Ki. Thus I remember certain sayings of your own as to one who would find a great treasure in the land of Goshen and thereafter suffer some temporal loss, and—I forget the rest. Man, cease smiling at me with your face and piercing me through with your sword-like eyes. You can command all things, what boon then do you seek from me?"

"To lodge here a little while, Prince, in the company of Ana and Bakenkhonsu. Hearken, I am no more Kherheb. I have quarrelled with Pharaoh, perhaps because a little breath from that great wind of the future blows through my soul; perhaps because he does not reward me according to my merits—what does it matter which? At least I have come to be of one mind with you, O Prince, and think that Pharaoh would do well to let the Hebrews go, and therefore no longer will I attempt to match my magic against theirs. But he refuses, so we have parted."

"Why does he refuse, Ki?"

"Perhaps it is written that he must refuse. Or perhaps because, thinking himself the greatest of all kings instead of but a plaything of the gods, pride locks the doors of his heart that in a day to come the tempest of the Future, whereof I have spoken, may wreck the house which holds it. I do not know why he refuses, but her Highness Userti is much with him."

"For one who does not know, you have many reasons and all of them different, O instructed Ki," said Seti.

Then he paused, walking up and down the portico, and I who knew his mind guessed that he was wondering whether he would do well to suffer Ki, whom at times he feared because his objects were secret and never changed, to abide in his house, or whether he should send him away. Ki also shivered a little, as though he felt the shadow cold, and descended from the portico into the bright sunshine. Here he held out his hand and a great moth dropped from the roof and lit upon it, whereon it lifted it to his lips, which moved as though he were talking to the insect.

"What shall I do?" muttered Seti, as he passed me.

"I do not altogether like his company, nor, I think, does the lady Merapi, but he is an ill man to offend, Prince," I answered. "Look, he is talking with his familiar."

Seti returned to his place, and shaking off the moth which seemed loth to leave him, for twice it settled on his head, Ki came back into the shadow.

"Where is the use of your putting questions to me, Ki, when, according to your own showing, already you know the answer that I will give? What answer shall I give?" asked the Prince.

"That painted creature which sat upon my hand just now, seemed to whisper to me that you would say, O Prince, 'Stay, Ki, and be my faithful servant, and use any little lore you have to shield my house from ill.'"

Then Seti laughed in his careless fashion, and replied:

"Have your way, since it is a rule that none of the royal blood of Egypt may refuse hospitality to those who seek it, having been their friends, and I will not quote against your moth what a bat whispered in my ears last night. Nay, none of your salutations revealed to you by insects or by the future," and he gave him his hand to kiss.

When Ki was gone, I said:

"I told you that night-haunting thing was his familiar."

"Then you told me folly, Ana. The knowledge that Ki has he does not get from moths or beetles. Yet now that it is too late I wish that I had asked the lady Merapi what her will was in this matter. You should have thought of that, Ana, instead of suffering your mind to be led astray by an insect sitting on his hand, which is just what he meant that you should do. Well, in punishment, day by day it shall be your lot to look upon a man with a countenance like—like what?"

"Like that which I saw upon the coffin of the good god, your divine father, Meneptah, as it was prepared for him during his life in the embalmer's shop at Tanis," I answered.

"Yes," said the Prince, "a face smiling eternally at the Nothingness which is Life and Death, but in certain lights, with eyes of fire."

****

On the following day, by her invitation, I walked with the lady Merapi in the garden, the head nurse following us, bearing the royal child in her arms.

"I wish to ask you about Ki, friend Ana," she said. "You know he is my enemy, for you must have heard the words he spoke to me in the temple of Amon at Tanis. It seems that my lord has made him the guest of this house—oh look!" and she pointed before her.

I looked, and there a few paces away, where the shadow of the overhanging palms was deepest, stood Ki. He was leaning on his staff, the same that had turned to a snake in my hand, and gazing upwards like one who is lost in thought, or listens to the singing of birds. Merapi turned as though to fly, but at that moment Ki saw us, although he still seemed to gaze upwards.

"Greeting, O Moon of Israel," he said bowing. "Greeting, O Conqueror of Ki!"

She bowed back, and stood still, as a little bird stands when it sees a snake. There was a long silence, which he broke by asking:

"Why seek that from Ana which Ki himself is eager to give? Ana is learned, but is his heart the heart of Ki? Above all, why tell him that Ki, the humblest of your servants, is your enemy?"

Now Merapi straightened herself, looked into his eyes, and answered:

"Have I told Ana aught that he did not know? Did not Ana hear the last words you said to me in the temple of Amon at Tanis?"

"Doubtless he heard them, Lady, and therefore I am glad that he is here to hear their meaning. Lady Merapi, at that moment, I, the Sacrificer to Amon, was filled—not with my own spirit, but with the angry spirit of the god whom you had humbled as never before had befallen him in Egypt. The god through me demanded of you the secret of your magic, and promised you his hate, if you refused. Lady, you have his hate, but mine you have not, since I also have his hate because I, and he through me, have been worsted by your prophets. Lady, we are fellow-travellers in the Valley of Trouble."

She gazed at him steadily, and I could see that of all that passed his lips she believed no one word. Making no answer to him and his talk of Amon, she asked only:

"Why do you come here to do me ill who have done you none?"

"You are mistaken, Lady," he replied. "I come here to refuge from Amon, and from his servant Pharaoh, whom Amon drives on to ruin. I know well that, if you will it, you can whisper in the ear of the Prince and presently he will put me forth. Only then——" and he looked over her head to where the nurse stood rocking the sleeping child.

"Then what, Magician?"

Giving no answer, he turned to me.

"Learned Ana, to you remember meeting me at Tanis one night?"

I shook my head, though I guessed well enough what night he meant.

"Your memory weakens, learned Ana, or rather is confused, for we met often, did we not?"

Then he stared at the staff in his hand. I stared also, because I could not help it, and saw, or thought I saw, the dead wood begin to swell and curve. This was enough for me and I said hastily:

"If you mean the night of the Coronation, I do recall——"

"Ah! I thought you would. You, learned Ana, who like all scribes observe so closely, will have noted how little things—such as the scent of a flower, or the passing of a bird, or even the writhing of a snake in the dust—often bring back to the mind events or words it has forgotten long ago."

"Well—what of our meeting?" I broke in hastily.

"Nothing at all—or only this. Just before it you were talking with the Hebrew Jabez, the lady Merapi's uncle, were you not?"

"Yes, I was talking with him in an open place, alone."

"Not so, learned Scribe, for you know we are never alone—quite. Could you but see it, every grain of sand has an ear."

"Be pleased to explain, O Ki."

"Nay, Ana, it would be too long, and short jests are ever the best. As I have told you, you were not alone, for though there were some words that I did not catch, I heard much of what passed between you and Jabez."

"What did you hear?" I asked wrathfully, and next instant wished that I had bitten through my tongue before it shaped the words.

"Much, much. Let me think. You spoke about the lady Merapi, and whether she would do well to bide at Memphis in the shadow of the Prince, or to return to Goshen into the shadow of a certain—I forget the name. Jabez, a well-instructed man, said he thought that she might be happier at Memphis, though perhaps her presence there would bring a great sorrow upon herself and—another."

Here again he looked at the child, which seemed to feel his glance, for it woke up and beat the air with its little hands.

The nurse felt it also, although her head was turned away, for she started and then took shelter behind the bole of one of the palm-trees. Now Merapi said in a low and shaken voice:

"I know what you mean, Magician, for since then I have seen my uncle Jabez."

"As I have also, several times, Lady, which may explain to you what Ana here thinks so wonderful, namely that I should have learned what they said together when he thought they were alone, which, as I have told him, no one can ever be, at least in Egypt, the land of listening gods——"

"And spying sorcerers," I exclaimed.

"——And spying sorcerers," he repeated after me, "and scribes who take notes, and learn them by heart, and priests with ears as large as asses, and leaves that whisper—and many other things."

"Cease your gibes, and say what you have to say," said Merapi, in the same broken voice.

He made no answer, but only looked at the tree behind which the nurse and child had vanished.

"Oh! I know, I know," she exclaimed in tones that were like a cry. "My child is threatened! You threaten my child because you hate me."

"Your pardon, Lady. It is true that evil threatens this royal babe, or so I understood from Jabez, who knows so much. But it is not I that threaten it, any more than I hate you, in whom I acknowledge a fellow of my craft, but one greater than myself that it is my duty to obey."

"Have done! Why do you torment me?"

"Can the priests of the Moon-goddess torment Isis, Mother of Magic, with their prayers and offerings? And can I who would make a prayer and an offering——"

"What prayer, and what offering?"

"The prayer that you will suffer me to shelter in this house from the many dangers that threaten me at the hands of Pharaoh and the prophets of your people, and an offering of such help as I can give by my arts and knowledge against blacker dangers which threaten—another."

Here once more he gazed at the trunk of the tree beyond which I heard the infant wail.

"If I consent, what then?" she asked, hoarsely.

"Then, Lady, I will strive to protect a certain little one against a curse which Jabez tells me threatens him and many others in whom runs the blood of Egypt. I will strive, if I am allowed to bide here—I do not say that I shall succeed, for as your lord has reminded me, and as you showed me in the temple of Amon, my strength is smaller than that of the prophets and prophetesses of Israel."

"And if I refuse?"

"Then, Lady," he answered in a voice that rang like iron, "I am sure that one whom you love—as mothers love—will shortly be rocked in the arms of the god whom we name Osiris."

"*Stay*," she cried and, turning, fled away.

"Why, Ana, she is gone," he said, "and that before I could bargain for my reward. Well, this I must find in your company. How strange are women, Ana! Here you have one of the greatest of her sex, as you learned in the temple of Amon. And yet she opens beneath the sun of hope and shrivels beneath the shadow of fear, like the touched leaves of that tender plant which grows upon the banks of the river; she who, with her eyes set on the mystery that is beyond, whereof she hears the whispering winds, should tread both earthly hope and fear beneath her feet, or make of them stepping stones to glory. Were she a man she would do so, but her sex wrecks her, she who thinks more of the kiss of a babe than of all the splendours she might harbour in her breast. Yes, a babe, a single wretched little babe. You had one once, did you not, Ana?"

"Oh! to Set and his fires with you and your evil talk," I said, and left him.

When I had gone a little way, I looked back and saw that he was laughing, throwing up his staff as he laughed, and catching it again.

"Set and his fires," he called after me. "I wonder what they are like, Ana. Perhaps one day we shall learn, you and I together, Scribe Ana."

So Ki took up his abode with us, in the same lodgings as Bak-enkhonsu, and almost every day I would meet them walking in the garden, since I, who was of the Prince's table, except when he ate with the lady Merapi, did not take my food with them. Then we would talk together about many subjects. On those which had to do with learning, or even religion, I had the better of Ki, who was no great scholar or master of theology. But always before we parted he would plant some arrow in my ribs, at which old Bakenkhonsu laughed, and laughed again, yet ever threw over me the shield of his venerable wisdom, just because he loved me I think.

It was after this that the plague struck the cattle of Egypt, so that tens of thousands of them died, though not all as was reported. But, as I have said, of the herds of Seti none died, nor, as we were told, did any of those of the Israelites in the land of Goshen. Now there was great distress in Egypt, but Ki smiled and said that he knew it would be so, and that there was much worse to come, for which I could have smitten him over the head with his own staff, had I not feared that, if I did so, it might once more turn to a serpent in my hand.

Old Bakenkhonsu looked upon the matter with another face. He said that since his last wife died, I think some fifty years before, he had found life very dull because he missed the exercises of her temper, and her habit of presenting things as these never had been nor could possibly ever be. Now, however, it grew interesting again, since the marvels which were happening in Egypt, being quite contrary to Nature, reminded him of his last wife and her arguments. All of which was his way of saying that in those years we lived in a new world, whereof for the Egyptians Set the Evil One seemed to be the king.

But still Pharaoh would not let the Hebrews go, perhaps because he had vowed as much to Meneptah who set him on the throne, or perhaps for those other reasons, or one of them, which Ki had given to the Prince.

Then came the curse of sores afflicting man, woman, and child throughout the land, save those who dwelt in the household of Seti. Thus the watchman and his family whose lodge was without the gates suffered, but the watchman and his family who lived within the gates, not twenty paces away, did not suffer, which caused bitterness between their women. In the same way Ki, who resided as a guest of the Prince at Memphis, suffered from no sores, whereas those of his College who remained at Tanis were more heavily smitten than any others, so that some of them died. When he heard this, Ki laughed and said that he had told them it would be so. Also Pharaoh himself and even her Highness Userti were smitten, the latter upon the cheek, which made her unsightly for a while. Indeed, Bakenkhonsu heard, I know not how, that so great was her rage that she even bethought her of returning to her lord Seti, in whose house she had learned people were safe, and the beauty of her successor, Moon of Israel, remained unscarred and was even greater than before, tidings that I think Bakenkhonsu himself conveyed to her. But in the end this her pride, or her jealousy, prevented her from doing.

Now the heart of Egypt began to turn towards Seti in good earnest. The Prince, they said, had opposed the policy of the oppression of the Hebrews, and because he could not prevail had abandoned his right to the throne, which Pharaoh Amenmeses had purchased at the price of accepting that policy whereof the fruits had been proved to be destruction. Therefore, they reasoned, if Amenmeses were deposed, and the Prince reigned, their miseries would cease. So they sent deputations to him secretly, praying him to rise against Amenmeses and promising him support. But he would listen to none of them, telling them that he was happy as he was and sought no other state. Still Pharaoh grew jealous, for all these things his spies reported to him, and set about plots to destroy Seti.

Of the first of these Userti warned me by a messenger, but the second and worse Ki discovered in some strange way, so that the murderer was trapped at the gate and killed by the watchman, whereon Seti said that after all he had been wise to give hospitality to Ki, that is, if to continue to live were wisdom. The lady Merapi also said as much to me, but I noted that always she shunned Ki, whom she held in mistrust and fear.

CHAPTER 15

The Night of Fear

Then came the hail, and some months after the hail the locusts, and Egypt went mad with woe and terror. It was known to us, for with Ki and Bakenkhonsu in the palace we knew everything, that the Hebrew prophets had promised this hail because Pharaoh would not listen to them.

Therefore Seti caused it to be put about through all the land that the Egyptians should shelter their cattle, or such as were left to them, at the first sign of storm. But Pharaoh heard of it and issued a proclamation that this was not to be done, inasmuch as it would be an insult to the gods of Egypt. Still many did so and these saved their cattle. It was strange to see that wall of jagged ice stretching from earth to heaven and destroying all upon which it fell. The tall date-palms were stripped even of their bark; the soil was churned up; men and beasts if caught abroad were slain or shattered.

I stood at the gate and watched it. There, not a yard away, fell the white hail, turning the world to wreck, while here within the gate there was not a single stone. Merapi watched also, and presently came Ki as well, and with him Bakenkhonsu, who for once had never seen anything like this in all his long life. But Ki watched Merapi more than he did the hail, for I saw him searching out her very soul with those merciless eyes of his.

"Lady," he said at length, "tell your servant, I beseech you, how you do this thing?" and he pointed first to the trees and flowers within the gate and then to the wreck without.

At first I thought that she had not heard him because of the roar of the hail, for she stepped forward and opened the side wicket to admit a poor jackal that was scratching at the bars. Still this was not so, for presently she turned and said:

"Does the Kherheb, the greatest magician in Egypt, ask an unlearned woman to teach him of marvels? Well, Ki, I cannot, because I neither do it nor know how it is done."

Bakenkhonsu laughed, and Ki's painted smile grew as it were brighter than before.

"That is not what they say in the land of Goshen, Lady," he answered, "and not what the Hebrew women say here in Memphis. Nor is it what the priests of Amon say. These declare that you have more magic than all the sorcerers of the Nile. Here is the proof of it," and he pointed to the ruin without and the peace within, adding, "Lady, if you can protect your own home, why cannot you protect the innocent people of Egypt?"

"Because I cannot," she answered angrily. "If ever I had such power it is gone from me, who am now the mother of an Egyptian's child. But I have none. There in the temple of Amon some Strength worked through me, that is all, which never will visit me again because of my sin."

"What sin, Lady?"

"The sin of taking the Prince Seti to lord. Now, if any god spoke through me it would be one of those of the Egyptians, since He of Israel has cast me out."

Ki started as though some new thought had come to him, and at this moment she turned and went away.

"Would that she were high-priestess of Isis that she might work for us and not against us," he said.

Bakenkhonsu shook his head.

"Let that be," he answered. "Be sure that never will an Israelitish woman offer sacrifice to what she would call the abomination of the Egyptians."

"If she will not sacrifice to save the people, let her be careful lest the people sacrifice her to save themselves," said Ki in a cold voice.

Then he too went away.

"I think that if ever that hour comes, then Ki will have his share in it," laughed Bakenkhonsu. "What is the good of a shepherd who shelters here in comfort, while outside the sheep are dying, eh, Ana?"

It was after the plague of locusts, which ate all there was left to eat in Egypt, so that the poor folk who had done no wrong and had naught to say to the dealings of Pharaoh with the Israelites starved by the thousand, and during that of the great darkness, that Laban came. Now this darkness lay upon the land like a thick cloud for three whole days and nights. Nevertheless, though the shadows were deep, there was no true darkness over the house of Seti at Memphis, which stood in a funnel of grey light stretching from earth to sky.

Now the terror was increased tenfold, and it seemed to me that all the hundreds of thousands of Memphis were gathered outside our walls, so that they might look upon the light, such as it was, if they could do no more. Seti would have admitted as many as the place would hold, but Ki bade him not, saying, that if he did so the darkness would flow in with them. Only Merapi did admit some of the Israelitish women who were married to Egyptians in the city, though for her pains they only cursed her as a witch. For now most of the inhabitants of Memphis were certain that it was Merapi who, keeping herself safe, had brought these woes upon them because she was a worshipper of an alien god.

"If she who is the love of Egypt's heir would but sacrifice to Egypt's gods, these horrors would pass from us," said they, having, as I think, learned their lesson from the lips of Ki. Or perhaps the emissaries of Userti had taught them.

Once more we stood by the gate watching the people flitting to and fro in the gloom without, for this sight fascinated Merapi, as a snake fascinates a bird. Then it was that Laban appeared. I knew his hooked nose and hawk-like eyes at once, and she knew him also.

"Come away with me, Moon of Israel," he cried, "and all shall yet be forgiven you. But if you will not come, then fearful things shall overtake you."

She stood staring at him, answering never a word, and just then the Prince Seti reached us and saw him.

"Take that man," he commanded, flushing with anger, and guards sprang into the darkness to do his bidding. But Laban was gone.

On the second day of the darkness the tumult was great, on the third it was terrible. A crowd thrust the guard aside, broke down the gates and burst into the palace, humbly demanding that the lady Merapi would come to pray for them, yet showing by their mien that if she would not come they meant to take her.

"What is to be done?" asked Seti of Ki and Bakenkhonsu.

"That is for the Prince to judge," said Ki, "though I do not see how it can harm the lady Merapi to pray for us in the open square of Memphis."

"Let her go," said Bakenkhonsu, "lest presently we should all go further than we would."

"I do not wish to go," cried Merapi, "not knowing for whom I am to pray or how."

"Be it as you will, Lady," said Seti in his grave and gentle voice. "Only, hearken to the roar of the mob. If you refuse, I think that very soon every one of us will have reached a land where perhaps it is not needful to pray at all," and he looked at the infant in her arms.

"I will go," she said.

She went forth carrying the child and I walked behind her. So did the Prince, but in that darkness he was cut off by a rush of thousands of folk and I saw him no more till all was over. Bakenkhonsu was with me leaning on my arm, but Ki had gone on before us, for his own ends as I think. A huge mob moved through the dense darkness, in which here and there lights floated like lamps upon a quiet sea. I did not know where we were going until the light of one of these lamps shone upon the knees of the colossal statue of the great Rameses, revealing his cartouche. Then I knew that we were near the gateway of the vast temple of Memphis, the largest perhaps in the whole world.

We went on through court after pillared court, priests leading us by the hand, till we came to a shrine commanding the biggest court of all, which was packed with men and women. It was that of Isis, who held at her breast the infant Horus.

"O friend Ana," cried Merapi, "give help. They are dressing me in strange garments."

I tried to get near to her but was thrust back, a voice, which I thought to be that of Ki, saying:

"On your life, fool!"

Presently a lamp was held up, and by the light of it I saw Merapi seated in a chair dressed like a goddess, in the sacerdotal robes of Isis and wearing the vulture cap headdress—beautiful exceedingly. In her arms was the child dressed as the infant Horus.

"Pray for us, Mother Isis," cried thousands of voices, "that the curse of blackness may be removed."

Then she prayed, saying:

"O my God, take away this curse of blackness from these innocent people," and all of those present, repeated her prayer.

At that moment the sky began to lighten and in less than half an hour the sun shone out. When Merapi saw how she and the child were arrayed she screamed aloud and tore off her jewelled trappings, crying:

"Woe! Woe! Woe! Great woe upon the people of Egypt!"

But in their joy at the new found light few hearkened to her who they were sure had brought back the sun. Again Laban appeared for a moment.

"Witch! Traitress!" he cried. "You have worn the robes of Isis and worshipped in the temple of the gods of the Egyptians. The curse of the God of Israel be on you and that which is born of you."

410

I sprang at him but he was gone. Then we bore Merapi home swooning.

So this trouble passed by, but from that time forward Merapi would not suffer her son to be taken out of her sight.

"Why do you make so much of him, Lady?" I asked one day.

"Because I would love him well while he is here, Friend," she answered, "but of this say nothing to his father."

A while went by and we heard that still Pharaoh would not let the Israelites go. Then the Prince Seti sent Bakenkhonsu and myself to Tanis to see Pharaoh and to say to him:

"I seek nothing for myself and I forget those evils which you would have worked on me through jealousy. But I say unto you that if you will not let these strangers go great and terrible things shall befall you and all Egypt. Therefore, hear my prayer and let them go."

Now Bakenkhonsu and I came before Pharaoh and we saw that he was greatly aged, for his hair had gone grey about his temples and the flesh hung in bags beneath his eyes. Also not for one minute could he stay still.

"Is your lord, and are you also of the servants of this Hebrew prophet whom the Egyptians worship as a god because he has done them so much ill?" he asked. "It may well be so, since I hear that my cousin Seti keeps an Israelitish witch in his house, who wards off from him all the plagues that have smitten the rest of Egypt, and that to him has fled also Ki the Kherheb, my magician. Moreover, I hear that in payment for these wizardries he has been promised the throne of Egypt by many fickle and fearful ones among my people. Let him be careful lest I lift him up higher than he hopes, who already have enough traitors in this land; and you two with him."

Now I said nothing, who saw that the man was mad, but Bakenkhonsu laughed out loud and answered:

"O Pharaoh, I know little, but I know this although I be old, namely, that after men have ceased to speak your name I shall still hold converse with the wearer of the Double Crown in Egypt. Now will you let these Hebrews go, or will you bring death upon Egypt?"

Pharaoh glared at him and answered, "I will not let them go."

"Why not, Pharaoh? Tell me, for I am curious."

"Because I cannot," he answered with a groan. "Because something stronger than myself forces me to deny their prayer. Begone!"

So we went, and this was the last time that I looked upon Amenmeses at Tanis.

As we left the chamber I saw the Hebrew prophet entering the presence. Afterwards a rumour reached us that he had threatened to kill all the people in Egypt, but that still Pharaoh would not let the Israelites depart. Indeed, it was said that he had told the prophet that if he appeared before him any more he should be put to death.

Now we journeyed back to Memphis with all these tidings and made report to Seti. When Merapi heard them she went half mad, weeping and wringing her hands. I asked her what she feared. She answered death, which was near to all of us. I said:

"If so, there are worse things, Lady."

"For you mayhap you are faithful and good in your own fashion, but not for me. Do you not understand, friend Ana, that I am one who has broken the law of the God I was taught to worship?"

"And which of us is there who has not broken the law of the god we were taught to worship, Lady? If in truth you have done anything of the sort by flying from a murderous villain to one who loves you well, which I do not believe, surely there is forgiveness for such sins as this."

"Aye, perhaps, but, alas! the thing is blacker far. Have you forgotten what I did? Dressed in the robes of Isis I worshipped in the temple of Isis with my boy playing the part of Horus on my bosom. It is a crime that can never be forgiven to a Hebrew woman, Ana, for my God is a jealous God. Yet it is true that Ki tricked me."

"If he had not, Lady, I think there would have been none of us left to trick, seeing that the people were crazed with the dread of the darkness and believed that it could be lifted by you alone, as indeed happened," I added somewhat doubtfully.

"More of Ki's tricks! Oh! do you not understand that the lifting of the darkness at that moment was Ki's work, because he wished the people to believe that I am indeed a sorceress."

"Why?" I asked.

"I do not know. Perhaps that one day he may find a victim to bind to the altar in his place. At least I know well that it is I who must pay the price, I and my flesh and blood, whatever Ki may promise," and she looked at the sleeping child.

"Do not be afraid, Lady," I said. "Ki has left the palace and you will see him no more."

"Yes, because the Prince was angry with him about the trick in the temple of Isis. Therefore suddenly he went, or pretended to go, for how can one tell where such a man may really be? But he will come back again. Bethink you, Ki was the greatest magician in Egypt; even old Bakenkhonsu can remember none like to him. Then he matches himself against the prophets of my people and fails."

"But did he fail, Lady? What they did he did, sending among the Israelites the plagues that your prophets had sent among us."

"Yes, some of them, but he was outpaced, or feared to be outpaced at last. Is Ki a man to forget that? And if Ki chances really to believe that I am his adversary and his master at this black work, as because of what happened in the temple of Amon thousands believe to-day, will he not mete me my own measure soon or late? Oh! I fear Ki, Ana, and I fear the people of Egypt, and were it not for my lord beloved, I would flee away into the wilderness with my son, and get me out of this haunted land! Hush! he wakes."

From this time forward until the sword fell there was great dread in Egypt. None seemed to know exactly what they dreaded, but all thought that it had to do with death. People went about mournfully looking over their shoulders as though someone were following them, and at night they gathered together in knots and talked in whispers. Only the Hebrews seemed to be glad and happy. Moreover, they were making preparations for something new and strange. Thus those Israelitish women who dwelt in Memphis began to sell what property they had and to borrow of the Egyptians. Especially did they ask for the loan of jewels, saying that they were about to celebrate a feast and wished to look fine in the eyes of their countrymen. None refused them what they asked because all were afraid of them. They even came to the palace and begged her ornaments from Merapi, although she was a countrywoman of their own who had showed them much kindness. Yes, and seeing that her son wore a little gold circlet on his hair, one of them begged that also, nor did she say her nay. But, as it chanced, the Prince entered, and seeing the woman with this royal badge in her hand, grew very angry and forced her to restore it.

"What is the use of crowns without heads to wear them?" she sneered, and fled away laughing, with all that she had gathered.

After she had heard that saying Merapi grew even sadder and more distraught than she was before, and from her the trouble crept to Seti. He too became sad and ill at ease, though when I asked him why he vowed he did not know, but supposed it was because some new plague drew near.

"Yet," he added, "as I have made shift to live through nine of them, I do not know why I should fear a tenth."

Still he did fear it, so much that he consulted Bakenkhonsu as to whether there were any means by which the anger of the gods could be averted.

Bakenkhonsu laughed and said he thought not, since always if the

413

gods were not angry about one thing they were angry about another. Having made the world they did nothing but quarrel with it, or with other gods who had a hand in its fashioning, and of these quarrels men were the victims.

"Bear your woes, Prince," he added, "if any come, for ere the Nile has risen another fifty times at most, whether they have or have not been, will be the same to you."

"Then you think that when we go west we die indeed, and that Osiris is but another name for the sunset, Bakenkhonsu."

The old Councillor shook his great head, and answered:

"No. If ever you should lose one whom you greatly love, take comfort, Prince, for I do not think that life ends with death. Death is the nurse that puts it to sleep, no more, and in the morning it will wake again to travel through another day with those who have companioned it from the beginning."

"Where do all the days lead it to at last, Bakenkhonsu?"

"Ask that of Ki; I do not know."

"To Set with Ki, I am angered with him," said the Prince, and went away.

"Not without reason, I think," mused Bakenkhonsu, but when I asked him what he meant, he would not or could not tell me.

So the gloom deepened and the palace, which had been merry in its way, became sad. None knew what was coming, but all knew that something was coming and stretched out their hands to strive to protect that which they loved best from the stroke of the warring gods. In the case of Seti and Merapi this was their son, now a beautiful little lad who could run and prattle, one too of a strange health and vigour for a child of the inbred race of the Ramessids. Never for a minute was this boy allowed to be out of the sight of one or other of his parents; indeed I saw little of Seti in those days and all our learned studies came to nothing, because he was ever concerned with Merapi in playing nurse to this son of his.

When Userti was told of it, she said in the hearing of a friend of mine:

"Without a doubt that is because he trains his bastard to fill the throne of Egypt."

But, alas! all that the little Seti was doomed to fill was a coffin.

****

It was a still, hot evening, so hot that Merapi had bid the nurse bring the child's bed and set it between two pillars of the great portico.

There on the bed he slept, lovely as Horus the divine. She sat by his side in a chair that had feet shaped like to those of an antelope. Seti walked up and down the terrace beyond the portico leaning on my shoulder, and talking by snatches of this or that. Occasionally as he passed he would stay for a while to make sure by the bright moonlight that all was well with Merapi and the child, as of late it had become a habit with him to do. Then without speaking, for fear lest he should awake the boy, he would smile at Merapi, who sat there brooding, her head resting on her hand, and pass on.

The night was very still. The palm leaves did not rustle, no jackals were stirring, and even the shrill-voiced insects had ceased their cries. Moreover, the great city below was quiet as a home of the dead. It was as though the presage of some advancing doom scared the world to silence. For without doubt doom was in the air. All felt it down to the nurse woman, who cowered close as she dared to the chair of her mistress, and even in that heat shivered from time to time.

Presently little Seti awoke, and began to prattle about something he had dreamed.

"What did you dream, my son?" asked his father.

"I dreamed," he answered in his baby talk, "that a woman, dressed as Mother was in the temple, took me by the hand and led me into the air. I looked down, and saw you and Mother with white faces and crying. I began to cry too, but the woman with the feather cap told me not as she was taking me to a beautiful big star where Mother would soon come to find me."

The Prince and I looked at each other and Merapi feigned to busy herself with hushing the child to sleep again. It drew towards midnight and still no one seemed minded to go to rest. Old Bakenkhonsu appeared and began to say something about the night being very strange and unrestful, when, suddenly, a little bat that was flitting to and fro above us fell upon his head and thence to the ground. We looked at it, and saw that it was dead.

"Strange that the creature should have died thus," said Bakenkhonsu, when, behold! another fell to the ground near by. The black kitten which belonged to Little Seti saw it fall and darted from beside his bed where it was sleeping. Before ever it reached the bat, the creature wheeled round, stood upon its hind legs, scratching at the air about it, then uttered one pitiful cry and fell over dead.

We stared at it, when suddenly far away a dog howled in a very piercing fashion. Then a cow began to bale as these beasts do when they have lost their calves. Next, quite close at hand but without the

415

gates, there arose the ear-curdling cry of a woman in agony, which on the instant seemed to be echoed from every quarter, till the air was full of wailing.

"Oh, Seti! Seti!" exclaimed Merapi, in a voice that was rather a hiss than a whisper, "look at your son!"

We sprang to where the babe lay, and looked. He had awakened and was staring upward with wide-opened eyes and frozen face. The fear, if such it were, passed from his features, though still he stared. He rose to his little feet, always looking upwards. Then a smile came upon his face, a most beautiful smile; he stretched out his arms, as though to clasp one who bent down towards him, and fell backwards—quite dead.

Seti stood still as a statue; we all stood still, even Merapi. Then she bend down, and lifted the body of the boy.

"Now, my lord," she said, "there has fallen on you that sorrow which Jabez my uncle warned you would come, if ever you had aught to do with me. Now the curse of Israel has pierced my heart, and now our child, as Ki the evil prophesied, has grown too great for greetings, or even for farewells."

Thus she spoke in a cold and quiet voice, as one might speak of something long expected or foreseen, then made her reverence to the Prince, and departed, bearing the body of the child. Never, I think, did Merapi seem more beautiful to me than in this, her hour of bereavement, since now through her woman's loveliness shone out some shadow of the soul within. Indeed, such were her eyes and such her movements that well might have been a spirit and not a woman who departed from us with that which had been her son.

Seti leaned on my shoulder looking at the empty bed, and at the scared nurse who still sat behind, and I felt a tear drop upon my hand. Old Bakenkhonsu lifted his massive face, and looked at him.

"Grieve not over much, Prince," he said, "since, ere as many years as I have lived out have come and gone, this child will be forgotten and his mother will be forgotten, and even you, O Prince, will live but as a name that once was great in Egypt. And then, O Prince, elsewhere the game will begin afresh, and what you have lost shall be found anew, and the sweeter for it sheltering from the vile breath of men. Ki's magic is not all a lie, or if his is, mine holds some shadow of the truth, and when he said to you yonder in Tanis that not for nothing were you named 'Lord of Rebirths,' he spoke words that you should find comfortable to-night."

"I thank you, Councillor," said Seti, and turning, followed Merapi.

"Now I suppose we shall have more deaths," I exclaimed, hardly knowing what I said in my sorrow.

"I think not, Ana," answered Bakenkhonsu, "since the shield of Jabez, or of his god, is over us. Always he foretold that trouble would come to Merapi, and to Seti through Merapi, but that is all."

I glanced at the kitten.

"It strayed here from the town three days ago, Ana. And the bats also may have flown from the town. Hark to the wailing. Was ever such a sound heard before in Egypt?"

CHAPTER 16

Jabez Sells Horses

Bakenkhonsu was right. Save the son of Seti alone, none died who dwelt in or about his house, though elsewhere all the first-born of Egypt lay dead, and the first-born of the beasts also. When this came to be known throughout the land a rage seized the Egyptians against Merapi who, they remembered, had called down woe on Egypt after she had been forced to pray in the temple and, as they believed, to lift the darkness from Memphis.

Bakenkhonsu and I and others who loved her pointed out that her own child had died with the rest. To this it was answered, and here I thought I saw the fingers of Userti and of Ki, that it was nothing, since witches did not love children. Moreover, they said she could have as many as she liked and when she liked, making them to look like children out of clay figures and to grow up into evil spirits to torment the land. Lastly, people swore that she had been heard to say that, although to do it she must kill her own lord's son, she would not on that account forego her vengeance on the Egyptians, who once had treated her as a slave and murdered her father. Further, the Israelites themselves, or some of them, mayhap Laban among them, were reported to have told the Egyptians that it was the sorceress who had bewitched Prince Seti who brought such great troubles on them.

So it happened that the Egyptians came to hate Merapi, who of all women was the sweetest and the most to be loved, and to her other supposed crimes, added this also, that by her witcheries she had stolen the heart of Seti away from his lawful wife and made him to turn that lady, the Royal Princess of Egypt, even from his gates, so that she was forced to dwell alone at Tanis. For in all these matters none blamed Seti, whom everyone in Egypt loved, because it was known that he would have dealt with the Israelites in a very different fashion, and thus averted all the woes that had desolated the ancient land of Khem. As for this matter of the Hebrew girl with the big eyes who chanced to have thrown a spell upon him, that was his ill-fortune, nothing more. Amongst the many women with whom they believed he filled his house, as was the way of princes, it was not strange that one favourite should be a witch. Indeed, I am certain that only because he was known to love her, was Merapi saved from death by poison or in some other secret fashion, at any rate for a while.

Now came the glad tidings that the pride of Pharaoh was broken at last (for his first-born child had died with the others), or that the cloud of madness had lifted from his brain, whichever it might be, and that he had decreed that the Children of Israel might depart from Egypt when and whither they would. Then the people breathed again, seeing hope that their miseries might end.

It was at this time that Jabez appeared once more at Memphis, driving a number of chariot horses, which he said he wished to sell to the Prince, as he did not desire them to pass into any other hands. He was admitted and stated the price of his horses, according to which they must have been beasts of great value.

"Why do you wish to sell your horses?" asked Seti.

"Because I go with my people into lands where there is little water and there they might die, O Prince."

"I will buy the horses. See to it, Ana," said Seti, although I knew well that already he had more than he needed.

The Prince rose to show that the interview was ended, whereon Jabez, who was bowing his thanks, said hurriedly:

"I rejoice to learn, O Royal One, that things have befallen as I foretold, or rather was bidden to foretell, and that the troubles which have afflicted Egypt have passed by your dwelling."

"Then you rejoice to learn a falsehood, Hebrew, since the worst of those troubles has made its home here. My son is dead," and he turned away.

Jabez lifted his shifty eyes from the floor and glanced at him.

"Prince," he said, "I know and grieve because this loss has cut you to the heart. Yet it was no fault of mine or of my people. If you think, you will remember that both when I built a wall of protection about this place because of your good deeds to Israel, O Prince, and before, I warned, and caused you to be warned, that if you and my niece, Moon of Israel, came together a great trouble might fall on you through her who, having become the woman of an Egyptian in defiance of command, must bear the fate of Egyptian women."

"It may be so," said the Prince. "The matter is not one of which I care to talk. If this death were wrought by the magic of your wizards

I have only this to say—that it is an ill payment to me in return for all that I have striven to do on behalf of the Hebrews. Yet, what else could I expect from such a people in such a world? Farewell."

"One prayer, O Prince. I would ask your leave to speak with my niece, Merapi."

"She is veiled. Since the murder of her child by wizardry, she sees no man."

"Still I think she will see her uncle, O Prince."

"What then do you wish to say to her?"

"O Prince, through the clemency of Pharaoh we poor slaves are about to leave the land of Egypt never to return. Therefore, if my niece remains behind, it is natural that I should wish to bid her farewell, and to confide to her certain matters connected with our race and family, which she might desire to pass on to her children."

Now when he heard this word "children" Seti softened.

"I do not trust you," he said. "You may be charged with more of your Hebrew curses against Merapi, or you may say words to her that will make her even unhappier than she is. Yet if you would wish to see her in my presence——"

"My lord Prince, I will not trouble you so far. Farewell. Be pleased to convey——"

"Or if that does not suit you," interrupted Seti, "in the presence of Ana here you can do so, unless she refuses to receive you."

Jabez reflected for a moment, and answered:

"Then in the presence of Ana let it be, since he is a man who knows when to be silent."

Jabez made obeisance and departed, and at a sign from the Prince I followed him. Presently we were ushered into the chamber of the lady Merapi, where she sat looking most sad and lonely, with a veil of black upon her head.

"Greeting, my uncle," she said, after glancing at me, whose presence I think she understood. "Are you the bearer of more prophecies? I pray not, since your last were overtrue," and she touched the black veil with her finger.

"I am the bearer of tidings, and of a prayer, Niece. The tidings are that the people of Israel are about to leave Egypt. The prayer, which is also a command, is—that you make ready to accompany them——"

"To Laban?" she asked, looking up.

"No, my niece. Laban would not wish as a wife one who has been the mistress of an Egyptian, but to play your part, however humble, in the fortunes of our people."

"I am glad that Laban does not wish what he never could obtain, my uncle. Tell me, I pray you, why should I hearken to this prayer, or this command?"

"For a good reason, Niece—that your life hangs on it. Heretofore you have been suffered to take your heart's desire. But if you bide in Egypt where you have no longer a mission to fulfil, having done all that was sought of you in keeping with the mind of your lover, the Prince Seti, true to the cause of Israel, you will surely die."

"You mean that our people will kill me?"

"No, not our people. Still you will die."

She took a step towards him, and looked him in the eyes.

"You are certain that I shall die, my uncle?"

"I am, or at least others are certain."

Now she laughed; it was the first time I had seen her laugh for several moons.

"Then I will stay here," she said.

Jabez stared at her.

"I thought that you loved this Egyptian, who indeed is worthy of any woman's love," he muttered into his beard.

"Perhaps it is because I love him that I wish to die. I have given him all I have to give; there is nothing left of my poor treasure except what will bring trouble and misfortune on his head. Therefore the greater the love—and it is more great than all those pyramids massed to one—the greater the need that it should be buried for a while. Do you understand?"

He shook his head.

"I understand only that you are a very strange woman, different from any other that I have known."

"My child, who was slain with the rest, was all the world to me, and I would be where he is. Do you understand now?"

"You would leave your life, in which, being young, you may have more children, to lie in a tomb with your dead son?" he asked slowly, like one astonished.

"I only care for life while it can serve him whom I love, and if a day comes when he sits upon the throne how will a daughter of the hated Israelites serve him then? Also I do not wish for more children. Living or dead, he that is gone owns all my heart; there is no room in it for others. That love at least is pure and perfect, and having been embalmed by death, can never change. Moreover, it is not in a tomb that I shall lie with him, or so I believe. The faith of these Egyptians which we despise tells of a life eternal in the heavens, and thither I would go to seek that which is lost, and to wait that which is left behind awhile."

"Ah!" said Jabez. "For my part I do not trouble myself with these problems, who find in a life temporal on the earth enough to fill my thoughts and hands. Yet, Merapi, you are a rebel, and whether in heaven or on earth, how are rebels received by the king against whom they have rebelled?"

"You say I am rebel," she said, turning on him with flashing eyes. "Why? Because I would not dishonour myself by marrying a man I hate, one also who is a murderer, and because while I live I will not desert a man whom I love to return to those who have done me naught but evil. Did God then make women to be sold like cattle of the field for the pleasure and the profit of him who can pay the highest?"

"It seems so," said Jabez, spreading out his hands.

"It seems that you think so, who fashion God as you would wish him to be, but for my part I do not believe it, and if I did, I should seek another king. My uncle, I appeal from the priest and the elder to That which made both them and me, and by Its judgment I will stand or fall."

"Always a very dangerous thing to do," reflected Jabez aloud, "since the priest is apt to take the law into his own hands before the cause can be pleaded elsewhere. Still, who am I that I should set up my reasonings against one who can grind Amon to powder in his own sanctuary, and who therefore may have warrant for all she thinks and does?"

Merapi stamped her foot.

"You know well it was you who brought me the command to dare the god Amon in his temple. It was not I——" she began.

"I do know," replied Jabez waving his hand. "I know also that is what every wizard says, whatever his nation or his gods, and what no one ever believes. Thus because, having faith, you obeyed the command and through you Amon was smitten, among both the Israelites and the Egyptians you are held to be the greatest sorceress that has looked upon the Nile, and that is a dangerous repute, my niece."

"One to which I lay no claim, and never sought."

"Just so, but which all the same has come to you. Well, knowing as without doubt you do all that will soon befall in Egypt, and having been warned, if you needed warning, of the danger with which you yourself are threatened, you still refuse to obey this second command which it is my duty to deliver to you?"

"I refuse."

"Then on your own head be it, and farewell. Oh! I would add that there is a certain property in cattle, and the fruit of lands which descends to you from your father. In the event of your death——"

"Take it all, uncle, and may it prosper you. Farewell."

"A great woman, friend Ana, and a beautiful," said the old Hebrew, after he had watched her go. "I grieve that I shall never see her again, and, indeed, that no one will see her for very long; for, remember, she is my niece of whom I am fond. Now I too must be going, having completed my errand. All good fortune to you, Ana. You are no longer a soldier, are you? No? Believe me, it is as well, as you will learn. My homage to the Prince. Think of me at times, when you grow old, and not unkindly, seeing that I have served you as best I could, and your master also, who I hope will soon find again that which he lost awhile ago."

"Her Highness, Princess Userti," I suggested.

"The Princess Userti among other things, Ana. Tell the Prince, if he should deem them costly, that those horses which I sold him are really of the finest Syrian blood, and of a strain that my family has owned for generations. If you should chance to have any friend whose welfare you desire, let him not go into the desert soldiering during the next few moons, especially if Pharaoh be in command. Nay, I know nothing, but it is a season of great storm. Farewell, friend Ana, and again farewell."

"Now what did he mean by that?" thought I to myself, as I departed to make my report to Seti. But no answer to the question rose in my mind.

Very soon I began to understand. It appeared that at length the Israelites were leaving Egypt, a vast horde of them, and with them tens of thousands of Arabs of various tribes who worshipped their god and were, some of them, descended from the people of the Hyksos, the shepherds who once ruled in Egypt. That this was true was proved to us by the tidings which reached us that all the Hebrew women who dwelt in Memphis, even those of them who were married to Egyptians, had departed from the city, leaving behind them their men and sometimes their children. Indeed, before these went, certain of them who had been friends visited Merapi, and asked her if she were not coming also. She shook her head as she replied:

"Why do you go? Are you so fond of journeyings in the desert that for the sake of them you are ready never again to look upon the men you love and the children of your bodies?"

"No, Lady," they answered, weeping. "We are happy here in white-walled Memphis and here, listening to the murmur of the Nile, we would grow old and die, rather than strive to keep house in some desert tent with a stranger or alone. Yet fear drives us hence."

"Fear of what?"

"Of the Egyptians who, when they come to understand all that they have suffered at our hands in return for the wealth and shelter which they have given us for many generations, whereby we have grown from a handful into a great people, will certainly kill any Israelite whom they find left among them. Also we fear the curses of our priests who bid us to depart."

"Then *I* should fear these things also," said Merapi.

"Not so, Lady, seeing that being the only beloved of the Prince of Egypt who, rumour tells us, will soon be Pharaoh of Egypt, by him you will be protected from the anger of the Egyptians. And being, as we all know well, the greatest sorceress in the world, the overthrower of Amon-Ra the mighty, and one who by sacrificing her child was able to ward away every plague from the household where she dwelt, you have naught to fear from priests and their magic."

Then Merapi sprang up, bidding them to leave her to her fate and to be gone to their own, which they did hastily enough, fearing lest she should cast some spell upon them. So it came about that presently the fair Moon of Israel and certain children of mixed blood were all of the Hebrew race that were left in Egypt. Then, notwithstanding the miseries and misfortunes that during the past few years by terror, death, and famine had reduced them to perhaps one half of their number, the people of Egypt rejoiced with a great joy.

In every temple of every god processions were held and offerings made by those who had anything left to offer, while the statues of the gods were dressed in fine new garments and hung about with garlandings of flowers. Moreover, on the Nile and on the sacred lakes boats floated to and fro, adorned with lanterns as at the feast of the Rising of Osiris. As titular high-priest of Amon, an office of which he could not be deprived while he lived, Prince Seti attended these demonstrations, which indeed he must do, in the great temple of Memphis, whither I accompanied him. When the ceremonies were over he led the procession through the masses of the worshippers, clad in his splendid sacerdotal robes, whereon every throat of the thousands present there greeted him in a shout of thunder as "Pharaoh!" or at least as Pharaoh's heir.

When at length the shouting died, he turned upon them and said:

"Friends, if you would send me to be of the company that sits at the table of Osiris and not at Pharaoh's feasts, you will repeat this foolish greeting, whereof our Lord Amenmeses will hear with little joy."

In the silence that followed a voice called out:

"Have no fear, O Prince, while the Hebrew witch sleeps night by night upon your bosom. She who could smite Egypt with so many plagues can certainly shelter you from harm;" whereon the roars of acclamation went up again.

It was on the following day that Bakenkhonsu the aged returned with more tidings from Tanis, where he had been upon a visit. It seemed that a great council had been held there in the largest hall of one of the largest temples. At this council, which was open to all the people, Amenmeses had given report on the matter of the Israelites who, he stated, were departing in their thousands. Also offerings were made to appease the angry gods of Egypt. When the ceremony was finished, but before the company broke up in a heavy mood, her Highness the Princess Userti rose in her place, and addressed Pharaoh:

"By the spirits of our fathers," she cried, "and more especially by that of the good god Meneptah, my begetter, I ask of you, Pharaoh, and I ask of you, O people, whether the affront that has been put upon us by these Hebrew slaves and their magicians is one that the proud land of Egypt should be called upon to bear? Our gods have been smitten and defied; woes great and terrible, such as history tells not of, have fallen upon us through magic; tens of thousands, from the firstborn child of Pharaoh down, have perished in a single night. And now these Hebrews, who have murdered them by sorcery, for they are sorcerers all, men and women together, especially one of them who sits at Memphis, of whom I will not speak because she has wrought me private harm, by the decree of Pharaoh are to be suffered to leave the land. More, they are to take with them all their cattle, all their threshed corn, all the treasure they have hoarded for generations, and all the ornaments of price and wealth that they have wrung by terror from our own people, borrowing that which they never purpose to return. Therefore I, the Royal Princess of Egypt, would ask of Pharaoh, is this the decree of Pharaoh?"

"Now," said Bakenkhonsu, "Pharaoh sat with hanging head upon his throne and made no answer."

"Pharaoh does not speak," went on Userti. "Then I ask, is this the decree of the Council of Pharaoh and of the people of Egypt? There is still a great army in Egypt, hundreds of chariots and thousands of footmen. Is this army to sit still while these slaves depart into the desert there to rouse our enemies of Syria against us and return with them to butcher us?"

"At these words," continued Bakenkhonsu, "from all that multitude there went up a shout of 'No.'"

"The people say No. What saith Pharaoh?" cried Userti.

There followed a silence, till suddenly Amenmeses rose and spoke:

"Have it as you will, Princess, and on your head and the heads of all these whom you have stirred up let the evil fall if evil comes, though I think it is your husband, the Prince Seti, who should stand where you stand and put up this prayer in your place."

"My husband, the Prince Seti, is tied to Memphis by a rope of witch's hair, or so they tell me," she sneered, while the people murmured in assent.

"I know not," went on Amenmeses, "but this I know that always the Prince would have let these Hebrews go from among us, and at times, as sorrow followed sorrow, I have thought that he was right. Truly more than once I also would have let them go, but ever some Strength, I know not what, descended on my heart, turning it to stone, and wrung from me words that I did not desire to utter. Even now I would let them go, but all of you are against me, and, perchance, if I withstand you, I shall pay for it with my life and throne. Captains, command that my armies be made ready, and let them assemble here at Tanis that I myself may lead them after the people of Israel and share their dangers."

Then with a mighty shouting the company broke up, so that at the last all were gone and only Pharaoh remained seated upon his throne, staring at the ground with the air, said Bakenkhonsu, rather of one who is dead than of a living king about to wage war upon his foes.

To all these words the Prince listened in silence, but when they were finished he looked up and asked:

"What think you, Bakenkhonsu?"

"I think, O Prince," answered the wise old man, "that her Highness did ill to stir up this matter, though doubtless she spoke with the voices of the priests and of the army, against which Pharaoh was not strong enough to stand."

"What you think, I think," said Seti.

At this moment the lady Merapi entered.

"I hear, my lord," she said, "that Pharaoh purposes to pursue the people of Israel with his host. I come to pray my lord that he will not join himself to the host of Pharaoh."

"It is but natural, Lady, that you should not wish me to make war upon your kin, and to speak truth I have no mind that way," replied Seti, and, turning, left the chamber with her.

"She is not thinking of her king but of her lover's life," said Bakenkhonsu. "She is not a witch as they declare, but it is true that she knows what we do not."

"Yes," I answered, "it is true."

CHAPTER 17

The Dream of Merapi

A while went by; it may have been fourteen days, during which we heard that the Israelites had started on their journey. They were a mighty multitude who bore with them the coffin and the mummy of their prophet, a man of their blood, Vizier, it is reported, to that Pharaoh who welcomed them to Egypt hundreds of years before. Some said they went this way and some that, but Bakenkhonsu, who knew everything, declared that they were heading for the Lake of Crocodiles, which others name Sea of Reeds, whereby they would cross into the desert beyond, and thence to Syria. I asked him how, seeing that at its narrowest part, this lake was six thousand paces in width, and that the depth of its mud was unfathomable. He replied that he did not know, but that I might do well to inquire of the lady Merapi.

"So you have changed your mind, and also think her a witch," I said, to which he answered:

"One must breathe the wind that blows, and Egypt is so full of witchcraft that it is difficult to say. Also it was she and no other who destroyed the ancient statue of Amon. Oh! yes, witch or no witch, it might be well to ask her how her people purpose to cross the Sea of Reeds, especially if Pharaoh's chariots chance to be behind them."

So I did ask her, but she answered that she knew nothing of the matter, and wished to know nothing, seeing that she had separated from her people, and remained in Egypt.

Then Ki came, I know not whence, and having made his peace with Seti as to the dressing of Merapi in the robes of Isis which, he vowed, was done by the priests against his wish, told us that Pharaoh and a great host had started to pursue the Israelites. The Prince asked him why he had not gone with the host, to which he replied that he was no soldier, also that Pharaoh hid his face from him. In return he asked the Prince why *he* had not gone.

Seti answered, because had been deprived of his command with his other officers and had no wish to take share in this business as a private citizen.

"You are wise, as always, Prince," said Ki.

It was on the following night, very late, while the Prince, Ki, Bakenkhonsu and I, Ana, sat talking, that suddenly the lady Merapi broke in upon us as she had risen from her bed, wild-eyed, and with her hair flowing down her robes.

"I have dreamed a dream!" she cried. "I dreamed that I saw all the thousands of my people following after a flame that burned from earth to heaven. They came to the edge of a great water and behind them rushed Pharaoh and all the hosts of the Egyptians. Then my people ran on to the face of the water, and it bore them as though it were sound land. Now the soldiers of the Pharaoh were following, but the gods of Egypt appeared, Amon, Osiris, Horus, Isis, Hathor, and the rest, and would have turned them back. Still they refused to listen, and dragging the gods with them, rushed out upon the water. Then darkness fell, and in the darkness sounds of wailing and of a mighty laughter. It passed, the moon rose, shining upon emptiness. I awoke, trembling in my limbs. Interpret me this dream if you can, O Ki, Master of Magic."

"Where is the need, Lady," he answered, awaking as though from sleep, "when the dreamer is also the seer? Shall the pupil venture to instruct the teacher, or the novice to make plain the mysteries to the high-priestess of the temple? Nay, Lady, I and all the magicians of Egypt are beneath your feet."

"Why will you ever mock me?" she said, and as she spoke, she shivered.

Then Bakenkhonsu opened his lips, saying:

"The wisdom of Ki has been buried in a cloud of late, and gives no light to us, his disciples. Yet the meaning of this dream is plain, though whether it be also true I do not know. It is that all the host of Egypt, and with it the gods of Egypt, are threatened with destruction because of the Israelites, unless one to whom they will hearken can be found to turn them from some purpose that I do not understand. But to whom will the mad hearken, oh! to whom will they hearken?" and lifting his great head, he looked straight at the Prince.

"Not to me, I fear, who now am no one in Egypt," said Seti.

"Why not to you, O Prince, who to-morrow may be everyone in Egypt?" asked Bakenkhonsu. "Always you have pleaded the cause of the Hebrews, and said that naught but evil would befall Egypt because of them, as has happened. To whom, then, will the people and the army listen more readily?"

"Moreover, O Prince," broke in Ki, "a lady of your household has dreamed a very evil dream, of which, if naught be said, it might be held that it was no dream, but a spell of power aimed against the majesty of Egypt; such a spell as that which cast great Amon from his throne, such a spell as that which has set a magic fence around this house and field."

"Again I tell you that I weave no spells, O Ki, who with my own child have paid the price of them."

"Yet spells were woven, Lady, and has been known from of old, strength is perfected in sacrifice alone," Ki answered darkly.

"Have done with your talk of spells, Magician," exclaimed the Prince, "or if you must speak of them, speak of your own, which are many. It was Jabez who protected us here against the plagues, and the statue of Amon was shattered by some god."

"I ask your pardon, Prince," said Ki bowing, "it was *not* this lady but her uncle who fenced your house against the plagues which ravaged Egypt, and it was *not* this lady but some god working in her which overthrew Amon of Tanis. The Prince has said it. Yet this lady has dreamed a certain dream which Bakenkhonsu has interpreted although I cannot, and I think that Pharaoh and his captains should be told of the dream, that on it they may form their own judgment."

"Then why do you not tell them, Ki?"

"It has pleased Pharaoh, O Prince, to dismiss me from his service as one who failed and to give my office of Kherheb to another. If I appear before the face of Pharaoh I shall be killed."

Now I, Ana, listening, wished that Ki would appear before the face of Pharaoh, although I did not believe that he could be killed by him or by anybody else, since against death he had charms. For I was afraid of Ki, and felt in myself that again he was plotting evil to Merapi whom I knew to be innocent.

The Prince walked up and down the chamber as was his fashion when lost in thought. Presently he stopped opposite to me and said:

"Friend Ana, be pleased to command that my chariots be made ready with a general's escort of a hundred men and spare horses to each chariot. We ride at dawn, you and I, to seek out the army of Pharaoh and pray audience of Pharaoh."

"My lord," said Merapi in a kind of cry, "I pray you go not, leaving me alone."

"Why should I leave you, Lady? Come with me if you will." She shook her head, saying:

"I dare not. Prince, there has been some charm upon me of late that draws me back to my own people. Twice in the night I have awakened and found myself in the gardens with my face set towards the north, and heard a voice in my ears, even that of my father who is dead, saying:

"'Moon of Israel, thy people wander in the wilderness and need thy light.'

"It is certain therefore that if I came near to them I should be dragged down as wood is dragged of an eddy, nor would Egypt see me any more."

"Then I pray you bide where you are, Merapi," said the Prince, laughing a little, "since it is certain that where you go I must follow, who have no desire to wander in the wilderness with your Hebrew folk. Well, it seems that as you do not wish to leave Memphis and will not come with me, I must stay with you."

Ki fixed his piercing eyes upon the pair of them.

"Let the Prince forgive me," he said, "but I swear it by the gods that never did I think to live to hear the Prince Seti Meneptah set a woman's whims before his honour."

"Your words are rough," said Seti, drawing himself up, "and had they been spoken in other days, mayhap, Ki——"

"Oh! my lord," said Ki prostrating himself till his forehead touched the ground, "bethink you then how great must be the need which makes me dare to speak them. When first I came hither from the court of Tanis, the spirit that is within me speaking through my lips gave certain titles to your Highness, for which your Highness was pleased to reprove me. Yet the spirit in me cannot lie and I know well, and bid all here make record of my words, that to-night I stand in the presence of him who ere two moons have passed will be crowned Pharaoh."

"Truly you were ever a bearer of ill-tidings, Ki, but if so, what of it?"

"This your Highness: Were it not that the spirits of Truth and Right compel me for their own reasons, should I, who have blood that can be shed or bones that can be broken, dare to hurl hard words at him who will be Pharaoh? Should I dare to cross the will of the sweet dove who nestles on his heart, the wise, white dove that murmurs the mysteries of heaven, whence she came, and is stronger than the vulture of Isis and swifter than the hawk of Ra; the dove that, were she angry, could rend me into more fragments than did Set Osiris?"

Now I saw Bakenkhonsu begin to swell with inward laughter like a frog about to croak, but Seti answered in a weary voice:

"By all the birds of Egypt with the sacred crocodiles thrown in, I do not know, since that mind of yours, Ki, is not an open writing which can be read by the passer-by. Still, if you would tell me what is the reason with which the goddesses of Truth and Justice have inspired you——"

"The reason is, O Prince, that the fate of all Egypt's army may be hidden in your hand. The time is short and I will be plain. Deny it as she will this lady here, who seems to be but a thing of love and beauty, is the greatest sorceress in Egypt, as I whom she has mastered know well. She matched herself against the high god of Egypt and smote him to the dust, and has paid back upon him, his prophets, and his worshippers the ills that he would have worked to her, as in the like case any of our fellowship would do. Now she has dreamed a dream, or her spirit has told her that the army of Egypt is in danger of destruction, and I know that this dream is true. Hasten then, O Prince, to save the hosts of Egypt, which you will surely need when you come to sit upon its throne."

"I am no sorceress," cried Merapi, "and yet—alas! that I must say it—this smiling-featured, cold-eyed wizard's words are true. *The sword of death hangs over the hosts of Egypt!*"

"Command that the chariots be made ready," said Seti again.

****

Eight days had gone by. It was sunset and we drew rein over against the Sea of Reeds. Day and night we had followed the army of Pharaoh across the wilderness on a road beaten down by his chariot wheels and soldiers, and by the tens of thousands of the Israelites who had passed that way before them. Now from the ridge where we had halted we saw it encamped beneath us, a very great army. Moreover, stragglers told us that beyond, also encamped, was the countless horde of the Israelites, and beyond these the vast Sea of Reeds which barred their path. But we could not see them for a very strange reason. Between these and the army of Pharaoh rose a black wall of cloud, built as it were from earth to heaven. One of those stragglers of whom I have spoken, told us that this cloud travelled before the Israelites by day, but at night was turned into a pillar of fire. Only on this day, when the army of Pharaoh approached, it had moved round and come between the people of Israel and the army.

Now when the Prince, Bakenkhonsu, and I heard these things

we looked at each other and were silent. Only presently the Prince laughed a little, and said:

"We should have brought Ki with us, even if we had to carry him bound, that he might interpret this marvel, for it is sure that no one else can."

"It would be hard to keep Ki bound, Prince, if he wished to go free," answered Bakenkhonsu. "Moreover, before ever we entered the chariots at Memphis he had departed south for Thebes. I saw him go."

"And I gave orders that he should not be allowed to return, for I hold him an ill guest, or so thinks the lady Merapi," replied Seti with a sigh.

"Now that we are here what would the Prince do?" I asked.

"Descend to the camp of Pharaoh and say what we have to say, Ana."

"And if he will not listen, Prince?"

"Then cry our message aloud and return."

"And if he will not suffer us to return, Prince?"

"Then stand still and live or die as the gods may decree."

"Truly our lord has a great heart!" exclaimed Bakenkhonsu, "and though I feel over young to die, I am minded to see the end of this matter with him," and he laughed aloud.

But I who was afraid thought that *O-ho-ho* of his, which the sky seemed to echo back upon our heads, a strange and indeed a fearful sound.

Then we put on robes of ceremony that we had brought with us, but neither swords nor armour, and having eaten some food, drove on with the half of our guard towards the place where we saw the banners of Pharaoh flying about his pavilion. The rest of our guard we left encamped, bidding them, if aught happened to us, to return and make report at Memphis and in the other great cities. As we drew near to the camp the outposts saw us and challenged. But when they perceived by the light of the setting sun who it was that they challenged, a murmur went through them, of:

"The Prince of Egypt! The Prince of Egypt!" for so they had never ceased to name Seti, and they saluted with their spears and let us pass.

So at length we came to the pavilion of Pharaoh, round about which a whole regiment stood on guard. The sides of it were looped up high because of the heat of the night which was great, and within sat Pharaoh, his captains, his councillors, his priests, his magicians, and many others at meat or serving food and drink. They sat at a table that was bent like a bow, with their faces towards the entrance, and Pharaoh was in the centre of the table with his fan-bearers and butlers behind him.

We advanced into the pavilion, the Prince in the centre, Bak-enkhonsu leaning on his staff on the right hand, and I, wearing the gold chain that Pharaoh Meneptah had given me, on the left, but those with us remained among the guard at the entrance.

"Who are these?" asked Amenmeses, looking up, "who come here unbidden?"

"Three citizens of Egypt who have a message for Pharaoh," answered Seti in his quiet voice, "which we have travelled fast and far to speak in time."

"How are you named, citizens of Egypt, and who sends your message?"

"We are named, Seti Meneptah aforetime Prince of Egypt, and heir to its crown; Bakenkhonsu the aged Councillor, and Ana the scribe and King's Companion, and our message is from the gods."

"We have heard those names, who has not?" said Pharaoh, and as he spoke all, or very nearly all, the company rose, or half rose, and bowed towards the Prince. "Will you and your companions be seated and eat, Prince Seti Meneptah?"

"We thank the divine Pharaoh, but we have already eaten. Have we Pharaoh's leave to deliver our message?"

"Speak on, Prince."

"O Pharaoh, many moons have gone by, since last we looked upon each other face to face, on that day when my father, the good god Meneptah, disinherited me, and afterwards fled hence to Osiris. Pharaoh will remember why I was thus cut off from the royal root of Egypt. It was because of the matter of these Israelites, who in my judgment had been evilly dealt by, and should be suffered to leave our land. The good god Meneptah, being so advised by you and others, O Pharaoh, would have smitten the Israelites with the sword, making an end of them, and to this he demanded my assent as the Heir of Egypt. I refused that assent and was cast out, and since then, you, O Pharaoh, have worn the double crown, while I have dwelt as a citizen of Memphis, living upon such lands and revenues as are my own. Between that hour and this, O Pharaoh, many griefs have smitten Egypt, and the last of them cost you your first-born, and me mine. Yet through them all, O Pharaoh, you have refused to let these Hebrews go, as I counselled should be done at the beginning. At length after the death of the first-born, your decree was issued that they might go. Yet now you follow them with a great army and purpose to do to them what my father, the good god Meneptah, would have done, had I consented, namely—to destroy them with the sword. Hear me, Pharaoh!"

"I hear; also the case is well if briefly set. What else would the Prince Seti say?"

"This, O Pharaoh. That I pray you to return with all your host from the following of these Hebrews, not to-morrow or the next day, but at once—this night."

"Why, O Prince?"

"Because of a certain dream that a lady of my household who is Hebrew has dreamed, which dream foretells destruction to you and the army of Egypt, unless you hearken to these words of mine."

"I think that we know of this snake whom you have taken to dwell in your bosom, whence it may spit poison upon Egypt. It is named Merapi, Moon of Israel, is it not?"

"That is the name of the lady who dreamed the dream," replied Seti in a cold voice, though I felt him tremble with anger at my side, "the dream that if Pharaoh wills my companions here shall set out word for word to his magicians."

"Pharaoh does not will it," shouted Amenmeses smiting the board with his fist, "because Pharaoh knows that it is but another trick to save these wizards and thieves from the doom that they have earned."

"Am I then a worker of tricks, O Pharaoh? If I had been such, why have I journeyed hither to give warning, when by sitting yonder at Memphis to-morrow, I might once more have become heir to the double crown? For if you will not hearken to me, I tell you that very soon you shall be dead, and with you these"—and he pointed to all those who sat at table—"and with them the great army that lies without. Ere you speak, tell me, what is that black cloud which stands before the camp of the Hebrews? Is there no answer? Then I will give you the answer. It is the pall that shall wrap the bones of every one of you."

Now the company shivered with fear, yes, even the priests and the magicians shivered. But Pharaoh went mad with rage. Springing from his seat, he snatched at the double crown upon his head, and hurled it to the ground, and I noted that the golden *uraeus* band about it, rolled away, and rested upon Seti's sandaled foot. He tore his robes and shouted:

"At least our fate shall be your fate, Renegade, who have sold Egypt to the Hebrew witch in payment of her kisses. Seize this man and his companions, and when we go down to battle against these Israelites to-morrow after the darkness lifts, let them be set with the captains of the van. So shall the truth be known at last."

Thus Pharaoh commanded, and Seti, answering nothing, folded his arms upon his breast and waited.

Men rose from their seats as though to obey Pharaoh and sank back to them again. Guards started forward and yet remained standing where they were. Then Bakenkhonsu burst into one of his great laughs.

"O-ho-ho," he laughed, "Pharaohs have I seen come and go, one and two and three, and four and five, but never yet have I seen a Pharaoh whom none of his councillors or guards could obey however much they willed it. When you are Pharaoh, Prince Seti, may your luck be better. Your arm, Ana, my friend, and lead on, Royal Heir of Egypt. The truth is shown to blind eyes that will not see. The word is spoken to deaf ears that will not hearken, and the duty done. Night falls. Sleep ye well, ye bidden of Osiris, sleep ye well!"

Then we turned and walked from that pavilion. At its entrance I looked back, and in the low light that precedes the darkness, it seemed to me as though all seated there were already dead. Blue were their faces and hollow shone their eyes, and from their lips there came no word. Only they stared at us as we went, and stared and stared again.

Without the door of the pavilion, by command of the Prince, I called aloud the substance of the lady Merapi's dream, and warned all within earshot to cease from pursuing the people of Israel, if they would continue to live to look upon the sun. Yet even now, although to speak thus was treason against Pharaoh, none lifted a hand against the Prince, or against me his servant. Often since then I have wondered why this was so, and found no answer to my questionings. Mayhap it was because of the majesty of my master, whom all knew to be the true Pharaoh, and loved at heart. Mayhap it was because they were sure that he would not have travelled so far and placed himself in the power of Amenmeses save to work the armies of Egypt good, and not ill, and to bring them a message that had been spoken by the gods themselves.

Or mayhap it was because he was still hedged about by that protection which the Hebrews had vowed to him through their prophets with the voice of Jabez. At least so it happened. Pharaoh might command, but his servants would not obey. Moreover, the story spread, and that night many deserted from the host of Pharaoh and encamped about us, or fled back towards the cities whence they came. Also with them were not a few councillors and priests who had talked secretly with Bakenkhonsu. So it chanced that even if Pharaoh desired to make an end of us, as perhaps he purposed to do in the midnight watches, he thought it wisest to let the matter lie until he had finished with the people of Israel.

****

It was a very strange night, silent, with a heavy, stirless air. There were no stars, but the curtain of black cloud which seemed to hang beyond the camp of the Egyptians was alive with lightnings which appeared to shape themselves to letters that I could not read.

"Behold the Book of Fate written in fire by the hand of God!" said Bakenkhonsu, as he watched.

About midnight a mighty east wind began to blow, so strongly that we must lie upon our faces under the lea of the chariots. Then the wind died away and we heard tumult and shoutings, both from the camp of Egypt, and from the camp of Israel beyond the cloud. Next there came a shock as of earthquake, which threw those of us who were standing to the ground, and by a blood-red moon that now appeared we perceived that all the army of Pharaoh was beginning to move towards the sea.

"Whither go they?" I asked of the Prince who clung to my arm.

"To doom, I think," he answered, "but to what doom I do not know."

After this we said no more, because we were too much afraid.

****

Dawn came at last, showing the most awful sight that was ever beheld by the eye of man.

The wall of cloud had disappeared, and in the clear light of the morning, we perceived that the deep waters of the Sea of Reeds had divided themselves, leaving a raised roadway that seemed to have been cleared by the wind, or perchance to have been thrown up by the earthquake. Who can say? Not I who never set foot upon that path of death. Along this wide road streamed the tens of thousands of the Israelites, passing between the water on the right hand, and the water on the left, and after them followed all the army of Pharaoh, save those who had deserted, and stood or lay around us, watching. We could even see the golden chariots that marked the presence of Pharaoh himself, and of his bodyguard, deep in the heart of the broken host that struggled forward without discipline or order.

"What now? Oh! what now?" murmured Seti, and as he spoke there was a second shock of earthquake. Then to the west on the sea there arose a mighty wave, whereof the crest seemed to be high as a pyramid. It rolled forward with a curved and foaming head, and in the hollow of it for a moment, no more, we saw the army of Egypt. Yet in that moment I seemed to see mighty shapes fleeing landwards along the crest of the wave, which shapes I took to be the gods of Egypt, pursued by a form of light and glory that drove them as with a scourge. They came, they went, accompanied by a sound of wailing, and the wave fell.

But beyond it, the hordes of Israel still marched—upon the further shore.

Dense gloom followed, and through the gloom I saw, or thought I saw, Merapi, Moon of Israel, standing before us with a troubled face and heard or thought I heard her cry:

"Oh! help me, my lord Seti! Help me, my lord Seti!"

Then she too was gone.

"Harness the chariots!" cried Seti, in a hollow voice.

CHAPTER 18

The Crowning of Merapi

Fast as sped our horses, rumour, or rather the truth, carried by those who had gone before us, flew faster. Oh! that journey was as a dream begotten by the evil gods. On we galloped through the day and through the night and lo! at every town and village women rushed upon us crying:

"Is it true, O travellers, is it true that Pharaoh and his host are perished in the sea?"

Then old Bakenkhonsu would call in answer:

"It is true that he who *was* Pharaoh and his host are perished in the sea. But lo! here is he who *is* Pharaoh," and he pointed to the Prince, who took no heed and said nothing, save:

"On! On!"

Then forward we would plunge again till once more the sound of wailing died into silence.

It was sunset, and at length we drew near to the gates of Memphis. The Prince turned to me and spoke.

"Heretofore I have not dared to ask," he said, "but tell me, Ana. In the gloom after the great cliff of water fell and the shapes of terror swept by, did you seem to see a woman stand before us and did you seem to hear her speak?"

"I did, O Prince."

"Who was that woman and what did she say?"

"She was one who bore a child to you, O Prince, which child is not, and she said, 'Oh! help me, my lord Seti. Help me, my lord Seti!'"

His face grew ashen even beneath its veil of dust, and he groaned.

"Two who loved her have seen and two who loved her have heard," he said. "There is no room for doubt. Ana, she is dead!"

"I pray the gods——"

"Pray not, for the gods of Egypt are also dead, slain by the god of Israel. Ana, who has murdered her?"

With my finger I who am a draughtsman drew in the thick dust that lay on the board of the chariot the brows of a man and beneath them two deep eyes. The gilt on the board where the sun caught it looked like light in the eyes.

The Prince nodded and said:

"Now we shall learn whether great magicians such as Ki can die like other men. Yes, if need be, to learn that I will put on Pharaoh's crown."

We halted at the gates of Memphis. They were shut and barred, but from within the vast city rose a sound of tumult.

"Open!" cried the Prince to the guard.

"Who bids me open?" answered the captain of the gate peering at us, for the low sun lay behind.

"Pharaoh bids you open."

"Pharaoh!" said the man. "We have sure tidings that Pharaoh and his armies are slain by wizardry in the sea."

"Fool!" thundered the Prince, "Pharaoh never dies. Pharaoh Amenmeses is with Osiris but the good god Seti Meneptah who *is* Pharaoh bids you open."

Then the bronze gates rolled back, and those who guarded them prostrated themselves in the dust.

"Man," I called to the captain, "what means yonder shouting?"

"Sir," he answered, "I do not know, but I am told that the witch who has brought woe on Egypt and by magic caused the death of Pharaoh Amenmeses and his armies, dies by fire in the place before the temple."

"By whose command?" I cried again as the charioteer flogged the horses, but no answer reached our ears.

We rushed on up the wide street to the great place that was packed with tens of thousands of the people. We drove the horses at them.

"Way for Pharaoh! Way for the Mighty One, the good god, Seti Meneptah, King of the Upper and the Lower Land!" shouted the escort.

The people turned and saw the tall shape of the Prince still clad in the robes of state which he had worn when he stood before Amenmeses in the pavilion by the sea.

"Pharaoh! Pharaoh! Hail to Pharaoh!" they cried, prostrating themselves, and the cry passed on through Memphis like a wind.

Now we were come to the centre of the place, and there in front of the great gates of the temple burned a vast pyre of wood. Before the pyre moved figures, in one of whom I knew Ki dressed in his magician's robe. Outside of these there was a double circle of soldiers who kept the people back, which these needed, for they raved like madmen and shook their fists. A group of priests near the fire separated, and I saw that among them stood a man and a woman, the latter with dishevelled hair and torn robes as though she had been roughly handled. At this moment her strength seemed to fail her and she sank to the ground, lifting her face as she did so. It was the face of Merapi, Moon of Israel.

So she was not dead. The man at her side stooped as though to lift her up, but a stone thrown out of the shadow struck him in the back and caused him to straighten himself, which he did with a curse at the thrower. I knew the voice at once, although the speaker was disguised.

It was that of Laban the Israelite, he who had been betrothed to Merapi, and had striven to murder us in the land of Goshen. What did he here? I wondered dimly.

Ki was speaking. "Hark how the Hebrew cat spits," he said. "Well, the cause has been tried and the verdict given, and I think that the familiar should feed the flames before the witch. Watch him now, and perhaps he will change into something else."

All this he said, smiling in his usual pleasant fashion, even when he made a sign to certain black temple slaves who stood near. They leapt forward, and I saw the firelight shone upon their copper armlets as they gripped Laban. He fought furiously, shouting:

"Where are your armies, Egyptians, and where is your dog of a Pharaoh? Go dig them from the Sea of Reeds. Farewell, Moon of Israel. Look how your royal lover crowns you at the last, O faithless——"

He said no more, for at this moment the slaves hurled him headlong into the heart of the great fire, which blackened for a little and burned bright again.

Then it was that Merapi struggled to her feet and cried in a ringing voice those very words which the Prince and I had seemed to hear her speak far away by the Sea of Reeds—*"Oh! help me my lord Seti! Help me, my lord Seti!"* Yes, the same words which had echoed in our ears days before they passed her lips, or so we believed.

Now all this while our chariots had been forcing their way foot by foot through the wall of the watching crowd, perhaps while a man might count a hundred, no more. As the echoes of her cry died away at length we were through and leaping to the ground.

"The witch calls on one who sups to-night at the board of Osiris

441

with Pharaoh and his host," sneered Ki. "Well, let her go to seek him there if the guardian gods will suffer it," and again he made a sign to the black slaves.

But Merapi had seen or felt Seti advancing from the shadows and seeing flung herself upon his breast. He kissed her on the brow before them all, then bade me hold her up and turned to face the people.

"Bow down. Bow down. Bow down!" cried the deep voice of Bakenkhonsu. "Life! Blood! Strength! Pharaoh! Pharaoh! Pharaoh!" and what he said the escort echoed.

Then of a sudden the multitude understood. To their knees they fell and from every side rose the ancient salutation. Seti held up his hand and blessed them. Watching, I saw Ki slip towards the darkness, and whispered a word to the guards, who sprang upon him and brought him back.

Then the Prince spoke:

"Ye name me Pharaoh, people of Memphis, and Pharaoh I fear I am by descent of blood to-day, though whether I will consent to bear the burdens of government, should Egypt wish it of me, as yet I know not. Still he who wore the double crown is, I believe, dead in the midst of the sea; at the least I saw the waters overwhelm him and his army. Therefore, if only for an hour, I will be Pharaoh, that as Pharaoh I may judge of certain matters. Lady Merapi, tell me, I pray you, how came you to this pass?"

"My lord," she answered, in a low voice, "after you had gone to warn the army of Pharaoh because of that dream I dreamed, Ki, who departed on the same day, returned again. Through one of the women of the household, over whom he had power, or so I think, he obtained access to me when I was alone in my chamber. There he made me this offer:

"'Give me,' he said, 'the secret of your magic that I may be avenged upon the wizards of the Hebrews who have brought about my downfall, and upon the Hebrews themselves, and also upon all my other enemies, and thus once more become the greatest man in Egypt. In turn I will fulfil all your desires, and make you, and no other, Queen of Egypt, and be your faithful servant, and that of your lord Seti who shall be Pharaoh, until the end of your lives. Refuse, and I will stir up the people against you, and before ever the Prince returns, if he returns at all, they who believe you to be an evil sorceress shall mete out to you the fate of a sorceress.'

"My lord, I answered to Ki what I have often told him before, that I had no magic to reveal to him, I who knew nothing of the black arts of sorcery, seeing that it was not I who destroyed the statue of Amon in the temple at Tanis, but that same Power which since then has brought all the plagues on Egypt. I said, too, that I cared nothing for the gifts he offered to me, as I had no wish to be Queen of Egypt. My lord, he laughed in my face, saying I should find that he was one ill to mock, as others had found before me. Then he pointed at me with his wand and muttered some spell over me, which seemed to numb my limbs and voice, holding me helpless till he had been gone a long while, and could not be found by your servants, whom I commanded in your name to seize, and keep him till your return.

"From that hour the people began to threaten me. They crowded about the palace gates in thousands, crying day and night that they were going to kill me, the witch. I prayed for help, but from me, a sinner, heaven has grown so far away that my prayers seem to fall back unheard upon my head. Even the servants in the palace turned against me, and would not look upon my face. I grew mad with fear and loneliness, since all fled before me. At last one night towards the dawn I went on to the terrace, and since no god would hear me, I turned towards the north whither I knew that you had gone, and cried to you to help me in those same words which I cried again just now before you appeared." (Here the Prince looked at me and I Ana looked at him.) "Then it was that from among the bushes of the garden appeared a man, hidden in a long, sheepskin cloak, so that I could not see his face, who said to me:

"'Moon of Israel, I have been sent by his Highness, the Prince Seti, to tell you that you are in danger of your life, as he is in danger of his, wherefore he cannot come to you. His command is that you come to him, that together you may flee away out of Egypt to a land where you will both be safe until all these troubles are finished.'

"'How know I that you of the veiled face are a true messenger?' I asked. 'Give me a sign.'

"Then he held out to me that scarabaeus of lapis-lazuli which your Highness gave to me far away in the land of Goshen, the same that you asked back from me as a love token when we plighted troth, and you gave me your royal ring, which scarabaeus I had seen in your robe when you drove away with Ana."

"I lost it on our journey to the Sea of Reeds, but said nothing of it to you, Ana, because I thought the omen evil, having dreamed in the night that Ki appeared and stole it from me," whispered the Prince to me.

"'It is not enough,' I answered. 'This jewel may have been thieved away, or snatched from the dead body of the Prince, or taken from him by magic.'

"The cloaked man thought a while and said, 'This night, not an hour ago, Pharaoh and his chariots were overwhelmed in the Sea of Reeds. Let that serve as a sign.'

"'How can this be?' I answered, 'since the Sea of Reeds is far away, and such tidings cannot travel thence in an hour. Get you gone, false tempter.'

"'Yet it is so,' he answered.

"'When you prove it to me, I will believe, and come.'

"'Good,' he said, and was gone.

"Next day a rumour began to run that this awful thing had happened. It grew stronger and stronger, until all swore that it had happened. Now the fury of the people rose against me, and they ravened round the palace like lions of the desert, roaring for my blood. Yet it was as though they could not enter here, since whenever they rushed at the gates or walls, they fell back again, for some spirit seemed to protect the place. The days went by; the night came again and at the dawn, this dawn that is past, once more I stood upon the terrace, and once more the cloaked man appeared from among the trees.

"'Now you have heard, Moon of Israel,' he said, 'and now you must believe and come, although you think yourself safe because at the beginning of the plagues this, the home of Seti, was enchanted against evil, so that none within it can be harmed.'

"'I have heard, and I think that I believe, though how the tidings reached Memphis in an hour I do not understand. Yet, stranger, I say to you that it is not enough.'

"Then the man drew a papyrus roll from his bosom and threw it at my feet. I opened it and read. The writing was the writing of Ana as I knew well, and the signature was the signature of you, my lord, and it was sealed with your seal, and with the seal of Bakenkhonsu as a witness. Here it is," and from the breast of her garment, she drew out a roll and gave it to me upon whom she rested all this while.

I opened it, and by the light of torches the Prince, Bakenkhonsu, and I read. It was as she had told us in what seemed to be my writing, and signed and sealed as she had said. The words ran:

"To Merapi, Moon of Israel, in my house at Memphis.

"Come, Lady, Flower of Love, to me your lord, to whom the bearer of this will guide you safely. Come at once, for I am in great danger, as you are, and together only can we be safe."

444

"Ana, what means this?" asked the Prince in a terrible voice. "If you have betrayed me and her——"

"By the gods," I began angrily, "am I a man that I should live to hear even your Highness speak thus to me, or am I but a dog of the desert?"

I ceased, for at that moment Bakenkhonsu began to laugh.

"Look at the letter!" he laughed. "Look at the letter."

We looked, and as we looked, behold the writing on it turned first to the colour of blood and then faded away, till presently there was nothing in my hand but a blank sheet of papyrus.

"Oho-ho!" laughed Bakenkhonsu. "Truly, friend Ki, you are the first of magicians, save those prophets of the Israelites who have brought you—Whither have they brought you, friend Ki?"

Then for the first time the painted smile left the face of Ki, and it became like a block of stone in which were set two angry jewels that were his eyes.

"Continue, Lady," said the Prince.

"I obeyed the letter. I fled away with the man who said he had a chariot waiting. We passed out by the little gate.

"'Where is the chariot?' I asked.

"'We go by boat,' he answered, and led the way towards the river. As we threaded the big palm grove men appeared from between the trees.

"'You have betrayed me,' I cried.

"'Nay,' he answered, 'I am myself betrayed.'

"Then for the first time I knew his voice for that of Laban.

"The men seized us; at the head of them was Ki.

"'This is the witch,' he said, 'who, her wickedness finished, flies with her Hebrew lover, who is also the familiar of her sorceries.'

"They tore the cloak and the false beard from him and there before me stood Laban. I cursed him to his face. But all he answered was:

"'Merapi, what I have done I did for love of you. It was my purpose to take you away to our people, for here I knew that they would kill you. This magician promised you to me if I could tempt you from the safety of the palace, in return for certain tidings that I have given him.'

"These were the only words that passed between us till the end. They dragged us to the secret prison of the great temple where we were separated. Here all day long Ki and the priests tormented me with questions, to which I gave no answer. Towards the evening they brought me out and led me here with Laban at my side. When the people saw me a great cry went up of 'Sorceress! Hebrew witch!' They broke through the guard; they seized me, threw me to the ground and beat me. Laban strove to protect me but was torn away. At length the people were driven off, and oh! my lord, you know the rest. I have spoken truth, I can no more."

So saying her knees loosened beneath her and she swooned. We bore her to the chariot.

"You have heard, Ki," said the Prince. "Now, what answer?"

"None, O Pharaoh," he replied coldly, "for Pharaoh you are, as I promised that you should be. My spirit has deserted me, those Hebrews have stolen it away. That writing should have faded from the scroll as soon as it was read by yonder lady, and then I would have told you another story; a story of secret love, of betrayal and attempted flight with her lover. But some evil god kept it there until you also had read, you who knew that you had not written what appeared before your eyes. Pharaoh, I am conquered. Do your will with me, and farewell. Beloved you shall always be as you have always been, but happy never in this world."

"O People," cried Seti, "I will not be judge in my own cause. You have heard, do you judge. For this wizard, what reward?"

Then there went up a great cry of "Death! Death by fire. The death he had made ready for the innocent!"

That was the end, but they told me afterwards that, when the great pyre had burned out, in it was found the head of Ki looking like a red-hot stone. When the sunlight fell on it, however, it crumbled and faded away, as the writing had faded from the roll. If this be true I do not know, who was not present at the time.

We bore Merapi to the palace. She lived but three days, she whose body and spirit were broken. The last time I saw her was when she sent for me not an hour before death came. She was lying in Seti's arms babbling to him of their child and looking very sweet and happy. She thanked me for my friendship, smiling the while in a way which showed me that she knew it was more than friendship, and bade me tend my master well until we all met again elsewhere. Then she gave me her hand to kiss and I went away weeping.

After she was dead a strange fancy took Seti. In the great hall of the palace he caused a golden throne to be put up, and on this throne he set her in regal garments, with pectoral and necklaces of gems, crowned like a queen of Egypt, and thus he showed her to the lords of Memphis. Then he caused her to be embalmed and buried in a secret sepulchre, the place of which I have sworn never to reveal, but without any rites because she was not of the faith of Egypt.

There then she sleeps in her eternal house until the Day of Resurrection, and with her sleeps her little son.

It was within a moon of this funeral that the great ones of Egypt came to Memphis to name the Prince as Pharaoh, and with them came her Highness, the Queen Userti. I was present at the ceremony, which to me was very strange. There was the Vizier Nehesi; there was the high-priest Roi and with him many other priests; and there was even the old chamberlain Pambasa, pompous yet grovelling as before, although he had deserted the household of the Prince after his disinheritance for that of the Pharaoh Amenmeses. His appearance with his wand of office and long white beard, of which he was so proud because it was his own, drew from Seti the only laugh I had heard him utter for many weeks.

"So you are back again, Chamberlain Pambasa," he said.

"O most Holy, O most Royal," answered the old knave, "has Pambasa, the grain of dust beneath your feet, ever deserted the House of Pharaoh, or that of him who will be Pharaoh?"

"No," replied Seti, "it is only when you think that he will not be Pharaoh that you desert. Well, get you to your duties, rogue, who perhaps at bottom are as honest as the rest."

Then followed the great and ancient ceremony of the Offering of the Crown, in which spoke priests disguised as gods and other priests disguised as mighty Pharaohs of the past; also the nobles of the Nomes and the chief men of cities. When all had finished Seti answered:

"I take this, my heritage," and he touched the double crown, "not because I desire it but because it is my duty, as I swore that I would to one who has departed. Blow upon blow have smitten Egypt which, I think, had my voice been listened to, would never have fallen. Egypt lies bleeding and well-nigh dead. Let it be your work and mine to try to nurse her back to life. For no long while am I with you, who also have been smitten, how it matters not, yet while I am here, I who seem to reign will be your servant and that of Egypt. It is my decree that no feasts or ceremonials shall mark this my accession, and that the wealth which would have been scattered upon them shall be distributed among the widows and children of those who perished in the Sea of Reeds. Depart!"

They went, humble yet happy, since here was a Pharaoh who knew the needs of Egypt, one too who loved her and who alone had shown himself wise of heart while others were filled with madness. Then her Highness entered, splendidly apparelled, crowned and followed by her household, and made obeisance.

"Greeting to Pharaoh," she cried.

"Greeting to the Royal Princess of Egypt," he answered.

"Nay, Pharaoh, the Queen of Egypt."

By Seti's side there was another throne, that in which he had set dead Merapi with a crown upon her head. He turned and looked at it a while. Then, he said:

"I see that this seat is empty. Let the Queen of Egypt take her place there if so she wills."

She stared at him as if she thought that he was mad, though doubtless she had heard something of that story, then swept up the steps and sat herself down in the royal chair.

"Your Majesty has been long absent," said Seti.

"Yes," she answered, "but as my Majesty promised she would do, she has returned to her lawful place at the side of Pharaoh—never to leave it more."

"Pharaoh thanks her Majesty," said Seti, bowing low.

Some six years had gone by, when one night I was seated with the Pharaoh Seti Meneptah in his palace at Memphis, for there he always chose to dwell when matters of State allowed.

It was on the anniversary of the Death of the Firstborn, and of this matter it pleased him to talk to me. Up and down the chamber he walked and, watching him by the lamplight, I noted that of a sudden he seemed to have grown much older, and that his face had become sweeter even than it was before. He was more thin also, and his eyes had in them a look of one who stares at distances.

"You remember that night, Friend, do you not," he said; "perhaps the most terrible night the world has ever seen, at least in the little piece of it called Egypt." He ceased, lifted a curtain, and pointed to a spot on the pillared portico without. "There she sat," he went on; "there you stood; there lay the boy and there crouched his nurse—by the way, I grieve to hear that she is ill. You are caring for her, are you not, Ana? Say to her that Pharaoh will come to visit her—when he may, when he may."

"I remember it all, Pharaoh."

"Yes, of course you would remember, because you loved her, did you not, and the boy too, and even me, the father. And so you will love us always when we reach a land where sex with its walls and fires are forgotten, and love alone survives—as we shall love you."

"Yes," I answered, "since love is the key of life, and those alone are accursed who have never learned to love."

"Why accursed, Ana, seeing that, if life continues, they still may learn?" He paused a while, then went on: "I am glad that he died, Ana, although had he lived, as the Queen will have no children, he might have become Pharaoh after me. But what is it to be Pharaoh? For six years now I have reigned, and I think that I am beloved; reigned over a broken land which I have striven to bind together, reigned over a sick land which I have striven to heal, reigned over a desolated land which I have striven to make forget. Oh! the curse of those Hebrews worked well. And I think that it was my fault, Ana, for had I been more of a man, instead of casting aside my burden, I should have stood up against my father Meneptah and his policy and, if need were, have raised the people. Then the Israelites would have gone, and no plagues would have smitten Egypt. Well, what I did, I did because I must, perhaps, and what has happened, has happened. And now my time comes to an end, and I go hence to balance my account as best I may, praying that I may find judges who understand, and are gentle."

"Why does Pharaoh speak thus?" I asked.

"I do not know, Ana, yet that Hebrew wife of mine has been much in my mind of late. She was wise in her way, as wise as loving, was she not, and if we could see her once again, perhaps she would answer the question. But although she seems so near to me, I never can see her, quite. Can you, Ana?"

"No, Pharaoh, though one night old Bakenkhonsu vowed that he perceived her passing before us, and looking at me earnestly as she passed."

"Ah! Bakenkhonsu. Well, he is wise too, and loved her in his fashion. Also the flesh fades from him, though mayhap he will live to make offerings at both our tombs. Well, Bakenkhonsu is at Tanis, or is it at Thebes, with her Majesty, whom he ever loves to observe, as I do. So he can tell us nothing of what he thought he saw. This chamber is hot, Ana, let us stand without."

So we passed the curtain, and stood upon the portico, looking at the garden misty with moonlight, and talking of this and that—about the Israelites, I think, who, as we heard, were wandering in the deserts of Sinai. Then of a sudden we grew silent, both of us.

A cloud floated over the face of the moon, leaving the world in darkness. It passed, and I became aware that we were no longer alone. There in front of us was a mat, and on the mat lay a dead child, the royal child named Seti; there by the mat stood a woman with agony in her eyes, looking at the dead child, the Hebrew woman named Moon of Israel.

Seti touched me, and pointed to her, and I pointed to the child. We stood breathless. Then of a sudden, stooping down, Merapi lifted up the child and held it towards its father. But, lo! now no longer was it dead; nay, it laughed and laughed, and seeing him, seemed to throw its arms about his neck, and to kiss him on the lips. Moreover, the agony in the woman's eyes turned to joy unspeakable, and she became more beautiful than a star. Then, laughing like the child, Merapi turned to Seti, beckoned, and was gone.

"We have seen the dead," he said to me presently, "and, oh! Ana, *the dead still live!*"

That night, ere dawn, a cry rang through the palace, waking me from my sleep. This was the cry:

"The good god Pharaoh is no more! The hawk Seti has flown to heaven!"

At the burial of Pharaoh, I laid the halves of the broken cup upon his breast, that he might drink therefrom in the Day of Resurrection.

Here ends the writing of the Scribe Ana, the Counsellor and Companion of the King, by him beloved.

LEONAUR

ALSO FROM LEONAUR
AVAILABLE IN SOFTCOVER OR HARDCOVER WITH DUST JACKET

TROS OF SAMOTHRACE 1: WOLVES OF THE TIBER *by Talbot Mundy*—When his ship is taken and his crew slaughtered Tros of Samothrace is captured by Imperial Rome.

TROS OF SAMOTHRACE 2: DRAGONS OF THE NORTH *by Talbot Mundy*—Tros of Samothrace burns for vengeance and has declared himself the implacable enemy of Rome.

TROS OF SAMOTHRACE 3: SERPENT OF THE WAVES *by Talbot Mundy*—Tros, his allies and the forces of Rome have drawn apart to prepare for the conflict to come.

TROS OF SAMOTHRACE 4: CITY OF THE EAGLES *by Talbot Mundy*—As Tros of Samothrace continues in his attempts to confound Caesar's plans for the invasion of Britain, he journeys to the Eternal City to seek the aid of its great leaders—and Caesar's opponents—Cato, Pompey and the Vestal Virgins themselves!

TROS OF SAMOTHRACE 5: CLEOPATRA *by Talbot Mundy*—Cleopatra—Queen of Egypt—is a formidable character ever ready to play the game of intrigue, betrayal and shifting loyalties to suit her own objectives. Blood will surely be spilt and once again Tros finds himself inexorably caught up in monumental events that threaten his life and those he loves.

TROS OF SAMOTHRACE 6: THE PURPLE PIRATE *by Talbot Mundy*—The epic saga of the ancient world—Tros of Samothrace—draws to a conclusion in this sixth—and final—volume. Julius Caesar has been assassinated and Queen Cleopatra of Egypt finds herself in a perilous position and desperate for allies to secure her power.

THE ILLUSTRATED & COMPLETE BRIGADIER GERARD *by Sir Arthur Conan Doyle*—These are the adventures of Conan Doyle's incomparable French hero-the finest swordsman in the Light Cavalry-Etienne Gerard. Arranged for the first time in historical chronological order, his many enthusiasts can now properly appreciate his colourful career as he fights, loves and blunders his way through the Napoleonic epoch-from his earliest adventure as a young blade determined to reach his lady love despite the unwelcome attention of her fathers bull-through many campaigns and special missions-to the bloody field of Waterloo, the downfall of his beloved Emperor and beyond. This is the complete collection of these classic stories. What makes this edition exceptional is the inclusion of nearly 140 illustrations-mostly by the famed military artist William Barnes Wollen-which accurately portray the spirit of the stories and the uniforms and scenes of the events they portray.

LEONAUR

ALSO FROM LEONAUR

AVAILABLE IN SOFTCOVER OR HARDCOVER WITH DUST JACKET

GARRETT P. SERVISS' SCIENCE FICTION *by Garrett P. Serviss*—Three Interplanetary Adventures including the unauthorised sequel to H. G. Wells' *War of the Worlds--Edison's Conquest of Mars, A Columbus of Space, The Moon Metal.*

JUNK DAY *by Arthur Sellings*—". . . . his finest novel was his last, *Junk Day,* a post-holocaust tale set in the ruins of his native London and peopled with engrossing character types . . . . perhaps grimmer than his previous work but pointedly more energetic." *The Encyclopedia of Science Fiction.*

KIPLING'S SCIENCE FICTION by *Rudyard Kipling*—Science Fiction & Fantasy stories by a Master Storyteller including 'As East As A,B,C' 'With The Night Mail'.

THE COLLECTED SCIENCE FICTION AND FANTASY OF STANLEY G. WEINBAUM: THE BLACK HEART by *Stanley G. Weinbaum*—Classic Strange Tales Including: the Complete Novel The Dark Other, Plus Proteus Island and Others Stories included in this Volume The Dark Other (novel) Proteus Island The Adaptive Ultimate Pymalion's Spectacles.

THE COLLECTED SCIENCE FICTION AND FANTASY OF STANLEY G. WEINBAUM: STRANGE GENIUS by *Stanley G. Weinbaum*—Classic Tales of the Human Mind at Work Including the Complete Novel The New Adam, the 'van Manderpootz' Stories and Others Stories included in this Volume The New Adam (novel) The Brink of Infinity The Circle of Zero Graph The Worlds of If The Ideal The Point of View.

THE COLLECTED SCIENCE FICTION AND FANTASY OF STANLEY G. WEINBAUM OTHER EARTHS by *Stanley G. Weinbaum*—Classic Futuristic Tales Including: Dawn of Flame & its Sequel The Black Flame, plus The Revolution of 1960 & Others.

THE COLLECTED SCIENCE FICTION AND FANTASY OF STANLEY G. WEINBAUM INTERPLANETARY ODYSSEYS by *Stanley G. Weinbaum*—Classic Tales of Interplanetary Adventure Including: A Martian Odyssey, its Sequel Valley of Dreams, the Complete 'Ham' Hammond Stories and Others Stories included in this Volume Mars A Martian Odyssey Valley of Dreams Venus Parasite Planet The Lotus Eaters Uranus The Planet of Doubt Titan Flight on Titan Pluto The Red Peri Io The Mad Moon Europa Redemption Cairn Ganymede Tidal Moon.

SUPERNATURAL BUCHAN by *John Buchan*—Stories of Ancient Spirits, Uncanny Places & Strange Creatures.

LEONAUR

ALSO FROM LEONAUR

DARKNESS AND DAWN 1: THE VACANT WORLD by *George Allen England*—A Novel of a future New York.

DARKNESS AND DAWN 2: BEYOND THE GREAT OBLIVION by *George Allen England*—A Novel of a future America.

DARKNESS AND DAWN 3: THE AFTER GLOW by *George Allen England*—A Novel of a future America.

BEFORE ADAM & OTHER STORIES by *Jack London*—In Leonaur's three volume The Collected Science Fiction & Fantasy of Jack London, his SF and fantasy novels and shorter works are brought together for the first time. Stories included in this Volume Before Adam The Scarlet Plague A Relic of the Pliocene When the World Was Young The Red One Planchette A Thousand Deaths Goliah A Curious Fragment The Rejuvenation of Major Rathbone.

THE IRON HEEL & OTHER STORIES by *Jack London*—In Leonaur's three volume The Collected Science Fiction & Fantasy of Jack London, his SF and Fantasy novels and shorter works are brought together for the first time. Stories included in this Volume The Iron Heel The Enemy of All the World The Shadow and the Flash The Strength of the Strong The Unparalleled Invasion The Dream of Debs.

THE STAR ROVER & OTHER STORIES by *Jack London*—In Leonaur's three volume The Collected Science Fiction & Fantasy of Jack London, his SF and fantasy novels and shorter works are brought together for the first time. Stories included in this Volume The Star Rover The Minions of Midas The Eternity of Forms The Man With the Gash.

MR MUKERJI'S GHOSTS by *S. Mukerji*—Mr S. Mukerji works very diligently in an office. It is not very interesting work, but Mr Mukerji has another far more diverting interest. He is an expert in ghosts and stories of ghosts. It is the height of the British Raj and Mr Mukerji is in an ideal position to discover stories about the 'sahibs' of India as he is about the Indians themselves.

KIPLINGS GHOSTS by *Rudyard Kipling*—These 12 pieces encompass all of Kipling's ghost stories, many of which are set in his familiar world of British India. They are complemented by supernatural tales of deadly curses and werewolves.

www.ingramcontent.com/pod-product-compliance
Lightning Source LLC
Chambersburg PA
CBHW020923020726
47495CB00002B/320